PRAISE FOR **ADVENTURES OF V**

With a few brush strokes, Reid creates a whole world. It's like magic –
the reader is sucked into that world, instantaneously. V swirls us into an
extravaganza, a detailed, delightful, dystopic, alien, familiar future – primal,
ferocious, and gratifying.
– Susan S. Senstad, author of *Milk and Venom* and *Music for the Third Ear*

Vivacious, vampish, victorious, voluptuous, vibrant, villainous … An
eternal 19-year-old, gorgeous vampire, monster-vixen named "V" – a pagan
Goddess, reborn as a super-heroine beauty who lives off the blood of the
bad, to rescue the souls of the good. Irresistible hijinks!
– Ed Cowen, producer, impresario

A wild ride into adventure, fantasy, and chills, V gifted me with glimpses of
arcane current and historical knowledge. Not for years have novels been as
much fun and enlightening.
– Chuck Shamata, actor

Utterly engrossing, rich, dark, and deep, Gilbert Reid creates worlds within
worlds of vivid, bold adventure.
– Bernice Landry, artist

Gilbert Reid's prose is so sensuous and evocative! When he takes you down
unfamiliar paths, and into situations that excite suspension of disbelief, you
follow him because the energy of V's personality is so witty and alluring, she
charms you into the universe the author has created. Vivid, complex, wildly
imaginative.
– Diana Leblanc, actor, director

PRAISE FOR OTHER BOOKS BY GILBERT REID

PRAISE FOR *SON OF TWO FATHERS*

This epic, suspenseful love story set in the 1500s in Venice is filled with the dangerously wicked intrigue and counter-intrigue, with delicious atmosphere, texture, and, most importantly, historical context ... It is a rich tapestry of history, intrigue, and, of course, love.
– Lynne Deragon, actor

Deep knowledge of Italian history and culture, told with ribald humor, scandalous intrigue, and page-turning drama.
– Sandra Martin, author of *A Good Death*

Son of Two Fathers offers readers thrilling moments laden with suspense, scalding tension, and unpredicted twists and turns of plot – thoughtful explorations of subjects as diverse as visual art, theater art, philosophy, political history, and Jewish history. Readers interested in history will enjoy this book. Readers interested in Jewish history will delight in it.
– Mordechai Ben-Dat, *The Canadian Jewish News*

A dazzling kaleidoscope of vivid characters and settings, a perfect summer companion for anyone with a taste for adventure and romance.
– David Calderisi, director, actor

PRAISE FOR OTHER BOOKS BY GILBERT REID

PRAISE FOR *LAVA AND OTHER STORIES*

Very powerful, poetic and nasty and tough.
– Anna Porter, publisher, writer

The writing is terrific. The characters are glamorous, decayed, old, young, loved, unloved. Reid inhabits each one. His raw, elegant prose, his vivid and sensuous images leave one breathless, with recognition and terror.
– Diana Leblanc, actor, director

The women, how they speak, what they confide, and omit, what they expose about each other! It's as if only sexuality happened that summer.
– Susan S. Senstad, author of *Milk and Venom* and *Music for the Third Ear*

PRAISE FOR SO *THIS IS LOVE: LOLLIPOP AND OTHER STORIES*

Reid's stories are in the great traditions of Alice Munro or Mavis Gallant.
– Margaret Macmillan, historian, writer

Powerfully rendered and suspenseful.
– Joyce Carol Oates, critic, publisher, writer

An unerring and compelling examination of aggression and compassion.
– *The Vancouver Sun*

One of the 100 best books of the year.
– *The Globe & Mail*

PANDEMIC

BOOK 2
THE GATEWAY

ADVENTURES OF V: VOLUME 4
"The Goddess is back. Her hour has come."
– Jules Cashford

PANDEMIC

BOOK 2

THE GATEWAY

by

GILBERT REID

TWIN RIVERS
PRODUCTIONS

Issued in print and electronic formats
ISBN 978-1-7771580-3-3: *Pandemic Book 2, The Gateway:* Paperback
ISBN 978-1-9994790-9-1: *Pandemic Book 2, The Gateway:* EPUB
ISBN 978-1-9994790-8-4: *Pandemic Book 2, The Gateway:* Kindle
ISBN 978-1-7773141-3-2: *Pandemic Book 2, The Gateway:* Amazon paperback

Cover and text design by Counterpunch Inc. / Linda Gustafson
Illustrations by Niki9door

 Published by
Twin Rivers Productions
20 Bloor Street East
PO Box 75070
Toronto, Ontario, M4W 3T3

To receive a free book or novella, sign up at:
https://gilbertreid.com

For Trisha Jackson and Ramsay Derry

Truly, it is in the darkness that one finds the light.
– MEISTER ECKHART

The wound is the place where the Light enters.
– RUMI

I am what I wanted and I want what I am.
– MEISTER ECKHART

CONTENTS

Cast of Characters xv

PROLOGUE   Stars And Stripes   1

PART ONE   Andromeda-II   3

PART TWO   A Spreading Wave 123

PART THREE The Gateway 179

PART FOUR   Shangri-La   321

Aftermath   481

Coda   483

CAST OF CHARACTERS

Aaloka – 9-year-old Indian girl, from Mumbai

Aimi Hosokawa – Japanese scientist, friend of Sabrina Jacobs.

Alex Wolf – Chief Research Scientist at Andromeda Corporation

Annette Brighton – US navy officer

Anthony Garcia – spy, sent to monitor Kate Thornhill

Anton Fabritz – Swiss industrialist and inventor

Ashley Samos – lecturer in art history, married to Doctor Kevin Harris

Ben Kamu – Kenyan genius AI programmer

Bill Brothers – anchor of the Volpe Network "This PM" show

Billy Wayne Penn – long-haul truck driver

Callida Galeazzo Montezemula Ruspolis – rich, beautiful Mexican

Captain Allan Anderson – US Navy officer

Carlos Andreas Stout – Mexican media billionaire

Charlie Parr – grizzled, veteran war cameraman and photographer

Claire V Jacobs – cult fashion designer, master of the Cyber Universe

Cletus Buck Kettle – mercenary with Black Murk Security

Colonel Jefferson Siebert – Marine Colonel

Dmitry Dwarf – reincarnation of Dmitry Pavlov, of the eternal Evil Spirit

Doctor Kevin Harris – expert in lobotomizing prisoners

Doctor Ra'shae Mansoor – 28-year-old molecular biologist

Ed Ross – Secret Service Agent

Father Michael Patrick O'Bryan – V's dead Jesuit friend and mentor

Father Patrick O'Connor O'Bryan – Father O'Bryan's nephew

Federico Harvey – US Navy officer

Freddy – another name for the murderous Reptile Man

Gail McCoy –world-famous country-and-western singer and model

General Arthur Godwin Wells – retired US Army, expert on strategy

George Apostolou – host of the radio show "Our Greatest Fears"

George Kennedy – President of the American Bar Association

Greg Erdman – author of books about aliens, hybrids, and SINs

Gus Wallach – head of security at Bio-Frontier

Guy Vargas – US Navy helicopter pilot

Helen Guerrera – a lawyer, Chief Counsel for Andromeda Corp

Henry Cheng – 25-year-old molecular biologist, CEO of Bio-Frontier

Ingrid Carlstrom – Captain Olsen's Executive Assistant on the *Eden*

Irene Selander – Swedish novelist, wife of Anton Fabritz

Isis – Isis a reincarnation of Asherah, goddess and V's companion

Jed Baker – Cambridge UK criminologist, friend of Sabrina Jacobs

Joseph Humility Ebenezer Jackson – vice president of the USA

Kaitlin Wagner – an 18-year-old university student, plus her cat, Fluff

Karl Emmanuel Corcoran – a right-wing libertarian pundit

Kate Thornhill – Professor of Physics at MIT, Nobel Laureate

Katherine du Bois Hughes – president of the USA

Larry Bilodeau – thirty-six-year-old inveterate bachelor

Laura Giordano – lawyer, one of V's human identities

Magnus Olsen – Norwegian Captain of the *Eden of the Seas*

Marie-José Duval – waitress in the Café de Paris, on the *Eden*

Marit – beautiful SIN (Synthetic Individual), works for Sabrina Jacobs

Mark Tobin – liaison between *Andromeda II* and the US Navy

Mary Loo – Billy Wayne Penn's girlfriend

Michelle Bruni – Art history student, friend of Ashley Samos

Mike Collins – mercenary with Black Murk Security

Monica Fabritz – Swiss citizen, 19, completing her Ph.D. in physics

Norma Cheng, molecular biologist, wife of Henry Cheng

Professor Dinko Milinkovic – a left-wing, anti-capitalist pundit

Puppet Master – an incarnation of the Eternal Force of Evil

Renée Scott – Press Secretary to the president

Reptile Man – hybrid and mindless killer

Rufus Mudcock – billionaire owner of the Volpe Network

Sabrina Jacobs –CEO of Andromeda Corporation

Sally – Rufus Mudcock's long-time executive assistant

Samantha Andrews – reporter for Volpe TV's "This PM" show

Sana Kapoor – liaison: Atlanta Center for Disease Control

Sarah James – Secret Service Agent

Séamus Heaney – owner of the Blue Fin Marina

Sergeant Eve Schmidt – Marine Sergeant

Shelly Nixon – Executive producer of Volpe TV's "This PM" show

Sherriff Doug Serra – Sheriff in a small Florida municipality

Sonia Davis – The president's National Security Advisor

Virginia Lilly – actress, star of B series cult films

Wang Fang – Fang is Chinese, a star acrobat in La Cirque de la Mer

Wang Fei – Fei is Chinese, a star acrobat in La Cirque de la Mer

V – Reptilian hybrid, half-human, half-alien, and superheroine

PROLOGUE – STARS AND STRIPES

"Now, let me say this!" Centered in the glare of floodlights on the hoverjet platform at the stern of *Andromeda II*, Katherine du Bois Hughes, president of the United States, glowed, glamorous and warlike – her head shaved, her skin lustrous, and dressed in boots, tight black jeans, and a skintight black T-shirt. "Let me say this – We will not cower! We will not hide! We will not submit! We will fight! All of us together, we will fight without pause, without fail. We will fight, however long it takes. And we will win! Do not doubt this for a moment! Victory will be ours! Victory will be yours! God Bless America and God bless all the nations of the Earth – and God Bless all of you, whoever you are, whatever you are, and wherever you come from! Thank you!" Clapping and cheers and whistles thundered from the deck. The president bowed, waved, flashed a huge smile, and stepped away from the microphone, out of the floodlights, into the shadows.

"Hail to the Chief" echoed over the speaker system. The giant Stars and Stripes, brilliantly lit up, floated gently in the wind.

Fireworks from the *Deng Xiaoping IV*, the Chinese missile launcher, and from *Andromeda II*, reflecting the colors of the flag, burst over the dark brooding waters of the Atlantic.

And, defying the dark immensity, defying the dangers, the flag, Old Glory, gently rippling in the breeze, spread out to its full magnificent extent.

PART ONE – ANDROMEDA II

CHAPTER 1 – BABEL

"Madam President, welcome to *Andromeda II*." Doctor Sabrina Jacobs reached out her hand. A white dove, perched on Sabrina's shoulder, fluttered and cooed.

"Thank you, Doctor Jacobs." Without an instant's hesitation, the president grasped the hand of her archenemy, Sabrina Jacobs, the CEO of Andromeda Corporation, the woman who symbolized biotechnology; the woman who was the creator of wonders and terrors. The president glanced at the dove. "You have a mascot."

"She landed a few minutes ago and seems to have adopted me." Sabrina stroked the bird's feathers. "May I present Lieutenant Mark Tobin, US Navy? He is our liaison with the US Fleet."

"Lieutenant Tobin," the president favored the handsome young officer with the irresistible Katherine du Bois Hughes smile. Finally, she was able to speak to one of her own people! At last! This was a foothold. This was a beginning. Now, she could begin to reclaim America for the constitution, for truth, justice, and democracy.

"Madam President!" Mark Tobin saluted. "We have just managed to establish contact with Admiral Morrison-Rodriguez on his flagship, the aircraft carrier, *Dwight D. Eisenhower*. We can put you in contact with him right now, if you wish. By the way, his daughter, Adrianna, is doing her Ph.D. in marine biology – and she is here, on *Andromeda II*."

"Yes, I would like to talk to the Admiral. And his daughter, I imagine, will help attest to my bona fides – after all, there is considerable confusion as to whether I am alive or dead."

"You are clearly very much alive." Mark Tobin smiled.

"But, first, Doctor Jacobs, Lieutenant Tobin, perhaps I should receive an update on the situation. When I talk to the Admiral, I want to know what

I'm talking about. V and I have been cut off for almost five hours. I imagine things are moving fast."

"They are, indeed, Madam President," Mark Tobin nodded, "Doctor Jacobs and I and members of Doctor Jacobs's staff have prepared a briefing for you."

"Wonderful! Let's do it," said the President.

A Tower of Babel – that was Katherine's first impression of the communications center of *Andromeda II*. She glanced around. People of every color and race were shouting, talking, arguing in dozens of languages: English, Mandarin, Swahili, French, German, Japanese, Russian, Korean, Spanish, Hebrew, Bengali, Arabic, and Vietnamese. Walls of screens showed multilingual feeds from all over the world, with breaking news from Moscow, London, New York, Shanghai, Cairo, Cape Town, Nairobi, Mexico City, Delhi, and …

A bell rang. Silence fell. Sabrina stepped forward. "Hello, everybody! May I present the president of the United States. The president would like to meet all of you, in person, so we will do a walk-around, I believe they call it."

And, so, the president, with Sabrina and Mark Tobin at her side, plunged into the milling crowd of experts, technicians, scientists, and communications teams.

The president stared and smiled. The whole scene was amazing! At the center of the action seemed to be a female hybrid, a black and red hybrid.

"Oh, God," thought the president, "she's almost my double, or I'm almost her double." This sleek voluptuous creature was introduced to the president as "Claire – Claire V. Jacobs."

"But I've met you!" Katherine took the reptile's claw in her hand. "You are the designer, Claire V. Jacobs! You were at the White House. We had a very interesting conversation."

The sleek black reptile grinned. "Yes, I'm the very same, but looking a bit different tonight, Madam President, as you can see!"

"As a human, you are blond and blue-eyed!"

"Yes, that is definitely me!"

"When did you …?"

"I've always been a hybrid, Madam President. I was cloned from V's DNA. I came out of a test tube. I've been a hybrid from the beginning."

"Cloned?"

"I'm the guilty party, Madam President," Sabrina put her hand on Claire's silken lustrous reptilian shoulder. "V knew nothing about it and was furious.

Her basic law was not to make any creatures like herself; this basic law was laid down to protect humans from creatures like V. V was protecting us from V."

"When she found out about me, V was going to kill both of us," volunteered Claire, "me and Sabrina – wham, bang – dead!"

"Is that true?" said the president, glancing at V.

"It is," said V, smiling at Claire.

"But then V fell in love with Claire," said Sabrina, "and so, luckily for me, she decided to spare me too. I must add, Madam President, that I too am a hybrid, like V and Claire – it's a long story – and that in our demon or reptilian mode, Claire and I are twins."

Katherine gazed into Claire's golden reptile eyes and took a deep breath. She was learning almost too much and in too short a time. But, then, people always said she was a quick learner. *Oh, my world has changed!* She sighed and smiled at the beautiful scarlet-and-black hybrid and Claire smiled back.

When the introductions had been made, they all gathered around a large table in the center of the communications room. The president asked Sabrina to chair the meeting.

"Thank you, Madam President. Claire and Ben have been following what communications and information we've been able to get out of Florida and the mainland. They will give you the overview."

Claire, her scarlet-and-black scales glowing, and Ben, the Kenyan computer and intelligence-gathering genius, gave a quick summary of the news out of Florida. They began and finished each other's sentences. The zombie virus, they explained, was spreading fast; nothing seemed to be able to stop it; almost everyone who got close to it was infected within seconds; the cases of immunity were extremely rare, perhaps less than a quarter of one percent; the zombies were beginning to show more organization and determination, a determination to spread the disease. And the zombies did seem to be under the direction of some sort of central directing intelligence. But it was unclear what or who this controlling intelligence was. In Washington, there was confusion. The vice president had ordered the destruction – by conventional missiles and by nuclear weapons – of the *Eden of the Seas* and *Andromeda II*, but, somehow, some sort of interference in the electromagnetic field – possibly a space-time machine of some kind – had stopped these attacks.

"How do you know all this?" The president leaned back in her chair and stared at the two – the sleek black hybrid and the Kenyan expert.

Claire and Ben explained the electronic intelligence, how they were accessing a flood of classified communications, and they outlined their theories regarding a "Puppet Master" who was controlling the zombies.

"The Puppet Master thing is just a theory, so far," said Ben.

"Yes, just a theory – we need more information to confirm it," said Claire.

"And we're working on that," said Ben.

"Yes, we're working on that," said Claire.

"I can give you a bit of the scientific background to the plague, now, if you wish, Madam President."

"Yes, certainly, thank you."

Sabrina explained what was known about the Zombie Plague, what it did, how it was transmitted, how the contagion started, what kind of bacterial agent it might be, and how they were trying to pin down its nature and cure it both on *Andromeda II* and at Bio-Frontier.

Nobel Laureate Kate Thornhill – her brilliant black-and-white mask shining, looking like a human zebra – gave a quick backgrounder on the physics behind the electronic storms. She talked about the possible nature of the – hypothetical – space-time machine which had been distorting signals in southern Florida and frustrating the efforts by the vice president to nuke *Eden of the Seas* and *Andromeda II*. "But whatever their intentions and whatever or whoever is doing this, Madam President, they have powers far beyond our technology. So we must proceed with the utmost caution. No country on earth possesses this kind of technology, Madam President, and it is still mysterious why both the *Eden* and *Andromeda II* have been spared. It looks rather like our enemies are trying to protect us, but why …? We don't know."

Sabrina added that Captain Olson of the *Eden of the Seas* had seized back control of the bridge of the *Eden* and was taking the ship as far out to sea as possible to reduce the danger of more zombies escaping the ship.

Lieutenant Tobin leaned forward. "We are in contact with Captain Olson. *Eden of the Seas* is being escorted by ships of the US Navy, staying, of course, at a safe distance. But we have not informed the vice president of this fact."

"That, I think, is very wise, Lieutenant Tobin. Thank you," said the president.

Mark Tobin nodded his thanks. And then he summed up plans for the president's return to American soil: A US navy hover-jet would rendezvous with *Andromeda II* in about three hours. It would take the president to Admiral Rodriguez's flagship, the aircraft carrier, *Dwight D. Eisenhower*, and from there, if the president wished, she could broadcast to the American people.

"Yes, I want to do that," said the president, "I want people to know that I am alive and that I am back in command and that, as commander in chief, my orders – not those of the vice president – are to be obeyed."

"Then it is proposed that, as soon as possible after your arrival on the aircraft carrier, you go directly back to Washington."

"Yes, I agree, Lieutenant Tobin. That is exactly what I must do. I must go directly back to Washington – to the White House, and there I will take back control of the government, try to right some wrongs, and, above all, I will use whatever power I have to defeat this epidemic."

"Are there any other questions?" Sabrina glanced at the president; then, she looked around the table. "Is there anything else, any other point, anyone wants to bring up? Anything relevant? Even marginally? Anything the president should know? Don't be shy! No? Good. Madam President." Sabrina bowed towards the president.

"Well, all I want to say is," the president looked around the table, seeming to gaze, individually, at each person, "Thank you! Thank you, all of you! And this: we all know we have a long, difficult, dangerous fight in front of us, but, if all of us pull together and work together, we will win, and right and justice for all will triumph. Thank you."

As they left the command center, Sabrina turned to the president. "There is more to it than we have made public. Claire and Ben and I can brief you."

The president, Mark Tobin, V, Claire, Ben, and Sabrina slipped into a small, secure, sound-proof conference room.

"There's more that we discovered about the outbreak," said Ben, nodding at Claire. "It's information that, for the moment, should be shared with as few people as possible."

"That's right," said Mark Tobin.

"Yes, there is more," said Claire.

"I'm listening," said the president.

Claire explained how she and Ben had hacked into the vice-president's encrypted communications and how they discovered that the vice-president was behind the plot.

"Oh, my God," said the president.

"Wow!" said V.

"But the vice president has been double-crossed," said Claire.

"Double-crossed? How?"

"The people who organized the attack – provided the yacht and the biological weapon – have bigger plans. As a result of the double-cross, *Eden* didn't stay out at sea, as the vice president intended. Instead, it crashed into Miami. The zombies have gotten off the ship. That's how the plague spread to Florida. Now, the zombies are acting on instructions to spread it as far as possible and as fast as possible."

"So, he really intended to kill me – to kill all of us, and thousands of innocents!"

"Yes, it certainly seems so," said Sabrina. "He also targeted *Eden* and *Andromeda II* with nukes, but something – not necessarily a friendly something, as Kate pointed out – seems, for now at least, to be protecting us."

Claire turned her glowing reptilian eyes towards the president. "We have the tapes and recordings of the vice president's conversations, Madam President, if you wish to hear them."

"No, if you say it is so, I believe it."

"Thank you, Madam President," Claire and Ben said in unison.

"You have been following this, Lieutenant Tobin?"

"Yes. We've been working together moment-by-moment from the beginning. I listened to the tapes. We decided that only a few people should know about the vice president's role."

"That's very wise," said the president.

"The only other people – outside this room – who know about the vice president's role are Kate Thornhill and her guard-assistant, Anthony Garcia. And they can be trusted, absolutely."

"Renée Scott warned me against the vice president," said the president, thinking of Renée, whom she had last glimpsed on the balcony of the Eden, about to jump, and hoping that Renée, somehow, had survived.

Sabrina caught the thought. "Yes, Madam President, Renée Scott is alive and well. The whole group is alive and well. Agent Sarah James, Alex Wolf, Helen Guerrera, Marie-Josée, Ed Ross, Fei and Fang, and the others, have found refuge at a company affiliated to us, in Miami. They are working, right now, on developing a vaccine against the zombie virus – the company is called Bio-Frontier. They are coordinating directly with us, and they are our best hope – probably our only hope – for a vaccine."

"Thank God," sighed the president.

CHAPTER 2 – A SIN

When the briefing was over, and after the president had spoken to Admiral Morrison-Rodriguez and met his daughter, Adrianna, who turned out to be a charming, brilliant young woman, the president turned to Sabrina. "I could use the next few hours to rest – it has been a strenuous day and night, and the next twenty-four or forty-eight hours are going to be equally busy."

"Of course, Madam President. I've had my own suite prepared for your use."

Sabrina took the president to the suite – which was guarded by two Royal Marines and which had been prepared to welcome the president and allow her to catch an hour or two of sleep – or even just of rest – before boarding a US navy hover-jet for the aircraft carrier, *Dwight D. Eisenhower*.

"And this is Marit," said Sabrina. "She will be available for anything you might need."

"Madam President, I will be at your service."

"Delighted to meet you, Marit," the president shook the young woman's hand. The young woman looked Nordic, perhaps Swedish. She was extraordinarily beautiful. She cannot be completely human, the president thought, blinking at the girl. No, she could not be merely human; she was too perfect.

"I am honored to serve you, Madam President."

"Well, I shall leave you two now," said Sabrina, "Madam President." Sabrina bowed and left the suite. Outside, at the door, the two Royal Marines saluted.

"The shower is here, Madam President," said Marit. "The controls are here. You push this button, and I will come immediately. Refreshments are in the refrigerator. Coffee will be made automatically, on your command, just here, on this panel. You can tell it what you want – espresso, latte, normal coffee, etc. The list of possibilities is here. A change of clothes – all your size, I believe – is available here. And these screens give you full access to world communications, though, as you know, electromagnetic disturbances are causing a wee bit of havoc – particularly as regards any information coming out of Florida."

"A wee bit of havoc," the president repeated, smiling. "You have a nice way of putting things, Marit."

"Yes, understated hyperbole – I'm told it's a weakness of mine," Marit looked down for a second, as if she were shy. "The US Navy hover-jet that will take you to the aircraft carrier *Dwight D. Eisenhower* should be here in three hours. So you have time to rest." She smiled and stood waiting in case the President had other orders.

"Marit, may I ask you a question?"

"You may ask anything, Madam President."

"What is the meaning of your name, Marit?"

"It is Swedish for 'beautiful,' Madam President. I did not choose it, obviously."

"Well, it is very apt, Marit. You are very beautiful."

"Thank you, Madam President."

"May I ask – are you human or are you a …?"

"I am what used to be called a BIOC, or Biological Creation, Madam President." Marit smiled a bright, friendly, faultless smile. "But as I know you are aware there is a new term for my generation, 'Synthetic Individual.' The Acronym is SIN."

"SIN – how … Well, I guess it's apt, in some ways."

Marit laughed. "Well, yes, in my case even more so, Madam President, because I was originally designed to give pleasure, sensual pleasure, and I believe that such activities are often referred to as 'sin' in some human religious traditions."

"Ah, tell me – about being designed for pleasure." The president sat down on the edge of the bed and removed one of her boots. Ah, to relax, finally, to relax, and to learn, to learn so much in such a short period of time!

"It was not always easy," Marit knelt beside the bed to help the president remove the second boot. "You see, humans often do not know what they really want. But I suppose you are aware of that too, Madam President. I imagine that, with your experience, you are a connoisseur of human weaknesses – and strengths."

"Yes, I guess I am – I had to be – I never thought about it that way."

"In any case, Sabrina gave me a very hard case as a sort of test – it was an experiment, and it ended tragically I am afraid."

"A hard case?" the president lifted off her T-shirt; she had decided that there was no need for modesty in front of such a creature as a SIN, and who was clearly a very pleasant and intelligent young woman – a "person." She sighed. How far she had come in the last few hours! Now she was finally ready to have that discussion about justice for SINs and hybrids with Renée, the discussion Renée had stubbornly insisted they must have. "Sit down, Marit, tell me," said the president, unbuckling her belt and pulling off her jeans.

"Really?" Marit was still kneeling. "I am to sit down?"

"Yes, sit down. Tell me your story – it will be my bedtime tale," the president lay back on the bed, her head propped up by the pillows.

"Well, Madam President, this is the story ..." Marit sat down in a chair that was very close to the bed, next to the president. "I was initially created about five years ago."

"Five years ago?"

"Yes. Five years – they are continually tinkering with me, so I am much more flexible now than I was in the beginning. And, of course, since I'm a biological creature or device, not mechanical or silicon based, my neural networks are naturally self-generating and respond to inputs, so I learn from experience; it's a continual set of feed-backs, new perceptual patterns, new skills, and new feelings too, I think. In short, I learn something new every day, even every minute."

"Of course," said the president, her eyes fluttering, half closing. "You learn. I too am learning, something new ... every day."

"One day, shortly after I finished my initial trials, Sabrina called me into her office. Sabrina, you know, is always pushing the limits. We must go further and faster in experiments with human nature, she tells everybody, if we are to save the human race. She believes some sort of apocalypse is coming and humans have to develop technology – and biological and psychological resilience – so as to be ready. She calls it transcendence, going above and beyond the limits – some people call it the singularity – in any case ..." Marit closed her eyes. It was all as clear as yesterday, her adventures trying to bring happiness to one human being – a man called David Stanford Adams III. She was sitting between Sabrina and Aimi Hosokawa when ...

... She was sitting between Sabrina and Aimi Hosokawa and being sagely quiet, her hands folded in her lap, her legs pressed together, listening, waiting to see what her mission would be, and how difficult it would be.

"In any case, Marit," Sabrina said, "You will find it interesting, I think, and a bit of a challenge."

Just as Sabrina said this, Marit's mission, the man, her chosen man, David Stanford Adams III, entered the room. He looked nervous. He kept twisting his hands in front of him. Marit could see it clearly. Those hands, pale and sparsely hairy with thick black hairs, were wet with nervous sweat.

"Sit down, David," said Sabrina.

"Ah, thank you." He sat down, but he almost missed the chair. Marit was tempted to laugh. In fact her lips did sketch out a smile, and Sabrina, always alive to everything – after all she was a hybrid and she could read thoughts, even Bio-Creation or SIN thoughts – gave her a gentle poke in the ribs, and sent the mental message, "Be kind, Marit. David is very timid, and he has a great many, well, complexes."

Sabrina was twirling a pencil. "Are you sure you want to do this, David? You don't have to, you know."

"No, I want to do it. I've never lived with a woman, a real woman, so now I will learn."

"Well, David, Marit has been designed to please you and to give you pleasure, conversational pleasure, sexual pleasure, pleasure in her beauty, so she will cater to your wishes. But she's not a machine, you know, she's a living being. She will, I'm sure, develop needs and opinions of her own – in fact, I suspect she already has needs and opinions of her own."

David Stanford Adams III's lips trembled, but he was brave. "Yes, I am ready; I am ready for opinions." He cleared his throat and glanced nervously at Marit.

She flashed what she hoped was an efficient smile, a glorious, friendly, all-forgiving smile.

"Good," Sabrina too smiled, thinking if Marit the Love SIN survived David Stanford Adams III, she could survive anything.

"What do you think, Marit, and how do you feel?"

"I am feeling very well, and you, Sabrina, how do you feel?"

"I feel exceptionally well today, Marit. So, now, formally, I would like to introduce you to David Stanford Adams III."

"Hello, David Stanford Adams III, it is a pleasure to meet you," Marit stood up, reached out her hand, and David Stanford Adams III shook it. She noticed, deciphering his mental reactions, that he now realized that her hand was warm and dry and soft as silk and that her handshake was firm and frank and not trembling or sweaty or clammy or nervously self-conscious and awkwardly indecisive like his handshake, and, since he didn't know when to let go, and since he wanted to hold onto her hand forever because it felt so good, he just held on. Marit was puzzled as to what to do since her program on human etiquette dictated that handshakes were to end rather quickly, but David Stanford Adams II either did not know this, or he had decided for some reason to break the rules, though she did not understand – referencing the backup grammar of human communications – why he would do such a thing, or what his intentions could be, so she merely tightened her smile ever so slightly, kept her candid blue eyes steady, looking directly into the eyes of David Stanford Adams III, and she gave an ever so slight tug on his hand, an ever so gentle effort to liberate her hand, indicating that, perhaps, if he did not have an overwhelming impelling reason for hanging on to her, he should let go, and, finally, with an amorous sigh, he did.

"Well now that you have been introduced," said Sabrina, "you can begin your life together – and may it be a long and prosperous and happy one." She gave both of them a brilliant smile, and to Marit, she sent the mental message, "Good luck, darling. And if you get in trouble – don't hesitate! Call Aimi or me."

That evening …

"Do you wish me to unbutton your shirt, David Stanford Adam's III?"

"Ah, uh, I don't know, I mean …"

"You look uncomfortable, David Stanford Adams III. I would be pleased to unbutton your shirt, if it gives you pleasure."

"Ah, I don't know, but I guess, yeah, sure, go ahead …"

With deft slender fingers, Marit opened one button after another. She knew she smelled good, spicy, and sweet, like soap and fresh lemons and sunshine. She knew that her straight blond hair tumbled down in a perfumed veil across her forehead and that this might be attractive to the male of the human species. She crossed her eyes slightly, intent on focusing on the buttons.

"You have a beautiful chest, David Stanford Adams III," she said, running her warm fingers up and down his chest underneath the half-open shirt.

"Ah, yeah, I guess, I mean – I do?"

"Are you pleased, David Stanford Adams III? Are you pleased that I am touching your chest? Does my presence give you pleasure?"

"Call me David," David said, swallowing, "just call me David." He had never had such a perfect perfumed creature – human or not – close to him, perhaps his mother, but his memories of his mother were foggy: she and his father had died in a boating accident just short of David's fifth birthday. And, even before the accident, his mother, who had grand social ambitions, had been notably absent from little David's nursery.

"Of course, David Stanford Adams III, I shall call you David. What would please you most, David Stanford … I mean, David … what would please you most, a massage, a dry martini, or a conversation by candlelight or a combination of all three?"

"Ah, gosh, I don't know."

"Here, David, while you consider the possibilities and prioritize, let me lift off your shirt."

"Ah, I don't know, I mean …"

She didn't wait for an answer, but she lifted off his shirt.

David swallowed again. He felt ashamed of his nakedness, particularly since Marit was fully dressed. "I have bad skin," he said.

"Your skin is beautiful, David, but for middle age residual adolescent acne, undoubtedly an endocrine problem, and a few wandering black hairs and blackheads, a collapsed rib cage, and excessive pallor and all related problems – Andromeda Corporation's face mask magic recipe and Andromeda Corporation's M-45 Body Cream and Andromeda Corporation's Z-342 muscle regenerator offer ideal solutions. They will cure your skin in no time, puff out your chest, and make you darkly hairy or smooth and hairless, a sleek ephebe or a Tarzan of the Jungle, as you prefer, it's all up to you. All the great Bollywood and Hollywood actors and actresses swear by these Andromeda Corporation product lines."

"Oh, gosh, I don't know," he had wrapped his arms around his chest, which was strange Marit thought since he had no breasts to speak of; there was nothing whatsoever to see or to hide.

"Do not worry about cost, David."

"No, well, gosh …"

"I come equipped, David, with a gift pack of Andromeda Corporation beauty products and sexual products and vitamin supplements and a lifetime membership in the Andromeda Corporation body regeneration club. Here, let me apply the face mask. But it would be better, perhaps, David, if you were naked."

"I don't like to be naked alone," David said, swallowing.

"Of course, David, would you like me to be naked too?"

"Ah, I don't know, I mean …"

"Would you prefer that I undress myself, David, or would you like to be the one to remove my clothes?"

"Huh, I don't know. I've never ..."

"It is not so hard," she said, "See this strap here – this bit of equipment is called a bra, I believe, David. Well, you can use your fingers, your right hand, and you can slip it off my shoulder, and then you can do the same to the other, and then ..."

Shortly afterwards, David Stanford Adams III was lying on his back, with a clay-like face mask hiding his features – he looked like he had escaped from the Venice carnival – and with Marit, naked, straddled over his midriff applying a massage to his chest and stomach muscles.

"You are a fine specimen of a human being, David," said Marit.

"I like it when you call me David," David said, and then, as an afterthought, "But," he swallowed, "if you wish to call me Master, call me Master."

"Master, yes, I shall call you Master, Master."

"Ah," David let out a sigh, slightly cracking the clay-like carnival mask.

"Now, Master, if you wish to turn over, I will massage your back, Master." Marit was in fact having fun. It was like having a toy. Anything she wanted him to do, he would do, when she figured how to give him sufficient courage to do it, that is.

David turned over.

"I shall use Andromeda Corporation's Skin Toner Bio-Mark # 13 on your back, if you wish, Master."

"Yes, do use Skin Toner Bio-Mark # 13 on my back," said David, as he thrilled to the feel of her silky-smooth, muscular, naked thighs closing tight around his waist, and of her moist warm intimacy lowering itself onto the small of his back. He wondered: Can she have babies? Does she feel pleasure?

"Good, Master. Skin Toner Bio-Mark # 13 is a very fine product, even a miracle product, if I may allow myself, Master, to say so. It will clear your skin of all blemishes," Marit kneaded David's shoulders. "The effect will last for several months, perhaps years."

David sighed. His embarrassment was fading away. This creature would do anything for him and would probably allow him to do anything to her – if he had the courage to do anything at all, and if he could figure out, too, what precisely it was he wanted to do.

Later ...

"Now what do you wish, Master?"

David Stanford Adams III stared at her. He had never seen or been with such a beautiful creature; in fact, he had never had any creature at all, except the nice lady in the hotel years ago, who had been paid for by V and by Alex Wolf. That lady had offered to realize all his most intimate desires. But with that lady, his desiring machine had stalled, sputtered, and gone on the blink, or the fritz, sending out futile impotent sparks, and they had ended up having dinner, which was very fine but not the same as having one's every darkest most contorted desire fulfilled in the intimacy of a pre-paid hotel suite.

He stared at Marit.

Marit smiled at him, patiently waiting.

"The problem is," he said, swallowing and perspiring, "the problem is – I don't ever know what I want. I've never known what I want. Only when people tell me what I want, do I sometimes know what I want, and not always even then, if you see what I mean."

"You don't know what you want, Master?"

"No, I never know what I want – even when people instruct me."

Marit kept her smile focused, tightening her facial muscles, looking at him wide-eyed, blinking, feeling her mind was going to implode. She ran a few algorithms; the programs faltered, so she applied a fallback meta-program, a program to analyze the programs and to come up with some answer, any answer! Let us try this, one of her higher-level cognitive functions declared: It's a risk, it might not work, but nothing ventured, nothing gained. "So, you don't know what you want, Master?"

"Yes," David Stanford Adams III stuttered, wondering what was coming.

"Well, what you want, Master, is this: You want to take a hot shower, Master, a hot shower with me, the two of us stark naked, and with lots of bubbly creamy luscious soap and we will drink iced Cognac while we are in the steamy bubbly soapy shower. Does that sound acceptable?"

She saw doubt and fear flicker in his eyes.

"Master!"

"Ah, uh, golly, I don't …"

"This is an order, Master," she whispered, emitting sparks of fire from her ice-blue eyes.

"An order," he gulped.

"Yes," she said, defying the algorithms, breaking the first-level codes, relying on a fifth-level meta-linguistic program that allowed for – indeed, encouraged – role reversal. "It's an order!"

"Good," said David Stanford Adams III. "That makes things easier."

"We must put the Cognac in plastic glasses, Master, to avoid any unfortunate accidents. Broken glass can inflict nasty cuts on human flesh, you know."

And so it was that David found himself being soaped down – and soaping down – this most exquisite and delightfully imperious bio-woman – or SIN – in a steamy hot shower; she was a creature that could only have been dreamed up by a man – or woman – in quest of perfection.

"Are you pleased, Master? Please say you are pleased!"

"I am pleased, Slave," he said, "I am pleased."

"It gives me supreme pleasure," she said, raising an eyebrow in surprise. Golly, her meta-program was saying, he's taking the initiative! "When you call me 'slave,' Master, it gives me a little shiver – a ticklish *frisson* – right here!"

David blushed, calling her "slave" had been a bold move, a true expression of those dark fantasies, those twisted baroque bits of theater, he had often harbored when out on the road and bedding down alone between cold clammy sheets in lost dead-end motels during his lifelong bootless quest for the big deal, the jackpot, the gold at the end of the rainbow, and true passion and glorious sex, none of which had, until now, shown the slightest inclination to be found.

"Now, you know, Master, those sparse strands of hair combed across the top of your head, they are not perhaps what you need to increase your sex appeal as a Phallic God that appeals to all women and all creatures of this universe."

"They aren't?"

"No, Master, no."

"No?"

"Master, I propose we shave your head, if you agree, of course, Master."

"Huh, I don't know."

"It is an order, Master."

"Oh, if it's an order, Slave, then …"

"Good, Master! Your slave is delighted that you agree. Drink some Cognac, Master!"

"Yes." David Stanford Adams III drank some Cognac.

"Bow your head, Master." And she applied shaving cream, the gel kind, to his noggin, slush, slush, slush, the touch of her hand was creamy and soft and strong and masterful and utterly delicious.

David bowed his head in obedient ecstasy, as she used his razor to get rid of all traces of hair and, lo and behold, David Stanford Adams III began to resemble a new man, reborn, a new creature emerging out of the ruins of the old David Stanford Adams III.

"Now we shall eat," she said.

"Eat?"

"Yes, Master, eat."

Soon, within mere weeks, after obligatory courses of Andromeda Corporation body tone, Andromeda Corporation suntan, Andromeda Corporation muscle builder, and a diet of three-hour-long daily walks, and no junk food, only Andromeda Corporation super food, the new David Stanford Adams III was a sexy beast, shaved head, muscles, strong chest, tanned, and tough.

He was reborn, and he was in love, and for the first time in his life he was truly happy.

"And so, Madam President, we lived happily for several months. I reported to Sabrina and David reported to Sabrina and we went to see her together, too, so that she could see how we functioned as a couple, but you know, David had a job, in security, so we traveled, and we were one day in a town where they didn't like BIOCs – or SINs – and word got around about me, and after we had been there about a week, three men – vigilantes – came to our motel room, and while I was in the shower singing to myself; they meant to kill me. David fought them – but he really didn't like to hurt people, and he couldn't bring himself to punch back the way he should have punched back – and they beat David, and they hit him, while two of them held him, they punched him, and punched him, and then they stabbed him, and when I heard something I came out of the shower and I saw what was happening and – well, I am pretty strong, Madam President, and I am well-trained in self-defense – I tore them away from David, and I broke their arms and jaws and hands. But it was too late. David died in my arms, but he did say, just as he was dying, with the blood trickling from the side of his mouth, he did say, and he repeated it four times, he did say, that he loved me."

She stopped.

Loved me …

He loved me …

He, a human being, a real human being, loved me.

There were tears in Marit's eyes.

The president was asleep, sprawled on the bed.

Gently, Marit removed the president's socks. She pulled a bed cover over the president, and, with her eyes still wet, she tiptoed out of the room. She told the two Royal Marines on guard that she would come back every fifteen minutes to check on the president and she gave them her Tab Number.

"Yes, ma'am," said the two marines, saluting.

"I can bring you coffee if you would like," said Marit.

"Absolutely, ma'am, we would, ma'am. Thank you, ma'am!" and when she disappeared, the older marine turned to the younger, "Well, are you in love with her, then, lad, or not?" And the younger said, "Difficult to settle for a real woman, once you've met one of those."

"Indeed," said the older marine, "And this one is kindness itself."

It was four o'clock in the morning.

On the mainland, America's Zombie Dawn – due in about four hours – was about to fire up the eastern skies: Miami and Fort Lauderdale were almost entirely in the hands of the zombies.

Organized resistance had ceased.

But people were in hiding, almost everywhere, and many of the suburbs had not yet been touched by the plague.

CHAPTER 3 – BLACK OPS

In a corner of the Communications and Control Center, next to Claire and Ben's workstations, V, her black baseball cap tilted over her forehead and still in black jeans, black T-shirt, and black boots, was leaning back in a swivel chair with her legs stretched out and her feet up on a table.

She was going through the analyses Kate Thornhill had made of the electromagnetic and gravitational anomalies in the Florida area, and of the probability they were dealing with a space-time machine of some kind. If this was the case, it was a machine which no human science could build; or even, at humanity's present stage of knowledge and development, conceive. Something like the Crystal, something only aliens could build – V frowned. This did not look very good.

Which aliens would do such a thing?

Surely not *her* aliens!

And *why* would the aliens do such a thing?

And … hmm, she tossed a few of the papers down on the desk, and then she sat up straight and shuffled them into a neat pile. It was all very perplexing. She was sure Marcus would come – eventually – and enlighten her.

Claire turned her demon snout for a moment from the computer screens she was absorbed in and said, "V, I've found it. Here's the solution to your Monica Fabritz problem."

"Monica Fabritz …?"

"The Swiss girl kidnapped – you believe she was kidnapped – by the Reptile Man. Remember: The Anti-Christ Caper – you know, all tied up with the Apocalypse, the End of the Beginning, the Beginning of the End, that sort of thing. It's probably linked to what's happening now, and probably linked to the Puppet Master. Remember?"

"Show me!" V stood up, leaned over Claire's desk, and took a deep breath, feeling instinctively reassured by all the bustle and activity. All around them people were busy – Kate Thornhill, her smitten guardian, Anthony Garcia, who'd been given some security analysis job; Ted and Audrey, the little extra-terrestrials; God only knew what they did, but they often came up with start-ling bits of information which they shared through Kate; Ben Kamu, Claire's partner; other teams who, with Sabrina, were working on spectrum analysis of the zombie fluid glimpsed on video feeds and they were coordinating this with Bio-Frontier, and others …

Chaos – creative chaos.

Claire flicked her forked tongue out of her mouth, and curled it up, licking her snout. "I just got this an hour ago. This document links two things – the zombie outbreak and the birth of the Anti-Christ."

"The Apocalypse," said V, remembering – no, *seeing* – the words scrawled in blood on the school bus in Texas, and in the barn where Liz Shaw had been slaughtered – and it has been painted in blood in the Lewis household too.

"Right, the Apocalypse." Claire drew in her tongue, and blinked at V with heavy-lidded, golden, reptilian eyes. "I think the zombie plague and the Rep-tile Man are two parts of the same strategy: to bring about the apocalypse and the end of the world – as we know it, of course. I imagine the world itself, the planet Earth, will get on quite well without humans."

"Remember, love, we are human too," said V.

"Oh, sorry, I keep forgetting!" Claire turned her snout up in a pert reptile grin. "In any case, dear V, you were right! Monica Fabritz is alive. But you were wrong too: The Reptile Man doesn't have her – the Government does!"

"The Government?" V sat down. Claire handed her a printout.

"This was heavily encrypted. It took Ben and me a good ten minutes to turn it into prose."

"Thank you, both of you," said V.

Ben, from his desk, glasses poised high up on his forehead, sketched a courtly bow. "You are welcome, V."

"And, V," said Claire, "the clock is ticking: the magic baby is due to be born just about right now."

"That would be right," said V, "the timing is right, yes."

"And they are going to lobotomize the mother!"

"Lobotomize? What?" V recoiled in horror; it was one of her greatest fears.

"Yes, there's a … a Doctor Kevin Harris, the expert … in …"

"Does the president know about this?"

"No," said Claire, "I'm sure she doesn't. This is a 'black' operation; it is being carried out by a rogue organization. Also, there is the deniability factor …"

"If you don't know, you can't lie, and so you can't be caught out in a lie, so the underlings don't tell their bosses what they are doing, thus protecting the boss from incrimination and self-incrimination," murmured V. It was an old trick, and one resorted to by governments and bureaucracies – and corporations – all over the world.

"Exactly, ignorance, for VIPs, is bliss," said Claire, "and, in any case, however much she hated us or hates us, I doubt very much if your new friend and best bosom buddy, the president would have approved something like this."

V read the document:

TO: THE DIRECTOR – BLACK OPS
FROM: HOMELAND SECURITY BOPS – SUBCOMMITTEE 3-D
"ULTRA TOP SECRET: FOR YOUR EYES ONLY:

Monica Fabritz (hereafter known as "the Subject"), the 19-year-old Swiss national, who was a guest in the Lewis home – where all other humans present were killed and dismembered – and who was completing her Ph.D. in mathematics and physics at Princeton University, was in fact not killed in the attack on the Lewis family.

Monica Fabritz (The Subject) was abducted by the killer – the so-called "Reptile Man."

Monica Fabritz (The Subject) was found two weeks after the attack sitting, naked, badly bruised and scratched and lightly bitten, and complaining of a horrible headache, on a beach on a sandbar off the Florida Coast.

Luckily the Subject was found by a retired Intelligence officer (Black Ops) who had gone out to the sandbar to fish; he contacted Black Ops Home Land Security immediately.

The Subject was immediately taken into custody – and not allowed to contact or see or communicate with anyone.

No one knows the Subject is alive.

In the interests of National Security, the fact that the Subject is alive has been classified ultra-top-secret.

Several points are of worthy of note:

First, the Subject is Pregnant: Medical examinations have shown that the Subject was impregnated by the creature – the "hybrid" – similar to the creature in the Vermont, California, and Texas incidents; in fact, DNA results indicate it is the same creature or a clone.

Second, the "hybrid" is indeed a half-alien, half-human hybrid. DNA analysis also demonstrated that half of the creature's DNA – male line – is in fact, with a high degree of probability, non-terrestrial; nothing like it is known on the planet earth (see note below regarding Andromeda Corporation and its alleged experiments with "alien" DNA, rumors of a hybrid subject known as V, and rumors that some intelligence agencies use hybrids, notably this mythical V, as hired help, assassins, and as intelligence operatives. We do not have independent corroboration of such speculation, but it is not to be dismissed).

Third, Homeland Security's Bioterrorism Sub-Committee 14-B, Research Unit-4, has decided that the Subject's pregnancy will be carried to term. This decision has been confirmed by Black Ops Subcommittee 5-DZ. The Subject – it is fully conscious, not at all docile, and, unfortunately, is very articulate – strongly dissents from this decision. The Subject insisted on its right to abort the fetus. The Subject's request has been refused.

Fourth, the Subject's DNA has been altered by her "intercourse" with the creature, possibly by the act of insemination itself, possibly by some sort of "injection," possibly a bite or a scratch. In consequence, the Subject, though initially human, is now an alien-human hybrid.

The exact mechanism by which this transformation was effected is, we believe, still unknown to human science. (One caveat: see the note on the role of Andromeda Corporation, below)

The Subject has not – repeat, not – been informed of this change in its DNA.

The Subject's hybrid status means automatic re-classification from "human" to "non-human", pursuant to paragraph 212, Section A-1, Anti-Bio-Terrorism Law 23456B.

In consequence the Subject has no legal status and no rights under American law and has ceased to exist as a 'human subject' or 'human being.'

Hereafter, pursuant to the linguistic and lexical requirements and rules regarding human-hybrid and human bio-construct or human-SIN interaction as specified in paragraph 214, Section A-32, Anti-Bio Terrorism Law 23456B, regarding the re-classifications of beings from human to non-human status, the Subject will be referred to in documents not as "she" but as "it."

In interactions with the Subject, terminology reserved for humans will be maintained in order not to raise suspicions of the Subject – it is excessively intelligent and perceptive – that it has lost its human status. It will be referred to, when it is present, as "you" or as "she," to give the Subject the impression that, in some regards at least, it is still being treated as a "person."

The Subject has been placed in top secret high-security isolation.

The Subject's family and the Swiss authorities have been informed that the Subject is dead. Ashes have been sent to Switzerland for disposal. The American Ambassador attended a funeral service and offered the condolences on behalf of the United States Government.

[NOTE: European and Swiss law do not provide mechanisms for re-classification from "human" to "non-human" so that the Swiss Government – if aware of the Subject's existence – would still consider the Subject to be a human being, a person, and to enjoy full rights as a Swiss citizen in continuation with her former biological and civic identity; this would be true notwithstanding whatever changes have occurred in the Subject's genetic makeup as a result of intercourse with the alien-human hybrid.]

Further:

The Subject has clear memories of events which at first it was willing to share.

The Subject is lucid and extremely angry; it refuses to cooperate, and insists it be allowed to talk to its family and to the Swiss Embassy. It has asked for books – on mathematics and physics mostly, and a few novels, and for access to the Internet.

These requests have been refused – sensory and intellectual deprivation is being used for disciplinary and security purposes: no light, no sound, and minimal ability to move.

The subject is not being sedated for fear of damaging the fetus or compromising observations of the Subject and the effects of the Subject's "altered" DNA.

The subject is now manacled, is being fed intravenously, and is under constant electronic and visual monitoring. It is, once a day, allowed ordinary food, under strict supervision, and is allowed to walk around in a high-security room, under constant guard and supervision.

So far, the injection of the alien hybrid's DNA has not resulted in any observable changes in the Subject's body morphology or chemistry – or behavior.

The "alien" aspects of the subject therefore remain, up to this point in time, "latent."

In order to assure the Subject's docility and cooperation, a decision is pending on whether to totally or partially lobotomize the Subject, using chemical or surgical-electrical methods or a combination of said methods.

Such an intervention would not, experts assure us, compromise development of the fetus. The committee is divided on the question of whether this course of action is advisable or not. UPDATE NOTE: The pregnancy is approaching term; this has caused an acceleration of certain biological processes. Transformation into an alien hybrid seems likely in the near future –hours, days. It has therefore been decided to PROCEED WITH LOBOTOMIZATION IMMEDIATELY.

GENETIC NOTE: The Subject is a superb athlete, its ancestors have generally lived into their nineties or over 100 years, and its intelligence is in the highest quintal and multi-faceted; so that, if the half-alien creature intended to breed with the best the human race can offer, he – or it – could not have chosen better – our loss is the alien's gain.

POLITICAL NOTE: The Subject's family is a very rich, very old Swiss-Swedish family, father's side Swiss, mother's side Swedish, active in banking, pharmaceuticals, and medical research, and Swiss and Swedish politics, with extensive connections in Germany, France, and Spain, as well as in the United States, the UK, and China. If the Subject's continued existence became known, there would undoubtedly be a major diplomatic incident and a public relations disaster for this country and its anti-terrorist campaign.

NOTE ON ANDROMEDA CORPORATION: Andromeda Corporation has long been involved in cutting-edge biological research and research in various nanotechnologies and also in the integration of nano and biotechnologies. Andromeda Corporation is rumored to have access to alien – non-terrestrial – DNA and it is rumored that several hybrids have been created by Andromeda Corporation. As mentioned above, several intelligence organizations are rumored to have knowledge of the source of this alien DNA, the sample or prototype, but requests for clarification have been met with obfuscation or downright refusal to divulge any information. The CIA refuses to cooperate on information sharing as do the British, French, Chinese, and Russian intelligence organizations, and certain elements in the FBI. German intelligence and Italian intelligence refuse even to entertain inquiries. It is rumored that one highly regarded 'agent' – a paid assassin – rumored to be female – is in fact an alien-human hybrid and that this agent, quite possibly the mythical V, has been operational for many years – even decades – on behalf of various allied and non-allied governments.

V looked up. "And where is Monica Fabritz being held?"

"Ah," said Ben Kamu. He handed V a map and another print-out. V glanced at it: "The Everglades Agricultural Research Institute?"

"It's a cover name. It has nothing to do with agriculture. It took us a bit of digging. But that's where the lady – aka 'the Subject' – is, or was, as of last night when we tracked the last message out of there," said Claire.

"The zombies might get to the place today or tomorrow," Ben pointed at the map. "We've been trying to piece together a picture of their progress. It's spotty, because most communications are down or intermittent. We've been using drones and nano-drones to relay radio messages, and to pick up information, and to establish contact with Bio-Frontier and Alex and Helen."

"Well ..."

"At the Everglades Agricultural Research Institute," said Ben, "they are planning to lobotomize Monica Fabritz just before the baby arrives – they don't want maternal feelings to trigger any mother-child attachments and they are afraid the stress of the birth or birth pangs might trigger the alien side – cause her to morph and become reptilian, super-strong, and super dangerous."

"Like us," said Claire, "and certainly, for them, if she morphed, she would be difficult to handle."

"Not totally stupid on their part."

"No, but they are evil bastards who deserve to be exterminated, in my humble opinion," said Claire, with a reptilian grin, golden eyes gleaming, the slit maroon-black pupil dilating.

"Re-educated, maybe," said Ben.

"You're an idealist, Ben," said Claire, giving him a friendly flick of her forked tongue.

"And you," said Ben, stretching and yawning, "secretly, deep down, you, Claire, are a softie, a marshmallow!"

"Touché," said Claire, flapping her reptilian lids; she adored flirting with Ben, and sometimes she thought that …

"Get me a hover-jet," said V, "I'm leaving and I'm leaving now."

CHAPTER 4 – HELL

The President kicked off the bed covers, she turned over, she flipped onto her side, she kicked out – she was dreaming.

It was Hell. She was in a place like Hell. Maybe it really was Hell. The waters were burning, the oil slicks spreading, the air stank of sulfur; a reptile-demon, V, was grinning down at her and had pinned her down spread-eagled on her back in the oily smoky sulfurous slime.

"I am God," she was saying, "I am the pathway to God."

"Really?" said V. V jumped up and sat on the edge of the dinghy – now they were in a black dinghy somehow, in a sulfurous burning lake.

"I open people's souls." the president heard herself saying, "I pry their souls open with my knife, my words are my scalpel; so finally they really know who they are, who they are in God's world, which is our world, I open their eyes."

"To what do you open their eyes?"

"I open their eyes to themselves, to their true selves."

"To their *true* selves?" The V demon grinned.

"Yes."

"Pshaw! Fiddlesticks! There is no *true* self." The V demon bared her fangs and jumped on the President, pinning her down between reptilian super-muscular thighs. "Each person is a hodgepodge of selves, bits and pieces, flotsam and jetsam, wreckage and lifebuoys, dinghies and battleships, voices from the dark, hollering, screaming, and sometimes laughing. It's wreckage. It's chaos. The self is like an onion. You peel away all the layers, and there is nothing left, just peeled layers, and then a void. There is nothing essential to know, no center, nothing to reveal!"

"No, there is a true self – the eternal soul, clear as crystal, sparkling like a diamond," cried the president, "If people are going to live, they need to find themselves, their true center, their eternal soul."

"Maybe you're the Devil, not God!" The V demon grinned and hopped up and down, riding on the president.

"Bitch!" screamed the president. And, as she screamed, she morphed, turning into a python-like snake, at least eight feet long, a foot thick; she squirmed under the strong-as-steel muscular thighs of the V demon.

"Slut!" Demon V grinned, tightened her grip. "After all," the V demon hissed, "the self, if it exists, is not God; you are not revealing God, you are revealing … knowledge … knowledge of good and evil. You are offering the forbidden fruit. You are the serpent!"

The president reared her serpentine snout, hissed, opened wide her snake jaws, fangs dripping poison …

The V demon roared with laughter. "Yes, you are the creepy-crawly slippery belly-crawling, slimy creature who persuaded Eve to eat that wicked apple!" V seized the serpent's jaws with her claws and snapped the jaws shut, locking them tight together; venom dripped from between the sealed serpentine lips.

"Ah, got you!" V the demon exulted.

The president-serpent tried to yelp, tried to hiss, tried to bite, but she was muted, gagged, paralyzed in the grip of V the demon. With her jaws clamped shut, the president-serpent, purveyor of deadly, sinful, fatal, self-knowledge, bucked, twisted, tried to spring free, tried to coil her scaly body, and bounce away – nothing doing. Nothing worked. The demon laughed, bent down, and kissed the serpent on the snout, and let her go: "You are free! You are fallen! You are free to creep and crawl on your belly forever, and to slither in shame and cower under rocks and scout the barren soil for foul things to devour."

The president, turned over, groaned …

A nightmare, I'm having a nightmare.

Now the sea is flat and infinite and a wall of flame, floating on the water, is drifting to the west; a ship has sunk; America is burning, madness is spreading.

Two slippery scaly bodies rise out of the water. In a moonlit silver spray of droplets, they flip over the edge of matte-black dinghy, and slide, with a wet, slapping, slithery, seal-like sound, down onto the dinghy's soft rubber deck, the reptilian feet morphing from flippers into foot-claws.

"Want to fight?" says one demon.

"Yep, I want to fight," says the other demon.

Splash!

Splash!

Into the depths they go.

"Madam President, Madam President!" Marit was standing over her. "Madam President!"

"Yes, oh, yes, Marit! Oh, my God, I was having a dream – a nightmare, an awful nightmare."

"It was only a dream, Madam President," said Marit, "The hover-jet will soon be here to take you to the carrier task force – it will be here in about 15 minutes, Madam President."

"Oh, my God, and I need a shower," said the president, sliding out of bed.

"I'll make coffee and prepare a quick snack while you shower, Madam President." Marit smiled her most reassuring smile.

"Thank you. Do you dream, Marit, do you have nightmares?"

"Sometimes, Madam President, sometimes I dream."

"What do you dream of?"

"Oh, that is strange, Madam President. I dream of David, of David Stanford Adams III."

"David Stanford Adams III?"

"Yes, he was, well, he was my man," Marit looked down. "He loved me; he said he loved me – and, you know Madam President, he was a human person, a real human, one hundred percent human – and he said he loved me."

The shower was hot and wonderful and made the president feel human again – once again human and civilized, and it was strange, but as she showered, she thought that she recognized the name, David Stanford Adams III, and then she remembered. Yes, though she was asleep, she did remember bits and pieces; Marit told her a story and what kind of story was it? Oh, yes, it was a love story; it was Marit's love story.

"The jeans and T-shirt, I think, Marit," the president said, coming out of the shower, a towel wrapped around her. She kissed Marit on the cheek, and said, "I am sorry, Marit, I am sorry about David Stanford Adams III."

"Oh, Madam President, thank you! You can't know how much that means to me."

"You loved him, didn't you, Marit."

"I did, Madam President, yes, I did," Marit's eyes glistened; she was almost about to cry – as a SIN you were not allowed to mourn or expected to mourn. Most people didn't realize that you suffered anguish and loss and loneliness, just like anybody else, so people did not offer their shoulders for you to cry on, people did not tell you how sorry they were, people did not go out for a drink with you, or cook you a meal, people did not even think of it, and, now, to have words of comfort and understanding spoken by ... by the president! It was wonderful; it was almost too much.

CHAPTER 5 – SAMANTHA GOES LIVE

Tough-as-nails, battle-scarred cameraman Charlie Parr had found a refuge – for himself and for Sam. After gorgeous, super-keen, TV reporter Samantha Andrews caught the zombie thing and Charlie taped her up like a mummy, she had lain quiet, not causing too much trouble. And – thank the gods! – Charlie himself had not caught the damned thing!

Penthouse South-B-1 was ideal. It was empty. The refrigerator and cupboards were well-stocked. It had its own private rooftop swimming pool. The pristine water sparkled, lit by the pool lights and rippled by a slight breeze.

In the kitchen, Charlie found a large transparent garbage bag and he put it over his head and shoulders. He added more tapes around Samantha, taping her legs tighter together. She struggled feebly but didn't resist, and he laid her down on a metal-frame single bed in what must have been the kid's room.

He pulled the blinds down, so the room was in shade.

"Just lie quiet, Sam, okay, just lie quiet."

She whimpered once. It sounded like she was agreeing with him. She didn't move, so he figured she was okay; she was breathing and, for the moment at least, she was calm. Out of sight, out of mind, he figured. If she couldn't see him, she wouldn't bite him.

He went into the bathroom, stripped off, and took a hot shower, soaping down, closing his eyes and envisaging the last few hours – worse, somehow, than any of the battlefields he'd been in.

At least in war, when you were dead, you were dead.

Well, not always – sometimes the badly wounded lingered between life and death for a long time; and sometimes the maimed, their lives transformed into hell in a split second, would linger for years or decades – burnt beyond recognition, without arms or hands or legs, without a mind, or blind, or without hearing, or with their minds so fucked up that it was like they were trapped in hell itself; and of course they were forgotten, many of them, tucked away, invisible, in special institutions, lawns outside, sunny days outside, darkness inside: after a brief fanfare and all the pious words, people really didn't like to see the victims of the wars, the heroes who had fought to protect them, or who had fought, innocently, for some less glorious cause; seeing the mutilated remains reminded people of their guilt, of their responsibility – they had elected the people who started the wars, or who stumbled into them, who chose, for some goddamn reason, to undertake the slaughter, or, who, more simply, just fucking well failed to prevent it.

Charlie had known quite a few people – men and women – whose lives had been ended or destroyed by war and he had often come close to being terminated himself. He had been in an armored car when it was blown off the road, opened up like a tin can by an Improvised Explosive Device – those infamous IEDs – and Charlie was the only guy to come out of that particular tin can alive, and in fact, not only alive, but intact, though for a few weeks he had a trembling in his hands that he only got rid of by drinking scotch, and so he was always drunk when holding the camera but – luckily – it didn't show, and then after a little less than two months the trembling went away, and his hands were as steady as a rock again, and he put the scotch back in the cupboard. And then there was the time he, and a journalist, a feisty gal called Armanda, and their driver were kidnapped and the driver was murdered by the kidnappers, and the journalist was raped, and he, Charlie somehow, he was left alone, just handcuffed, chained, and left in a back room with a bucket for a toilet. He was a worker, like them, the kidnappers told him. As a cameraman, he was a member of the proletariat. Fuck the proletariat, thought Charlie, and after a week he managed to break the chain away from the wall, sneak out of the back room while the guard was dozing and while out in front of the building the others were arguing – he could hear them shouting. He managed to get the journalist – lying tied up and blindfolded in her own filth on a cot in another room – somehow managed to get her out of the place alive, climbing through a window, scrambling down a ravine, and across a creek, and into scrubland. She was not in very good shape after the rapes and the beatings – four front teeth gone, one eye blind – and he only found out about the rapes when they were on their way to the airport, after hiding for four days in the bush. It was a lucky escape, and he figured it happened because the kidnappers – a miserable gang of local tribal Jihadi bandits who thought they were holy revolutionary cowboys – were fighting among themselves about what to do – shoot all their prisoners now or later. Yeah, Armanda, a cute kid, gutsy, kind, intelligent, talented, and – well, she was never the same again.

So that was it: He was going to try to keep Samantha safe, somehow, and get her out of this damned fix. Maybe this zombie condition was reversible; maybe Samantha could be made whole again. He damned well hoped so!

Charlie came out of the shower with a deliciously soft white fluffy towel wrapped around his thin, hard, tanned waist, and walked through the living room and out the sliding glass doors, and stood on the terrace, next to the brightly shining swimming pool, and looked at the city and at the ocean.

I could use a smoke, he thought.

Quit, years ago.

In the city, buildings were burning, sirens were wailing; smoke rose in waves and drifted across the sky. One whole section to the south was veiled in heavy clouds of smoke. Charlie could see the flames.

But here, where they were, the electricity was still on. Charlie went inside, made himself a fresh coffee, ate a couple of spoonfuls of crunchy 100% – no hydrogenation – organic – at least that's what it said – "organic" – peanut butter, and went to his jacket and got out his U-Tab web phone.

He tested the thing. Yeah, pure miracle, it seemed to still be working. He tapped in the number. "Hey, it's me. Yeah. She's still alive. She's a gutsy kid. Have you heard if there's any cure to this thing? No, or you don't know, which is it? You don't think so. The Government says a vaccine will be coming shortly? Well, they would say that, wouldn't they? Okay, well, what should I do? Wait? Okay. Am I going to tell you the story? No. Not now, maybe later. Good-bye." Charlie looked at the U-Tab for a few seconds as if it were a filthy, evil thing with a will of its own.

He went into the kids' room and saw that Samantha was squirming, but gently, slowly, trying to work her way out of the duct tape.

Charlie wondered if she needed water, if she needed food, if she needed to pee, if she needed to shit, but he thought, there was no way he could get close to her, and if he caught the damned thing, well, then, they were both done for. He looked in the medicine cabinet. But there was nothing that he could use to tranquilize her, and if he tried it would be dangerous and there'd be no way he could know it would work. He shook his head. The way she was, maybe even taking Aspirin would kill her, damn it!

He went into the room, sat down next to the bed, and sat close to her. He wanted to hold her hand, but that wasn't a good idea either.

After about five minutes, he went out of the room, turned out the light, and he got a book from a bookshelf – a dog-eared paperback of Ernest Hemingway's "A Farewell to Arms" – he frowned, strange to find such a book here! – and a fold-up chair from the rooftop terrace – glancing for a second at the brilliant swimming pool, under the terrace lights, the peacefully rippling water – and he came and sat down in the corridor next to the bedroom door and he started to read. Old sentences, old phrases – some of them he knew by heart.

Then he thought about it, set Hemingway aside, and got the old-fashioned transistor radio that he had spotted sitting on the kitchen shelf. He turned it on, and listened to the news, full of static, and intermittent – a stream of horror stories. He listened with one earphone, keeping the other ear clear, just in case.

The thing was spreading; there seemed to be no way to stop it.

Some commentators, in the north, were speculating that the only way to stop it would be to nuke Florida.

"Yeah," said one of the pundits, "But everybody has a grandmother in Florida – nuking Florida would be political suicide."

"Political suicide," Charlie muttered, "political suicide – what an obscenity! Who cares about political suicide?" He was beginning to think that maybe if the human race did perish it would not be such a bad idea.

Fuck!

No, Charles James Parr, he told himself, don't let yourself become a cynic, you are no different from the others, and you are no better than the worst of them; we are all in this together, every goddamn one of us; and thinking that the human race would be better off dead is definitely an evil thought. We've come this far; we should survive; we must survive, goddamn it! He half closed his eyes; and the images came unbidden: he'd covered wars in Africa and wars in the Middle East, he'd seen women with their arms and breasts chopped off, women who were raped while they were dying and after they were dead. He'd seen priests and nuns disemboweled because they had tried to protect their parishioners or tried to protect the hospital where they worked. He'd seen journalists with their writing hand cut off; he'd been there in Moscow, and one of the first on the scene, when a woman journalist was shot in the elevator of her apartment building because she'd exposed what the local political thugs were doing – her head bloody against the mesh wire of the elevator cage, ash blond hair, long, streaming down, soaked in blood, blue eyes wide open, beautiful eyes, startled, wide open, beautiful even in death. He'd seen drones and missiles vaporize kindergarten kids, wipe out wedding parties, and incinerate buses full of pilgrims – men, women, and children. He'd seen kids who'd been purposely addicted to drugs and recruited into child armies, turned into perpetually stoned, cold-eyed, child soldier killers, at age eight, ten, twelve, and thirteen. Up close, he'd seen kids torn apart by fragmentary bombs and by barrel bombs and by shrapnel grenades, containing ball bearings, nails, and pebbles, and disguised as toys; he'd been on a bus that was hit by a missile and had seen the kid beside him – an eighteen-year-old – decapitated; he'd seen … Yes, and he didn't want to think about it: He'd seen and he'd found his own girlfriend, a twenty-three-year-old French girl, Michelle Lesauvage, a doctor with Doctors without Borders, disemboweled, her abdomen, from vagina to belly and heart, one open, folded-back, gaping wound, lying in her tent when the rebels from …

Her eyes were open – wide open.

He had knelt by her side and closed them.

Enough …

After Michelle died, Charlie had decided then that he'd had enough of foreign parts, of far-flung adventures – the hotel rooms, the bars, the one-night stands, the dusty roads, the jungles with leeches, mosquitoes, cotton-mouths – of being a cameraman on assignment … It was the final straw. There'd been the armored car, Charlie climbing out of the wreckage, holding the camera, shooting the smoking twisted metal, the bodies, raw red meat blackened by fire, gaping mouths, eyes still open, but not seeing anything – the road where it happened, the stinking hot, blindingly brilliant, desert all around; there'd been the raped journalist Armanda, sitting beside him in the car to the airport, stony-faced, saying, with a lisp from the missing teeth and swollen tongue and chapped, broken lips, and the one bloodied and broken eye, and without looking at him, "They raped me, Charlie, they held a knife to my neck and they raped, me, and they pushed the barrel of a pistol into me and they said they were going to pull the trigger. Charlie, some of these guys were fifteen years old, I mean, some of these guys, Charlie, they could have been my little brother." Charlie held out his hand, pressed her hand, and she leaned towards him, and he put his arm around her. Finally, she slept. At the airport they sat at a small table and drank coffee. She didn't say anything more.

He'd come back to the States for the simple domestic life.

So, now, what was the situation? He looked around. He was in a luxury penthouse and everything seemed calm, almost too calm. The risk was that they would get trapped up here, or that he would catch the thing out of the air, or maybe the building would be invaded by zombies, or maybe a stove was left on in some apartment and the building would catch fire …

The radio was whispering in his ear. "The vice president has ordered all bio-tech firms to stop research immediately. Troops have been sent to … The Reverend Paul Coughlin declared that the plague is God's message to humanity. Our pride, he said, is being punished. The plague is a divine sign that …"

Charlie dozed, his head falling forward on his chest, or lolling sideways on his shoulder. He would jerk it upwards, waking himself up, sweating in horror, his stomach a knot of fear, and then he glanced over, and saw that Samantha was still there.

The radio was still whispering in his ear – nonsense and more nonsense. He shut it off.

He began to doze again, his eyes shut, opened, shut, and his head lolled, and then he was asleep – and as he slept the zombie plague spread.

"Charlie," he heard the voice, "Ghhhhhrrrr, Charlie, gghhhr, ghhhhrrrr, Charlie!"
He snapped back awake.

Samantha had levered herself up and was half sitting against the back of the bed, and against the wall with its big poster of a startled cartoon duck – who was wearing sunglasses – sitting in a cartoon deck chair. "Sitting Duck" it said. There were bullet holes drawn on the cartoon wall behind the duck. Samantha's legs were still taped together, and her arms taped to her sides. Her eyes were still taped shut and most of her hair appeared to have fallen out; but, maybe by eating the tape, she'd evidently chewed her mouth free – it was dribbling green goo.

"Charlie …" she said, weakly, and then growled and bared her teeth.
"Yeah, Sam, what is it?"
"Grrhhhh … ah … Grrrh," green goo spilled from her mouth, "Aim camera and mike, Charlie … Grrhhhh … story … Grrhhhh … from inside … Charlieeeee."
"You want me to shoot you like this, Sam?" Charlie had gotten up out of his fold-up chair and had pulled a transparent plastic garbage bag over his head.
"Yesssss, Charliiieeeee, grrrrhhhhhhhh. Important … Ghhhhhrrrr … must know … people … grrrrh … must know …"

"Okay … Okay, Sam. I'll set it up and let you know when I'm ready. Do you want me to take off the blindfold …?"

"Grrrhhhhhh … only … only … if not dangerous … grrhhhh … yeee … grrrrh …" more green goo dribbled, but at least didn't spray, "only if not dangerous for you, Charlie," Samantha managed to breathe out, one brief string of articulate words.

"Okay, Sam. Look, I suggest we start with you blindfolded, it's more dramatic, and then I'll take the blindfold off, and that way they'll see how tough this is. Before you start, I'll give the background of what happened to you, Sam, is that okay?"

"Grrhhhh … Grrhhhh … grrrrh … okay … Grrrrhhhh … yes … okay … good … grrrhgggh … great … idea, Charlie!"

Charlie set up the camera and he set up the directional mike and he snuck over with a big plastic bag covering everything but his hand – he had put on the rubber gloves he'd found in the kitchen, and he pinned a lapel mike to what remained of Sam's dress.

Then he phoned in. "Shelly, Bill, we are ready to go live again, if you are interested. This is Sam's decision."

"What, she's not infected?" Shelly sounded almost indignant.

"Oh, yeah, she's infected alright, she's a zombie you'll be glad to know, but she's fighting back. She wants to give the inside story of what it's like to be a zombie. The zombie's own story. Right, Sam?"

"Grrrhhhhhh … grrhhhh … yes, Charlie, right, ghhhhhrrrr."

"I'll give some background, Shelly, and then I'll turn it over to Sam. Right now, she's blindfolded, but I'm going to take the blindfold off. She'll start talking with the blindfold on, then I remove it, and she'll report from where she is …"

So, with the camera rolling, and broadcasting, live …

Charlie, from off screen, the camera showing only the child's drawings and the sitting duck poster with the cartoon bullet holes on the wall above Samantha, gave the background: What their mission was; what they had seen in the streets; how Sam had been infected, how brave she had been, and how they had escaped. "Now," he said, "Sam has sacrificed herself to discover the truth. Samantha Andrews is a zombie, and she's going to tell the zombie story, from the inside." The camera swung slowly down, revealing Sam, propped up, taped down, arms taped to her sides, legs taped together, just her mouth and cleavage showing, her eyes taped shut, while Charlie ended by explaining how they'd found an empty apartment, that he had taped Sam down and had protected himself with plastic bags, and now Sam was ready to report from the inside of the head of a zombie.

"Sam, it's all yours now, I'm rolling."

"Grrrhhhh … Hi, this is Samantha Andrews, reporting … ghhhh," more bright goo splashed and sprayed from her mouth, "gghhhhhrrrr, reporting, hungry, oh, so hungry, grrrrrhhhh, from Miami … to bite, want to bite, gghhhhhhrrrr, want to … devour … ghhhhrrrr, to devour Charlie … to devour anybody … human flesh … worst thing are the voices …"

"I'm coming in, Sam, I'm going to take the tape off your eyes …"

"Grrrhhhh … yeah … grrhhhh … be careful, Charlie, be grrrhhhhh careful."

Charlie appeared on screen, covered in a transparent plastic garbage bag, well, actually two plastic garbage bags, and wearing the long sleeved rubber gloves.

He tore the tape off Samantha's eyes.

Her eyes glowed phosphorous green and she had no pupil or iris that could be seen. Jesus Christ Almighty, thought Charlie.

He retreated behind the camera.

"Grrrrh … grrrhhhhh … Thanks, Charlie … gruuuu …worst thing … are the … voices … the voices in my head … grhhhhh … telling me … what to do … I don't want them … grrrrh," she slobbered and splashed green goo, "I don't want them … telling me to … grrrhhhhh … kill … It tells me to kill … grrhhhh snarl splash … one voice really … calls itself … calls itself …"

"What does it call itself, Sam?"

"Calls … grrhhhh … yeewwoooohhh … Ahhhh … calls … itself … Puppet Master, the Puppet Master … our God, the Puppet Master … Dmitry, it calls itself Dmitry the Puppet Master …"

Within minutes, Charlie Parr and Samantha Andrews were world-famous. Samantha reported every little quiver of feeling. She spurted green goo, she dribbled from her nostrils, she stuck out her tongue and wagged it, she screamed to be let go, her eyes glowed green like green glutinous jelly, what little was left of her hair continued to fall out, she wiggled and tried to break free, sometimes Charlie, wrapped in his plastic, had to go in and wrap her up with more duct tape.

And all the time, Samantha kept reporting what was going on in her head, what she was feeling. "We are all puppets, we are all puppets, going to destroy, going to destroy, that's the voices talking, the voice, it tells me, Grrhhhh, kill, kill, kill, eat, eat, eat, and we are Dmitry puppets, Apocalypse, Dmitry puppets, grrrhhhhh, and we will change it all, grhhhhh, grhhhhh, slobber, slobber, slobber, Apocalypse, Dmitry Puppet Master says, Apocalypse, the End, Puppet Master says, Kill them all, kill them all, kill them all … kill all humans … kill … kill … kill."

"Dmitry Puppets, Dmitry Puppet Master," said Charlie. "Did you get that Bill, Shelly?"

"We got it. What does it mean?"

"Grrrhhhhh," Sam spit out a wave of green goo, "Death, Dmitry. Grrrhhhh, means Death … grrhhhh … Death for all … Dark God … grrhhhh … the Dark God … Apocalypse, End of Beginning … Ghhrrrhhh – Beginning of End …"

"Dark God, Sam?"

"Dark … grrhhhh …" Samantha spat out a long ropy, bubbling, thick, string of green goo, it landed on her chest and legs, and wiggled this way and that, as if it were alive, "Dark … God … Darkness … Infinite … Inside me, Charlie, it's inside me, inside me … Help, Charlie, help!"

"Okay, Sam, nothing's going to happen … you'll be okay."

"The Dark God … Charlie … The Dark God … it's grrhhhh … grrhhhh … eating me from within, Charlie, going to consume us all, Charlie, eat up everyone into darkness and slavery and death … grrhhhh and kill, kill, kill … grrhhhh … the Puppet Master will kill everything, Charlie, even the plants that grow … grrhhhh and the great earth itself, Charlie, even the great earth itself … grrrhhhhh …"

"Did you get that, Bill?"

"I got it."

"Two seconds, you are on – two, one …"

Bill Brothers turned towards the camera. "Our courageous reporter, Samantha Andrews, in the front line in America's battle against terror, is giving us, ladies and gentlemen, extraordinary and invaluable information. As a zombie, Samantha has direct insight into the mind – or minds – behind this extraordinary attack on America, an attack, ladies and gentlemen, not only against America, but against the whole human race. Samantha said, and I quote, 'The Dark God is going to consume us all; it is going to eat up everyone into darkness and slavery and death; the Puppet Master will kill everything, even the plants that grow and the great Earth itself, even the great Earth itself.'" Bill Brothers just stared at the camera, a bead of sweat rolled down the side of his forehead. He blinked. The truth was that – perhaps for the first time in his adult life – Bill Brothers was experiencing a real emotion. He cleared his throat; his eyes glistened. "We are talking, here, ladies and gentlemen, about the Apocalypse," he cleared his throat again, "We are talking about Armageddon, ladies and gentlemen, we are talking about the decisive battle between Good and Evil," he regained momentum, his voice deepened, "And America, as always, is in the front line of the fight – for good, against evil. We are the citadel, ladies and gentlemen, we are the City upon the Hill; we are the beacon of hope – for all mankind. We must not and we will not fail!" Bill Brothers paused, knowing his voice was about to break – to think, that his beautiful Samantha had been reduced to a mummified, half-mad, drooling freak! He cleared his throat. "And, now, a message from our sponsors: Paradise Food for Dogs and Cats – and ferrets, if you have a ferret."

Two cowardly cartoon dogs and one feisty cartoon cat now took over the screen. In a small oval, a ferret provided the American Sign Language commentary.

CHAPTER 6 – DOCTOR HARRIS

Who the fuck are those people on the road? Doctor Kevin Harris Ph.D. D. Sc., etc., etc., hated obstacles, any obstacles. He was already late. He glanced at his watch. They couldn't be those zombie creatures, not out here, not this far north.

"What are those people?" he said out loud.

"I don't know, Doctor, but they don't look friendly." Henry Black was Doctor Harris's usual driver – Henry was impeccable, always on time, always precise, never made a fucking mistake, not like everybody else, not like all the other fucking incompetent fucking losers.

"Maybe we'd better take a detour."

"There's no detour we can take, Doctor, not out here."

Doctor Kevin Harris was headed to the Everglades Agricultural Research Institute, deep in the Everglades.

His task – which he delighted in – was to carry out an operation that had been planned for months – a contingency response to an event that had been amply foretold, and which he, personally, had predicted. Why the powers-that-be had not decided to act much earlier, was beyond Doctor Harris's comprehension.

It should have been done long ago – the dangers of waiting were just too great. Bureaucrats are fucking idiots!

The overdue phone call giving the green light for the operation had come – finally and at last – just this morning, and Doctor Harris had answered it himself. His wife, Ashley Samos – she'd insisted on keeping her maiden name – was out in the backyard, already, doing her exercises – Ashley was lying on her back stretching out her arms, high in the air, bracing her pelvis – on the rubber mat she had bought for the purpose.

Ashley was eighteen years younger than Doctor Harris and she was seven months pregnant with their first child and he was very proud, Doctor Kevin Harris was, of having such a beautiful young wife: her milk-chocolate skin glowed, her dark eyes smoldered, her jet-black, lustrous hair shone, and she was so happy, bearing the child, that she ran her hands over her swollen belly so often, and got a dreamy look. "Oh, Kevin, I am so happy, you have made me so happy!"

She was determined the child would have the best upbringing, and she was determined too that she would keep her shape and her beauty, for her husband.

Doctor Kevin Harris, who grew his hair long and who wore colorful shirts and liked to run on the beachfront every evening towards sunset and thought of himself as at least twenty years younger than he was, could now feel the surge of pride – pride in possession – as he watched her through the window doing her exercises, very carefully, and, just behind her was the bright cobalt blue of the swimming pool, barely rippling in the morning light, and the green of the well-watered lawn and the flowers she tended so carefully. Life was good.

Doctor Harris said to the voice on the phone – a very high-placed person in the Security Establishment – that, yes, he could do it, certainly, he could perform the lobotomy on "the Subject" this evening when he got out to the Institute, all the chemicals were there, and he had prepared the procedure and he had all the information – the scans, the X-rays, the MRIs, the analyses – he needed to do it, and, no, he really wouldn't need an assistant, it would be quite simple, really, it merely involved several injections and a highly targeted use of ultra-high-frequency sound, ultra-high vibrations, an excavating remote controlled nano-drone, and radiation, focused on the areas in the fontal cortex that were to be destroyed, and the center of all volition and decision-making would be eliminated; and, he said, "Once I have given her the anesthetic it will be quite simple."

No fuss, no bother.

"All I need is one male nurse in attendance," he said, "Duff Brent will do if he's on duty tonight; he can also control the anesthetic dosage."

"This has become urgent, Doctor Harris."

"Yes, I understand, the time is near. I'll get to the Institute at about 11:00 o'clock tonight."

"This will work, won't it, doctor?"

"Certainly, the subject will feel no emotion, and will have no will-power or decision-making ability. She will be a living doll, passive and blank, a puppet.

We will be able to control her every move. We can insert a remote-control mechanism into what's left of her brain. So, if she undergoes the change, then she is ours, a mere tool, an instrument. She will be a robot – she will not be dangerous at all."

"*It*, Doctor Harris, remember – we call the subject *it*."

"Yes, of course, *it*," Doctor Harris frowned; he clenched his fists; fury rose; he fought it back; he must not – *must not* – lose his temper; making any mistake, or even *seeming* to make a mistake, whatever it was and however trivial it was, was extraordinarily annoying; he was excessively proud of his intelligence. "*It* will be a mere instrument, putty in our hands, sir; *it* will be putty in our hands." Now, he permitted himself a small giggle – a beautiful woman, reduced to a living doll – how sublime!

"Good luck, Doctor Harris. You will give me, personally, a full report."

"Yes, of course."

"Verbal – nothing is to be written."

"Yes, of course."

The line went dead. It was clearly encrypted. Doctor Harris hung up the phone and stood absolutely still in the kitchen for a moment staring, absent-mindedly, out the window.

Ashley was stepping slowly, gingerly, into the pool, holding on to the railing. She had a fixed routine. She would swim up and down for twenty lengths, then she would climb out and towel herself down, very carefully, and then she would change, putting on one of those long flimsy spaghetti-strap pleated crepe dresses she wore, in a bright colors, perhaps canary yellow, perhaps russet red, perhaps indigo – they set off her perfect complexion and exquisite chocolate-latte coloring strikingly – and she would sit down and begin to work on her thesis: Her books and papers were lined up on her desk and she had written down, as she always did the night before, a list of the things she intended to accomplish today: Complete the notes for tonight's lecture on Picasso, prepare next week's lecture on Piero della Francesca; make notes on Sigmund Freud's essay on Leonardo …

Ashley was a treasure. Doctor Harris was very proud of having acquired her – he had spotted her in the Metropolitan Museum in New York two years ago. She was staring at a small Greek statue; he stared at her; her silhouette and figure were an intriguing glimpse of perfection; she became aware of his presence, she turned, he saw her, and … on his part, it was instant desire, desire to possess, and lust, absolute lust, at first sight. He must penetrate, he must subdue, he must defile, this virginal wonder.

It took a lot of persuading to get Ashley to fall in love – every technique and trick in the book – because she was wary, extremely intelligent, and afraid of being hurt.

He picked up the cup of coffee he had been drinking – Ashley had prepared his breakfast before beginning her exercise routine.

He walked out to sit down in a deck chair and just watch her swim up and down.

She greeted him with a small wave and continued swimming. Doctor Harris closed his eyes. Tonight, in a crucial way, he would make history: he would neutralize an alien invasion. Yes, you could actually put it that way: He would neutralize an alien invasion.

Tonight, he would perform an operation on another young woman, a young woman wrapped in secrecy, a young woman who was no longer entirely human, a young woman the world believed was dead; a young woman who was known merely as "The Subject."

"It," not "she" – how pedantic and evasive those mealy-mouthed, dithering, procrastinating bureaucrats were!

He picked up the U-Tab and glanced at the news: "This Evening President du Bois Hughes is to visit Miami. After giving a speech to the American Bar Association on the world's largest and most luxurious cruise ship, the *Eden of the Seas*, President du Bois Hughes will ..."

Ashley had no idea what work Doctor Harris did. She thought he was involved in cutting-edge research on the medical implications – the dangers for humans – of working with hazardous materials, fertilizers, chemical fodder for animals, and so on. She had no idea how vital his work was to national security.

"*It,*" not "*she*" – how ridiculous!

The "it," the "Subject," had once been human; but now she was half-alien, a hybrid; but she had not yet morphed into her hybrid form.

It was presumed the hybrid form would be like the Reptile Man – extremely strong, extremely dangerous – a killer without a mind or conscience, a deadly machine to be neutralized and mastered.

It was essential therefore that the young woman's mind be "neutered" – obliterated – before *she* did morph because it was highly likely that, once *she* had morphed, it would be impossible to control her.

In the last few days there had been signs that her physiology was speeding up, that changes were taking place, and there were indications that these little "tremors" were warnings of changes to come.

Such a speedup in the subject's metabolism was natural as her time approached, Doctor Harris had pointed out, and could have been predicted, and indeed he had predicted it, and he had urged the authorities to make a preventive strike – early lobotomy – to preempt the danger – but of course the idiots shillyshallied, and delayed, pissed time away, and hummed and hawed – and now the time was short; maybe there was no time.

The creature was due to have her baby – any day now. What was her name when she was human …? Ah, yes, Monica Fabritz … Swiss, a foreigner, not even American!

Monica Fabritz – good-looking too, exceptionally so, and intelligent, well, IQ in the stratosphere somewhere, oh, well …

"*It*," not "*she*" …

His driver, Henry Black, had come to pick him up at ten o'clock that evening. A terrorist attack had taken place a few hours before and the news was not good. The *Eden* had been infected by some sort of biological weapon, the President was reported dead, and the *Eden* had crashed into the shore, and these zombies, or whatever they were, were wandering all over the place. Ashley was at the University, delivering her Picasso lecture, Doctor Harris left her a message telling her to get home right away and not to leave the house, to lock the doors, and not to let anyone in.

"Who the devil are those people on the road?"

"I think they are … well, doctor, they are not normal. Look at the way they walk."

"Zombies, they are those zombie things …"

"I'm going to try to make a dash for it, Doctor; this is a fast car; we'll make it."

"You're sure?"

"As sure as I can be of anything, doctor." Henry gunned the SUV, and he headed straight for the line of zombies; they were advancing like strange puppets; their arms were dangling in front of them, hanging loose; they had baleful faces, they were foaming at the mouth, and spewing god knows what liquid.

Wasn't there something about the zombie thing being infectious?

Maybe they shouldn't get near them, maybe they should turn back, maybe they should …

But it was too late.

CHAPTER 7 – MONICA

The low-flying Andromeda Corporation hover-jet skimmed over ocean then sand, then forest. V looked out the window. When Claire showed her the document – Ultra Top Secret – that she and Ben had extracted from secret government files, V had been annoyed – to put it mildly. Monica Fabritz was pregnant, she was a hybrid, and she was a prisoner of the Government, and they were going to lobotomize her. Over my dead body, thought V. Lobotomize! She would save the woman and save the baby.

The Anti-Christ …

It meant something, but she wasn't sure what.

A baby is a baby is a baby is a baby …

The air glowed with fires in Miami and Fort Lauderdale.

The zombie plague was spreading, getting close to the breakout point, after which …

The matte-black stealth supersonic hover-jet had flown in from *Andromeda II,* keeping as close to the ocean and then to the ground as it dared – in order to minimize the possibility radar detection. It skimmed over power lines, abandoned warehouses, treetops, sand dunes, and lampposts.

The hum of the hover-jet, its quiet almost imperceptible vibrations, took V back to one of her road trips across America. She really did love the Great Republic, the United States of America, that strange utopian crazy dreaming cruel mad imperious violent giant of a transcontinental nation.

How long ago had it been, two years, or three …?

She had been driving for hours, late at night, lulled by the hum of the motor, the feathery whispering of the wind against the windshield, and the endless sleepy unspooling of the pavement and that single hypnotic broken white line flashing in front of her, and she was listening to George Apostolou and his syndicated night program: "Our Worst Fears."

It gave V a perverse pleasure, a delicious little frisson, that she was one of "Our Worst Fears." This was delicious, this was delectable! She grinned. *It is all about me! I am the monster they fear!* She reached out and took a sip of coffee from the thermos. It was a vast and desolate desert where she was, flat land, stretching away, and it was – she glanced at the car clock – two o'clock in the morning – the motel was still three hours away.

She would sleep in the shadows, curtains pulled tight shut, all the livelong day, while the sun blazed outside and people went about their business; and then, when night came, she would hunt.

Just driving across America was an adventure, on the road, in a road movie, on the loose, tasting the absolute freedom of endless limitless ever-receding frontiers, the motor humming softly, listening to those wild intimate crazy voices in the night.

The relentless focus of the headlights was mesmerizing, as it tunneled in, on an endless onrushing stream of sage bush, with the dusty shoulder of the road and a few scraggly trees flashing by.

V was entering the dead zone, a place where all agriculture had dried up and given up and the people had moved out, leaving behind the expanding dust bowl – the ghost towns, decaying silos, empty wooden houses, vacant barns, rusting farm machinery, oil derricks, and fracking towers.

Streams of dust and little eddies of dust swept across the road, whirling up in the headlights – ghosts.

It was then, out in this emptiness, that V had turned on the radio, wondering what weird station she might be able to pick up in the haywire static-ridden atmosphere.

She loved the random chaos of old-fashioned American nighttime radio, all those voices from far away, and she remembered, decades before, almost a century before, listening to radio at night, AM radio from far away, interrupted by flashes of static, and in those days she could tell that the static was emitted by lightning flashes, and by tracking the static – the number and quality of the bursts – she could tell, she could feel in her gut, how far away the thunderstorm was, how it was moving over the land, sweeping over the forests and mountains, and tumbling, in thunderous downpour chaos, over ridges and hills and escarpments, and gliding, a dark watery curtain illuminated by great flashes of light, over lakes and rivers, and how it was headed her way, coming closer and closer, as the rusty sporadic bursts of static got more frequent, and she had a feeling in her mind, in her gut, of the lay of the land, of the vastness of America, of the mountains, rivers, canyons, plains, and the strata of soil and rock and sediment and granite and limestone and schist and glacial rubble, the geological violence, the sheer explosive energy, underlying it all, and she had a feeling, too, deep inside, for the invisible stresses and strains of the earth's crust, the fractures and micro-fractures, the shards and fragments, pushing, straining, pulling, and the vast continental and oceanic plates, slowly moving, slowly building up tension, fiery tension, and she had a visceral sensation, too, of the plants, grasping at the soil with their tendrils and roots, reaching for the sun, drinking up water and soil and air, splitting rocks, and she had a dizzying awareness, too, of the masses of air moving, hot and cold fronts, thunderous and rainy, clear and dry, high pressure and low, moving towards her, and sweeping across the land – America!

She wondered, often, during those long hot electric nights, lying naked on top of a hard flat motel bed, with a fan in the window turning slowly, creating a slow lazy whirring fluttery breeze, she often wondered where this feeling came from, this feeling for the land, this visceral, sexual, erotic drunken love, and this passion, this visceral stirring in her gut and in her belly, and in her loins, this whirlwind of sensuality that was a physical thing, a presence, a spirit, in her mind. America! And she felt them moving around her and within her, all those immense terrestrial forces, forces beyond human understanding. It was America, it was Earth, it was the planet, and she was in love with it.

Now, more than a century after those first nocturnal serenades, the radio again spoke and it was George Apostolou, a deep mellow voice, a little gravely, but warm and soothing, a voice you could trust, and it said …

"Are you afraid?" The voice paused. The silence in the car suddenly struck V as ominous, heavy with the little presences of emptiness, of absence, of nobody being there, with just the soft sound of the car motor and of the dark asphalt and of the night wind against the windshield.

Then, the voice, George's voice, answered itself. "*I'm* afraid. I'm afraid of the things in the night, of the things that move, of the things that think, and of the things that grow, that grow silently, secretly, slowly."

The wind buffeted the windshield, the motor purred, the pavement rumbled underneath the wheels, disappearing into the past.

"They are watching us, those things that grow, that grow silently. And I'm afraid, friends, I'm oh so afraid, of the lies, of all the lies. The airwaves are filled with lies, the papers are filled with lies, the streets are filled with lies, the lies our politicians tell us, the lies our so-called leaders tell us, all our leaders, our so-called pundits, our business leaders, our political leaders and those who would call themselves our spiritual leaders – all lies – and all liars."

Again, the voice paused.

"And even, my friends, the lies we tell ourselves. Yes, my friends, I am afraid. I am deadly afraid. I am afraid for you, I am afraid for me, and I am afraid for this great Republic of ours which we call our home. I am afraid for the City upon a Hill. I am afraid for all our beliefs and all our hopes."

The wind rippled against the windshield. A moth or bug, a quick blur of light and dark, a life, an ephemeral life, splattered, squish, against the glass. The white intermittent center line, faded now, rushed out of the darkness. From right and left, non-stop, scrub, and clumps of brush, and banks of yellow drifting sand rushed towards V, zipped by, and faded into yesterday.

"Fear is wisdom, my friends, fear is wisdom. Fear is our advanced warning system, it's our radar, it's our sonar. Fear sees far. Fear sees deep. So, let your fear speak, my friends, let your fear speak, unleash your terror – give voice to your fears and let the truth be known!"

The voice stopped and there was a musical interlude while V thought, "Gosh, this guy is really good. He's making me afraid of myself. I'm one of the monsters of the night; maybe I should phone in and tell him what I am!"

"We are back, my friends, and our first caller tonight is from Harold Sibelius in Kansas. Hello, Harold, you say you've studied the trees and that the trees think, and are watching us ..."

"Yes, George, we are related as you know to all living things, and there are forms of consciousness, possessed by living things, that escape us, we don't notice what is right in front of us and all around us. We're being watched, and we are being judged."

"Who is watching, who is judging us, Harold?"

"The trees, the plants, all the living things – they form a kingdom, they communicate, they watch, they listen, they judge."

"How's the judgement falling – are we guilty, are we innocent?"

"Guilty as hell, George, we are guilty has hell. We are the rapists of the planet and all that lives on it. We are fouling our nest, George, and everybody else's. Let me just give you an idea of how we are destroying the various foundations of our existence!"

Foundations of our existence, true, true, certainly true, mused V, her hands light on the wheel, her eyes blinking, dazed by the whirring luminous passage of time, of the night ...

A flickering red neon sign – *Motel: Vacancies* – The sign was spraying sparks and dangling, half-broken, from a billboard; it surged up, swept by, and disappeared. Behind the sign, out in the darkness, was the low-lying, burned-out hulk of what had once been a motel.

The road without end streamed towards her – hardly any other cars; just from time to time a pickup truck; and that was all, just asphalt, streaming towards her.

Time sped by – streaming asphalt, a white broken line …

"I'm talking with Walter Bush from Little Rock. Now, what were you saying, Walter?"

"Well, George, I was saying that scientists tell us electromagnetic waves – radio waves and light waves – they say travel through a vacuum; there is nothing there; but, I ask you, is there really nothing there? How can any form of energy be transmitted to a void where there is nothing? Now, I think that what is there is Dark Matter, and that this Dark Matter, which we can't see, and which makes up maybe 90 percent of the mass in the universe, why this dark matter, I think is alive, it is the reverse of the Holy Spirit, George, it is the Dark Spirit, the Dark God, which shadows us and our world, it is the manifestation of the Dark Side, George, it is the Dark God, it is Satan, George, it is …"

A small town surged up – it looked totally deserted – and then it was gone, facades of buildings, one dilapidated mall, a small church – it all seemed one-dimensional, a stage set, not a real town.

Maybe it wasn't a real town.

If you are alone for hours on the road, a hallucinatory sensation of unreality settles in. Everything looks fake, a façade, a stage set, décor for some western or horror flick.

More miles and miles of asphalt went on, streaming towards her.

"Now, here's a subject to reflect on," said George Apostolou, in his soothing, deep voice. "Those new earthquakes and tremors in Yellowstone National Park, do they presage a volcanic eruption? Even after the events of 2027, few people stop to think, but here in the United States, we are sitting on one of the largest super volcanoes on the planet. Last time it exploded, and it was just, relatively speaking, a hiccup for the super volcano …"

V pulled over and stopped, in the middle of nowhere.

She opened the door, got out of the car, and stretched. She walked up and down. The air was warm. The night was dark. Somewhere far away she heard something that sounded like a coyote. She sniffed the air – just sand and sagebrush and empty air and, aside from the coyote, no sound at all except the air itself moving slowly over the desert.

She got back into the car and pulled out onto the road and stared again at the onrushing asphalt, at the broken white line. George Apostolou was still on the air.

"Now, I want to ask you, George, because I do have my suspicions and I do have my reasons: are people really people or are they really just pods, facsimiles, masks?"

"I don't know, Karen, what do you think?"

"I think we've already been invaded, George, we have the aliens in our midst. They are all around us, George, and they pretend to be people. I mean even your best friend, George, she could be an alien."

"Now, let me ask you, Karen, are the aliens benign, and friendly, or are they evil?"

"Well, look at this, George, we have a beautiful planet here, it's a planet fit for living on, and it is full of riches, George, so these intergalactic wanderers they will be looking for a place to settle down, to exploit. I think Professor Greg Erdman has pointed this out in his books."

"Yes, Professor Erdman is often a guest on this program."

"That's right, George, well, Professor Erdman is a great man – a prophet not honored in his own country, if I may be so bold."

"You may, Karen, you may be so bold."

"Well, George, if the aliens have technology, George, they will be predators, not herbivores, not cud-chewing cows, no sir, they will be warriors, exploiters, conquerors, they will have the same adventurous spirit that made us humans into the warriors, exploiters, and conquerors that we are – and, George, they will have no mercy. Why should they have mercy on us? I mean, after all, George, have we shown any mercy to the other species that inhabit the planet? No, George, we have not! We have enslaved them, exploited them, and massacred them. So, I expect the aliens will do the same to us ..."

The gentle rhythms of the hover-jet shifted slightly, just a nuance, but V woke with a start – she had been in a reverie, back a few years before, travelling all night, virtually all night, driving across the desert, listening to one of her favorites – George Apostolou on "Our Worst Fears."

Gus Hurst, the crew member sent to watch over her, nodded. "It's time, V. We're almost there."

The hover-jet was slowing down; it came to a standstill fifty feet above a dirt side road deep in the Everglades. It hovered, almost soundless, below the line of almost all radar devices.

V went to the door and looked down.

The country road was a white scar though the dark flesh of thick vegetation. Its dust reflected the burning glow that was in the night sky, and around it was darkness – the swamp of the Everglades, fecund, teaming with life, full of alligators, pythons, cobras, pelicans …

V checked the hook that linked her to the cable. She pulled at it and tugged. The clip was solid, locked tight.

Gus gave her a thumbs-up. She returned it with a thumbs-up and stepped out of the hover-jet into the glowing damp night. The cable tightened. V swung away from the door, hanging, for an instant, in space.

The cable unspooled. V raced down towards the ground.

She was in human mode and was wearing her standard camouflage patterned brown-and-black make-up, her black skin-tight combat catsuit, black combat boots, and her black waterproof backpack, a light submachine gun over her shoulder, and a pistol and stun gun at her waist.

"Good luck," whispered Arnold, the pilot, through her earphone.

"Thanks, you too," she transmitted, a mental message.

V landed, softly, knees bent, crouching, on the road, the dust stirred up around her by the hover-jet downdraft and by the gentle touchdown of her boots. She stood up straight, unhooked herself from the cable, looked up, and waved the hover-jet off. The cable zipped upwards, Gus waved, and the hover-jet door slid shut.

The hover-jet lifted slowly away, becoming, within seconds, virtually invisible, and then it went supersonic and disappeared, leaving behind only a sonic boom that seemed to come from nowhere.

V stood absolutely still, surveying the scene. The side road was dark, no lights of any kind. Tall reeds and grasses grew on both sides. The air smelled of flowers, rotting vegetation, and stagnant water, fetid and fecund marine life, alligators, pelicans, reptile flesh and riotous vegetation. It would take her about ten to fifteen minutes to get to her target. The Everglades Agricultural Research Institute was about two miles away.

In reality the Everglades Agricultural Research Institute was a cover for a top secret government installation where scientific black ops were carried out, research that officially did not exist, and where, at present, they were holding the "Subject," the Swiss girl impregnated by the renegade or maverick hybrid – a hybrid created by God only knew who ...

Dmitry Pavlov?

But he was dead.

The Dmitry Puppet Master ... whatever that was?

Had Dmitry Pavlov somehow resurrected himself?

Was it the ghost of Dmitry? Was such a thing possible? And behind the ghost of Dmitry, what lay behind the ghost of Dmitry?

The Dark God? What or who the hell was the Dark God?

Perhaps the girl, this Monica Fabritz, also known as "The Subject," now a hybrid herself, would offer some clues.

V ran at a quick trot along the road, her boots stirring up little clouds of soft dust. Her senses were honed and on high alert – watching for monitoring devices, booby traps, electronic trip wires, alligators, zombies, or hostile humans ...

And also – for the Reptile Man ...

Twenty-eight-year-old Doctor Ra'shae Mansoor stretched. She wiggled her shoulders. Her muscles were stiff, and she was exhausted. She yawned, settled back in her chair, crossed her legs, and uncrossed her legs, pushed her chair away from her desk, and glanced at her watch. It was almost dawn. The relief shift had not come. Doctor Hamilton, Director of the Institute, had not been heard from since yesterday evening; text messages were not returned; his voice mail had ceased to function; his GPS locator had gone dead.

And it got worse – since 9:00 pm yesterday, Washington had not replied to requests for orders or guidance; there was nothing but silence.

None of the night staff – nurses, doctors – had shown up.

Only a few guards were present.

And Doctor Kevin Harris was coming tonight – of all nights! And he was going to perform the lobotomy.

The lobotomy had been declared urgent!

This was something Doctor Mansoor had opposed and fought and risked her career to prevent. But there was no way she could stop it. The "powers" had decided. She had considered resigning; but then she thought that would make no difference – so she would hang on and see what she could do to prevent the worst from happening.

And now – what would happen?

Internet connections – wireless and not – had failed about half an hour ago, and she had not heard from her husband or her mother – who was baby-sitting the kids – since yesterday at noon.

She'd phoned her husband, but his phone just rang and rang, and finally the voice mail came on. She left a message. He did not call back.

Her old-fashioned cellphone still worked.

She picked it up and tried again.

"Sorry, but all our circuits are busy; please hang up and try again."

She tried her mother, once again, one last desperate time.

"Sorry, but all our circuits are busy; please hang up and try again."

Texting gave the same result: no result.

"We are experiencing network difficulties; please try again later."

Ra'shae believed in keeping calm, no matter how bad a situation got; but she was desperate. Fear gnawed at the pit of her stomach. She should get in the car and just drive to Miami and see what was happening. But she couldn't leave.

The Directive was clear: "Abandoning one's post for whatever reason is equivalent to high treason and is punishable by death."

All night, the news had gotten worse and worse. The zombie virus, whatever it was, was spreading – and spreading faster and faster.

Earlier, when communications still existed, on one channel there had been a woman reporting who had apparently been turned into a zombie – there she was, wrapped up like a mummy, propped up, bubbling away, looking absolutely awful, she was spewing out green stuff, her eyes glowed, she'd lost most of her hair. She looked like death itself.

Ra'shae stared at the screen – now blank – occasionally it flickered on; and there was that brave zombie girl, still reporting; then it flickered off.

What in the world was going on out there?

Not knowing, was worse, she was sure, than knowing.

The power supply had become intermittent, so Ra'shae had asked the guards – there were four of them – to turn on the emergency generators; she could hear the low, reassuring background hum; but the lights were dimmer than usual, and it gave to the laboratory and her office a ghostly livid sheen that she didn't like, not one bit she didn't.

The air-conditioning had failed early last night, before everything else, which was strange, so Ra'shae had turned on the little gray metal fan she had on her desk; it swung back and forth making a purring sound, sending out a gentle breeze that was cool against her forehead. It stirred the pages of the document she was reading, rustling the edges of the paper. Anyway, she couldn't concentrate; she couldn't focus – "Alien DNA structures as Parasitical Invaders." The gist was that the aliens were a sort of disease, that being a hybrid – like "the Subject" – was like being infected; that it was a new form of plague; that …

Ra'shae was not at all convinced; she was tempted to think, in her more fanciful light-hearted moments, that perhaps humans were the disease, the parasite.

Or neither …

She looked at her half-full coffee cup: the coffee was by now lukewarm; if she drank any more of that, she'd explode. And, thinking of exploding, reminded her that she wanted to pee, she wanted to pee badly.

She'd been sitting there, alone, for hours.

The second nightshift scientist, Doctor Denis J. Platt, should have arrived at least two hours ago. But there was no sign of him; he hadn't texted, he hadn't phoned.

Ra'shae had tried his line – nothing but static, not even the voice mail; a text she sent bounced back, "delivery impossible."

And then – Ra'shae was worried, more than worried, about her family. Her kids, Amin, age six and Tabia, age nine, were with their grandmother just outside of Miami; this zombie thing was getting too close.

Surely mother had the sense to keep everybody locked indoors!

It was pure anguish – waiting like this, isolated, out in the middle of nowhere, sweating in the heat, unable to do anything, dying to know …

She swiveled her chair around and glanced at the screens that monitored the Subject: well, the Subject was certainly not asleep: brain activity was intense: frontal lobe activity was high, it was probably running through mathematical formula or the laws of physics or something like that; the kid was a genius and was trying to stay sane by exercising her mind. Muscle spasms were continuing – well, they were not muscle spasms, the Subject was using the restraints to do isometric or resistance exercises; the Subject was determined to stay in shape. The Subject was nineteen years old; she was disciplined, strong-minded, and, as Ra'shae knew, very, very tough.

Ra'shae rubbed her eyes and yawned. It was a dreadful situation. The Subject was a prisoner in what, for her, was a foreign country – no appeals, no due process, no lawyers, nobody – isolated, alone, thrown into this prison, manacled down, incommunicado, buried alive.

Yesterday afternoon, about three, before the catastrophe happened, Ra'shae had accompanied the guards when they took the Subject for a walk – up and down a few concrete corridors – and allowed the Subject to go to the bathroom and shower. The Subject had been very friendly, flashing its big smile, and it had asked Ra'shae about her kids, about her husband, about her research. It said that It wanted to have kids one day, and then It stopped and said, "Of course, that's silly isn't it, I'm pregnant, so I am going to have a kid, I guess we might as well call it a kid, but I'm not sure. I really don't know what is growing inside me." Ra'shae answered the questions about herself, she didn't comment on the Subject's allusions to the Subject's pregnancy, which was due, in fact, overdue; generally, Ra'shae tried to obey the Directive, which emphasized, insisted, that none of the staff develop any feelings of empathy for or identification with the Subject.

At about midnight – before the communications breakdown – Ra'shae had received the notice that they were going to lobotomize the Subject. Doctor Harris – that odious violent presumptuous man – was on his way. Then, once the lobotomy had been completed, they were to evacuate the Subject. If they were not able to evacuate the subject in time, before the zombies arrived, and if the zombies did arrive, then the instructions were to eliminate the Subject – to eliminate the Subject by any and all means.

This would be a tragedy, Ra'shae thought, since all the research and all the care – and all the expense – would have been for nothing. They would never learn what made the alien-human hybrid tick, they would never know …

And, besides, Ra'shae, if she allowed herself to glimpse the truth, had to admit she was fond of the Subject, really liked her, and even admired her, and would have liked, had circumstances been different, to become her friend.

She sighed. Okay, I've got to pee – Now! She stood up, stretched again, flexed her muscles – stiff from sitting still so long – and walked down the corridor to the washroom; she went into the cubicle, pulled down her skirt and panties, and sat down, and took her time and was amazed at the gush that came from her. I really needed that! She sighed. It was almost dawn and – whatever the Directive said – she was going to drive to Miami and get her kids, Amin and Tabia. She would make herself another cup of coffee – one for the road … They could shoot her afterwards, if they wished to do so.

She walked back to the office and went straight to her desk. Oh, oh, something was wrong. The little row of red lights was flashing – blink, blink, blink.

This meant that some of the links were broken – or disconnected – from the Subject's body.

Ra'shae glanced up at the monitors. The mind monitor machine was absolutely flat: no brain activity whatsoever – had the Subject died?

She hesitated.

Perhaps she should call the guards. No, she'd check herself. She turned on the microphone. She didn't want to startle the Subject. "I am going to turn on some lights, and I am going to come in to see if you need anything, is that okay?"

She turned on the lights.

The bed-platform was empty.

The Subject was gone. The straps that held her down had been ripped away and were dangling from the bed-platform. The sheets had been tossed aside. The hospital gown was lying on the floor in shreds. The monitoring cables were dangling free. The monitors inside the lab were blinking blank. The gurney had been turned over. The Intravenous drips were smashed, their stands turned over. The door into the lab was open. It looked like it had been torn off its hinges.

Ra'shae pushed a button and clicked the microphone. "Code Red!" she cleared her throat, "Code Red!"

And then she heard a rustling sound behind her – and a gentle cough – and she turned and looked and …

A few minutes earlier, 19-year-old Swiss citizen Monica Fabritz, aka the Subject, had been lying rigid with fear on the operating table which functioned as her bed. She was shackled down in the dark and could barely move.

She closed her eyes, then opened them: I'm going crazy, I'm going crazy and I can't stop it! And nobody will help me!

She had started worrying about her sanity two or three days earlier.

I'm losing it, she thought, I'm absolutely bloody losing it! She wondered why she hadn't gone totally insane earlier on. The way she was being treated was outrageous. She had seen the whole Lewis family, her friends, and her best friend, Sarah Lewis, slaughtered by … by that beast … and then she had been kidnapped and held and … well, raped … raped repeatedly … by that beast …

And then, abandoned by the beast, and picked up by the US Authorities, she had tried to cooperate. She had begun by telling them everything she knew, and for her pains she had been put in solitary confinement, and then transported, at night, shacked and blindfolded, in an armored vehicle, to an unknown location – though she had figured it out – it was in Florida someplace and she had been held incommunicado, and then tied down, again shackled, and deprived of books, of conversation, of people, of the Internet – of light, of movement, and of her freedom – totally.

The Swiss Embassy she was sure knew nothing.

Her family thought she was dead.

She was sure of it.

These people – they made her blood boil – assured her that her family knew she was okay and that she was just undergoing prolonged "observation." All lies, she was certain, all lies, all hateful lies. They were going to kill her. That was their plan: She would just "disappear" – forever.

She was furious and she was terrified.

Then, three days ago, the voice started talking to her. It said, "Kill them all, Monica! Kill them all, when you can, kill them all."

She didn't like hearing voices in her head.

She suspected that it was some diabolic form of psychological warfare her captors had decided upon. Perhaps they were piping in the voices. Perhaps they had some mechanism for projecting voices into her mind, some form of neurological suggestion. "They want me to go insane, that's what they want: they want me to go totally absolutely fucking nuts."

This made her even more furious – even more terrified.

Trapped in darkness and manacled down, she tried to think of things she knew; she evoked and visualized places she had been, friends, family; she told herself stories and anecdotes; she tried to play them on her inner screen, like little imaginary movies. She exercised different muscle groups by straining against the straps and steel.

The voice said, "You don't know who I am, do you, Monica?"

"No, I don't know, and I don't care. Go away!"

"I'm afraid I can't go away, Monica." The voice sounded like a precociously aged little old man-child, ancient and infantile, a monstrous creature that was not yet born, that was waiting to emerge into the light; it was like an ancient satanic fetus, a diabolical hobgoblin, an unclean thing.

"Oh? Why can't you go away?"

"Because I am part of you now, Monica, and you are part of me."

"I don't want to have anything to do with you whatever you are."

"I am afraid that is not possible, Monica. You belong to me now, whatever you decide doesn't matter. You belong to me."

"Fuck off!"

"You belong to me!"

"Shut the fuck up! Fuck off! Go away!"

The voice stopped and Monica let out a sigh of relief – wondering too whether she had been talking in her mind or out loud and whether the instruments were picking up this little performance or not – and she realized that she was trembling and that her body was covered in sweat – gooey sweat – she was wearing only one of those little hospital gown things and nothing else – and she imagined that all the little instruments in the control room would be abuzz with gossip about her going insane, about her talking to herself, and so on, and on, and on.

And then, that same day, something else happened which really scared her, but which was, in a weird way, exhilarating. She began to hear what other people were thinking; she began to understand what the instruments were doing. She began to feel and sense that everything was, to her at least, transparent. She could hear things and feel things through the walls, in the corridors, in the other rooms.

And she began, too, to be very conscious of people's bodies, of the blood circulating in people's bodies, of their smells, of their perfumes. It was, she knew, a very hygienic environment, antiseptic and sterile, or at least that was the intention. They didn't want anything to infect her and to compromise the fetus developing within her. But she caught every whiff of everything, and, yes, she began to hear thoughts, well, she thought they were thoughts – other people's thoughts. Maybe this was just the beginning of madness. Maybe she was going crazy! Maybe it was incipient psychosis. She listened to the thoughts, like bits of dialogue heard over a radio.

"Amin has the colic. I must phone Mustapha ..."

"Doctor Mansoor shows symptoms of developing empathy for the Subject; perhaps it would be advisable to shift her to a less sensitive ..."

"Doctor Hamilton is very concerned about the pregnancy – we are at term and ..."

"We are nurturing the Anti-Christ in this little hothouse. I hope you realize that, Doctor Hamilton. The Director is very concerned about ..."

"The subject shows accelerating physiological changes."

"Lobotomy should be performed as soon as possible."

"Doctor Harris will perform … He's eager to … He has promised … putty in our hands …"

"The Subject shows no sign, so far, of morphological transformation."

"You can't count on that, the Subject is …"

"Subject," Monica thought, "what Subject? Who is this Subject?" She mulled. She licked her lips. She was feeling dehydrated. She'd better ask them to give her water or adjust the drip. She thought some more: "The Subject" – what strange terminology … And then it dawned on her that the Subject, well, *the Subject* was her! Of course, it couldn't be clearer! How stupid of her not to see it!

Morphological transformation – what the fuck was that about?

The birth of the Anti-Christ?

Her belly was swelling up … no doubt about …

I'm giving birth to the Anti-Christ? A monster, yes, but the *Anti-Christ*! These people are nuts, absolutely frigging totally bonkers – what evil assholes!

Lobotomize … who … No, they couldn't … Oh, yes, they could … Oh, yes, they would … That was something they would certainly be capable of doing!

I am the one they are going to lobotomize – this Doctor Harris … He is a crazy guy, that guy, and not a nice guy, not at all; in fact, he is an absolutely evil psycho. She had seen through him, and heard through him: He was an egomaniac who disguised his craziness under a 'cool' exterior – long hair, bright shirts, baggy khaki shorts, ostensibly friendly, casual, on first name basis with everybody, the guards, the cleaning women, the doctors, and, even … with her.

"Hey, Monica, how are you doing?"

"Not well – I want out of here – or at least I want books, I want …"

"Now, Monica, it's hard, I know, but it's for your own good."

She listened in to their thoughts and to their conversations and she began to get a pretty clear picture of the situation. The alien – the beast – Monica called him 'Freddy' after an ancient series of horror films she had watched with her father late one night in Zurich – had impregnated her. Well, she knew that. But he had also, they seemed to think (And they should know, they had been doing all those tests) injected her, or something, or contaminated her, so that her DNA had been altered and she was now a *hybrid*, whatever that was. Was she a hybrid of human and Freddy? And she also picked up that she was now no longer considered human and was to be referred to, out of her hearing of course, as "it."

"*It*" – fuck, these people! They were even crazier than she thought.

But, worse …

On reflection, much worse …

A hybrid, I am a hybrid? A hybrid – like Freddy?

This was not amusing.

Lobotomy … that was even less amusing.

Scheisse! Shit! Merde! Cazzo!

I have to get out of here!

Henry Black, Doctor Kevin Harris's driver was a determined and skillful man and he knew that he didn't have any choice – the road behind them, he'd noticed, glancing in the rearview mirror, was blocked with zombies; and he knew that Doctor Harris was in a great hurry and on a vital mission regarding national security. So Henry tried to run the car past the zombies in front of the car, but once he got the car through the front line of zombies, there were more zombies, and these second line zombies wouldn't get out of the way, and so Henry drove them down. One of them bounced up on the hood of the car and splashed a sort of green goo all over the windshield, and the body, leaving this smear behind, dropped off and rolled away, and Doctor Harris was shouting at Henry saying "You damned fool, you are going to get us killed," and Henry said, "I'm just trying to do my job, Doctor Harris, there are zombies behind us and zombies in front; I couldn't have gone back because the road was already blocked behind with zombies."

More zombies slammed into the car.

Henry swerved, swerved again.

One of the zombies threw a metal bar which smashed into the windshield just in front of Henry, and the air-conditioning was still on, ribbons of green stuff, like a fog, then, turning to a mist, flooding into the car, and Doctor Harris said, "Turn the damned air-conditioning off, will you!"

Henry began to vomit.

"Oh, for God's sake, Henry! Now is not the time to be sick, man!"

The car was skidding sideways, Henry's hands limp on the steering wheel. The car skidded, skidded, tires squealing, and then smashed against a concrete ditch barrier, bounced, and scraped along the barrier and then stopped.

Doctor Harris was pissed off, more than pissed off. It was disgraceful – Henry letting him down like that.

You can't trust anybody!

Henry had collapsed sideways. His eyes were glazed, and his mouth was open, and he was making funny bubbling sounds.

Doctor Harris looked out the back window and saw that the zombies were approaching fast. They were clumsy, but they were quick, they looked like cartoons; but it was clear they were deadly dangerous. A couple of them were carrying lengths of pipe or iron bars and one of them Doctor Harris noticed, was carrying an axe.

Where the hell do zombies get axes?

"Hey, Henry," he said, "wake up, Henry!"

Doctor Harris swore. He had to do everything his goddamned self! Fuck, even Ashley sometimes burned the goddamn fucking toast and let the fucking coffee get cold, even though he'd told her a million fucking times how he liked his fucking toast and coffee – and then there's the bed, the sheets have to be tight, goddamn it, tight, pulled tight, and the towels, sometimes Ashley would leave a wrinkle in a towel hung up on her rack – unbelievable! He'd thought she was perfect at first, but she was not goddamn perfect – she was a fallible bitch, a cunt, a fucking whore, like all the others.

He unbuckled his seat belt, opened the door, and got out of the car.

He was going to push Henry over to the passenger side and take over the driving. But then he saw that Henry was drooling some sort of green fluid and making weird jerky movements. Henry's eyes, which had been closed, opened, and they glowed, they glowed like a goddamn jelly fish, they glowed like one of those genetically modified Portuguese Man-of-War Doctor Harris had seen once when he was swimming off the coast of the Bahamas. "You are sick, man, you are sick," Doctor Harris said. It was disgusting. Doctor Harris did not like illness. Illness was a form of moral failure, like old age. Just seeing an old person waddling along the fucking sidewalk, weaving back and forth, taking up all the fucking space, slowing down the rushing important pedestrians, made Doctor Harris seethe. Old age and illness were forms of stupidity, for losers, definitely for losers. And this was worse than sickness, this was being a zombie! Zombies are fucking losers! Well, fuck this! He grabbed Henry by the arms and pulled Henry out of the car. Henry struggled to get up, foaming more green bubbles, looking really like he'd come out of a horror video game, his dark skin all crumpled up, like it was putty, or some sort of warped Halloween mask. Henry's white shirt was stained green; it burst open and a tentacle shot out and wrapped itself around Doctor Harris's wrist and another shot out and grabbed for Doctor Harris's arm. What the fuck was this? The guy was turning into a vegetable! "Henry you have let me down, you have let the side down, Henry, I'm really sorry about this." Somehow Doctor Harris ripped the tentacles from his wrist and sleeve and kicked Henry in the crotch. Henry's crotch exploded in gooey tentacles that burst through his trousers, as if they were fueled by acid; the trousers, the cloth, just disintegrated. Doctor Harris guffawed. "Henry, ha, ha, ha, you gotta get a better tailor, man, ha, ha, ha," and he turned to see that the zombies were quite close now, and one, the one with the axe, rushed forward, moving very fast for a zombie, and brought the axe smashing down, just missing Doctor Harris – by a hair's breadth – and burying the head of the axe in the car door. "You bastard," said Doctor Harris as the zombie grabbed Doctor Harris by the throat and squeezed. Doctor Harris was aware of the other zombies gathering around, and it occurred to him, that he, Doctor Kevin Marc Harris MD Ph.D. D. Sc., might die at the hands of these abortive monsters, these freaks, these mindless beasts, these absolute losers, and such a death – indeed any death at all – would be ironic, and would be unworthy of Doctor Kevin Harris, who by all rights should be immortal. He pulled the axe out of the car door, and he swung it around so that it hit the zombie's legs, and the zombie, whose hold on Doctor Harris's neck was weak, yelped, spurting more pestilent goo, let go of Doctor Harris's neck and fell down. Doctor Harris swung the axe again, and this time he lopped off the zombie's head – the zombie looked like he had been a fireman, to judge by what remained of his uniform. Doctor Harris swung the axe again, off went one leg, and again, off went another leg, "Ha, you see what a real man can do!" He turned to the other zombies, "Come and get me you idiots, come and get me," holding the axe with one hand he crouched, arms and legs spread, ready for the fight. Three of the zombies shambled forward. Harris brought them down, each with a single stroke of the axe. The other zombies, about ten yards away, hesitated. "All right then, all right then," said Harris. He retreated to the car. He kicked Henry – the remains of Henry – the head was still more or less intact, a mask now, but the eyes were still human, partially human, glowing, flickering green now a bit, but still human, and the mouth said, "Please, Doctor, don't leave me!"

"Eh, Henry, what did you say, there, what did you say?" Doctor Harris leaned down, mimicking compassion, thinking this fucker deserves death, put me in danger, the low IQ idiot did, imperiled the mission, he did, loser, definitely a loser.

"Don't leave me! Please, doctor!"

Doctor Harris laughed. "Sorry old bean, gotta go, I have promises to keep you know, I can't tarry, I can't linger, I can't stay, maybe see you around, bye-bye Henry, toodeloo, survival of the fittest, Henry, think Charles Darwin, Henry, think dinosaurs, think asteroids!"

Harris climbed in, slammed the door – Thank the bloody stars the goddamn thing still shuts, and, ah, and even locks – after that bloody axe hit it.

He put the axe on the seat beside him, the handle towards him, ready for action. He turned the key, noticed the blue-and-white Virgin Mary fob.

Kitsch, fucking kitsch!

The engine started, roared.

Zombies were climbing onto the car, clamoring at the back window, pounding on the sides of the car, clambering onto the hood.

"Hey, hey, hey!" Harris gunned the car, swung the wheel, skidded away from the concrete barrier, the zombies toppled off.

One clung to the hood, its face pressed against the window, it was a woman, fuck – even the women were in on the act!

He swerved again.

She was still holding on – splayed spread-eagled on the hood, not much hair on her head, but what there was of it was streaming over her face, green eyes glowing, and mouth, goddamn half her teeth were missing, mouth spouting that godawful green goo.

He slammed on the breaks.

The car skidded and shudder to a stop, tires screaming. The woman shot off the hood, cartwheeling down onto road – ending up in a heap, a bright bag of bones in the headlights.

He gunned the motor, accelerated, drove over her – bump, bump, and bump.

The bumping didn't stop.

"Damn!" She must have gotten stuck under the car – or bits and pieces of her must have – because the bump-bump-bump went on for a long time, but then it ceased, and the going was smooth, and he took a deep breath, checked that his kit for the operation was intact. Yes, looked like it hadn't suffered at all, thank my fucking lucky stars! One first-class lobotomy coming up!

He turned on the radio, "... has declared a national state of emergency ... wide-spread arrests of scientists and engineers have been reported ... unconfirmed reports state that the zombie plague has already entered the state of Georgia, but we don't have any independent confirmation of that ... Meantime ..."

He switched the babble off and wondered if he could get to the Everglades Agricultural Research Institute in time to perform the lobotomy.

He didn't want to think what would happen when the zombies reached the Institute, if they were headed that way, and, maybe, by design or by accident, released the Subject.

Above all, he didn't want his experiment to be interrupted: he was eager to demonstrate just how much of the Subject's personality and intelligence he could eliminate, just how effectively he could reduce her – oops, sorry, "*its*" – intelligence and still keep *it* – ah, "*it*" – alive.

Turn "*it*" into a pure elemental animal – the bare minimum of consciousness so it would obey orders – and later he could insert a control mechanism: push a button, give a command, just say a word, and it would be executed, total control of its feelings, pain, pleasure, and orgasms …

It would be a human robot – entirely in his control.

This was all the more exciting since "*it*" was an extraordinarily intelligent and very beautiful young woman – to reduce such a divine being to slavish drooling servitude, well, that was something worth waiting for.

And, as a docile slave, she would be of immense use to science – and, personally, to Doctor Kevin Harris. Her tastes and behaviors could be redesigned to his specifications.

He stepped on the gas.

Monica Fabritz was dripping sticky sweat. She was submerged in pure, helpless, paralyzing terror. Yes, they intended to lobotomize her – by now she was sure of it. That horrible slimy Doctor Harris was on his way, she could feel it in her bones; she somehow, mysteriously, knew it was so!

Madness and idiocy were things she feared almost more than anything else.

It was all building up to a climax, in more ways than one: she felt a pang, a rhythmic thrust, it must be a contraction: this must be the beginning.

Ouch!

Ouch!

And – ouch!

What a night – all hell had been breaking loose and the usual night staff had not appeared and Doctor Mansoor was still on duty and was very unhappy because … because, as Monica now knew with dawning certainty, Doctor Mansoor was worried about her husband Mustapha and she was worried about her children, Amin and Tabia, and she was worried about her mother Hoda – and because she couldn't get through to them; all the communications were down – Internet, land-line, cell phones, U-Tabs – everything.

And the electricity flickered off a couple of times.

Monica felt it in her bones; it was an image of impending chaos; she felt everything; her consciousness was expanding, encompassing vast stretches of the world. The great world system where everything was linked to everything else at the speed of light, where there was always a backup for anything that went wrong, the great world system – she saw it like a sort of multi-dimensional fluid matrix in her mind – the great world system of human civilization was under huge strain, and it looked like it was breaking down, some parts of it were breaking down, because … because …

… because zombies were on the loose. The images flashed into her head.

Zombies?

What the hell? Zombies?

Zombies?

Nobody told her about zombies!

Monica caught some of the images – from Doctor Mansoor who had been glancing nervously at the monitors earlier in the evening; from Doctor Mansoor who had been thinking of the Beretta 9mm she kept in the top right hand drawer of her desk, thinking of using it, either to defend herself from the zombies, or, if the zombies did arrive, to end it all.

Now, nothing: the TV and Internet connections had failed.

And there was something else in the air.

Something Monica sensed.

Something dark and terrifying was coming.

Freddy – Freddy was coming to get her.

Freddy wasn't much for talking – in fact, he didn't seem to be able to talk, no, that was not true, he had said "Monica," at the very beginning, unless it was an illusion or hallucination on her part, she remembered him, saying "Monica", only that one time, and, once or twice, he had looked at her and said, "Sorry," like he was sorry, for what – for killing people, for tearing them apart, for raping her, for keeping her prisoner? He liked eating, though, mostly people, draining them dry, absolutely dry, and then disposing of the bodies; strangely, he knew how to cook, and he cooked for her, before and after raping her …

"Sorry …"

"Sorry for what, Freddy," she thought. "Sorry for what?"

She did not want to meet Freddy ever again. She was certain that for Freddy she was merely a vessel. He was coming for the unborn child. Well, the unborn child was almost here. It was nine months almost precisely, and her belly had swollen up like a pirate galleon's sails when the southeaster was billowing and blowing full. The little Anti-Christ, if that's what he was, was about to be born. God – is he going to look like mother or father? And is he going to tear me apart with his claws and fangs coming out of my womb, or is he going to behave and be born like a normal baby? She had no idea whether it was a he or a she but she found it hard to believe that Freddy would spawn a girl child. She envisaged a snake-like monster, a coiled serpent uncoiling, issuing from her womb, crawling out between her legs. Ugh!

Still, she wanted to run her hands over her belly, but, of course, she couldn't. She couldn't touch herself anywhere. She was tied down, shackled, handcuffed, and ankle cuffed. What the hell did they think she was going to do?

She licked her lips. I'm hungry. I want a banana – a banana I can peel and then eat chomp, chomp, chomp, a bite at a time, and I want ice cream, yes, ice cream, maybe chocolate and vanilla, that I can lick and bite into and that will dribble over my fingers – and I wouldn't mind a coffee, a good strong Italian coffee. I know they have bananas and I know there is ice cream in the freezer and I know that Doctor Mansoor – she is rather pretty and I do think, in spite of everything, that she rather likes me and, in spite of everything, I rather like her – I know that Doctor Mansoor has her own little coffee machine, it makes good coffee too, in her office. Boy, am I hungry!

I would kill for a banana.

She closed her eyes – no need really to keep them open, she couldn't see anything anyway as she was blindfolded and the room was pitch black except for some blinking lights on the instruments – and she imagined being free, she imagined sitting on a cedar log fence, eating a banana, gossiping with Sarah Lewis about their professors at Princeton, just as they had been doing the day before Freddy turned up, sitting on a cedar log fence, snowflakes coming down around them, sitting there gossiping and laughing, a few hours before Freddy came – and cut a swath through the Lewis farmhouse, and tore Sarah limb from limb, literally, limb from limb. Please, whoever runs the universe, will you send Freddy to Hell forever, forever, and forever!

She felt a stirring and a sharp pain.

Oh, no, she thought, maybe the moment has come.

She thought – I should push the button and alert Doctor Mansoor. Of course, Doctor Mansoor is not a medical doctor, not an obstetrician. And, then, Doctor Mansoor has gone for a pee, and she will probably sit in the washroom having deep thoughts, or stare at herself in the mirror and worry herself sick, as she is now doing, over her kids, her husband, and her mother, and wonder, as she is wondering, whether her whole family has been transformed into zombies … It was weird being plunged into Doctor Mansoor's mind like that. And then, the zombies … zombies!

Zombies, what a strange weird idea, as if Freddy the Reptile Man were not enough strangeness!

Another spasm came, and then, in that very instant, she felt a tingling all over her body, a strange sensation, like ants were racing all over every inch of her flesh, and she felt a trembling, and she shivered and she felt something like beads of sweat breaking out all over her skin, and a chill, and then a rush of heat, like a fever, and then it was as if she had lost consciousness, briefly, maybe just or a second, but how could she judge time in this non-environment of "low level sensory deprivation" as their psychologists called it when she overheard them, and then she was awake and everything, smells, sounds, even sight, even sight behind the blindfold which had slipped up now she noticed and she could see beneath it – everything was sharper, more vivid. She could hear all the computers humming and she even seemed to have a sense of what they were humming about, the blinking lights of the instruments were much brighter, the room, suddenly, was visible, it was like in a reddish tone. It's like I'm seeing infra-red, she thought, this is bloody strange, and another spasm came, and, instinctively, without thinking about it, she tried to reach for her swollen tummy, and – snap! – the wrist constraint broke, and – snap! – the other wrist constraint broke, and she thought, what the hell is happening? She felt her belly, and, yes, it was swollen, but it felt strange, rough and smooth, not simply smooth, it felt like scales, my God, she thought, like smooth scales, like Freddy, like … a reptile … like … a hybrid, and the phrase came back to her, "the Subject has not yet undergone morphological transformation," and she remembered the person mentioning that "the Subject's DNA has been transformed," so, she thought, with a mixture of thrill and horror, so, now, maybe, "the Subject" has in fact undergone "morphological transformation," or is this a bad dream, but, no, it didn't feel like a dream. It didn't have the unwilling uncontrollable fatalistic drift of a dream. She kicked with her feet and – snap – the ankle straps flew away. She tore off the blindfold and she struggled to sit up and she sat on the edge of the bed – more an operating theatre platform than a bed – and she tore off the monitoring wires and she slipped out of the rags of the hospital gown – somehow it seemed to have exploded or disintegrated into confetti-sized strips – She hated those bloody revealing, undignified hospital gowns – and she stood up and was glad to see that she could stand up. And so now I am a monster, she thought, looking down at her swollen breasts and swollen belly, a reptilian monster, a reptile-mammal! And when had proto mammal-reptiles, our common ancestors, last roamed the earth, and when had mammals and reptiles split up, going their separate ways, well, maybe about 250 million years ago, so maybe Freddy is a throw-back – and me too for that matter, a reptilian killer from the deep backward abyss of time! Oh, boy!

Wow!

Gosh and Golly!

"Merde!" she whispered, "Unglaublich, schrecklich!"

A monster, a reptile …

A killer …

She went to the door of the lab and turned the handle and was mildly surprised to find that just by pulling on it, rather gently – she ripped the metal armored door off its hinges.

Wow!

This was utterly, scientifically impossible!

But …

After passing through a short corridor, she was out in the observation booth, which was also Doctor Mansoor's office; it was hot; a little gray metal fan was turning on Doctor Mansoor's desk, and rustling some papers, but Doctor Mansoor was not there – still in the bathroom down the hall no doubt – but in a separate alcove in Doctor Mansoor's office, Monica spotted the refrigerator and the coffee machine.

Monica didn't even think about what she had become. She went into the alcove, flipped a button to turn on the coffee machine – and chose "double espresso macchiato" thinking – Is espresso okay if you are pregnant, in the last stages of pregnancy?

While the machine hummed, she opened the refrigerator. Yes, a banana, a bunch of four bananas, the skins had turned dark. She snapped off one of the bananas and glanced around – yoghurt, vanilla flavor low-fat, and cheese, and a salad in a plastic package – carrot sticks, celery sticks, etc.

Hmm! She shut the refrigerator door, unpeeled the banana – Oh, it was just right, firm and not yet chalky – and went over to Doctor Mansoor's desk – she opened the top right hand drawer and took out the Beretta 9mm pistol that she knew was there from reading Doctor Mansoor's mind and monitoring her fears. The Beretta was loaded. Good!

She picked up the report that Doctor Mansoor had been reading and she took it and the Beretta 9mm back to the alcove and jumped up and sat on the shelf, next to the sink, letting her legs dangle, just below a large bookshelf filled with technical volumes, and she perused the article – "Alien DNA structures as Parasitical Invaders."

She thought, "Fuck me, excuse my French or my Swiss German or my Italian, or my High German, or whatever, but Fuck Me" – and, finally, she looked down, examining herself for the first time: bright blue or cobalt scales. Fuck!

The realization was slowly dawning that something new, and irrevocable and exceptional and infinitely bad had happened – and it had happened to her – to Monica Fabritz.

She took a bite out of the banana. Well, it certainly tasted good. Her claws, she noticed, were just as agile as human hands, and much stronger.

Should I use the Beretta 9mm to kill Doctor Mansoor – or should I just tear her apart and drink her dry?

Good question.

Her fangs tingled – they were itchy, itching for action …

Fangs …?

Morbid and wicked thoughts, Monica, morbid thoughts!

She glanced at the Executive Summary of the article. "Am I the parasite," she wondered, "or is the thing that transformed me, the DNA code or modifier, is that the parasite?"

The coffee was ready. Monica slipped down off the shelf, her foot-claws making clickety-clack on the ceramic tile floor, took the pre-filled cup, and holding it between her claws she slipped back up onto the shelf, pushing a couple of books out of the way.

The shelf was partly hidden from the door to the observation booth; so, in the first instant at least, she would be invisible to Doctor Mansoor when the good doctor came into the room.

Little lights above Doctor Mansoor's desk were blinking – indicating that the "Subject" was no longer in the position she was supposed to be, shackled down in the dark.

Anger surged.

The voice came again. "Kill them all, Monica, kill them all, tear them apart and drink their blood, drink every last drop of their blood."

Monica felt a rush of excitement, and a tingling in what she realized must be, yes indeed, in what must be her fangs – fangs like Freddy. Yuk! And double Yuk!

"Fuck off," she said, "Fuck off, Go to Hell! Do not bother me!"

"You'll regret your disloyalty, Monica."

"What are you and who are you?"

"I am your master; I am your creator, Monica."

"Fuck off!"

"You should get down on your knees and worship me, Monica. I have given you the gift of eternal life."

"Fuck off!"

Monica sighed, took a sip of the coffee – well sip was not exactly the word she realized, it was more like she lapped and sucked it up with her tongue – fangs – she knew she had fangs though she had not yet checked in a mirror – make delicate sipping a difficult balancing act, lips and tongue versus fangs – but the coffee was excellent and she sniffed, her nostrils quivering, every molecule of coffee giving her a sensual pleasure that was beyond anything she knew, and, it was true, the idea of blood was exciting, the vision of herself, whatever she looked like and, yes, she had not yet looked in a mirror and had no intention of doing so, the vision of herself, bright cobalt reptile, crouched over a victim, tearing into a human body, ripping it open, and sucking all the blood out of it, yes, it was quite exciting and, she thought, this must be vampire or reptile pornography – images to titillate, images to send you towards an orgasm of the taste buds. The thrill travelled up and down her belly and down her thighs. She said, "Well, thanks for eternal life, but I don't intend to worship you, Mister, so piss off, please, and leave me alone."

"You are ungrateful, Monica, very ungrateful."

"Yes, I am ungrateful. Tough bananas!" Monica took another slurping delicious suck of the coffee.

Monica heard the door of the bathroom open and close; she heard Doctor Mansoor's high heels – the lady always insisted on being very elegant – and she heard the door to the office open.

Her muscles tensed. She was ready to spring. She took a bite from the banana and she didn't move. This will be extremely interesting, she thought. One claw edged towards the Beretta 9mm.

Eating Doctor Mansoor might indeed be a pleasure – a tender morsel, a beautiful human, a deliciously sensual woman: yum, yum, yum …

"Kill them, kill them all – drain their blood to the very last drop," the voice exulted, riding on the crest of Monica's bloodlust.

"Piss off!" Monica told the inner voice, thinking, I do not like to be bossed around – I never did, and I never will!

Doctor Ra'shae Mansoor went straight to her desk and sat down and then she saw all the little red lights blinking and she realized that the Subject was no longer where she should be.

Doctor Mansoor flicked on the lights in the lab.

The operating table was empty – chaos, overturned drips, ripped up shackles, a torn-off armored door …

My God!

And – the subject was gone! Doctor Mansoor pushed the alarm. Bells began to ring, lights to flash, and a mechanical voice said, "This is lockdown, this is lockdown, code red, code red."

Doctor Mansoor then noticed the smell of fresh coffee and of ripe banana and she noticed too, in the same instant, that the paper "Alien DNA structures as Parasitical Invaders" was no longer on her desk and Doctor Mansoor felt a chill run down the back of her spine and she started to turn in her chair …

Oh My God!

As she turned towards the kitchen alcove, Doctor Mansoor saw … .

Sitting on the shelf, Monica Fabritz felt the human female's fear, the human female's terror, she felt the woman's sudden rush of adrenaline, the rising pulse and pressure of her blood; it was, yes, it was very exciting! Blood, blood, blood!

Yum, Yum, Yum …

Freddy rose out of the swamp, dripping water and mud. He leapt to the dusty shoulder of the road, and crouched in the soft dust, with mud and water trickling from his claws. He was alone, always alone, and he was frightened too, frightened in a strange way he had not experienced before. He didn't know what he was frightened of; but …

Something was coming, something dangerous.

And he didn't know what it was.

He saw the headlights in the distance. A column of military vehicles racing along the hardtop that led to the experimental station – The Everglades Agricultural Research Institute – that was where, he somehow knew, that was where they were keeping his creature and his child; he had come to liberate his creature – the female who belonged to him – and the baby – and take them to a cave that he had found; in reality, it was a hollow in an old abandoned building deep in the Everglades and there they would not be found, not until they were ready to come out and feast. He would care for them. They would be his and his alone.

And they would feast together and eat of human flesh.

They would commune, under the sun, under the moon.

They would hunt, the female, the child, and he …

The voice told him there were dangers ahead; that the humans wanted to destroy his baby, his son, and, even, perhaps, his female; and that he had to act quickly and now. The voice told him, too, that there was another danger, a danger that was difficult to describe, but that it was close.

It was the greatest danger.

It was female, a woman, and the greatest danger.

The headlights were closer now; the column of vehicles, five of them, was racing towards him – coming on fast.

He had to decide quickly: Were these vehicles an immediate threat and if they were, what should he do about it? As the headlights approached, he moved off into the shadows, the lead headlights just catching sparkling reflections off his metal gray scales.

He crouched now, ready to spring.

"They have come to destroy your son," the voice said.

What? They have come to destroy my son – No, it cannot be allowed.

"Kill them," the voice said, "kill them all – each and every one."

It was a convoy, a military convoy, coming fast.

"Kill them, kill them, now! Kill them!"

Still ten miles to go, and …

"What the fuck," muttered Doctor Kevin Harris, there was a fucking road block up front, fucking stupidity! Doctor Harris decided to swing the car around it. After all, it was just a few oil barrels burning. Oh, damnation! A couple of trees had been cut down and were lying across the road. Bodies were sprawled here and there. Looked like humans, looked like soldiers. He didn't see any of the fucking zombies.

He tried to drive around the oil drums, but he clipped one of the drums and it toppled over and flared up and suddenly half the fucking car was on fire. Driver's side, for Christ's sake!

He slammed on the brakes, turned off the engine, cars could blow up if they caught on fire – couldn't they?

He unbuckled his seat belt, slid over to the passenger seat and tried to open the door.

The fucking door wouldn't open. It must have been damaged when they hit those fucking zombies, or when the fucking zombies attacked the car, or maybe when that fucking zombie wacked the car with the hammer. He slammed against the door with his shoulder. He kicked the door. He jerked the handle. It came off in his hand.

Jesus!

I don't deserve this! Do I deserve this? No, I don't deserve this. He slammed himself against the door.

The flames licked inside the car, filling it with smoke. He could see smoke coming from the hood and under the hood. He coughed. His eyes stung, filled with tears.

I don't fucking believe this!

Then the whole thing exploded. A huge flash and he was covered in flame and the explosion blew out the door and blew him out the door and he was tumbling, over and over, a ball of fire, on the ground, on the roadside, a ball of fire and flesh, rolling on the asphalt, blinded by flame – the pain of it – his clothes on fire, his hair on fire, his skin on fire. He thought, Fuck, I'm being burned alive.

He was covered in oil, burning oil.

He rolled, kicking, screaming, kicking, on the asphalt, rolling over and over. It didn't want to go out, the fucking fire, it fucking well didn't want to go out, the clothes, the hair, the skin, still burning, still sizzling and smoking and flaming. His chest and arms were on fire.

Screaming – was that him, screaming?

He staggered to his feet, he staggered forward, a living column of flame, he made it to the concrete barrier that lined the side of the road, he grabbed it – Oh, the pain, the fucking pain – he rolled over it, still a ball of flame, and he crawled staggering, rolling, to the ditch and he splashed into it – mud and water, not much water, but at least it was water and he rolled in the stuff, mud, guck, and slime, trying, praying, screaming that it would go out.

It sizzled and hissed and he lay at last in the muddy water staring up at the night sky, humid and bright like candy floss with the reflected purple and rose of flames, the burning car sending columns of fire into the air, and the oil barrels, still burning. The stench of burnt hair and burnt flesh was overpowering.

There was a giant flash and the car must have really exploded and a flare of metal, raining metal, sparks and ashes slashing down. He closed his eyes and rolled over on his belly face down, arms over his head to protect that vulnerable but marvelous brain of his – that brain of unrecognized genius – from yet more damage. Then it was quiet and he turned over scraping the muck out of his eyes and realizing that most of his hair had been burned off and he tried to sit up and God it hurt but he managed and his clothes had been burned off, but by God he still has his prick and balls, it looked like, anyway, curled up between his legs, but so tender, hard to tell, with all that much, picking the skin raw flesh peeling off

His nose – most of his nose was gone!

No matter, one can smell – sniff, sniff, sniff – without a nose, ha, ha, ha!

He had to get to the Institute, he had to do that Swiss bitch, he had to do the lobotomy, he had to turn that snotty privileged bitch into a mindless beast, he had to finish the experiment, with finesse and with delicacy, he had to remove her brain, the brainy part, ha, ha, ha, of her brain, the brainy part, ha, ha, ha …

But the car no longer existed.

All his kit had been destroyed.

Ah, no matter! He could improvise – if he could get to the Institute. He could use a needle; he could insert it and twirl it around a few times, whisk it like he was whisking whipped cream, scoop out the part of the prefrontal cortex, he could use the electroshock equipment. It would be less precise, and more painful, but she would be drugged anyway and when she woke up she wouldn't even have any idea of how to complain or who or what she was, she would be in no position to complain, to whomever, in any case nobody would listen to her because she would definitely be a thing, not a person.

Call her *it* not *she* – fucking politically correct sniveling bureaucrats!

Part of the pleasure of the whole thing was calling her "she."

Probably "she" would have to be spoon-fed.

She's going to have to wear diapers. Let her go naked – shit herself, sure, like that, a real show! Keep her in a cage! With straw on the floor! He began to laugh, ha, ha, ha ... What the fuck am I laughing at? I've got to get there first.

And, in the void, I can chemically redesign her personality!

Make her libidinous – irrepressible, needy, worshipful ...

A thing of beauty!

Fuck!

What was that?

A hulking figure came out of the mist.

A zombie!

Harris tried to get up. He managed to stand but it was fucking difficult. He'd have to run or see if he could hide, or maybe use fire to fight them off. The stupid fucks were probably afraid of fire, stupid fucking fucks, ha, ha, ha.

Got to survive, got to get to lobotomize the bitch, ha, ha, ha.

He fell down again, on his belly. Fuck!

He clawed at the slime, and crawled out of the ditch, slithering on his belly. Oh, fuck, it was painful. His guts were being ripped out. He had to get over the fucking cement barrier. He growled: Use your brains, idiot, your brains – they've always been your strong point, use your brains – you always were the smartest guy in the room.

Strips of flesh were peeling away – raw flesh underneath – strips of flesh crisp like deep fried crispy bacon, reels of the stuff.

Barbecue man, Barbecue man, I'm the barbecue man! He thought of the barbecue last week. He felt his cheek – peels of flesh falling away, baring the teeth, like a fucking skull, he could feel the teeth and gums, open to the air, fancy that, no lips, no lips to kiss or be kissed with, fucking stupid, ha, ha, ha! He crawled, he stood up, half stood up, staggered, moved to the barrier, thinking how at that last barbecue, last week, he'd bullied that poor stupid cow Ms. Anderson, a dithery fucking spinster, told her that her thesis was ridiculous, that it was pure unadulterated shit, which was not true, rather the reverse, it was brilliant and original, the poor cow. In front of fucking everybody, he told her that she was an ugly overweight fat fucking useless bitch, shouted that she was a stupid cunt – yes, in front of everybody too, she was in tears, really stupid ugly cunt, really ugly. Ashley had looked at him as if she was sending a dagger though his heart and he thought, "Good, now Ashley, the fucking spoilt bitch, can see how dangerous I can be!" If you are dangerous, unpredictable, a real son-of-a-bitch, they respect you. They let you do anything. Terror is a real fine teacher! Ashley, the bitch, the disloyal bitch, had gone to the Anderson cow and held her and then gone off with her and the two of them had sat in a corner talking all night. For two days Ashley refused to say a word – she had shut him out completely, absolutely. In fact, lately, she had become somewhat perfunctory in her attentions, a tad cold, a touch distant, a trifle snobbish and frigid. Fucking cunt bitch, doesn't know what side her bread is buttered on … I'll show her!

When I get back, I'll show her, ah, ah, ah!

She'll grovel, she'll grovel, naked, and she'll beg, ha, ha, ha.

His vision was blurry. One eye had melted out of its socket – drooled down the decayed cavern of his cheek – Hey, I can feel the cheekbone – well, fuck that, double fuck that, you can see out of one eye! Goddamn fucking right!

Even though, in truth, the one remaining eye, badly singed, was blurry too.

The zombie was standing there, arms dangling, mouth hanging open, staring at him. What the fuck are you looking at, you stupid cunt!

He screamed, "What the fuck you looking at!?"

He climbed onto and toppled over the concrete barrier coming down on all fours, on the asphalt; the burned-out car body, smoldering flickering, the oil drums, the stench …

Oh, the pain!

He saw his U-Tab lying on the pavement – must have fallen out of his clothes when he had been thrown out of the car, yeah, when he still had clothes, ha, ha, ha … He was the crispy-fried man, naked, on his hands and knees. He stabbed at a button on the U-Tab. The Tab lit up.

The zombie walked forward, slowly, with what looked like deliberation.

Fuck, the zombie had something in his hand.

It looked like, he blinked his one eye; it looked like it looked like, a miniature pointed pickaxe …

A pickaxe …

A miniature pickaxe …

The pickaxe came in a single swing of the arm of the zombie and its narrow razor-sharp point smashed into Doctor Harris's forehead and into his skull.

Ugh!

A flash of blinding light.

The Apocalypse.

Then nothing.

Doctor Kevin Harris crumpled down and curled up.

The zombie stared at what he had done. He looked down at the body, at the axe implanted in its forehead. He wiped his nose – which was drooling loops of sticky goo – looked away and forgot about the body lying on the pavement and about the axe and about swinging it and about everything else. He turned, grunted, wiped his nose, spat, and shambled away, shoulders hunched, arms swaying loosely, dangling, and headed into the swamp.

Doctor Kevin Harris lay on the pavement, now sprawled on his back, his one eye staring straight up at the flame-licked sky but not seeing much of anything, not anything that had a name – names had ceased to exist. The axe stuck out of his head like a strange animal's horn – turning him into a sort of devilish unicorn.

The U-tab, face up, flickering on the pavement, was saying, "Hi! This is Ashley Samos, please leave a message. Thank you!"

Doctor Harris rolled on his stomach and grabbed at the object, whatever it was, that was making that strange noise which was a human voice though the thing that Harris had become no longer recognized the human voice or any voice for that matter. He growled and he picked it up between burnt stubs of fingers. One finger and a thumb fell off. He growled again, drooling slobber. He brought the U-Tab to his teeth. "Gurrmph," he growled. He licked it. He sniffed it. He gnawed at it. It was hard, unyielding. He snarled. It was not something to eat or suck on, so he dropped it and stomped on it. He made a yowling sound, a keening slobbering yelp that rose like an inhuman yodel to the inflamed candy-floss sky.

The U-Tab said, "Your time is up. Ashley Samos thanks you for your message!" Then it went dark.

The shaggy burned-out creature stood for a moment, growling, sobbing, slobbering, drooling, turning, round and round, in a hunched, bestial circle wondering, dimly and without words, where it should go now.

The pain, the nameless pain, was great.

Unspoken was the thought, not a thought, really, just a feeling, just pain, pain, and more pain. Must hide from the pain! Must hide!

Shambling off, head down, the small axe sticking out of its forehead, one eye seeing dimly through a blur, arms dangling, the creature headed towards the swamp. Nameless things would greet it there, its brothers, its sisters.

Doctor Harris had the mark of the Beast upon him – he had devolved, spinning backwards through millions of years, to a time before human time began. Under the flaming scarlet sky, the unnamable wordless thing he had become growled and snarled and slobbered, stumbling its way into the darkness.

CHAPTER 8 – COLONEL SIEBERT

V decided what the heck, she would waste no time trying to break into the Everglades Agricultural Research Institute, so, when she came to the electrified link metal fence and the watch towers, she would just plain leap over the whole thing, and this meant that she had better change into her reptilian self – it had much more bounce. She frowned. She would probably scare the hell out of people and, alas, maybe hurt some soldiers.

She stripped naked and packed everything, neatly folded, into her backpack. Closing her eyes, she morphed in an instant – just a shimmering blur – into her sparkling turquoise-green reptilian self. The process felt like a pleasant summer breeze passing over her naked body. It was, in a minor way, voluptuously sensual, a surrogate for sex or for a good sauna or massage.

She sometimes regretted that she was stuck with one color scheme – turquoise and green, with gold, yellow, and red accessories or decorations, which accessories were her claws, eyes, and tongue – even if, admittedly, her present mix and pattern was rather stylish and varied. She occasionally wondered if she should ask Sabrina and Alex about color and pattern variation, alternatives, and if they could be added to her general design. Maybe Claire could act as consultant and design a new tailor-made bespoke reptile look, or perhaps a kaleidoscope effect, like Kate Thornhill's dancing dervish tattoos, always changing unless she ordered them to be still. Well, such considerations were minor, in the present circumstances, with the end of civilization impending. The question of vampire and reptilian aesthetics could be raised after all of this was over – if there was any after.

If the enemy won, and the image of the Dark God kept flickering into her consciousness, if it won, there would be no more human race to save.

And – no more food!

If there were no humans, she would starve to death.

With no sinners to save, there could be no salvation!

Father O'Bryan SJ, where are you when I need you for a quick theological consultation, eh? Dead, the poor Jesuit, dead and buried these many years, though she had, half in jest, offered him eternal life, saying, "How will I live without you, Father?" And he, gently refusing her offer, and pouring them both another shot of Bushmills, had said, "You will do very well without me, V, and, in any case, in spirit, I shall always be with you." Ah, Father O'Bryan, Father O'Bryan!

She vaulted over the sixteen-foot-high fence and landed softly, almost in slow motion, on the small lawn – neatly cut grass, they must have a fine budget – in front of the "Everglades Agricultural Research Institute," and almost at the same instant as her claws touched down, and as she flipped down into her on-all-fours-ready-for-action-crouch, and was about to leap again, bells went off and an alarm sounded, and V thought, hmm, that seems too quick to be just for me, something else must be happening. A guard came running from one of the guardhouses, he wasn't even looking at her, he was running towards the main building, but then he saw her and he stopped, muttered "Jesus Christ," and began to swing his automatic weapon towards her. It was an MP-5K PDW, V noticed. *Oh, so naughty!* V leaped clear over him, so he swung around, watching her go overhead, and then swinging around to meet her with the butt of his submachine gun since she was now behind him and within two feet of his face, and V said, "You are damned good, soldier," and grinned – well, it was a reptilian grin – at his nice fresh tanned handsome face – and she in that instant knew his background and his thoughts and how he liked his spaghetti cooked – his maternal grandmother was Italian – and she grabbed the weapon, and being careful not to break his arm, she tossed it away, and in one powerful motion she pushed him down, though he was young and devilishly strong and had really quick reflexes. She leapt onto him, straddling his midriff and pinning down his wrists, "Very impressive, young man, and, yes, your grandmother's *spaghetti all'Amatriciana* is indeed splendid, though I only know from hearsay since my diet, alas, doesn't include Italian food."

"What in the hell are you?"

"Good question, soldier."

"Are you a demon from hell – a hybrid?"

"Bingo," said V. She pulled the stun gun from the side of her back pack. She pushed it against the young man's neck, but held back from pressing the trigger, "A hybrid, that's what I am."

"What are you going to …?"

"Look, I'd love to talk, darling, I really would. I like you. But I'm in a bit of a hurry right now and don't have time." She lowered her snout to within an inch of his face and whispered, "Some other time I'd love to have a cozy, intimate chat!"

"What the hell are you going to …?"

"This will give you a bad headache, my sweet, but nothing worse than that. Still, you are a very pretty fellow! I apologize! I am sorry to knock you out like this!" She pulled the trigger. The young man jerked once, twice, three, four times, and lay still.

It was cruel, V thought, but it was also quite pleasant, feeling the handsome young man and his muscular body jerking – one, two, three, four times – as she held his midriff locked in a vice between her thighs. Perhaps another time, in another universe, if it were not you, if it were not me, if we were other than we are, if we were young lovers, perhaps returning to our hotel room from a walk along the Seine, then these youthful spasms would be a different matter entirely, and even more enjoyable, my dear. She leaned down and kissed the young man's cheek. It was warm under her reptilian lips; it was smooth with just a hint of stubble under her reptilian tongue.

"V – Get back to the business at hand!"

"Yes, yes, my conscience, you are quite right!"

She leapt up – leaving the young man sprawled on the grass – and she shot up into the air – one clean air-borne arc of twenty yards – arriving at the main door, which, just at the instant she landed, banged open, and three guards came running out, as she flattened herself against the wall. She jumped behind them – zapped them all, one after the other, with the stun gun: zap, zap, zap …

Oh dear, my poor chaps!

They were all so young, so tanned, so handsome!

It was all over so quickly it was hardly any fun at all.

V had never collected boy toys, but it now occurred to her that it might be an amusing hobby to take up, for a short time at least. Her usual taste in men ran to older guys, guys with more experience, guys who had something interesting to say, guys who had refined the techniques and attitudes of tenderness and the rituals of courtship, though, she had to admit, the youngsters could surprise you sometimes and they had such appetizing bodies and such corpuscular energies and …

Such warm, hot blood!

The zap would keep the lads down for about thirty minutes, which should be enough time for what V had to do – capture and liberate the hybrid girl.

Then she felt, she smelled, she sensed *terror – pure terror …*

Terror, pure terror, it was inside the building somewhere.

She ran into the building, down a well-lit corridor where lights were flashing.

"This is lockdown; this is lockdown, code red, code red, code red."

Alarms were ringing: Buzz, buzz, buzz, buzz …

"This is lockdown, this is lockdown; code red, code red, code red."

Colonel Jefferson Siebert, Ph.D., MD, seven army medals and one air force medal, thirty-seven years old, 215 pounds of muscle, steely blue eyes, strong jaw, not a single cavity, always shaved his head: it meant there was no fuss no bother and no need to talk to barbers or listen to the mostly inane conversations that went on in the most desultory time-consuming fashion in most barber shops military or civilian, you would think that people had nothing better to do with their time, and Colonel Siebert believed, firmly believed, no, he knew, he knew that time was precious, that we were only on this earth, in this life, for so long, and that there were important things to be done, and too many things to be learned, to waste time on frippery and frivolities.

He was staring out the armored windshield of the Yong Sheng V Light Armored Vehicle going 75 miles an hour along a narrow hardtop road through an alligator infested swamp to a godforsaken outpost known to the world – well, it really wasn't known to the world at all under any name whatsoever, come to think of it – as the Everglades Agricultural Research Institute – and inside that Institute was one of the most important discoveries that mankind had made – inside that building was a half-alien, half-human hybrid, and the creature was pregnant with what might be the first of a race of half-alien, half-human hybrids and a mortal danger, so the experts at the briefing said, to the future and very existence of humanity.

Colonel Siebert's orders were to evacuate the hybrid and if that was not possible – the zombie menace was approaching from the south – to eliminate the hybrid and its unborn child and to incinerate the remains taking all precautions not to be contaminated by said hybrid and said fetus.

He was chewing this over, literally clenching his jaw, when he caught sight of something, just a flicker, out of the side of his eye, just a glimmer, on the edge of the road, about 150 meters in front of the Yong Sheng V on the right hand side, and he said to the driver, slow down, sensors, right, one o'clock to three o'clock, and the sensors flashed – "bio-form" – and the driver, Sergeant Miranda Gonzalez, a twenty-three-year-old combat veteran, a feisty, Spanish-speaking brunette, said, "It's a life form, sir, bio-form, size of a human or a large kangaroo," and the Colonel said, "Kangaroo? Okay, now, slower, and, Gunner, turn the Gatling to the sector, and use high intensity floodlights, ready to go on my signal." The Colonel didn't like surprises on the side of the road, he'd seen too many men, women, and vehicles torn apart by improvised explosive devices, gutted by short range bazookas, turned upside down by little bits of plastic buried in the soft dust or the soft tar of roads, in cities, in the country, in the deserts, so: "Flood it with light, and prepare to fire."

The gunner, a fresh-faced jug-eared twenty-one-year-old from backwoods Kentucky who went by the name of Claibe J. Coates, said, "Aye, aye, sir!" Colonel Siebert thought, with an inner smile, that all the members of his team, each and every one of them, had character, were quirky individuals, with wit and grit and stamina, "Kangaroo," from a woman who had never been to Australia, and the naval "Aye, aye," from a guy who'd probably never set foot on a ship, but that was good, it was a team and bigger than its parts, all for one, and one for all, and he said:

"Okay, lights!"

The lights flooded on, and the visual was startling – a guy who looked like a reptile – yes, kangaroo did come to mind, goddamn it, and he realized, in the same instant, that this was Reptile Man, it must be, the killer hybrid, and, with the thought, what's it doing here, came the answer! It's after its victim, it's after its child, and came the second thought: What to do about it, should we try to kill it, capture it, and before he could give the order – and he was not sure which order – the Gatling homing in on the thing and the missile launcher – electronic cross-hairs focused on the image – but the thing leapt, it just sort of rocketed out of there, up into the air, out of the glare of the lights, straight into the sky, and then, wham, it came down on top of the armored Yong Sheng V and it ripped open the roof – Wham, Rip, Screech!

Colonel Siebert wrenched himself around, took out his sidearm and fired upwards. The creature had Claibe in its claws, and pulled Claibe out of the vehicle, and threw the body, minus the head it seemed to Colonel Siebert, over the side of the vehicle, just a flash of part of a body going down beside the 6-ton Yong Sheng V, which was now spinning sideways on the hardtop, as the creature, and Colonel Siebert was emptying his revolver into the bastard's gut but it didn't seem to make a bit of difference, the creature leaned down and grabbed at Miranda, slashing her jugular, blood spurting everywhere, and splashing into the Colonel's eyes, and the Yong Sheng V skidded sideways, Miranda's head bobbing up and down as if it were no longer attached to her body, and Miranda's hands, white-knuckled – the Colonel, wiping the blood from his eyes, somehow noticed – Miranda's hands, white-knuckled, still gripping the wheel.

The Colonel leaped up and grabbed the thing by one of its legs, and he tried to climb up its body, he was going to drag the thing down and finish it off with a knife, a knife might just do it, and he felt the thing grab him, deep claws, striking into his flesh, and haul him up through the twisted metal, and suddenly in the glare of headlights from the other vehicles, still racing onwards, nobody had yet realized what was happening, there they were, the two of them, face-to-face on top of the Yong Sheng V which was still skidding – and the colonel crouching, ready to spring, said, "What the hell are you? Who the hell are you?" and the creature just stared at him, its fangs and its claws dripping blood, its eyes glowing, impenetrable, and then, suddenly, the Yong Sheng V hit the ditch, bounced into the air, the Colonel thinking, "I didn't realize we were going so fast," and the two of them went flying, and the Colonel had, at that instant, grabbed the thing by the arm, and it held onto him too, and they landed, smashing down through reeds and long grass, in the mud, and the Colonel lay breathless for a second, his arm over the arm of the reptile, and then he staggered to his feet, the whole scene, the reeds, the mud, the long grass, the watery pools – and alligators, probably, thought the Colonel – and the Reptile Man, already standing, glittering gun metal, all his scales, and his flinty eyes, all lit up by vehicle headlights, like the two of them were on a goddamn movie set, thought the Colonel, and he reached for his knife and the thing said, "Sorry, Colonel, sorry," and then, "Good-bye Colonel," it was clear as a bell, "Sorry, Colonel, sorry," and then, "Good-bye, Colonel," and it leapt into the air and was gone.

Colonel Siebert stood there, covered in mud, shaking, gripping the knife, ready to strike, feeling sick and empty – it was his fault, his fault for hesitating, even an instant, his fault, but then he realized, and he knew, instinctively, he knew that the Gatling gun and the missile launcher would have been too slow, too late, would have meant nothing, so …

There was nothing he could have done.

Damn, damn, damn!

When the Colonel came out of the swamp, the vehicles were all stopped, the headlights on bright, with floodlights swinging over the surrounding swamp, soldiers out with weapons drawn – automatic rifles, machine guns, grenade launchers, and the motors were running, and his second, Sal Freemont, came trotting up, wiping his forehead, and said, "Are you okay, sir?"

"Yes, I'm okay," he looked down the road. Claibe's body was laid out, with his head sitting next to it.

"Put Claibe in your vehicle, Lieutenant, please," and Colonel Siebert walked over to his own vehicle. It was lying on its side, smoking, sparks striking off, gasoline leaking.

It's going to go up any minute, he thought. He climbed onto the side of the overturned Yong Sheng V. He looked down through the open, smashed, door.

Miranda's body was sprawled down in what had been his seat, against the far window, her face and hair splashed with blood, soaked in it. The air had the metallic smell of fresh blood and of electrical sparks and of gasoline and of gunpowder.

Colonel Siebert climbed down into the vehicle. He crouched – it was crowded, hardly any space at all, turned on its side like this – he crouched and he put his arms under Miranda, awkward, sprawled limp like that, slippery, covered in blood, and he lifted her up. "Colonel, sir," it was Sergeant Schmidt; she was up on top, looking down, lit up by the headlights. "Colonel, sir, it's going to blow, sir, any second it's going to blow."

"I know that, soldier, here, help me," and he lifted Miranda up, and pushed her limp body, neck three-quarters severed, her head lolling back, hair, heavy with blood hanging down, and Sergeant Schmidt took hold, and the Colonel climbed up, and, together, they got Miranda out of the open door, and then they climbed down and got her away from the overturned Yong Sheng V, and the Colonel said, "Now, Sergeant Schmidt, we've got to hurry. If that thing is here, it's here for some reason, and that reason must be inside the laboratory. I think it's here for the same reason we're here!"

And just as he said this, just as he was about to climb into Sergeant Schmidt's vehicle, the overturned Yong Sheng V burst into flame and then exploded, with a huge thunderous upward whoosh, and a wave of heat hit the Colonel like he'd been slapped in the face. It lit up the whole countryside, swamp, narrow hardtop, dusty muddy shoulder. It looked as if it were high noon.

"Okay, that's that," said the Colonel, and he settled himself next to Sergeant Schmidt – who took over the driving – Lieutenant Freemont sitting behind them. It was a lighter, faster Yong Sheng VI.

The motors roared and they were on their way.

Doctor Ra'shae Mansoor sat in her chair, her fingers gripping the hand rests, her knuckles turning white, her mouth open, and her heart beating so hard she could hear it hammering against her temples.

Sitting on a shelf in the alcove next to the refrigerator, with her legs crossed, and one clawed foot rocking back and forth, was a reptile woman, she was very pregnant, she was holding a banana, and she was chewing. She stared at Ra'shae and her fangs, which were quite prominent, seemed to shine in the dull observation room lights, and her tongue – which was bright red – flicked out of her mouth several times. She was licking her lips, or what passed for lips. The scales were a bright blue – cobalt, actually, the color of the deep blue sea.

Beside the reptile woman was Doctor Mansoor's Beretta 9mm.

Neither of them said anything for what seemed to Ra'shae an eternity. Seconds clicked over on the electronic clock – one, two, three, four … The reptile took a bite out of the banana.

Ra'shae was thinking that her kids, if they survived the zombie plague, would probably have to grow up without their mother. She had read the detailed and highly confidential reports of what the hybrid reptile man had done and she was terrified. This creature would probably do the same.

"I stole a banana," said the reptile, "I hope you don't mind." Its voice had a bit of a lisp and a pronounced hiss, "And I've borrowed your pistol. I didn't want you to do anything rash."

Ra'shae swallowed. "No, no," she cleared her throat. "I don't mind."

"I also made some coffee," the reptile woman slid – heavily, awkwardly – off the shelf. "Would you like some?"

"Yes, ah, yes, I would." Ra'shae felt the sweat pearling on her back, on her forehead.

"Good. That's nice." The reptile woman, or the Subject, pushed a button. "How do you like it? No, let me guess, cappuccino, lots of foam, not too hot, at about 130 degrees Celsius. Is that right?"

"Yes," Ra'shae again cleared her throat. "That's right."

"Good." The reptile woman popped a capsule into the machine, pushed a few buttons, and turned towards Ra'shae and then she strolled forward, coming quite close, her eyes gleaming. "Now, Ra'shae, do you mind if I use your first name?"

"No, no, not at all."

"Good. So, Ra'shae, you may call me Monica, if you wish."

"Yes, of course, Monica." Ra'shae trembled. She felt the violence within the creature, the tremendous violence, the contained anger, the rage – and the strength – and the blood thirst.

Ra'shae swallowed. Thoughts and images raced through her head: The creature is smiling at me, but she could tear me into bloody shreds in less than a second and – she wants to, she's dying to do it!

Ra'shae saw herself, in one brief flash image, a shredded mass of flesh, her face, a mask detached from the skull.

"Having a name is less impersonal than being called 'it' or 'the Subject,' don't you think, Ra'shae?"

"Yes, you are right."

"Coffee's ready! Don't get up! You sit there. I'll bring it." And the reptile woman – her tummy was certainly heavily swollen – she was ripe, more than ripe – went to the machine and took the cup, carefully, between her claws, and, with her back still turned to Ra'shae she said, "Yes, Ra'shae, your thoughts are quite accurate. I am very angry, I am extremely violent, I am very dangerous – there is a voice urging me to kill every human being I meet – and I am very thirsty – and, yes, it is a very bloody picture you have just imagined: You disemboweled, your face – and it's a very pretty face behind those thick horn-rimmed glasses – torn off, or half torn off, which would be more effective, leaving a memory, a trace of the beauty that once was, before the disfigurement." Monica turned around, tilting her head to one side, and smiled and brought the coffee to Ra'shae.

"Thank you, Monica." Ra'shae's hand was trembling, but less than before. She took the cup. She took a deep breath.

Monica went back to the alcove, took the pistol, and grabbed a stool - one of those stainless steel stools on little wheels – and rolled it over close to Ra'shae.

She sat down on the stool, with the Beretta in one claw, and with her face close to Ra'shae's face. "I'm going to have the baby, Ra'shae, and I'm going to have it now, soon, I can feel it, the contractions have begun, and they are getting stronger." She reached out a claw to steady herself against the desk. "I think I might even faint."

"Oh, my God," said Ra'shae. "We don't have a doctor, nobody is here ... We ... I've never delivered a baby; I know nothing about ..."

"I want you to promise, Ra'shae, that you will not harm me – or the baby."

"I promise."

The reptile woman gazed at her and then said, "Good. So now we'll have to work together. And, you may need your pistol."

She pressed the Beretta into Doctor Ra'shae Mansoor's hand.

Colonel Siebert stared at the brightly lit narrow hardtop racing towards him; he glanced at the dark flat Everglade landscape, at the night sky glowing with the distant fires of Miami and Fort Lauderdale. It seemed to him that at any instant that creature, the metal gray reptile hybrid, could spring out of the darkness, rip the armor off the armored cars, and rip apart some young man or young woman, and Colonel Siebert felt a personal responsibility for all those young people, and he was determined that, if the opportunity came, he would kill, somehow kill, that murderous monster. He did wonder, though, about why the hybrid had spared him. *He could have killed me in an instant.* And why had he apologized, saying "Sorry, Colonel, I'm sorry," before leaping off into the night?

This brought up the question of the hybrid woman and her unborn child. What to do about them? The Colonel's inclination was now to eliminate, no, let's not be euphemistic, to kill, no, since she was partly human, originally human, and innocent, she had not gotten herself into this predicament, the *real* word to use, the Colonel muttered to himself, was "murder," the wisest thing, given the vicious nature of these hybrids, was to murder the girl and her unborn baby – otherwise this female hybrid would undoubtedly kill humans and the baby hybrid would kill humans and he, the Colonel, would have all those future human deaths on his conscience.

"Pardon, Colonel?" said Sergeant Schmidt.

"No, nothing, just talking to myself," said the Colonel.

The lights of the Everglades Agricultural Research Institute were just in front of them, the column of vehicles swerved around a bend in the road and there were the metal gates of the Institute itself.

"Slow down, we'll ask permission before we barge in," said the Colonel.

Caution, this time, was the better part of valor. He had no idea what was going on inside the Institute. And radio communications with Headquarters had ended in a blitz of static half an hour ago. They might be headed into a trap.

No communications from Washington or from Fort Myers or Miami either. Radios and satellite communications seemed knocked out, and even the GPS was wobbly, and, yeah, right now, as he was watching, it signed off, fizzled out, and was gone.

The lead vehicle stopped three yards short of the gate.

The lights lit up the metal grid, the guardhouse, the road inside the compound, and the neatly cut grass of the lawn.

The Colonel drew his weapon, got out of the vehicle, and walked up to the guardhouse. It was empty. He pushed the button for communications – no answer.

Then the Colonel saw the bodies lying on the grass, five or six men, still in uniform, lying as if dead – probably dead.

The Colonel got back in the vehicle. "Listen up," he said, "we are going in. We drive through the gate; then vehicles fan out, 'A' vehicle and 'B' vehicle stop facing inward towards the buildings. 'C' and 'D' vehicles swing around, on either flank: distance 30 yards outwards from the 'A' and 'B' arc, facing outwards. Watch out! We have bodies of guards. They look like friendlies, on the ground – so let's not run over them – but, once out of the vehicles, approach them with care."

The vehicles rushed through the gate, smashing it aside and then they swung around so that they could confront dangers coming from within or without.

The Colonel now reached into the inner pocket of his flak jacket for the sealed envelope that had written on it "To be opened only on arrival at the Everglades Agricultural Research Institute." He focused on the single sheet, illuminated in the reading lamp of the armored vehicle:

"Colonel Siebert: Your *real* – secret – orders are to eliminate the hybrid woman and her child – or fetus – and to eliminate all the members of the staff of the Everglades Agricultural Research Institute – EARI – who are present, including scientific personnel and all guards and maintenance and auxiliary staff – everyone without exception is to be eliminated.

Any other persons found in the Institute or its vicinity must also be eliminated.

The bodies should be burned and the building demolished so that nothing remains but ash. Explosives and gasoline are in storage building B in the Institute compound.

Good luck, Colonel, I know you will carry this mission to successful completion. General Karl Hoffmann.

PS: Note: Jeff, this order – which I don't like – was signed personally by the vice president in virtue of the emergency powers he assumed this evening."

"Fuck!" The Colonel squinted at the scene, lit up in the headlights, the guards were lying near the door; one guard was lying close to the guardhouse and the smashed gate.

He folded the letter up, put it back in the envelope, and slipped it back into his vest and he climbed out of the vehicle. "Let's see what we've got."

He walked over to the guard lying on the grass near the guardhouse and he crouched down. The young man was lying face up his eyes were closed, it looked like he was sleeping, and the Colonel noticed the pulse in the man's neck, and he felt the man's forehead, temperature normal, and he saw the tell-tale red mark on the young man's neck. Stunned, the young man had been stunned.

Whoever came through here it was certainly not the killer hybrid.

The Colonel looked up. His men were in position, some of them flattened against the building – its blank walls were without windows – some of his team were lying on the ground, their weapons pointed outwards, at the ready – submachine guns, handheld missiles, high precision pistols with killer hollow-head dum-dum bullets.

They were nervous, waiting for orders.

The Colonel stood up slowly, surveyed the scene, and he said to his second, "I'm not sure what we are facing here. We've taken no hostile fire yet and the guard here has been stunned – whoever did this didn't want to kill him."

"The others have all been stunned too, sir," said Lieutenant Freemont, "Pulses normal, eye readings and neuro readings indicate no permanent damage, sir. They'll probably be out for another twenty or thirty minutes."

"Let's go in slowly," said the Colonel. He rubbed his chin, "I don't want anybody shooting just to shoot. We'll talk first and shoot after, unless we see our reptile friend, him shoot on sight. Use the hollow-head bullets on that guy, or the flamethrower." He paused. "Okay, I'm going in first."

V sniffed the air. This was definitely enemy territory. As she made her way down the corridor in the Everglades Agricultural Research Institute, she was wary and edgy – ready to kill anyone who stood in her way; the place seemed totally, eerily, empty; then, she heard voices, around the corner and through a door, in someone's office.

She tensed, claws extended, fangs gleaming, stun gun drawn, ready to spring into action.

She peeked around the corner. A cobalt-colored hybrid, a reptile woman, who was very pregnant, and an Indian woman in a lab coat were sitting close together, knee-to-knee, drinking coffee. V entered the room.

"Well, ladies, is this a coffee club or what?"

Monica Fabritz and Ra'shae Mansoor turned towards the door.

Standing in the doorway was a spectacular reptile woman – she gleamed and glittered, turquoise and green, with golden eyes.

"Oh, my God," whispered Ra'shae, reaching for the Beretta.

"What is this, another Freddy?" hissed Monica, baring her fangs, flexing her claws, ready to spring up and tear the intruder apart.

The reptile woman was wearing a backpack and holding in her hand what looked like a stun gun. "Hello," she said.

"Hello," breathed Ra'shae, still holding the coffee cup half way to her lips, one hand cradling the Beretta.

"Hello," hissed Monica, narrowing her reptile eyes; the vibes were good, but ...

"You are Monica, I presume, also known as the Subject," said the newcomer, "And you must be Doctor Ra'shae Mansoor." V stepped into the room.

Monica stood up – at first she had been terrified. But now she sensed that this new creature was friendly, that she was not a homicidal machine, not like Freddy; that she was here, in some strange way, to help.

"I'm going to have the baby," Monica said. She was trembling.

"She's going to have the baby," Ra'shae said.

"I know."

"Now, I mean now," said Monica.

"Oh," V said, her eyes widened, "You mean like now, really now – like *now, now*?"

"Yes," said Monica. "Now, now – like right away."

"Bloody Hell!" V frowned; she was not sure she approved of babies – particularly this baby! And as for assisting at a birth ...!

"We need hot water," said Ra'shae, "They always ask for hot water, lots of hot water. At least I think they do."

"In the movies," said V, clenching a clawed fist. What the devil were they going to do?

"Yes, in the movies, I really don't know," said Doctor Mansoor, "I've had children, but it was always in the hospital and –"

"Hot water, then," said V, "lots of hot water."

"And towels, I think," said Ra'shae, putting the Beretta down, "I read somewhere about towels."

"Oh, God," Monica suddenly cried out, "it's starting, it's starting again, Ohhhhh, Ohhhhh, Ohhhhh!"

Colonel Jefferson Siebert motioned with his hand, and whispered, "We'll go in here. I'll take the lead."

"Yes sir."

"I want four of you right behind me – Kathy, Sam, Salvo, Anne. The rest cover the situation out here under Lieutenant Freemont. Sergeant Schmidt, you do liaison – if something happens, you come straight to me, right."

"Yes, sir," she said.

The colonel entered the building and advanced cautiously down a corridor. Alarm lights were flashing, the ordinary lights were fading or on power-saving dull mode, the female electronic voice saying "This is Lockdown, this is Lockdown. Code Red! Code Red!"

Colonel Siebert walked forward slowly, keeping close to the wall, Corporal Anne Laverne closest, the other soldiers strung out behind her. Colonel Siebert was not happy. He did not like the idea of eliminating – killing, murdering, yes, let's use the honest word – "murdering" – the guards and the scientific personnel and he even had doubts now about murdering the hybrid and, most of all, he didn't trust the vice president, the man was a self-righteous fanatical religious nutbar under the influence of crooked preachers and unscrupulous or crazy mountebanks who wanted to bring about the Apocalypse and so-called Rapture as fast as possible so that the Lord's Kingdom could be ushered in tomorrow or, at latest, the day after tomorrow, and all those who were saved, the chosen ones, would be saved and, as for the rest, they would be cast into the depths of Hell; in the Colonel's humble and very personal opinion – which he had the good taste never to express – these people were absolute idiots and criminals; some of them were rascals, certainly, many of them were fools; most of them were both. Bottom line: the vice president was not to be trusted. Besides, the president might not be dead, the Colonel was not convinced she was dead, and he felt there was something fishy and deeply suspicious about the whole terrorist attack and particularly about the way the vice president immediately and radically took over, fired half the Cabinet, and started arresting people, it smelled like a coup d'état.

Things were not right.

The Colonel turned a corner and stopped. He didn't believe his eyes. He was face-to-face, with – with, damnation, with what exactly?

Monica felt like she was being ripped apart. "Press down," Ra'shae Mansoor was saying, "press down with your abdomen, press down."

Monica pressed and pressed and pressed. It seemed to her that the little monster inside her was stubborn as hell, that he did not want to be born, that he was fighting her all the way, that he was in fact the Anti-Christ and that his first act, even before being born, would be to rip her apart, and even this super-strong new body, this spectacular muscular reptilian body, was clearly too weak a vessel to contain the baby, whatever he was. She pushed and pushed, holding her sides with her claws, trying to pull together every ounce of strength she had, and now he was there, at the gates, and she thought her belly and vagina and thighs would explode, would be ripped apart. How in the world had women done this through the centuries! She wanted to howl, to scream, to hiss, to gnash her fangs, but she gritted her fangs instead, she clenched her jaw, she clenched her claws, she held on, she was not going to give in, she was going to expulse this creature into the world, she was going to survive, damn it, and, then, once the deed was done, then she would see what she had become and what she would do with this new creature that she had become.

"That's it keep pushing …"

Colonel Siebert had just come around a corner when he saw it – the enemy – or whatever it was … damnation!

Colonel Siebert levelled his pistol at the creature.

It was carrying two buckets of what looked like steaming water and it was one of the most beautiful things – creatures – the Colonel had ever seen. It looked like a work of art, a statue carved out of some exotic glittering metal, voluptuous, iridescent – perfect.

And – it was a goddamn hybrid!

It was a goddamn female hybrid!

It was a reptile woman, for Christ's sake!

Under the dull flickering fluorescent ceiling lights – flashes of static filled lurid air – and in the institutional gray of the corridor, the creature glowed, positively glowed – turquoise, green, and a touch of scarlet and gold. Yes, it looked like a woman, but of course it wasn't a woman, it was a hybrid, a hybrid of beautiful and exquisite form. The creature was, as they used to say in an earlier century and during one of the old great wars, "stacked."

It was aware of him, he realized. He raised one hand so as to warn the four soldiers behind him to stay back and to be silent.

Now it turned and looked at him, but it didn't drop the bucket or seem alarmed, instead it looked at him steadily, its gold serpent eyes gleaming; it was just a second, though it seemed much longer to Colonel Siebert, and in that second his finger tightened on the trigger because he knew how quickly such a creature could move and how deadly and strong it was – and then it smiled – how he knew it was a smile he would never figure out and somehow too he knew it was a friendly smile – and it said, with a slight and very polite English accent, "Colonel Siebert, would you mind awfully if I ask: Are you by any chance a medical doctor?"

The Colonel hesitated, shoot now and talk later, or wait, take a chance, trust to his gut instinct – and his gut instinct was, for some weird reason, telling him to trust this woman-like thing; he kept his finger tense on the trigger, but he did not pull it. He did ask himself how the creature knew his name, but if he and she – or it – did talk, then he would ask it, and see if it would tell him the truth. He was beginning to think of "it" as a "she" and a mighty attractive "she" in her own way, in the reptilian line, if you were into that sort of thing, and he thought that he must have played too many holographic video comic games with super heroes and super heroines in patterned cat suits when he was a kid and that this unfortunate formative experience had left him with a weirdly eclectic and kinky sense of what was attractive and of what was, for him at least, undeniably sexy.

"Why?" he said, "Why do you want to know?"

"We have a problem."

"A problem? We?"

"Monica, the hybrid, is having a baby, I know nothing about these things, nor does Doctor Mansoor, and, well, I dare say any help would be greatly appreciated, Colonel."

"I am a doctor, yes, but not an obstetrician." Colonel Siebert advanced a few steps.

"I read minds, Colonel, that's how I knew your name. I apologize for the intrusion into your mind, but I had to know whether you intended to shoot me – or not."

Colonel Siebert signaled to his men – two men and two women – to advance. "Don't shoot," he said to them. "Okay," he said to V, "Show me."

"Thank you, Colonel. Just follow me," V started to walk down the corridor. "My name is V, by the way."

"What are you, exactly?"

"I'm a hybrid, Colonel, half-alien, half-human. In fact, I'm the original one, the prototype."

"We met a hybrid. He killed two of my people."

"That is horrible. I am very sorry. When?"

"Twenty minutes ago, on the road here."

"I have been hunting him down – once, after the bus incident in Texas, I thought I had tracked him down, maybe even had him cornered. But he got away. He is very strong, very clever, and very deadly."

"He certainly is strong." The Colonel had caught up with V and was now walking beside her. He still had his pistol out.

"By the way, Colonel, President Katherine du Bois Hughes is still very much alive. I don't think she'd approve of the order signed by the vice president to kill everybody here. I know you don't want to do it. I think you are right."

"What?" Colonel Siebert wondered how this creature knew, of course, she could read minds, and so …"

"I can provide proof later, if you wish," said V.

The Colonel heard his people behind them.

"Holy Cow!"

"Do you see what I see?"

"Colonel, are you okay?"

"I'm fine. Corporal Laverne, join me, will you. The rest of you, stay back, cover the corridor in both directions." The Colonel decided this was one to play by ear; he would follow his gut instinct.

"Yes, sir."

When Colonel Siebert and V – followed by Corporal Anne Laverne – came into Ra'shae's office, Monica – all cobalt blue scales with a red lozenge on her forehead – was lying on her side on the floor on a thick bed of clean towels that Ra'shae had gotten from the storeroom, Monica's hips were propped up on a pillow, Ra'shae was kneeling behind her, supporting her back, saying, "Push, push, push," in a rhythmic almost hysterical way. Monica hissed, baring her fangs, "I am pushing, ugh, ugh, ugh, damn it, I am pushing, ugh, I'm pushing as hard as I bloody well can!"

"Ladies, this is Colonel Siebert," said V, "He's come to help us; he's a doctor. This is very convenient, but he's not an obstetrician, I'm sorry to say."

The Colonel gazed at the scene and then glanced at V. "Can you retract those pointed nails on your claws?"

"Yes, Colonel, I can." V retracted the nails and showed him her claws, appropriately defanged.

"Good, I want you to do this. Wash your hands – your claws – then ..."

"Right, yes, sir!"

"Be thorough. Where's the soap?"

"On the second shelf, in the kitchen niche, there behind you," said Ra'shae, "Colonel, I'm Doctor Mansoor, Ra'shae Mansoor, and this is ... Monica."

"I'm pleased to meet you, Colonel," Monica breathed out, "Ahhhh! Oh, God, how do people manage to have babies!?"

V washed her claws in the mini-kitchen sink– being very thorough and going up beyond the elbows – and stood ready.

With Corporal Laverne standing guard at the door to Ra'shae's office, Colonel Siebert knelt down, and put his hand on Monica's forehead. "How do you feel, Monica?"

"Pissed off, thank you for asking, Colonel: I'm pushing and pushing, but the little ..." Then suddenly there was a pop, a gush, a rush, a flood of water, and Monica murmured, "Oh, oh, oh, oh ..."

"The water has broken; the cervix is well dilated, and soon we'll see the baby's head," said the Colonel, he glanced up. "V, you take it from here. I'll give you instructions if you need them."

"Me?" said V.

"Yes, you," said the Colonel.

"Oh, well." V rolled her serpent eyes and knelt on the soft bed of fresh towels, Monica turned slowly onto her back, V saw the baby's head, it was a little dome of scales of cobalt blue and V thought, well, that answers one question! I was wondering whether the little rascal would come out in human or alien form and I guess now I know. I truly hope he is not the Anti-Christ! That would be very embarrassing for the hybrid cause – and I would have some very hard questions to put to my dear alien father, Marcus.

V began to guide the baby's head, very gently, forward, saying, "Keep pushing, but gentle now, Monica, gently, gently, gently," and the baby's head came out, slowly, in little gentle wave-like movements. V took a deep breath, she hadn't delivered a baby since, well, since the fourteenth century, and she had forgotten – or repressed – everything she'd learned on that occasion. "Good, that's it, that's it!"

"Oh God, oh God, oh God, oh God," groaned Monica, her claw clutching Doctor Mansoor's hand.

"It will be okay, Monica, everything's okay," said Doctor Mansoor, "I know what it's like. I've been through it twice myself."

"And you're still a functioning person, my God," groaned Monica, starting to laugh, "How do you do it? Oh, oh, oh, oh, that *hurts!*"

"Colonel, we have a problem," a soldier came running into the room, breathless. V glanced at her. The newcomer was a young woman, deeply tanned, her blond hair pulled back in a severe bun, the visor of her camouflage cap low over her forehead, her blue eyes, visible through clear Polaroids, opened wide as she took in the scene.

"Jesus Christ Almighty," she murmured, eyes widening further. Colonel Siebert was kneeling next to a … well, a sort of bright blue reptile woman that was apparently having a baby, with the help of an Indian woman and a, well, a sort of turquoise reptile – woman: a hybrid, two hybrids. What the hell was going on?

"Yes? What problem, Sergeant Schmidt – the hybrid?"

"No, sir, zombies, sir, zombies, they're coming down the road, they are coming out of the Everglades, sir, lots of them."

V turned towards the Colonel, "Colonel, you have to get your people inside. The zombies are very contagious. I've seen them up-close, you have to avoid any contact whatever with them." V turned her attention back to Monica's baby, concentrating, guiding the baby gently, gently, and gently putting pressure on the base of the vagina, gently pushing and the baby, it was like it was coming out in little oscillations, little wavelets, and the baby was turning on its side, sliding out, slippery and gooey and warm, and the head was now free.

"Sergeant Schmidt, use the missile launcher to try to blow away as many as possible – from a considerable distance – at least twenty yards. And our hybrid friend here is right: no close contact, understood? If those things get close, retreat – understood?"

"Yes, sir!"

"Empty the vehicles of weapons. Then tell the men to withdraw into the building, block the entrance; place two men with a flame-thrower and with hand-held missile launchers in the corridor. Get someone to man the monitors that cover the outside and all entry points. Where are the monitors, Doctor Mansoor?"

"Next room to the left," said Ra'shae. "Colonel, there is a large garage, and it's empty, you could back the vehicles in there, that way they might be protected – and avoid contamination. It has armored steel doors, closed from the inside."

"Good," said the Colonel, "Could you show Sergeant Schmidt?"

"Yes, of course," said Ra'shae.

"Go with Sergeant Schmidt then, and get all vehicles inside." Colonel nodded at Schmidt. "Then, once the vehicles are safe, go with Doctor Mansoor and check all weak points, get Doctor Mansoor to show you everything, all points where the zombies might get in. Corporal Laverne, you stay here as liaison. Understood?"

"Yes sir!"

"I'll be outside shortly."

"Yes, sir!"

"Now you can stop pushing, Monica," said the Colonel, "now you can stop pushing; the head is out, the baby and V are doing the work now."

V guided the little wiggling struggling creature out of the womb, its two arms were free now, and sticky, covered in a web of goo, then, suddenly, the baby slipped and slithered up into V's hands; it was free.

"Oh, mein Gott, lieber Gott," sighed Monica, "Oh … mon Dieu, c'est mieux … Oh … quelle histoire … merci, merci … danke … grazie … thank you …"

V took a warm wet towel, and glanced at the Colonel.

He said, "Yes, clean the nose and the mouth. Make sure it can breathe."

V cleaned away the mucus, the fluid and membrane from the baby's mouth and nostrils, and then she lifted the umbilical cord, which was around the baby's neck, over its head. The baby gurgled and squealed.

"I think you've done this before," said the Colonel, glancing at V.

"Centuries ago, Colonel, centuries ago," V said. "The zombie thing is very contagious – and … Oh, my God! There are those poor guys I stunned outside, can someone get them in, is there still time?"

"Corporal Laverne, go and tell Sergeant Schmidt, tell her to see if the men can get those unconscious guards inside. Tell them to hurry; and stay away from the goddamn zombies!"

"Yes, sir!"

She disappeared.

"I'm going now. You can finish without me, V"

"Colonel," said V, glancing up at him with her big golden eyes, "I'm immune to the zombie thing. When I'm finished here, I'll come and help. I can fight them directly."

The Colonel looked at her and nodded. She was indeed a most stunning creature. What a weird turn of events, he had come on a mission of extermination, he hated the hybrids, and from everything he had seen and heard about them he knew he was right to hate them, but now he was in fact, for the moment at least, in alliance with a hybrid, and she had said she was the prototype, the original, hybrid, so she was the daughter of the original alien, she was the beginning of the alien invasion of earth if that was what it was, and she must know more about all of this than anyone else alive. He said, "I presume you have a human form too."

"Yes, I do," said V, "I'll show it to you, later, but be careful, Colonel, very few people are immune to the zombie virus. You don't want to become a zombie."

"I'll be careful," and he was gone.

V cut the umbilical cord, held the baby in her claws, held it upside down and gave it a slap and it started to cry, not an unpleasant cry, it was a boy, and it didn't yet have fangs. V cleaned it.

Monica said, "Let me see, it's a boy, isn't it, and it's a hybrid."

V held the baby up

Monica sighed, "It looks like … Well, it's beautiful!"

V lowered the baby into Monica's arms and then, using a hot wet towel, V cleaned Monica's belly and legs and between her legs.

Ra'shae came back from showing the soldiers the layout of the Institute and she and V knelt, side by side, and wrapped Monica and the baby in clean white towels.

V stood up. "Monica, Ra'shae, I have to go. Otherwise, everybody is going to become a zombie."

CHAPTER 9 – PILLARS OF ASH

The zombies had come stumbling down the road leading to the Everglades Agricultural Research Institute; some had come directly through the Everglades, some had been eaten by alligators, their legs snapped off, but the torsos still struggling, crawling through the mud until the alligators came to get the remains, and the remains seemed still to struggle, and some alligators seemed repelled by the zombies and vomited up the remains, and then stayed away from the wiggling torsos that were making their way through the slime of the jungle or swimming, a primitive breaststroke, through shallow water, some had fallen into quicksand, flailing in the dark, not knowing what was consuming them, gurgling as they went under, and then those which remained came to the Everglades Agricultural Institute. Some staggered through the smashed, half-open gate. But most, for some reason, tried to climb over the wire link fence that protected the Institute; some were caught in the wires, the thick oversized twined barbed wire that curled along the top of the fence, and some were electrocuted when they got to the highest wires, a double strand of high voltage cable, and, hit by an enormous jolt, they were either projected back, off the fence into the darkness, or they hung there, sizzling, sending off sparks, jerking and dancing as the electricity drove masses of energy through their nervous systems, which had become like half-dead wiring in a mad and diseased and rotting body; but some of them, climbing the fence, getting tangled in the barbed wire and then freeing themselves and getting hit by a huge jolt of high tension high voltage electricity, sparks flying and sizzling and the smell of burnt flesh on the air, were projected over the fence and into the yard of the Everglades Agricultural Research Institute, and these zombie missiles got up, shook themselves, and foaming green foam and bubbles at the mouth, staggered forwards, with green pus oozing from their burns and cuts and wounds, and staggered forward, hands out in front of them, green eyes glowing, now that it was almost dawn the light was beginning to show in the eastern sky, but still the green eyes were weird and scary thought Sergeant Eve Schmidt as she ran forward to get the unconscious guard who had fallen close to the gatehouse.

She shouted to Private Joe Stickler to cover her, and he came running beside her, and said, "Sergeant, I'll cover you anytime," and she said, "Yeah, I know Joe, thanks for that," and Joe knelt with his flamethrower aimed at the advancing zombies, while Schmidt, the fence lights glinting on her blond hair, on the tightly wound bun of spun gold, and on her tinted Polaroid glasses, knelt down and pulled the guard to his feet, a handsome young guy she could see, and began to carry him back towards the building while Joe let loose a wave of flame – a great whoosh of heat and brightness – that caught three zombies who were just coming through the smashed gate, and, as Eve glanced back she saw a zombie, a woman with large sagging breasts and a T-shirt, well, the rags of a T-shirt saying 'I Love New Orleans,' and the woman was hanging, baked by electric shock, dancing like a puppet afflicted by the Saint Vitus Dancing disease, shreds of her shorts smoking and burning, and she was dancing, jerking up and down, arms and legs madly jerking, and Eve thought, Christ, that woman was somebody's mother or sister or wife, and she turned away just in time to see a zombie racing towards her …

… and she shouted to Joe, "Joe, now here!" and he swung around and whoosh the zombie was caught in the full blast, turning to a charcoal statue, a statue of ash, that disintegrated in front of their eyes. Eve caught the reflected blast of heat full on and felt it singe her hair and the visor of her cap, and now she was running, with the big heavy handsome young guard, still out cold, over her shoulder and she got to the door and lowered him down, and said, "Take him inside, right away," to Private Phil Belluz, who stared at her wide-eyed, a look of terror on his face. He said, "Yes, sir," and he grabbed the guard and carried him over his shoulders inside the Everglades Agricultural Research Institute. Eve Schmidt spun around, her pistol, loaded with dum-dum hollow-headed bullets, in her fist, and saw Joe Stickler retreating, blasting away at the zombies and she saw that one of them had come from the side and was about to leap on Joe and she zapped the zombie, and its head exploded and luckily none of the green sparkling goo that sprayed out of the exploding head hit Joe, and she shouted, and it was strange to shout, she was surprised at the sound of her own voice, because this battle was going on silently, and the zombies were ghostly quiet and then Eve felt someone touch her on the shoulder and it was the turquoise hybrid reptile woman and the colonel was right behind the hybrid and the Colonel said, "Let her take over now, Eve, let's bring Joe back in, Lieutenant Freemont has got the vehicles stored safely, all the guards are accounted for, and the hybrid is immune to the zombie disease so she can fight this fight," and the hybrid said, "Yes, that's right, Eve. I could use your pistol and the flamethrower if the Colonel gives me permission," and the Colonel who was squinting at the army of zombies – now maybe about twenty or thirty of them – said, "Yes, permission granted." And he added, "Christ Almighty, these are people, I mean these are folks, ordinary folks, and we are killing them, ordinary Americans, for Christ's Sake," and V said, "Yes, they are Colonel, but until we find a cure they are … well … you can see what they are, and as I said, it is very infectious." Eve said, "You know how to use this?" And V said, "Yes, it's got hollow-headed bullets, right, but the flame-thrower, I think that is even better." "Okay," said Eve, and, as Joe Stickler came back towards them, his back was towards them, and at the last minute he turned around and saw V and his eyes, behind his goggles, went wide and he said, "Fuck Me, what is that, what is that thing?"

"That thing is a hybrid, Joe," said V, "one of those things you've heard about and seen – the bad one – that's what I am, Joe, a hybrid, but I'm a friendly hybrid, Joe."

The Colonel said, "Give her the flame-thrower, Joe."

Joe still staring said, "What? Are you guys, hostages? Has this thing hypnotized you, what's going on?"

"No, Joe, it's that she's immune to the zombie disease, so she can go out and look after them," the Colonel said, "and her name is V."

V said, "Thanks, Joe," as Joe, still looking at her wide-eyed, turned over the flame-thrower and V, slinging the strap over her shoulder and hooking the tank on her back, said, "I'll be back. I'll have to be quarantined for a bit. Ra'shae told me they have a shower and decontamination chamber at door D-2, so I'll go in that way and be decontaminated before I come back to you, just in case, and," she added, "since these zombies are people – or were people – I'm going to try to persuade them to go away, just to go back to where they came from, maybe later they can be cured."

She headed out across the ground towards the zombies who, strangely, had stopped or slowed down, and V shouted, "Go away! Go away! Head back! Get out of here!" She transmitted the same message, mentally, over and over, with all her strength. One of the zombies, a tall skinny man, clothed, partly, in the ragged remains of a bus driver's uniform, hurled himself at her, and V let him have it with the flamethrower.

He went up in tower of flame and then, when she turned the flame-thrower off, the statue of ash stood there for a moment and then fell apart, like something ancient suddenly dragged out of a crypt and exposed to the air – and poof, he was gone … dust and ashes.

Another zombie approached, staggering towards V. He was tall, with glowing green eyes and steel-rimmed glasses; one lens looked blind, with a white, star-shaped crack; the frame was crooked, bent and unhooked, hanging crazily, from one ear. He had a pale long face, flesh that looked putty-soft, the bulging folds of a triple chin, and he was bald except for wisps of blond hair flattened back and greased down at the sides. He was dressed in old-fashioned faded blue denim overalls, and V realized, reading the bits and pieces that were left of his mind, that he was a rich retired Wall Street banker who had pretended to like the earth and who had taken up gardening as a status symbol and so he would have something to talk about at the club. There were still traces of dirt on his hands and under his fingernails. Drifting like clouds in his dead mind were isolated fragments of images, island-like remnants of a dying personality – a rusty red wheel-barrow crusted with dirt and sparkling with rain drops and turned on its side in a narrow gravel path in an overgrown garden; a Granny Smith apple he had taken one crisp bite of just yesterday, and its bittersweet after taste, like all the freshness of spring; then too, memories of the way he had been seduced by the simplicity of the garden. It had become not the quirky sign of status it had been in the beginning, but a true love, a passion, almost a religion; thirty-six hours ago, he was on his knees, cupping a flower in his thick fingers, thinking, "Oh, the wonder of it!" Then, in a flash, like lightening lighting up a dark landscape, the garden was gone, and V felt the sensations the banker experienced when he put his arms around his wife, the hard hollow and the bony spine between her shoulder-blades, she was so fashionably skinny, such an elegant, good-looking, and talented woman, and the way touching her like this always made him think, though he loved her, it always made him think, when he put his arms around her, it always made him think, with horror, of the bones beneath the flesh, the skeleton beneath her beauty, and of death.

"Stop," V said, sending the strongest message she could straight into the fog bank that was his mind.

"Stop!"

"Stop!"

No, he didn't stop; he shambled on, his arms outstretched, hands dangling, long fingers, like flaccid meat hooks.

"Stop," V shouted, concentrating all her mental strength, "Stop!"

The banker shuffled forward, his green viscous eyes, becoming brighter and brighter, and seeming to bore into her soul.

"Sorry," muttered V. She pulled the trigger.

In the bright quick flash of the flamethrower the banker-gardener flared into a screaming pillar of fire, then a column of crisp black ash; then, as the whoosh of fire finally passed, the smoking glowing flesh and the ash disintegrated, fell away, flakes drifting, then – nothing.

The other zombies hesitated.

One large woman with long baleful face spit out a stream of green foam, but it missed V, and she blasted the wave of foam away with a wall of pure fire.

It sizzled, disintegrating into a cloud of ash and steam.

The woman stood, uncertain, "Bahhhh," she said, "Bahhhh," and she backed up slightly. Then, with their eyes all flickering green flames, they began, all of them, to chant, in chorus, "Bahhhh, Bahhhh!" They stood still, like machines that had been turned off.

V repeated her message, "Go back! Go back where you came from! Go back! Shoo! Skedaddle!"

They stood uncertain.

V let out a blast of fire – whoosh! – aiming it close, but not right at, a small group who looked like the skeletal zombie remains of teenagers. One girl had a yellow T-shirt with a funny face goofily sticking out its tongue, and scarlet hot pants; another was a punk rocker retro twentieth century nostalgic, or what was left of him, with lots of metal piercings and heavy eye shadow. Another looked like the school jock; in fact, that was all he was wearing: a skimpy thing that looked very much like a blood-stained jock-strap. His perfectly sculpted, heavy shoulder muscles were sepulcher white and stained with blood and green goo and blue veins were visible underneath the marble-white flesh.

"They're just kids," V muttered, as she tightened her grip on the flamethrower.

In each of them she could see the ghost of the person that had once been, and might be again, but if they only survived.

"Go back," she shouted, "Get out of here!"

Some of the green eyes blinked, staring at her, eyelids fluttering. The jock-strap gave her the finger. Well, some of his personality obviously survived!

"Shoo! Shoo! Get out of here! Go!"

They hung there, hollow scarecrows, hesitant, uncertain.

"Go back!" she roared, "Get the fuck out of here!"

Slowly, the creatures began to withdraw, leaving behind the ash and char-coal statues, and the bodies hanging on the wire, one still dancing an electric jig, his trousers ballooning out, knees bending, legs jerking, head bouncing back and forth – shaking, *Yes, No, Yes, No* – and arms flailing as if he were waving or skipping to a convulsive jitterbug and an inaudible tune, jungle rock or the electro-blues. The fence sprayed out yellow sparks.

The zombies stumbled away, like shadows.

V walked along the fence blasting with the flamethrower all the dangling trapped zombies hanging on the fence including the sad dancer of the jig, until all that was left was ash. It was unpleasant, tragic even, but the possibil-ity of contagion was even less pleasant.

With a withering wall of flame, she blasted into oblivion all the spots and gobs of green goo that she saw – luckily there weren't many.

She went to the gate and dragged it shut, and used a dangling chain to tie a knot and lock it; well, it looked like it was locked; that would have to suffice for the time being. She glanced around – all clear!

It was almost dawn. The birds were twittering, and the zombies, shrinking away now, were disappearing down the narrow hardtop road. They seemed insubstantial, unreal shadows, in the silver-gray and pinkish-yellow light of the rising sun.

All the smells were suddenly more alive, and V breathed in the air, only slightly tainted by the smell of scorched and burnt flesh.

She headed back to door D-2 which was locked shut. "Open the decon-tamination chamber, please."

Luckily, Doctor Mansoor knew how the thing worked. "Yes, V!" Doc-tor Mansoor said through the speaker and she turned the decontamination machinery on and the door slid open, and V stepped inside. The door slid shut. V was in the decontamination chamber.

Well, V thought, I am very trusting! They could poison me in here! Through the glass she had seen Doctor Mansoor and the Colonel and she was re-assured. She trusted them both, strangely; well, not so strangely; after all, she could – in spite of some interference – read their minds and sense their intentions.

The gas and liquid decontaminant streamed over her and she scrubbed and scrubbed, and showered and showered, thinking that the stuff hadn't even touched her, so all of these precautions were probably unnecessary. It went on for almost five minutes, until she declared, "Okay, that's enough!"

She went through the airtight double doors and isolation chamber into the drier, a narrow air-tight transparent enclosure with high speed fans and heaters.

It dried her with a stream of antiseptic and disinfectant air that fluttered and cascaded down over her body, warm, like being buffeted by a tropical wind.

Then she was dry – whew!

The final airtight door slid open and she carefully stepped out of the drying chamber. She was back inside the Everglades Agricultural Research Institute. "I could use a coffee," she said, with a hissing reptilian sigh, seeing that the person waiting for her was that attractive blonde, Sergeant Eve Schmidt.

"What are you?" said the Sergeant. "What are you, really?"

V hesitated. The sergeant had a crisp jaw line, perfect honey tanned skin, intelligent skeptical blue eyes; she radiated a sense of tense wiry competence, a woman who would know what had to be done and who would do it; on a battlefield she would smell of clean salty sweat; in a bedroom she would smell of soap and sunlight and shampoo; the sergeant had had a man, V pictured him, clicking into the recesses of Sergeant Schmidt's mind, the man, Miroslav Atan, had been the love of her life, but he had been killed, a few feet away from Sergeant Schmidt, crouched behind some scrub, during a firefight, just a stupid low-level skirmish, with Mexican guerrillas, shot in the forehead, dead before he hit the ground, just as he was saying, "Honey, we'll soon be out of here and then we can …" Such a stupid, tragic waste …

"What are you?" Eve Schmidt repeated.

"The future," said V, her golden eyes glowing. "I'm the future." She laid her claw on Eve's shoulder and added, "And we – together – you and I – are the future."

The gentle squeeze of the alien claw – the feel of it, remained behind, on Eve Schmidt's shoulder; it was like an echo, like an imprint. V was gone, running down the corridor, leaving Sergeant Eve Schmidt to wonder what the hybrid had meant by that "We are the future – and together."

Eve took off her cap and ran the palm of her hand across her forehead; it had seemed, weird as that might be, it had seemed like the hybrid had been making a declaration of – well, of friendship, and maybe – of love.

"God Almighty," whispered Eve Schmidt. The hybrid's golden eyes, and the pressure of its claw still echoed in her mind. Eve narrowed her eyes, ran the tip of her tongue along her lips, and put her cap back on, pulling it down tight so the visor, along with the glasses, shielded her eyes.

Inside Doctor Mansoor's office the monitors showed the zombies retreating, just faint figures, shambling away as the dawn light spread over the Everglades.

"Well, it looks like V solved that problem." Colonel Siebert was holding the baby wrapped in a warm towel and wondering at the situation he found himself in – a go-by-the-book military man in alliance with hybrids and holding a hybrid baby. He would never have thought it possible. He frowned.

The infant looked like a normal human baby except for the golden eyes and the blue scales. It was holding onto the Colonel's thumb with one of its small pudgy hands that had not yet become claws. "He looks healthy," said the Colonel, "though it's difficult to tell. I've never seen a hybrid baby before."

"Neither have I," said Monica, "I've never seen a hybrid baby before – Christ, before tonight I'd never even seen a hybrid – except of course, Freddy. And now ..."

"And now ...?" said the Colonel.

"And now I am one, for God's sake! What a weird thing!"

"Confusing, I imagine."

"You can say that again, Colonel!" Monica had already showered and she felt totally normal, except of course she was not normal at all, she was no longer herself, no longer Monica Fabritz, her sense of vision had expanded, her sense of smell was hyper-acute, her ability to intuit what others were thinking was almost magical; she was a hybrid alien-human, apparently, and she was the mother of a hybrid alien-human: a little guy from outer space, product of a rape, and the son of a monster. To her extremely well-organized and logical Swiss mind, this was all a bit too much.

When she'd come out of the shower, Monica had taken a deep breath, screwed up her courage, and, for the first time, she had looked at herself in a mirror. She stared at herself for a long time. There were some signs of the old her, some traces in the contours and lineaments of the face, but not much.

The golden eyes and the bright blue – cobalt – scales, the fangs, the forked tongue, the red lozenge in the middle of the forehead, it was all utterly strange as if she were dressed up and disguised in some incredible Hollywood makeup and prosthetics for carnival or for some wild party in Zurich's underground scene or in Venice at carnival time. "Hey, Monica Fabritz," she said to the image in the mirror, "Are you still alive? Are you inside there somewhere?"

The image spoke the question but didn't answer – the golden eyes stared, the fangs were bright; the face in the mirror was stranger than a stranger: the eyes, though they were her eyes, were impenetrable.

"So, you don't know if you are still alive, dear Monica Fabritz?" she said to the image and then she splashed water on her face and looked up at the enigmatic dripping reptilian mask. It smiled back at her.

Ra'shae Mansoor came into the bathroom and held out a towel. "How do you feel?"

Monica took the towel and pressed it against her face – against the mask, the carnival caricature. When she took the towel away, the mask stared back from the mirror. It smiled, and the big gold reptile eyes blinked. "I feel okay." She patted the mask that was now her face and turned to Ra'shae. "But I don't know who you mean when you say 'you.' I don't know what I mean when I say 'I.' I mean, look at me; what am I? Who am I?"

Ra'shae gazed at her. "I think you are still the person you were, still the girl you were, Monica Fabritz, nineteen years old, student, Swiss, and a whizz at math and physics – maybe now you have a few extra powers – like our new friend, V."

"Thank you Ra'shae, but I'm not so sure I am still me."

Colonel Siebert was saying, "He certainly looks healthy. And – I think he's hungry."

"I'm to nurse him?" Monica gazed at the baby. "Yes, I think I'm ready – milk, milk from mother's breast, that's what he needs. I didn't want him, I didn't think I could love him, but now he's here I claim him – he's mine."

And, strangely, she felt a rush of love, of possessiveness, of need, and a surge of warm heaviness in her breasts, an insistent liquid pressure, almost an ache, and she was suddenly eager to claim what had come from her flesh, what she had been holding in her body, what had made her suffer so much in his coming into the world, and she reached out to take the baby.

"We haven't even named him," said Ra'shae.

"So, here we are," V entered the room and, noticing a shadow above them, she shouted, "Watch out!"

The skylight exploded.

CHAPTER 10 – FREDDY

Freddy, the murderous hybrid, plunged down in a rain of showering glass and bits of metal grid and pieces of steel framework and just as Colonel Siebert was holding the baby out to Monica, Freddy grabbed the baby out of Colonel Siebert's arms, and it was so fast that Colonel Siebert didn't see what was happening but instinctively he did grab Freddy by the arm, and then by the leg as the hybrid tried to leap, and then Freddy smashed the Colonel against the wall, and Colonel Siebert fell down, wondering if his neck was broken, but getting up almost right away, unsheathing his pistol, ready to fire, but worried that the bullets might hit the baby, and V leapt at Freddy and grabbed him but Freddy kicked free, and just as Eve Schmidt came running into the room – she'd heard the racket, the explosion of glass, the shouts – her pistol drawn and ready to fire, and Monica had recovered and she leaped towards the skylight …

V shouted, "Colonel, you stay here, Monica, you stay here! I'm going after him. I'll get the baby back!" She leaped through the shattered skylight, and was gone and …

… and found herself on the flat roof of the Everglades Agricultural Research Institute. She glanced around. There he was – Freddy, a silhouette against the rising sun, leaping off the roof, in one giant jump. It took him across the yard, out of the Institute and into the tangled jungle of the Everglades.

V leapt behind him, running, vaulting, clearing the electric fence in one bound, landing in a crouch on all four claws, springing through the air again, and, within a few leaps she was closing in on Freddy. Freddy was slower because of the baby. Following him, V splashed into the mud and water, pushing through vines and undergrowth, through reeds, and jumping past an alligator that leapt, its jaws wide open, to get her, but it missed, and V, whose blood was up, was tempted to stop, flip the alligator over, rip it apart, and give it a lesson in manners, but she had to keep focused on her mission, "Keep focused, V," she told herself, and she zipped past a cottonmouth that lunged at her, but again missed, "Okay, fellow reptiles, get out of my way!"

V leapt, clearing a huge moss-covered log, a tangle of vines, and a cluster of bushes, and came down, softly, almost in slow motion, next to Freddy, he was cradling the baby, trying to protect it. He kicked at V, catching her in the midriff and knocking her backwards into the trunk of a tree. She bounced back, and went into a crouch, facing him, blocking his path – Where the hell was he going, anyway, and what did he want with the baby? He hissed at her, baring his fangs, cradling the baby.

V, crouching, hissed back. "Give me the baby!"

Freddy hissed and growled.

"Why do you want the baby, Freddy, you don't want the baby, what would you do with a baby, how would you feed it?"

He growled and hissed, and pawed at the ground.

V stood up and walked towards him calmly, "Freddy, darling, I am your sister, you know that, and I am also your mother, darling, because the DNA that made you, it came from me, so give me the baby, I know what you are feeling."

In fact, she had no idea what this creature was feeling – its mind was closed off, protected, or maybe it didn't have a mind, now that was a dangerous idea, a hybrid with no mind! She gazed at him. He was not at all bad looking, this hybrid. His sleek muscular body and gray metal scales glittered in the golden light that filtered through the trees, the oleander, and cypress, and ferns. His bright golden eyes stared at her.

He bared his fangs, hissed, and took a step towards her.

V tensed. Now what were they going to do? Neither of them, it seemed, wanted to hurt the baby, so how could they fight or wrestle?

She was eager to fight. She wanted to tear the creature's head off. She wanted to know what went on inside his brain. She suspected his mind – if you could call it that – might be a gateway to the Evil Monster, to the Dmitry Whatever It Was, to the Puppet Master, perhaps even to the Dark God, whatever that was. She was within two feet of Freddy. "Freddy, give me the baby." She saw a flicker of recognition in the creature's eyes and he hissed.

He said, "She calls me that."

"Who calls you that?" asked V, knowing the answer, but relieved to be suddenly facing a creature who could at least talk.

"She, the creature; the human I had; the human I want. The human I want."

"If you want her, Freddy, you love her."

"Freddy wants human, loves human."

"Well, if you love her, Freddy, then you should give her the baby." V frowned. How will we arrange visiting rights? "If you want her and love her, you must give me the baby, so she can have the baby, then she will love you," said V, thinking, I am lying. Monica hates you with all her guts. "You are a killer who killed her friends in front of her eyes. You are a rapist. You tortured her. You held her prisoner. You raped her, raped her again and again."

"I am not me," he said, "I am not me."

V hissed, baring her fangs, clenching her claws, coming closer, "Who are you then, Freddy, who are you?"

He blinked. His reptile eyelids closed, as if he were about to go to sleep.

V tensed all her muscles, ready to leap. Yes, he was entering a trance. Maybe, now, she could seize the baby and run!

But his eyes fluttered open. He spoke, but his voice was different, cadaverous as if coming from a great distance, a giant voice, like the voice of a god, and the voice said, "I will destroy you all, and I will kill the baby, and I will kill you too, V, especially you!"

"Who the hell are you? You are not Freddy."

The voice, coming it seemed from far away, became suddenly high and childlike, "I want you, V, I want you, ha, ha, ha, you are me and I am you, I want you and I will get you and take you and have you, ha, ha, ha, and I am going to kill the baby," it said, chanting, "I am going to kill the baby, ah, ah, ah, and then it laughed, a deep resonant enormous laugh, "I am going to kill the baby", and I am going to take you, take you, V, forever and ever and ever."

V was thinking: It – this monster – was going to put this scheme of killing the baby into action – and now!

She leapt at Freddy, extended her claws, and snatched the baby, and leaped back to the other side of the clearing, cradling the baby in her arms and noticing that it reached for her breasts and seized a nipple in its tiny hands, just as …

… just as Freddy's eyes fluttered shut and then opened again, and he howled, and V turned and ran, and as she ran like the wind, her heart was pounding in fear, not for herself, but for the tiny creature she was holding.

"Okay," she said to the baby, "we are going to make it, we are going to get you safe and sound back to your mother," and she could hear, as she leapt through the swamp, giant risky strides, never knowing, because the reeds hid everything, what she would be landing on, and she could hear behind her Freddy racing behind her and then ...

She was suddenly outside the swamp, on a flat muddy patch, a clearing, hot golden sunlight streaming in at a low angle, the air rich with perfumes and insects dancing in the smoky beams of light, and she saw a picnic table, an old gray weathered wooden picnic bench, with benches attached, and she thought, no, I can't put him down on that, because he'd fall off, and she then thought, under the table looks safe, and she bent, looked, no life forms, no dangerous life forms, no snakes, scorpions, spiders, bugs – and she put the baby down and he, his little golden eyes blinking at her, let go reluctantly, and she said, "I'll be right back, baby," thinking how bloody idiotic people – no, hybrids – became when faced with a baby, it's as if the heart melts and the mind goes gooey and mushy, yuk, but she knew she couldn't help herself – sigh! – and she turned, swinging around, already crouching, already poised in the ready-to-wrestle, ready-to-fight position, and Freddy was standing there, staring at her, and he didn't move so she slowly stood up, and she said ...

"Well, Freddy, you can talk, so talk, talk to me, Freddy, you and I are the same thing, you know, I am closer to you than the voice, I am closer to you than the Puppet Master whatever he is."

And Freddy said, "Love."

"Love? Love what, love who?"

"Love you, love her, love child," he said. "Love human."

"Yes, Freddy," V sighed, "love is a fine thing."

"He wants baby."

V stepped forward and put her claws on Freddy's shoulders, "the Puppet Master, the Puppet Master wants the baby?"

Freddy nodded. There were beads of sliver liquid at the edge of his eyes – tears! "Yes, but ... He wants you, V. He wants you – more than baby."

"He wants me – me?"

"You he wants, much wants, he wants you more than any other."

"He wants me?"

"Yes."

"Okay, he shall have me – and I shall have him."

"You know not what you say."

"I do know what I say. Freddy, where is the gateway, how do I get to the Puppet Master?"

Freddy sniffled, his tongue flicked out, "*Flight of Fancy*, the yacht, the yacht with the poisoned balloons, the yacht is the Gateway, he wants you to go there, meet him …"

"The Puppet Master wants me to go there – to the yacht?"

"Yes," said Freddy.

"Well, tell him I shall go there," said V, "but, right now, I am taking the baby with me, back to its mother."

"I come with you," said Freddy.

V frowned. My God, what should she do now? She turned to the table. The baby had already come out from under the table and was crawling over the muddy ground towards her; less than an hour out of the womb, and already much more precocious and mobile, she thought, than a human baby – *oh, boy, oh, boy, oh, boy!*

V knelt and picked up the baby, cradling it in her arms. "But Freddy, you have killed people; you have killed a lot of people. The people, the humans, will not want to see you. They will want to punish you if they see you. They will want to kill you."

"I don't care. I will die," said Freddy.

V hesitated. "Come then," she said. She could kill him, of course. But it would be difficult and messy and might put the baby in danger – and, perhaps Freddy could be saved – or made useful.

They began to walk back towards the Everglades Agricultural Research Station.

"You are me and I am you," said Freddy.

"Yes," said V, wondering at it and yet knowing what he meant. And she was also wondering: Could she turn this creature, this monster, her brother, her son, against the Puppet Master, could she tame him, help him?

"Do you eat normal food, Freddy or do you need to drink blood?"

"I eat normal food," he said, "I like normal food, I cooked for the woman and I made her cook for me, she was angry and I thought I will make her one of us, she will become like me, then she will have to love me, and like me, and she will be mine, and she will cook for me. I eat normal food, not like you, V."

"Yes, nobody is like me, I guess, I'm the evil one."

"No, I am here because of you," he said,

"Because of me?" V said.

"Yes, because of you."

"Why, Freddy, why because of me?"

"Because I am bait," Freddy said, "I am bait – that is the word. And when you go to the *Flight of Fancy* you will enter another world and you will fulfil your destiny."

"My destiny?" said V, "And who is the creator of my destiny?"

"You," said Freddy, "But he loves you. The Evil One loves you. He wants you. He wants to consume with you without end. You are the goddess, he says, if he consumes you, he becomes the god."

"Who loves me? Goddess? Who wants to become a god?"

"Puppet Master."

"The Puppet Master loves me – me?" said V and she thought, core blimey, what the …? This is grotesque! Yuck! Ugh! This is ugly. I don't like this! I don't like this one bit. "He wants me?"

"Yes. Possess you. He wants possess you, ah, *to* possess you."

V cradled the baby closer. Its little hands were warm, stroking her scales. By now, the morning sunlight was bright, shining on the walls of the Everglades Agricultural Research Institute. They were walking side by side, too, like old friends. What a strange thing! V sensed that in Freddy there was good, as well as evil, and that the evil was an emanation of the Puppet Master.

"A friend of mine, Father O'Bryan, used to talk about possession by the Devil," said V, thinking out loud.

"What?"

"Nothing, Freddy, nothing; perhaps we can talk about it later."

V thought that maybe destiny was what she was holding cradled in her arms it was making a cooing sound, the baby was. V looked down, hissed *coo, coo, coo,* and held it closer. It reached for her breasts with little fingertips; it tickled her right nipple, then pinched it, but not hard.

So, *Flight of Fancy* it is for me, she thought, as she caressed the baby. It made a gurgling sound, its eyes bright, focused on her.

"You're sure you want to surrender to the humans, Freddy?"

He looked at her. "Yes, they can destroy me. My work is done."

Suddenly, V could see into his mind, and what she saw there was very interesting. "You are letting me in, I see, Freddy."

"Yes, I am letting you in, V, I am letting you in."

The first to see them was Sergeant Eve Schmidt. She had gone up to the roof of the Institute as lookout, with four soldiers manning submachine guns and rocket launchers.

"Jesus Christ," she said, "Look at that!"

The two gunners lying on the roof beside Sergeant Schmidt looked up and saw V walking next to the one they had come to know as Freddy, the hybrid that had killed two of their comrades, two of their closest friends, and that had kidnapped and raped the young Swiss woman, Monica Fabritz. Eve put the binoculars to her eyes. "She's got the baby; she's holding it her arms. Hold your fire, guys, let's wait and see what she – what they – have to say. But keep them covered." Eve tugged at her cap, pushing the visor down, and she took the megaphone.

"V, are you approaching as friendlies?"

"Yes, Sergeant Schmidt, we are approaching as friendlies."

"Can you assure us that … the creature … won't cause problems?"

"Yes," shouted V, "I guarantee for him. He wants to surrender."

"I'm coming down," said Eve, "Corporal Burgess, you're in command."

"Yes, sir."

Eve climbed down the steel service ladder on the side of the building and walked slowly out in the humid dawning light across the flat grassy space, towards V, the baby, and the killer hybrid known as Freddy. Eve's hand was curved close to her holster, fingers itching to act, not that she was under any illusions as the efficacy of ordinary bullets against Freddy – or V.

"Well," she stared at V and motioned her chin towards Freddy. "What does he want?"

V cradled the baby close. "He wants to see Monica, Eve, and he wants to surrender, isn't that right, Freddy?"

"Right; that is right, I'm sorry, Sergeant Schmidt, that I killed your friends."

"Yes, you did," said Eve, staring at him through her dark tinted glasses, the rising sun glinting off the lenses. "And not only them, you killed a whole lot of people," she paused, "I suppose handcuffs and that sort of thing would not be useful." She turned to V.

"Not very useful," said V, "but symbolic maybe."

"Will you accept handcuffs, Freddy?" Eve Schmidt thought the handcuffs would be useless; but they would reassure the troops and it would indicate that Freddy was agreeing to surrender and to be a prisoner; her thought was that they should handle Freddy with great consideration and care and lots of tact – or kill him immediately. If he became hostile, he would be too strong to contain. Out of the corner of her eye she noticed V, who was carefully cradling the baby, flash – with a nod – approval of the gentle, diplomatic approach.

"Yes, I accept handcuffs, Sergeant Schmidt," Freddy bowed his head and meekly put his claws behind his back.

"Thank you, Freddy." Eve went behind him, thinking, I may be an idiot, but for some reason I trust V entirely; I would trust her with my life, and I guess, right now, I am trusting V with my life. She clipped the handcuffs around Freddy's wrists, and tightened the handcuffs lightly, but not so they would be uncomfortable – he could break them anyway – and she clicked them shut.

"You are welcome, Sergeant Schmidt," said Freddy.

"Let's go," said V. "The baby's hungry."

The sun had risen above the trees; the mist was fading; the air was fresh and birds were singing. The air was full of smells and noise, the fecund rhythm of life.

It was the second day of the zombie plague.

"No way," said Monica, cradling the baby. "No way! I will not forgive him!" She turned to Colonel Siebert. "Colonel, you lost two of your people, two of your friends!"

"It's not a question of forgiveness, Monica, it's, well, it's ..."

Monica turned towards Freddy who was standing with his head down. "You do realize, Freddy, you have killed people, many people, the kids in the school bus in Texas, the whole Lewis family, and I'm sure you've killed many others."

"Yes, many others, I killed many others," breathed Freddy, his voice low, his head down, "many, many others."

Colonel Siebert stood with his arms crossed, watching. It was unbelievable, one hybrid, though she was mentally thoroughly human, putting another hybrid on trial, the killer hybrid who had massacred two of his marines, too of his closest friends, two people who depended on him, and ...

Monica's golden eyes blazed. Her fury, all the suppressed anger, boiled up. It thundered through the veins of her new, ultra-powerful, deadly, sleek alien body; like a fever it invaded every muscle and tendon, it was pure uncontrollable rage, extending down to the tips of her claws and her fangs, all eager for action, all eager for revenge, all eager to kill; and at the same time, with the coolness of her extremely analytic, highly-trained, Cartesian Swiss intelligence which had always been able to rise above things, always been able to see the big picture, always been able to detach itself from her own passions and fears, and with the coolness of her very Swiss – calm and methodical

– approach to every vital question, she saw the logic in the Colonel's argument, and in V's: Freddy could be useful; and, in a sense, Freddy too was a victim. "And, you held me prisoner, Freddy, and raped me, raped me over and over, and over, and you turned me into – well, into what I am now!"

Monica stopped; she looked around; she handed the baby to V.

"Oh, enough, enough hatred," Monica said. She stepped up to Freddy and reached out. She put her claws on his shoulders. "Okay, Freddy, for my part, for what happened to me, for what you did to me, I forgive you – if it makes you happy, I forgive you. I have heard the voice too, I have heard the Puppet Master, so I can understand, I can understand a little bit of what happened to you, of what you are." She was staring at him, fixing his downturned eyes with her brilliant serpent eyes. "Look at me, Freddy." He looked up. He held her gaze. "You must promise me, Freddy …"

"Yes, Monica."

"You must promise never hurt anyone else ever again, Freddy – promise me!"

"I promise, Monica, I promise you all, I will never hurt anyone else again."

"And promise to obey Colonel Siebert. That is the most important thing. That will override everything else. You promise?"

"Yes, I promise, Monica, I promise to obey Colonel Siebert."

"Good, Freddy." Monica withdrew her claws from his shoulders, "I will hold you to it, Freddy!" She leaned forward, and kissed him on the forehead, "Now, I have done," she said, and took the baby from V.

"Thank you, Monica," Freddy lowered his head.

Colonel Siebert walked up and down. "I'm going to be frank with you. I don't know what we should do. Freddy is so powerful – you are so powerful, Freddy – that we really cannot contain you. So, by taking you prisoner as we have – and it was absolutely the right decision, Sergeant Schmidt – we have to accept your word you are going to behave. Now, you have killed and killed …"

"Yes."

"How can you guarantee you won't kill again?"

"He is gone."

"Who is gone?"

"The Puppet Master; he made me kill."

"So you were, ah, possessed, as Monica told us," Colonel Siebert glanced at Monica and then at Freddy. "That's what made you do the things you did."

"Yes, he created me; he possessed me; he wanted me to do those things."

"How can you guarantee he won't come back?"

"My work is done. He has abandoned me. He is gone. He will not come back. I am empty, now, an empty vessel. Now he wants her." Freddy nodded at V, "He wants her. It is love and it is hate. It is his obsession. He wants her. He wants V. He wants her power. He wants his revenge. He wants to consume her and destroy her and love her. She is a goddess, and he wants to be a god, he wants her. He wants to possess her, to *be* her."

"Yes," said V, "the Puppet Master spoke to me, through Freddy. For some reason he is obsessed with me. He wants me – why exactly, I don't know – but I am going to go to meet this Puppet Master, whatever he or it is. As for love and possession and being like a goddess ..." V shrugged her shoulders and brushed the thought away with a sweep of her arm.

"Well," Colonel Siebert, hands on hips, looked around, "Okay, I am going to take a risk here, if all agree, we will keep Freddy with us, and we will see that he faces whatever justice the government decides upon. Do you all agree?"

"Yes, we agree Colonel."

"Freddy, do you agree?"

"Yes, Colonel Siebert, I agree. I am your prisoner. I will obey you in all things."

Twenty minutes after Freddy's surrender, the *Andromeda II* hover-jet eased its way down onto the law on the Everglades Agricultural Research Institute to pick up V – and Monica and her baby and carry them back to *Andromeda II*.

"While I remain on the mainland, I want eyes and ears with you, V, if you agree," Colonel Siebert said.

"I agree. You want someone to liaise between us. That is an excellent idea."

"Sergeant Schmidt," said the Colonel, turning to Eve Schmidt. "Would you be so kind as to accompany V and Monica and the baby back to *Andromeda II* and stick with them and, as soon as you can, report back to me. I am particularly interested in the president's whereabouts and her plans."

"Yes, sir!" Sergeant Schmidt saluted.

Within minutes the hover-jet was in the air.

PART TWO – A SPREADING WAVE

CHAPTER 11 – COLLAPSE

By noon of Day Two, the zombie plague was spreading exponentially. People, the people who were still people, panicked, and ran, shot or poisoned themselves and their families, or jumped from balconies of buildings; they fled through the streets, they hiked into the Everglades, and everywhere they tried to get to their cars.

The zombies seemed to love parking garages and underground parking lots and trapped many escapees just as they were trying to get away.

The zombies even managed to block the exit to some above ground and underground parking garages by causing smash-ups right at the exits and ticket booths.

People desperately scrambling out of Fords and Toyotas and BMWs and Mercedes were morphed into zombies before they knew what hit them and then they began to eat their wives, or husbands, or the family dog, or their children, or mothers-in-law, whether these had morphed into zombies or not.

It was a mess.

Government services and other organizations collapsed in a welter of confusion and mutual recrimination – though individual police and fire units did their heroic best trying to stop the spread of the zombie plague, some police units firing at the mobs of zombies, trying to slow them down, and retreating tactically, wisely, block by block, street by street, just steps ahead of the plague, as the zombies advanced spitting infectious goo, spraying venomous spittle, and biting anything and anybody they met.

The zombies were fruitful and multiplied.

Three units of the Greater Miami fire department used hoses to delay the zombies and tried to put out a few of the fires that the zombies, mostly through zombie carelessness, had set off or caused.

But fire hoses did not really stop the advance of the zombies, so the fire trucks, like the police units, retreated, and then retreated again, leaving fires raging, and, in some cases, spreading from block to block, and then, resisting all the way, the police and fire brigades – what was left of them – abandoned the built up areas altogether and tried to block routes out of the city, routes north and west and south; they knew that if the zombie plague got to the western coast of Florida or if it escaped from the peninsula then all chances of stopping it would be lost.

Many of the police and firemen and women paid for their courage with their lives. Others were transformed into zombies and joined the invasion.

The vice president had gone on television – several times – to say that the president was dead, that he had assumed full powers, and that "This thing, like the plagues inflicted upon Ancient Egypt, is a Divine Judgement upon all of us, and will work its way out, cleaning away the wicked, the dross, the chaff, and the garbage; and that perhaps, in hastening, as it seemed to be doing, the Final Day of Judgement and the Rapture, this was a good thing for all. The ways of the Divine," said the vice president, deepening his splendid resonant voice, "the ways of the Divine are mysterious and inscrutable and not to be sullied by the petty, carping judgement of mere fallible presumptuous mortals."

The vice president added, in an improvised press conference, that it was a posse and cabal of evil scientists, only interested in getting grants, or godless biotech companies defying the Divine Edicts of God, that had created this monster in the first place, so that he was not going to rely on these so-called scientists, those pagans, those soulless, relativistic, unprincipled, effete, latte-sipping libertines, those atheistic unbelievers, to try to counter the spreading disease. "We shall rely on prayer," he said, "and on prayer alone."

CHAPTER 12 – ASHLEY

Ashley Samos scarcely dared breathe. She was barefoot and naked except for panties and a silk spaghetti-strap pajama top and she was curled up on her side lying crammed into the narrow dusty cobwebby crawlspace under the wooden toolshed just beside the swimming pool.

A few inches from her face were the feet, the bare, filthy feet, streaked with blood, gore and green goo, of two of the zombies that had come crashing through the front window into the house when Ashley was still in bed, bleary-eyed, and worried sick about Kevin.

She hadn't caught a wink of sleep all night.

Ashley had tried and tried to get Kevin on the U-Tab. At first, she got static, or at best, she got his voice mail. She left the message, four times: "Please, Kevin, ring or text me when you can. And, darling, be careful, please be careful!"

Then she got nothing. Then, finally, she got a message; it was from his U-Tab. It was horrible, a mixture of groans and slobbering and animal noises, grunts and gnawing. She had listened to it, over and over again. It was his voice – but it was also the voice of a slobbering beast: *Grrrhh, grrhhhh …*

She replayed it, and replayed it, and replayed it.

Kevin had become a zombie – or worse.

He was probably wandering in the Everglades or in the city somewhere, helpless, mindless, a cannibalistic, bestial, shaggy, slobbering thing.

Her heart shrank in horror.

She had thought about it and thought about it; but there was no way, in the present chaos, that she could find out where he was and go to help him.

Ashley saw it as part of her mission in life, one of her missions in life, to save what was best in Doctor Kevin Harris from what was worst – and the worst had recently been getting worse and worse, and more and more noticeable. He was becoming crueler every day, and not only to her. Her girlfriends intuited how nasty he was becoming, though Ashley never talked about it, never talked about the brutality, the bullying, the relentless sarcasm, the racist taunts he aimed at her: "Mongrel, black bitch, black whore, low IQ African idiot"; the arrogance towards everybody and everything was growing. The girls said, "Leave him. You are beautiful, talented – and above all, good, you are a good person, leave him."

But Ashley thought he could be saved, and she would save him.

Now salvation would probably be impossible.

In any case, in the next few minutes she and her unborn baby would probably die, or worse, if the zombies got them.

Her whole world – and everybody else's she realized – had turned upside down in a few hours: the zombies were everywhere.

Nowhere was safety to be found.

The two zombies next to the toolshed were grunting and snarling as they shuffled past her hiding place towards the pool. If they went to the other side of the pool, they would easily be able to see her curled up under the toolshed; and what would happen if they saw her?

She lay absolutely still. She had to control her breathing. She absolutely had to control her breathing. Focus, Ashley, focus!

She concentrated on a tiny black ant, its antennae quivering, its little head bobbing up and down. It was trying to drag a fragment of dried up, curled up brown leaf along the pavement – the ant was staggering this way and that underneath the load. How strong the ant must be! She wondered what thoughts – if you could call them thoughts – went through the ant's mind as it struggled with the huge unwieldy object. In the ant world at least, everything seemed normal. A leaf was a leaf was a leaf …

The zombies were joined by a third zombie. She heard growling and slobbering. They were fighting; it sounded as if they were fighting. One of them fell down, or was shoved down, just beside Ashley's hiding place. His head was less than a foot away – he was fighting somebody who was on top of him, green goo splashed out in every direction. God, Ashley thought, I am going to catch this thing! I am going to become a zombie! God, what will this do to the baby?

She held her breath. She closed her eyes, and just for an instant, and she was back in the lecture hall, giving a lecture in her series on "Violence and Continuity in Culture," just before the news of the terrorist attack came in.

"So," Ashley – wearing a splendid high-waist, freely flowing dress of orange crepe that complemented the chocolate sheen of her skin – was standing just next to a projection of Pablo Picasso's painting, *The Young Ladies of Avignon,* with about thirty students staring up at her and she was saying, "So, to sum up, Pablo Picasso's creativity worked by destroying. He took a hammer and an axe to tradition. He destroyed to create. His mind worked the way capitalism has been said to work, by 'creative destruction' – abolishing and hacking apart the old to create the new. He smashed traditional European forms. But in destroying them, he also took the bits and pieces, from many traditions, European, African, Hispanic, Pre-historic, and he shuffled them, rebuilt with them; by borrowing and stealing, here and there, pell-mell, he cobbled together something new, he practiced cultural and visual *bricolage* – or, if you like, *cultural appropriation* – by tinkering with and combining odds-and-ends, using the flotsam and jetsam of various traditions, and so he freed up his own perceptions, and his own talent, and created new languages or idioms, new ways of seeing, for other artists, and for all of us, and freed up the whole tradition of Western art. Destruction of course has deep roots and an important role in creativity – and even in the creation of the self: when we are children, and growing up, we adopt models, ideas of who and what we are, and then we destroy those models so we can transcend them – or integrate them into something larger, into a new form of civilization, or into that ongoing construction site we are pleased to call the *self*. So, there is something capriciously and violently childlike in Picasso's method – a little boy delighting in destroying all his toys. And, speaking of the self, we often see Picasso himself, represented within the frame of his paintings, sketches, and drawings, adopting a variety of models for himself: the clown, the harlequin, the monkey, the quixotic knight errant, the bull-fighter and the bull, or even the painter, as so many surrogates, perhaps, for himself, or bits and pieces of that self, imaginary projections. As for women, he idealizes them, he petrifies them into monumental forms, or he smashes them, fragments them, breaks them into pieces, and turns them into primitive mask-like icons, jagged saw-like slashes, serrated knives, as in one of his most famous paintings, seen just behind me here, painted in 1907, and which is generally called *The Young Ladies of Avignon*, though Picasso himself called it *The Brothel* or *Le Bordel*, which means 'brothel,' in French, but which also means, in French, 'chaos, mess, or disorder' – so he was being, let's say, ironic about his own iconoclasm, his own breaking of the idols. He was telling us that, on one level, this whole thing is a joke. Well, I'm anticipating. Let's continue next week. We'll be looking at how Paul Cézanne and Henri Matisse influenced Picasso and, generally, the revolutions in 20th Century art. Has anybody got any questions?"

Almost every hand in the room shot up and this was usual with Ashley's lectures, which were extremely popular. She was modest, but, in the faculty – and beyond – she was a rising star.

"Yes, Michelle."

"Ashley, do you think that this creative destruction, as you call it, was motivated by hatred – say, of women? And what do you think about the problem of cultural appropriation in Picasso's work? You alluded to it, but you didn't really analyze it."

"Those are very good questions, Michelle. They touch on de Kooning's work too. I think that probably Picasso's feelings of violent, even raging ambivalence, towards women were part of –"

Alarm bells went off.

In the distance sirens wailed.

"Okay, let's wait," Ashley said, "And see what's going on."

The loudspeakers sputtered into life: "Ladies and gentlemen, this is Bob Manguel, Dean of Faculty. I regret to announce that there has been a terrorist attack on the cruise ship *Eden of the Seas* and that the president of the United States, Katherine du Bois Hughes and hundreds of others are presumed dead. We have been informed that the attack may be part of a larger series of attacks. We are closing the faculty and we are cancelling all lectures and seminars until further notice. I advise everybody to go home to their families or to return to residence and stay in your rooms. Lock your doors. The Faculty and University websites and speaker systems will keep you updated on our plans. Be safe and God bless America!"

"The president is dead? It can't be! Oh, this is awful, this is terrible!" Ashley steadied herself by putting a hand on the lectern.

It was chaos. All the students were taking out their U-Tabs to see what they could learn, to contact families and friends.

"Everybody," said Ashley, "We'd better find out what is happening. We'll meet again when we can."

Amazingly they all clapped. Voices shouted out, "That was a great lecture, Ashley!" and "We love you Ashley!"

"Thank you," she said, tears in her eyes. Ashley was one quarter Greek, one quarter Danish, and half black – and the president for her was a special heroine, a vicarious friend, a model, and an inspiration. "God bless you, everybody, each and every one."

With Michelle – one of her best students – at her shoulder, Ashley looked at the news on her U-Tab: it was not good. Reuters said the news was unconfirmed but that reliable sources had declared, "The president is almost certainly dead. The chemical or biological attack has infected 98 to 99 percent of those who have come into contact with it. Rumor has it that people are being transformed into zombies."

"Zombies?" said Ashley.

"Zombies?" Michelle's blue eyes widened, "Look at that! Jesus Christ!"

The U-Tab screen showed images taken by U-Tabs and cell phones on the *Eden of the Seas*, short clips of people foaming at the mouth, of bodies exploding, of bodies flying through the air, one image of a guy gnawing on a woman's leg, a leg without a body, of people who looked like they were changing into plants."

"This is unbelievable," said Ashley, "Look at that ... I mean ..."

"God, it's terrifying, I mean, is this real?"

"I'd better get home," said Ashley, "and so should you!"

"Yes, you're right," said Michelle.

"Good luck to us all," said Ashley, "I hope we can get together next week."

Michelle dared, and gave Ashley a quick soft peck on the cheek.

"Thanks, Michelle. Keep safe!"

"You too, Ashley, keep safe!"

Ashley watched Michelle disappear around a corner – a last wave, a blown kiss – and then as she headed down the corridor towards the exit, Ashley kept saying over and over in her mind, "The president can't be dead; she can't be dead; she can't be dead."

As Ashley came out onto the parking lot, the sun had just disappeared; the sky had darkened to a deep shade of blue and was already turning to black; the palm trees were lit up in sharp relief by the lights from the building. A gentle hot breeze came across the asphalt. It touched every inch of Ashley's skin, pasting the orange crepe dress to her body, to sculptural, beautiful, swelling belly. All in all, Ashley was a perfect female human, in all her glorious fecund fragility. Self-consciously, Ashley ran her hands over the swelling belly. She looked around. There was no one. Strangely, the parking lot was already empty, ghostly, vaguely threatening.

Feeling vulnerable, and suddenly afraid, she looked around. I'm a fool, there is nobody here – there is nothing to fear.

She got to her car, the last one left in the lot. It was an ancient electric tiny two-person bug of a thing, silver in color, which she had bought three years before, second hand. She put her books and computer – she was old fashioned and actually carried a netbook around – on the passenger seat.

She slid in behind the wheel, pulled the door shut, and sat there – a sinking feeling in the pit of her stomach. It couldn't be – the president could not be dead – and yet ...

She pulled out her U-Tab and tried to get Kevin.

She got his voicemail.

She left a message for him to call her as soon as he could.

She scanned the news on the U-tab screen; all news feeds were concentrating on the bio-terrorist attack on the *Eden of the Seas*. And, yes, there were the images, still more images of people being turned into zombies; how horrible!

She took a deep breath, turned on the engine, and drove home – through deserted streets, home to an empty house and no news from Kevin.

Zombies ...

Now, trapped under the toolshed, she opened her eyes and lay as still and quiet as she could.

The zombie struggling on the ground, lying on the flagstones, turned on its side. Its green phosphorescent eyes, eyes like bulging, pulsating jellyfish, stared straight at Ashley.

The creature was – it had been – a man, a middle-aged white guy, unshaven, with wrinkly jowls, a twisted, fleshy mouth, and crooked unclean, badly stained teeth. The zombie coughed, spitting a loop of green slime that splashed over Ashley's face.

Ashley wiggled farther back into the crawl space. Yuk! Now I'm going to be a zombie myself! Damn it! Warm goo dripped from her lips and nose. She wiggled and wiggled. She'd try to get out the other side, come out behind the toolshed.

The zombie had lost interest and was thrashing and bouncing on the flagstones – another zombie, on all fours, was gnawing at its ear.

Ashley pushed back and back and levered herself out the other side of the toolshed. She stood up in the narrow space between the tall white wooden fence and the shed. She wiped at her face – her fingers came away covered in green slime. Yuk! She looked around. She could try to climb over the fence, but where would she go? Zombies were everywhere.

She waited; the zombies did not come.

She peeked around the corner of the toolshed. If she got into the tool shed, she could get the electric saw, or the electric-powered hedge cutter, or an axe, Kevin adored deadly weapons in the guise of garden tools. Ashley disapproved of his arsenal of toys. They made her nervous – they were so many murders or accidents, just waiting to happen.

As she stood there, watching and pondering her options, more zombies came, filing in from the street, down the side of the house.

The garden was filling with zombies. It was a zombie convention. One of them spotted her, made a yowling sound. They all turned their baleful green eyes, and then it happened. They all came shambling towards her.

She made a dash for the back gate – it led into an alleyway. If she could make it, maybe she could find an open garage, and lock herself in, or just outrun them. They were not fast, but there were too many of them.

Just as she reached the gate, pulling on the latch, the zombies closing, reaching out their arms in that weird limp-wristed, slightly fey way, the gate opened, pushed by zombies. There were more zombies, zombies in the alleyway.

Ashley started back.

She was trapped.

A zombie reached for her, his fingers catching the spaghetti strap, almost ripping off the pajama top. He spurted a spray of goo. It splashed over the side of Ashley's face.

Damn, double damn! Ashley turned, ran, and took a running leap, a deep breath, and plunged into the pool head first and dove to the bottom of the deep end. Swirling around in the water, she clawed at her face to get rid of the mask of goo. Soon it was gone, but she was out of air, almost out of air. Above, through the rippling water, she saw the zombies, staring down at her. The sun was high. It must be two o'clock. It was shining down, the sun, brilliant ripples in the water, and putting a halo of white light around each zombie.

Angels …

Angels of death …

She came up in a mighty splash, gulped air, and swam, keeping as far from the side of the pool as she could. The zombies stood, lined up, at the edge of the pool, staring at her. She swam towards the shallower end, where she could just barely stand, and still keep away from the edge of the pool.

The zombies stared. Some snarled. All dripped green goo. Some had baleful, even mournful expressions; and some had no expression at all. Mrs. Henry Elliot, from next door, who must be eighty, was naked. Half her hair had fallen out, her shrunken, sagging, skin-and-bones body glowed, coated in a weirdly luminous sheen of green goo; and from her shoulders grew thick clusters of what looked like feathers, as if, thought Ashley, she were sprouting angelic wings. Ashely covered her mouth. She was going crazy! She wanted to laugh. Doctor Andrews, who was a fanatical golfer and who lived across the street, was wearing pajama bottoms, vertical blue stripes on white, and a knotted blue cloth belt; his chest and pajama bottom were stained with blood and gore and goo; he had lost all his hair and he was missing one arm – just a stump, sticking out and dripping some sort of fluid, and looking like it was growing something … a bright green tendril … a plant. Then there was the reverend Hubert Fish, who must have caught the zombie virus or whatever it was at the church; he was wearing his clerical collar and nothing else – only one black shoe and one white sock. His face was gray, and his teeth were fangs and his tongue was hanging out – it looked very long – and dripping the green drool that seemed to Ashley to be an integral part of being a zombie. Standing on tiptoes neck deep in the water, Ashley glanced around – there must have been fifteen zombies, evenly spaced around the pool, all staring at her, all waiting – but waiting for what?

There was– no way out.

Well, damn it, if they waited, she would wait, and wait, and wait!

At least the water was warm.

They seemed to be afraid of the water; she hoped they bloody well were afraid of the water.

So far, too, she had noticed no change in herself – she rubbed at her nose; no green snot to be seen; she pulled at her hair, no hair came out.

So far, so good! But how long were they going to stay there? It was eerie. They were silent now, not fighting, not growling, just standing, just staring, all those bulging green eyes focused on one thing – on her.

One of the zombies spat into the pool – a large gob of gluey stuff, zombie phlegm. The gob stretched out, became a long worm, and, looking like a snake, began to wiggle its way towards Ashley.

Ashley plunged under water, swam to the bottom, and swirled around to see what the thing was doing. The green snake of snot was following her – as if it were alive.

Wiggle, wiggle, wiggle …

Ashley swam to the deeper end: yes, the thing really did look like was coming after her. God! It was determined to get her – and her baby.

Her baby … Oh, God … she had to save her baby!

CHAPTER 13 – MY ZOMBIE LOVE

George Kennedy had slept a fitful sleep lying fully dressed – in jeans and a neatly pressed blue shirt open at the collar – on top of the sheets in his suite on the *Eden of the Seas*.

Now, it was past noon, and he was feeling groggy and so he decided to make himself another coffee. Soon he would be out of coffee; that was a dire prospect.

He had snacked from the fridge. He had nibbled at the fruit he'd taken from under the stiff plastic in the gift vase. He had listened to Captain Olsen's announcement – made by a friendly zombie girl no less. The captain had regained control of the ship and intended to take it out to sea. George had heard the ship tear itself away from the shore – an ear-splitting grinding, screaming, god-awful screeching – and reverse out into the harbor, and swing slowly around and head for the open sea.

He had gone out on the terrace of his luxury suite and watched the shore recede – sure enough, Captain Olsen had kept his word; he had managed to get the ship away from shore.

Sometimes the U-Tab worked, mostly not. The office had called from Chicago – the partners had stayed up all night, apparently making contingency plans – a number of members of the firm were presumed dead on the *Eden of the Seas* – and they were tracking the progress of the zombie plague; the legal and insurance implications were immense, and horrifyingly complex!

His U-Tab rang.

Gosh, it was working again!

It had been dead for much of the night – and for almost all the morning.

He flipped it open.

It was Flora from the Chicago office. "There's a rumor," she said, "that the vice president intends to nuke *Eden of the Seas*; in fact, he may already have tried, maybe even a couple of times, but something – our sources tell us – went wrong."

"Jesus – what won't the man do next?"

"Well, if he tried once, he may try again."

"True. There are a lot of people on this boat," George was not really frightened of dying; he felt he had died already, and he had certainly lived a good life, a privileged life, and, if he died, well, he died, it would be sooner, rather than later, but still, "There are a lot of people, and the man should think about that."

"Zombies, not people," said Flora.

"Well, Flora, the zombies are people – were people – and maybe they will be people again, if we can find a cure, or if this thing burns itself out."

"In any case, the vice president is also rumored to want to nuke Florida, the whole of the south."

"That man is –"

There was a knock at the door.

"Just a moment, Flora, there's somebody at the door."

"Somebody …?" Flora said, "Don't go to the door, George! Ignore it! For God's sake! Ignore it! My God, he's going to open it," she said to people in the office in Chicago, people who had all passed a sleepless night, not only working but also wondering about friends, family, loved ones. "The damned fool is going to open the door!"

George Kennedy was already on his way to the door. He peered through the old-fashioned fish-eye peek hole.

He recognized her. She had changed – blood, and green gore, and foam at the mouth and glowing green eyes; her hair all a mess, but it was her, it was still her.

George Kennedy opened the door. "Hello, darling," he said.

CHAPTER 14 – LARRY BILODEAU

In a northern suburb of Miami, thirty-six-year-old inveterate bachelor Larry Bilodeau opened one bleary blood-shot eye, blinked its heavy lid once, then twice. The digital clock beside his bed blinked back – in red letters: "14:27"

Jesus Christ!

It was afternoon already!

Jesus Christ! He had slept in – again. Well, it didn't matter. Nobody was waiting for old Larry; there was no office to go to; no appointments to keep, no work to do, not today anyway.

And God, what a headache!

Larry had treated himself to an all-night session of microwave pizza, beer, then more pizza, and popcorn, and wine, three bottles of wine, and films from his very own private pirated downloaded collection of Virginia Lily films, which he alternated with spicy porno clips, so he could imagine Virginia Lily – *boy, was she hot* – in the steamy sex scenes played by actresses – well, they really weren't actresses, they were whores and sluts of course – who, however pretty and however young, didn't have a zillionth of the sex appeal of Virginia fucking Lily; but if he took the situation, and replaced, in his mind, the slut with Virginia Lily, well, then …

Virginia Lily starring in – Larry Bilodeau's dreams!

Larry burped.

He burped again – garlic and anchovies – ah, that was good!

The room was dark: no light was allowed in. The outside world was something Larry liked to keep out – out where it belonged – out, definitely out.

On the rug, invisible, lay two pizza boxes, five empty bottles of beer, two bottles of wine, and one overturned empty maxi supersize tub of buttered popcorn.

Larry remembered hearing sometime in the night sirens somewhere far away wailing about something; he shut them out, putting on his sound-excluding earplugs – which he was still wearing. These things were nifty and allowed in only those sounds that Larry wanted in – and all he wanted to listen to were the soundtracks of the films – films of the divine Virginia Lily.

Virginia Lily – her long legs, her sexy voice, her heroic deeds, and her skimpy, skintight costumes were his absolute ideal. Sometimes Virginia Lily even disguised her beauty by becoming monstrous – a long dead glamorous ghoul, oozing maggots and overgrown with fungus, climbing out of the tomb to search for her true love; or turning into a panther woman with fangs and coated in sleek black fur; or a film star who'd been preserved for seventy years in a celluloid museum come back to life as a celluloid vampire …

Orgasmic, positively orgasmic!

And the upturned upper lip and that little gap between her two front teeth – that little gap always gave Larry a feeling of, well, a feeling of ecstasy, and, sometimes, if he concentrated just a tiny bit, a first-class erection.

Virginia Lily leaping fearlessly from a tall building – to save the foolish daredevil kid that was trapped on the collapsing 20-story-high construction crane!

Virginia Lily swimming out from under the capsized luxury yacht, dodging the evil thug who was going to encase her naked and alive in concrete in a nasty rusty old oil drum and drop her in the deep blue sea.

Virginia Lily cast away alone on that mysterious tropical island inhabited by freakish but brainy and sadistic apes who had invented a fiendish time machine …

But why was the little gap between her two front teeth so alluring? Why was the upturned lip so enticing?

These things were mysterious.

These were things to dream about; this was Larry's religion and obsession.

When she glanced towards the camera, Larry felt that Virginia was looking at him, straight at him; that somehow she knew, she absolutely knew, that he was there, right there, in front of her, sprawled naked in bed, staring at her, and, of course, caressing his erection, and imagining …

If I had the energy, I'd be a stalker, Larry mumbled, and sometimes, in fact, he did fantasize about tracking the star down, taking her prisoner, and …

Larry struggled to get himself disentangled from his sheets, all criss-crossed and knotted up and sweaty in spite of the air-conditioning from his passions of the night before and also stained with wine, beer, butter, and tomato-based pizza sauce plus a variety of melted cheeses that had spilt over from the pizzas ...

He stood up, turned on the very low bedside lamp; it cast a dim, amber light over the rubble. Larry's head throbbed. He needed the old hair-of-the-dog.

He adjusted the sound-excluding Exile Plug ear pods, tuned in to Antique Hard Metal Rock from his Music Library; and, with real and metaphorical drums hammering in his head, he staggered into the kitchen.

He stood dazed for a moment. Why the hell did I come in here? It was too bright. Any light was too much light. He opened the frig door. Boy, it stank! He really should clean it out – someday, maybe ...

Balancing on bare feet, his paunch projecting heroically, like an over-sized bay-window, Larry stared at the possibilities: beer, white wine, or, outside, on the kitchen counter, room temperature Southern Comfort.

Larry's head spun. He swayed. The kitchen, lit by bright fluorescent lighting, swayed with him. Damn! It was going to capsize. His vision went blotchy and dark, a color image singed by fire from behind, turning into charcoal, the world fading. Blood hammered in Larry's temples, overwhelming the hard metal rock. His stomach rose.

He grabbed the bottle of Southern Comfort, filled a tumbler almost to the brim, popped in two ice cubes – watched the amber nectar slosh and brim over – and threw it back.

"Ah!"

Larry stood in the kitchen, swaying, his bare feet planted on the floor, his body a swollen shambles, but still functioning, yeah, man, you bet – still working, still chugging away, the old carcass, still pumping along, still pulsating with horny testosterone! Boy! Was he horny! Hangovers, Larry had often observed, had a special twisted, horny, morbid, fantasy-laden side effect! Hangovers, underneath the dreaded headaches and cobwebby head fog, awakened and liberated the underlying, creepy reptilian mind. To every cloud, there is a silver lining.

He topped up the tumbler and, flipped out the light, and padded his way back to the bedroom, popped three aspirins, swallowed the whiskey, and tumbled down onto the bed.

He ordered the ear pod to shift to the theme song of *Dank City*, Virginia Lily's latest vehicle. That's what they called it, right, *vehicle* ... If you are going to charm a lady, you must be up on the in-speak. Well, that would be for later.

What had he planned to do today? "Yes, Larry old man," he muttered, "what were you going to do today?"

Ah, yes, mow the lawn!

Yes, mow the lawn!

Larry had recently purchased a nifty little gizmo so that he could ride around the lawn and mow the lawn – it was so much more satisfying than having a robot do it.

You got to smell the grass!

When Larry got dressed and went out into the garden it was well after three o'clock; sirens were wailing, gun shots echoed in the suburb, and shouts and screams could be heard everywhere.

But Larry didn't hear anything. The Exile Plug ear pods kept out all sounds – except those Larry chose to hear. Portable paradise!

The sun was shining; the high hedges kept out any hint of the outside world and, unplugged from the Net for the last twenty-four hours, Larry was oblivious to what might be happening around him – he was floating in his own world of sound: *Dank City* – and a world of dreams.

Virginia fucking Lily!

Larry sat down in the lawn mower saddle, pushed the button, and the machine began to move over Larry's perfectly manicured lawn, carrying Larry along for the ride. *Giddy up little pony, giddy up!*

CHAPTER 15 – VIRGINIA CAGED

Thirty-five-year-old Henry Cheng, CEO of Bio-Frontier, which was a prized sub-contractor for Andromeda Corporation, stared through the bullet-proof microbe-proof plate glass of the air-tight isolation lab at the strange creature which had once been film star Virginia Lily.

The creature was bald and hairless, except for a rigid bright green crest up the center of its skull; it had glowing green bug eyes, its skin was a lustrous shiny, patterned green, and from time to time it drooled a green fluid which it wiped away with a cloth or with the back of its hand – it was scary, and it was unbelievable!

Virginia Lily – his absolute favorite!

Henry remembered swooning for her. Just two months ago, his wife Norma had said, "Boy, Henry, I must admit, I'm jealous. But she sure is damned beautiful, and feisty, no doubt about it!!"

They had just come out of an old repertoire cinema, a fresh breeze off the sea, a beautiful evening; the film was that old classic, *Zombies from the Crypt of Hollywood.*

Now here she was, this beautiful human female, totally hairless, except for that bright green crest that ran from her forehead to the nape of her neck, and with those big green glowing eyes, bright green skin, and with slime dribbling, in spurts, from time to time, from her nostrils and mouth.

She was sitting in the isolation cube, this zombie who was not a zombie. In fact, she looked like one of the zombies or monsters that in her movies she always managed to defeat.

She was dressed in a little skimpy semi-transparent hospital gown, might as well have been naked, and she was sitting on a little hospital stool, as if everything was perfectly normal, calmly playing chess with the ten-year-old kid, Jake.

Jake was also dressed in one of those skimpy little hospital gowns, but he looked as normal as a kid could look. His tousled brown hair flopped down over his forehead. With blue eyes, and freckles on his nose, he looked like a real kid, the old-fashioned bright, polite, funny kind of kid you saw in those old Norman Rockwell American paintings from the mid-20th Century, the sort of kid who'd sit on a stool in a drugstore in 1952 slurping a milkshake.

Jake and Virginia, well, they behaved, it seemed to Henry Cheng, like they'd known each other for a hundred years. The two of them were joking and dueling on the chessboard. And they were as calm as calm could be, in the isolation chamber in the isolation ward.

"Yes, indeed, she's a cool lady," said Norma, standing next to Henry, her hands deep in the pockets of her white laboratory coat.

Henry turned to Norma and kissed her. "Yes, she is, but then so are you, my love."

"The test results should be ready in a few minutes," Norma said, returning the kiss, "Then we can probably let them out of that cage."

"Good," said Henry, "They've been very patient – this is a horrible situation."

"And we are not out of it yet," said Norma.

"No, we aren't. Not by a long shot."

When Alex Wolf had turned up at the back door, in the middle of the night, boy, was that a relief. For the previous nine hours, Henry had felt himself – and Norma and their skeleton staff – under siege.

Sabrina Jacobs had gotten in touch at 19:10 hours, just after the terrorist attack, when it became clear that this was a biological chemical attack and that it might involve something like the Mind Slug.

Sabrina had asked Henry to get ready to do some lab work, if he could manage it, and to make available Andromeda Corporation's universal decontaminant – hopefully good against the Mind Slug – for a rescue operation that they might have to carry out.

Henry had said, "Yes, Sabrina, we can do that – we'll prepare lots of decontaminant, if you can deliver it."

Half an hour later, an Andromeda Corp hover-jet had turned up – floating here, low, over the back lot – and hauled up twenty large cylinders of decontaminant.

A little later, communications failed – no more news from Sabrina or from *Andromeda II*.

Henry began to fear the worst.

The *Eden of the Seas* had hit the shore at 20:30 hours. Henry and his wife and the skeleton staff he'd been able to assemble had followed the whole thing on television and from the reports they'd gotten from family and friends – with video feeds and cell phones. Many of those family and friends had now become zombies or were dead or missing.

At 22:48 hours, most of the video feeds and cell phones went dead. A few cameras kept showing bits of sidewalk, or a kitchen sink, and one was lying on second base in the Jeb Bush high school playground. The sounds and occasional sights were horrible.

But then most of the batteries died and most of the satellite and relay tower connections had sputtered into silence or been interfered with. The images and sounds disappeared, one by one.

There was just static, static everywhere. Could it be a giant electromagnetic storm, or was it something else, something more sinister?

Henry figured that he and his wife and the skeleton night staff were safer in the company's laboratories than at home. There was no reason for people – or zombies – to come here. Bio-Frontier was in an out of the way place, an abandoned industrial park, far from any heavily populated area.

In fact, Bio-Frontier was located in a former port area which was now a derelict isolated part of the city, mostly boarded up old factories and ware-houses that dated from decades ago and which were surrounded by unused railway tracks, pitted roads with the asphalt breaking up, crumbling into tarred gravel and sand, and grass and plants poking up, pushing out, and taking over, and shuttered buildings.

The company was housed in an old industrial warehouse and it had thick concrete and steel walls and very few windows, though there were loading docks and high-security entrances equipped with decontamination chambers.

Inside the armored cocoon of the big old warehouse, Henry's company was extra modern and minimalist in design.

The company was equipped with emergency generators, out back in a sep-arate building, and with a kitchen and supplies and with some very basic sleeping quarters – a couple of rooms of bunk beds – with showers and bath-rooms attached – so that if Henry and his staff ended up working all night, and it often happened, they could manage quite comfortably.

It was like a little Noah's Ark – they could survive here for a time.

The initial 19:10 call from Sabrina had put them on high alert – most of the staff had already gone home for the night but Henry Cheng and his wife, Norma Wu, had decided they'd better stay at the company – and they got a small group together, the few they could contact and who were willing to come. And there was Gus Wallach, head of security, who did night shift at Bio-Frontier.

Bio-Frontier was one of the best equipped labs in the country for emergency biological research – and so, if they got samples of the virus – the Mind Slug pathogen – whatever it was – then they could try to see what could be done about it – hopefully something.

Henry felt self-conscious toting a pistol but, even in this isolated spot, right now, with what was happening, he was worried about mobs, and looters, and he was most worried about ... well, what could you call them, zombies, it was like a horror film, but all the elements for every horror film ever made were being invented in scientific laboratories, as Henry well knew, every day.

When the buzzer rang and the alarm beeped, Henry broke out in a sweat. Somebody was outside. Outside was a hot humid night with smoke and the smell of the burning city in the air.

The monitor, when the floodlights went on, showed a naked tanned guy – he did have a towel around his waist – with a shaved head and next to him was a woman with a shaved head draped in the Union Jack, yes, the Union Jack. And behind them stood what looked like a female zombie – no hair except for a stiff vertical crest, green eyes glowing, and, then, beside her, a kid, who looked normal and who was dressed in a T-shirt and jeans.

Henry turned to his wife, "What in the world?"

Norma, holding her cup of coffee, squinted at the monitor. "I don't know. They don't look infected – except for the zombie."

"No," said Henry, "If we answer they'll know we're in here."

"They may be looters."

"They're not dressed like looters."

The buzzer rang again.

"Oh, my God," said Norma, almost spilling her coffee, "That's Alex Wolf and Helen Guerrera!"

Henry stared at the monitor; he pushed the button; and he spoke to the microphone. "Alex, Helen, is that you?"

"Yes, Henry, it's us."

"Thank God," murmured Norma.

And so, for Henry Cheng and Norma Wu the second part of the saga began – the battle for survival – and for salvation.

CHAPTER 16 – ALEX

Well, finally, the tests were done. Virginia and Jake were out of that glass cage, and Jake could get some shut-eye. Virginia Lily found herself sitting on a fold-out chair at a table in a conference room across from Alex Wolf, her single crest of hair standing straight up from the middle of her hairless scalp, her phosphorous green eyes glowing, her skin a bright, radiant, patterned green. She was sipping from a cup of black coffee M-J had just given her and watching over Jake who was fast asleep in a corner of the room on a fold-out camp bed. Jake was now, once again, dressed in his freshly laundered and pressed jeans and T-shirt.

"He's cute," said M-J.

"Yes, he is," said Virginia.

Half an hour earlier, M-J had come to their room and said, "Hey, Jake, hey, Virginia, you will be delighted to know your clothes have been decontaminated and cleaned and dried!"

So, Virginia was now dressed in the lime-green T-shirt and skintight hot pants and scarlet flip-flops Jake had kindly bought for her way back when they had gone shopping together. "Poor kid," she said, "He's been awake for at least twenty-four hours."

"You guys are heroes," said M-J. "If you want more coffee, just call. I'm in the kitchen!" And she headed off on her rounds.

"She's an angel of mercy," said Virginia, "always so cheerful."

"What about you, Virginia?" Alex Wolf was wearing a baseball cap and laboratory overalls with the Bio-Frontier logo. He took a sip of coffee. "How do you feel?"

"Me?" said Virginia, "I feel perky."

"Perky?"

"Yes, and except for this green goo I still seem to be producing, I feel like myself. Mind you, I know I don't look like myself!"

"Come to the lab, and I'll show you what we've been doing."

"Right," Virginia got up off the stool and came to the door of the storage room, "But I'm going to leave the light on and the door open, in case Jake needs me."

"You two have been through a lot."

"So has everybody," said Virginia, thinking, Jake is mine now, at least until we get out of this mess, and I'm responsible for him; and thinking, yes, it's been quite a night and quite a day.

When they first got to Bio-Frontier, Jake and Virginia had been told to go in by a special entrance, which they had done and, once inside, they had found themselves in an extra-strict and isolated decontamination chamber, where they had been told to take off all their clothes, "Close your eyes, Jake!"

He didn't close his eyes but kept them wide open. He was tempted to say "Awesome," but he felt it might not be tactful to do so, besides he was, just a bit, embarrassed by his own nakedness. And then, still stark naked, they had been sprayed with disinfectant, over and over, and then they were given those little hospital-like gowns, those little white shirt things that open at the back, and they'd been placed in isolation, in a sort of glass cage, where they could be observed but not infect anybody else.

"Just a precaution," Alex Wolf and Henry Cheng had explained through a thick pane of glass.

"That's okay," Virginia had said, glancing at Jake and he'd nodded and said, "Yeah, that's okay. That's cool!"

In the glass isolation cage, Jake and Virginia had played chess on the little chess board from Virginia's Porsche and that had been disinfected along with them. Jake was a real sport; he hadn't complained once – and it had been sort of cute, Virginia thought, being prisoners together, a bonding experience. The chess game, too, had been a real challenge, and lots of fun. She almost forgot they were more or less naked, in the middle of the Apocalypse, and trapped in an isolation-observation chamber.

"Your move," Jake was staring at the board: Virginia could see he was beginning to blink; the poor kid was exhausted; soon he'd droop over the chess set and slide off the stool and onto the floor.

"Okay, let's see, Jake," said Virginia; her hand was poised over the rook, no, she moved her hand to the bishop, no, she moved it again, hovering over a vulnerable little pawn.

"You are teasing me, Virginia!"

"No, I'm thinking deep and hard. I'm not as fast as you are, Jake."

"Liar," Jake grinned, "you're a sort of genius."

"Ah, you flatter me, kind sir!" she made her move. "The problem is – you're the one who is the genius, Jake, so I've really got to think really, really hard!"

Jake frowned: playing chess with Virginia was really challenging, and lots of fun. Jake was biting his lip, concentrating, really concentrating.

The air coming into the isolation room was cool and had no smells, no smells whatsoever; it was creepy, Jake thought, really creepy; but he'd agreed to the whole thing, so whatever happened he was going to have to take responsibility for it. He had to protect Virginia.

Jake had said, "Anywhere Virginia goes, I'm going too."

So both of them spent all that time sitting playing chess in the isolation chamber, and people were looking at them through two layers of thick bullet-proof plate glass: the little girl, Aaloka, looked at them, the tall naked girl M-J – though now she was dressed in overalls and a baseball cap – looked at them, and the – cool – black reptile woman looked at them with her gold eyes and narrow black snout and waved a yellow-pointed claw and he and Virginia waved back and Virginia even blew a kiss to the reptile woman and got one back.

Awesome!

Jake thought it was all pretty cool except for the fact that he had had to take off all his clothes. But that was less embarrassing than it otherwise would have been because Virginia had to do it too – which was awesome – and because Alex and Helen and the group with the reptile woman – Sarah James was her name, Jake had learned – they didn't have much in the way of clothes either and some of them – like M-J who turned out to be French and from Paris or something – didn't have any clothes at all, not at the beginning anyway, and M-J didn't seem to care about it, not having any clothes, and she said she sort of preferred, when she could, to make do with little or nothing in the way of clothes, so that made Jake feel better and more relaxed about being naked or near-naked. Now all the others had got some laboratory overalls and things, or jeans and T-shirts or white laboratory coats and everybody looked like a construction worker or a scientist in a scientific laboratory – and, of course, that was right, and really appropriate and awesome, because they were in a real scientific laboratory.

Most of the clothes, he caught glimpses of the clothes people were wearing through the plate glass windows, most of them didn't fit very well and so they all looked sort of goofy. M-J was probably right. No clothes would be awesome too.

Yeah, definitely, the coolest one, next to Virginia of course, was the black reptile woman Sarah – and that little girl Aaloka who said she owned the reptile woman and called her "Black Dragon" – and maybe M-J who at the beginning didn't have any clothes on and who winked at him and who didn't seem bothered by anything that happened and always smiled; she was really cool too. They were all friends now it seemed to Jake, all part of a team, all part of the crew of a little boat caught in a very big storm.

"That was a good move, Virginia! See! You do know what you are doing!"

"You are a true gentleman, Jake," Virginia gave him a big bright phosphorescent wink and coughed up a big gob, which she caught in her hand and plopped into a little bucket they had placed just beside her.

So, dressed in those skimpy little medical gowns people wore in a hospital, skimpy little things that barely tied up at the back, they were playing chess and waiting for the results of some tests.

Alex Wolf and the doctor called Henry – Henry Cheng – had taken samples of the green slime that dribbled from Virginia's nostrils and mouth and also, they'd take hair from Jake and Virginia, spit samples from Jake and blood from both of them.

It was like being at the center of some huge drama.

It was cool and frightening at the same time, it was like being in a space ship with the acid-dripping alien and its giant double jaws hiding somewhere in the metal tubing or in the ventilation system, and Jake and Virginia, in the isolation chamber, were the fish swimming in their own private polluted little virus-infected ocean or pool which was contained in the steel and plate glass walls or maybe they were the exotic monsters, the enemies of humanity, the creepy-crawling things that might look human but weren't, like alien pods, and all that was possible. But Jake didn't feel like he was a creepy-crawly thing and he didn't think Virginia was a creepy-crawling thing either though she did look weird but he'd gotten so used to her glowing green eyes and bald head and crest standing up in the middle and her green glowing skin, and the dribble coming from her mouth – and the big gobs she spat out from time to time – that it seemed entirely normal and even beautiful.

Virginia said, "Well, here we are, and I don't know how long we are going to be here."

She spoke into the microphone. "Any idea how long Jake and I have to stay in here?"

"I don't know," said Alex Wolf, "It shouldn't be long. Are you guys thirsty or hungry?"

"I'm starving," said Jake.

"Okay we'll send in sandwiches and some water," Alex said, and in a few minutes sandwiches and water were delivered by the tall girl. "Call me M-J," she had said when they first met. She winked and waved through the glass. The sandwiches and water bottles came through a slot, with a triple barrier and a vacuum in between.

"You're slobbering less now, Virginia," Jake said.

"Well, thank you, Jake, that is a very elegant and flattering and kind thing to say to your zombie girlfriend."

"You're very welcome, zombie girlfriend," said Jake with a big grin.

Virginia ran her hand self-consciously over her skull and over the stiff crest of hair in the middle. "I'm not sure this fashion will catch on."

"You look like a punk rocker from ancient times," said Jake, "I saw pictures in a comic book." He was opening his ham-and-cheese sandwich.

"Maybe you could set up a public relations campaign to say this is the new way to be beautiful," said Virginia, biting into the Swiss and Gruyere on whole wheat. She was wondering if her former life was over, if her career was over, and she was thinking, if we get out of this, I want to keep Jake, he has no parents, and he probably doesn't have grandpa any more, maybe I can adopt him, if I don't die, if he doesn't die, if we don't die.

As if he had read her thought, Jake said, "I'm an orphan, you know."

"Yes, Jake, I know."

"Grandpa said I could only stay with him for a few weeks. Then I'd have to go. He said he was too old and cantankerous and ill-tempered to look after a kid."

"Well, I'm sort of an orphan too," Virginia said, wondering at how quickly she had fallen for this kid, head-over-heels! And she'd never even wanted kids! Kids were too fragile, too vulnerable – hostages to fortune, somebody had said, and Virginia was afraid, terrified, something would happen to her kid – and if it did, she would … absolutely die …

"You are?"

"Maybe, Jake," Virginia said, chewing on her sandwich, "Maybe we can find a way to stick together – I mean after all this is over – just maybe." She didn't want to get his hopes up – or her own. She was terrified she would lose him.

"Wow! That would be great!" It was just what Jake was hoping she would say but he didn't want to come out and ask because he had no idea whether Virginia wanted the same thing and he had no idea whether such a thing was even possible.

"It might be complicated," Virginia said, her green phosphorescent eyes glowing at him, "but we'll figure a way. The law is complicated."

"We'll figure a way." Jake felt he could overcome the law. In videos and films, he'd seen lots of people overcome the law.

"So, where were we?" Virginia looked down at the chess set.

"Cool, I'm going to beat you!"

"I'm not so sure of that, Jake, I'm not so sure," said Virginia, concentrating, but with her mind echoing the thought, "You've inspired me to great heights of endeavor, Jake."

She made her move.

"Ah," said Jake.

And she said, "Mom and dad died when I was twelve and so I went away to school and then I went straight to university and drama school and then I started working right away. I had a boyfriend and he was sort of my family, but he died."

"Gosh, so you have nobody. You're like me."

"Yes, we are a jolly old pair – perfect for each other!"

Jake was looking down, staring, concentrating on the chess board. Virginia gazed at him. He was so beautiful!

Virginia didn't tell Jake that her father, who was a real estate mogul, had believed, at one point, that he was going bankrupt, and he had felt he didn't have any hope of getting out of it, and he was manic-depressive anyway so any bad news could trigger a spiral of self-hatred, a spiral of hopeless despair, and an orgy of guilt – and a bout of drinking – and so he came home one day, it was a sunny day, and Virginia was out at the swimming pool, sitting at a little fold-up table, staring at the water, the sparkly bright blue water, and trying to figure out how to solve a problem in algebra, like, you've got to eliminate the fractions so you multiply both sides by the smallest common denominator and, she remembered, as long as you do the same thing to both sides of the equation, whatever you do, you don't change the fact that the two sides are equal, and so …

She was trying to understand the logic behind what she was doing: why it worked. It was one of her characteristics which sometimes annoyed her teachers – she always wanted to know the *why* of things.

She looked up and her dad was standing there – he was a really handsome man and she was madly in love with him and wanted to marry somebody exactly like him, even down to the moods which she sometimes caught a glimpse of – and he had a drink in his hand which was probably whiskey she thought from the golden color, and he was just standing there looking at her as if he wasn't seeing her, so she said, brightly, "Hi, Daddy."

"Hi Daddy," she said, and then, again, "Hi Daddy!"

And he just stared at her as if he hadn't seen her, as if she didn't exist, and she felt a cold shiver of fear and of … well … of non-existence, as if she had disappeared, as if she had become invisible, as if she were guilty of something, something horrible, but she didn't know what, something she had done that had made Daddy turn her into nothing, and in one swallow he drank down his whiskey, went back into the house and Virginia got up from the chair, leaving the textbook on the table, bright pages under the sun, so bright they were almost unreadable, and she heard bangs in the house – bang, bang, bang – and she went into the house just in time to see daddy shout at mommy and mommy shout back and say, "No, no, don't, please, don't, please Fred, don't, don't do it," and Virginia saw that daddy had something dark in his hand, and she saw it was a gun and she understood the bang, bang, bang had been shots – and he was holding it pointed at mommy, and Virginia wanted to scream out, Don't, and the gun went off and Virginia screamed "Don't" and then daddy turned and he saw her – this time, now, he really saw her – and he came running towards the door where she was standing, still out in the sunlight, just beyond the shadow cast by the overhang, and he wasn't daddy anymore and she could see in his eyes he was going to shoot her too and she ran, past the pool, and down into the rose garden, hearing a shot, and feeling something whizz past, brushing her shoulder, and she crawled under the bushes and crawled towards little door that led into the Hoffman's garden next door, and she got down on all fours and crawled through the fence, through the little door for the dogs to go through – and she heard shots whiz through the bushes, bullets brushing the trees, smashing through the leaves, smashing into the wood, smashing into the fence, with flakes and splinters of wood flying everywhere, and she was on her belly, crawling in the mud and leaves, and then she was staggering to her feet on the other side of the fence, in the Hoffman's yard, and she ran, keeping herself down, bent double so the daddy who was no longer daddy wouldn't see her if he looked over the fence and she ran, doubled over trying to make herself small, past the Hoffman's swimming pool, up the steps of broad flagstone terrace, and into the kitchen of the Hoffman's house where Concetta the maid was preparing lunch, laying out the cutlery and already there was a big bowl of salad, and Concetta looked up and she said, "Virginia Lily, you are all muddy, darling, what are you doing here, what's happened?" and Virginia said, "Daddy killed mommy and he wants to kill me and maybe he will come here and kill everybody and we've got to hide," and Mrs. Hoffman came into the kitchen and said, "What were those bangs, it sounded like gunfire," and Virginia said, "It's daddy, call the police!" And Mrs. Hoffman said, "That can't be right, Virginia." And then there was another shot. And Mrs. Hoffman said she was going to look. And Virginia said, "No, don't! Daddy's gone crazy. He'll shoot you."

Mrs. Hoffman went anyway, with Concetta and Virginia trailing behind her.

There was silence, just the birds singing.

Mrs. Hoffman opened the bigger gate that joined the two gardens, "I don't hear anything," she said, "It seems quiet. I'm sure, Virginia, you were imagining things and …"

Then Mrs. Hoffman stopped talking and just stood there.

Concetta took Virginia and held her close.

Daddy was floating face down in the pool in the middle of a big stain of dark red blood that looked black in the middle of the sparkling water and little wavelets because the afternoon breeze had come up and you could feel it on your skin and hear it moving in the leaves.

Later, people were standing around Virginia, the women's dresses fluttered in the breeze, the men stood silent; some of the women spoke as if Virginia wasn't there.

"The child shouldn't be here."

"Get her away, somebody get her away."

"Take her inside."

Mommy was lying face up with her eyes still open in the kitchen and the maid, Bianca, was lying face down in the laundry room with a hole in the back of her neck and lots of red and gray stuff.

Gandolfo, the golden terrier, was lying across the threshold of the media entertainment room. Virginia didn't see any blood; but he didn't wake up when she touched him, and he felt cold. Virginia shivered. It made his fur seem dirty and greasy and dead and, yes, underneath him there was blood, a smear of blood on the marble floor, dog's blood.

The police and a woman in a uniform came who asked Virginia lots of questions; Virginia felt it was like an exam – she was always a good student. She tried to give the right answers. The woman seemed pleased. She nodded and smiled. Virginia noticed that the woman had nice bright teeth and the beautiful skin that some of the women who spoke Spanish always seemed to have. It looked like honey.

She wanted to go and sit in the policewoman's lap and lay her head against her honey skin, but she knew that was the sort of thing babies or little children did and she was not a baby or little child – not any more.

Then there was lots of yellow tape all over the house and in the yard and around the pool. The sun was shining, but the air seemed cold to Virginia. She shivered. She heard her teeth chatter; then they stopped.

Lots of people came to the funeral

Virginia didn't want to cry but she finally did when she put her hand on her father's coffin which was closed, and her mother's coffin was closed too.

And Bianca's coffin was closed in the other funeral home where everybody spoke Spanish.

People knelt and said, in Spanish, "Is this the little girl?" And they hugged her, and touched her, and she sat in the front row with Bianca's three children, and when they stood up, they held hands, and she held hands with the little girl, Carmelita, and the little girl was crying, and Virginia hugged her and stroked her hair and told her not to cry, "There, there, don't cry," thinking, "She's like a doll, so neat, so small," and thinking, "I'd like to keep her, I'd like to keep her all for me!"

Funny thing was, afterwards, well, funny when you looked at it, or thought about it, the funny thing was: her father was not bankrupt at all; he had misread an ambiguously worded email, that was all that had happened, but it was enough, as Virginia understood much later, when she was an undergraduate, it was enough because of his depression and because of the drink and because of the self-disgust, and so, when everything was liquidated, Virginia was a very wealthy young teenager and she had no siblings and no grandparents or relatives except one eccentric old lady who told her that she, Virginia, was the cause of it all, that her mother never should have accepted the Devil's seed and borne the Devil's child, a wicked girl whose beauty made her even more wicked, like Jezebel. Virginia looked up Jezebel online and decided she liked Jezebel.

Virginia went to a boarding school and a lawyer – a young woman with a very brisk manner – looked after Virginia's "affairs," and, when she came of age, Virginia's fortune was large, very large indeed. It gave her security – so she could take risks – and taking risks made her career possible – but, once her career began, she hardly touched any of the money, determined to be her own person, pay her own way, and make her own fortune. But she did make sure Bianca's children – particularly little Carmelita – got the best possible education and help in starting their own careers.

"So, it's just us, Jake," Virginia had said, looking at him with those strange buggy glowing green eyes.

"Just us, together, to the end of time," Jake answered, quoting a line from one of her movies, *Romance in the Glacier* where Virginia was an alien frozen in the ice in her crashed spaceship – from 250,000 years ago – but revived when an expedition came upon her and the leader of the expedition fell in love with her and even touching her was dangerous and ...

Though Virginia looked really weird, her smile was so warm and her touch so smooth and gracious, that Jake felt he'd known her forever, and when she put her arm around his shoulders, he fell back gently against her thinking it was not at all a sissy thing to do, but maybe the thing a real man would do, because he would protect her and she would protect him, and they were partners and they would always be with the good guys against the bad guys wherever they met them.

They stayed that way for maybe a minute, and then Virginia released him and said, "Okay, where were we, partner?"

"Your move," said Jake.

"Oh, you've done it again, Jake," said Virginia, concentrating, "You've almost got me – but, hmm, but – not quite!"

Five moves later, Jake did whisper, as if he couldn't believe it himself, "Checkmate!"

"Yes, gosh, golly, you have got me trapped Jake, I think, I think, I think ..." And finally, Virginia said, "Yes, I surrender. You're the champ!"

Jake was so happy! He instantly fell asleep – and only woke up so he could get dressed and leave the little isolation cube for a more friendly conference room that had been converted into a temporary extra bedroom.

Then he was out again – like a light.

"So, Virginia," Alex was saying, "this is how we are running the tests," and he indicated to Virginia a series of computers attached to various instruments.

"Looks impressive," said Virginia, feeling more like the old Virginia Lily now that she was in her lime-green T-shirt, hot pants and scarlet flip-flops.

"It is. Henry and Norma have state-of-the-art equipment and they are the best there is in this field."

"So, tell me – what are you guys doing, exactly?"

"We've analyzed the DNA sequences of everybody."

"Everybody?"

"Yes, we're not just testing you and Jake. We have an almost ideal population here to experiment with. We have different types of people. We have you – and you are immune but not entirely: you've got symptoms but not the important, deadly symptoms. And – this is important – you aren't from our tests infectious. People can't catch it from you. We have Jake who has no symptoms, and that may be because he's naturally immune, or it may be because you sneezed on him – and, in some sense, 'vaccinated' him. We have Renée Scott and Steve Clark and Allison Trent and Wang Fei and Wang Fang – the Chinese twins – and our little girl, Aaloka, who are all human beings and who seem to be naturally immune; we have Marie-Josée, who's a synthetic individual –"

"M-J's a SIN?

"Yes, she's a new model, built in Paris, but – actually cutting-edge, far beyond anything anybody else has done, almost I think a fluke. I hadn't seen – or even imagined – such an advanced version was possible until I analyzed her DNA. Only Andromeda Corporation's Marit is anywhere near her level."

"M-J is fun. I like her," said Virginia, running her hand over her smooth skull. There I was exchanging wisecracks a few minutes ago with M-J – who seemed to have taken over the canteen – and I had no idea I was talking to a SIN!

"Yes, she's highly intelligent and very resourceful. She's entirely a person as far as I'm concerned, mentally, emotionally, she's exactly like you or me or the others. But as she is a SIN, she is immune, presumably because she doesn't have the weaknesses, the chinks in the armor most biologically natural people have. Her immune system is special, or her DNA just doesn't let the virus lock on or penetrate. We're not sure. I want to talk to her 'creator', who is also her legal father, Henri Duval, in Paris, but we haven't been able to get through."

"And then you have …?"

"Yes, then you have people – well, hybrids – like me …"

"You're a hybrid, Alex?" If she had had eyebrows, Virginia would have raised them. "You don't look like a hybrid. You don't look like Black Dragon."

"Yes, I'm a hybrid and so is Helen – and so is Ed Ross, the Secret Service guy. We can turn into those reptile things, when we wish to, and then we look like Sarah, but with different color schemes."

"Wow, or, as Jake says, awesome!"

"Ed Ross and Sarah were turned into hybrids to make them immune to the zombie virus. It was the only way we could get them off the *Eden*. Now we hybrids are immune, presumably, because we have extra defense mechanisms added by our alien element. Or, again, maybe like M-J, because there's no access point, no entry point, for the virus."

"Wow," said Virginia again, slurping back more slimy goo, her big green eyes glowing, "you have almost everything you need right here."

"We're lucky that way, yes," said Alex, "but I think you, Virginia, are the key. You are generating a sort of fluid that might just allow us to create a vaccine; your immune system has reacted against the virus and has neutralized it in some way. So we have a detailed breakdown of your immune reaction and the anti-bodies it has created and we've been comparing it with the DNA maps and models of the zombie virus – or Mind Slug as it used to be called – that Sabrina Jacobs has been sending us from her research ship *Andromeda II*."

"And," said Henry Cheng, who had just joined them, "We are trying to manufacture a large sample of the antibodies you produced and then we are going to test it."

"Test it – how?" Virginia turned her glowing green eyes towards Henry.

"On some zombies," said Henry, gazing at her. Even as a zombie Virginia Lily was a stunner.

"Zombies – where are you going to get the zombies?" Virginia wiped some bubbling green foam from her lips, "Sorry, this is disgusting."

"I think they are coming to get us," said Henry.

"Yes," said Alex Wolf.

"What do you mean, coming to get us?"

"A huge crowd of zombies is gathering about a mile away – and they are headed here, or so it seems," said Alex. "Some of the perimeter monitors have spotted them."

"Oh, boy," said Virginia.

"We're pretty well defended," said Henry Cheng, "but, still, it is going to be an interesting evening."

"Who's in charge of defense?"

"Sarah is the senior officer, so she's been elected to coordinate our defense; she was suggested by Renée Scott who, as the President's Press Secretary, represents the White House," said Alex, "Sarah will work with the head of security here at Bio-Frontier, an old time security guard who has worked for Henry for a long time, a guy called Gus Wallach."

"He's a totally solid guy," said Henry. "He knows the buildings like the back of his hand."

"So Black Dragon is head of the defense force," said Virginia. The world was stranger, and stranger. Here she was, heroine of stage, screen, and Internet, turned into a bald, glowing-eyed, green-skinned, dribbling monster, and federal Special Agents were reptile dragons, and charming young French women were SINs. And they were all working together.

"Yes," said Alex, "Aaloka's Black Dragon."

"She owns you all, Aaloka, doesn't she?" said Henry Cheng, smiling, "I heard her call you Gold Dragon – and Helen is …"

"Right," Alex laughed, "Helen is Silver Dragon."

"Aaloka's a rich girl. Poor Jake's only got one zombie to boss around," said Virginia.

"Well, at least the kids are having fun," said Henry Cheng, "but even if we have a team of dragons, keeping out the zombies is not going to be easy!"

CHAPTER 17 – BATTLEGROUND

Aaloka was fast asleep, in a corner, on a couch, in one of the conference rooms, tucked under a blanket. In the same room, a meeting was underway.

"So, the zombies are coming from the south, and we have weak points here and here and here." Sarah James – Black Dragon – was leaning over a layout and security plan of the Bio-Frontier, her two yellow and black claws planted on the schematics.

"Yes, that's right, those are the vulnerable points, those old windows, the loading dock, and the executive offices that have plate glass windows, and the reception area, which is open; there is a grill we can close, though." Gus Wallach's finger was moving over the schematics: the entry points to the plant – the possible weak points – the security camera set up, what was covered and what wasn't.

"So, we'd better put the hybrids up at that end," said Sarah, turning to Gus, and giving him her best reptile-hybrid smile.

"I figure, yes, the hybrids are the strongest, and from what you say, Sarah, they – you – are immune." Gus Wallach smiled at the reptile lady. Gus was an old-timer, a bachelor, with a large white handlebar moustache, stained with blonde remnants, and his white hair pulled back in a ponytail – but in spite of his bohemian appearance, Gus was unfailingly methodical, a go-by-the-book and study-up-on-the-latest-technologies man, which didn't exclude, he thought, using flair, imagination, intuition – Gus believed in check lists *and* in gut instinct. In his books, the two complimented each other.

"You know, I still can't believe it," he said, shaking his head and staring at Sarah's reptilian snout, gold eyes, and fangs.

"I can't believe it myself, Gus," Sarah grinned. "It's almost as new to me as it is to you. This time yesterday, I was still a human being."

Their little army was something the likes of which Gus had never seen, nor even imagined. Hours before, his eyes had opened wide when he first saw the rest of the ragged motley crew arrive, about twenty minutes after the zombie woman, Virginia Lily and her kid, Jake, and Alex Wolf and Helen Guerrera.

"Yes, we'll let them in," Henry Cheng had said, "However weird a group they are – they are with Alex and Helen."

So, Gus had opened his arms and said, "Welcome, welcome one and all!" And he watched them come in through the loading dock door.

First, there was Sarah – now their Commander in Chief – a black scaly hybrid reptile lady with the little Indian kid, Aaloka, cute as a button, riding on her back, and calling her mount "Black Dragon."

Second, there was a tall French girl called M-J, who when she came through the door was not wearing a single stitch of clothing and who turned out – she told him herself – to be a SIN and who made Gus feel, inveterate bachelor that he was, that he might like to take her home with him, cook her a good meal of his home-made spaghetti carbonara – matched with a good bottle of Gavi di Gavi – and introduce her to his collection of fish – he had Betta fighting fight, Balloon Kissing Gourami, and a giant pike and ...

Third, there were the two Chinese girl acrobats, Fang and Fei, who came through the door clutching what looked like table napkins, trying to cover themselves, not very successfully, he had to admit, and they were really cute too, just kids, both of them still at college.

Fourth, there were a couple of very muscular guys, Ed Ross, a Secret Service guy, nice guy but a bit shy, and Steve Clark, an ex-Marine, secret agent, and a woman, Allison Trent, expert in communications apparently, all federal Special Agents, like Black Dragon; but Black Dragon was some sort of special Secret Service agent, and who outranked them all – so everybody agreed that, even if she was Black Dragon and a hybrid, she and Gus should coordinate this little war they might be getting themselves into.

And then, finally, there was, my God, there was Renée Scott, the President's Press Secretary that Gus had seen on television, must have been a hundred times. She was an ultra-cute, stylish number, and quick as all get out, always keeping her good humor no matter how pesky those journalists got. She was the one who said that, according to her, Black Dragon should be in charge of security.

Nobody objected to that – after all Renée Scott was the White House speaking – and so a sleek red-and-black reptile-woman became their commanding officer, which indicated to Gus that the world was changing faster than he would ever have imagined.

So, with everybody with shaven heads and more or less naked, like refugees from a deluge, Gus had greeted them with the words, "My, my, it's Noah's Ark all over again!"

"You can say that again," the reptile woman answered, "I'm Sarah, and this is Aaloka, who's up on my shoulders here."

"She's Black Dragon," said the little girl, "And she's *my* dragon."

"She is indeed your dragon. I can see that," said Gus.

"Your moustache is beautiful, a classic handlebar, I believe," said the tall French girl, with a bright smile and no effort to hide her nakedness – apparently, no inhibitions whatsoever, "I'm Marie-Josée or M-J for short."

"Well, you are all welcome," said Gus, stroking his white handlebar moustache, and feeling a flush of pleasure, and he said, "Showers are available. And we have clothes, not very elegant clothes, but clothes for all of you – the fit may be a bit rough, but, better than nothing, I suppose. Black Dragon doesn't need clothes, I imagine."

"No, this is my uniform," said Black Dragon, "for now at least."

"She's cute, don't you think," said M-J.

"M-J's my biggest fan, after Aaloka of course," said Sarah, putting Aaloka down gently, so the little girl's feet landed, softly, on the floor.

"Well, let us get started. The showers are over there," and Gus indicated the way.

"A quick shower for everyone, and then we'll review the security situation, if everyone agrees," Sarah Black Dragon said. No one disagreed.

Gus felt protective of everybody and of the plant itself. Bio-Frontier had become his true home. He liked to take the night shift so he could catch up on paperwork and talk to Henry and Norma who often worked nights.

Gus was in the building when the terrorist attack alarm went off, and he said he would stay on. "My fish can survive happily without me for at least a week – even more."

The rest of the security staff didn't show up. All those Gus was able to contact said they were busy trying to save themselves or their families and Gus told them he understood and that they should take care – hide, find some place to hide. "Lock yourself, in! Don't go out!" For many of them, Gus suspected, the realization of the insidious nature of the danger would have come too late.

They were probably either dead or they were zombies.

Gus Wallach handed out weapons to the night staff. "Just in case," he said, and he explained how the pistols and stun guns worked. "I'm not sure these bullets are much use against zombies," he said, glancing at a TV monitor, "But something's better than nothing, I guess."

CHAPTER 18 – MANHATTAN

In New York City, Day Two of the Zombie Apocalypse began as a hot, steamy, sunny, smoggy Manhattan stinker.

In the 78-story New York Headquarters Volpe Octopus Building, it was ten hours since they had lost contact with Charlie and Samantha.

When contact was lost, the switchboards were lit up with calls and the servers were flooded with texts asking: "Where are they? What's happened? Please save Sam!"

But, since then, there was nothing to say. There was no news. The monitors and links gave out just hiss and static and noise and no images or no voice. Charlie's U-Tab kicked into voice mail: "Hello, there, this is Charlie Parr. I can't talk to you right now. Please leave a message."

Then there was nothing – not even the voice mail.

"All communications are down in the area of south Florida," said Shelly Nixon who was briefing the production team, a weary, bleary-eyed group of survivors. "Land lines, satellite connections, cell phones, everything is down. Sometimes fleeting images come through – for instance – this came through on from somebody's U-Tab." She pointed at the screen. It showed a zombie eating what remained of a … it looked like a fireman … a guy wearing a fireman's helmet; the zombie was munching on a forearm. There was a palm tree and what looked like rising smoke in the background. It looked like a parking lot. Then the image flickered off. "That's just five seconds of image," said Shelly, "Probably somebody or something kicked the U-Tab and it took the shot and somehow the shot got transmitted through the blockade or whatever it is."

"So what about Sam and Charlie?" asked one of the young interns, Olivia Madison. She was a bright skinny blonde from Portland, Oregon; she seemed to live for work and work alone.

"They may be still alive. I hope they are, Olivia. I hope Charlie manages to get through all the static and tell us how they are."

In the studio, Bill Brothers was interviewing top security expert Paul Stratford on the breakdown of communications.

"What is the possible cause of this collapse of communications?"

"Well, Bill, you may remember the events of 2027."

"I do – one of the greatest catastrophes to hit our planet."

"Yes, it was, it was. Well, at that time, while the earth was hit by a wave of tremors and earthquakes, eruptions and tsunamis, it also experienced a massive electromagnetic disturbance which cut or reduced communications all over the planet."

"Yes."

"We are seeing similar phenomena now."

"Electromagnetic disturbances …"

"Yes. But now the disturbance is on a local level, confined to southern Florida and to parts of the Caribbean – not global as it was in 2027."

"Is this related to the terrorist attack on the *Eden of the Seas*, the attack on the president, and the zombie plague?"

"I believe it must be. The coincidence is too great."

"So we are under attack."

"I believe we are, yes."

"Who is attacking us?"

"I have no idea, Bill. But I will say this: whoever is attacking us is using weapons that no nation on this earth is known to possess."

"So this could be an alien attack, part of an alien attack."

"Yes, it could."

"But why would the aliens just attack Florida?"

"I have absolutely no idea, Bill. We'll have to ask the aliens – wherever they show themselves."

"Thanks, Paul. Now, let's have a roundup of the news, said Bill Brothers, right after this message from our sponsors."

The commercial break began by touting something that made you smell like a dream so that all your friends would be envious of your new designer odor, and your girl, your guy, passers-by, your neighbors, and your pet would not be able to resist you. The image sequence showed Virginia Lily emerging from a bubble bath, spraying herself with the magic product, then being overwhelmed by a crowd of frenzied suitors, men and women, and including dogs and cats and ...

"What? You want more pundits?" Bill Brothers wiped his forehead. He needed a shower; he was sticky everywhere, under his arms, in his crotch, and down his legs. He rubbed his chin. Scratchy – he needed a shave. Damn! The producers had decided they wanted him to have a five o'clock shadow, and the disheveled unkempt look of a guy who'd spent more than one sleepless night. That was easy enough – he'd been on the air for almost 20 hours straight now.

Weirdly, too, he was suddenly beginning to recognize his loss – Samantha was almost certainly dead. Emotion always came as a delayed reaction to Bill Brothers. Usually, if he cried at all, he cried years after the fact – the death of a child, the death of his first wife from cancer, the time when – he was eleven years old – his dog was run over by a car – and the emotion usually hit him, many years later, when he was alone, maybe in the middle of the night, or walking along the street, or waiting for a flight, or checking into a hotel, and usually the sense of loss, welling up, hit him, right then, for no reason he could discern; and even then he didn't believe it. He didn't believe he could ever really feel anything for anybody – sometimes, in rare moments of reflection, he wondered – Why was that?

"Yes, more pundits, we need more pundits," Shelly Nixon was staring at him, "We don't have much hard news with all the connections to Miami down, so we'll fill with pundits."

"Fuck pundits," said Bill Brothers, "We don't need pundits. We've got reality – why do we need pundits?"

"We need pundits," said Shelly Nixon, touching her hair. "We absolutely need them – besides, these guys are on the payroll. And, Bill, an even more important point is this: Rubber Duck – "Rubber Duck" was Shelly's pet name for the Big Boss billionaire media magnate Rufus Mudcock, owner of Volpe Global Octopus – Rubber Duck just sent me a text, I quote: 'Where are my fucking pundits?'"

"So pundits it is," said Bill Brothers.

Bill Brothers smiled at the first pundit.

"So Professor, what is the answer to the zombie plague.

The Professor – Karl Emmanuel Corcoran – was a clean-cut young man in an expensive bright blue suit, with a flower in his buttonhole and a handkerchief in his vest pocket, and he was an expert on policy from the Free Capitalism From its Chains Foundation. "Now, Bill, if the Government would just reduce taxes and get out of the bio business – in fact, get out of all business – then we wouldn't have zombie plagues, or reptile men on the loose, and ordinary Americans could spend their own hard-earned dollars on the things they need and desire, and not have to worry about these zombies and taxes and accountants. Government is the problem, Bill, not the solution! Say, if you have government inspecting restaurant kitchens for rats and turds and dead cats and horse meat and so on, well, then the chefs and kitchen staff get lazy and the risk of rats and plagues and turds and dead cats and horse meat and so on increases exponentially. It's called 'moral hazard,' Bill. If government only withered away, people could go into the kitchens, sniff around and check under the stove for the rats and turds and dead cats and horse meat themselves, and then the zombies would die on the vine, Bill. Without subsidies and without government, Bill, there would be no zombies, and that's God's own truth!"

Bill swiveled around to face the other pundit; this pundit had a long gray wild beard and his gray hair, what was left of it, tied back in a pony-tail, "And Professor Dinko Milinkovic, what do you have to say – what is the answer to zombie plagues and reptile hybrid murders?"

"Well, Bill, I'd say that unleashing neoliberal deregulated capitalist rapaciousness and greed is not the answer, Bill, I'd say what we need is more regulation, regulation with real teeth. Make the bastards pay for their crimes! Big business has bought government, that is clear, and I'm afraid the United States of America is no longer a democracy; it is a plutocracy, an oligarchy, a corporatist cabal, money rules, money buys Congress, money buys the regulators; and money even buys the Presidency. The profit motive creates zombies, Bill, no doubt about it. We are in the last stage of Capitalism, Bill; that is clear: big corporate financial capitalism without conscience or soul. The filthy rich reign over us all – and they bring us plagues, oil spills, financial disaster, reptile men, and zombies. Each time these fat cats create a problem, we the people pay for it. Global capitalism creates zombies, no doubt about it. It appropriates bodies, our bodies and our minds, it colonizes our gray cells, and it floods our mind-time, turning us into zombies. If we want to protect freedom, we should regulate, regulate, regulate. And I think, too, we should nationalize companies in strategic and dangerous fields – oil, energy, biochemistry, electronics, banking, automobiles, toothpaste, baby oil, coffee beans, movies, nightclubs, and peanuts … and all other logos. The Fat Cats rule; the poor people – the workers, the peasants, the students, the pensioners, they are the ones who pay, always. Capitalism is incurable, Bill. We should nationalize Andromeda Corporation."

"Andromeda Corporation is not an America-based company."

"Much of its research is done in America. We should seize its assets here and make them work for humanity, not for the selfishness of a few fat cats – like that Jacobs woman."

When he'd finished with the two pundits, Bill Brother's wiped his brow, splashed water on his face, and, back in the studio, went for a one-on-one with another pundit – retired General Arthur Godwin Wells.

"Well, General, let's look at the situation," said Bill Brothers pointing to a large mobile graphic map.

"Absolutely, Bill."

"The situation map shows here that zombies have now invaded the Florida Keys, and there are reports of zombie infiltrations as far north as West Palm Beach. On the other hand, so far the west coast of Florida, Naples, Sarasota, and Tampa seem not to have been infected – so far."

"Yes," said the General.

"General, what do you say?"

"Well, Bill, zombies do not fight fair and do not play by the rules of war."

"Does anybody?"

"Good point, Bill, good point; but we try, we try. All you can do is try, Bill."

"So, what's to be done against these zombies?"

"The problem with your zombie, Bill, is you get too close to him – or her – and you become one. We saw that with Samantha."

"Right, so …"

"Distance, you gotta keep your distance."

"So you try long-distance weapons – missiles, bombs, helicopter gunships, and so on."

"Yes, that's what you do, Bill, and that's what the government has been trying to do."

"Trying?"

"Well this is pretty hush-hush and I'm sticking my neck out but as you know there has been a lot of electronic interference."

"Yes," said Bill, "all communications are down."

"Well, Bill, that is making our defense effort every difficult: Now, this is just rumor, but I have heard that missiles have been blown up, helicopter gunships have been blown up and a couple of missiles I've been given to understand have simply disappeared and maybe even a Stealth Wedge V. There seems to be some sort of electronic shield protecting this zombie invasion, this zombie beach-head."

"What about the attack on the beach, the Karl Rove Beach? It seems …"

"Bill, I am risking my neck again. I was privileged to see some footage – secret confidential footage – of the attack on the beach, low level strafing by our very own US helicopter gunships with heavy Gatling gun type machine guns, more than a thousand rounds a minute, and napalm and cluster-bombs. It doesn't take much imagination to picture the effect all that can have. And, tragically, I don't think those were zombies, Bill, those were people; those were people trying to escape."

"My God, General, are you accusing …?"

"I'm not accusing, Bill, I am observing. As for judgements and accusations, we have to wait for the full facts to come out … but I will tell you this: I have had, through local contacts, confirmation that those were people on the beach, not zombies."

"If this is true, General, it is a tragedy."

"It certainly is, Bill, a tragedy within a tragedy."

"General, let's continue, after the break."

Cartoon dogs and cats squabbled over Scrabble Paradise Dog Food, "the food you can use for your cats, your dogs, and your fish – and, in a pinch, during the end-of-the-month-blues for your little ones. Kids and the unemployed and the irredeemably deservedly poor gobble it up."

"So, General, fighting the zombies – why is it so difficult?"

"Well as we said if you get close you catch the thing, and you become a zombie. But then there is the other problem, Bill."

"Which is …?"

"These zombie folk are very resilient – they bounce back – you can even cut the head off, and they refuse to die."

"Let's see the *Eden Paradise Promenade Café de Paris* tape again, so folks can see what you mean, General."

"Right, now, Bill, as you can see in this tape, the zombie's head was literally cut off – this feed is from earlier on, from a security webcam on the *Eden of the Seas*, before we lost communication with the *Eden*'s security system, and it shows, you can see her here now, it shows this young lady in a sort of French maid's costume ..."

"She's a waitress at the Café de Paris on the *Eden*."

"Right, well, this young lady – a very attractive young lady I must say – she has a meat cleaver and she's being attacked by these two zombie folk wearing chef's hats ... those white floppy toque things ... Now, note here, she lops off both arms – I mean both arms – of one of the zombies, and he just pauses a second or two, and then he comes after her again. And meanwhile ..."

"There's the other zombie ..."

"Yes, meanwhile there's this other zombie – also in one of those toque things – see, there he is – and he comes storming at our young lady and she lets him have it, and, this is extraordinary, Bill, I mean, just look at this, with one hit – Whack! – she cuts off his head ..."

"She has a great backhand stroke, General."

"Absolutely, Bill, I would love to have her with me on the court; this is one talented young lady, yes, I'd certainly want her on my side of the net. Now, the head is gone ... bouncing out, freeze that frame please, and replay, thank you, as you can see, Bill, the head, looking startled, bouncing out, off to the left, still wearing the chef's hat, I believe technically it's called a toque, Bill, and then off screen ... But ..."

"Yes ..."

"But, Bill, the key thing here is, that zombie, without the head, he comes charging at her again, and in fact, now both of them are after her, and she, wisely, skedaddles."

"We don't know what happened to her, do we, General?"

"No, unfortunately, we have lost track of this heroine. She may have been killed later. She may have become a zombie herself. Or she might – these are very rare cases – she might be immune in which case if she could fight or hide, she might still be alive. Now, I hope we find out, Bill, but maybe we will never know."

"Now, General, that brings up an interesting point – immunity. Not very many people are immune."

"No, Bill, best estimates are 1 or 2% of the human population. So if this thing really gets loose – well, Bill, we are goners!"

"But SINS, biologically created individuals or synthetic individuals as they are known, there's a rumor that they are immune ..."

"Bill, I was hoping you wouldn't ask me about that," the General put on his most charming self-deprecating grin, the grin he'd used as a student, selling pirated DVDs and Encyclopedia-Tabs door-to-door. The General was a very handsome man.

"Why?"

"Because … well, I believe that, yes, SINs are immune. We have reasons to believe they are immune. In fact our young lady warrior there, she might well be a SIN, I think, the most advanced version, cutting-edge stuff, possibly designed by Andromeda Corporation, or that French-German consortium, Henri Duval's EURO-BIO."

"Why do you say that?"

"Well, I think she probably was – or is – immune. She showed no decrease in performance or strength, no sign she was catching the zombie thing. So that would raise the probability that she's a SIN. And then there's the, well, the physical perfection."

"She's very beautiful."

"Yes, she is, sort of flawless – she is somebody's idea of perfection, which would suggest that, just possibly, she was designed – not the result of genetic hazard, luck-of-the draw like the rest of us."

"So, why didn't you want me to ask you about SINs?"

"Well, because – and I'm a minority here and I'm retired so I'm speaking only for myself – but I think we should have more of them."

"More SINs."

"Yes, they could be our first line of defense. If you had a couple of hundred like that young lady – armed with more than just a meat cleaver – I mean you see her earlier in the clip looking around – desperately I might add – for something she could use to defend herself – she had to improvise – but, say, if we had a couple of hundred like that girl and they were armed with electric saws, or pistols or rifles with explosive softhead bullets, well, we could kiss goodbye to those zombie folk in no time."

"And why did you not want to talk about this?"

"Well, Bill, as you may know, there is a witch hunt on for SINs and for the scientists who make them."

"Yes, I'm not sure I would qualify it as a *witch hunt*," Bill Brothers blushed and shuffled his feet nervously; he was terrified that the Security and Ortho-dox Establishment, the STASI or KGB or STARR Commission might come knocking at his door or storming into the studio – and then if they were mad at him, these Occult Powers, if they looked into the details of his life, they could raise possible charges of harassment from his diddling or fooling around with Samantha though it was consensual but, even if she was a consulting adult with a postgraduate degree, in a sense, her position could be construed as her working for him, thus under him, thus inferior, thus vulnerable to the old quid pro quo, consensual sex slavery, in which case under paragraph 245-H-B of Code 75 of …

"Well, Bill, in my eyes, it is, yes, a witch hunt – totally unjustified, dangerous, unpatriotic, premature, unscientific, and against the basic concepts of human rights and plain good sense for which this nation should stand and for which it usually has stood, thanks be to God, throughout its history. The Founding Fathers were rationalists, Enlightenment Men, for God's Sake! This is America after all and courage not fear is our hallmark – or should be."

"You are a man of strong opinions, General."

"Well, Bill, now what I'm really worried about is my priest might refuse me the sacrament next Sunday, for my approving of artificial life forms and giving rights to them and all."

"You are a believer, General."

"Yes, I am, Bill, and I believe the Good Lord gave us minds and we should use them. I have many friends who are of different faiths – Jewish, Muslim, Hindu, Buddhist, or who are not believers at all, agnostics, atheists. We all share, I think, a sort of awe before the fact of just being here, the utter joy of sharing this wonderful planet, the ecstasy and privilege of each moment here. There are many ways, I believe, to confront the mystery and joy and pain of being alive, of being here, of existing, the wonderful privilege of just plain existing … My way, personally, is to worship the God of tradition, of the tradition from which I come. That's what I want to defend, the right for each of us to find our own way, Bill, and I want to defend that – freedom of conscious and expression and speech – with whatever it takes. And if a young lady like the one we've seen there, if she can help us, well God bless her!"

"Thank you, General."

"Thank you, Bill, it's been a privilege, as always, and I want to add a special thanks to your people, to Samantha and Charlie; they are in the front line. They are saying like it is: the truth, the unvarnished, old-fashioned truth. Their courage is extraordinary! I salute them. They are the stuff of which this nation was built. They are heroes."

CHAPTER 19 – RUFUS MUDCOCK

Somewhere, high above the Pacific Ocean in a private jet, the monitor screen flickered, went blank, and then came on again. Bill Brothers appeared, disappeared. He was saying: "As you know folks, we have lost contact with Charlie Parr and Samantha Andrews, but we are sure to re-establish contact soon. There are burst of interference which are … interrupting satellite communications … and even … landlines … those old fashioned … seem to … trouble … electro … magnetic … we …"

A suave off-screen voice declared: "We are having trouble with this broadcast. We shall be back to you in a moment."

Bill Brothers disappeared in a screen of old-fashioned hissing snow. Most other communications systems were also down.

Rufus Mudcock – aka Rubber Duck – who had his teeth in a chocolate croissant and who was sitting in front of the monitor screen that had suddenly gone blank, got on his Universal U-Tab intending to scream, "What the fuck is happening? What the fuck are you idiots doing?" But there was no connection. No connection to anything.

And his private jet, flying over the Pacific, somewhere between Tokyo and Honolulu, was suddenly flying blind.

The pilot said, "Mr. Mudcock, ladies and gentlemen, we've just lost contact with Japan and with Hawaii, and with all GPS systems. We are returning to manual controls and visual navigation as of now."

Sally, Mudcock's Executive Assistant, said, "Would you like a drink, Rufus?"

"Damned right I would, Sally. The usual, thank you!"

"Coming right up, Rufus," she said, and sidled away, her slit skirt showing a handsome bit of tanned thigh; she was a good girl, was Sally, and she'd been with him, how long, oh, God, it must be fifteen years now, good-looking, discreet, with, he supposed, her own life, but always ready to work, no matter what time of day or night, and so it ended up being 24/7. Hmm! Maybe she didn't have a life after all. He must look into it.

Rufus Mudcock looked out the window – down below there was nothing but the ocean, the endless ocean.

"You know, Sally," said Rufus Mudcock, as Sally returned bearing the Chivas Regal, "The world is a very big and mysterious place."

"Yes, Rufus, it is."

"Things happen, you know, Sally, things happen."

"Yes, they do, Rufus."

"I liked that general – no nonsense – he says it the way it is."

"Yes, he does, Rufus."

"If you say it the way it is, Sally, you get screwed; maybe not right away, Sally, but eventually, you get screwed. Remember that, Sally – you heard it from me."

"The general is rich, Rufus, and retired, and has no children."

"Right, Sally, thanks for reminding me. That's why he can tell it the way it is – he has no hostages to fortune; the general is a free man."

"There aren't very many free men – or women, Rufus."

"No, there aren't, Sally; you are right. Freedom is a dream that died a long time ago."

"Would you like me to top the Chivas up, Rufus?"

"Yes, Sally, indeed I would. Thank you, thank you."

Below them there was only the ocean, inhuman and vast and – though filled with human junk – seemingly untroubled by human dreams – or human nightmares.

CHAPTER 20 – SHELLY NIXON

Shelly Nixon was in the corridor behind Studio Five, under flickering fluorescent overhead corridor lights, leaning against the wall, smoking a cigarette, tapping the floor with one high heel of her Prada patent leather stilettos.

"You're smoking." Bill Brothers came up and stared at her – good-looking broad, she still was, with her narrow, deeply tanned face, dark, haunted, burnt-out eyes, wiry nervy body, with those perfect small firm cupcake tits, that he could see though the white silk T-shirt, nipples pressing darkly, "I thought you gave up."

"Yeah, I'm smoking."

"It's illegal."

"I don't give a fuck."

"You should be happy, eh, Shelly, this is your triumph – Samantha turned into a hideous zombie, probably dead, and we've got the highest ratings in the whole wide world."

"Piss off, Bill."

"Okay, I've got to go back anyway. We're back on in ten minutes – if we are on, that is, and if we aren't on, we'll pretend."

"Right, in ten minutes, I'll be there."

"Right," Bill Brothers hesitated, she looked desolate and vulnerable, lines and shadows under her eyes, vulnerable, sad, needy, and therefore sexy; he showed concern, the fatherly patrician concern he put on so well, deepening his voice slightly. "Are you really okay, Shelly, really?"

She looked up at him, grimaced as the smoke curled out of her mouth, and passed like a veil in front of her eyes, thinking, now Pretty Big Boy sees me as prey, giving me the big, doe-eyed look, the stealthy hunter, "Yeah, I'm okay, Bill, thanks, I'm really okay."

She watched Bill Brothers walk down the corridor, shoulders bent, a big, tall, fine-looking man, dressed by the best tailors, his complexion and hair exquisitely cared for, usually impeccably groomed, soigné, très soigné, always smelling of expensive cologne and aftershave. She wondered whether the man had any feelings or any thoughts at all: A straw man, a hollow man, the mere husk of a man, the poet must have been thinking of Bill Brothers when he coined those images – but of course the images were created a century and more before Bill Brothers was born, and yet …

Poetry is eternal.

"Fuck," she muttered, gazing at the cigarette, smoke curling upward. She wondered why the fuck they painted these corridors in gloomy vomit gray-green, why the fuck they left all the pipes hanging out, why the fuck they used flickering dull fluorescent lights that made you think you were a ghoulish, ghostly, pale, vitamin-starved convict on death row counting the days until the electric chair or the fatal needle put an end to the dreariness and boredom and suspense: corridor lighting to vomit by.

She stubbed the cigarette out by pressing the glowing flame hard into the palm of her hand, murmuring inwardly "ouch" and gritting her teeth but making no noise, no complaint, not a sound. Her eyes watered from the pain.

"Fuck this!" She walked into the washroom, stared around as if dazed; white, bright, ceramic, a line of cubicles, a line of metal sinks, and a line of mirrors.

She flushed the crumpled cigarette down the toilet and washed her hands and dried them – noting the red circular mark where she'd burned the palm of her right hand. She stared at the red mark. "Serves you right, you bitch!" She looked at the face in the mirror and repeated, "You bitch, you bitch, you bitch," quietly, letting her voice run down into a whisper. "You fucking bitch!"

The face in the mirror was thin and tanned and had lines running down the cheeks – prominent cheekbones throwing a shadow. The lips were thin but sensual and dark and precisely delineated, the teeth were even, carefully redesigned, bright white against the tan – good teeth, perfect teeth, yes, the dentists and dental hygienists always said so. The eyes were narrow, slanted slightly upwards at the sides and dark and it looked like the pupil and iris had been smudged together, blood vessels had broken in the extra clear whites, not many, but still; the leaden circles under the eyes – well-earned leaden circles – were darker than before. Her hair, naturally curly, was greasy now, a sort of mousey-gray black. The forehead was high, and, strangely, almost entirely without wrinkles. Nice neck, too, she thought, long, tanned, graceful, not ropy and creased and wrinkled, not yet. Her breasts and nipples showed, and her ribcage, pressing against the elastic white silk T-shirt; the leather belt was tight around the slim waist; the jeans were tight too. "Boy, am I tight! I'm a very tight girl!" She splashed water on her face and let it drip and run, rivulets down her cheeks, running off her chin, down her neck. She splashed more water over her face and then, hands on the sink, leaning towards the mirror, she stared into her own eyes, "You killed that kid, you bitch, you utter bitch, you killed that kid as surely as if you had taken a gun and put it to the side of her head and pulled the trigger, you killed that kid for nothing, for absolutely nothing, for your own stupid vanity and sense of hurt over a guy who is not worth the little finger on the kid's left hand, who is not worth a copper penny, who is not worth … a guy who is a hollow man, a straw man, a nothing man, and you, you bitch, you stupid bitch, you fucking stupid bitch, you killed Samantha for that." She splashed more water, violently, over her face, over her head, smoothing down her hair, greasing it down against her skull, violently, more water, more water, and more water. She was dripping wet, water streaming down; her hair was plastered close to her skull.

She got a paper towel and she started, very slowly to dry her face. She remembered – and it was the first time she had thought about it in a long time – how, when Samantha first came to work at the network, the girl had been so eager to learn; how Samantha had adopted Shelly as her guide, and how Shelly had been flattered by the girl, by her attentions, by her intelligence, by her eagerness to learn – and by her beauty. And Bill Brothers moved in. And Samantha had no idea there had been an affair between Bill and Shelly, she even confided in Shelly … and so … hatred and jealousy and bitterness and revenge … had begun.

A buzzer buzzed. "Shelly Nixon, please, Come to studio!"

"I'm on my way," said Shelly, to the empty bathroom, "I'm on my way." She sighed, "Fuck! And I was in love with the kid; I didn't even know it, and I was in love with the kid!" She rolled up the paper towel into a ball, stuffed it down garbage slot, and left the washroom.

In the corridor she said, out loud, "Samantha, if your soul is out there any-where, know this: I killed you and I killed Charlie. If you have any influence, Sam, send me to hell; send me to hell forever and ever and ever, Sam, it's the least you can do."

In the washroom, the mirror was still dripping water.

CHAPTER 21 – SALLY

"That kid, Samantha Andrews, she's a spunky little thing," said Rufus Mud-cock, sipping the Chivas carefully, with the edge of his pursed lips, and glancing out at the clouds far below.

"She is, Rufus," said Sally.

"I met her once, liked her, sexy as all get out, ambitious too."

"Yes, Rufus," said Sally who was checking for links to the outside world – there were none, not for the moment.

"If she doesn't make it, maybe try to do something for her family, if she has a family; lots of kids these days, they don't have families."

"I'll make a note of it, Rufus," said Sally, typing into her personal electronic memory bank: "condolences; funeral; commemorative broadcast with clips from Samantha's earlier reporting; pension; does Samantha Andrews have a family? Check!" She paused, "Then there's Charlie, Charlie Parr."

"Tough son of a bitch – I got drunk with him once in Kabul."

The jet bounced. Rufus almost spilt some of the Chivas on his neatly creased trousers. "That was some bounce! I wonder what's happening."

"Sorry for that, folks," the pilot's voice said, "We are experiencing unusual air turbulence, and radar and GPS coordinates have returned but are a bit wonky at the moment. We've had bits and pieces of communication with Hawaii and Tokyo and Los Angeles – but there is lots of interference. Satellite communications are wonky too."

"Wonky?" said Rufus.

"Yes," said Sally, "And he also says wanker, bonkers, blimey, on the fritz, holy moly, gosh, golly, jerrycan, and I'm all knackered."

"He's a regular lexicographical museum," said Rufus, looking out at the cloudless stratosphere, "What does he think he is, Australian?"

"He thinks he's a poet," said Sally, "an aspiring poet."

"God help us," said Rufus.

"I'll be right back," said Sally, and she got up and headed along the aisle toward the kitchen, thinking that it was time for Rufus to have his morning snack.

The plane jumped again, up 300 feet, and then plunged down, perhaps 2,000 feet.

Rufus, who was strapped in, lost consciousness.

Sally, who was just going towards the kitchen, fell sideways, knocked her head on an armrest, but managed to grab on and cushion her fall. She lay in the aisle, blinking, holding on for dear life, staring at the ceiling, seeing papers and one laptop computer flying, and a – plastic – glass of Chivas Regal hit the ceiling – and it fell, like it was in slow motion, splashing her in the face with the whiskey, and she realized that the pilot had left the mike open.

"Steady, steady as she goes," the pilot muttered.

"What the hell was that," said the co-pilot.

"Out of the blue," said the pilot.

"No warning, what the hell," said the co-pilot, "Look at that! What the hell is that?"

"Looks like a waterspout," said the pilot, "Hey, folks, how are we doing?"

"Thanks, I think we're okay," Sally said into her lapel mike. She carefully levered herself into a sitting position, and, holding on to the armrests and overhead racks, she got up and made her way back to Rufus.

He was sitting there, eyes closed, still breathing, dribble trickling from the corner of his mouth. Sally took a serviette from the tray, bent over, was about to wipe away the dribble when she glanced out the window and saw it – towering up in the clear blue sky was what looked like a tornado, like the tornadoes she'd seen as a kid in Colorado, but this was a tornado of water, it was waterspout, and, God, it must be miles and miles and miles high – and wide, my God, it was hard to tell.

Rufus opened his eyes. "I had a dream, Sally. I dreamed we were all dead, everybody was dead; the whole world was dead. But you were alive, Sally, you were alive, standing on a street corner, waiting for a bus that never came."

"We're both alive, Rufus, but look at that." Sally pointed out the window.

The huge waterspout towered up; but it was not alone. There were others behind it – a phalanx of giant waterspouts advancing across the sunny blue sparkling ocean.

"Well, I'll be …" said Rufus.

"Folks," said the pilot's voice, "We're going to make a run for it! Hold onto your hats! This is going to be one hell of a ride!"

"Buckle up, Sally," said Rufus Mudcock, "I can't afford to lose you!"

"Whoopee," cried the pilot.

"Calm down, man," said the co-pilot.

PART THREE – THE GATEWAY

CHAPTER 22 – FOG

At precisely 3:32 pm, a wall of thick impenetrable fog suddenly appeared out of nowhere on the radar on *Andromeda II*.

The rotating radar on the *Eden of the Seas*, two hundred kilometers west of *Andromeda II*, also detected it.

The wall of fog grew, and grew, denser and denser, a wall of moisture, hanging over the sea, glittering in the sunlight, a wall of vapor.

Then there were thunderclaps, out of the clear air, thunderclaps resonating under the blue, blue sky.

"Something is happening, Magnus, something is happening," said Ingrid Carlstrom. She stared at him, her glowing green eyes – with flashes of blue – staring at him, featureless eyes, merely glowing blobs in that ravaged beautiful face.

"Yes, Ingrid," said Magnus Olsen, "something is certainly happening." He turned to stare at the radar – something like a huge blob was forming to the east, then there were the thunderclaps, huge shuddering echoing flashes of light – and the rolling deafening thunder following them.

Wham!

Darkness fell. In an instant it was night. The lights on the bridge went on automatically. In the newly garish light, Captain Olsen looked around. The bridge was a picture of carnage. The wheel and half the command console had been blown away. Bits of twisted metal stuck out, wires dangled, computer screens were shattered. The windows and walls were smeared in blood and covered in a spider-web-like web of green goo. Dead bodies lay everywhere. Some had been hacked to pieces, some seemed to have died when they were on their way to becoming vegetables, some were wearing, on their grotesquely distorted faces, grimaces of horrible pain – like souls cast down to hell, mouths stretched in a silent scream, like souls in the last circle of Dante's Inferno.

Outside, now, it was pitch black, though a minute ago it had been three o'clock in the afternoon in a perfectly bright and cloudless day. Magnus shook his head. This was something beyond imagining.

A great flash of lightning hit the bow of the *Eden* and left a burning image in Magnus's eyes – and a tremendous clap of thunder shook the windows of the bridge. Bolts of lightning danced, arcs of brilliant electricity, among the masts and railings and fixtures of the shattered bow of the *Eden*.

"I am frightened, Magnus," Ingrid was staring at him.

"So am I, Ingrid," said Magnus.

"Please hold me, Magnus. I am a zombie, Magnus. I am a zombie, but, still, I am afraid."

"Certainly, I will hold you, Ingrid," said Magnus.

She pressed herself against him, and he felt her warm, lithe young body – not cold, not icy, not limp, like you would expect one of the living dead to be – but strong, young, pliant. Her body pressed against his body and he put his arms around her and he realized for the first time how tired he was. He felt like an old man. He would not be able to keep going for very much longer, though it had not been such a long time at all, and in the past he had often done stints of 48 or even 64 hours or even more, much more, on the bridge without flinching, with only coffee and an occasional sandwich to keep him going. But now it seemed, well, it seemed like it was too much, too much was happening! He pulled himself together and he stroked Ingrid's head – no hair, virtually no hair, left – and he murmured, "It will be all right, Ingrid, it will be all right. We shall get through this, you and I. We shall overcome."

Another giant bolt of lightning lit up the bow of the *Eden of the Seas*. It illuminated the interior of the bridge like a blow torch. As he blinked against the light, Magnus Olsen saw the contorted bodies and faces, the dead zombies and their victims. He wondered how many others were dead on the *Eden* – the monitors showed most of the zombie activity had quieted down – some were feasting on the dead, others were wandering aimlessly, some were slowly morphing into vegetation. Captain Magnus Olsen wondered when, if ever, this trial, whatever it was, would come to an end.

"We shall overcome, Ingrid, we shall overcome," he repeated. She was breathing quieter now, calmer now, close to him, oh, so close – her life, her young, warm, palpitating life, pressing against him.

Her hand crept up the side of his face and stroked his cheek.

"Magnus, oh, Magnus," she whispered, her face hidden in his shoulder.

CHAPTER 23 – DARLING

"Grrhh, grrrh, what was that, man?"

When a flash of lightning bolted out of the clear blue afternoon sky and lit up the terrace-balcony and its deckchairs, the light so bright it looked like the canvas deckchairs had been X-rayed, leaving a negative image imprinted on George Kennedy's eyeballs, and when a few seconds later thunder rolled through the *Eden of the Seas*, shaking the chandelier in their luxury suite, George Kennedy's wife started up from the bed where she was lying, drowsy in a half-zombie, half-human state, and she said, growling, and slurring her words, "Grrhh, what was that, man? No, darling. You are my darling."

"I have no idea, darling," said George, who had just turned away from the coffee machine which he'd set to brew an extra-strong pair of cafe lattes. "A lot of strange things have been happening, darling. This is probably another one of them."

He rubbed his eyes to get rid of the afterimage, and he went to the sliding glass doors and pulled shut the thick lightproof curtains. George Kennedy did not want anything to disturb Vickie. She'd been through enough in the last few hours.

When the knock on the door came, George had been on the phone to his Chicago office, trying to sort out the legal and personnel implications of the disaster on the *Eden of the Seas*. All the other members of the firm who had been on the *Eden* had almost certainly perished or had been transformed into zombies – at least that was the conclusion George and his colleagues reached after trying to reach them on their U-tabs. "Don't open the door, George, don't open the door!" Flora had been shouting on George's U-tab, and then he heard her, faintly, turn to the people in Chicago and say, "The damned fool is going to open the door!"

He peered through the old fashioned peephole, and he recognized Vickie, his wife, she was wearing no bra, torn remnants of panties, and that was about it; her eyes glowed bright phosphorous green. She was covered with blood and with that green goo the zombies seemed to exude everywhere.

He opened the door.

She stood there, "Grrrh," she said, "Grrrh."

"Come in, darling," he said, and he went to her and put his arms around her, and, after a moment's hesitation, her arms went around him – he was wearing a bathrobe and nothing else except boxer shorts – and she laid her head against his shoulder, and she murmured, gurgling, "Grrrh!" but very softly.

She smelt of blood – the coppery tang – and George had a vivid flashback vision of Vickie, on hands and knees, eating her manicurist.

He led Vickie into the suite and closed the door behind him and locked it carefully. "I'll make some coffee, darling."

"Grrrh," she stood still, barefoot, naked, covered in gore, his beautiful, elegant, always impeccably groomed wife of thirty years.

Unlike so many zombies George had seen, and glimpsed, too, on his U-Tab when it was receiving anything that was not buried in static, Vickie had not lost her hair. It was ash blond and shoulder length, and now it was plastered to her skull.

George picked up his U-Tab, "Hi, Flora, Vickie's back. I'll call you later."

"George …" the voice began, but George had already signed off.

He took his wife and led her to a chair and sat her down. She looked up at him. "Grrrh?"

George leaned down and kissed her, chastely, on the lips, "I think perhaps, after a strong cup of coffee, a hot shower would do us both good."

"Grrrh!" Her phosphorescent green eyes blinked at him.

While George prepared the coffee – a matter of pushing a few buttons and of waiting for a second or two – he wondered at how beautiful Vickie was, even now, even covered in blood and gore and green goo and with her blond hair plastered down around her face and down the nape of her neck, and how slender she was; and he thought that he was a very lucky man and that somehow he would bring her through this. The coffee, fine thick and aromatic, dripped into the two cups. George Kennedy was one of those men who seem very courageous – and even foolhardy – and that was because he could not really imagine any harm coming to him. He had a secret conviction that he was invincible, and, while he knew, and constantly reminded himself, that this conviction was entirely foolish and utterly unfounded, he still could not rid himself of the courage that came from being – invincible, invulnerable, favored, perhaps, by some god or just simply, by blind fate or stupid luck. So, being conscious of all this, George was perhaps really courageous, really brave, however much he mocked his own courage.

"Here, darling, Vickie." he knelt before her and offered her the coffee.

"Grrrh," she pronounced, with a sort of "thank you" lilt to the *grrrh*. She took the cup and lifted it to her lips, and drank the coffee.

"Now, Vickie, darling, let's take a shower." He stood her up and he let his bathrobe fall away, and he led her by the hand to the bathroom, and he turned on the shower, and checked for the temperature, and he gently pulled off the frayed string that was all that was left of her panties – she let him do it, passively, raising first one foot, then the other, and he pulled off his boxer shorts and he said, "Let's do this together, okay?"

"Grrrh?" she looked up at him.

"Yes, Grrrh," he said.

She smiled – my God – she smiled! "Water," she said.

"Yes, water," George said, "Come on, my love, let's do it, let's be together." And together they stepped into the bubbling perfumed waterfall.

The water cascaded down over them. George kissed her on the lips, the glowing green eyes, blinking through the water, watching him. He reached for the shampoo, and he began, gently, and then more vigorously, to shampoo her hair, as she leaned against him, close to him, and she whispered, "Grrrh, water, grrrh, man."

He cleaned her thoroughly and himself and then he dried her and then he dressed her in her white silk bathrobe and she let him do it, staring at him all the while with those green eyes and then he fed her, spooning soup from the miniature freezer that he heated on the suite's stove. And he made her drink more coffee. Strangely, she would lift the cup to her lips and drink, but she didn't know how to feed herself – or didn't want to feed herself – so George lifted the spoon to her mouth, said, "Open," and she opened her mouth, and he gently pushed the spoonful into her mouth.

"Grrrh, man." She blinked at him.

"Yes, darling."

"What was that, man?" She glanced towards the curtained windows, as lightning flashed, and thunder roared.

"I don't know, darling, thunder, maybe a storm coming."

"Grrrh," she said, "Grrrh – hold me, man."

More lightning flashed, thunder rolled, enormous waves of thunder. The *Eden of the Seas* shuddered, and then continued, speeding on its way, getting as far from land as possible.

CHAPTER 24 – EVE SCHMIDT

The thunder hit *Andromeda II* like a shock wave.

Out of the blue sky, it came – WHAM!

The ship trembled.

"Ouch, ouch, and ouch!" Claire tore off her earphones, put her claws to her head, and rolled her chair back, away from the computer. "Ouch, ouch, it almost burst my head! What in the world was that?"

WHAM!

Another roll of thunder. The lights flickered. The computer screens blinked. Red lights flashed. The Royal Marines up on the gangway looked around nervously. All the scientists and technicians stopped working and stared.

Something weird, really weird, was happening.

Kate Thornhill looked up. Claire, with her claws pressed against the side of her head, looked like she was in pain. "Claire, are you okay?"

"Yes, yes, I'm okay – but it was like being electrocuted," Claire glanced at Kate. Wow! How beautiful Kate was! For the last few hours, Kate had been in a stable pattern of black-and-white stripes, like a zebra; one thick black band, framing her eyes, made her look like a raccoon, or a cartoon bandit. It was wild and exotic, the way Kate's skin patterns worked. Claire tilted her head to one side. She should persuade Kate to come to the next Paris or Milan fashion season. Just think – Claire V Jacobs presents "A Nobel Prize-winning Zebra!" Kate certainly had the figure to strut stuff down the runway!

"Would you consider coming to Paris and modeling, with Gail McCoy and me?" Claire tilted her snout upwards, bared her fangs, and displayed her cutest, most alluring reptilian smile, "Please, pretty, pretty please!"

"Sure, why not," said Kate, and turning to Anthony Garcia, she winked, "She wants to show me off, I'll bet – the zebra woman!"

"Well, I think it's a perfectly charming idea," said Claire.

"I said I'd come," said Kate, laughing, "I'm serious! I've always wanted to be a model! Besides, I think the time for hiding is over, don't you, Anthony?"

"Definitely," said Anthony Garcia, fully realizing, for the first time, how much he was in love. "You should hide no more."

"There's a wall of mist out there that looks like a wall of steel," said V, who had been out on deck with Sergeant Eve Schmidt. They had arrived on *Andromeda II* with Monica and the baby only half an hour ago. Coming into the Communications and Control Center, V and Sergeant Schmidt were both still blinking from the bolt of lightning that had come, literally, out of the blue.

"We've been watching it on the radar," said Kate.

"And there is something else," said Ben Kamu, "Look at this!"

"What?" said Claire; she rolled her chair back to the computer screen.

"An object, something, it looks like a boat, inside the mist – and the fog is beginning to roll back."

WHAM!

Another bolt of lightning – and crack of thunder – echoed inside the Communications and Control Center.

"Can you get a closer profile of that?" said V, leaning over Ben's work station.

"I can try," said Ben.

"That looks like ..." V leaned closer.

"It's *A Flight of Fancy*," said Claire, whose mind was linked into all the sensors of the radar and the computer systems and all the drones they had flying and whose nervous system had become one with all the electronics carried by *Andromeda II*. All of which meant that Claire was, in a sense, an integral part of the world electronic mind with all its sensory extensions. "It's *A Flight of Fancy*."

"The Gateway," said V.

"That's your invitation to meet the Puppet Master?" Eve Schmidt glanced at V.

"Yes," said V.

"I'm coming with you," said Eve Schmidt.

"You are welcome to," said V. "You are our liaison, and Colonel Siebert wanted you to see everything. Well, you'll see everything."

"The US Navy wants to have a look first," said Ben, who had been monitoring communications. "They want to use the helicopter gunship that they've docked with us."

"They shouldn't do that," said V.

"They insist."

"Let them do it," said Sabrina, who had just come into the room, "They will explore, see what's there, look for dangers, and then you can go, V, and enter the Gateway, if that is what it is."

"Well, okay," V frowned. "But they should just look. They should definitely not get close to *A Flight of Fancy*, and above all they should not put anybody on the yacht."

"I'll tell them," said Sabrina, turning to the officer standing beside her, "and Mark Tobin, their liaison officer here, will certainly tell them. I'm not sure they'll listen."

Mark Tobin nodded. "I've already warned them. They insist on going ahead – they have their orders."

"Well, what will be will be! If they do it, it will be their responsibility."

Sergeant Eve Schmidt leaned against a desk and sipped a cup of fresh, excellent coffee – nursing it along so it would last – and contemplated the Command and Control Center of *Andromeda II*.

It was an awesome place, a vast room in the middle of *Andromeda II's* superstructure, it was at least four decks deep, with a very high roof, and it contained maybe thirty or forty people, working in front of screens of various sizes. On the gangway, two stories up, that ran around the whole room, there were armed troops, carrying submachine guns. She recognized them as British Royal Marines plus a couple of People's Republic of China officers. She had worked with guys like them – the Brits and the Chinese – in the Middle East. It'd be interesting to compare war stories; they probably knew people she knew. She also wondered why there weren't more Americans. She frowned. The United States damned well should be here – this place was essential!

V, who was not far away, caught the thought. "It's rotational. Usually, there are Americans, but the new administration, until now, has not been friendly, and they have suspended cooperation, but there is an American liaison officer, Mark Tobin, from the US Navy. He's almost always here. In fact, there he is – over there."

"Great," said Eve, "I'm glad we're not entirely out of the picture!"

For Marine Corps Sergeant Eve Schmidt, it had been a fascinating couple of hours. She and V and Monica Fabritz and the baby had been picked up, just outside the Everglades Agricultural Research Institute by an Andromeda

Corporation hover-jet that was clearly some sort of extremely advanced stealth aircraft since it seemed to have gone unnoticed by whoever was jamming everything around southern Florida. Then, too, it was flying very low, dangerously low and fast for such an aircraft.

It was weird to find herself in the small hover-jet, skimming over the palm trees and magnolias and then over the ocean, with a strange crew: three hybrids – Monica, her hybrid baby, and, of course, V, all three in reptile form, and one human pilot, a smooth, handsome Brit called Arnold, who seemed to be a special ops sort of guy, and herself, one human Sergeant, namely Eve Schmidt of the United States Marine Corps.

Colonel Siebert had only agreed to let Monica and the baby go with V on condition that Eve Schmidt accompanied them as the Colonel's representative. The Colonel wanted to know what was going on, and, as Eve suspected, he had picked up on the fact that V liked and trusted Eve and that the feeling was for some reason, which Eve herself didn't understand, mutual.

Eve was to report back from *Andromeda II* and tell the Colonel that all was well, and she was to confirm that the president of the United States, Katherine du Bois Hughes, was indeed alive and well and not a prisoner or being coerced in any way.

Not only did Eve get proof the president was alive. She actually met the president – who was in the Command and Control Center when Eve and V arrived on *Andromeda II*.

When Eve entered the Center, the first person she noticed was the president, and she was shocked – well, maybe shocked was not the right word – by the way the president looked.

Head shaved and dressed in a black T-shirt, black jeans, black baseball cap, wearing black combat boots, Katherine du Bois Hughes looked like a very fit Special Ops trooper.

She also looked younger and even more beautiful than Eve had imagined, even after seeing her on countless TV and Internet broadcasts. Her skin positively glowed.

Sometimes there is nothing like the real thing.

"I'm delighted to meet you, Sergeant Schmidt," the president said, shaking Eve's hand, "I understand you and V captured the reptile man."

"It was V's work, Madam President," said Eve, "We just took possession."

"Ah, yes, V, remarkable person, isn't she?"

"Yes, she certainly is," said Eve, thinking, how weird, the president is famous for hating hybrids – those "alien invaders" – and now she refers to V as a 'person,' and she seemed to be pals with them – including that gorgeous black-and-red number at the center of all the action. But then Colonel Siebert and Eve herself and her fellow Marines had also had what she might call a revelation, yes, a revelation of sorts, or a conversion, concerning hybrids.

"Stay with me, Sergeant," said the president, "Interesting things are happening." They were standing in front of a screen in what Eve Schmidt recognized, as she paused and looked around, was a beyond-cutting-edge ultra-modern communications and control center. Some of the equipment seemed more advanced than any she had ever seen.

It also contained perhaps the weirdest assemblage of human beings and non-human creatures Eve Schmidt had ever seen. There was a woman who was striped black and white like a zebra. The stripes covered her face and body; there was the black-and-red female hybrid reptile, who seemed to be some sort of special computer and Internet genius that they all respected; and there were people of almost every nationality and race – she heard English, Spanish, German, Mandarin and Cantonese, French, Swahili, Russian, Somali, Japanese, Korean, Bengali, Portuguese …

"Young Claire here," said the president, indicating the sleek black female hybrid, who had her snout glued to a huge computer screen and whose claws hovered over but did not touch the keyboard, "and her partner Ben Kamu – next to her – have located the boat that carried out the terrorist attack on the *Eden*. It's a yacht, *A Flight of Fancy*."

"Hi Sergeant, I'm Claire," said Claire, looking up. She had cute red markings on her snout. "*A Flight of Fancy* just popped up out of nowhere. It wasn't there thirty minutes ago – nor was it anywhere near that we could see."

So, now, a few minutes after *A Flight of Fancy* appeared, the US navy declared that it wanted to go and visit *A Flight of Fancy*.

Eve agreed with V and with Mark Tobin and Sabrina – and with the Chinese commander who was speaking from his missile launcher just five hundred yards astern *Andromeda II* – that going near the yacht was dangerous for humans and should be left to hybrids.

Eve was more than a little apprehensive as she followed the action on the screens. There it was. The US Military helicopter approached *A Flight of Fancy*, it examined the yacht with an array of sensors, and with drones. The yacht seemed to be deserted, abandoned, totally without life, a ghost ship; and then they decided to lower two troopers onto its deck.

The two went into a cabin.

They disappeared, no sign of life, no communications, nothing.

The drone that was with them disappeared too – and it stopped transmitting.

"Not good," muttered V.

"The helicopter is coming back now for refueling," said Ben Kamu, "We are the closest – so they are coming here."

"V can hitch a ride with them," said Claire.

"But why was *Flight of Fancy* not located earlier?" Eve said, feeling that she was barging in; but, well, that had never stopped her before.

"It was hidden or deposited here, through another one of those time-and-space-and-gravitational anomalies we've been seeing," said the striped black-and-white human zebra, glancing, with a smile, at Eve. "I'm Kate Thornhill from MIT, by the way, and you'll have to excuse my color scheme, it's rather active at the moment. Usually, I keep it hidden."

"*What* gravitational anomalies, and what does that *mean*?" Eve decided that, since they were treating her as part of the team, she would act as part of the team.

"Something or someone is twisting the very fabric of our universe, the space-time matrix, the underlying laws or rules that seem to make it work. The gravitational field is shifting and the electro-magnetic and thermal fields – energy in general – is being transformed – warping and twisting – in very strange ways," said Kate, "and this explains, in part, the breakdown of communications – whatever is going on is jamming everything."

"Strange as it may seem," said Claire, glancing up, her golden eyes shining, lights reflecting off her jet-black scales and scarlet markings, "It may be also be a sort of time machine."

"Yes, Claire. I agree. I'd go further. I think it is a time machine, among other things." Kate paused and glanced at Eve. "And it's far beyond our technology – or the technology of anybody on earth for that matter."

"Yes," said Ben, turning to Eve. "Just imagine! *A Flight of Fancy* may have been sailing around in a different time, past or future, or a different, slightly different, universe, or, even, just in a different place on this planet now, but was instantly transported here. That is why it just appeared about half an hour ago."

"It's an invitation," said V, "It's the gateway."

"You are to go and confront the Puppet Master," said Eve, "that's what Freddy told you, that's what his mind told you, right?"

"Yes," said V.

"Freddy?" said Kate.

V turned to Kate. "Freddy is the name Monica Fabritz gave to the reptile man, the reptile man who kidnapped her and raped her – and also killed all her friends. She named him after a monster in some old horror movies."

"Oh, of course," said Kate, "*Freddy* – I remember those films! They were scary, really scary!"

"Sergeant Schmidt," said an extraordinarily pretty young blonde, whose name badge said 'Marit', "Sergeant Schmidt, the president is about to leave; but she would like to see you for a moment before she goes."

CHAPTER 25 – LINK

Colonel Jefferson Siebert held the earphone away from his head.

There was static on the line, but still, the message was getting through.

"So, Sergeant Schmidt …" Colonel Siebert ran his hand over his shaved skull, "you are telling me that the president is alive." The Colonel was still in Doctor Mansoor's office in the Everglades Agricultural Research Institute, with Doctor Mansoor, two other soldiers, and Freddy, who was sitting quietly in a corner, lost, it seemed, in his thoughts.

"Yes, I spoke with her, I met her, it is her, she's here on *Andromeda II*, and she is alive and well."

"What … are …?"

"Sorry, sir, I didn't catch that."

"What are the president's plans?" The Colonel wiped the sweat from his forehead. With the failure of the air-conditioning, the atmosphere in the Everglades Agricultural Research Institute had become very heavy. The small gray metal fan on Doctor Mansoor's desk moved back and forth, creating a tiny but welcome breeze. "What are her plans?" the Colonel repeated, trying to ignore the bursts of static. The snapping fizzling sound reminded him of old-fashioned radio sets he'd experimented with as a kid. The static made you aware of vast invisible forces jolting and snaking their way through the atmosphere, through the universe. "What are her plans?" he repeated again, while nodding back at Doctor Mansoor – whom he now called Ra'shae – who'd gestured that she was going to make some more coffee – for him, for the two soldiers who were with them, and for Freddy. They were beginning to consider Freddy as if he were almost part of the team. He'd been very cooperative and had even come up with a couple of suggestions on security. All of this was unorthodox, to say the least, but, then, the situation was unorthodox.

"Yes, thank you, Doctor Mansoor, I would like some," Freddy said, glancing up at Doctor Mansoor with his mysterious reptile eyes. "Thank you."

"Sergeant Schmidt, can you hear me?" the Colonel stood up and walked around. Their work was done here at the Everglades Agricultural Research Institute. He had to find out what was next – and he had to find out whether he would be court-martialed for not following orders and not killing everybody at the Institute. He smiled grimly. Well, so, if he were court-martialed, he'd take up basket weaving in prison. No, even better – he'd work on a Ph.D. in physics, unless, of course, they shot him.

"Sergeant Schmidt ...?" the Colonel frowned; this was a wacky system, but at least it was a system. You had to hand it to that Sabrina Jacobs and her team. *Andromeda II* was using a series of high-flying miniature drones as temporary mobile relay stations to establish communications to Florida, bypassing all the standard land and satellite systems, which had collapsed. The Andromeda system wasn't perfect, but it worked, most of the time, with lots of static and frequent break-up; but at least this way, there were some communications!

"Colonel ..." Eve's voice came in a burst of static; then it was clear. "Colonel, yes, I hear you! You asked, what are the president's plans? She's transferring by helicopter to the *Dwight D. Eisenhower* – in about ten minutes. Then, I think, she's going to broadcast to the nation, and head for Washington."

"Well, thank God for that," said Colonel Siebert.

"I'll put her on, sir," said Eve Schmidt.

"Put who on, sergeant?"

"The president, sir, the president."

"Oh, yes," the Colonel rolled his eyes, and gestured at the soldiers, "Certainly, of course, put the president on, thank you, Sergeant."

"Colonel Siebert," said the president, "Congratulations on liberating Monica Fabritz and her child and congratulations on capturing the reptile man – I believe he is called Freddy."

"Thank you, Madam President, as you know, we had help – to put it mildly."

"Colonel Siebert, I intend to return to Washington shortly, immediately after I have shown myself to the American people and assured them that I am alive."

"You certainly sound alive, Madam President."

"Thank you, Colonel, it was a close call, but I am alive, and I can thank some of the people here for that – and hybrids, I might add. All of this, and the fact that you were helped by V and everything regarding the hybrids, including

Monica and the baby, should be kept totally confidential for the time being. The American people have had too many shocks in the last few hours. I will make the truth known as soon as I can, though, I assure you of that, Colonel."

"Thank you, Madam President. I'll give my men and women strict orders that everything we have seen and done is top secret – until you give the word, Madam President."

"Thank you, Colonel. Now, one of the front lines in our war is against the Puppet Master, the force or creature that directs the zombies, and V is preparing to meet or confront him – or it – shortly, we believe."

"So, I understand," said the Colonel.

"The other front is against the zombie virus – the search for a vaccine and a cure."

"Yes," said the Colonel.

"There is a company which Doctor Jacobs believes is the closest to developing a vaccine against the zombie virus."

"Good news!"

"Yes, good news. It's not far from you, Colonel. It's our best – well, really, our only – hope. It's called Bio-Frontier. They may need extra troops and protection. Sergeant Schmidt and Doctor Jacobs will be sending you the coordinates and other information. My press secretary, Renée Scott is at Bio-Frontier, as is Doctor Alex Wolf, Chief Research Scientist of Andromeda Corporation, and Andromeda's Chief Counsel, Helen Guerrera. Both of them work closely with Doctor Jacobs. There are several hybrids, including Alex and Helen, at Bio-Frontier, and a Secret Service agent, Sarah James, who has been transformed into a hybrid – she is coordinating defense at Bio-Frontier, so when you get there you can coordinate with her. She is, I've been told, in reptile form – and looks something like V or Monica or Freddy – She has our full confidence."

"Yes, Madam President, I'll coordinate with Agent James," said Colonel Siebert, thinking, a Secret Service agent who has been transformed into a hybrid, well, well, well …

"V who is here with me suggests that if you run into zombie attack, use Freddy as part of your defense – since he is immune – if you judge you can trust him, that is. V says that, according to her, you can trust him."

"We'll judge that, Madam President, as circumstances dictate. From what I've seen I have great faith in V's … ah … judgement so unless something else intervenes, we will follow V's suggestion. Freddy has been very cooperative so far – even helpful."

"Colonel Siebert, I'm leaving now for the *Dwight D. Eisenhower*, and then for Washington, where I hope to see you when this battle is won. Good luck, Colonel Siebert! Be careful, and Godspeed. I'm putting Sergeant Schmidt back on the line."

Eve took the phone from the president, and stood in the middle of the room while the president and V listened in.

"Sergeant Schmidt," the Colonel said, "I want you to go with V on her mission to the Puppet Master; I'd like to have a representative on this mission, and you are the person on the spot – unless the president has you earmarked for another mission."

"No, the president doesn't need me, and she has cleared me for the mission with V," Eve said and glanced at the president and V.

The president nodded.

V nodded.

"Yes, sir," said Sergeant Schmidt, "The president confirms that; and V agrees. I will accompany V on her mission. Now, Colonel, here are the coordinates of Bio-Frontier." And Sergeant Schmidt gave the Colonel the coordinates and details regarding the location and defenses of Bio-Frontier.

"Thank you, Sergeant," said Colonel Siebert, glancing at his notes, and calculating how long it would take for him to get to Bio-Frontier.

"Thank you, Colonel," said Sergeant Schmidt.

"Well, good luck to all of you," said Colonel Siebert. Then static took over and the communications went dead. The Colonel turned to his people and to Freddy. "We have a new mission. It's a vital one. So could everyone please get ready to move out."

Everyone went into immediate action.

"Ra'shae," said the Colonel, "I think you should come with us. There is nothing for you to do here. We'll leave a small guard with the Institute, but for you, it will be safer to be with us, and it will be easier to locate your family if you're with us."

"Thank you, Colonel. I'm grateful. I'll come with you."

"Freddy, are you with us on this one?"

"I am with you, Colonel."

On *Andromeda II*, the strains of "Hail to the Chief" faded as the presidential helicopter disappeared from view. Everybody who had been on deck hurried back to their work.

Merit lingered a little longer, her hand on the railing. She gazed at the point where the presidential helicopter had disappeared. She put her hand to her cheek, where the President had kissed her – not once, but twice.

She sighed and turned back to check on her work schedule and see what tasks she had been assigned. Life was more and more interesting – and more and more of a challenge. Marit was sure she was up to it. Just yesterday, Sabrina had said, "The sky's the limit for you, Marit. The sky's the limit." Marit left the sunshine, and hurried below deck to help Sabrina with some urgent work that had to be finished before the day was over.

Outwardly, now, *Andromeda II* and the Chinese missile launcher, *Deng Xiaoping IV*, seemed to be back to normal, calmly sailing through the deep blue sea. In the distance, was the elegant silhouette of a yacht, shimming in the sunlight, *A Flight of Fancy*.

CHAPTER 26 – MONICA REMAKE

On *Andromeda II*, Monica Fabritz gazed into a mirror, contemplating her new body, her reptilian alien incarnation. Hmm! She frowned and turned this way and that. Her fangs were a bit too long and too pointed. The bright cobalt blue scales were a trifle garish. She was, after all, Swiss, and instinctively classical and conservative in her sartorial tastes. But, otherwise, looking into the full-length mirror on the back of the foldout wardrobe door in the suite provided for her on *Andromeda II*, she thought that, for a newly minted reptile-girl, she didn't look too bad. The ensemble was glamorous, sort of, in a weird, comic book, Pop Art sort of way.

"It takes getting used to, doesn't it?" said Sabrina, who was holding the baby. "It did for me."

"Really?" Monica blinked at Sabrina. "I didn't know you were a hybrid."

"It's a long story, but, yes, I'm a hybrid."

"Well, you are right, it does take getting used to," Monica ran one claw up and down the side of her face. A reptilian face stared back at her from the mirror. The golden eyes, which had at first seemed so enigmatic, now seemed, somehow, to be familiar; they made sense; they had an expression she could read.

"Soon it will be natural." Sabrina stood beside her. "You'll move back and forth between the human you and the reptile you, and hardly notice the difference."

"I tried to turn back – to become human – but it doesn't work. I'm stuck in this, ah, this outfit, this new version of me."

"I was stuck too – locked-in, I called it – for almost three years," Sabrina sighed. "And I do remember what it was like."

"Three years! Oh, God!" said Monica. "Where am I going to live for the next three years, in a zoo?"

"I'm sure you'll be reversible much sooner, maybe in a week or two." Sabrina handed Monica the baby.

"But there's something I have to do, and I have to do now," Monica held the baby to her breast, as it reached for her nipple. "I have to tell my parents I'm alive."

"Well," said Sabrina. "We could contact them and …"

"But they will want to see me, on the video phone, and, well, how can I show them what I have become – they will have a heart attack!"

Sabrina inspected the young woman. She was a handsome hybrid. And she was holding the first hybrid baby, the beginning, perhaps, of a new world. Maybe it was the beginning of the end of the old world – though Sabrina hoped not. She loved the old world, the human world, with its frailty and resilience, its variety, its mortality.

"Yes, you will certainly present them with a … shock." Sabrina stood back and leaned against a dresser. "But I have an idea – I know your father and your mother. I have met them several times. I think I have an idea which might make all this, well, acceptable to them."

"You are an angel, Sabrina! If you can do that, it would be a miracle," said the reptile girl. She turned and kissed Sabrina on the cheek – a soft fluttering brush of the long reptile tongue.

Sabrina blushed.

CHAPTER 27 – DEPARTURE

The US Navy helicopter gunship had just refueled and was about to take off from *Andromeda II*.

V, still in reptile mode, stood on the deck of *Andromeda*, in the soft sea breeze and gentle downdraft from the helicopter's slowly turning blades. She turned to Sabrina. "I'm worried about you, Sabrina. You look exhausted."

"I'm fine," Sabrina smiled, "but I am worried too – I am worried about Claire. She's glued to the computer systems. She's integrated her mind totally into the Web and her body into the electromagnetic field. Each shock in the system is a shock to her body and mind. She's determined to go as far as she can. She hates the Puppet Master with a fury I've never seen before. I'm afraid she's going to kill herself – Kate and Ben and I have warned her. But she just keeps at it."

"Claire is pretty strong."

"She's also headstrong."

"That is true – I wonder who she inherits that from?"

"Me, I'm sure," smiled Sabrina, "it must be part of me that I implanted in her that has made her pig-headed. It certainly couldn't come from you!"

"Absolutely – it certainly couldn't come from me!" V grinned and put a friendly claw on Sabrina's shoulder.

"I would never forgive myself if something happened to Claire," said Sabrina.

V, with the back of one claw, carefully wiped a tear away, a tear that was traveling down Sabrina's cheek.

"And I, dear Sabrina," said V, "will never forgive myself if anything happens to either of you."

Sergeant Eve Schmidt stood a bit apart, listening to the dialogue, and gazing at the warm friendship between the two creatures, V and Sabrina, both hybrids. But one was in reptilian, the other in human form. Eve stamped her foot. She was eager for action, toting a backpack and a submachine gun. To V, she signaled with her chin: *It is time.*

V nodded. "Good-bye, Sabrina, my sister, my love. Look after Claire; but look after yourself too. I'll be back soon." V kissed Sabrina on the cheek and she walked away, turned and waved, and joined Eve Schmidt, and they both boarded the helicopter gunship, which, only seconds later, lifted off, tilted away, and sped over the ocean, heading south, heading towards *A Flight of Fancy* and V's rendezvous with the Puppet Master – and, perhaps, with the "Dark God" whatever that might be.

Sabrina watched the helicopter until it disappeared. She had masked from V the fact that twice Claire had fainted. She had hidden from V that fact that she, Sabrina, had taken over some of Claire's computer penetration powers in order to "spread the load." It was horrible. It was like being swept into a vortex that sucked every atom of energy out of her body.

The helicopter was a speck on the horizon.

V was by far the strongest – she was unique.

If anyone could confront the Puppet Master and whatever forces were behind him, it would be V.

The president had left only a few minutes before.

Now *Andromeda II* was relatively quiet – the calm before the storm. The afternoon sun glittered on the ocean waves, breaking the light apart into a million diamond-like sparkles. Sabrina ran her hand along the warm railing, closed her eyes, and turned her face to the sun and to the warm breeze – oh, whatever happened, life was so good, so delicious, so fabulous ...

Life should go on forever!

Sabrina sighed, opened her eyes, and, seeing Marit beckon for her, she headed back to the Communications Center. She stopped, with her hand on the door, and frowned and muttered, "I think I can do anything. I think I'm immortal, but, of course, I'm not. None of us are."

"Did you say something, Sabrina?" Marit raised a beautiful eyebrow, concern in her blue eyes.

"No, nothing, Marit. Nothing – let's go. There is work to do."

CHAPTER 28 – A FLIGHT OF FANCY

Boy, this is a weird and spooky place! V was alone, standing on the sunbaked deck of the terrorist yacht, *A Flight of Fancy*.

The rappel rope she had shimmied down had dropped her from the helicopter gunship. And the rope itself was cast away – so as not to allow any contamination to sneak its way up into the helicopter. The rope spiraled down, making a neat, snake-like coil on the highly polished wooden deck of *A Flight of Fancy*.

With her, V had brought an ultra-miniature radio and camera, which were strapped to her head, one camera facing forward, the other back, and both with widescreen capability, plus a set of sensors on a wrist band separate from her GPS tracer. She also had a sensor which, it was believed, could spot the zombie virus.

Those on board the helicopter could see what V was seeing, and they could hear what she was hearing. And, if communications held up, Claire and Sabrina and the others on *Andromeda II* would also see and hear what V saw and heard. And, beyond *Andromeda II*, the information flow would be transmitted to Admiral Rodriguez's carrier group where the president would land shortly.

The wooden deck was still warm from the sun, though the sun was now low in the sky. Soon, it would be night. The deck felt pleasant under the panther-like padded soles of V's foot-claws.

But, beyond the tactile comfort of the varnished wood, there was something eerie about *A Flight of Fancy*. It was a sensation of suppressed, barely contained, vibrant energy that V didn't like. It was insidious and treacherous with bad vibes, definitely bad vibes.

A Flight of Fancy was spotless.

It was as if it had been freshly polished and was brand-new, painted, and varnished, and waxed to perfection.

But there was something ghostly about it, as if, sailing on the sea, without crew or passengers, as far as V could sense, *A Flight of Fancy* was unreal.

An illusion …

V frowned. Maybe the boat didn't exist – maybe it was just a mental hologram, a psychotic construct, conjured up to ensnare them, to trap them – to trap her!

It was, Freddy's mind had told her, the threshold, the gateway.

But it was the threshold or gateway to what?

"Okay, I'm here," said V, "Now we shall see what we shall see."

V shielded her eyes from the lowering sun, and watched as Captain Anderson's helicopter gunship rose in the air, and backed off to about half a kilometer away.

She spoke to the mini microphone that hovered close to her snout.

"Can you hear me?" she asked.

"Roger. I've got you, though there is static."

V hoped the people in the helicopter would be safe. Something tricky and dangerous was lurking here, close by. She had grown very fond of handsome Captain Alan Anderson, and Guy his gallant pilot and, of course, of her old friend, since this morning, the blond, tanned, beautiful Marine Sergeant, Eve Schmidt.

"Okay, I'm going in the cabin, now," said V, thinking back. Something was in here; something that was, probably, not at all nice.

When she and Eve Schmidt boarded the helicopter, V was in demon form – ready for action. Eve gave V the once over and nodded. "I'll bet Captain Anderson will find you pretty – ah – alluring!"

"Only if he's addicted to comic books and video games."

"You're too modest," said Eve.

The look on Captain Anderson's face was worth the price of entry. "Hello, ah, V, I'm Captain Allan Anderson. I'm delighted to meet you."

"Captain Anderson," said V, extending a claw. Yes, indeed, Captain Anderson was a very cute piece of male human flesh. He was blond, tanned, with very even, very white teeth, clear blue eyes, a high forehead, and a splendid body glimpsed through his uniform.

She caught a similarly perceptive thought from Eve. She blinked and caught V's glance and V's thought, and smiled, proving to V that human-hybrid communication could be instantaneous. "So, what's the situation?"

"It's not good," said Captain Anderson, frowning. What was this weird reptile animal with a voluptuous female human body and bright green and turquoise scales and gold and black serpent eyes and who could speak English? She – or it – was wearing a waterproof Special Ops backpack, sporting a shoulder holster with a Beretta 9mm pistol, and carrying a white canvas sailor's tote bag, tied at the top with rope, and that she put down on the floor of the helicopter. Wow! But this weird creature came recommended by the president of the United States herself and she also came accompanied by a Marine Corps sergeant, an exceptionally good-looking blonde – 'Eve Schmidt' the name badge said – who looked like she wouldn't brook any nonsense, not even from a fully-armed hybrid.

"Sergeant Schmidt," Captain Anderson had said, saluting, and then formally shaking hands.

"Captain Anderson." Eve Schmidt saluted, shook his hand, and let the suggestion of a smile flicker on her lips.

Captain Anderson cleared his throat and looked V straight in the eye, though V could see he was finding it hard to do so because he couldn't see anything there, just the amber light and the dark maroon lozenge-like slit that seemed to sparkle. Was she mischievous? Was she evil? Was she without a soul or anything like a soul – was he looking into the void?

"Yes, Captain?" said V, "You were about to give us an update on the situation. You inspected *A Flight of Fancy* … and?"

Captain Anderson shook himself out of the spell. "Yes, sorry, I guess I'm just adapting to this – ah – this new alliance we seem to have concluded with – ah – with you hybrids. We didn't really seem to know you existed a few days ago."

"It does take getting used to," said V.

"It sure does," said Eve, "but this girl is good, Captain, I can assure you."

"Well, then," said Captain Anderson, as the helicopter lifted off *Andromeda II*, and began to speed towards its destination, "the situation is this. The yacht *A Flight of Fancy* appeared on our radar at 15:00 hours. It appeared just after those huge flashes and thunder bolts; and it appeared, apparently, out of nowhere. The event was registered by the radar on your ship, *Andromeda II*, and on the Chinese missile launcher. We all picked it up at the same time."

"Yes," said V, "*Andromeda II* spotted it when you did, and the Chinese."

"We only had this one helicopter gunship in our little – well, our little battle group, so we were sent to fly over *A Flight of Fancy*. It appeared to be drifting and unmanned. There was no sign of life on board.

"Nobody?"

"Nobody. So, it was risky with the possibility of the virus being on board, but on orders from the flagship I sent two of our people down there –"

"Yes, we know," said V. She glanced at Eve Schmidt; Eve knew that V and Sabrina and Lieutenant Tobin had warned the navy, but …

"Yes, I was not happy with the decision. The two volunteered for the mission – they rappelled down, got to the deck, looked around, went into the cabin, and then they just disappeared. We lost communications. The drone went dead too and disappeared."

"Right …" V frowned, glancing at the glittering sea. At that moment, *A flight of Fancy* came into view – below them.

"So, there it is!" said Eve Schmidt. She put her hand on V's glittering turquoise arm.

The yacht, *A Flight of Fancy*, was out there, in plain sight, peaceful, on the twinkling water, the sun shining down brightly.

"It looks innocent doesn't it," said V.

"So, it just appeared out of nowhere," said Eve, squinting out of the window, "And you lost two of your people."

"Yes," said Captain Anderson, "That's the way it went. As you know, *A Flight of Fancy* had just appeared out of nowhere. The water around it was strangely calm, as if welling up from the deep, but there were ripples around the ship, as if it had just landed, gently, from somewhere, else, ripples moving out from the sides of the ship, and a sort of shimmering light seemed to radiate from it. So, there we were, staring at it – and we'd just lost communications with our base ship. We had been ordered to board her. And Corporal Annette Brighton asked me, 'Captain, what do you think?' I hesitated. Then I said, 'It looks peaceful; it looks harmless; we'd better have a look. We're the only ones here who can do it.' And so, Annette Brighton and Federico Harvey volunteered to rappel down to *A Flight of Fancy* had have a look. They slipped into their biohazard suits. We're a specialized unit, so we have those things on hand."

"Annette and Federico," said V, echoing the names.

"They are two of my best people," Captain Anderson looked V in the eye. "We were in the Yemen wars and in the Fifth Somali war and the third Mexican civil war together."

"Right," said V, "good people, tough, intelligent."

"Exactly – when they went down to it, the sunlight made *A Flight of Fancy* look innocent, beautiful even. But, you know, where the sun is shining people die."

"Yes," said V.

"So down they went. We pulled the rope back up, without letting it touch the deck of *A Flight of Fancy*. And Annette and Federico were standing there on the deck, both in their biohazard suits.

"And then …?"

"Looks clean," said Annette Brighton. She was taking measurements for any known bioweapons. There seemed to be no traces of anything.

She and Federico Harvey went forward. And they went up to the wheelhouse.

"All clear, here, Captain," said Annette.

"Yep, and it looks like the yacht is steering itself," said Federico, "And all the sails are neatly folded. Somebody took the time to do this – no signs of panic."

Captain Anderson glanced at V and then at Sergeant Schmidt. "Both Annette and Federico had their weapons out and both were equipped with cameras and mikes which showed us, up here in the gunship, what they were seeing down there. So, having scoured the deck, and finding everything peaceful and normal and no sign of a living soul, and having hollered, 'Hello, hello, anybody home?' Annette and Federico went up to the bridge, which was covered."

"They went up to the bridge, so inside," V repeated, frowning. Really bad idea! Sergeant Schmidt glanced at her. They were, it seems, thinking exactly the same thing: Going inside anywhere was not a good idea. If you hadn't seen the weirdness up close, you were not prepared to confront it.

Captain Anderson cleared his throat. He looked down. Then he looked at V, the hybrid, staring her straight in the eye. "At first, everything seemed okay, shipshape, impeccable even, a very neat cabin, and then – fizz, fizz, fizz – we lost audio and visual connection with them. There was a blank, just flickering screens and static.

"Last thing we heard was Federico, saying 'Hello, what the hell are …?' It sounded like a question, but to what, or to whom it was addressed – maybe just to himself or to Annette – we don't know. The vital signs link – where we get real-time pulse, temperature, cerebral activity, died too. Gone! The miniature drone ceased transmitting at the same instant. There was nothing, just nothing! We tried to send in more miniature drones, mini-drones, but they ceased to communicate, and they exploded or disintegrated just as they approached the yacht."

"So, *A Flight of Fancy* has a protective force field of some kind," said V.

"Yes, it must be something like that. The last mini drone we sent just refused to go into or onto the boat. It hived off, hovered, and then it dove into the ocean. It committed suicide, in effect."

Eve Schmidt bit her lip. "So, somehow the force field or some other device hacked into the drone's command and nervous system, took over, and ordered it to dive."

"Yes, I think it must have been something like that," said Captain Anderson.

V looked out the window. *A Flight of Fancy* was drifting along, its sails furled, on the sparkling late afternoon sea, like a dark shadow against the brilliance. It was a good-looking boat. But was more than a boat – it had become more than a boat. Physically it was a stylish, antique yacht, a throwback to the early twentieth century: it had wooden decks, and the wheel was at midships level, it had three masts and obviously powerful motors too. It could probably sleep twelve people, maybe more.

"A pretty little thing," said Eve Schmidt.

"Yes," said V. She flipped through the U-tab intelligence file. "*A Flight of Fancy* is registered in Panama and belongs to the Mexican billionaire, Carlos Andreas Stout. He was found dead, with his mistress; they were poisoned three days ago by their morning coffee. The boat slipped out of a marina in the Dominican Republic four days before the billionaire died."

"It looks harmless enough," said Captain Anderson, "but there is something there, something in there."

"Yes," said Eve Schmidt, "a ghost ship."

"Yes," said Captain Anderson, "a ghost ship – or a ship with a ghost in it."

"A ghost that has killed probably thousands of people," said V.

"Who, I wonder, wants to bring about the end of the human race?" said Eve Schmidt, looking at the Captain and at V.

"That, I guess, is the question," said Captain Anderson.

"We will soon find out," said V, "maybe."

Now, standing on the deck of *A Flight of Fancy*, V adjusted the camera strapped to her headband. If the communications links held through the wild variations in interference, Captain Anderson and Eve, in the helicopter, and, farther off, Claire and the others on *Andromeda II*, and, farther away still, Admiral Rodriguez in his flagship, *Dwight D. Eisenhower*, would see what V was seeing and hear what she was hearing.

V glanced around, letting the cameras get good coverage. "I don't see any bodies here on deck. The sensor doesn't indicate any zombie virus. It all appears perfectly in order – spit-and-polish and spick-and-span. The wood-work is superb, just as Federico and Annette said. This is a fine boat."

"But there's something you don't like, V," said Eve Schmidt; she had become attuned to V's moods, undertones, nuances.

"Yes, there is a malevolent energy, or something. You should back off farther, at least a mile, maybe more; there is some sort of force lurking here. I have no idea what it is."

"Roger that, we'll back off."

"Now I'm going to go up to the bridge. How are the images?"

"Clear, very clear."

"Here goes! I'm going down below."

V climbed up to the bridge and entered.

"Oh, oh, what have we here?"

Lying on the highly polished wooden floor, just at the head of the stairs, was a body. V knelt next to it. It was a young woman, lying face up. Her jet-black hair was cut short, but with bangs that went down to her eyebrows; she was beautiful in a delicately boyish Hispanic way. Her large dark eyes were open, staring. She had dark, finely textured skin, and neatly delineated lips. Yummy! The girl looked positively delicious. She was wearing a simple tan-colored tunic, with a rope knotted at the waist. It looked like something from ancient times. In her fist she was holding a pistol-like object, obviously a weapon of some kind.

V pried the young woman's fingers apart and took the weapon. "I don't know what this is, Captain Anderson, Sergeant Schmidt. I've never seen anything like it before."

V turned it over, so Eve and the Captain could get a good look – and beyond them the situation room on the *Dwight D. Eisenhower* and the communications center on *Andromeda II*.

"Never seen anything like it," said a technician from somewhere

– *Andromeda II* or, more likely, the *Dwight D. Eisenhower*, "It looks very sophisticated, whatever it is."

V slipped the weapon into a pocket on her backpack.

She turned her attention to the body. The young woman showed no evident trauma, and no signs of infection from the zombie virus, no green traces around her nostrils, and no green crud or dried foam on her lips. Her skin and features were perfect, almost too perfect. V wondered if she were perhaps a new kind of SIN.

"She looks dead, but she feels warm," said V. V felt for a pulse. There was no pulse. She extended a mental probe. There was no mind activity she could discern.

The girl's eyes were open, beautiful, dark, staring. V pressed her claw gently over the lids and closed the eyes. The body felt alive, smelt alive, beautifully alive, but it wasn't.

"This is puzzling. I think she is in some way alive, but all the objective signs, except temperature, indicate that she's dead." V applied the bio-measures pad. It was designed to pick up any vital signs, pulse, temperature, neurological activity. "Captain, on your instruments, do you see any signs of life?"

"No, no, I don't. The only anomaly is temperature."

"Yes," said V. "This is creepy." She frowned. Something was not right. "It's strange. It feels weird." She stood up, and went into the next cabin.

There, lying on the floor, were two bodies. Well, they were skeletons, lying near the communications and computer center of the boat – the two skeletons were in US Navy uniforms. "Captain, do you see what I see?"

There was a pause, a burst of static, and then, "Yes, V, those look like –"

"They look like your people." V knelt by the two bodies.

"Yes, that's Annette and Federico, to judge by the uniforms."

Captain Anderson stared at the screen. The two bodies looked like ancient, freshly disinterred, highly polished skeletons. Or they looked like the sort of anatomical skeleton used in an artist's studio or medical lecture hall. There was no flesh, nothing except glittering white bone, picked lean. And they were still wearing their uniforms. These were his people, his friends.

V knelt next to one body. She held up the dog tag, so it was visible to the camera: *Annette Brighton*. The skull appeared perfect, picked clean. The woman's collar was crisp with starch. The dog tag was sparkling clean, as if it had just been polished.

"Yeah, that's Annette," said the Colonel, his voice made fuzzy by another burst of static.

"It's as if all the soft tissue was vaporized," V said, "There's no smell, no trace whatsoever of soft tissue. I'm just going to turn her over if you don't mind, Captain."

"Go ahead. Do it."

A double burst of static rippled across the audio. The video images skipped and skipped again. Anderson glanced at Eve Schmidt, "Do you think we're going to lose her?"

"No, not V," said Sergeant Schmidt.

Static flashed again; the camera images flipped, dissolved, flipped, and then returned.

"A lot of weird electromagnetic activity," said Guy, the helicopter's pilot.

V turned the skeleton over. It was surprisingly light. V was afraid it might fall into bits and pieces if the connective tissue was gone, but the skeleton stayed intact, as if wires were holding the bones together. "There is no trace of fluid," she said, "no blood, no suppuration, no signs of putrefaction, or organic decay, not on her uniform, not on the floor."

"What about the other body?"

V knelt by the other body and lifted the dog tag: *Federico Harvey*. The uniform was in perfect shape, as if it had been freshly cleaned and ironed, which perhaps it had.

"Whatever did this, Captain, it didn't touch the dog tags or damage the cloth or the belts or the metal buttons, unless they were killed and the flesh removed and then their clothes were put back on, but I don't see the point of that; or how it could be done."

Captain Anderson clenched his fist.

"You okay, Captain?" said Eve Schmidt.

"I'm okay, it's only that …"

V went to the *A Flight of Fancy's* communications desk. The navigation machinery was elaborate and ultra-modern. Behind its antique façade, the yacht was loaded with state-of-the-art equipment. V set down an instrument box and attached her instruments to the computers, to the radio sets – and there were several of these – they too looked ultra-high-tech.

V plugged in her U-Tab so that the information from the yacht's computers could be automatically uploaded and transmitted. She said into the microphone, "Captain, are you receiving, Claire, are you receiving this stuff?"

"Yes," said the Captain, watching the information scroll down on the screen as a massive number of programs and data files were uploaded.

"Yes, V, I am receiving," said Claire from *Andromeda II's* Command Room, "and it looks like this radio – the yacht's radio and communications systems. This radio has recently been tuned to a station which lies … in the Republic of …" A sizzling burst of static downed out Claire's voice.

"The Republic of what, Claire …?"

A burst of static filled their earphones.

"The Republic of what …?"

"Come in! Come in!" shouted the Captain.

"Did you hear her, Captain?"

"No, she was interrupted."

"Hello Claire?"

"Yes, V, I said the Revolutionary Republic of … bust of static … I'll analyze the messages. But I think they got there from …" Another burst of static cut Claire off.

"Somebody is playing games," said Eve Schmidt.

"Yes, that's right. Somebody is playing games, Captain," said V, "Somebody is blocking us – very selectively"

"Oh, oh, look at that," said Eve Schmidt.

The Captain shouted, "V, there is somebody – or something – somebody behind you."

"Yes," said V, "I've got it, thank you, Captain."

V turned. The dead woman was standing behind her. She was smiling; her dark skin seemed to glow.

"Hello, V," she said.

"Hello," V said.

The girl took a step forward. "The Puppet Master wanted you to come, you know, and he was hoping to be here to meet you in person. But he couldn't be here, so he sent me."

"Really?" said V, "And so …"

CHAPTER 29 – ZURICH

On *Andromeda II …*

"We have the line to Europe," said Sabrina. Monica handed the hybrid baby to the famous country-and-western singer, Gail McCoy, who took it with pleasure.

"Okay, little guy, here's my finger, here it is." Gail was curious about the little fellow. The baby closed its small claws around her finger and held on.

Sabrina had borrowed Gail from Claire's design studio, thinking that Gail McCoy – indisputably human and world-famous – could be useful in solving a problem regarding Monica Fabritz and her new status as a hybrid.

"I don't know if I can do this," said Monica, holding the U-Tab in her claw and staring at it, "They will want to see me. What if they want to see me? Yes, they'll certainly want to see me … and I'm a monster – this thing – me – is not their daughter."

"I think I have a trick that will convince your father that you … are you," said Sabrina Jacobs.

"A trick?" Monica widened her reptilian eyes. It would be impossible for her father to accept the "new" Monica! She was sure of it. She had just been staring at herself in a mirror, and feeling a tingling in her fangs, hunger, hunger for blood, and she had stroked the fangs with her long forked tongue, thinking, yes, they are hungry, they are telling me things about what I have become – a reptilian monster, a drinker of blood. I am no longer human.

She ran her claws over the finely patterned scales of her face, the red lozenge up above her snout, the nostrils that quivered with hunger, the eyes – Oh, God – the eyes. How could her father recognize her in this creature if she couldn't recognize herself?

"Well, your father," Sabrina was saying …

It was just before eight o'clock in the evening in Zurich, Switzerland.

Anton Fabritz had a white scar across his right eyebrow from an ice clamp that had sprung off a rock face when he had leaped across a crevasse to catch Monica, his daughter, who was then thirteen, when it seemed she was about to lose her grip, and tumble down … perhaps 500 feet – to an icy death. Monica had shared with him – and he with her – so many adventures.

Each time he looked in the mirror – and not only then – Anton thought of his daughter; nine months, a little more than nine months, nine months and twelve days, dead.

Monica …

Anton Fabritz had a trick he employed at the end of his working day – he would empty his mind, as much as possible, and he would close his eyes, and, for a few brief moments, he would remind himself of the most essential things in his life – his wife, a few friends, the memory of his daughter, his responsibility to shareholders, workers, customers, partners. Work, for Anton, was one form of social responsibility; wealth was a privilege, and it had to be justified, continually. This was easy to say, he mused, but hard to practice – the temptations and conflicting pressures were so many.

Then, he would swivel around and face the view from his window – this evening, it was sailboats on darkening water with low hills in the distance. Nature was greater than humanity, he would think, greater and more mysterious. Humans were a small particle in the natural universe, an ingenious species in a small niche on a small planet rotating around a middling star in a small galaxy in a small cluster of galaxies in …

He was in his ultra-modern study overlooking Lake Zurich. The screen on one side of the studio showed scenes of disorder in Miami and Fort Lauderdale.

"Doctor Fabritz, your guests will be here in five minutes," said Teodora, his Executive Assistant, peeking in at the door.

"Thank you, Teodora."

"Doctor Fabritz …"

"Yes, Teodora?"

"Irene says she has a headache and isn't feeling well and …"

"Thank you. I'll talk to her."

"Good evening, Doctor Fabritz."

"Teodora, are you free this evening?"

"Yes, Doctor Fabritz."

"Perhaps, if you like, you could join Irene and me in greeting our guests – it might make things easier, as a precaution."

"Certainly, Doctor Fabritz, it will be a pleasure"

Anton Fabritz liked his new assistant, Teodora Kalinowski; she was very efficient, and he was training her to take over one of the subsidiaries of Fabritz Industrial Holdings Incorporated; she was the daughter of one of his associates and old friends, and she had trained in Milan at the Bocconi University – a business degree – as well as scoring a first in history at Oxford.

Anton swiveled his chair and looked out over the lake. He swiveled back, looked at the rows and rows of books on the wall opposite – so much to know and so little is known – and then he looked at the 42-inch screen on the wall. Most of the images from Florida were now ten hours old. A sort of electronic blackout had fallen over much of the state. The experts had no convincing explanation of why this was happening.

Anton's eye was caught by the photo stand on his desk, the image of his daughter, of his only daughter, Monica.

"Move, Monica, move," he said.

The image came alive "Hi Dad," the girl said, "Hey, look at us," and a series of holograms showed Monica and her mother walking down a street in Manhattan, shopping, then in the Metropolitan Museum, then in Berlin at a cafe, and then just Monica, at a fairground, "Oh, whoopee, this is great, Dad, this is great," in their country place in France, then in Paris strolling in the Luxemburg Gardens, then on a visit to India, and images of Monica making her valedictorian speech at her graduation ceremony, the top, obviously, but modestly, of her class, "Our first duty is to the truth," she said, "As young scientists in training we must remember ..."

He could reach out and touch her – and he did.

But of course, the image was just empty air – an illusion.

And, once touched, it broke apart into sparkling fragments, confetti, sequins, like pieces of a glorious rainbow – and faded.

Anton Fabritz stood up. He was a trim, tanned, handsome man, forty-eight years old, an accomplished mountain climber and underwater enthusiast, with a Ph.D. in optical engineering, and a taste for opera and for theatre, and German and French literature. He turned away from the fading image of Monica – bits of tinsel hanging in the air – and he stood for a moment looking out over the lake.

Nine months and twelve days ago ...

The reptile man had taken her, Monica, so much life, and then nothing – an urn and a handful of cold ash.

He had gone to America himself to pick up the ashes and he and his wife had scattered the ashes over the Mediterranean.

Once, on a sailing holiday, Monica had said, "That's what I would like to happen, that my ashes be scattered here, in the water, far out to sea, with the sun shining."

It was just off Capri that she had said it; and it was there that, on a brilliant warm sunny day, Anton and Irene had scattered the ashes.

The reptile man …

Anton had asked Sabrina Jacobs – they sat on several boards of directors together – about the reptile man and she had told him that, yes, the DNA was of the same strain they were experimenting with – Anton did not know about V, though he had met her several times in her human version, Laura Giordano – but how the DNA had been obtained to create the reptile man, Sabrina said, she did not know.

And now, this new tragedy; it must be some sort of biological weapon.

It turned people into wild beasts, puppets, zombies …

He glanced at the screens – they showed buildings burning, people running, a girl wrapped in duct tape reporting on what it felt like to be a "zombie" – she was a damned brave and spunky girl that one, and the cameraman who was with her … Samantha … Samantha Andrews and Charlie, Charlie Parr. They were names to remember. He wondered if they were still alive – the text said there had been no contact with the pair for the last ten hours.

The German text streamed under the images of chaos: "These images of fighting north of Miami are over three hours old. Much of southern Florida has been incommunicado for the last three hours due to an electro-magnetic storm of unprecedented ferocity. Some messages have managed to get through but … There has been no definitive world on President Katherine du Bois Hughes. She is presumed dead. Meanwhile, vice president –"

Anton Fabritz clicked off the stream of images and went downstairs and into his wife's studio-office. She was standing by the window. Irene Selander a tall slender woman, in a long dress, looking out at the lake, holding a drink – whiskey, to judge by the tumbler and the pale gold tint.

"Anton," she said, as he entered, "Anton, I just can't face people tonight. I just can't face them. Nothing seems to mean anything anymore, I can't …"

"Now, now, now …" Anton took her in his arms. Irene and Monica had been more like sisters than mother and daughter – they looked alike, they thought alike, and though, sometimes, they fought like two wild cats, they made up instantly and seemed to love each other even more deeply after each spat. Anton sometimes wondered who was mother and who was daughter. "Now, now," Anton said, "I know, I understand, you don't have to come if you don't feel you can, but, on the other hand, you very much like …"

"We still have the line open to Europe," said Sabrina, "I don't know how long we'll be able to keep the connection open."

"When will happen if they see me? I'm a monster – this thing is not their daughter." Monica was tempted to chew her claw-nails. She frowned. It was not like her, fretting like this. Before Freddy, she had been so decisive, so quick, with no doubts, no regrets. But a lot had happened: Freddy and the murders, the repeated rapes, her imprisonment, her transformation, and the baby …

"You're not a monster," said Gail McCoy. Sabrina had asked Gail to help because she knew that Gail was cool and calm, and she was fully human, and she was used to dealing with Claire in hybrid form. Gail, Sabrina calculated, would be invaluable. Also, her modeling and singing career had made her famous, a sort of touchstone for humanity – an icon of what it meant to be human. She would be a reassuring presence, a sort of guarantee, even for someone as sophisticated as Anton Fabritz.

"You might just talk to them, without visuals," said Sabrina. "But your voice is not exactly …"

"Yes, my voice is not the same," said Monica, emphasizing the lisping reptilian hiss. "I sound like a snake."

"I told you I have an idea," said Sabrina, "I know your father; we have spent quite a bit of time together. He knows what I'm like, and your mother too – she and I have seen lots of each other; so, I have an idea: I think it will help convince them that you are you."

"An idea?" said Monica.

"Yes, I'm going to perform a magic trick."

Monica hesitated, she frowned, she paced up and down, a bright cobalt reptilian panther; finally, she turned to Sabrina. "Okay, boss, if you say you can convince dad that I'm his daughter, let's try it!"

Sabrina stood up, "Let's talk to Doctor Anton Fabritz."

Anton Fabritz was being his impeccably polite self, "Well, general, what do you think of …?"

"I believe there is a distinct danger of civil war," said the general, "and if that happens, then all bets are off in the Republic of …"

Desert had just been served. Irene Selander was delighted that Anton had insisted on her coming to the dinner and she was delighted too that he had asked Teodora to join them – the conversation was interesting, and Teodora relieved any pressure to play the hostess by picking up the slack. She was a fine young woman, thought Irene, with a pang, while smiling at the general, a Russian billionaire who was in partnership with Fabritz industries, and watching Teodora charm the general's wife. Anton was in deep conversation with the general and with Paul Heinrich, one of the American scientists who had worked with Anton on new developments in nano-laser technology, programming molecules to …

A servant entered. "It's a call from Sabrina Jacobs, sir. She says it is extremely urgent."

"Extremely urgent?"

"Yes, Doctor Fabritz."

"Will you excuse me for a moment, Paul, General, ladies and gentlemen? I shall be back in an instant."

Anton hurried down to his studio, flipped on the lights, and pushed the button and found himself staring at Sabrina Jacobs.

"Hello, Sabrina, what is this about?" he said, looking at the screen. Sabrina Jacobs looked very much her elegant self, if perhaps a bit tired, dressed in T-shirt and jeans. Is it about the crisis in Florida?"

"Only indirectly, Anton," said Sabrina; she seemed very serious, even nervous.

"Tell me."

"Anton, you know me quite well. You've known me for years."

"Yes."

"Do you trust me?"

"Yes. Absolutely."

"I'm going to show you something."

"Okay, fine, show me," he paced around impatiently. Anton Fabritz did not like people who played games; and he did not like to waste time – or to abandon his guests, even if they were in very capable hands – Irene and Teodora.

"I am going to undress," said Sabrina, "to show you what I have to show you, I'm going to have to undress."

"What?" Anton looked around. Anton had never been involved in scandal; his family had never been involved in scandal; as a pillar of the Swiss establishment, he was allergic to even just the idea or slightest whiff of scandal. Was this being taped? What did Sabrina want?

"I'll put a towel in front of me, Anton. I know you are sensitive."

"Good, well, that at least is something, Sabrina," Anton tried to smile, "I'm a timid fellow, you know – and happily married!"

"What I want to show you is this," said Sabrina. "I am a hybrid."

"What?"

"A hybrid."

"But …" Anton had gone pale. It was a so-called hybrid, the reptile man who had …

Someone – an extremely good-looking young woman – appeared on the screen with Sabrina. Was it Gail McCoy, that model CVJ used in its last two campaigns? Yes, it was! – Gail McCoy held a towel in front of Sabrina, so just Sabrina's shoulders and neck and face were visible. "This is Gail McCoy, Anton. I believe you've heard of her."

"Yes, yes, of course, hello, Ms. McCoy."

"This won't take a moment, Doctor Fabritz," Gail McCoy said, looking at the screen, and somehow, straight into Anton's eyes. Gail had a very pleasant accent from somewhere in the American south, or was it from the Appalachians?

Sabrina, the towel barely covering her breasts, said, "I am a hybrid and I'm going to show you the – well, a sort of magic change."

"Sabrina, I don't know what you are trying to …"

Then, in a flash, it happened, she was … She became a … reptile. Gail McCoy pulled the towel away.

"My God, Sabrina!" Anton staggered backward; it was a physical blow.

"It's still me, Anton," Sabrina's voice now had a slight lisp and a hissing sibilant edge to it; her fangs gleamed, and her golden eyes sparkled in the coal-black face, bright red markings on the snout.

"Yes, it's still her," said Gail, who was standing next to Sabrina, "I can attest to that, Doctor Fabritz."

"I need a moment, Sabrina. I need a moment to adjust …"

"Take your time, Anton."

Anton sat down. He stared at the screen. In an instant – unless it was some kind or trick – the beautiful woman he knew as Sabrina Jacobs had transformed herself into a … into a monster, into the female version of the reptile that had killed his daughter. He had heard rumors about Sabrina, for years, but he had discounted them – unbelievable, impossible, monstrous!

He took a deep breath. But now … she was, yes, she was a monster. But why was she doing this? Why was she revealing herself in such a dangerous way?

Finally, he felt he was able to speak.

He stood up and approached the screen, "But," he paused; it was difficult to use her name while addressing this, this creature, "Sabrina, why are you telling me – and showing me – this … this thing, this side of you … why now …?"

"Because, Anton, the reptile man …" her reptilian face seemed to fill the screen, the gold, snake-like eyes, the glittering black scales, the red marking above her eyes, the white fangs, the tongue – the forked tongue – that was so bright, so red.

"God, yes, the reptile man …" Anton took a deep breath; his heart flooded with grief and rage, "Yes, the reptile man …"

"He didn't kill Monica, Anton."

"What?"

"Monica is alive; she is well, she has had a baby – she is here, beside me, close to me, and, like me, she is, mentally, very much herself, Anton; but Anton …"

"Yes …" Anton Fabritz sat down again; his stomach tightened; he gripped the armrest; his knuckles turned white. What horrible thing – besides death – had happened to his daughter? He was aware of every sound, of his own breathing, of his own heart. He was aware of the solid old 19th Century mansion around him, of its staircases and rooms and windows and terraces, of the woodwork and stonework, of the plumbing, of the garden and heated swimming pool, of the mist slowly rising off the pool into the summer evening … Everything that was solid seemed to melt into nothing – into ghostly fog. The air-conditioning seemed suddenly not to be working. He was sweating. No, it was cold; the sweat under his shirt was turning to ice. He felt a horrible chill. He steadied his breathing, "Go on, Sabrina, go on."

"The reptile man changed Monica into a hybrid – well, a different color scheme from me; but she is for the moment like me, like what you see before you. She will be able to change back soon and be her old self. I'm sure of it, but for the moment … she is locked into this reptilian form … like me," Sabrina opened her arms: as if to say, "this is what I am, look on me, you mortals, and ..."

"It doesn't matter," said Anton, "Tell her it doesn't matter what she is or what she looks like."

"Monica?" said Sabrina.

The camera angle swiveled slightly and, standing beside Gail McCoy, Monica appeared, and the camera zoomed in on her. "Hi Dad," she said.

"Monica," Anton hesitated, ever so slightly, absorbing the fact this creature – this bright cobalt reptile with a red lozenge between its brilliant gold serpent eyes – was his daughter. "Thank God!" he swallowed, "This is a miracle. Are you okay, are you alright?"

The reptilian face grinned; it seemed to Anton a grin.

"Yes, I'm okay – decked out for carnival, as you can see!"

"What happened? Sabrina said ..."

"The reptile man killed the Lewis family; but he kidnapped me. For some reason the American authorities reported that I was dead."

"But ..."

"The reptile man, I call him Freddy after that monster in those old films we watched, remember ... that time we were staying outside Paris and ..."

"Yes, yes, I remember, the old films from the 20th Century, those horror films."

"Right, Freddy Krueger."

"Yes, you used to get so frightened."

"Yes," Monica hissed, "I'd come running into your and mommy's bedroom and I wouldn't want to go back to my own room."

"Yes," said Anton, thinking, My God, this really is Monica, this really is our daughter, this is ... unbelievable.

"Freddy kept me for about two weeks, and he ... well ... he raped me ... he wanted to get me pregnant."

"And he did, he did get you pregnant?" Anton was thinking, how am I going to explain this to Irene? Well, she's intelligent, she's tough, she will ...

"Yes, I had a baby, just earlier this morning. In fact, I only turned into what you see, into this creature, last night ... Until last night I was my usual self. So, I'm getting used to it myself. Gail – Gail, can you show dad, his ... ah ... his grandson, please?"

The camera panned, and Gail McCoy, who was carrying a small cobalt-colored reptilian humanoid baby, came up to Monica and carefully handed the baby to her, saying, "Here's the little guy. He's being very well-behaved, Doctor Fabritz."

"Here he is, Dad," said Monica, cradling the baby and displaying him for the camera. "Here is my son."

"Well, well, hello there," said Anton, swallowing. "He looks healthy."

"Yes, and he certainly is hungry," said Monica, gazing down at her hybrid child. "He can't get enough, can you little fellow?"

The baby was grasping at her breast.

"So, what do we do now?" said Anton, thinking of the immense implications – and dangers – of what he had just seen.

"Dad, Sabrina thinks I should stay here – with the baby – on *Andromeda II*, until we sort things out, until I can change back into a human being – and you and mom can come to visit me, if you wish to of course, anytime, maybe after this emergency in Florida is over. What do you think?"

"Yes, I think that, if that is what Sabrina thinks, that is a good idea. Sabrina obviously has . . . ah . . . experience with this kind of situation. I will speak to your mother this evening, right away, and then, as soon as possible, hopefully in the next day or two, we – both of us – will come to see you. Sabrina?"

"We will be honored to have you and Irene," said Sabrina, "and we are honored to have Monica. She is a very, very brave young woman."

"Monica, I love you, I love you very much," said Anton.

"I love you too, Dad," Monica smiled, waved, and she held up one of the baby's claws, so that it could wave too.

"Goodbye, Monica," Anton said, "Until tomorrow."

"Goodbye, Daddy, Monica waved. "Until tomorrow!"

The screen went dead.

Anton Fabritz sat very still for a moment.

He glanced at his watch, he stood up, he straightened his tie, he walked over to the window and he looked out over the lake, dark now, with lights glittering on the far shore, and a boat of some kind, just in front of the window, not far away, silently moving towards shore; it all seemed so normal, so solid, so prosperous, so Swiss: and, on the streets behind him, world-famous banks, insurance companies, the offices of leading pharmaceutical companies, high-tech, precision engineering companies, bio-tech companies, luxury goods companies, many of the finest commercial and technological creations and accomplishments of the human race. He took a deep breath, and went back to the dinner party, apologized for his absence, smiled at everyone, and took up the conversation where he had left off.

"You were saying, General, a possible civil war ..."

"Yes, Anton, the situation is explosive in several of the Central Asian Republics and I dare say that ..."

Later, when their guests were gone, Anton told his wife.

He showed her the automatic backup of his conversation with Sabrina and Monica.

Irene sat very still for a second or two and then she said, "That's Monica. Inside she hasn't changed at all. That's Monica! When can we leave?"

"In a few days, I hope, in a few days," said Anton; he put his hand on his wife's arm.

Then they talked, they talked – much of the night.

Irene laid her hand on his hand. Then she released his hand and stood up and walked to the window where already there were glimmers of dawn; she frowned, her mood had changed, "Our daughter is now an alien, Anton," she said, "An alien, or part alien – no longer human."

"It wasn't her choice," said Anton.

"Who – or what – will we be embracing, Anton, who or what will we be embracing when we welcome our daughter home? And – that, that child, that thing, that ... monster that has come out of her womb, that blue, scaly thing, what is it, Anton, what is it?"

"Irene ..."

"And what shall we do with it, Anton? How shall we dispose of it?"

"Irene ..."

In the far distance, faintly, Anton heard a tram, one of the early morning trams. A normal workday was about to begin in Zurich, Switzerland.

On *Andromeda II*, Sabrina Jacobs, now once again human, was staring at Monica's baby, as Gail McCoy handed it back to Monica.

"He's hungry already," said Gail, "aren't you, little guy?"

"You know," said Sabrina, "This is the beginning of something, you know, this is the beginning of something absolutely new."

Monica took the baby and cradled it, "Yes," she said, looking down at the baby that blinked up at her with adoring reptilian eyes, "Yes, the beginning of something new – but of what?"

CHAPTER 30 – ISIS

V stood very still, gazing at the apparition.

The dead woman was standing there, smiling; her skin glowed. "Hello, V," she repeated. "As I said, the Puppet Master wanted you to come. He wanted to meet you here in person. But he couldn't be here, so he sent me."

"Well, then," said V.

"My God," said Captain Anderson.

"Cool," said Claire, from *Andromeda II*, her voice echoing, "and the Dead shall rise again, and the slain shall wake and walk again. Wow, Lazarus, a female Lazarus, did you see that?"

"This is a very interesting time we are living," said Eve Schmidt to Captain Anderson, "It might just turn me into a mystic!"

"Yes, interesting times," breathed the Captain.

"Just what are we dealing with here?" muttered Admiral Rodriguez from the *Dwight D. Eisenhower*.

V said, "I thought you were dead."

"I am dead – well, in a manner of speaking. Or I was dead. It's hard to explain. Now I am no longer dead."

"What's your name, then?"

"My name is Isis."

V held out a claw, "I am pleased to meet you Isis." The girl accepted the claw. Her hand was warm. "You don't look dead, Isis, and you don't feel dead."

"My life is in your mind, V. You will give me life, real life, life eternal."

"Oh," said V, smiling and leaning back against the yacht's communications console. "But others see you too – so you are real, not just a figment of my mind."

"I know," Isis said, "I am real, but I am not real."

V said, "This is all very metaphysical and interesting, Isis. But who wanted me to come, Isis, can you tell me?"

"Him, he wanted you to come."

"Him? Who is he?"

"He had a name once," said Isis, brushing a stray strand of hair away from her eyes. V thought: Yes, she is perfect; she is too perfect, too perfectly sculpted, to be human, or merely human.

Isis returned V's smile. "Now, he is new, he is renewed, but he is unhappy in his present state. As I said, he is the Puppet Master – the master of the zombies."

"Oh," said V, thinking, so this is the Puppet Master, or his representative. She was trying to read the girl's mind but there seemed to be nothing there, only a deep black empty space or a thick velvet curtain that blacked out all attempts to get inside and do a reading.

"Your friends in the helicopter are in danger," Isis stared straight at V, "imminent danger. They must leave, now."

V said, "Captain Anderson, did you hear what Isis said? I think the message is serious."

"Yes, we are drawing back."

"As fast as you can," said Isis, "As fast as you can!"

"Go as far as you can, Captain. Don't worry about me. Go back to your ships. I'll get out of here somehow."

"Be careful," said the Captain.

"V, if you get yourself killed, I will never forgive you," said Claire.

"So, Isis, what should we do now?" said V.

"Now, V, we will –"

WHAM!

FLASH!

A huge explosion of energy burst upon the world. The cabin and everything in it, and the yacht itself disappeared in a burst of blinding light. The ocean trembled, dissolving into a myriad of silver sparkles and then into – nothing.

WHAM!

FLASH!

V closed her eyes, slammed her claws against her ears and struggled desperately to concentrate, to stop her brain from exploding, her body from flying apart in little sparkling, smoking bits.

On *Andromeda II*, the impact projected Claire twenty-five feet across the room; she smashed into a wall and slithered, all limp, a rag doll, down to the floor, where she lay in a heap, stunned and blinking. Two of the master computers blew up – sparks and bits of metal and plastic and tangles of wire flying everywhere. Claire picked herself up; smoke curled from her ears, and tendrils of smoke flowed off the points of her claws. "Whew!"

On *A Flight of Fancy* – or the ghost of *A flight of Fancy* – V kept her eyes squeezed shut. She was being deafened, torn limb from limb, vibrated to death. The yacht shook and trembled as if it would fly apart into a million pieces.

Capitan Anderson's helicopter spun out of control, turning around and around, hurtling down towards the sea.

Then it all ceased.

The pilot gained control of the helicopter.

"Exciting," said Eve Schmidt.

"What in the hell was that?" said Captain Anderson.

"A rehearsal, I reckon," said Eve Schmidt, "a trial run."

V took her claws away from her ears. "So, Isis, what was that? Whatever it was, it was very impressive!"

"I am sorry. I apologize. It happened before I realized it would happen. The Puppet Master is angry; he is losing control of himself, and of the force, of the energy that powers the gateway."

"A gateway? Where is it? And to where?"

"The gateway is in the lost temple to the ancient gods and the new gods."

"And you, Isis, you carry the name of an Egyptian goddess, so what is the connection?"

"The connection is rebirth. I am reborn from death, just as you are. You kill, and others die, so that you may be reborn and live, continually reborn and live and live again, and they live on in you, all the dead, centuries of dead, their voices are in you. Then, there is the force of darkness."

"The force of darkness?"

"Yes." Isis pushed her bangs away from her forehead and spoke as if she were reciting something from memory. "He is a misshapen product of hell, an incarnation of the lack of love; he is an infernal mixing of DNA, his body is a mismatch of parts, his destiny is night, he is jealous and vindictive and he will pursue us to the ends of time, and it is he who wishes to sacrifice you – all of you, and all of humanity. He wishes to lord it over humanity – but only when humans have been reduced to mindless beasts." Isis changed her tone from oracular to confidential. She smiled. "He's a vindictive wicked little bastard, really! I don't like him at all!"

"Are you listening, Claire, are you listening, Captain?"

"Yes, yes, we are."

"So, Isis, who are you?"

"I died a long time ago – centuries ago, I believe, perhaps millennia. Even the dust of my body had been scattered to the four winds, the molecules and atoms migrated everywhere, and they have fallen as rain and they have floated as dust and they have grown in plants and they have become embedded in the muscles of wolf and coyote and of a wise man who strode the dusty sacred roads of India, a Brahman who made his pilgrimages and who strode naked, streaked with paint and holy colors, who begged with a begging bowl, and leaned upon his staff at the side of the many dusty roads he traveled and he saw the redcoats march in lines and the maharajas defeated and he saw flags rise and fall and he prayed at sunset and bathed in the holy waters and then, at last, he too was turned to ashes and dust on the holy steps of the Ganges, and I was there with him, as I was with countless others. And so here I am now, having known all this, my atoms like those of all of us born like the very elements themselves – like iron and copper, oxygen and carbon – in the furnace and forge of the stars, and destined to die, too, in the heart of the sun, our very own star, but now I am here, and you are my sister, and you must be sacrificed, be ready to be sacrificed, to be truly my sister and to save me, and then out of the valley of darkness – out of the valley of death – we will come, together, if only for a time, and your younger sister, too, the black-and-red reptile known as Claire, I need her too to feed his hunger, to liberate us all. She will die – and perhaps be reborn, and your other sister too, the one known as Sabrina, the great hunger desires her sacrifice too. She will die, and, perhaps, she too will be reborn."

"Oh," said V, claws on her hips, "so we are to be sacrificed?"

"Yes, it is not my doing, and it makes my heart sad."

"And the two skeletons – were they sacrificed?"

"The two, the man and the women, who are now bones, I am sorry about that. It was a mistake, an accident. I didn't mean to do it. I did not know my strength. I am new, once again new, having just been reborn, and I have much to learn. My heart is heavy with sadness for the young man and the young woman and, if I could bring them back, I would do it, but I cannot, not now at least, for such is the nature of time, when we are inside it, when we are prisoners of it, such as we now are, it only allows us to travel forward, not backward, and we must enter the mysteries to free ourselves, to free ourselves totally. Then I shall see if I can arrange for rebirth of the two people I have slain without willing or intending to do so."

"Okay," said V, with a touch of impatience. V, who was herself very mysterious, even to herself, was excessively impatient with other people's mysteries, and mystical or metaphysical talk – stuff about time going forwards and then switching into reverse – made her antsy and gave her the willies. She knew this was a weakness, like her pride, her hubris, her overconfidence. But, still, it made part of her want to whirl around like a whirling dervish and whirl and whirl and whirl away into a cloud of unknowing. The world overflowed with baloney; and V was allergic to baloney. "Okay, Isis," she said more softly, lisping slightly. "What happens next?"

"This boat, *A Flight of Fancy*, will soon die. It will become a ghost – only to be reborn – as the gateway opens – then you, we, shall enter the time beyond time."

"A ghost? *A Flight of Fancy* will become a ghost?" V put her claw on a smooth warm ledge of teak trim; it felt so solid, so reassuring.

The yacht began to vibrate ... everything trembled.

"What is happening?" V felt as if her body was dissolving.

"We are about to die."

"Die?"

"In a manner of speaking, V" said Isis.

"In a manner of speaking, you say?" V huffed and puffed and stamped the deck hard with one foot-claw. "All this is very obscure. You are a very annoying young woman, Isis! You speak in riddles."

"I shall try to correct that," said Isis, tilting her head to one side and giving V an adorable grin. "You are funny when you are angry, V. I didn't realize I'd like you so much!"

"I am funny, am I?" V crossed her arms across her chest – in her annoyed schoolmarm pose. Isis deserved a good spanking.

"The threshold is here."

Everything vibrated, the wooden deck turned into a blur, V seized Isis by the hand. "Okay, wicked child, tell me: what is really happening?"

"The threshold is here."

"Yes, fine, but the threshold to where?"

"Your guess is as good as mine," said Isis, holding tight to V and still smiling, though her features were becoming a blur. "I have no idea."

"Oh, that is reassuring!" V's body was vibrating like a tuning fork. Her fangs chattered. It was not a pleasant experience. Her heart was pumping like crazy; it was about to burst. Isis's features exploded into a smear. "Captain Anderson, can you hear us?" V was beginning to think that this whole idea was … crazy, maybe even … dangerous …

There was nothing but static.

The yacht vibrated like mad and the decks and masts and the ocean itself became unreal, transparent, just lines, a sketch, and the wood disintegrated into floating fragments, bits of paper blown by the wind. V fell, hand in hand with Isis, through space, an infinite dark abyss of space. Then they were swept upwards in a tornado of light, round, and round, and round, and then downward, and waves splashed up out of nowhere and …

There was a blinding flash of light.

WHAM!

FLASH

Then, there was nothing, absolutely nothing.

NOTHING!

"Claire you are taking this too far," Ben Kamu was standing behind Claire, his hand on her shoulder. "You're going to kill yourself!"

The computers trembled. Smoke rose from the mainframes. A few computer screens had already exploded showering glass all over the Control Room.

"I'm going to take some of the computers off line," Ben said, "Otherwise, when this thing blows, we won't have anything left."

He flipped switches on a bank of five computers, isolating them. "Claire!" he shouted, "Let go of it, pull back – it's too dangerous!"

"Piss off, Ben, darling," she hissed, "I'm going to follow this to the end of the line. This is unique. This is unprecedented. Whatever is happening here, I've never seen anything like this in my whole life!"

"I'm going to get Sabrina!" Ben was worried sick – and furious. "Claire – you are risking your life!"

"Piss off, love," she hissed, her snout glued to the screen, "I know you mean well, but …"

"Okay, I'll piss off," said Ben. He headed off to find Sabrina. Maybe she could talk some sense into the girl. Boy! Was Claire pig-headed! Well, Sabrina could be very persuasive, so just maybe …

"Ben's right, Claire," said Kate Thornhill from the next console, "You should slow down, maybe detach for a few minutes, you are right inside the network, your mind is flowing with the electromagnetic field. If this thing blows, it's your whole brain, your whole body which is at risk!"

"You'll be fried, Claire!" shouted Ben, from the Communications Center doorway, as he headed for Sabrina's office.

Claire muttered under her breath, "Something is happening, something dangerous, and I am not going to let V go, I am not going to let V go, I'm not going to let V go."

"You don't have to let ..." Kate started to say, looking at Anthony Garcia and the others in despair, "You don't have to let V –"

WHAM!

There was a huge explosion. Light, blinding, eye-searing light, filled the room; Claire's chair disintegrated into a thousand floating, smoking fragments.

WHAM!

Claire exploded – she was projected high in the air; she flew backwards across the room, smashing into the wall, up on the balcony, smashing through the railing – leaving twisted metal in her wake and narrowly missing a Royal Marine, who, miraculously had just ducked down to pick up a piece of paper, and then Claire fell, smashing down, first onto the gangway, and then she rolled over, bounced off, under the smoking gaping railing, and fell straight down, crashing onto the computers below, then she bounced again, like a rubber doll, and fell flat on the floor, and lay still.

People were blinking from the flash of light and covering their ears and bending their heads from the echoing shock wave; then, waking up, coming to themselves, they saw Claire, lying, inert, still, on the floor, and they rushed towards her. Sabrina ran into the room with Ben Kamu, "What happened, what happened?"

"It's Claire!"

Sabrina ran to Claire and knelt beside her.

Kate was already there and two Marines.

"There's no pulse, ma'am, no pulse at all," said one of the Marines, a medic, looking up at Sabrina. "There's no breath, no pulse, no heartbeat."

"Try!"

One of the Marine's had grabbed the defibrillator. They tried it – bang, bang, and bang!

Nothing!

Claire, the elegant reptile girl, the world-famous fashion brand, the model, lay, as still as death, smoke streaming from her nostrils; steam rising from her ears – her golden eyes open, staring.

"Claire cannot die!" shouted Sabrina, "Claire does not die. It is not something Claire can do! I won't allow it! Stand back!"

Sabrina threw herself full length on Claire's body.

"Sabrina …!" Kate shouted.

"What is she doing?" asked Anthony Garcia.

"She's trying to heal Claire. She's using her healing power. Hybrids have a sort of healing power, but when somebody is already … gone … I don't know if it's possible," Kate turned away and buried her face in Anthony's shoulder, "This is awful!" She looked up at Anthony, "What in the world is happening?"

Anthony had no words; he stroked Kate's hair.

Sabrina, lying full length on Claire, was giving Claire the kiss of life. But it was a kiss of life that was passing from every pore, from every nerve, from every fiber of Sabrina's being, from every corpuscle, from every cell. Sparks flashed around the two of them; miniature lightning bolts leaped between Sabrina and Claire. Smoke rose. Sabrina's T-shirt burst into bright red flame.

"She's going to kill herself," said Anthony.

"Oh, God, Oh, God!" Ben Kamu twisted his hands.

"It's impossible; she's trying to do the impossible," said Kate.

Sabrina's clothes exploded – shreds of jeans, a belt buckle and a belt flew across the room, smashing against a computer screen. Her T-shirt flared up, bright red, flaring off sparks, flames whooshed and vanished. The T-shirt collapsed in a veil of ash.

WHAM!

A blinding flash, an eye-searing bolt of lightning shot up from Sabrina, engulfing her and Claire, wrapping them in pure fire. It was like looking into an explosion of the sun. People closed their eyes, covered their eyes, ducked behind desks, flattened themselves on the floor.

Anthony screamed. He was blinded. He couldn't see anything, just brightness and then blackness. Total dark, he thought, total dark! Now I'm blind.

He felt Kate tighten her grip on his arm, and he heard her whisper, "Oh, God, oh, no, oh, no, Sabrina!"

He heard Ben Kamu say, "Oh fuck, oh, no, oh fuck!"

Anthony blinked. His vision was returning, black and white and blurry, like an old-fashioned film negative. He wondered if he'd ever see clearly again.

He blinked again. His eyes filled with tears.

Burning, he smelt burning, like human flesh had been scorched. He rubbed his eye with his one free arm, the other was holding onto Kate.

"Help me, Anthony," he heard Kate whisper, "Help me." He blinked again. Then it was clear, it was becoming clear, the room, the people standing around, their eyes wide open their faces in shock. A woman screamed, "Oh, no, no, no, no!"

A man cried out, "God Almighty, it cannot be."

Ben Kamu stood there, a statue, his arms limp by his side, his mouth open, staring; he said, "My God, my God, my God …"

Two women held each other, shielding their eyes so they wouldn't have to look, they wouldn't have to see.

Anthony blinked again.

Then he saw.

Claire, the black reptile, with the cute red snout, lay there, apparently dead, mouth open but not breathing; she was as immobile as stone; the golden reptile eyes open, the arms flung out, limp, the claws open, half curled, facing upwards.

And there, where Sabrina, the super woman, had been … was …

"Come, help me," said Kate, looking up at Anthony, "Come, we must help her."

There, where Sabrina had been was … an ancient crone.

A creature that was so old she appeared to beyond age, beyond humanity, a withered, shrunken …

"This can't be happening, this can't be," Anthony whispered.

There, where Sabrina Jacobs had been, was a naked, bent, hag-like creature, a witch from the wild heath or forest in a Shakespearean tragedy, a fairy-tale horror. Her hair, and there were only a few strands of it left, was white as snow, fine as gossamer. Her skin hung in folds. Her shanks and buttocks drooped. Her breasts sagged; they were empty paper-mâché sacks, the elongated wrinkled russet-colored nipples hanging straight down. Her face was riven with deep creases and folds, collapsed as if it had melted. This new creature was deadly pale, pure white, almost marble white. Pulsating veins of waxen blue showed beneath the yellowed parchment that was her skin. Her bones stuck out, and under the sagging tits, the bones of her ribcage pushed out from the skin like a birdcage caught in a spider's web. Her clouded eyes, white with cataracts, dripped thick tears – a gummy white fluid – and the tears flowed down the riven drooping cheeks. She was naked and seemed a thousand years old. She turned around and around and around, as if dazed, her head bent, her mouth open, her teeth broken and yellowed and crooked. She seemed confused.

"Come, Anthony," said Kate, "we must help her."

"Yes," said Anthony, as if waking from a dream – or nightmare, "Yes."

"Sabrina," said Kate, reaching out her arms.

"Kate," said the broken voice, a whispered cackle, "Kate … ha, ha, ha … Kate …"

"Sabrina …"

"I know … I know …"

"Sabrina, let us take you to your suite. You can't …"

"No, no," the ancient crone held up one skinny arm, "No, no …" She waved Kate away with the claw-like hand with its twisted skeletal fingers, long yellow nails.

"But Sabrina …"

"I know what has happened, Kate, I know what I have become," the voice was stronger now.

"Sabrina, you can't …"

"No matter, what becomes of me is not the point!" The old hag coughed, wiped the phlegm away with the back of her claw-like hand.

"But Sabrina …"

"Ben," Sabrina held up a bony hand, "Ben," she coughed, and bent over deeper, trembling, visibly struggling to stay on her feet, "There is work to be done, Ben, set up that backup system you were preparing."

"Yes, Sabrina, right away." Ben stared at her, bowed, and went to work.

"Now, Kate," Sabrina said, peering at Kate from ancient gummy eyes, "Thank you, Kate, and thank you, Anthony, but you have work to do! Kate you must continue your calculations."

"But without Claire …"

"Yes, without Claire," the hag coughed, and coughed again, wiping away a fistful of thick dark phlegm, "without Claire nothing will be possible. But Claire will live – Claire will live."

"But …" Kate glanced over at Claire. The girl-reptile lay immobile, unnoticed now in the confusion when all eyes were turned towards Sabrina.

"She's blinking," shouted Ben Kamu, "Claire is blinking!"

Sabrina limped, almost hopped, it was like she was a creature that had to go on four legs; she supported herself with her bony hands, scrambling across the floor like a crab. She knelt beside Claire. "Claire," she whispered, the raspy broken voice coming out of the small frail ancient creature was surprising.

Claire's red forked tongue flicked out between her lips, "Mommy," she said, "You put me in a cage. I don't want to be in a cage."

"You are no longer in a cage, my darling," Sabrina managed to whisper.

"Mommy, I love you; why don't you love me?"

"I do love you, Claire, I do love you."

"You do love me? Really?"

"Yes, I love you. I shall love you forever."

"Oh, Mommy! I love you! I love you so!"

"I'll be in my suite," said Sabrina to Ben. She stood up and hobbled, half crawling, half scurrying, towards the door of the Command Center. At the door, she turned to Kate, "Don't tell Claire what happened to me. She must not know. Tell the others not to say anything, block your thoughts!" she gasped.

And then, Sabrina, or what was left of her, went out the door.

The others stood still in shock.

Claire, still lying on the floor, blinked her gold reptile eyes, "Mommy," she said, "Mommy, where are you? Why have you left me in darkness, Mommy? Why have you put me in a cage? Why don't you love me, Mommy? Why have you abandoned me?" Then she screamed, "Mommy!!!!"

Kate knelt by Claire.

Ben Kamu said, "If she doesn't get back to herself, we can't rebuild the code, we won't be able to get V and the others back – that is, if we can get them back at all."

"Claire!" Kate put her hand on Claire's arm.

The blank reptile eyes stared up at her, the claw grabbed Kate's arm and held on. "Where is Mommy," Claire sobbed, "Where is Sabrina?"

When the fresh air and sunlight hit her, Sabrina shivered and trembled. Every bone in her body – her new-old body – ached. The breeze was fresh; the sun was hot; it slammed into her skin and seemed to burn right through the flesh to the bones. A few lonely strands of white hair fluttered in the breeze. She groped for them with a skeletal hand. Her naked mottled skull glowed white under the afternoon sun. The deck burned under her bare feet.

She hobbled to the railing, her body lurching left, then right, then left, then right again. "Unsteady as she goes," she muttered. "Sabrina, you are just skin-and-bones, Sabrina, you are a pathetic old rag, yes, a bag of bones." She spat into her hand and looked at the puddle of phlegm, and the ancient, mottled, wrinkled, arthritic claw. "Ugh!"

She grasped the railing with one skinny, aged claw; the pale gray bony fingers and knuckles were splattered with vivid, dark, age spots.

She curled the fingers around the smooth metal of the railing, holding on desperately; she was afraid she would fall and break apart like a badly made toy.

"A pile of bones," she muttered, "a pile of bones."

She took a deep breath.

"So, this is what mortality is like."

The warmth of the sun was a comfort; the warm smooth sensation of the railing under her hand was ecstasy, the crisp sparkling of the water was divine, a blur of warm dancing light. She closed her eyes. She loved being alive, she really loved being alive – She didn't want to die, no, she didn't.

Ian, the son of Ian, the old engineer on *Andromeda I*, now himself a solid sixty-year-old, came along the deck. He saw the naked old woman grasping the railing. He stopped dead in his tracks: God, she was ancient. She looked like a skeleton draped in a thin membrane of skin. Where had she come from? Who was she?

"Hello," he said, hailing her with a doubtful smile.

"Hello," croaked the crone.

"Who are you?"

"You don't recognize me, Ian?" The crone turned towards him and spoke – it was a phlegm choked voice – thick saliva dripped from her drooping lips; the lips sagging outward, drooling silver. It sparkled like spider milk in the reflected light of the waves.

Ian looked closer; the milky clouded eyes, he could see, had once been crystal blue; the sparse strands of brittle hair had been blond, there was one thick gold lock of hair, sparkling, a mockery, just above her left ear. The shrunken shoulder-blades, the withered hanging breasts … A beautiful woman, withered, melted, dissolved, by time – but it had happened in a few minutes.

He had seen her an hour ago!

They had shared a joke about troubled times!

"Sabrina?"

"The same," she croaked. "Yet different, Ian, as you can see," with the back of her hand she wiped away a dribble of saliva and dabbed at a milky tear which was moving slowly down her withered cheek.

"I can't believe it!"

"Well, it is true, my friend. It's me."

"My God, what happened, lass, what happened?"

"Help me to my office, Ian, and I shall tell you the tale."

He took her arm. She was so frail. Her bones could shatter in an instant.

"Claire," she croaked in her broken voice, "Claire has to be saved."

"Claire?" said Ian, "Tell me – what happened to Claire?"

"You see the shadow on the water, Ian," Sabrina reached out one skinny arm and pointed at the horizon where a veil of mist hung like a thick wall of haze.

"The time-shift zone," said Ian, "or at least that's what somebody just said it might be; I came up to see for myself."

"Yes, the time-shift zone; that is what it must be," Sabrina clung to his arm, afraid to slip and fall, "When the shift took place, Claire had integrated her mind into the electromagnetic and gravitational fields, so the time-shift, the implosion of time, hit Claire directly – it overcharged her mind, and her body. It exploded her, literally, mental bits and pieces, scattered everywhere, that's all that was left – and then …"

"Yes?"

"It seemed she was dead. But she cannot die, Ian, she must not die. She is my child, Ian, and the destinies of millions of others, perhaps of humanity itself, depend upon her."

"So, you used your healing power."

"Yes, I did," the withered old face – a drooping and lopsided melted mask of the beauty that once had been – grinned slyly up at him from the shrunken, crooked body. "I used everything I had, Ian, everything I had – except for a sliver of life, just enough to stay and make sure that Claire recovers, and V wins the day. What you see is what remains, it's the husk, the shell of what once was me – but still is me, mind you," she cackled, "I'm not done yet, Ian, not by a long shot," and she wiped a spool of silver drool from her chin, "And you know what, Ian …?"

"Tell me …"

"I'm going to be one wicked old lady, really evil. I'm going to try everybody's patience, Ian! They will all loath me!"

"That's not possible, Sabrina!"

"Ha, ha, ha, ha, just you wait and see, Ian, ha, ha, ha, just you wait and see!"

"No, you can't mean that!"

"I'm going to drive Claire mad! I'm going to put them to the test."

"The test of what? What test?"

"The test of love – Can they still love me when I'm a crone, a monster?"

"That's perverse, Sabrina!"

"I am perverse, Ian."

"Well, I have heard rumors," said Ian.

"Ha, ha, ha, yes of course you've heard rumors, Ian. Who knows, Ian, who knows what madness lurks in the heart of darkness, what folly in the dancing nymph, what shadows in the hearts of men – and women too, ha, ha, ha! This will be fun. I'm a trickster at heart, Ian, a prankster, I like drama. Old fashioned soap opera is my element, Ian! They'll make me walk the plank, Ian, ha, ha, ha! They'll make me walk the plank, ha, ha, ha, ha!"

"Walk the plank?"

"Ha, ha, ha, yes, Ian, splash, Ian, splash! Ha, ha, ha!"

And with a wave and a ghastly crooked smile, Sabrina Jacobs, eternally young Nobel Prize Laureate, disappeared, cackling, limping, with a waddling spider-like walk, into her suite, and slammed the door.

Ian stood very still in the sunlight – the cackle certainly did sound wicked. Had Sabrina been driven mad by her transformation? Or was she reverting, in a new guise, to the habits of the past, when she was in love with Dmitry Pavlov, and was known to be one of the most perverse women and lovers in the world. Had love driven her mad?

Well, years ago, when he was a feisty young man, Ian had read the steamy magazine articles and newspaper reports from those days and he had seen the photos.

And now for the world-famous beauty to come to this ghastly end! Ian leaned on the railing and stared into heart of the sunlit brilliance – it was something too horrible to contemplate. He turned and saw Marit. She was hurrying along the deck. "You heard?" he said.

"Yes. I am going to her. I am going to her now," said Marit.

"Yes, lass, if anybody can help her and comfort her, it will be you. Good luck! Do everything you can!"

"Thank you, Ian! I will," said Marit, and she disappeared behind the door to Sabrina's suite.

Ian stood for a moment by the railing. What was that silver sparkle he had seen in the beautiful SIN's eyes? Yes, it was tears, definitely tears.

Claire was half-conscious. Kate Thornhill was trying to revive her; Ben Kamu glanced away from Claire at the radar screens.

Empty!

He looked again – yes, the radar antennae were still turning; everything seemed normal, and, yes, there, on the edge of the screen, Ben could see the *Eden of the Seas* and its US Coast guard escorts; and close to *Andromeda II*, the Chinese missile ship was clearly visible.

But the yacht, *A Flight of Fancy*, was gone.

Even the tiny speck that had been the helicopter gunship was gone too.

To the south, the ocean was empty, absolutely empty.

V and her companions had disappeared.

"Kate," said Ben, "Kate …"

CHAPTER 31 – COMMANDER IN CHIEF

In the Volpe Octopus Empire building in New York City, Shelly Nixon was swallowing a coffee – with a handful of vitamin B energy pills – and watching, bleary-eyed, and tearfully to tell the truth, a rerun of Samantha Andrews, the brave zombie girl, reporting on what it was like to be a zombie, and reporting, too, on the foul plot of the evil Puppet Master, on his plan to enslave the human race. By now the poor kid was almost certainly dead, and dead because of her – because of Shelly Nixon!

Other monitors showed replay scenes of continuing chaos in Miami, Fort Lauderdale, on the Florida Keys, and there were scattered reports of zombie sightings elsewhere – northern Florida, South Carolina, Texas; the zombies were getting organized, it seemed they were spreading – and spreading fast.

With the back of her hand – and thinking of Samantha – Shelly wiped away a tear. Damn, she thought, I look like an idiot, they'll think I'm an idiot and a sissy – they'll walk all over me ...

In her earphone a voice suddenly spoke, "Shelly, we have a call from the US Navy carrier group *Dwight D. Eisenhower*, off Virginia somewhere. They are commandeering all networks, cable, and Internet, everything ..."

"*Commandeering*? In the name of what are they commandeering? *How* can they commandeer? How *dare* they commandeer?" Shelly wiped away a tear and sharpened her voice.

"They say, in the name of the president of the United States of America," said the voice – and Shelly realized it was Nicole down in the liaison and chase-producer's office, a sharp no-nonsense kid, on short-term contract.

"What?" Shelly paused, thinking, but the president is dead. "Okay, let's switch to their feed, right away."

"Right, Shelly, right away!"

On the screen appeared an image of the aircraft group Dwight D.

Eisenhower, a dozen warships, on the sparkling sea, then the image centered on the huge aircraft carrier, the *Dwight D. Eisenhower* its towers and radar and radio antennae and rotating discs rose up. It was brilliant under the afternoon sunlight – a beautiful, almost sublime, image of military might.

"Oh, God," thought Shelly, "Can it be?"

"Ladies and gentlemen," a deep masculine voice said.

The image changed; the screen was filled with a huge American flag, undulating gently in the breeze; a moment of silence, only the sound of the flag, gently flapping. Then, the music began – "Hail to the Chief."

"Oh my God," breathed Shelly.

Now, the image was a long shot; there was an honor guard lined up on the deck of the aircraft carrier.

And, inspecting the guard, walking beside an admiral – was that Admiral Rodriguez? Yes, it was! – beside the admiral, was a tall black woman, in black jeans, military boots, black T-shirt, and wearing, a baseball cap!

"Oh, my God," breathed Shelly, "it's her, it's really her!"

"Hail to the Chief" continued.

"Oh, my God," breathed Shelly; she wiped away her tears; she spoke into a mike, "Get the General! Get Bill! Get them on deck right away, we need them on the floor right away, and get our White House person, I want her reaction. Who's following the vice president? And get what's his name who has been following the arrests of scientists and SINs! I want everybody ready to go!"

"Hail to the Chief" was still playing; and the deep voice said, "Ladies and Gentlemen," the voice paused, "the president of the United States …"

"Hail to the Chief" continued. The images of the president now zoomed in. She was shaking hands with sailors, she was talking to them, they were talking to her. She was laughing.

"Ladies and gentlemen, in a few moments, the president of the United States … will speak to the nation."

"Hail to the Chief" continued. Now the sailors were crowding around the president; now they were throwing their hats in the air; now there were cheers.

"Ladies and gentlemen, in a few moments …"

The president, waving, and even blowing a few kisses walked away from the sailors and then, there she was, suddenly, in front of the flag.

You could hear the giant flag, the Star and Stripes, gently undulating in the breeze, the light wind, the sunlight, the ocean, the great steel might of the ship: everything was tangible in the image.

The president stepped to a podium that suddenly appeared next to her in front of the flag. She looked directly at the camera. The camera zoomed in for a close-up.

The music ended with a flourish.

"Hello," the president said, rather gravely, the sun gleaming on her skin, and then she flashed her widest smile, "Hello America, and hello my fellow Americans! Well, for one thing, I'm alive. For another, I am well. And for a third – I've had a haircut," she lifted off the baseball cap, put it down, and ran her hand over her skull, "I was in contact with the zombie virus, I was lucky. Unlike so many others, I survived – and, to be decontaminated, to be sure none of the virus was sticking to my skin, I had to have a shave – a close shave!" she smiled, paused, and then changed her expression to one of grim warlike determination, "The United States has been subjected to – is now being subjected to – at this very moment – a massive terrorist attack. This attack is unprecedented in its scale and method. This attack is directed against not only us, not only against the United States of America, but against every nation on earth and against all of humanity. From this moment, the battle is engaged; and we, the American people, we, the citizens of earth, will win!" She paused. "In a few moments I will be returning to Washington to resume my work as president – and as commander in chief. In the coming days, I will ask for your help, your patience, and your understanding. Now, in this decisive moment, in this moment of maximum peril, I ask for your prayers. As I said, we are in the midst of a tremendous battle; it will not be easy; it may not be short; but – do not doubt this – do not doubt this for an instant – we will win. Thank you, God bless you, all of you; and God bless America!"

The president saluted and stood to attention.

The "Star Spangled Banner" echoed across the decks of the *Dwight D. Eisenhower*.

The huge Stars and Stripes undulated slowly in the breeze.

"Okay," said Sally Nixon, "Let's get Bill and the General to give us their take on the President's return and give me that line up of reports from the field. And try again to get Sam and Charlie! Work, people, work!"

Out in the desert, where she had just landed and where she was being led, blind-folded, hooded, in a chain gang of 50 other high-profile prisoners, and with ankle chains and handcuffs, shuffling along, barefoot, in the dust, and hardly able to breathe because of the stifling air under the hood, gluey sweat coating her face, and dribbling down her chin and throat to her chest, also hot in the bright orange prisoner's uniform, sweltering hot, boiling hot, and wanting desperately to pee, Sonia Davies, the president's National Security Advisor, heard a female guard whisper, "Take heart, honey, your trials may be coming to an end, the president is back. Don't answer me! Don't say anything, the super is watching!"

To judge by the voice, it was the same guard who, putting on the blind-fold and hood, and attaching the chains, had glanced around and whispered, "This ain't gonna last, Ms. Davies, this is crazy, and it ain't gonna last. So, keep your faith, honey, you keep your faith!"

Sonia didn't say anything. It was too good to be true: the president back! She shuffled along, feeling the tug from the chains of the person in front of her – she had no idea who it was – pulling on her, and feeling the pressure of the person pushing behind her – she had no idea who he or she was either. We're anonymous, she thought, we're anonymous, unsexed, and dehuman-ized and with no voice and no identity, no gaze and no presence; we're mute, blind, and shackled, we've become things, not people, not even animals.

"Keep moving! Keep moving!"

The line of prisoners, heads bowed and hooded, snaked along in a dusty valley. The temperature was about 100 degrees; the humidity was high and rising; it was sweltering. Virtually the only sound was the clinking of chains and the muted shuffling of feet. They were heading towards a site where a large pit had been dug just two hours before by two small bulldozers subcon-tracted by Black Murk Security.

"Keep moving! Keep moving!

Sonia thought; should I just pee? Should I just let the pee run down my leg? Oh, God, I want to, I so much want to! But, no, I'm going to resist – resist for just a bit longer. When you give up, and you lose your dignity, your ene-mies have won.

"Keep moving! Keep moving!"

"The Star-Spangled Banner" was still echoing in the room, one hundred feet below the White House.

The vice president sat very still. He said nothing. Every person at the big table had turned to look at him. The air-conditioners hummed. The screens showed various scenes – the *Dwight D. Eisenhower* seen from a distance, the giant American flag slowly, powerfully, peacefully, waving in the breeze; one screen showed a freeze image of the president smiling; another screen showed a ten-minute-old feed – taken from a Coast Guard helicopter – of the *Eden of the Seas*, escorted by several US coast guard ships, sailing in the late afternoon sunlight, looking, in spite of its crumpled bow, like the miracle of engineering that it was; some screens were empty, either black or showing just static and snow – since connections to southern Florida were still down and many communications satellites had ceased to function or had been rendered blind by the electromagnetic storms that were engulfing south Florida and part of the Caribbean.

The vice president glanced around the table. That evil smart-ass Indian woman, the medical liaison expert, Sana Kapoor, gold earrings dangling, crisp jacket shining, full lips impeccably glossed, was looking straight at the vice president with her large dark eyes, expressionless, and twirling her gold-plated Mont Blanc pen.

Fred Hansen, Kapoor's sycophantic egghead ally, was doodling something on a piece of paper and studiously avoiding looking at the vice president.

The Chairman of the Joint Chiefs was looking at the vice president anxiously, wondering if the vice president would be able to help save the Chairman's ass, or whether it would be best to jettison any pretense of allegiance to the vice president as quickly as possible, jump off the sinking vice presidential ship, like a rat, and hope that the president …

"Wonderful news," the vice president finally said, "wonderful news and the Lord be praised for He has in His infinite wisdom and goodness brought our dear, dear president back to us. But for now …"

He was wondering if he should rescind the secret orders he had sent out to execute a certain number of the president's key supporters, people like that testy stubborn National Security Advisor, Sonia Davies, and several hundred other obnoxious folk who stood in the way of the Lord's work. Why, they were being walked to the execution site right now, not knowing it, of course, not knowing they were about to die, for ignorance is bliss, even for the wicked to whom the most just of punishments – the death penalty – was about to be meted out.

Then there was another itchy little thing, of course, how much did the president know?

"For now," he said, "until the president returns to Washington, we continue as before." He smiled. With luck, enough of the good work would be accomplished and finished, a done deal – a *fait accompli,* as the evil perfidious Frogs say – before the president knew what was happening and before she could reverse course – and save all those evil misbegotten scientists and bureaucrats who would all be dead already; all their evil knowledge and science gone – poof – forever gone! And it would be far too late to bring them back. And the Lord be praised!

"Let's adjourn for a moment," said the vice president, making a sacred teepee of his long, distinguished fingers, just in front of his nose, "For a session of private prayer and contemplation."

CHAPTER 32 – RUFUS

"That damned woman has more lives than a cat," said Rufus Mudcock, watching the clip – communications had spurted into life again and just long enough for the president's speech on the *Dwight D. Eisenhower* to come through.

Rufus was still feeling queasy from the narrow escape his personal jet, Mudcock VII, had had from the wandering jungle of giant waterspouts that had suddenly blossomed in the middle of the Pacific Ocean, but somehow the crazy pilot, who sang "Singing in the Rain" while doing it, managed to wiggle and swerve and dance his way through them, and avoid sudden death for the whole crew and all the passengers, and now the sun was shining again, and the horizon looked simply like the horizon, a glowing glorious blue-white haze hanging over the ocean, and that was all, which was as it should be.

"Yes, Rufus," said Sally, "Personally, Rufus, I am glad she is back."

"I am too, Sally, I fought against her and I am known as a mean son-of-a-bitch ornery reactionary backward billionaire – and I am, in fact, as you well know, a mean son-of-a-bitch ornery reactionary backward billionaire – but I think that the vice president, charming as he is, and with a gift of the gab that can skin a cat alive, is a wacko true believer end-of-the-world madman who would take us all straight down the path to the Apocalypse."

"You've come to that conclusion, have you Rufus?"

Rufus shot his personal assistant a look. "I have, Sally."

"Good, Rufus, I approve."

Rufus had to smile at Sally. She was an impertinent wench, respectful as all get out, but then suddenly, and without warning, she'd speak her mind and be as stubborn as a mule. He respected her for it. "You may not believe it, but sometimes old dogs like me learn new tricks, Sally. Personally, I want to have no truck with the Apocalypse. I like this life and I'd appreciate sticking around for a few more years – or even decades – and continuing to be a mean son of a bitch and ornery reactionary bastard. Well, that woman, the president, she inspires confidence – she's got a solid head on her good-looking shoulders!"

"She did look good," said Sally, "I like the new haircut."

"It looks good, Sally, it does, like she's a soldier going into battle, and there is a positive glow about the lady."

"So, maybe there's hope, Rufus," said Sally, getting up to prepare a snack, "Maybe this zombie thing can be beaten back!"

"Where there's life, there's hope, Sally," Rufus watched Sally sway down the aisle. She was a good piece of womanhood, she was. He sighed, looked out at the brilliant Pacific Ocean – sparkling under the sun. It stretched away like infinity, glowing, the light of the sky and water mingling in a single brilliance. Even lust felt trivial, faced with these immensities, he thought, but, now, considering Sally, he mused, if only he were a mere forty years younger!

He looked back down at his fold-out desk and started to go over merger plans he was developing for integrating his bio-information-processing company with his new startup for secure data storage in space capsules and underground on the moon ... He tapped a pencil on the paper, looked out the window, and wondered, vaguely, if Sabrina Jacobs and Andromeda Corporation might be open to some sort of link-up deal, some joint projects in the bio-data field, there might be some profitable synergies to be found if they ...

Bill Brothers was haggard and unshaven, his tie was undone and his striped blue-and-white custom-made Savile Row shirt was soaked in sweat and hanging open; he peered at the computer screen, glanced up at the camera, where the little red light told him he was on air, and said:

"Coming just a few seconds after the president's speech, we have reports just of a huge shock wave – a sort of sonic boom – that hit several ships at sea, out in the Atlantic, just off the Florida coast; but there is no direct news from southern Florida itself, which seems to be covered by a sort of electro-magnetic dome which is isolating it from the outside world; and now, we have ... what? We have what?"

"We have Charlie on line," said Shelly Nixon's voice, "He and Sam are back."

"I don't believe it!" Bill glanced up. In spite of the lights he could see Shelly's face in the control room and goddamn if tears weren't streaming down her face, or maybe it was just the reflections of the studio lights; but, no, goddamn it, Shelly was crying, the bitch was crying! He turned with a weary smile to the camera.

"Well, ladies and gentlemen, we once again have Charlie Parr and Samantha Andrews, in a Volpe Octopus Net exclusive broadcasting direct, and live, from Miami Florida. Hello, Charlie, hello Samantha …"

All communications had been down for hours, but Charlie Parr was, even if he had to admit it himself, an ingenious son-of-a-gun. He had spent at least five hours out on the terrace, next to the pool, experimenting with the small transmission disk he always had in the van.

There was an old Europe-India joint-venture satellite which, once upon a time, had carried exotic channels and which had some open receivers for rogue or random or emergency transmissions.

Maybe nobody has thought of this old antique – few people ever used it; most people thought it was dead; and, in most resource catalogues, it wasn't listed, not even as backup.

Maybe the evil genius who had shut everything down, maybe the electromagnetic whatever it was had forgotten about this one – it had an unusual orbit and …

The company or a series of companies that sent up the satellite had gone bankrupt and disappeared from history.

It took lots of tries and some very fine tuning, but then his little disk was locked on!

Bingo!

He got it.

And the satellite was still functioning!

Maybe somebody didn't notice the bills weren't being paid; or, maybe, just maybe, somebody was keeping the thing alive, paying the bills, secretly, for secret purposes. Well, whatever …! It was good news!

Sam had recorded more of her zombie thoughts and Charlie had compressed them into a very short burst of a signal which he sent up into space, and the signal was picked up, still compressed, routed to London along one retransmission line, to Montreal along another, and from there, if his luck held, it would be bounced to New York, to the Volpe World Octopus Building.

It worked!

And now, with this background check done, they could again go live.

He went into the darkened bedroom. "How you feeling, Sam?"

"Grrhhhh, good grrhhhh, Charlie, grrhhhh, the t … t … tuna sandwich was grrrh great, Charlie, grrrh, snarl, thanks."

"You're welcome, Sam!" Charlie adjusted the camera. "Are you ready to report again, Sam, I've got the connection. Just say the word and I'll get us to New York!"

"Ready," said Sam. She was still tied up in duct tape like an Egyptian mummy, but they had risked an experiment and while communications were down, Charlie had stripped away the duct tape and released Sam and she had gotten up and stretched and she had taken a shower and looked at herself in the mirror, "Grrrh, grrrh, goddamn awful," she growled, "grrrh, horrible," with slime spilling out of her mouth, "How can you stand to look at me, Charlie?"

"You are beautiful, Sam, still beautiful, always beautiful."

"True … grrhhhh … grrrh … gentleman, Charlie, grrhhhh, old-fashioned, truly gallant, Charlie, gggghhhhhh."

While Charlie worked on setting up a connection Sam had toweled herself and then dried in the sun and had coffee and sandwiches, sitting on the terrace wrapped in a large towel.

Then she had insisted that Charlie wrap her up again, since "Grrhhhh, it's not safe, Charlie, I might go grrrh wild, he's trying … the Puppet Master is trying grrrh … grrrh … all the time … grrhhhh he's trying to take over … so better taped up, Charlie, better … grrhhhh … taped up."

So dressed in protective plastic bags, Charlie had taped her up, but neatly this time, like a proper Egyptian mummy, right up to her collar bone. Her eyes glowed and she sprayed and dribbled slime but now she looked well wrapped – and very respectable.

Charlie remained careful, but he was by now pretty sure he was immune and so he wasn't as worried as before – though he kept telling himself that the most dangerous moment is when you think the danger has passed, when you let your guard down – that's precisely the moment the gods or the fates put the screws to you.

"Well, Bill," said Charlie, from off screen, with the camera trained on Samantha, "We've been holed up here watching the end come, Bill. In this building many of the occupants have become what look like potted plants, as you can see here," and Charlie fed New York with the horrific images – creatures half-human, half-vegetable, some dead rotting zombies, some dead, eviscerated humans – he had taken when he had wandered, furtively, very carefully, up and down the service stairs. "No local communications seem to be working – telephone, radio, Internet, there is nothing, absolutely nothing. There are fires down in the street. Lots of buildings are burning. And I was out an hour ago and did not see a single living person though I did see quite a few zombies who were feeding on each other or just lying on the street or sidewalk. Just as I got back, we were hit by a shock wave, Bill. It smashed lots of windows. I thought it was a bomb. But I see no sign of a bomb. And, Bill, there is a strange haze, lying off the coast here. It glows. It looks like a wall, a wall of air or water or light or something. And one thing I saw which really frightened me, Bill, was a zombie driving a car. They are mobile, now, Bill, they are mobile. But Sam's got the inside dope, so I think I'd better turn it over to Sam who is, as everybody knows, in the front line of our fight with the Puppet Master."

"Thanks, gghhhr, grrhhhh, Charlie ... Hello ... America ... this is ... grrrhhh Samantha Andrews ... the final ... battle begins ... the hole ... the gateway is open ... the Puppet ... grrhhhh. The Puppet ... grrrhhhhh the P ... P ... P ... Puppet Master ... is w ... w ... winning ... now ... cars ... planes ... trains ... buses ... breakout of ... zombie puppets ... Grrhhh ... also known as ... Dmitry puppets ... is now ... Puppet Master ... wants ... domination ... over race ... human race ... reduced to human slaves reduced to beasts ... grrrhhhhh ... slobbering ... slaves ... final battle about to begin ... but far ... far from here ... time vortex ... grrhhhh ... time vortex ..."

"What do you mean by time vortex?" said Bill Brothers.

"Grrrhhh ... shock wave ... was door ..."

"A door?"

"A door for the Goddess."

"The Goddess?"

"Yes, grrhhhh, a door ... Goddess grrhhhh and now ... now ... grrrhhh Goddess ... now ... grrrhhh now ... oh, now, oh, it's horrible, Charlie, it's horrible, oh, No, no, no, it's HORRIBLE, unbelievably HORRIBLE" and Sam screamed, "HELP, Charlie, HELP!"

"HELP, Charlie, HELP!"

"The Goddess is gone, Charlie, the Goddess is GONE!"

"HELP, Charlie, HELP!"

And a geyser of green sprayed from her mouth and her head lolled sideways, her tongue hanging out, and her green glowing eyes closed, and she went into convulsions.

Charlie rushed to Samantha and as he did so he said, "Okay, we're wrapping this for now, I'll be back to you," and he said, "Sam, hey, Sam are you okay, Sam?" and he heard in his earphone Shelly Nixon say:

"Charlie, save her! For God's sake! Save her, Charlie! Please save her," and he could hear tears in the woman's voice.

"I'll try, Shelly, I'll try," and he put the connection on "mute" and "blind" but kept it open so that if he needed help from New York he could get it – though what help they could possibly give him he didn't know – and he knelt next to Sam and heedless of his own safety he felt for her pulse and he …

Bill Brothers turned to the camera. "Samantha Andrews is facing the true heart of darkness, she is facing something beyond horror, beyond naming and beyond comprehension, and she is showing her usual extraordinary courage. We wish her well and we will be back to Samantha Andrews and Charlie Parr as soon as we possibly can, to put you folks, with Volpe Octopus news, right there in the front line of the war against terror."

While he spoke these words Bill Brothers was aware of Shelly Nixon, tears streaming down her face, expressionless, stony-faced, muttering under her breath, a sort of prayer – a prayer for Samantha – and Bill Brothers was thinking that, yes, maybe Samantha was dead, was dying, and he was thinking that maybe, in the end, that would be the best result – she would be a heroine, she would be gone, she would be commemorated, mainly by him, and eulogized, while …

While, on the other hand, if Samantha survived, but possibly maimed mentally and physically, possibly having lost her beauty, then he, Bill Brothers – unless he could get out of it without losing face – would have to look after her, perhaps push her around in a wheelchair, perhaps sit with her on a park bench and watch her feed the pigeons, perhaps spoon tasteless gruel between her limp shriveled lips, into her slack mouth, gaze into her madness, into her dull and clouded eyes; she would no longer be an adornment, no be longer beautiful, with those long legs, sparkling eyes, quick wit, generous disposition, no, she would no longer be something he, Bill Brothers could rightly be proud of, but she would be a burden, a carrier of stigma, an invalid.

So perhaps it would be better if Samantha died, after all.

"We'll be right back, after this announcement from our sponsors," he said, smiling at the camera, and, when the little red light went off, he said:

"I need a fucking shower, I need fucking shave, and I need a fucking fresh shirt, will someone please hack out a bit of free time for me so I can feel like a human being!"

"Sam was talking about a goddess and a door, what did she mean?" said Shelly Nixon, half to herself.

"Who the fuck cares," said Bill Brothers.

CHAPTER 33 – BLACK MURK

South Florida – north of Miami.

"An outfit called Bio-Frontier is our next target," said Mike Collins.

"What about the president, then. Will she approve?"

"Sure, and it doesn't matter if the president is back or if she approves," said Mike, "We go ahead anyway; the president hates these bastards as much as the vice president does! We've got our orders, then, and don't you be mistaking it – we take out these evil bastards, these evil scoundrel scientists who created this zombie thing, and who want to destroy red-blooded Americans, but we'll destroy them first – all these bio-engineering fuckers, take it from me, they will go down and burn in Hell, they will, and we're the ones that are going to send them there!"

The five SUVs of the Black Murk Militia Group 234 – one arm of a private security and vigilante firm, Black Murk Inc., doing subcontract work – killing, rampaging, kidnapping, imprisoning, executing – for Orthodoxy – were one mile north of Bio-Frontier. The leader, in the lead SUV, had an old-fashioned paper and plastic map of the area. Bio-Frontier was one of the targets for the *purification* ordered by the vice president.

"Okay, we go get 'em!"

"Yeah, man, we go get 'em!"

The SUVs stormed down the empty road, all the militia guys nervously squinting out the windows on the lookout for zombies. They were terrified of the zombies, but felt it was their duty to serve America and the American people by attacking the true heart of darkness – the bio-tech companies where such monstrosities as the zombie virus were created, and hunt down the evil mad godless un-American scientists who created these atrocities. In any case, orders – with a list of targets – had come from Orthodoxy, orders signed by the vice president himself! It was now or never – take out the enemies of America!

Mike Collins decided the troops needed a bit of cheering. He shouted, and the others, through speakers, took up the refrain.

"Okay, we heard about the reptile man!"

"We heard about the Bio Creations!"

"We heard about the SINs!"

"And now, boys, we got the zombies!"

"Are we afraid? No!"

"Are they gonna stop us? No!"

"Death to all!"

"Death to all!"

They were armed with flamethrowers, with grenades, with pistols, with precision rifles and with bazookas to blast in the doors of company offices.

"Flame-throwers work against hybrids," said Mike Collins.

"Flame-throwers work against almost anything," murmured Cletus Buck Kettle; he half closed his eyes, hoping not to get seasick, the SUVs were skidding around a corner, up on two wheels, and then the column of SUVs smashed down, once again on four wheels, and raced down a narrow road in a disused and half-abandoned industrial park, wheels spitting up pebbles and bits of broken asphalt, and Cletus Buck Kettle, holding tight to the hand rest, his heart pumping, was fired up, eager to get into action, sweat sticking to his back, breathless with excitement. The moment before you went into a fight was to Cletus's mind like just before sex, eager anticipation mixed with terror, and he was thinking back on adventures of the past few hours, since the vice president had released all constraints, unshackled himself, as he put it, and unleashed the Black Murk vigilante forces hired by the Ministry of Orthodoxy. Last night was a fun riot! They had smashed into a small bio-technology firm located north of Miami, arrested all the night shift people there – three guys and five women – and sent them in chains for re-education to one of Orthodoxy's holding camps – then they had smashed all the computers, sabotaged all the cloud archives, and torched the building, which went up with a whoosh and sent lovely bits of burning wood and stucco and paper fluttering up into the night sky. They beat up one of the women; she said she had to get back to her family, she was not going to go to a re-education camp – fuck her! So they gave her a lesson she'd never forget, rearranging her face for her, so she'd be reminded how stupid and stubborn and unruly she had been every time she looked in the mirror for the rest of her life, if she had a rest of her life, which she probably wouldn't, the bitch! The thought made Cletus grin, and his grin was one of his attractive features, that big gap between his two front teeth seemed to drive some women, the right kind of full-bodied women Cletus really took a cotton to, crazy, really crazy.

They had attacked a vegetarian restaurant that was hiring SINs – women SINs, waitresses, and two female cook SINs – and they had killed the SINs – torching them, burning them alive, which was real fun, seeing them scream and burn up and melt and disintegrate, except for the bones, which looked like human skeletons and human bones, thinking of the suffering, but it wasn't of course real suffering because they were not true-blooded full citizens, not real American god-fearing folk or real folk or anything like that, I mean, they were just like pigs you roast or chickens you fry or lambs whose necks you slit, without suffering or feeling, the whole lot of them, because animals don't have souls as everyone knows and so are incapable of suffering and if they suffer who gives a shit anyway, eh, and the preacher had confirmed, once when Cletus asked him about it, that, soul-wise, machines like those SIN gals had no souls, no rights, and didn't suffer at all if you burned them alive, or they deserved it, if they did suffer, since they were instruments of the Devil, really, of the Anti-Christ. The team executed the two owners of the restaurant because it turned out they couldn't produce papers proving they were legal, besides, they were two Hispanic dykes and really didn't or shouldn't have any rights here in God's own country. Good-looking, though, particularly the young one, and Cletus wouldn't have minded having a prolonged interrogation session or two with her – like he'd done in one of those god-forsaken Arab countries – before putting the gun in her mouth and pulling the trigger, it took a real man to do that, by the way, what with all the blood and gore and the look in the woman's eyes, it was a real intimate thing, more intimate than most people get with their women, but in this case there was no time to savor the moment, because Collins said not to fuck around, that, Bejeus, Cletus, there was work to do, and he said, looking at Cletus with that grin he had – "Hey, Buddy, I know what you're thinking, but we don't have time" – and insisting, that they couldn't fuck around with those two bitches, so that was that – bang, bang, splat, splat, and blood and bone and gray matter splashed all over the frigging refrigerator that contained the soft drinks, stuff dribbling down like the sort of painting you could see in some museums the schoolmarm insisted on taking you to when you were a kid and then they were out of there, but Cletus did take one of those kids' drawings that were pinned up on the wall in the restaurant since it was real cute and showed the big sun with all its rays and mommy and daddy grinning, little stick people, out in front of the house which had six windows and a peaked roof – talented little gaffer, whoever drew it.

"Okay, ten minutes and we're at Bio-Frontier."

Buzzers began to buzz, beep, beep, beep, beep, and red lights were flashing.

"What's going on, Virginia?" Jake had just woken up and was rubbing his eyes and sitting on a bench. He yawned.

"I don't know, Jake, let's ask." Virginia put aside the book she had been reading – a detective novel, security chief Gus Wallach had lent her.

A mechanical voice began to repeat, "Security breach north sector, security breach north sector, security breach …"

Alex Wolf peeked in at the door, "It's the Orthodoxy militia, they've cut through the barrier at the edge of the industrial park and they are coming at us, towards the north side of the building. We have to stop them. If they get in here they will destroy everything and we'll lose the vaccine we have been making from your material, Virginia."

"The Orthodox militia, why in the world …?"

"The vice president put out a list of companies that are the work of the Devil and Bio-Frontier is on the list, so …"

"That man is the most complete evil stinking hypocritical idiot," Virginia put her arm around Jake. "What should we do?"

A huge crack of thunder echoed through the building.

Rain began to pour down, hammering the skylights.

"Where did that come from? The sky was clear a minute ago!"

Alex glanced at the sheets of rain. "I think the magnetic and gravitational anomalies are generating storms. The air pressure is changing and …"

Outside in the yard, beyond the single grilled window, the rain was pouring down, thicker rain it looked like than any rain Virginia had ever seen, and, shooting in exotic and isolated locations, she had seen plenty of massive tropical downpours.

Virginia got up, and stared through the window. The yard had turned to mud, rain splashing down like giant bullets. Yes, it was more than a tropical downpour. It was a Biblical deluge.

"Come on!" smiled M-J, peeking in at them, "We're off to war, apparently! Not only zombies, but also the militia – it seems everybody's out to get us!" She smiled again, a big mischievous grin, waved, and disappeared.

Virginia watched the little defense army stream past. There were the two young twins, Chinese acrobats, Fei and Fang, and the two Secret Service guys, and Helen and Alex and Renée, the President's Press Secretary, and a couple of lab technicians, all led by Gus Wallach and Black Dragon.

"We'd better get you to the other building," said Alex, "It has a deep bunker. You'll be protected there."

"I want to fight too, I hate those idiots," said Virginia.

"Yeah, let's fight," said Jake.

"No, you two have to get to the bunker," said Alex, "You are too valuable. You two are the only source for the vaccine."

"Militia," said Black Dragon, Secret Service Officer Sarah James, her gold snake eyes staring at the video screens, "Militia!"

"Right," said Gus Wallach, "five vehicles, entry gate six. They are faster than the zombies – the zombie army is still off a distance, that's what my intel says anyway."

Sarah looked around the table, "We have to assume the militia have bazookas, flame-throwers, grenades, some paralyzing gas, truncheons, straight razors, the usual shit those guys tote around," she paused, "These guys are cowboys, but they are fucking dangerous!"

"We have to stop them before they get into Bio-Frontier. They could disrupt the whole production process," said Alex, "and without a vaccine …"

"Without a vaccine, everybody is kaput," said Sarah, "Right?"

"Right," said Alex.

"Okay," said Gus. "The best place to stop them is between warehouse H and warehouse G," he pointed to a map of the industrial zone.

"Good," said Sarah, "Good – here, here, and here."

"Yes, those are the best points – good for an ambush. The buttresses on the buildings provide shelter for our people."

"Perfect," said Sarah, thinking Gus was good, no-nonsense, and he knew the ground, "Hybrids to the front line – everybody else is more vulnerable. M-J can you use a sniper rifle?"

"Gosh, I don't know."

"Well, you can try – I want you to take out the leaders, if and as soon as they step out of their armored cars. They have a special antenna sticking out of their battle vests, over the left shoulder, looks like it has a silly little knob on top, goes up about ten centimeters."

"Silly little knob on antenna, up about ten centimeters, over left shoulder," said M-J, and she took the high-tech sniper rifle Gus handed to her, unfolded it, straightened it, locked it, checked the sights, checked the loading mechanism, weighed it for balance. "Gosh!" She was startled. She absolutely knew how to handle the weapon – the movements were familiar – even automatic – and she didn't know how she knew how to do it or where and when she had learned how to do it.

"Part of being a SIN," said Sarah James, who had read M-J's mind and caught the perplexity. "You've had abilities programmed in that you're not aware of until you need to use them. Don't worry kid, it's okay: I somehow figured you'd know how to do this – and you are faster on your feet than most humans, even the best trained, so, if you don't mind, I'd like you to do this, be our snipper – eliminate their leaders."

"Yes, sir; no problem; thank you sir," said M-J, feeling that Sarah was being very kind; it gave M-J an uneasy eerie feeling, being the repository of talents and capabilities she didn't know she had and had no memory of acquiring.

"M-J, if you can disable or kill the leaders," Gus said, stroking his moustache, "the teams will be much less effective – these guys depend on the leaders' brains. As individuals, most of them are sheep."

"Right, as Gus says, that's key, cut off the leadership," said Sarah, "Okay, good, okay, now, I want the hybrids – that's me, Alex, Ed Ross, and Helen, to jump on the side of these armored SUVs, and take out the drivers. Now, we take out vehicles one and two – and the fifth vehicle. That will mean the other vehicles are blocked between the disabled vehicles. Now, if you can avoid killing the driver, him or her, so much the better, if not, kill them, don't hesitate. Too much is riding on this for hesitation and scruples."

"How do we do this?" said Helen; she knew she was a deadly predator, but she really hadn't practiced being a deadly predator, since she was a lawyer, and peaceful by inclination and all, and Alex hadn't had that much practice killing people either, whereas Sarah and Ed Ross were professionals.

"Okay, here's how," said Sarah, "On these vehicles the driver's door has an extra armored layer, it sticks out, you can grip it on the edge, and if you pull it off, the whole door comes because it's welded into the door's skeleton."

"Okay, right," said Helen, doubtfully.

"Grab the drivers and toss them out; and then pull off the steering wheel and the gears. We want to immobilize these guys, and we don't want them to get out in the open where they can use their flame-throwers."

"Then you could toss in tear-gas grenades," said Gus, "If this happens real fast, the guys inside the SUVs won't have their masks on yet – it'll keep them busy, they may panic and bail out without their flame-throwers and the other heavy stuff."

"Right, very good idea, Gus," said Sarah, "excellent idea."

"When they tumble out, we take them down," said Gus, "or get them to surrender."

"Ed, you deal with the two middle cars," said Sarah. "Allison and Steve, you hold down the control room with the monitors – you guys can tell me exactly where the dangers are and what you see."

"Right, good," said Steve; Allison nodded.

"Aaloka will stay with you in the control room. She will be safest there; and she will be in charge of keeping your coffee cups full and supplying you with donuts if for some strange reason you want donuts. Everything is in the control room. It will keep her busy and happy."

"Right!"

"The twins, Fang and Fei, you stand by with Steve and Allison and Aaloka; if our communications break down, then you can be runners, coming to me – I should be about here." She pointed to the map of the industrial park, "And you bring me the news. Okay!?

"Okay," said Fang.

"Hokey-dokey," said Fei. Finally, some action – things had been getting dull, cooking spaghetti and making sandwiches in the kitchen with M-J, though M-J was, of course, adorable and witty, and a super cook and the sandwiches were more than yummy.

Torrential rain poured down as the five Black Murk SUVs came careening around the corner, spitting up water and mud in their wake, and Mike Collins was saying, "Boys, this will be a walkover, this will be like eating our cake and having it too, and when we're finished here we'll … we'll … we'll … What the fuck!"

Suddenly, it had turned into night – totally dark – in one second, like somebody had turned off the lights, the outside lights of the warehouses flicked on; then it was light again, for an instant, a glimpse of blue sky, then it was darkest night again, darkest night and thunder, lightning, and the rain still pouring down.

"Now what in all blazes is that?" said Mike Collins.

Cletus was staring at the sudden darkness and at the rain and was about to say something – he didn't yet know what – when …

… when, suddenly, in a flash, from the buildings at the side of the road, a creature, what the fuck was it, Cletus had no idea, it came jumping down, maybe from the roof of the warehouse, maybe from behind one of the buttresses on the buildings, this thing, this monster, grabbed the driver's door – Cletus saw the shadow, the silhouette of the thing, like clinging to the door, but, before he could do anything, the thing had yanked the door off its hinges and the door went flying and Hank Stubbs, the driver, was yanked out, and thrown away like he was a paper doll, yeah, it was fucking unbelievable, Cletus saw Hank, flying through the air, smash against a warehouse wall, spread-eagled under a wall lamp, and then fall away, and the creature – fuck, it looked like a reptile woman – all glossy and black with gold eyes – tossed something into the SUV, a fucking grenade, and it bounced against the roof, and Cletus, who was trying to swing his submachine gun, put up his arm, instinctively, to shield himself, and the grenade exploded, and the SUV filled with gas, and Mike Collins was shouting, "Get out, get out," and Cletus, already half-blinded, his eyes full of tears behind his Polaroids, threw himself out of the SUV, the back doors now flung wide open, Dwayne Cooper jumping too, swearing, "Fuck! Fuck this!" and with the SUV still hurdling ahead, but swaying all over the goddamn place, rattling back and forth, and spinning now sideways, and Cletus bounced and rolled on the ground, watching the SUV spin away, smash against a wall and, WHAM, explode, and as he got up, crouching, ready to open fire, and running at the same time, he saw Mike Collins, silhouetted by one of the streetlamps, his vest and antenna making clear silhouette, Collins shouting, "Go round them, Cletus, go around the building," and the same instant Cletus saw a guy with a sniper rifle, a guy in worker's overalls and a baseball cap, no, it was a woman, something told him it was a woman, and she was taking aim, and wham, Mike Collins went down, just crumpled up, legs shot out from under him, and Cletus turned his submachine gun towards the sniper, "I'll get you, you fucking bitch," but when he completed the swing, she'd already ducked behind a pile of bricks, and between him and her one of the SUVs was swirling around in circles, it seemed, and smashed into a wall, and turned over on its side, exploded, and roared into flame, and Cletus realized all the SUVs had been hit the same way. Oh God, Cletus thought, and he saw the same woman, the woman in the fucking overalls, taking aim at Rosco Fernandez, now through a cloud of smoke and flame and in that instant Rosco was already down – hit by that fucking sharp-shooting woman – before Cletus could do anything about it – and all the SUVs were turned over on their sides, or smashed into walls, or stopped dead in their tracks, smoking, on fire, or filled with teargas, and the guys, God, the guys were wandering around like they were stoned, like they were in shock, and these creatures, these creatures, man, they were like snakes, they were snakes, they were reptiles – they were fucking hybrids, all glittery in scales, monsters with claws and eyes like snakes, like that famous fucking reptile man – they were taking down everybody, knocking them out, tossing them in the air, and, then there were others, working with the fucking reptiles, like the woman sharpshooter, he saw another enemy guy take aim, and, wham, another of our guys bit the dust, and another woman, another fucking women, and she took down Eddie Phillips, his face just exploded, Christ, "This is bad shit man," he muttered and he saw Ray Chester and Will Mendoza, still standing, looking dazed, looking like they'd had the shit kicked out of them, and he shouted, "Down here!" He beckoned, they followed, and they ran down a narrow side alley and Cletus thought maybe if he and the two guys could get in behind the Bio-Frontier building – down at the end of the fucking service road – he and Ray and Will could still blow the goddamn place up, and kill them some hybrids and SINs and evil fucking scientists while they were at it. They ran down the side of the building, and, Yeah, he spotted it, there was what looked like a weak point, a mental link fence and an outlying structure, and Cletus thought, we can jump up over that wall, get on top of that building and then maybe get access through the back way.

Just at that instant another huge bolt of lightning split open the sky, and landed, sizzling and cracking only a few hundred feet away, the darkness – the night – opened for a split second – and above them was blue sky – then the gap closed, again it was night. The rain poured down, doubly ferocious.

"What the hell is this?" Cletus turned to Ray and Will.

"I don't know, man! I ain't never seen shit like this!" Ray's eyes were as bright as fucking lanterns. "Not in my whole fucking life!"

"Don't look at me! I ain't no weatherman," said Will, rain streaming down his face, eyes blinking, made him almost look like he was crying.

"Okay," Cletus gave them both his most commanding stare, "day or night, rain or no rain, we go!"

Lightning flashed; it turned dark; rain poured down.

"Hey, Sarah," said Steve Clark, speaking into her earphone from the Bio-Frontier security room, "There's a second column of Black Murk SUVs on its way – racing to reinforce the other. About four clicks away."

"Damn," said Sarah James, blinking against the rain that, pouring down over her head, was flooding down, it was a Niagara-like waterfall; she blinked her reptile eyes, and wondered what the hell had happened to the weather; it was like somebody switched off the sun and they were in suddenly thurst into the deepest of nights. She had just thrown one Black Murk mercenary against the wall of a warehouse; his body fell, crumpled, to the ground; she figured he was out for an hour or two. She had just also torn a flame-thrower away from another Black Murk man, a burly overweight guy with a big belly and shaved head, and one brass earring, whom she now was holding down with one foot-claw; he was pinned down, rain pouring over him; and looking up at her with terrified eyes. "This will be messy," she said, "If there are more of them, it will be messy."

"Here's something that may help," said Steve Clark, "I'm patching through Colonel Jefferson Siebert."

"Okay," said Sarah, doubtful, "Colonel Jefferson Siebert?"

Then, in her earphone, she heard, "Agent James this is Colonel Siebert, the president has requested we back you up; we are entering the industrial park, in front of us we see a moving column of what look like Militia Black Murk SUVs. Are they friendlies?"

"No, Colonel Siebert, they are not friendlies."

"Do you want us to help?"

"Yes, Colonel, we need to stop them getting near Bio-Frontier."

"Right, we'll come up behind them. I'm going to send Freddy to keep them busy until we can dive into this little fight – it'll take us about three minutes."

"Freddy?"

"He's our hybrid, the reptile man, on our side now, for the moment at least."

"Okay, good, send Freddy."

"He's metal-gray, you can't miss him."

"Thanks, Colonel," said Sarah, "I'm pure black with a red snout; you can't miss me either."

"Roger that, Agent James," said Colonel Siebert; Sarah could have sworn there was a smile in his voice.

She picked up the Black Murk man, held him out at arm's length, and said, "Sorry, buddy," punched him out, and tossed him twenty yards where he fell against trunk of a tree, and rolled up into a plump fetus-like ball.

She looked around. There weren't many enemies left. Alex had tossed three guys her way, his gold scales shining in the lamplight that had come on automatically now that night seemed to have descended, must be just thick clouds, thought Sarah, and she noticed that Helen, all silver and reptilian in the night glow, had done pretty well too – she was just finishing off the guys who were cowering in one of the overturned SUVs.

M-J came out from behind some oil drums. "All leaders with funny little knobby antennae down, sir," she said, and saluted Sarah.

"M-J, you are my favorite SIN," said Sarah, "A SIN truly after my own heart."

"Thank you, sir, I like you too, sir," said M-J.

Sarah gave the SIN a friendly reptilian grin and put one of her claws on M-J's shoulder, "It's not over, M-J, more militia are coming, but this time we have help." She explained about Colonel Siebert.

"Goddamn rain!" It was like he was caught in an old black-and-white movie, whipped up and transformed into two dimensions, imprisoned in antique celluloid. Cletus didn't like it at all. It was dark as Hades. He climbed up the service ladder; it took him to the roof of the outer building, a sort of annex to the main building of Bio-Frontier. He signaled to Ray and Will to climb over the wall and get into the yard that separated the main building of Bio-Frontier from this armored-looking side building, which, he figured, probably contained high-security storage and maybe a safe-room. He could cover Ray and Will from the roof. And they could force their way into the main Bio-Frontier building. The way looked clear. But the goddamn rain and the goddamn night made it difficult to see.

Lightning flashed, not far away this time. The thunder rolled in like a tidal wave. It slammed into him like a punch in the gut. It rippled over the buildings, shaking everything – walls, fences, window; every damned thing trembled and shook.

It was like deep night – maybe two o'clock in the morning – with the rain pouring down and lightning flashing. Cletus looked down. It was fucking hard to see your hand in front of your face, the rain streaming down like it was and then –What the fuck! There, in the yard below him he suddenly realized was somebody – some bald asshole with a crest of hair who worked with Bio-Frontier obviously – the enemy!

Whoever it was, the bald guy with the crest was with a kid, with a boy, and so Cletus decided he was going to take out this Bio-Frontier punk Iroquois motherfucker, and he would take him out fast, no questions asked, no fucking questions asked: your fucking Iroquois hair-do is not going to save your ass, buster, you fucker, Cletus swore, no fucking way.

Virginia and Jake were hurrying across the space between the two buildings, towards what Alex had described as the "bunker."

"Okay, this looks good," Virginia started to unlock the door, and said, "Okay, Jake, my man, this is our bunker and we shall hold out here until we are called back –"

Then she spotted them: two dark figures, coming at her – they were militia men, they had slithered along the side of the building – just outside the range of the old overhead light bulbs whose feeble light was no match for the sudden torrent of rain and creepy darkness – it seemed like it was past midnight – and they were dressed in black and had knives and truncheons.

"Oh, oh, Jake, maybe we had better go back, beat a tactical retreat."

At that instant, as they stood in the door way, a militiaman they hadn't spotted dropped straight down from above, and slammed into Virginia, taking her down with him, and the two of them splashed down into the mud – wham!

Virginia turned over just as the guy was about to plunge a knife into her chest and her green phosphorous eyes glared at him, lighting up his face as if he had been exposed to a splash of phosphorous.

The militiaman – Cletus Buck Kettle – his face running with water – stared in horror – she was a fucking *she* with an Iroquois haircut and she was a fucking zombie with big glowing green bug eyes and she was going to turn him, Cletus fucking Buck Kettle, into a fucking zombie, Jesus Christ Almighty – and he hesitated, still holding the knife high over his head, and he hesitated just long enough for Virginia to slam his arm – wham!

The knife dropped, plop, straight down, into the mud. Cletus screamed, "This one's a fucking zombie!"

Virginia puckered up and spat a fat spool of glowing green goo straight into the man's eyes.

"Oh, my God, the freak has killed me, the zombie has killed me!" Cletus Buck Kettle rolled off Virginia and splashed down into the mud.

"Serves you right," said Virginia.

Cletus tried to stand up but couldn't; he was hysterical, and half-blinded by zombie goo and pouring rain. Screaming, he staggered away, fell on to all fours, crawling, and hollering, "The zombie has killed me!"

Virginia grabbed the knife he had dropped, leaped to her feet, and turned towards the other militia men. They stood there uncertain, hesitating, with Cletus down on the ground screaming. The other two guys didn't know what the hell to do, but Ray Chester made a quick dash and grabbed the kid – a hostage! The kid probably belonged to the zombie, he figured, she probably wanted to eat him or something, maybe cook him up in broth, or maybe just eat him raw, yeah, zombies probably ate raw.

Virginia turned towards him; her eyes were glowing phosphorescent green, flashing green fire.

Ray held a knife to Jake's throat. "I've got the kid, zombie, I've got the kid."

Virginia didn't even answer.

She leaped on Cletus.

He was still crawling, still screaming, "No, no, zombie, don't touch me, don't fucking touch me!"

She pinned him down, rolled him over, and as they rolled in the thick splashing mud, Cletus struggled, terrified, rolling away, screaming, "The zombie has fucking killed me!"

His pistol was half out of its holster. Virginia grabbed it, spun herself up in a double roll over, so she ended up, once again, on top of the Cletus.

She pushed the muzzle of the automatic between his eyes – thinking I'm damned glad I did my own stunts in *Dank City* – and she said very loudly, "I will fucking well shoot you unless your friend gives the kid back to me," and Cletus, staring at her green eyes, terrified, utterly hysterical, screamed, "You're a zombie, you are one of them."

"Fucking right I am one of them," Virginia shouted, "You know that already, and what I really like to do is to eat you guys alive and change you into pet zombies that I'll keep in my little zombie zoo."

Her bulging glowing green eyes stared down at him and she pressed the muzzle of the pistol tighter and she still kept an eye on the other two guys and was ready to swing the gun and shoot Ray Chester between the eyes if he showed the slightest indication that he was going to harm Jake.

Virginia was a crack shot.

The hours she had spent on the shooting range – preparing for *Naked in the Crypts of Rome* had honed her natural skill – quick reflexes and a keen eye.

The militia guy, boy, he had an evil smile, narrowed his eyes and said, "Fuck you, zombie! I'm going to kill the kid, anyway."

Virginia swung the pistol and shot Ray Chester between the eyes, and he fell backwards, his knife falling, leaving Jake standing there, his face as white as a terrified ghost, and the rain pounding down, plastering his black hair to his head, and, in the same breath, Virginia shot Will Mendoza, just above the bridge of the nose, and swung the pistol back to Cletus, pressed it between his eyes, and she said, "Now, I'm sorry, but unless you get the fuck out of here right now, I'll kill you too, and I don't like killing."

"Don't, zombie lady, don't shoot, please" Cletus said.

Virginia sprang off him. She looked down at the guy, pathetic and terrified. "Don't shoot, lady," he sobbed, "please don't shoot!"

"Lie down on your belly in the mud."

Cletus Buck Kettle did as he was told.

"Give me your belt."

Cletus did, struggling blindly to pull it through the loops in his pants, his face still down in the muddy water.

Virginia grabbed the belt, and looking around for other Black Murk men, she said, "Take off your clothes."

"What?" It was like a squeaky muffled sob from the mud.

"Take off your clothes, everything!"

Cletus did it, pulling off his pants, and hesitating at his underpants – what was she fucking going to do, spank him? She said, "Them too!" And he struggled out of his underpants, arching up his ass, so he could slip out of them.

When the Cletus Buck Kettle was stark naked, white and pathetic as a human worm, Virginia growled, "Now, run for it, get out of here!"

Watching Cletus go, climbing up over the fence, and down the other side, and then off into the rain and darkness, and scanning for other militiamen, Virginia went over to Jake and knelt in front of him.

Jake said, "You shot those guys, you shot them dead."

"Yes, I'm sorry."

"They're dead. They really are dead."

"Yes, I'm sure they are. Let's see, just to be sure," Virginia knelt next to the first militiaman and felt his pulse. She closed his eyes. She did the same for the second – no pulse, and so, she gazed for a second at his eyes, wide open toward the night, and running with rain that seemed like tears and she closed his eyes too. She looked up at Jake. She said, "Yes, Jake, I'm sorry, but they are both dead."

She stood up. Now I've done it, now he's seen I'm a killer, now I've lost Jake, now I've lost my only real friend. "Jake," she said, "Jake?"

His mouth was open; he was staring at her with wide eyes; he didn't say anything. It looked like he was in shock.

Now I've done it, she thought; her heart sank into darkness.

Jake threw himself into her arms.

The rain was still pouring down.

"We'd better go back and join the others," said Virginia. Green eyes glowing, she looked around, the pistol at the ready in one hand; with the other she held Jake tight. He was trembling and he was soaked. He whispered. "Never leave me, Virginia, okay, never leave me."

"I'll never leave you, Jake," she whispered back, "Never!"

Another buzzer was ringing.

"What next?" said Virginia, as the mechanical voice spoke over the loud-speakers: "Security breach, southern sector! Security breach, southern sector!"

"Well, we are in the southern sector." Virginia looked around, but she didn't see any militiamen, she didn't see any security breaches. "Okay, Jake, one more battle; we two will stick together forever, right?"

"Right," said Jake. He was still trembling. The rain had slicked down his hair; his face was crumpled up, as if he were about to burst into tears.

Virginia knelt by him and laid her hands on his shoulders. He was staring at her, looking straight into her eyes.

"Jake," she said, "Jake, Jake!" She was thinking that he was going into shock; that he was trying to find comfort looking into her eyes. Only he couldn't, he couldn't see anything or anybody in there. Nobody could look into her eyes; they were just bright green phosphorescent headlights, no pupils, no irises, no whites, just an empty surface glow. There was no way of looking into her soul, if she still had a soul, no way of seeing if she was still inside there or not. "Jake, you'll look out for me, and I'll look out for you – promise? I'm depending on you to save me if things get really bad, okay, you are my man!"

"Okay, yes, Virginia, yes, I'll save you," he said, and Virginia saw him stiffen his lip, and bite his lower lip, and his eyes focused, and he even smiled, and he said, "Yes, Virginia, I will."

"Great!" She stood up, her hands still on his shoulders, "Now, let's get back to the others."

The chain-link fence rattled. Jake and Virginia turned. A zombie – a god-damn zombie! – was suddenly there, only a few feet away. Where had he come from?

He was just above them on the chain-link fence. He had leapt to the top, and was about to leap over, right beside them. Virginia looked up and sneezed, a spectacular Roman candle sneeze, sending a spray of green goo right into the zombie's face. Automatically – part of her was still stuck in her polite, pre-monster, pre-zombie days – she said, "Sorry!"

"*Sorry!*" Jake grinned, "Virginia! *Sorry!*"

Wham! It was like the zombie had been shot. He yowled, careened off the chain-link fence, bounced in the mud, and landed face down in about four inches of watery mud where he jerked spasmodically once or twice, and then lay still.

"Is he dead?" Jake stared at the body.

Virginia peered through the fence. The body didn't move. One arm twitched. The zombie's face was under about three inches of water. "No," she said, "but he soon will be – if we don't move him, he'll drown."

"Is that good or is it bad?"

"Stay here. Keep watch! Scream if anybody gets near!" Virginia walked towards the fence, glancing back at Jake. "Are you okay?"

"Yes, I'm okay." The rain streamed down, running down inside his slicker and making a funny hollow echoing drumming sound in his ears.

Lightning flashed. Jake looked up. The clouds were like nothing he'd ever seen before. They were swirling in a vortex of light and darkness, like water swirling down a drain, it looked as if the swirling clouds were going to pick him up, sweep him up into the sky, twirling him around like a leaf, and he would get smaller and smaller – he actually saw himself up there, just a silhouette, arms and legs outstretched, a tiny cartoon stick-man version of Jake, whirling around like a piece of paper, and getting smaller and smaller and finally disappearing, so that he was gone and Virginia would think he had run away and she would never be able to find him, and she would think that he had abandoned her, abandoned and left her all alone, without even a word. He felt the whirling vortex was under his feet and in his stomach. The whole world was whirling around, and he was either going to fall down, and shrink away to nothing, and be lost in the mud and rain; or he would be swept upwards into the dark, through the clouds, through the night, towards the stars, and cease to exist, and be gone, be dead, no longer be Jake, no longer be anybody or anything, not even a tiny speck. Then he thought, No, this whirl is not going to get me. I'm here for Virginia. And she's here for me. Together forever!

Virginia had vaulted up the chain fence, over the top, and down the other side. It was like she was flying. She really didn't know what had gotten into her. She'd always been good at acrobatic stunts and at school she could do marvels on the trampoline – side flips and double flips – but for the really difficult and dangerous stuff in the movies and on TV she'd always had a double or a stuntwoman – or even a stuntman – the insurance companies and completion guarantee companies and the director insisted, since if Virginia were injured or killed, it would cost a huge amount of money and delay production – or sometimes they'd faked the difficult stuff with digital effects. But now it was like … well, it seemed effortless. It was scary really.

What had she become?

She strode over, splashing through the mud, looked down at the zombie, and in a spray of spatter and clayey gloop knelt by the body.

Pounded by the rain, the thick mud splashed up around her, got on her legs; her hot pants and her lime-green T-shirt, already soaked to transparency, were reduced to a mere ceramic glaze on her skin.

Carefully, Virginia turned the zombie over. His eyes were closed. His face was pale, unshaven, and puffy. Half his hair had fallen away.

"Wake up," she slapped his face, gently at first, then hard.

The zombie's eyes fluttered open. His eyes were bloodshot, gray, and had only a trace of green glow at the edges.

"Wake up. Can you hear me?"

His eyes went wide in terror. "What the fuck! Help! You're one of them!" He flailed weakly, trying to wiggle back through the mud, to escape from the creature kneeling over him.

"I'm one of what?" Virginia said, though she knew full well what he meant and she could imagine, looking into his terrorized eyes – eyes which, now, seemed fully human – what he was seeing: A zombie she-devil, her eyes glowing in the dark, hairless and glowing green, and just as she thought this, another flash of lightning lit up and sculpted her satin-green, hairless face, her skull, with the stiff crest of ghostly platinum-white hair in the middle, the glowing green pulsating light of her body. Boy, I'll bet I look like Satan himself, she thought and the thought made her smile, and some green goo dribbled from the corner of her mouth. I must remember, she thought, to keep my mouth shut.

"Don't bite, God, please, don't bite, don't bite me!"

"Can you get up?"

"Virginia!" Jake bellowed, "Virginia!"

"Get up? Why get up? What are you going to do?"

Virginia glanced back towards Jake. Zombies were climbing over the far side of the chain-link enclosure

"Virginia! They're coming!"

Two of the zombies were moving more rapidly than the others. They were headed straight for Jake – in a couple of seconds they would have him!

"So long," Virginia said to the guy who had been a zombie and who now just seemed to be a terrorized human being. "Get up and hide somewhere. It's dangerous out here!"

"What?" he shouted; his voice was stronger now.

Virginia vaulted back over the chain mail fence and splashed through the mud and rain. "Come on, let's go, Jake, let's go."

"Yeah," he said, shivering. "Let's go."

They ran towards the entrance to the main Bio-Frontier building and Virginia shoved Jake in the door, and then she paused, staring at the two zombies as they came shambling towards her.

Virginia sneezed, spraying out green goo. She looked at it, splayed like a web over her outstretched hand and fingers, thinking: Yuk – how gross! She turned to Jake. "Jake, I'm going to try something." She wiped her mouth, and concentrated: *I think I can, I think I can, I think I can …*

"What? What are you going to try?" Jake stood in the door, eyes wide, mouth open, under the lights, lit up like he was in a picture frame.

"I'm going to shoot those two guys down."

"Cool," said Jake; he was trembling watching the two monsters – one was a woman, the other was a man. They stumbled forward, getting closer and closer: How was she going to shoot them? What was she going to use? The militia man's pistol she still had in her hand?

Virginia had one hand on the door frame, and her legs were braced apart, in a fighting stance, so she could move real fast in either direction, spring out into the yard and attack or jump inside the door and slam it shut.

"Awesome," thought Jake. He had seen her strike that stance in the movies, when she was going to make a kung fu move or grab her sword and lop off the heads of the pirates or extra-terrestrials or leap from the mast of a pirate ship into the sea or onto the enemy galleon.

"Okay, here goes," she said. "Watch and learn, Jake, watch and learn."

Pursing her lips, churning her mouth, puffing up her cheeks, looking for a short instant like an eager monkey, or a nut-swollen chipmunk, Virginia puckered up, *I think I can, I think I can, I know I can!* And she spat a big bright round gob of green.

A big bright round gob of green …

It flew like an arrow, or, Jake thought, like a bright glowing green-yellow baseball, and it landed, smackeroo, wham, splash, boom, straight in the face of the woman zombie, and the gob exploded, spraying itself all over the zombie's face and head, coating her eyes, her forehead, and dribbling down, in a fine showering mist, like a small luminous Roman candle, onto what remained of her dress, a torn sort of white contraption – shoulders gone and front all shot to hell – that looked to Jake like those old-fashioned frilly white multi-layered wedding dresses he'd seen in the movies his mother would sometimes make him watch.

The zombie fell back howling, clawing at her eyes and at her face and then she fell down into the mud and rolled around like she was going crazy – well, she already was crazy – smashing her fists into the mud and rolling over and over and screeching, "No, no, no, ugghhhhaaaa!"

"Awesome, Virginia, awesome," said Jake. She was even better than in the movies. Her eyes glowed and her body shone green in the T-shirt and hot pants and she was bald and had that cool Mohawk hair that glowed silver-white in the lamplight. It was purely awesome!

The other zombie stumbled ahead. He was in a torn black tuxedo jacket that had a flower in the lapel, now soaked through-and-through, and he had no pants on, just ragged underpants, and no shoes but one black sock held up by a sort of suspender thing. He kept coming, stumbling a little, his arms dangling as if all the bones were broken,

"Wow!" Jake said, and turning to Virginia, "Can you do that again?"

"Sure, kiddo, just watch." Her eyes glowing, Virginia turned towards the male zombie, worked her mouth like a human cement mixer, like she was churning the goo up into a good solid mix and consistency.

She pursed her lips and let go another fiery green globule of glowing goo. Jake watched as it – Wow! – whammed right across the muddy field, through the falling rain, just like a miniature comet, leaving a faint misty trail behind, whizzing straight as an arrow, and then, bang, splat, it hit the tuxedo zombie square in the snout, and exploded in a great spray of luminous gooey mist, and the tuxedo zombie man fell back, clawing at his eyes, and howling, and he flipped over with a splash into the mud, and rolled around, thrashing, clawing, yowling, "Ghhhaahhhhaahhh!"

Both zombies were now rolling in the mud, clawing at their eyes, howling; it was gibberish, with a few human words here and there: "Help, no, God, help, I don't, No, I can't, it's over, I'm finished, this is not me, no not me …"

Virginia and Jake watched.

The two zombies became quiet and they lay as still as if they were dead, faces facing upwards but half submerged in the mud, under the pouring rain that pounded down on their faces, on their bodies, on the slime, on the pools that were spreading, and on the rattling chain of the chain-link fence.

"Okay, let's go in," said Virginia, wiping her mouth with the back of her hand.

She stepped over the threshold and closed the door and pulled the iron bar across the door and she turned to Jake, "Are you okay?"

"I'm okay, Virginia."

"Good."

"Virginia, you are really cool, just like you are in the movies."

"Jake, you were the general, I was just the artillery."

"Cool." Jake was staring up at her. He was pensive for a moment. Then he said, "Do you think they were getting married, I mean, the two zombies, they looked like …"

"Yes, maybe," Virginia frowned, "the bridal dress, and he was in a tuxedo, what remained of a tuxedo, could be … the dress was a bit elaborate for a bride's maid …" Virginia crouched down now, looking into Jake's eyes with her big blank phosphorescent eyes, and putting her hands on his shoulders. "Maybe, Jake, maybe we should …"

"Go out and maybe just see if they're okay?" Jake bit his lip.

"My thought exactly. It's crazy but …"

"Maybe we should, just see, I mean," said Jake.

"Yes, hmm, maybe," said Virginia.

"Yes, maybe," said Jake. He didn't want the zombies to die, particularly if it was their wedding day, and he was curious, too, to see what happened, and, then again, it was so much fun seeing Virginia in action, that he wanted to see her do it again. Maybe she could shoot down some more zombies. The battle had been too easily won. That, Jake thought, suddenly becoming very, very adult, was a pretty dangerous thought: If you get too proud and too sure of yourself, then maybe that is exactly when you get into deep trouble; and then he thought, boy, am I growing up fast, I think I'm really beginning to think like an adult.

"Okay, let's have a look." Virginia peered through the peep hole. She squinted. The two zombies were lit up by the outside lights. "Hmm, well, Jake, they are sitting there in the mud, and it looks like they are talking. I don't see any other zombies. I think maybe the others all ran away. But those two, it does look like they are talking."

"Maybe that means …"

"Yes, maybe that means they are no longer zombies," said Virginia.

"Elementary, my dear Watson."

Virginia looked away from the peephole and grinned at Jake. "Indeed Sherlock, indeed." She paused. "Okay, let's do this!"

"Yes."

Virginia pulled back the bar and cautiously, slowly, opened the door. She peeked outside. The two zombies were talking. Yes, it actually looked like they were talking. Virginia stepped out into the pouring rain. She looked like she was made of glowing green marble, Jake thought, as he watched the rain stream down Virginia's back under the bright security light.

"Keep close to me, Jake," she said, signaling him forward with an upraised arm as if they were two special ops soldiers in a video hologram game.

They walked over to the two zombies. And Virginia, said, "Don't be alarmed by my eyes, friends, I'm a fully rational human, or at least I think I am."

"Your eyes," said the woman, staring up at her.

"Yes, my eyes, well, I don't know how to change that, but they are what they are."

"Your eyes glow," said the woman, "Your skin glows, all green."

"She's okay," said Jake, putting his hand in Virginia's hand. "She won't hurt you."

The two zombies looked at Jake, and then, wide-eyed, the man zombie asked, "What happened? What happened to us?"

Virginia was wondering if she and Jake should trust the two zombies – well, maybe ex-zombies, or, maybe, Virginia thought, just super extra-clever disguised zombies, though somehow she doubted that such subtlety and duplicity were in the zombie repertoire, not yet at least, not until they had refined their act, but the last twenty-four hours had shown that whatever could happen, however improbable it might be, and however horrible, would probably happen, and that even things that couldn't happen, somehow had a tendency to come to pass in the most horrible way possible, with truly Old Testament Biblical ferocity. "What's the last thing you remember?"

"Ah, coming out of the church," said the man.

"Yes, coming out of the church." The woman put her hand, her muddy hand, in the man's muddy hand.

"So you did get married," said Jake. "Congratulations!"

Virginia glanced down at Jake, "Why, Jake, you are such a romantic fellow; I didn't realize!"

Jake blushed; even in the dim light and downpour, Virginia could have sworn he blushed. He squeezed her hand tighter.

"Then we saw a mob of people coming towards the church," said the man, and the woman said, "Yes, they were coming toward the church, and they looked really strange, they were all splattered with what looked like green paint!"

"Yeah," said the man, "green paint, and they walked in a really funny way, they were shambling, and stumbling, and their arms were hanging down by their sides, and they were coming from all directions, some people said it must be that zombie plague, but nobody'd taken that seriously, I mean, it was down in the south end of the city, but it didn't look so good, so we thought we'll get in the car quickly and drive away, and people were lined up throwing rice and confetti and Harry and Jack, was it Jack, darling?"

"Yes, honey, it was Jack," said the woman, "Jack Simpson, working on that car, tying on the tin cans, with Harry, Harry Turmel."

And the man said, "Yes, you're right, honey, I think it was Jack, they were kneeling down behind the car, it was a vintage Rolls-Royce highly polished and a sort of dark burgundy color, so they were kneeling down, tying on those tin cans, and all that silly stuff that people do at weddings, like the rice and the confetti and throwing things, and none of them were paying attention to the strange people with the green paint."

"No," said the woman, smiling dreamily, "And all the other people were all looking at us – just us!"

The man sniffled like he had a cold, and said, "And so, I said, I said, 'Hey, guys, there is something strange here, something's wrong,' and the minister, it was Mr. Cathcart, wasn't it, sweetie?"

"Yes," said the woman, "he's the man who married us, Mr. Reverend Philpot H. Cathcart Ph.D. in Divinity!"

"Yes, it was he," said the man, "How could I forget? And the Reverend Philpot Cathcart said 'Hey, they look like it's initiation day, maybe some college kids or something, maybe it's a film set,' Philpot said, 'Or maybe it's some sort of carnival!' But it wasn't carnival and there were no film trucks around and it's not the season for initiation, and then the creatures – they looked like zombies – they started to come faster, and some of them had glowing eyes, just like yours …"

"My name's Virginia; and this is Jake."

"Hi, Virginia," said the man, "it's still sort of spooky looking at those eyes."

"Yeah, but she's a heroine, she's … I mean she can do kung fu!"

"I'm Rob Rhys and …"

"And I'm Jean Corbett."

"She's keeping her maiden name," the man said.

"I'm keeping my maiden name."

They both looked at each other, covered in mud and half-naked and in rags and bruised as they were, they laughed and Jean leaned over and kissed Rob and Rob said, "Well, these zombies jumped on Jack. Jack was a quarter-back and he's a big guy, but fast, so he threw two of them off, and Harry Turmel started to grapple with another, and they fell down between the cars, and I was going to go to help them …"

He glanced at Jean Corbett, and she said, "And I put my arm on Rob's shoulder and I said, 'Don't go Rob, I don't like the look of this,' and by this time the crowd of zombies had caught up with the leading zombies, and they climbed and jumped over the cars, and the highly polished burgundy Rolls Royce – it was shining in the sun, oh, such a lovely perfect day – and they attacked the wedding party and then Jack and Harry came up from behind the fender and trunk of the Rolls, it was all polished, brilliant dark burgundy, sparking in the sun, with the sun sparkling on the steel and chrome and on that thing, what's that thing, darling, the …?"

"It's the hood ornament, darling, the 'Spirit of Ecstasy,' it's called," said Rob.

Jean Corbett nodded. "… and anyway, now they stormed up the steps of the church and the people were tumbling all over each other to get away. Caroline – my best friend – climbed on Rod's back, and Sally – my second best friend – tore her dress, it got caught in one of the bicycle racks at the entrance to the church, and the Reverend Philpot Cathcart said, 'My God! God have Mercy upon us!' But he didn't move, the Reverend, he just stood stock still with his mouth hanging open, and I said, 'Okay, Reverend, we've got to get into the church and we bar the doors and we keep these creatures out,' and the Reverend said, 'But, Jean, the Church should be open to all, divine mercy encompasses all,' and I said, 'But the Church is not open to the plague, Reverend, not to the plague' …"

"We really wanted a civilian marriage," said Rob, "but our families, well our families, they insisted, and then, because they can't stand each other …"

Virginia said, "Just a moment." She held up a hand and pointed. Two zombies were trying to climb the chain-link fence.

"Gob them," Jake's eyes lit up, "Virginia, gob them."

"What's gob them?" Jean stared at Virginia, wide-eyed.

"Gob them, Jake? You are a poet!" said Virginia, brushing back the bangs that were getting in Jake's eyes. She churned her mouth and she spat, two lightning-bolt baseball-sized planets – comets or meteorites of slime – one right after the other –zoom, zoom …

Wham!

Splash!

The two zombies fell backwards off the fence, clawing at their faces and yowling like banshees that had been cast down into the flames of Hell. They thrashed around in the mud, rolling over and over.

"Your story is exciting," said Virginia. "What happened next?"

Rob and Jean were staring at her. "What are you?" Rob said, clearing his throat.

"I'm a sort of antidote, I think," said Virginia. "Jake and I are testing it out. A few minutes ago, you were like those two – you were zombies."

"That's impossible …"

"No, it's not."

Yeah, you were zombies," said Jake, "Virginia spat that stuff at you and hit you smackeroo in the face and you howled and fell down just like those guys over there and then you … you woke up."

"Jake's right," said Virginia, "That's what happened."

"That would explain it, darling," said the bride.

"And so, yes, I guess that's right," Rob said, frowning, "I mean, we forced our way back into the church and we finally convinced the Reverend that it would be a good idea not to try to exercise sweet reason and Christian charity on the zombies, so we barred the door, but the zombies smashed it in, and one of the chief zombies was now Jack, he was spewing that stuff – like you just did, Virginia – and he was spewing it all over, and they came pouring into the church, and turned over the water bowl for the sacred water, and threw the stone bowl and the cup towards the altar and then they, those zombies, careened down the main aisle and climbed over the pews, and they were clumsy, and some fell down between the pews and got tangled up with the fold-out footstools, the ones that are there so you can rest you knees and kneel in comfort for the prayers, and they climbed, slobbering, onto the altar, and they trapped Sharon Tett, one of the bridesmaids there, and she was down on the altar, on her back, trapped, and this big hulking horrible zombie, drooling, and looking like the son of Frankenstein, he had her, and he bit her, and he bit off one arm, and then he lifted her up and let her fall away, down off the altar, onto the steps in front of the altar, and Jean and I were fighting them off with cushions we'd picked up from the choir stalls … And batting at them with the pillows, hoping they would go away, hoping it was all a nightmare."

"And it was meant to be the happiest day of our lives," Jean Corbett sighed.

"Yes, and that Rolls was really great! And I got a special deal on it!"

"Yes, and then you were bitten, darling, right by the altar."

"I was bitten?"

"Yes, you were bitten. Now, I remember. Suddenly I remember. And I thought without Rob I cannot live I want Rob to take me here, now, here in the church, and make me into a monster, so that if we die, we die together, and if we live, we will live as monsters together, and that is love …"

"I bit you?"

"Yes, I let you, and you bit me."

"Where, where did I bite you?"

"Right here, darling. It's the last thing I remember. It was like a kiss. And then I don't remember anything. Not until now."

"I think you should come with us," said Virginia. "What do you think, Jake?"

"Yeah," Jake bit his lip, and scrunched up his brow in deep thought, "I think they are okay."

"Come with you where?"

"Inside Bio-Frontier – that's what this building is, a bio-tech company. Don't worry. You'll meet people, ordinary people, well, more or less ordinary, but the good guys. We are with the good guys."

CHAPTER 34 – SURRENDER

The second column of Black Murk Mercenary Militia SUVs had just spotted the remains of the first column – SUVs upside down, SUVs lying on their sides, SUVs burning, and one SUV smashed and crumpled into the wall of one of the warehouses.

"Maybe we'd better, ah, think about this," said Dave Perry, the group leader and, just as he was about to give the order to retreat, the door on his driver's side was torn off its hinges and the driver – Rhett Diggins – was yanked out of his seat by something that looked like a metal gray reptile guy, oh, Jesus, it was the famous reptile man, and Dave was drawing his pistol when he saw coming out of a cross street the vehicles, armored vehicles, of what looked like a military column and at that instant, my God, a black female reptile, a sort of reptile woman, gleaming black, leaped through the empty door space, into the driver's seat, and turned her face to Dave – well her snout – with two big bright golden eyes – and red markings – and she said, pointing an automatic at David's forehead, "Hi, David, my name's Sarah James. I'm a Federal Agent, though I don't look like it. We'd like you to order your men to stand down, David, otherwise we, and Colonel Jefferson Siebert and his Marines, will wipe you out, and I personally, with great regret, would have to kill you. What do you think, David?"

David sat there, sweating, paralyzed, facing the reptile woman, in the SUV, with rain pounding down on the roof, in the dark, headlights now lighting up what was clearly a US Marine Corps vehicle, with more behind it, and a guy, yes, a Marine Corps Colonel, coming up, through the rain, walking as calm as could be, with his submachine gun cradled in his arm, and the heavy machine guns of his armored vehicle trained, it seemed, right at David's vehicle and the reptile woman aiming her automatic right at David's head.

"David?" the reptile woman prodded him with her pistol. She had a soft voice, with a hissing sibilant edge to it which was not unpleasant; her scales, wet from the rain, glowed and shimmered in the dashboard lights and reflections from the headlights.

The Colonel appeared at the side of the vehicle, "So what will it be?" he asked, fixing David Perry with a steely stare, and David was in no doubt that this guy was for real, he'd seen him give a lecture on tactics on TV, a broadcast direct from the military academy, brilliant lecture it was too, and while he was thinking this, the other reptile, the steel-gray-metallic one, appeared behind the Colonel, and he said, with that sort of hiss those creatures had, "All vehicles immobilized and accounted for, Colonel," and the Colonel, glanced back at him, and said, "Thanks Freddy, great work."

"Well, David," said the black female reptile, "You don't want to keep Colonel Siebert waiting, do you?"

"Okay, we'll stand down," said David; he took the microphone and ordered his people to stand down, and not to offer any resistance to Marines or to hybrids.

"Good," said Colonel Siebert, "And, I think that Agent James and I will perhaps have some missions for you and your men, David, so please stand by and be ready to go into action, and no nonsense, now, since we will know, and we will know right away," and the Colonel nodded at Sarah James, adding, "And it is a pleasure to meet you, Agent James."

"The pleasure is all mine, Colonel," said the reptile woman.

CHAPTER 35 – EUREKA

Alex Wolf, fresh from the battle zone and freshly morphed back into his human version, and Henry Cheng, still in his white lab coat, were conferring on progress in manufacturing a vaccine on the basis of Virginia's liquids and genetics and antibodies when Virginia and Jake arrived, having come through a five-minute session in the decontamination chamber, with the disheveled and mostly naked bride and groom, Jean Corbett and Rob Rhys, in tow.

"But we don't know if it will work," Henry was saying.

"That's true, and even if it does, a vaccine will only work for people who have not yet caught the virus, so we still have the problem of thousands and thousands ..."

"And we have the problem of delivery – I mean, with communications down, how are we going to ...?"

"Hello, Doctor Wolf, hello Doctor Cheng," said Jake, who was a very polite boy and believed – when he remembered them – in certain old-fashioned formalities.

"Hello, Jake – who are your new friends?" said Alex, staring at Jean and Rob.

"Hi Alex, hi Henry," said Virginia, "We think you should look at these two. A few minutes ago, they were full-fledged zombies and now ..."

"And now we are ourselves again," said Jean Corbett.

"Virginia gobbed them," said Jake.

"What?"

"I let them have it in the face with gobs of slime," said Virginia, wiping some more slime from her lips, "My mouth morphed into a howitzer. And, right away after the goo hit them, they fell down, as if they'd been sprayed with acid, and then they came to themselves."

"And it happened to another zombie too," said Jake.

"That's right," said Virginia, "I think what we have," and she held out of palm in which she'd pooled some of her drool, "what we have here is not a vaccine – though it might be that too – what it is, it's an antidote … a cure …"

"A cure," said Alex, opening his eyes wide, "A cure!"

"An antidote," said Henry Cheng, "A cure? I mean – it turns zombies back into humans?"

"I think so," said Virginia, and, glancing at Jake, "We think so."

"We think so," said Jake.

"It worked on us," said Rob Rhys.

"It sure did, honey," said Jean Corbett.

Henry Cheng stared at them. "So if we can make enough of this, and spray it on the zombies, then maybe we can turn the tide and beat this thing."

"Right," said Alex, "Even if this does work, it will be a race against time."

"Let's get to work."

"I hope we're not too late," said Alex, "I think this zombie thing is spreading like wildfire and if there are too many of them … well …"

"And Colonel Siebert and Sarah have got people – including the Black Murk SUV guys –who could start to deliver the antidote, who could go out and spray the victims," said Henry Cheng. "We'll have to rig up some spray equipment – and test it."

"Right, let's start planning now!"

"Jake – you and Virginia are heroes!" Alex shook hands with Jake and slapped him, gently, on the back.

CHAPTER 36 – CONTAGION

In the Volpe Octopus Net Building in midtown Manhattan Bill Brothers was beginning to look like a zombie himself; there were deep shadows under his eyes; his hair was even more mussed than before; and his five o'clock shadow was looking shaggy.

Shelly had told him, "You were right, Bill, the pundits are assholes. We don't need them. They are just peddling their little nostrums."

"But the General …?" said Bill.

"Yeah, let's keep the General," Shelly nodded, "He's excellent; he makes sense, has lots of insight. Keep him on with you. Besides, he has no family to worry about, so he can stay here, stick it out."

So, Bill Brothers and the General acted as joint anchors – reporting, live, on the end of the world. The General, who was 75, somehow managed to look crisp, neatly tailored, closely shaven, and fresh as daisy.

"Now we have reports from Houston, Texas," Bill stared at the camera, "We have reports that zombies have arrived in the outskirts of Houston, and, here, just south of New York, we have sightings as far north as New Jersey Turnpike. Here is a real time U-Tab report from a viewer."

The images showed zombies storming through a service station just off the Turnpike, in Bergen County, New Jersey.

"So, the zombie plague is on the edge of New York City, folks, this really is the end of the world," said Bill, his voice now raspy. He was imagining the zombies storming into the studio, biting the cameramen, turning everybody into a zombie, maybe even turning him, Bill Brothers, into a zombie. Such a thing was inconceivable!

The images from the Turnpike gas station showed the zombies milling around a zombie tourist bus at the Turnpike rest stop.

"This is obviously a hijacked tourist bus," said Bill. "What do you think, General?"

"Well, no, Bill, your conclusion might be a little hasty there. I don't believe it was hijacked. I believe the tourists, and tour guides, and the bus driver were all turned into zombies, see the driver's uniform there, that's the driver, the fellow who is eating the female cashier."

"Oh, yes, I see, General. He has his cap on."

"And not much else, either, Bill; but you will notice the Japanese and English and Spanish writing on the side of the bus."

"Tojo Corporation Bus Tours," said Bill, squinting.

"Yes, and all these particular zombies, you will notice, Bill, are Japanese, and the – see the zombie lady there, she is signaling to the other Japanese zombies to board the bus again, and she has the little hat and the little flag stuck on top of it, you know, that old-fashioned Japanese tourist guides use to indicate to their tourist flock who is the guide, and where they are supposed to go, and, yes, now they are boarding the bus. They are disciplined, organized, and very Japanese. They are headed our way, Bill, they are headed our way. The tourists were changed into zombies, so the tourist bus could be used as a delivery system. There is method behind this madness, Bill. This is not random."

"Oh, my God," said Bill, "the person, our viewer, who is still a person, who is holding the U-Tab, giving us this information stream from near the Japanese tourist bus, is now under attack, and running, and here the image gets jerky, as you can see, folks, and then the U-Tab falls to the ground and all we see are scuffling feet, and asphalt and one can of window washing fluid lying on its side, and somebody's arm ..."

"Yes, Bill, I can see it. The viewers, I believe, can see it."

"Yes, somebody's arm, I think a dead person, probably, General."

"Yes, I agree, Bill, it does look like the arm of a dead person."

"Now, Bill said, "here we have the security camera, a shot overhead, it shows the bus pulling out of the pit stop or gas station, and heading north."

"Yes, as we thought, heading towards New York City. I believe we are the target, Bill. We had better brace ourselves."

Bill squinted at a monitor, "There are reports that helicopter gunships have been sent to intercept the bus, but there is considerable confusion as to what, actually, is happening, and who is sending what where to do what."

"It's not a clear situation," said the General, "It's a typical case of the fog of war, Bill, we just don't know what the deuce is happening. It is not a clear situation at all."

"No, General, it isn't," said Bill, and he turned to the camera with a weary smile, "And now a message from our sponsors."

And, with a picture of film star Virginia Lily bathing in a pool, and suddenly surrounded by a posse of annoyingly importuning and admiring men, the voice, silken and soft, said, "Bio-engineered body odor can make you irresistible, so you've got to watch out, don't overdose, don't exaggerate ..."

"Now, we are back," Bill Brothers turned his five o'clock shadow towards the camera. "And, General, I must say, the situation is not rosy."

"No, it isn't, Bill."

"We have images from Houston, Texas, where zombies have gone on a rampage in a shopping mall, oh, this is tragic, General, this is tragic." Bill Brothers stopped to wipe his forehead, the air-conditioning in the studio had long since failed, "The zombies are on the loose in a toy store, the giant toy emporium, in the George Walker Bush Super Mall, and, well, the images are not suitable for broadcast, I'm afraid, not suitable for broadcast."

"The question is, Bill, the question is, from a logistical point of view, the question is this: how did the zombies get from Miami to Houston and to New Jersey in such a short time?"

Bill Brothers glanced at the computer monitor on his desk, "We have just had an unconfirmed report, it says here, General, it says here that the zombies landed in an airplane, that they landed at Houston Airport, General, that they landed at Houston Airport."

"So the zombies are now coordinated, and launching an all-out campaign, zombie naval, land, and air forces against the good people of these United States of America ... in the name of their Puppet Master," said the General, "this is total war, this is certainly total war, and it's a coordinated war, it's the Puppet Master's War just as your very brave Samantha Andrews warned us; she warned us it would be precisely this, planned and coordinated; the Puppet Master is obviously giving orders to his army, and he is giving them abilities too. It seems they can drive, and they can fly."

"It looks like it!" Bill Brothers felt he was beginning to stare death, even his own death, in the face. "Yes, it does look like this is a coordinated all-out nationwide attack! Can we contain it now, I wonder, General?"

"I doubt it, Bill. I doubt it – unless there's a miracle, some sort of miracle!"

The General was right. The zombie plague was spreading – like wildfire.

She was bright in the headlights and she was food that was clear – the running thing, the girl, was food. The girl, her legs pumping fast and flashing in the headlights, yes, she was food.

Larry Bilodeau was hungry: hungry for raw flesh – he'd been driving now for over half an hour, but he had no idea that time had passed and no idea who or what he was.

Headlights made a bright garish circle, while the white line and black asphalt streamed out of dark nothingness and straight into the dark nothingness that was Larry's brain.

And then he saw her, the girl on the side of the road, running. She had blond hair tied back in a ponytail and her legs and arms were tanned a nice shimmering gold or so it seemed in the brightness of the headlights and she was wearing white shorts and white socks and running shoes and a white T-shirt.

It looked like there was a cat clinging to her, or sitting on her shoulder; some sort of furry bundle. Maybe that was something to eat too.

The girl could be his meal, Larry decided, though there were no words in Larry's mind for "girl" or "cat" or "meal" or "running" or "socks" or "decision." Larry's name, though he no longer knew this, was Larry Bilodeau.

Now he was a cannibal and a zombie, and he was hungry.

The girl was alone and running, yes, running, along the shoulder of the road – nothing on either side of the road except Everglades, cotton-mouth killers, 20-foot, 200-pound Burmese pythons, and alligators.

The girl, her tanned legs flashing – yes, whatever she was, she was food.

Larry pulled past the running piece of food and then he slowed down, and he pulled over, the red pickup making a crunching sound on the gravel of the shoulder.

The sudden, mysterious rain and lightning and thunder had stopped.

The air was heavy and close; the night was dark.

A couple of hours before, in a northern suburb of Miami, towards dusk of "Day Two," shortly after having been bitten and spat upon while minding his own business on his very own neatly cut lawn by a wandering zombie loser, Larry Bilodeau – or the ghost of what once had been Larry Bilodeau – had come to a conclusion.

Northwest was the way he had to go – the voice said so.

The voice cackled and sparkled like static in Larry's head. It came like a flash of lightning, then it went, leaving darkness, only darkness; it called itself the Voice, or the Puppeteer, or sometimes, The Puppet Master. It didn't really matter what it called itself, it was a voice that had to be obeyed.

Larry peered out the windshield of the brand-new red pickup truck. He shifted the automatic into drive.

Larry was running on automatic himself.

He didn't know who he was or why he was going where he was going, he just knew he had to go – he had to drive and he had to keep on driving. And he also knew he had to bite anybody who tried to stop him or maybe sneeze and spit in their faces – which for some reason he didn't understand was even better: sneezing and biting and spitting were the absolute best!

He didn't put these thoughts into words because he really didn't have any words anymore and when he tried to think, and he did try to think, about what was happening to him, he found he couldn't.

Words – what are they?

His mind was a dark swirling galaxy of famished images.

And, now, he would get out of the nameless thing that was the pickup, his very own red pickup, and he would feed – on the running girl, on the flashing legs – he would feed, he would feed on it, on the running, glittering thing.

Six hours earlier, Larry Bilodeau had been deeply hung-over from the night before which he had spent – oh, how fabulous – alone getting a hard-on watching old movies starring his absolute favorite of all time, Virginia fucking fabulous Lily.

She battled vampires and aliens and intergalactic knights, in 3-D hologram. Larry alternated the high-class Virginia Lily drama and science fiction and horror, with stuff from the one of the sex channels – girls on girls mostly, and Larry would replace one of the girls with Virginia Lily.

Ah, the stuff of dreams!

Larry worked his way through the night eating frozen pizza he heated in the microwave, and as the night went on he had drunk two bottles of ice-cold Chardonnay, plus some whiskey.

And later, in the bright deadly sunlight which hurt his eyes, after he got out of bed at 2:00 p.m., he decided he would go out and mow his lawn, sitting on the little electric lawn mower that puttered back and forth over the green; it made the grass so neat it looked like a razor had been applied to the stuff. Keep everything in the garden disciplined, especially plants, was Larry's motto.

He was listening, the headache still echoing in his head, to some antique hard metal rock from the 20th Century, it was nostalgic stuff, put up to maximum volume in the ear buds of his antique retro iPod and he hadn't noticed that people were running up and down on the street just outside his hedge.

He hadn't listened to the news; he had been isolated in his own little castle, the world totally tuned out, gobbling pizza, sloshing down the Chardonnay, concentrating on his very own personal Virginia Lily-plus-pornographic-channel inspired hard-ons.

He didn't hear the sirens.

Even now, out on the lawn, he was concentrating, concentrating hard: he felt nature should be fully tamed, and that his hedge must be high, and squared off with electric sheers, so that the whole place looked like a lesson in geometry, and the streets outside and the rest of the world were invisible, intangible, fucking disorderly, to be kept at a distance, and not Larry's fucking concern.

There was a drummer hammering home the truth of true hard rock passion – boom, boom, boom, ripppppp, boom, boom, boom, rippppppp – in Larry's ears so that Larry was deaf and blind to everything else, and he was beating with one pudgy fist on the handle of the mower, which was purring along at a great rate, clipping, clipping, clipping that stroppy unruly undisciplined grass. There was something beautiful, too, Larry thought in the fresh green raw smell of newly amputated grass – it smelt, vaguely, like cow flaps, or animal shit, anyway, the pure essence of nature; Larry had once been forced by his father to visit a thing called a farm where they kept live animals from the past. It was, like, a museum. He found it boring; but he'd liked the smell of the shit – and he'd loved the squishy mud the things called pigs (he'd looked those pig things up on the Net) wallowed in; it looked and smelled enticing too, that sticky mud stuff, and Larry thought maybe someday, now that he was more savvy about the pleasures of perverse imaginings, and knew that anything could be fodder for the great mental machine that gave him those exquisite hard-ons, maybe someday he'd go back and have another look at that museum, reconsider the life and times of the pig. Maybe the pigs were onto something.

But for now, it had to be the vicarious pleasure of the subtle, shit-like perfume and bouquet of freshly cut, freshly shaved, freshly tortured grass.

Larry glanced up and blinked: What the fuck? A guy, a really weird looking guy, was stomping across the lawn, coming straight at Larry. What the hell was this? "This is my lawn, you freak, what the hell are you doing stomping across my lawn?"

Larry didn't like the look of the guy at all.

In fact, the guy looked like a ghoul from some midway freak show or late night old black-and-white horror movie starring Boris Karloff or Bela Lugosi that would give you the creeps and the shivers and make you hide under your blanket and squeeze your eyes shut. The guy looked like he'd come out of *Hollywood Vampires from the Crypts*, one of Larry's favorites, another Virginia Lily vehicle, but not meant for translation into real life.

The guy was real pale. His eyes were empty, and his arms joggled loosely at his sides like they were broken at the shoulders and elbows.

And the guy was clearly a slob, a loser, maybe a pervert. His belt was undone, the loop hanging loose, and his fly was unzipped, and his shirt was torn and open and covered in what looked like grease, but, when Larry took off his dark Polaroid glasses, the greasy color turned out to be crimson red, which made Larry do a double-take. Could that be blood?

As the guy came up to him, stumbling at the last minute, and looking down at his feet in a puzzled way, like, what are those fucking things doing there, Larry was getting off the lawnmower, wiping his hands on the back of his Bermuda shorts, and thinking, the guy may be dangerous, but he doesn't look very bright, and, while thinking that, and just as the guy looked up at him again, with baleful glowing green eyes, Larry slipped the ear buds out of his ears, and suddenly heard the silence of a summer's day, a few water sprinklers going, but then, above all, he heard something else, sirens in the distance, and screams, and gunshots, and, as he pulled the freshly sharpened garden sheers out of their holder on the side of the mower, a shiver went up and down Larry's spine like a sudden chill in the blazing heat of the day and a sort of underlying darkness opened up in the glaring brightness of the sun of the late afternoon with the light reflecting like silver off the leaves of the Oleander and Hibiscus, and Larry opened the garden sheers so that they were like a double pronged knife, awkward, Larry thought, tightening his grip, feeling a sudden surge of sweat on his palms, awkward, but, if handled right, deadly, and the guy just hung there staring at Larry with those baleful glowing eyes, and Larry said, "What the fuck do you want?"

The guy didn't say anything, he just lunged forward, and he sneezed, he sneezed right in Larry's goddamn face, he sneezed a spray of green snot, and, Larry screamed, "What the hell you doing, you idiot, you zombie, you freak, you, you, you trespasser, you!"

And Larry Bilodeau plunged for the guy and rammed one blade of the sheers straight into the guy's gut.

The guy looked down surprised, and let out a howl, and Larry was so surprised at what he had done, attacking the guy like that, "Christ, I'm a murderer, I just tried to kill a guy," that he let go of the sheers and the guy grabbed the sheers and pulled them out with a spurt of blood and the guy's belly was peeling suddenly open and a coil of intestine popping out – like a big dark clotted blood sausage uncoiling – with a smell of shit and something else Larry couldn't identify – and the guy howled again, and spurted out more of the green snot that splashed all over Larry, putting Larry into a cold fury, and Larry leapt on the guy and bit him in the neck and red blood spurted out, and Larry howled and growled and licked at the blood and bit some more, toppling, following the big shambling guy down as the guy, toppling sideways onto the neatly cut fresh-smelling recently watered grass, bit Larry's forearm. Fuck!

For some reason, at that exact instant, the sprayers went on and began to sprinkle both bodies, as they rolled in the grass, grappling with each other, splashed in blood and that green stuff, and bits of the guy's guts, and Larry was growling and snarling, and biting and pounding with his fists, and part of Larry's mind, a shrinking part, was wondering, was shouting, "Hey, Larry, stop, what the hell are you doing, Larry," and Larry asked out loud in a strange cavernous voice, "Who the hell is Larry?"

"Yeah, man, who the fuck is Larry?"

Time stood still for an instant … then …

"Grrrh!" Larry was gone.

The creature that had once been Larry stood up and looked down at the big man who was bleeding to death, the blood pulsating out in spurts, on a bright glossy green lawn, green foam bubbling at the guy's mouth, and the baleful green eyes that had stared at him now becoming even more empty, and the blood slowed to a trickle, and then it seemed to become thick and gluey …

Larry stood there and then he lost interest in the dying freak – there were no words to think about anything anymore or worry about anything just a buzzing silence and a voice inside the silence that somehow seemed to come from everywhere and which told him what he had to do.

"Drive, Larry, drive!"

Larry walked in a halting stumbling way to the garage and he put his hands in the pocket of his shorts and pulled out the keys and he got into the sparkling pickup that had just been cleaned and waxed, bright red it was, and he sat there, green goo dribbling from his mouth and nose though he didn't know that, and he sat there and waited, growling in his throat, and then the voice came again, the voice in his head, and it said. "Drive to Sarasota and bite people, bite everybody you meet, if you can't bite, sneeze!"

"Yes," Larry said in that new voice that came from the catacombs of his soul.

"That's the boy, Larry, spread the word! Spread the joy!"

"Yes."

"You are the man, Larry, you are totally the man." And the voice went on cackling in the background like some old record, like some scratchy old cyber disc, a kid playing at being an old man, or an old man playing at being a kid, a phlegm-filled voice that turned squeaky, and back again, "Proselytize, Larry, convert, preach to the pagans, Larry, convince!"

Larry put the key in the ignition, turned it, and the engine sprang into life. Larry drove out of the garage onto the street. He didn't notice the people running in the streets, the women screaming for help, he didn't notice the helicopters hovering overhead. He didn't hear the loudspeakers saying, "Stay indoors, lock your doors, pull your curtains; use your cell phones only for emergency calls. Tune to Station KJL on radio and KJL-2 on television; use U-tabs to receive the latest security information. Please stay calm!"

Larry didn't notice the woman who ran right in front of the pick-up screaming, "Mr. Bilodeau, Please help me, please stop, please help me, my husband George has gone crazy …"

Wham!

He hit her a glancing blow and drove on not even looking in the rearview mirror, as she fell, grasping the truck, her fingers and finger nails scratching along the fresh smooth paint of the pickup, and as she fell unconscious to the street with a broken leg and lay there, he didn't see her, but perhaps he was, for her, a blessing in disguise, since she was unconscious from shock or maybe from hitting her head on the asphalt and lay still, she was not noticed by most of the zombies who were now stumbling and groping their way through the Golden Palm Paradise Sea Side Estate, as they assumed she was dead already and not interesting, since only live, living, squealing, struggling flesh was enticing, or because they were attuned, like lions on the savannah, to movement, not noticing what is lying still, not realizing that it too is prey, that it too is meat, and so she didn't get bitten or sneezed at or spit upon, and when she came to herself, half an hour later, it was just past dusk and the street lights were going on and some of the automatic sprinklers were making that whish, whish, whish, sound that was so poetic and comforting in the twilight of the endless suburbs of America and she saw a shambling line of zombies moving away from her, towards the northern end of the suburb, and she lay still in terror, but none of them looked back, and she managed to stand up on one leg, and to stagger, pain shooting up her broken leg, blood seeping through her slacks, back to her house, a low-slung luxury bungalow, only remembering when she got inside that her husband George had turned into a monster who seemed to have stepped right out of a late night pulp movie, green foam gushing down his chin, tendrils springing out of his ears, and she felt a chill of terror that George would spring out of the hall closet and bite her and also a temperature shock from the air-conditioning which was still on, going full blast, and she almost fell back out the front door and down onto the flagstones, but George was gone, and the poodle, Lola, who was already crazy enough, had apparently not become a zombie dog because she was just her sloppy goofy hysterical self, licking Sarah's face and trying, vaguely, to comfort her.

Sarah lowered herself onto the sofa and drank a glass of bourbon Southern Comfort and thought, "Now I've got a broken leg and the world is coming to an end and this is a real fix I've got myself into." Then she remembered how she had caught a glimpse of Larry Bilodeau's face at the last minute, just before he ran her down, and she realized that he had become one of those, one of them, one of those things, one of the zombies. She flipped on the television and watched a rerun of the vice president, sweat beading his brow, and he wiped at it once, which didn't look good, it looked like the man was in a panic, and he said something about the terrible tragedy that has overtaken our nation, God judging sinners and punishing lax morals and unleashing His wrath on unseemly sexual hijinks and short shorts and neo-retro hot pants, and in the smaller images parading across the bottom of the screen or inset at the top she saw Miami burning, a big ocean liner or cruise ship rammed up against the seaside promenade and there was an image in one corner of a sort of mummy propped up on what looked like a bed and she, this mummy, though it was hard to tell what sex it was since it didn't have much hair and no eyebrows that Sarah could see, was talking at the screen, and Sarah clicked on that image and it enlarged to take most of the screen and, yes, it was the mummy talking, and it was a woman, it was that Samantha Andrews, that beautiful young reporter with the super-sized smile, or what was left of her, and she was saying, "Grrrhhh, move ... move ... west ... north ... spread ... spread ... the voice ... spread ... spread ... Grrrrrhhhhhhh ... Oh, God, Charlie ... I'm going to die ... ghhhhrrrr ... the voice says, spread, move, bite spit, growl, spew, spew, spit, spray, sneeze ... Grrrrrhhhhhhh ..." and a great gob of green came spinning out of the girl's mouth and went splat, right near the camera someplace, and a guy's voice from off screen said, "That's okay, Sam, keep talking, that's okay, you missed, and I've got a shield, so keep talking."

And the girl, "Gghhhr, slop ..." green goo dripping thickly from her mouth like a beard of green, and, "Grrrhhhhhh ... thanks Charlie ... Grrrhhhhhh ..."

Sarah turned the sound off, just leaving the screen on, and, coming out of a sort of shock she must have been in, she remembered she had trained as a nurse, many years ago, so she hobbled her way to the kitchen, cut off her slacks, and examined the break ... If I don't lose consciousness, she thought, maybe, just maybe ...

Just maybe I can fix this.

Just maybe I'll survive ...

And just as she had that thought, an image appeared on the overhead kitchen TV screen of a big ship, an aircraft carrier, and then an image of the American flag, and then of the President, Katherine du Bois Hughes, smiling, lifting a baseball cap, and talking ...

Then there was another image of the president, wearing that baseball cap, stepping out of a helicopter, at the White House, waving, and smiling.

But the TV was on mute.

So Sarah, working on the broken leg, didn't notice, didn't hear – "Hail to the Chief" and "The Star Spangled Banner." And then in any case it all turned to snow and hissing and the screens went dead and the air-conditioning fell silent and all the lights went off.

Food, Larry, food!

The running girl was food.

Larry Bilodeau pulled the pick-up, screeching, off the road, and onto the shoulder, splashing pebbles, coming to a stop about fifteen yards in front of the running girl.

The running girl was food, fodder, prey …

There was no thought-out calculation in Larry's move, merely the sense that if he were in front of her, she would come running into the trap, and he would catch her, and he could tear off her arms and legs and feast on them.

In his mind somewhere was the image of him biting at one of those smooth golden tanned arms, those wonderful thighs.

He would munch on that honey-colored flesh; he would break those fragile bones; he would slurp up that delicious blood.

The voice in Larry's head was furious, totally pissed off; it was yelling at him not to stop, not to bother with the girl, the voice was telling him to keep moving. He had to spread the word! "Spread the Word, the End is nigh! Larry, what the fuck are you doing?" the voice screamed, "Larry, this is not your mission, this is not true religion, Larry, you are to travel as fast and as far as you can, you are not to stop for a little snack on the way, Larry, you are making me angry. This morsel is not a morsel, Larry! You will get indigestion, Larry! Larry, the wrath of the Puppet Master shall be upon you! I'm very disappointed in you, Larry!"

Larry got out of the truck. If the old human Larry had caught sight of his new zombie self, he would not have recognized Larry Bilodeau.

The voice roared its displeasure. "You are being distracted by the pleasures of the flesh, Larry; this is evil of you, this is counter-productive, Larry, you have to get back on track, Larry, back on the straight-and-narrow, the pleasures of the flesh are spurious, Larry, they are irrelevant, even God, Larry, is against the pleasures of the flesh! You must concentrate, Larry, you have to spread the word, Larry, you have to proselytize, you have to carry the message! Think 'mission statement', Larry! Think 'prioritize'. Think 'business plan'. Keep your bearings, Larry. Where the fuck are your priorities, Larry? What the fuck are you doing, Larry?"

This creature that had once been Larry Bilodeau had been reborn out of the larva that once was Larry Bilodeau. It was a different creature, this new Larry, it hung there, loose-limbed, dribbling green fluid from both nostrils, two rivulets streaming from the downturned corners of its mouth, dark storm clouds and bright thunderbolts in what had once been its mind.

His greased back retro ducktail hairstyle – which he had specially done by

Henri who worked at Chez Federico in Miami – had been ravaged and now only one tail of the duck remained, and it consisted of a few heavy streaks of black hair, greased together in a sort of clumsy black gluey calligraphy against his chalk-white skull, whiter than white, as if Larry's skin had never seen the light of day, ever.

"Larry Bilodeau, I am very disappointed in you!"

"You are a loser, Larry, you are a fuckup!"

"Get back in the goddamn pickup, Larry!"

Larry's belly was hanging out, his shirt buttons had burst, and his shorts were sagging low and stained by blood and by green goo, a few tendrils had sprouted from his ears. His eyes were green, glowing, pulsating gently, and void of all signs of consciousness.

"Grrrhhh," he said, to the approaching girl.

She skidded to a stop, her eyes wide in terror. "Oh fuck," she said, "not another one." She darted sideways, across the ditch, leaped, in a quick straddle, over the concrete fence embankment, scrambled over the ditch, and disappeared into the trees, low scrub, then swamp, and, yes, she did have what looked like a cat – a small ball of fur with very bright eyes – on her shoulder.

She'd grabbed it so it wouldn't fall off.

Larry growled, and followed, heaving himself heavily over the concrete barrier. He stumbled getting down the slope, and then he stopped, breathing heavily, growling in his throat, his hunger getting stronger, and the voice saying, "Don't do this, get back in the fucking pickup, you dolt, you have to go west young man, you have to go west!" But Larry brushed the voice away like an annoying cobweb – it sputtered and flashed like distant lightning – and he staggered into the woods after the girl. She was moving fast. He could still hear her, and he smelt the air, and yes he could smell her, a spicy perfume, and he followed, slipping on the path, that led beside some sort of narrow canal, and the girl, he now saw, had stopped and she was moving carefully and she was watching something on the ground between her and Larry, and so Larry lurched forward, a step at a time, and the ground was slippery, and it was dark except for the moon that had come out, bright silver splotches, and Larry took one heavy step at a time, his own breathing sounding heavy and phlegm-clogged, and then the thing she was watching, made its move and came rushing at Larry, and it was a low slithery dark fast thing, an alligator though Larry didn't have a word for it, with big jaws open, ready to snap shut on Larry, and Larry knew enough, whatever was inhabiting Larry's skull knew enough, to jump aside, and move back, and so the alligator missed.

Whew!

Larry shambled backwards. He left the girl. She was standing there now, a silver sliver in the moonlight, holding a big stick, and the voice said, "See, that morsel was a waste of time, Larry boy, we've got bigger fish to fry, just think, a whole fresh city, full of fresh people meat, some of them will be old folks, not so spry, not so nimble, not so quick, as this morsel, so you will eat to your heart's content, Larry Old Man, don't worry, Be Happy, look on the Sunny Side Larry, Fortune smiles on the Bold, Larry Boy, Every cloud has a silver lining, It's just around the Corner, Early to rise, healthy, wealthy, and wise, Larry," and Larry, entranced by the tuneful voice that unspooled in his head, cranky and childlike, but somehow like soft soul music, from somewhere deep, somewhere dank and murky, somewhere sulfurous and smoky, and Larry shambled up onto road, and got back in the pickup, and started on his way.

"This is the opportunity of a lifetime, Larry, you can't miss this one, it's a limited time offer only, expires at midnight, Larry, get in on the ground floor, Larry, get on the fucking bandwagon while you can, Larry, otherwise you are a flatfooted, pussy-livered loser, Larry, and what I'm saying, I'm saying for your own good, Larry, and that's God's own truth, Larry! Floor it, Larry, floor the damned accelerator!"

It was about two minutes later that Sherriff Doug Serra saw the red pickup coming straight towards his roadblock.

Burned-out cars, trucks, and buses already lined the road, just at the entry to the little town of Belle Glade.

Victory so far – nobody had gotten past the barrier.

But they just kept coming – the zombies were determined to break out of southern Florida.

Doug Serra stared at the onrushing pickup, blinked the sweat away from his eyes, and wiped his forehead with an oily old cloth. It was clearer and clearer. He was fighting a losing battle. There was no way they could contain this thing.

His men didn't have any flamethrowers. But they'd listened to the radio and they'd heard some guy explaining that the zombie virus, that's what they called it, fuck what a name, the zombie virus, was extremely contagious, and the goo that transported it – bodily fluids, deadly bodily fluids – spittle, phlegm, maybe piss too, maybe sweat too, maybe even just droplets in the air if you got too close, and anything the slime had touched, they weren't sure yet, since this thing was new and ultra-contagious – while they were talking about this on the radio, a guy phoned in, a history nut, and he suggested Molotov Cocktails, and went into a long rigmarole about how the Russians had used them against Hitler's tanks in the Second World War, and Doug Serra thought that was a fine idea – bullets didn't do much, water hoses didn't work, and you couldn't get into hand-to-hand fight – but a Molotov cocktail, a bottle full of flaming gasoline, well, that might just do the trick, you throw it, and you run like blazes – and so the crates and boxes stacked up behind the kitchen of Frenchie's Alligator Bar & Grill had been emptied of the empty wine bottles and the bottles had been filled with gasoline and then corked up with gasoline soaked rags and then all you needed was a good baseball arm – underhand throw or overhand, didn't matter – and a lighter or a box of old-fashioned ecologically friendly wooden matches, and whoosh, a burst of flame, an explosion, Boom, and you got yourself a whole slew of fried zombies – without getting close enough they could spit on you or bite you or otherwise spread their poison.

So Mr. Comrade Molotov – Stalin's wartime Foreign Minister – was the answer, from far beyond the grave.

Of course, Sherriff Doug Serra, who had a Ph.D. in criminal psychology from a top-notch Internet University, a beautiful wife and two kids, was not happy with this. These zombies were ordinary American Christian folk, who just happened to have become zombie American Christian – or Jewish or Muslim or Hindu or Atheist – folk. They were American citizens with rights – theoretical rights – like everybody else.

"There but for the grace of God go I," Doug muttered to himself as he remembered the way his grandmother used to repeat that mantra whenever she saw some particularly unhappy or unfortunate individual, unshaven bearded hobos panhandling, or war veterans parked in wheelchairs and with-out limbs or eyes, or shameless girls who didn't know better flaunting their long legs in short-short skirts, or exhausted hookers flexing their leg muscles, or religious fanatics with paint on their faces and dressed in flimsy orange bed sheets who jangled their way along the tree-lined street chanting, Harry Christy somebody, "Harry, Harry, Harry … Harry Christy …"

There but for the grace of God go I.

Doug Serra sat for a minute in the patrol car, staring at the computer screen – staring at the U-Tab, staring at the photograph of his high school sweetheart and wife, Roberta, and their two kids, Lea and Rita, and thinking, "Roberta is now pregnant with our third kid, a boy this time, and God what sort of a world are we bringing these kids into!" He wanted to pray, but he had lost his faith a long time ago, and the words of the prayers he knew were empty and bitter on his lips and in his mind, and a part of himself hated himself for it, for this apostasy, this desolation. He sighed, "Well, may the fates and the gods be with us, Roberta," and the worst thing was he had not been able to get in touch with Roberta, the U-Tabs worked sometimes, then didn't work at all, and all he got from her mobile, and from their home number was static, not even the voice mail, not even a human voice, not even a message from the phone company, and he felt torn, he wanted to leave the whole thing, to leave his men – each man and woman on the barricade had family and friends and lovers they wanted to protect, but being here, stopping the zombies from getting through, this was the front line. This had to be done.

Here we stand; this we must do – there is no other way.

Doug Serra got out of the car. They shall not pass, he thought, they shall not pass. This is a battle we must not lose.

He stretched, wiggling his shoulders, suddenly realizing how stiff with tension his body was, a crick in his neck, aching shoulders. Damn it! What a situation! Anybody could become a zombie. It was pure luck, pure chance, or pure fate what became of you in this nether world, this vale of tears. And, yes, it was a damned exciting dangerous place, this weird and wonderful planet, Earth.

Why, the president herself had almost become one of the zombie folk, as she herself had admitted when she went on TV, and the signal, that signal, did get through, and there she was, earlier that afternoon, on the deck of an aircraft carrier, in a T-shirt and jeans, head shaved, looking like the heroine she was, and people had thought she was already dead, but then she re-appeared glowing with heath, raring to go, ready for the fight, and she had explained it on TV and radio and Internet from the aircraft carrier *Dwight D. Eisenhower*, the giant Stars and Stripes and the crisp waves glittering behind her, like she had emerged from the sea, like she, and the United States itself, had been reborn in the face of Death.

Yes, somehow, for a moment, the static had cleared, the interference had lessened, and like a miracle, she had risen from the dead like Lazarus. There she was – the woman herself!

Doug glanced at the screen set up beside his cruiser. They were doing a replay: the president had a shaven head and no eyebrows and she was wearing just jeans and the T-shirt and she had just told them of her close escape and she had explained her new hair cut was to make sure the decontaminant did its work, the virus being known to stick to any surface, in particular hair, and she was going back into the fight! She was a gutsy lady and sexy as all get out, and even sexier with the shaven head, those deep eyes and that black skin giving her a sort of extra glow and glamour in the brilliant afternoon ocean light, and behind her, floated the giant Stars and Stripes. "We will beat this thing!" she had said, "God bless you all, and God Bless America!"

The image froze – the music played: "The Star-Spangled Banner!"

Damned right, Doug thought, tears in his eyes, believer or not, God Bless America!

And beat this thing we will!

"Okay," he said, "turn on the floodlights."

The red pickup was close now.

Okay … Doug peered through his binoculars. The floodlights flashed on. The interior of the pickup cabin was lit up like it was center stage, targeted by a bank of klieg lights. Doug saw the guy's face clearly the green goo all over the guy's face, the empty greenish eyes, the …

A big red blinking sign lit up and flashed. STOP IMMEDIATELY!

PARADA IMMEDIATAMENTE

Sure enough, the pickup came straight on.

STOP IMMEDIATELY! TURN BACK!

PARADA IMMEDIATAMENTE

DÉ VUELTA DETRÁS

A trooper repeated the message through loud speaker, in English and Spanish.

Stop Immediately or we shoot!

STOP IMMEDIATELY! TURN BACK!

The pickup with the fat zombie just kept coming.

STOP IMMEDIATELY! TURN BACK!

"Okay boys!" Doug spoke into his old-fashioned short-range walkie-talkie and two guys wearing gas masks and plastic shields and bio-proof bodysuits ran out from the bushes and tossed their Molotov Cocktails, arcs of flickering yellow flame in the warm still night air, up they went and then down, perfect throw, perfect arc, and they smashed against the side of the pickup truck, one sailing right through the open window into the cabin, bouncing off the opposite door, and, there they were, breaking, shattering glass, and …

Whoosh!

As the flames exploded, and as they engulfed Larry Bilodeau, the voice spoke: "Hey, Larry, that's the way the cookie crumbles, I guess, eh, Larry, Tough titty, uh, Larry, now the shit hits the fan, Larry" the voice said, "Well, good night, Larry, sweet good night and happy dreams, Larry, happy dreams!"

For a split second, as he went up in a whoosh of searing flame – 500 degrees Celsius – maybe Larry Bilodeau remembered, for just a split second, or maybe more, who he was: Good old Larry Bilodeau, a barrel of laughs, and maybe he saw, just for a second, Virginia Lily, in *Dank City*, rising out of the flames, battling the bad guys, and sure to win.

Virginia – who could not die!

It took twenty-three seconds of screaming.

Then Larry Bilodeau wasn't anything or anybody anymore.

Mummified flesh, the authorities had discovered, was not contagious. But the best thing was to make sure that it was baked over and over and over again, just to be sure. The boys tossed some more Molotovs.

Whoosh, whoosh, whoosh! The pickup was burned and burned again. Then it was added to the roadside graveyard, shoved off the road by little yellow bulldozer usually used to dig trenches, sewer lines, small drainage canals.

"Here comes another one," said Doug, seeing the headlights in the distance. "Oh, oh," he said, "it looks like it's more than one."

The satellite feed, which was sometimes working and sometimes not, now worked, just for a flickering second or two, and it showed, in infrared, on Chief Serra's screen, a column of cars – A column! A fucking column! They were coming on fast. It might be humans, or it might be zombies. He had to remind himself that the zombies were humans too.

Whoever or whatever they were, he had to stop them. Even if they were humans, they might be carrying the virus.

How many cars, maybe twenty-five … yes, twenty-five!

This was not good.

The headlights were racing onward, getting closer. It would only be a minute or two now. "God help us!" Doug Serra wiped his forehead.

The big slobbery zombie in the red pickup was gone, but eighteen-year-old Kaitlin Wagner was still panting, still holding the big stick. She was watching carefully as the moon passed in and out of cloud cover – bright splashes of silver light, coming, going, coming – and going.

There were at least two alligators between her and the road. She could hunker down where she was, or she could try to make it to the roadway and keep going. If she went far enough maybe she could get away from the zombies or whatever they were, though she wondered if the whole world had turned zombie and maybe, on the whole planet, she was the only human being left.

She took a deep breath.

She stepped forward carefully.

That big black-looking log, with ridge of low bumps along its back, was an alligator, she was sure of it. Well, she'd skirt a little to the left and hope the creature left her alone.

She moved carefully, slowly, a step at a time.

The alligator made its move. God, those things could move fast!

What a day! What a night!

Whoosh! The alligator charged!

Run, Kaitlin, run!

Yes, what a day! What a night!

It had started like a normal day – sunshine through the window, and as Kaitlin got out of bed, she thought, Okay, today I am taking it all off, the whole frigging day off. I'm not going to type a single word. I'm not going to think a single thought! She had gone to bed early, had turned off her U-Tab, had put plugs in her ears and had slept the sleep of the just. Her thesis was on the "Uses of Biotechnology in Water Conservation and the Preservation of Water Tables." The computer sat reproachfully on her desk, orphaned, abandoned. When morning came, the sunlight lay like a fuzzy glowing blanket of gold over the part of her desk occupied by a big thick old dog-eared dictionary, and motes of dust, not many but enough, were floating like gold specks just inside the window. A book was propped on the reading stand, open at page 274. It was an old work by Doctor Sabrina Jacobs on regenerating coral reefs after they had been damaged by the excessive acidity of the oceans caused by the absorption of carbon dioxide from the atmosphere.

Kaitlin opened the window and took a deep breath. The air had that balmy, intense, moist, voluptuous, caress-my-skin and seduce-my-lungs quality which she loved about sea air and Florida air when it was not too humid but poised right on the knife-edge of just right. Just breathing was heaven!

Kaitlin made coffee in the espresso machine, liking the fact that she had an old-fashioned Italian-made contraption that let her do some of the work. She carefully measured in the freshly ground beans, and she carefully poured the water and screwed down the top.

She'd switched on the radio but got only static.

She'd tried her U-Tab and the Internet. The server must have been down. That was strange. It almost never happened.

When the coffee was ready, and after she had had a first sip, she showered and went out onto the little enclosed flagstone patio where nobody could see her, her own private space, and she sat down in the slouchy smooth canvas fold-up deckchair and let the air and the sun dry her off.

Then she dressed and went to meet her running group, the Everglade Ramblers.

They were all talking about some plague in Miami, but it was down at the south end and not here, up north, so life could continue, that's what they thought. In fact, real news, accurate news, was difficult to get and the city was full of rumors – but then people exaggerate. They are always getting excited and worked up about something.

Six of the group didn't turn up.

"Maybe we should just go home."

"Maybe it's safer if we stick together."

"They say this thing turns people into zombies."

"Did you see the images on the Internet?"

"No, I didn't."

They decided to shorten their run and then to check back, each one of them would head home earlier than originally planned, and so they began their run out along a pathway that skirted a part of the Everglades.

And that was how and when it happened.

They were about halfway through their run when two guys came lurching out from behind some bushes, oleanders which were fully in flower, and one of them grabbed Sue Leahy, who was second from front, wearing her trademark sexy skintight silver bio-breathe leotards. They coughed some sort of green goo all over her, tossed her down, and one of them tried to bite or rape her, it was hard to tell. Sue and the guy were thrashing, all tangled up, on the ground. The other weirdo jumped on Ken Burke, spun him around before Ken knew what was happening, Ken was a big guy, and he could certainly have handled the squirt who attacked him, but he was surprised, he didn't see it coming, so he just fell down, shouting "Ouch!" And the guy leaned over and spat, and then the same guy – and, God, he did look like a zombie – turned and grabbed for Lee Anne – and Sally Grossman punched him from behind, and he turned around, and spat a big gob of gooey stuff which went right past Sally's shoulder, then he turned away and ran, stumbling, after Lee Anne. Meanwhile Ken and Sue seemed to be having convulsions, and Kaitlin went to see if she could help, but when she bent over Ken she saw his eyes had gone funny, blank with a greenish tinge, and he was dribbling some sort of green liquid, and he growled and spat at her, and again the spittle missed, and Kaitlin backed away, and saw Sue getting up, a big gash in her arm from where the guy bit her, but now Sue was spurting the green stuff too. Kaitlin didn't know what to do – she wanted to help; but helping seemed damned dangerous. In fact, it seemed suicidal.

Sally Grossman had just kept running. She shouted, "Run, guys, run!" And she disappeared around a corner and was gone.

So, Kaitlin and Vickie Burton ran.

They ran towards the closest suburb, or housing estate. Where there were people, they could ask for help, they could seek refuge, they would be safe.

Vickie twisted her ankle just as they got to the suburb.

"Let's find a place to hide, any place."

The zombies, it turned out, were everywhere in the suburb, and they soon spotted Kaitlin and Vickie. As they closed in, Kaitlin helped Vickie limp along, with Vickie's arm slung over Kaitlin's shoulder. They skirted around a house, they broke in a back door – well, they didn't have to break in, it was open, wide open; but they shouted, "Is anybody here? Is anybody home?" Nobody was home, but the zombies were coming. They headed upstairs, Kaitlin helping Vickie, lurching from step to step.

They locked themselves in a bedroom

But somehow the zombies sensed they were there. Kaitlin pushed a bookcase against the door and then a table, but the zombies pushed in the door, began smashing through it.

"Go! I can't go, but you go," Vickie whispered.

"I can't leave you!"

Kaitlin smashed a zombie over the head with a wooden chair. It didn't seem to faze him one bit. He spit, and the gob went flying past her ear, except for a bit that got in her hair. Another zombie had grabbed Vickie by the foot and was dragging her. Vickie was screaming. "Go, go, go …!"

And then the zombie bent down and spat in Vickie's face and rolled over her and Vickie's shout became a scream and then a growl and then Vickie screamed, growling, foaming at the mouth, "Go, you bitch cunt slut Kaitlin Wagner or I will eat your fucking eyes out you bitch cunt always the best, the fastest, you bitch cunt, and ponytails are so passé you tasteless bitch cunt with your fake Irish name Kaitlin this, Kaitlin that, and, Oh isn't fucking Kaitlin so wonderful, Oh isn't fucking Kaitlin so intelligent, and you cunt Kaitlin I know you slept with Robbie, you bitch cunt, and the voice, the voice is telling me to kill you, and kill you I will unless you run like hell, so please run like hell, grrrh, because I love you, Kaitlin, I love you, Kaitlin, I love you, I love you more than you will ever know, more than anything in the whole wide world, you fucking traitorous too-good-to-be-true bitch grrrh, grrrh ...!"

With the scream echoing in her ears, Kaitlin pushed open a window and climbed out, terrified and fuming and appalled. Yes, goddamn it, I did sleep with Robbie Reiss, if a quick clumsy fairly unwelcome – I was just being nice and he was so desperate – fuck on the beach with my ragged old "I love New Orleans" T-shirt still on, and with the tide coming in, smelling all salty, and the breeze filthy with humidity and the sand wet and itchy and sticky and fucking uncomfortable under my back and backside, like sandpaper, if that could be called sleeping with anybody. Friendship certainly had its ups-and-downs, a real roller-coaster! Nobody really knows anybody else, even their best friends, even their lovers, she and Vickie having fooled around in bed one time – almost all night, it was – at camp when they were about 15 discovering delicious stuff that still, even now, when she thought back on it gave her shivers – her first and second truly interpersonal orgasms for one thing, and a woozy sort of tenderness and dissolving feeling – and made her want to ask Vickie if she thought about it ever, and if maybe they could do it again, but she hadn't ever dared. Oh, Kaitlin, how stupid of you! And now I discover Vickie hates my guts and she doesn't even like my ponytail, but also she screamed out a declaration of love which didn't sound like just the ordinary girlfriend "I like you" kind of love, no, it was something more, much more, much more desperate, much more passionate, but now too late, probably, almost certainly. So, yes, you never know anybody, maybe not even yourself, until the chips are down, and maybe not really even then, because lies are insidious and subtle and the layers of self-deception are endless, and the self in any case is divided, at war with itself, and even facing the abyss and death itself, you can keep on telling yourself lies, pride and vanity and self-righteousness and plain ornery stupidity at work, and so love is lost and all its immense unknown possibilities, and you remain a stranger to yourself, and so Kaitlin thought, half-consciously, mourning her friendship – and burgeoning love and lust and nostalgia – for Vickie Burton, who was utterly beautiful, even screaming hatred, even foaming at the mouth, and Kaitlin realized all this – all this turbulent topsy-turvy stuff – as she climbed out the open bedroom window, scurried across the tiled roof which was pitched at maybe a 45 degree angle as a precaution against heavy rains, and as she stood at the edge of the roof for a moment, and then jumped onto the white canvas swimming pool awning, tumbling down, sliding down, and then sliding to the edge, grabbing the rigid metal support rod, slipping over the side of the awning roof, hanging there for a second, and, letting go slowly, one hand at a time, she dropped to the ground, her feet touching down on the warm tiles, the sunlight bright in her eyes, and the water, cobalt blue, or chlorine green, sparkling up in little diamond-like wavelets and there was a cadaver, it looked like a cadaver, in ballooning Bermuda shorts, with the fat pale hairy legs of a thickset sedentary overweight middle-aged white guy, wearing white athletic socks and brown sandals, floating face down in the pool, and a baseball cap floating not far away and that was the owner, she guessed, or maybe some poor guy who'd just run in here to escape the way she and Vickie had.

Then, when she got out on the street, she didn't see any people, just zombie types wandering around with their eyes empty, shambling, strangely discombobulated.

Puppets without strings, she thought. They look like puppets without strings.

Maybe I'll wake up, maybe this is a nightmare.

She slipped in between some bushes and watched. There were no humans, just zombies, and they seemed to be wandering around aimlessly, now that there were no more humans to catch and eat or disembowel or convert to the zombie religion or whatever the zombies were intent on.

But I'm human.

So, I'm prey – I'm the hunted.

She was sweating heavily, she noticed, and the brilliant blue perfect day, with just a touch of a skin-caressing breeze, now seemed sinister and heavy with clammy menace. Even the palm trees, even the oleander looked dangerous, ponderously malevolent; even the plants were evil. Life itself was voracious; it consumed itself, it consumed everything; life was death.

It was maybe ten o'clock in the morning.

She slipped her U-tablet out of her pocket to see if finally, it would work, and she turned to the News Channel ... "So, this is a biological attack. Miami and Fort Lauderdale are at the epicenter of the attack. And the president was targeted and is almost certainly dead. Stay in your homes, the authorities are telling people, stay in your homes."

No fucking way, she thought. Her home was two blocks down and she could see the zombies wandering here and there. Her home would be a trap.

Where could she go?

She tried phoning friends. All the lines were blocked. The phone was not working, the voice said, "All circuits are busy, please try again later. All circuits are busy, please try again later."

Then it stopped working altogether – static at first, then nothing, not even static.

Mom, good old Mom, she thought, maybe I should go there. Her mom lived with a man, Ralph, of whom Kaitlin had to admit she did not entirely approve. Why beautiful talented women so frequently ended up with assholes, Kaitlin could not for the life of her understand, but it was true that a good man was a rare and seldom thing, and hard to find; in fact, the good guys seemed to belong to an almost extinct species – the dodos of the twenty-first century. Ralph Bedford was the sort of guy who didn't know very much, who didn't know or care that he didn't know very much; and who had an opinion on everything. How people could decide to be boneheads, decide to be intentionally stupid – and ignorant – was beyond her. His lack of curiosity was positively stellar. She'd decided that being pig-headed about one's own ideas and opinions was a perfect recipe for stupidity. If you weren't open to challenge, and you didn't question your own opinions and your own knowledge or beliefs, then you'd never learn anything new.

And old Ralph was pig-headed, no doubt about it.

He did, though, have very good taste in exotic beers; the fridge was always well-stocked. And dry white wines ... and smoked meats, he really knew his smoked meats!

But, even if it meant confronting old Ralph, blood was thicker than water. She had to find if her mother was okay. So, she headed for her mother's house. Her mother lived only a block away. Skirting from tree to tree, ducking from bush to bush, and sneaking from garage to garage, Kaitlin got to the bungalow – Florida Hispanic style. And, then, she hesitated.

It all looked very calm, deceptively, dangerously calm.

Kaitlin hugged herself. She was trembling. Her teeth were chattering. God Almighty! She was like an idiotic kid's cartoon – fear and terror, teeth chattering, cold sweat dribbling down her back, trembling limbs. Damn it! This had to stop! She jammed her fist into her mouth and bit down.

Maybe if she chewed gum it would help.

She slipped out the flat green package and popped two gum tablets into her mouth and chewed carefully, trying not to make a single sound, not even munch-munch.

There were three zombies standing uncertainly, hovering around, in a little circle in the middle of the street. They were two men and a woman. Their clothes had been reduced to rags – in fact, one of the men was naked, except for a blue sock and one brown shoe.

She skirted behind the next house, climbed over a fence, walked past yet another swimming pool, but this one didn't have any cadavers. She wondered if the zombies could swim, maybe jumping into a pool would be a last-minute desperate way of avoiding …

On the other hand, a pool would be a trap. They would just have to mill around, drooling that green goo, and waiting for you to get tired or cold or fall asleep and …

Crunch, munch, Ahchoo! Ahchoo! A splat of green goo!

And, abracadabra, you are a zombie too – or dead!

Or both …! The question occurred to her: Are these zombies dead or are they just sick? And if they are sick, is there a cure? And if there's a cure, will the damage left behind, from being a zombie, be permanent or will people be just the way they were before?

I'll bet nobody knows!

She climbed over the high fence that Ralph, when he moved in with Laura, insisted be built between the backyard and the neighbors – with the result that Laura lost two good friends, Terry and Sam Goldsmith, who saw the fence as a personal insult and who didn't like the way it cast a shadow on one side of their pool and on Terry's geraniums and roses, but, Hey, you know, true love demands sacrifices – right?

Kaitlin was anxious – how was her mother?

She didn't have to wait long to find out.

Her mother was on her hands and knees feasting on what remained of old Ralph.

"Hey, Mom," Kaitlin whispered.

Her mother looked up and growled, a string of fatty gristle hanging from her teeth, and blood and green goo dripping from her mouth. "Ghhhhrrrr," said mother. She was wearing the sunglasses with the big butterfly plastic white frames that she'd copied from an ancient collector's item Italian movie poster starring ... Kaitlin couldn't remember what movie it was ... it was really old ...

"So, Mom, are you okay?" Part of Kaitlin's mind was saying, "Can I get you anything? Salt? Pepper? Worchester Sauce? Maybe you'd like some ketchup or mashed potatoes and gravy with old Ralph's thigh-bone?" She wanted to laugh, she wanted to cry, she wanted to scream, she wanted to run over and hug her mother and say to her that everything would be all right; everything would be fine – just peachy-cream! She wanted to run like hell and get out of there.

Her mother stared at her, growling, dripping goo, and then she said, in a choked voice, "Kaitlin, run, grrrh ... grrrh ... Run like hell," and then she snarled, bared her teeth, spat a gob of green and went back to feasting on old Ralph.

Munch, munch, munch! Human teeth are not really made for tearing apart a freshly killed human body, but Laura seemed to be doing okay. It was a ghoulish slurping sound.

Whatever Ralph was, whatever he did, he didn't deserve that!

Ralph Bedford had been an actuary, vice-president of an insurance company. Kaitlin wondered if his actuarial tables had taken into account a cannibalistic zombie plague – the probability that you would be eaten, dead or alive, by your second spouse. No, probably the actuarial tables had not taken account of such an eventuality. She stared at her mother munching on human flesh. No, it was not a probable event, in the normal course of things. Normally, Laura wouldn't hurt a fly. She apologized if she killed a spider, and she'd even flirted, at one point, with the idea of becoming a vegetarian; industrial farming, she said, had made the lives of cows, chickens, turkeys, and pigs utterly horrible, their existence reduced to the equivalent of life-long torture.

Kaitlin sighed. Her mother had apparently forgotten she was there; she was busy feasting on Ralph's bones.

So long, Mom! See you later, maybe, maybe in another life!

Kaitlin turned to leave and saw her mother's cat, Fluff Ball, called Fluff for short which was probably a cat insult since he was a very independent tomcat, handy with his claws, and a terror to mice and snakes. He hissed at her. His hair was standing straight up. His fangs were bared. His eyes spat fear and hatred. She crouched, and she said, as gently as she could, "Hey, Fluff, did you catch it too?"

Fluff seemed to hesitate, then he looked away – it was marvelous how cats hate to lose face! They always looked away from embarrassing confrontations. Kaitlin waited. Fluff sniffed the air, then walked over to her and rubbed against her bare leg, purring.

From then on, Fluff was her partner.

When she snuck back over the fence, he squeezed under it. When she left the next yard, he followed. Fluff, evidently, had decided to stick with her.

"Okay, Fluff, if you want to stick close that's okay. I could use the company."

She decided she would try to head north, on foot, alone – alone except for Fluff if he stuck with her. And if she was on the road, maybe she could hitch a ride. The zombies didn't seem to know how to drive.

She rested part of the afternoon in a tool shed on the edge of the Everglades. It smelt of oil and tools and metal and sunburnt wood and fertilizer and seeds.

Fluff curled up in the crook of her arm and purred.

She was exhausted and had already walked miles.

She fell asleep and then woke up, slowly realizing that time had passed, and wondering, for a moment, where she was and what had happened and then she remembered. Fluff was crouched on her chest and was licking her nose – and then he gave it a gentle bite.

"Love bite, eh, Fluff."

She was starving and thirsty. But she had to keep moving – dusk was coming; soon it would be dark.

But then she discovered that she was wrong about the zombies not knowing how to drive. By early evening, it seemed the zombies had always known how to drive, or maybe they were just quick learners, because, now, at 8:00 o'clock in the evening of what Kaitlin figured must be Day Two of the Zombie Invasion, they certainly knew how to drive.

And so that big fat slob of a zombie had even stopped his pickup and jumped out and lumbered after her and chased her into the bloody swamp where …

Whoosh!

Now – the alligator was coming for her …

The alligator made a dash. Kaitlin sidestepped the charging beast, jumped, and almost fell, and kicked backwards as the alligator flashed by, then it whipped around, trying for her again, and she rolled away, got up and ran.

Fluff hissed and dashed in front of the Alligator. The alligator turned on Fluff, snapped its jaws, but missed. Fluff swerved, and swerved again, and leapt over the alligator, and zipped past it as it swung around, and she and Fluff ran for it, galloping, leaping over everything that got in their way.

Just as she and Fluff got back to the road, she saw them, a column of cars coming top speed, God, they must be doing 120 miles an hour, coming down the road …

She ducked behind a tree, just out of sight. Fluff curled around her legs. Yes, Kaitlin said, that's good. We have to stick together. We don't want those guys spotting us.

Then the cars were gone, just tail lights disappearing.

It was silent. The cat meowed.

Okay, Fluff, we are on the road again.

About a minute after the cars disappeared, Kaitlin saw what looked like a series of huge explosions, down the road, in the direction she was heading.

Oh, oh, she thought, the zombies must be up in front of us too.

Or maybe there's a road block.

Would the roadblock be manned by humans, or non-humans?

And maybe they've enforced quarantine on the whole area.

"Hey, Fluff, what do you think? Will they shoot us when they see us, or not?"

As the big long column of twenty-five cars came rushing onward at top speed, certainly at over a hundred, it was clear they were not going to stop. Doug Serra had no choice but to order the Molotov cocktail teams into action.

Two of his guys managed to hit the first three cars. The first two cars careened into each other, slewed sideways off the road, into the ditch, and threw two zombies out, flipped over, and then exploded in a huge whoosh of flame. The third car, also aflame, with the zombie driver burning up but still at the steering wheel, drove straight on, kamikaze style, smashed into the police barrier, sending the patrol cars careening across the road, opening a way through for the other cars, and then turning over exploding, and smashing into the ditch and concrete side barrier.

The rest of the column just streamed through the gap at over 100 miles an hour. Sheriff Serra and his team sprayed the cars with bullets from their automatics and threw a few Molotovs; but it did not seem to slow them down one bit.

The cars disappeared along the highway, heading north and west, and soon they were out of sight, the taillights disappearing …

Then they were gone.

It was the zombie breakout – they were headed towards Naples, Sarasota, Tampa, and Saint Petersburg …

Serra stood there, as if in shock. He had lost the battle. Who knew what the consequences would be? The line had been broken – the zombies were headed north and west, and as fast as they could go; soon the west coast of Florida would be infected – and then Georgia, Louisiana …

Serra wiped his forehead. Christ Almighty – maybe there was no way to contain this thing! The whole world would become a zombie world!

Then, there were the two zombies who had jumped or leaped or been thrown out of their cars – the ones hit by the Molotov cocktails – and they were lying on the ground looking like cadavers, their clothes smoking and sending off sparks; but they got up soon enough; and Serra shouted, "Don't go near them!"

It was too late.

Two of his men were infected within, well, it seemed like within seconds. And they charged and infected another of his men.

Serra ran to the box of Molotov cocktails; he was going to burn his own men alive, and he knew he had to do it – otherwise …

One of his men – Pete Craver – bit him in the arm before he could get to the box of Molotovs. Serra tossed Pete off, and managed to get his hands on two Molotov cocktails.

He lit them – fumbling with the lighter and tossed them straight at the line of four zombies approaching him.

One of his troopers, Jack Leblanc, still human, was pumping bullets into the zombies but that didn't stop them, the only thing that stopped them was fire.

Serra lobbed the Molotovs at the four zombies, but, even bursting into flame, they staggered on.

One of the burning zombies – Alyssa Velez – ran straight at Jack Leblanc and embraced him it looked like, grabbed him in a full body hug, pressing her lips to his, wrapping her arms around him, as the flames whooshed up, taking

Jack up with her in a pillar of flame.

Serra raced at Jack and tried to pull him away from Alyssa but couldn't. The flames were so hot he only managed to burn his hand and set his jacket on fire and then bullets exploded and Serra caught one in the chest, "Fuck, that is all I need," he thought, numbed, through the vibrating shock of pain, coming in sudden nausea-making waves; now there were three zombies converging on him, coming at him from three angles, he sprinted, feeling he was going to die and wondering why he hadn't become one of those things, not yet anyway.

He ran, using his flaming jacket as a protective cape, and got to the box of Molotov cocktails and he lifted two, touched them to his flaming jacket and threw them, scoring two bull's-eyes, two columns of flame, two pillars of burning flesh, there must be something about this in the Bible, he thought. Now there was only one zombie left, and that was his old pal Ed Rowan.

"Well, sorry, Ed old man, I can't let you eat me alive or turn me into one of the living dead." Serra picked up another Molotov cocktail and he lit it and he held it in his right hand, watching Ed stagger forward.

"Ed, look, Ed, I'm sorry, I really am sorry, but Christ Almighty, I have no choice, Ed, I have no choice."

Ed kept coming, shambling ahead, staggering, his arms stretched out in front of him like somebody groping in the dark, funny how some of these creatures were fast and some of them were slow. Ed's eyes were glowing green, a ghostly effect in the night, with the burning bodies still around them, and the blackened and burning carcasses of cars, and the smell of burning body fat, and fried skin, and sizzled hair, and spilt blood, and Serra thought of how he had always been able to depend on Ed Rowan, how they had gotten each other out of a dozen scrapes over the years, and he said a silent prayer for himself and for the soul of Ed Rowan, and he threw the bottle, and it exploded, and Ed just kept coming so Doug Serra backed away, and backed away, now feeling weak, feeling blood stream down his side, down his legs, feeling his strength drain away, that damned bullet must have done quite a bit of damage, and he backed up again, and he felt the hard metal of the one patrol car that was still undamaged, his own, by chance, the door, and the door handle and he reached out behind him to seize the door handle and Ed was still staggering forward, without a sound, without a whimper, a column of flame, a living or dead torch, it was hard to tell – were they dead or were they alive? Doug Serra clasped at the door handle, his hand slippery with blood. He felt dizzy and light-headed and for a single moment it all seemed a huge hilarious joke and he began to laugh and then everything went dark, even the man torch, the column of flame, his body, everything went dark and Doug Serra felt himself falling and his hand slipped down the smooth car door and then there was nothing, nothing at all.

"Well, Fluff, do we keep going or do we just hide here?"

Fluff had no opinion. He withheld judgement. He was looking up at her with his enigmatic cat eyes, but he certainly had been a hero cat. By leaping almost into its jaws, he had distracted the alligator and made it easy – well, relatively easy, for Kaitlin to escape the evil monster's clutches. Kaitlin took a deep breath. Well, the monster wasn't evil; it was just doing its alligator thing; it was in its nature, and all things in nature fulfil their destinies, as Aristotle perhaps would have put it.

Kaitlin had scrambled back up onto the road and then she and Fluff ducked down and hid again as the big long column of cars went racing past, and then she had seen the great flare of flame, and heard the explosions and the gunfire. Then it was all silent and still except the sound of flames; it was maybe, she thought, about a mile and a half away, maybe much less, just around a gentle bend in the road.

"I think, Fluff, that we should continue onwards, and see what we shall see, what do you think of that?"

Fluff meowed and Kaitlin knelt and picked him up and put him on her shoulder where he perched and seemed quite comfortable, keeping his balance as if he were an acrobat cat which he most certainly was.

When Kaitlin got to the police barrier, cars were still burning. There were dead, charred bodies on the road and on the shoulder of the road, and there was one police car that looked like it had not been damaged; it was hard to see through the smoke and in the dark.

Kaitlin approached the undamaged car cautiously. Maybe she could radio for help. What if there were still zombies, hanging about in the smoke and shadows?

An oil drum flared up and suddenly she saw him, a man, sitting on the asphalt, his back propped against the car. He was covered in blood. He held a pistol in his hand, and he was aiming it straight at her.

"You are one of them," he said. His voice was thick with phlegm. He coughed.

His eyes flickered with a green light.

Kaitlin glanced left and right: there was no cover that was close. She was outlined, she imagined, visible, an easy target, against the flames.

"I'm not one of them," she said, very clearly, "And neither is my cat."

"You cat?" he said, "Your cat?" The hand holding the gun wavered. A shot rang out. A spurt of asphalt kicked up and exploded just beside Kaitlin, pebbles and bits of tar hitting her legs. Fluff crouched lower and dug his claws into her shoulder. The man keeled over, in slow motion, and fell on his side.

Kaitlin stood stock still. That man just shot at me! That man just tried to kill me!

She hesitated – what to do?

The hesitation didn't last long.

"He needs help," she said to Fluff, "He's still a human being, and he needs help."

She walked towards the patrol car. Close to the man, there was a cadaver, a charcoal cadaver, burnt, all of him burnt, looking mummified, and Kaitlin said, "hello, hello," to the body that looked normal. Slowly, she approached.

Fluff tightened his grip on her shoulder and hissed. His hair went up straight; he arched his back.

Kaitlin stopped, thinking, cats know these things, cats sense things humans can't sense. But, still, if the man is hurt, and she took one step forward.

Fluff leaped from her shoulder and landed right in front of her and swung around and hissed at her. Then he turned again, and, cautiously, walked forward until he was right next to the human body. He sniffed; he meowed; and he turned to look back at her.

The man stirred. Kaitlin came forward, the man was trying to sit up, Kaitlin helped him – and then she looked into his eyes; they seemed to glow green; his mouth was dripping green goo … or was it just the light?

"Ugh," the wounded man said, "Ugh!" His eyelids fluttered and closed.

Kaitlin was kneeling next to him. Fluff had not run away so Kaitlin thought maybe it was not as dangerous as she thought it was. But she frowned. Are animals really that wise? Can instinct catch everything?

The man's shirt badge said "Doug Serra"

The man sneezed and a spray of green goo caught Kaitlin in the eyes and on her cheeks. She wiped it away with the back of her hand, thinking, "Well, now I've caught it, if I'm going to catch it." Blinking through the goo, she looked more carefully at the man: he was wounded and bleeding from the shoulder, blood was seeping through his shirt, a dark stain, spreading.

"Ugh," he said, "Ugh."

"You've been hurt," said Kaitlin, wondering at herself, talking to a zombie, a part zombie at least.

"Kill!" The man's eyes fluttered open. "Kill everybody!" He seemed to focus, the green tinge flicked in the blue of his eyes, "Kill everybody," he repeated, flecks of green foam bubbling on his tongue, dripping from his lips.

"What do you mean – kill everybody?" Kaitlin was still kneeling, her face close to his, and thinking that she definitely was an absolute idiot. He was one of them; he was going to leap up any second and bite off her nose or something worse.

"Kill them all," he breathed, his eyes seeming to focus closer in, the pupil narrowing in on her, "Kill, I had to kill them all."

"Them all – who?"

"My friends."

"You are hurt. You're bleeding. You need help."

"It's too late for me! *Madre de Dios*! They got past us. The zombies, they got past us," he coughed some more, and blood, lots of blood flooded out of his mouth. "And now I'm one of them. I feel it. I feel it inside, but … I'm going to …" His eyes closed. "*Estoy muriendo*."

Kaitlin unbuttoned his shirt; she had once taken first aid, but she really didn't know how to deal with a gunshot wound. His lungs were flooding, so he would choke on his own blood, she saw the wound, saw the blood, mixed with green slime that coated his chest. What in the world was she supposed to do?

She opened the door to the police car – cool and orderly inside; it seemed like another world, the computer screen glowed, a clipboard with notes sat on the passenger seat, a pen was attached to the clip board, beside the computer screen was a photograph of a woman and two children – his wife, Kaitlin figured, his wife and his kids – and she looked at the computer and at the radio and she pushed a few buttons and she said, "Come in, is there anybody, come in," and then she saw the button saying Mike and Speak, and she pushed it and she said, "Can anybody hear me," and a voice said, "Come in, Come in, yes, we hear you, Doug Serra's vehicle." Kaitlin said, "Doug Serra is wounded, I think he's dying."

"Who is this?"

"My name is Kaitlin. I was walking on the road, trying to get away from the zombies."

"Where are you?"

"We are on highway 93, I think, I'm not sure where, there is a long curve in the road."

"Continue."

"There was a road block here, but the zombies, I think it was zombies; they forced their way through, a column of cars, everybody here is dead except Doug Serra – and he is dying."

"What's wrong with him?"

"He's been shot in the chest, near the shoulder. Also, he's caught the zombie virus, I think, but he's not acting like a zombie."

"Take the U-Tab camera and show us. We've located you. We are sending, if we can, a helicopter."

Kaitlin spotted the U-Tab camera. She took it, turned it on, and took it outside and pointed the eye at Doug Serra's chest. The fires reflected on his chest, making the skin, the blood, the green sheen glow …

"Right," said the voice. "Now, Kaitlin, here's what you do …"

Kaitlin gently pushed Doug Serra into position, on his side, as the voice had instructed her. The voice had gone through the routine: in the trunk of the car there was a first aid kit, and, in the kit, there was a sort of plastic sheet material which would stick to the skin and seal punctures. Then there were steps to follow: Cut Doug's shirt off his body. Put the plastic sheet material over the wound, press it down, it will attach itself to the skin even if there is blood and gore and so on.

It did attach itself to the skin.

There was blood and gore.

Then she was to turn Doug Serra onto his side, with the wound on the downside, so that the lung on the uppermost side might not be filled with blood.

Then she was to wait for them.

They would be coming.

Yes, they would be coming, so they said.

They would be coming with a helicopter. They would get Doug Serra out of there; they would get Doug out. "He's one of our best men," the voice said, and he added, "Thank you for what you are doing, Kaitlin."

"You're welcome," said Kaitlin, embarrassed, not knowing what to say, how to respond. Doug Serra was on his side, he was breathing. The wound had stopped making the whistling sound; it seemed to be sealed. Little bits of green slime dribbled from the corner of his mouth. Kaitlin rubbed at her cheek, green goo peeled away, some of it was loose and powdery; some of it was rubbery and like a dry face mask and came away in thin sheets.

"You sure you haven't caught the zombie virus, Kaitlin?" said the voice.

"I haven't got it," she said, "I mean I sure don't feel like I've got it, and I looked at myself in the mirror and my eyes aren't green or anything and my cat is not afraid of me. But Doug Serra has got it; green goo is still dribbling from his mouth."

"I see, I see," said the voice, "Well, is that a fact!"

Kaitlin was curious about one point. "So – how are you sure your people won't get it when they come here in their helicopter. Everybody who goes near it seems to get it – well, so far I haven't but ..."

"You have a point, Kaitlin," said the voice, "you have a very good point."

"I must be immune, I guess."

"Yes, you must be immune. That is very interesting, Kaitlin, well, you just stay there, you just stay there, sit tight, and our people will come, and everything will be all right."

Something in the voice made Kaitlin uneasy – even suspicious, "Okay," she said, "I'll stay right here."

"Good girl. We'll be there shortly, Kaitlin."

And the connection ceased.

"Put our thinking cap on, Fluff, put our thinking cap on!" Kaitlin stood very still, picking some zombie goo out of her hair: If people were infected at the barrier and you sent a helicopter – maybe a helicopter gunship – what would you do? Would you land and take the nice infected people on board? Or would you ... bomb the hell out of the place?

"Fluff, we have a problem," she said, "I verily do believe we have a problem."

Fluff looked up at her and meowed.

CHAPTER 37 – JUDGMENT DAY

In the Volpe Octopus skyscraper in New York, the atmosphere – at first excited by the tragedy, by the stream of news, and by the spectacular nature of the zombie plague – was now gloomy and downbeat. People were beginning to think seriously of death, of their own death, of the death of their families, of their loved ones, and of their neighbors.

Yes, the zombie virus was spreading like wildfire and soon there would no humans left, so at least it seemed to Bill Brothers.

"Communications are very bad, General," Bill said.

"That's to be expected in a war situation, Bill," said the General who still looked tan and fit and fresh as a daisy, "and as I said, and as the president said in her speech, we are now being attacked, and this is a massive attack, using biological and electronic weapons – and real hard-wired weapons too, since we've seen our helicopter gunships shot down by ground-to-air missiles fired by zombies apparently, and so on."

"We are getting more reports of zombies on the west coast of Florida, and zombies in Texas and beyond, and zombies, as we have seen, at the gates of Washington and, as we already know, just outside New York City."

"It's going to get worse, Bill, before it gets better, that's what I think."

"Well, let's look at some footage from three hours ago …"

The vice president's good friend, spiritual counsellor, golfing partner, and business associate, the Reverend Raphael Honey Raphael, leader of the Second Coming Church of our Lord Jesus Christ of the Apocalypse, went on television and went viral on the net saying that, "The Final Day of Judgement is upon us. This is the Lord's Judgement, his righteous judgement. We deserve to perish, brothers and sisters, we deserve to perish."

He hammered on the pulpit; then he fell down and rolled around on the ground and hammered his fists on the hardwood.

"We deserve, Oh, Lord, to perish," he screamed.

A certain segment of the population – several hundred thousand perhaps – stormed out of their houses, rending their clothes, gnashing their teeth, and wailing about the Final Day of Judgement.

Some families, better prepared than others, carried out collective suicide, using poison in orange juice or ladled on ice cream or using pistols, kitchen knives, automatic weapons, and baseball bats. Children were not spared. Indeed, children were the first to be sacrificed.

Up on a stormy mountain side, the members of Evangelicals United for the End of the World and the Movement for the Quickly Coming of the Second Coming chanted.

"Hallelujah!"

"Hallelujah!"

Having failed to trigger a final total worldwide nuclear holocaust in the Middle East, which was the necessary prelude to the Rapture and Conversion of the Jews, the members of Evangelicals United for the End of the World and the Movement for the Quickly Coming of the Second Coming climbed high up on Mount Judd to give thanks for the new plague which appeared to be positively, deliciously Biblical in its proportions and consequences. If this wasn't the end of the world, then, well, nothing would be!

"The end is nigh," the preacher called out. "The end is nigh!"

They all fell to their knees, men, women, and children.

Clouds were gathering near the summit, beyond the tree line; the clouds darkened; lightning flashed; thunder rippled down the valley, and the day turned to night. And the preacher intoned:

"But all these things are merely the beginning of birth pangs. Then they will deliver you to tribulation, and will kill you, and you will be hated by all nations on account of my name.

For nation will rise against nation, and kingdom against kingdom; and in various places there will be famines and earthquakes."

Hallelujah! It did the cockles of the old heart good, and it warmed the soul, to see so many True in Christ, praying, prostrated flat on the ground or kneeling on their knees, up on the mountain top, praying for deliverance and salvation as the final annihilation of the planet Earth and all the ungodly creatures upon it approached at the speed of light!

"Hallelujah!"

"Hallelujah!"

Merry Apocalypse to all – and to all – a good night!

On *Andromeda II*:

Claire jerked and bounced up and down on the floor, as if traversed by a series of blinding electric shocks. Kate and Anthony knelt next to her, in the lamplight, as the lights in the Control Room were flickering, saying, "Claire? Claire? Claire?"

Claire vibrated like a violin string. Her fangs clattered. Her arms and legs lurched up and down. At any moment, she might bite off her tongue. It zipped in and out of her mouth like a snake that was being electrocuted.

"Claire!" Kate grabbed her by the shoulders.

Anthony gave Kate a glass of water. Kate put the glass of water to Claire's lips. The lips were trembling so much the water splashed up and spilled down Claire's chin and her fangs clattered against the glass almost shattering it.

Ben Kamu said, "Maybe a good stiff drink, something!"

"Yes," said Anthony, "A stiff drink and maybe some coffee too."

"Brew some coffee someone," said Kate, tears streaming down her face. She was still striped black and white like a zebra. "For God's sake: the child is dying!"

Ben brought a glass of whiskey. He handed it to Kate.

"Okay, Claire, you are going to drink this whether you want to or not!" Kate put the glass against Claire's lips, Claire's fangs clattered against it, shattering the glass.

"Goddamn," said Kate pulling the glass away; she grabbed Claire and looked at the reptilian lips: No, Claire hadn't cut herself.

"She didn't swallow any glass. I've got all the pieces," said Ben; he was down on his hands and knees.

"Let's try again," Anthony handed Kate a plastic glass filled with whiskey.

Kate pressed it to Claire's lips, the lips were chattering up and down, the fangs caught in the glass, splashed half the whiskey, and almost ripped the glass out of Kate's hand.

"Stroke her," said Ben, "Stroke her, Kate, stroke her, you know, make her purr. When she's stroked, she goes into this sort of state of … well, ecstasy, she can't control it!"

"Okay, anything's worth a try," Kate stroked the sides of Claire's head, and she murmured "Claire, Claire, Claire, we all love you," she kissed Claire, risking her tongue and lips against those chattering fangs which could cut her to pieces.

The chattering stopped.

Claire's reptile eyes blinked; she seemed to focus, and Claire returned the kiss, her tongue flickering against Kate's lips.

"I love you too, Kate," Claire said, "And I like your zebra color scheme and what are you talking about? And shouldn't we be working? And what is that whiskey for? Oh, never mind, I'll drink it." She took the glass of whiskey and downed it in one gulp.

"Wow," said Ben.

"So, what happened?" said Kate, "Do you remember?"

Claire looked puzzled, "What happened?"

"You were absent, you were trembling."

"Oh," Claire paused. Her reptile brow was furrowed in concentration, "What happened? Was I overwhelmed?"

"Overwhelmed?"

"I was far away. I wasn't here anymore. I was with V and with that woman she found on the yacht."

"They are gone."

"What's gone?"

"V, the yacht, the helicopter, they are gone."

Ben flipped on some screens, "See, Claire, the radar shows emptiness. And, here, the overhead satellite feed shows a wave of fog and of light and then nothing – the helicopter and the yacht are gone."

"Zoom in please. Can you see any floating wreckage?"

"I don't see anything."

"What about the GPS locator?"

"There is no GPS locator signal."

"What about the continual black box transmissions from the helicopter? It emits a stream of data in real time."

"It just stopped, just disappeared."

"Let's go back, see if we can listen to the feed just before the shock wave hit. Maybe we can see what happened."

"Okay – coming up!"

"Where the hell are they?"

"We can listen to the whole thing."

"Where the hell did they go?"

PART FOUR – SHANGRI-LA

CHAPTER 38 – THE GODDESS RETURNS

Sergeant Eve Schmidt knew she must be hallucinating.

Everything in the helicopter went blurry.

"Something is happening." She took off her Polaroids and wiped her eyes, "Something is …"

WHAM!

The sun shone brightly, the water sparkled, a brilliant blue, and the deep glorious sky was cloudless. The yacht *A Flight of Fancy* was perhaps two kilometers away, drifting on a calm afternoon sea, but everything, strangely, seemed unreal, too intense, too vivid, too technicolor, like an over-vivid video game; then …

WHAM!

"I think something is …"

A blinding light engulfed Captain Anderson, the pilot Guy Vargas, and Eve Schmidt. A wild vibration shook the helicopter, and then, in one instant, the world turned dark – suddenly it was deepest night …

The sun was gone.

The blue sky was gone.

The sparkling sea was gone.

WHAM

It was totally dark. "Oh, boy," whispered Eve Schmidt.

WHAM!

Out of the darkness, a flash of lightening thundered down, the bolt passed just next to the helicopter. The giant zigzag of light struck the ocean, sizzling into a huge whirl, a maelstrom, of foam.

"Oh, boy," Eve Schmidt closed her eyes. Her vision turned red, then purple, then a dazzling array of blood-shot pulsating stars.

The sizzling zigzag of light morphed into a huge circle of whirling light, a frenzied tumult of water and light, swirling down, swirling down, rising up, as a vortex of air, and then …

Eve Schmidt opened her eyes, and blinked.

The vortex formed itself into a towering tornado. Lit by the moon, it shimmered, twirling bands of silver and black. It touched down on the surface of the ocean and sucked up a mountain of water. Within seconds, the tornado became a waterspout that reached up and beyond the heavens. Turning and swirling, it swept towards the helicopter. The copter began to spin out of control.

"We're being sucked into it, Captain, into the waterspout" shouted Guy Vargas, the pilot, screaming to make himself heard over the roar.

"Go with the flow," said Captain Anderson, remembering an old story about a maelstrom he'd read; by giving into the inevitable, by inserting yourself into the roaring stream, sometimes you escaped it … Edgar Allan Poe, it must have been …

"Go with the flow?"

"Yes, dive into, follow the whirlwind."

"Okay, it's your funeral."

"Right! It will be our funeral together."

Eve Schmidt stared at the towering steel-gray tornado of water – it was beautiful, like a giant whirling snake or piece of cable and what was that light shining on it, it must be the moon – it was the moon.

And yet, a few seconds ago, the moon had been nowhere in the sky.

And it had been day, a few seconds ago, not night.

What about V? Where was she?

"What about V?" she said. Her earphones were filled with static; she pulled them off. Useless damned things!

"Just static, no reception," said the Captain. "And the radar doesn't show the yacht. In fact, it doesn't show anything!"

The helicopter moved more smoothly now, only ratting with random vibrations. But it was being sucked closer and closer to the towering swirling and monstrous blue-silver column of whirling water … Maybe we're going to drown, thought Eve Schmidt, maybe we're going to drown at altitude 500 or 1,000 feet.

Captain Anderson glanced down. The ocean was a cauldron of crisscrossing breaking waves, foam and froth, roaring steel-blue water, boiling, swirling, rising in monstrous …

A bolt of lightning split the column of water in two – two swirling masses of water peeled off. A series of bolts shattered the sea, shattered the air. It was non-stop explosion, flash, flash, flash …

Blinding light …

Captain Alan Anderson was not a praying man. But he closed his eyes and said a prayer to Whomever or Whatever governed the universe, asking that they be delivered from this chaos, which surely would destroy them all. He remembered the words of a prayer from his childhood. "The Lord is my shepherd and I shall not want … He maketh me to lie down in green pastures. He leadeth me beside still waters …"

A thunderous roar and a huge flash turned the insides of Captain Anderson's eyelids bright crimson, and then … silence …

And then there was a rising hush and then a hammering rushing sound, which the Captain clearly heard over the straining of the engine.

"Christ," the pilot muttered, "Christ Almighty!"

"A deluge," said Eve.

It was rain. The rain was hammering on the helicopter canopy.

The rain was terrific. It hammered against the helicopter rotor blades and against the canopy and cabin.

"I can't see a damned thing," the pilot shouted. "The instruments have gone crazy. The radar is going crazy."

"V, can you hear me?" the Captain pushed the communications button.

There was nothing, just static, bursts of static.

A huge flash of lightning burst upon them. It seemed to go on and on. The Captain closed his eyes – a burning redness welled up, under his eyelids.

"Oh, boy," said Eve Schmidt; the light had blinded her, a searing redness, blotches like blood on black velvet, "Oh, boy!"

Captain Anderson squeezed his eyes shut. The afterimage sparkled on his retina, the pilot and his helmet, and the controls, and the instruments, and lightning beyond the canopy and the sound of the rotors struggling against the deluge and then was there hail, it must be hail, a bang-bang-bang-bang rattling against the canopy; the rotors and engine screamed, straining to keep the helicopter aloft in a sudden surge of wind …

"Hail," said Eve Schmidt,"

"Golf balls," muttered the pilot.

"More like baseballs," said Eve Schmidt.

It sounded like the hammering hail might break the helicopter apart, wham, wham, wham, then there was a sudden surge of wind and Captain Anderson opened his eyes.

The wind dropped.

Without warning it was a calm night …

It was a starry tranquil night with a moon, and the shock was so great, when the rain and hail and wind ceased, that the helicopter shot up and almost flipped over, and then dropped straight towards the water – but pilot Guy Vargas regained control, and revved down the motor; the rotors slowed, and the sound was down to normal.

"Bravo," said Eve Schmidt, "That was cool."

"Whew," said Guy, "Thanks."

Captain Anderson shook himself. His teeth were clenched, his jaw was aching from the strain, and his hands were balled into fists, nails biting through his gloves.

He blinked.

The towering columns of whirling water were gone; and the ocean below, lit by the moon, was calm, just smooth rollers, the steel-blue ridges white with foam, the backs of the waves still pocked with marks of the falling rain; but there was no rain; the rain had ceased, just a few seconds ago, and now the marks of the rain disappeared too. Again, he looked down. The ocean was calm, just smooth rollers, under the moon.

"Tell me if I'm mistaken, Eve and Guy, but ten minutes ago, wasn't it about three o'clock in the afternoon?"

"Yes," said Eve, "It was just after three."

"That's right," said Guy, "actually I glanced at the time, and it was 15:13 when we went into that storm, or whatever the hell it was; it's now, by the same clock, 15:25. So 12 minutes ago we were bathing in that nice warm afternoon sunlight."

"And now it is night and the moon is up."

"Yes, Captain."

"It's a half moon. And last night we had …"

"Yeah, Captain, I get you – last night we had a full moon."

"So …" Captain Anderson frowned, "We've skipped a few days, which is impossible."

"I don't know what's impossible anymore, Captain, but there's something else."

"What?"

"We haven't got any communications and no GPS either from what I can tell and nothing here is broken."

They tried all the frequencies.

"There nothing there," said Eve.

"Let's try our reptile girlfriend, V."

"Hello V, are you receiving?"

Nothing!

"Hello V, are you receiving?"

They tried to contact the Admiral on the *Dwight D. Eisenhower*.

Nothing!

They tried to contact *Andromeda II*.

Nothing!

"Look at that," Eve Schmidt, "The radar shows an island."

"And this island has tall mountains." Captain Anderson peered through binoculars. In the distance he saw a vast mountain in the moonlight, rising above the other mountains; it was cone-shaped, and, caught by the moonlight, smoke was drifting from its summit.

"A volcano," said the captain, "We were nowhere near an island this size, or volcanoes or a major mountain range. Where the hell are we?"

"And, Captain, if you try the different radio frequencies, you'll discover ..."

"What?"

"There are no radio transmissions of any kind from anywhere, Captain."

"And there's something else ..."

"The yacht is there. It's still there. Or it's come back, or something."

"So, wherever we've gone, we've gone with the yacht!"

Now it was night.

V returned to consciousness, returned to life.

She found herself standing on the deck of *A Flight of Fancy*, locked in an embrace with Isis, holding the girl close, caressing her hair with her right claw, and whispering, "There, there, there, we will be fine, we will be okay, no harm will befall us!"

V shook her head and blinked. It was as if she were waking from a daze, or a deep sleep. It was night, not day – how had that happened?

Lightning flashed. Isis looked into V's eyes. Isis's dark skin shone in the electricity-charged air. Her eyes were wide, blinking. She buried her face in V's shoulder and tightened her grip on V's waist.

Another flash of lightning – a huge bolt of pure, burning, eye-searing, bluish white light, zigzagged down into the water, which boiled like a cauldron. Foaming waves towered up, dwarfing A *Flight of Fancy*. But the yacht itself did not move; it was a shimmering island of stillness in the tempest.

V blinked.

Yes, it was night.

A few seconds ago, it had been day.

V and Isis had been about to jump overboard – escaping from the disintegrating yacht – when A *Flight of Fancy* had, in the bright afternoon light, dissolved into millions of shimmering pixels, then into a scintillating fog, then into nothing, as did the world around it, the ocean and the sky and the sun itself, it all morphed into an iridescent void. V was certain that she and Isis would fall through the nothingness of A *Flight of Fancy* into the ocean, and then fall forever, though the veil of this strange place, into absolute nothingness. But she noticed, looking down at herself, as she reached out to Isis, and as Isis took her hand, that she and Isis were melting into insubstantial mist.

And so, as mist, V intermingled with Isis. Isis, at the last instant before the darkness, before the bolt of lightning, at the last instant, looking terrified, had seized V by the hand. "Don't leave me, please don't leave me!"

And so, they mingled, V and Isis, and, then, when they woke up, they were standing on the deck, holding each other in a tight embrace. They looked up. Rain came pounding down out of the dark night sky, pouring down, a deluge, soaking both of them, and, just as they took shelter in the cabin, soaked, absolutely soaked, the rain turned to hail that hammered down; and the two of them stood there, dripping, just inside the doorway, V and Isis, staring into each other's eyes, while the icy hammering continued on the roof of the cabin and as the lights inside the cabin automatically went on – after all, there were living creatures moving around inside the cabin, and it was night, and so the sensors automatically went into action – and, finally, the calm returned, Isis said:

"There is something I must do." And, with water still running from her short dark hair, little rivulets down her face, and her tunic soaked, Iris knelt by the two dead soldiers, Annette Brighton and Federico Harvey, two polished skeletons in their crisp neatly pressed uniforms, and she moved her hands over them, and as V watched:

The two skeletons glowed.

The glow engulfed them as if it were a flame.

The skeletal bodies were buried in a flashing glow and then ... then they were alive, rubbing their eyes, asking:

"What happened?"

"Who are you?"

They reached for their weapons which were no longer there, but stacked, neatly, at the side of the cabin.

"My name is Isis," she said, still kneeling beside them, water dripping from her tunic. "I am afraid I murdered you; but now you are alive."

"Murdered us?"

"Yes, I'm very sorry. I do apologize. I was distracted. You surprised me. I was frightened. So, I killed you."

"We were dead?"

"Yes."

"But now we're alive?"

"Yes."

Annette Brighton's eyes opened wide, "What in the world is that?"

"My God," said Federico Harvey, sitting up, staring first at Isis, and then, with horror, at the reptile woman standing just behind Isis; it was a turquoise and green and gold glittering creature – equipped with fangs and claws – and it was female, with large bright golden eyes, the eyes of a snake.

"*That*, as you so tactfully put it," said V, "is me." She tried to make her reptilian smile reassuring – though the fangs and forked tongue did make her initial charm offensives problematic, "I am a friend," she added, with a reptilian grin.

"Yes," said Isis, "She is a friend."

The radio sputtered into life. "V, are you there?" And from outside, in the air which had suddenly grown quiet and calm, they heard the helicopter coming close, hovering over the yacht.

V spoke into her miniature mike, "Yes, Captain Anderson, I am here, and Isis is here – and, well you won't believe this –"

"I will believe anything, V, anything."

"Isis has revived Brighton and Harvey."

"She did what?"

"She brought Brighton and Harvey back to life."

Captain Anderson said nothing for a long instant, then, "Could you give me Brighton, V? Thank you."

"Certainly," said V, and she held out the mike to Annette Brighton who staggered to her feet, looked down at herself, patted herself down, trying to decide whether she was real or not, whether she was dreaming or not, and she noticed that she was not wearing the bio-suit or the body armor she had been wearing when she landed on *A Flight of Fancy*, but that she was in her light summer uniform, clean and crisply ironed, as if it had just been put on, which made her think she was indeed dreaming. She took the tiny mike from V, and, staring at the humanoid reptile face, she said, "Thank you," and then she said, "Yes, Captain, it's me."

"And Federico?"

"He's here too, and there's this, well, this reptile woman. It looks like what people call a hybrid – you know: those mythical things that –"

"She's a friend," said Captain Anderson, "she's a friend."

"Yes, sir," said Annette Brighton, looking doubtful.

"Could you pass the mike to our reptile friend, Annette; by the way, her name is V."

"Yes, sir," Annette Brighton handed the mike to V. "Here," she said, her face still expressing doubt – even terror.

"Yes, Captain Anderson," said V, putting Anderson on speaker.

"V, there's an island," said Captain Anderson, "where no island was before. It has high mountains, and at least one volcano, so we have no idea where we are. Does your friend Isis have any idea?"

"Isis?"

"We have travelled through time and space to meet the Puppet Master," said Isis, "but I don't know when or where we are, Captain, except that it is very far and a very long time from our starting place and date."

"Do you know how long we are meant to stay here?"

"No, Captain, I'm sorry, I don't."

"We don't have infinite fuel, so we had better land the helicopter soon – so we are heading to the island. Try to follow us in the yacht."

"Yes, Captain Anderson, we'll do that," said V. "See you on the beach – perhaps the swimming is good."

"You are a demon with a sense of humor, I see, V," said the Captain.

"I try to keep people amused," said V, blinking her big snake eyes pleasantly at Annette Brighton and Federico Harvey.

The surf rolled gently in on a sandy beach. A line of foam shone white in the moonlight. "At least the moon is the earth's moon. Otherwise I'd have my doubts," said V. "We might be on another planet, in another galaxy, maybe in another universe."

"Yes, it is reassuring," said Isis. "It is the same old moon – the goddess Diana, or, for that matter, Isis."

"True," said V. "You are a moon spirit and a nymph."

"Thank you for the 'nymph'," said Isis. "I always wanted to be a nymph."

"A moon spirit," said Federico, thinking, this is a dream, this is a world full of crazies, or maybe of nymphs and dragons and tooth fairies.

"Yes, old myths, gods and goddesses," said Annette, pulling a sail around to capture the warm breeze that was blowing towards shore. She had already gotten used to working with the reptile-woman. V was strong and good at hauling sail and pulling up the anchor and generally seemed to know her way around a yacht.

They dropped anchor about seventy yards from the beach.

They lowered the yacht's boat.

V and Federico rowed them ashore, though the boat was equipped with what looked like a perfectly good motor. Rowing was quieter, more discreet, and would save fuel.

Guy had put the helicopter down on the beach, not far away, close to a cluster of palm trees. The beach was about 150 yards deep, with a few clusters of palm trees, and with 150 yards between the water and the tree line.

Captain Anderson, Guy, and Eve Schmidt were waiting for V and the others when the yacht's boat crunched up onto the sand.

"I wonder if we are at high tide," V said, examining the sand for dampness and for the usual line of flotsam and jetsam that indicated a high tide. The beach looked pristine and the sand, pure white, was fine and cool, lusciously easy on the soles of her reptilian foot-claws. She and Federico, helped by Isis and Annette, pulled the boat ashore, far up beyond the water's edge, and V tied the boat's rope to one of the palm trees.

"Where are we?" Eve Schmidt was staring at Isis – a girl who could kill people and then bring them back from the dead.

"I think, if we did travel through time, we must be back at least 200 years, before the invention of radio – probably much earlier than that – there seem to be no broadcasts of any kind," said Guy.

"Well, what do we do?"

"We have to get back."

"He did this," Iris gazed at Eve. "This may be an alternative universe, some sort of alternative universe."

"But *why* did Puppet Master do this?" Eve Schmidt felt she was by now an old hand at the struggle between the Puppet Master and humanity.

"To bring V to the Gateway," Isis pushed back her bangs. Her dark eyes blinked at Eve Schmidt.

"Why?"

"He wants V."

"Why does he want me?" V curled her reptilian lip.

"He's jealous, I think," said Isis. "Jealous of the Goddess."

"Jealous? Well, that's new!" said V. "Should I be flattered?"

"I'm not sure, darling V," said Isis, with a smile, "but I doubt it."

V took a lighter out of her backpack. They collected some twigs and fallen branches and made a fire. The humans and Isis ate some of the power bars that V always carried in her backpack to feed needy humans when she came across them in her hunting expeditions. V drank a small tube of coffee concentrate.

Federico Harvey crouched close to the fire and rubbed his hands. It had been an interesting day – or night, and even more so now, sitting by a camp fire with a female reptile who spoke excellent English and with a young girl in the sort of tunic a slave or servant may have worn in Ancient Greece or Ancient Rome and who seemed to be some sort of spirit and who had apparently murdered him and Annette and brought them both back to life and who seemed a really good and cheery sort of girl, maybe 14 or 15 or younger. It was all very intriguing. Besides which, it seemed that they were in some place that might not even exist. Other than that, it was paradise, his absolute dream of an ideal vacation spot.

"I'm changing into human form," V stood up, stretched, and yawned, "Just to sleep, if that's okay with you?" Her scales shone silver in the moonlight.

"We've never seen your human form," said Eve Schmidt. "I'll bet it's interesting."

"I hope you like it," said V, giving Eve a look.

Isis leaned towards Eve and whispered, "She really likes you."

V hitched her backpack onto her shoulders and walked away into the darkness, feeling suddenly a shy: being naked as a human was a quite different sensation from being naked in her reptilian form; being naked as the reptile was not really being naked at all – the scales were very stylish. In fact, she worried, sometimes, that she was forgetting her human self – it was so easy just to parade around in reptile format, particularly if no one else was about, and V was, in many ways, increasingly a loner.

When she was beyond the circle of the firelight, she slid out of her backpack, placed it carefully on the sand – so no sand would get inside – took a deep breath, and morphed into her human form – the process involved just a momentary whir, which stirred up a flurry of sand and created a nano tornado, and – abracadabra, presto – she was no longer the turquoise scaly reptile, but a pale, slender – and apparently human – female.

The soft breeze caressed her suddenly naked human skin. Being a vulnerable and sensitive human, she reminded herself, did have its upside. She truly did feel some things she didn't feel as a reptile coated in scales. The human epidermis was a sensitive all-encompassing organ and quite erotic when you got right down to it. It yearned to be touched, kissed, stroked, massaged, caressed, and coddled. Enough!

V took a deep breath. She allowed herself a second to revel in the fact that she was alive, that the moon was shining – wherever and whenever this might be – and that the sea was rolling in, that the sand was soft and still warm even now from the sun, delicious under her feet – and it was dry, too, she noticed, dry, which meant the storm and the rain which they had experienced out at sea, only a few miles away, or so it seemed, had somehow not reached here – and the perfumes of the plants and smell of the sea were so rich! She shivered from pleasure, pure sensual overload.

They must be above the tidal line, if there was a tide in this strange new world. If there was the moon, there must be tides. Or … maybe not … In this weird place, anything was possible.

She took a pair of black jeans, a black T-shirt, and sandals out of the backpack, and she pulled them on. She tightened the belt, put her pistol in its holster; and, hoisting her backpack over her shoulder, she walked back to the fire.

The captain and Guy, the pilot, and Eve Schmidt, Isis and Annette and Federico, looked up. Captain Anderson was tempted to whistle; but he just said, "So that's the human you."

"Yep," said V. She ran her right hand self-consciously over her closely shaven skull, dating from less than 48 hours ago, the shaving being part of the decontamination ritual after escaping from the *Eden*. She crouched down on her haunches. "This is the human me."

"You're not eating anything?" the captain said.

"No," said V.

"Do you mind if I tell them?" said Isis.

"No, Isis, go ahead. You seem to know a great deal about me," V stared into the fire. Her eyes were dark, the flames reflected in the glossy impenetrable blackness of pupil and iris.

"Are you sure?" said Sergeant Schmidt, who already knew the secret. She glanced from Isis to V and back again.

"Yes, Eve, I'm sure." V shivered. She felt happy and she felt afraid. But she was not sure what she was happy about or afraid of. "It's better that you all know what I truly am."

"V only drinks blood," said Isis. "She's, sort of, like a vampire."

Captain Anderson glanced at Isis and at Sergeant Schmidt and then at V. His clear blue eyes had gone round. "Is this true?"

V poked at the fire with a long thin piece of wood. "Yes, Captain, it's true. I drink human blood; that's how I survive." She looked up at the captain with a glance that was slightly abashed, slightly shy, and then she smiled, and, in that moment, Captain Anderson thought she was a stunningly beautiful creature whatever she was. "But, rest assured gentlemen and ladies," V said, "I am not hungry. I fed only a few days ago."

"That is reassuring," said the captain. He was remembering ghost stories and horror stories and comics he had collected when he was a kid. Just how dangerous, he wondered, was this creature? "When you bite people, do you turn them into ... well, into creatures like yourself?"

V was still poking at the fire. Ripples of light and shadow flowed over her face. "I can do that, but I don't do it – except in exceptional circumstances. My rule, my fundamental law, is to not create creatures like myself. But sometimes ..."

"But sometimes you are forced to do it," said Isis, "And you created a whole flock of hybrids the other day and they are like you and yet not like you."

V turned to her. "You, my young beautiful resurrected friend, you know a great many things. What are you exactly? Who are you?"

"I am your guide. I have in the past gone by another name. Many centuries ago, you were my mistress, my owner, and – my greatest friend."

"You are familiar. Something about you is familiar."

"Asherah is one of my names. You and I played Senet in the house of Marcus. I went with you from North Africa to Italy. In that time, I did not speak – except with my hands."

"You were deaf and mute."

"Yes."

"I held you in my arms when you died!"

"Yes. And V, you were – you are – my great love. For that reason, I think, I have been brought back – I am to tempt you, to guide you, to lead you into the trap. But now I am to be known as Isis."

"We shall call you Isis, then," said V, gazing into her eyes. "I loved you then, and I love you now. You were – you are – perhaps the greatest love of my life." V leaned over and kissed Isis on the lips. The kiss was returned, and it lasted quite a long time.

"Asherah," said the captain, "what – who – is Asherah?"

"Oh, it has been …" V gazed into space, "It has been …"

"Almost two thousand and six hundred years," said Isis, "since we were together."

"Ladies, what are these stories!" Captain Anderson laughed, "Two thousand six hundred years!"

"Yes, you are right, Captain," V smiled. "We must explain, though it will seem an incredible tale, I can promise you."

"I was V's servant, in North Africa, in greater Phoenicia, about 600 years before the birth of Christ, near the great city of Carthage that was destroyed – much later – by the Romans, 146 years before Christ. I was deaf-mute, in those days, and I was a servant in the home of a man called Marcus."

"Marcus: he was my mentor. He is my mentor."

"And he was – he is – your father." Isis glanced at V.

"Yes," said V, "He is my father. But, Captain Anderson, Asherah was also a goddess."

"Yes," said Isis, "Asherah is a name for one of the goddesses of the Phoenicians. We – the Phoenicians – originally lived on a strip of land in what is now Syria and Lebanon, between the mountains and the sea, next to what is now Israel. The Kingdoms of Israel were in those days our neighbors."

"Lebanon – beautiful country, the land of the cedar trees," V sighed, and threw a twig into the fire.

Sitting cross-legged and staring at the flames, Isis seemed to be in a trance, the firelight reflected off her dark eyes, as if she were blind, "Asherah's father – and perhaps her husband or mate – the tales of divine genealogies are confused and contradictory – was El, the supreme god, the protector of the Universe. And my brother, or perhaps my son – again, it's unclear – was Baal, a warrior god, god of thunder, god of harvests, god of the cycle of nature, of spring, and fertility. El was a cousin of Yahweh, the God of Israel, and perhaps a model for Yahweh, or an ancestral version of Yahweh, the God now worshipped by the Jews, Christians, and Moslems. Of course, the tribes fought for which God would rule and, in the end, the Hebrew gods won and we Phoenicians and our gods mostly disappeared. We were largely written out of history – like the Zoroastrians in Persia. It's a long story ..."

"A tragic story, perhaps," said V. "Sometimes I feel a hankering for the old gods and above all for the goddesses."

"Well, Yahweh got rid of all the goddesses. He was a bit of a masculine chauvinist ... ha ..." muttered Isis, staring into the fire. She looked up and grinned at everybody. Of course, she had to admit that, as a former goddess dethroned by the One God, she was a trifle bitter – and not at all objective.

But, in truth, Isis yearned for a world before the gods and goddesses, an animist world. And she told them how she adored the world that existed before the various personified divinities mopped up, vacuumed up, and monopolized the sense of the sacred, the radiant intrinsic glory of divinity, sucking it out of the tangible world, out of the trees, fountains, rocks, mountains, valleys, flowers, and animals, clouds and lightning and thunder and valleys, and out of everything. She yearned for a world teaming with epiphanies, a world where everything, and every sensation, every instant, every animal and plant, every creature, every stone, every grain of sand, was luminous with the sacred, glowing with mystery and promise: the rain, the wind, the snowy mountain tops, the trees, the grains of sand, and the pebbles on a beach ...

"Those girls were interesting, talking about the old gods and goddesses," said Captain Anderson, watching Isis and V walking, the two of them alone, far away, along the edge of the waves, silhouetted in the moonlight.

"Yeah," said Guy, "It was fun watching them strike sparks off each other."

"As for me," said Eve, "I was raised a Lutheran."

"Are you still practicing?" said Captain Anderson.

"No, not really, I'm more an agnostic, I think," Eve flashed him a beautiful smile. "But after today I'm willing to believe almost anything."

"I'm Catholic," said Federico, "but it was very interesting, what they said."

"I'm Jewish," said Annette Brighton, "I felt I should rush to the defense of Yahweh, but then I thought, no, it's better to let those two girls from ancient times have their moment. We can discuss it all later. We may be here for a long time. And, also, it was very nice of Isis to bring us back to life – I wouldn't want to rile her up."

"Yes, that was cool of her," said Federico, staring at the fire. Isis was pretty cool herself – maybe a bit young for him, of course. But her smile was to die for, her eyes were soulful and sparkled with humor, as if she knew and understood everything, seeing all sides of every question, forgiving every sin and form of misbehavior, her skin glowed like dark honey, her figure was slender, her lips … She looked like she'd be a lot of fun.

"Maybe we should get some sleep," said Captain Anderson. "We'll need to have somebody on guard at all times. We really don't know anything about the dangers that may be lurking about in this place."

Isis and V walked along the beach, just at the edge of the gently rolling surf, barefoot, their feet sometimes in the water, sometimes on the sand.

"Okay, so, you are my guide," said V. She took Isis's hand.

"Yes, I have come to take you to him."

"Why?"

"He wants to capture you."

"Why does he want to capture me?"

"I don't know."

"Ah, Isis, are you sure you don't know?"

"I swear, I don't know. But I will tell you this, whatever he wants you for it will not be good. He is evil, totally evil."

"And yet …"

"And yet, yes, he brought me back to life! And here I am!"

"Is he listening to us now?"

"No, sometimes he does, but now he is absent."

"Like God?" said V.

"Yes, if you like, he is absent like God." Isis kicked a spray of water onto V's legs, "Yours is a fallen world, V, and God – or whatever gods may still exist – have abandoned it – that is quite clear."

"Is the Puppet Master here? Where is he?"

"He is somewhere near. I'm not sure. You must defeat him, V, otherwise …"

"Otherwise, what?"

"Otherwise, all the humans will die."

"Die?"

"They will become beasts, no longer human."

"Like zombies, for instance."

"Yes, beast-like, like zombies, they will be craven, creeping, unclean, unthinking things, cannibals, pitiless, wallowing in filth, with no light of reason to guide them, no love or passion, no memories, no self-knowledge, no hope or health or salvation in them."

"Yuk."

"Yes, I agree – Yuk," said Isis, "I like humans; I was one once."

"Let's go back to the others," said V. "We must sleep."

"Yes, even goddesses must sleep," said Isis. She leaned close, kissed V on the cheek, and put her arm around V's waist.

V kept the first watch, lying down on her stomach, cradling a submachine gun, and facing towards the line of palm trees, the beginning of the forest, lying low so she wouldn't offer a silhouette against the flickering remains of the bonfire and the moonlight sparkling on the water. At the third hour, the captain woke up, and crawled over to her. "Do you ever sleep, Vampire?"

"I will sleep," said V, "If you keep watch."

"Then I'll keep watch, V, so you can sleep."

Isis was sleeping, on her side, next to Guy, the pilot. He put his arm around her; she opened her eyes for an instant and then closed them again.

V lay down next to Isis and quickly fell asleep.

Captain Anderson sat up, cradling his submachine gun. Feeling restless, he stood up, and walked on the beach, scanning the foaming fringe of the water. Out on the moon-lit waves, the yacht rode at anchor, a black silhouette, looking entirely like a normal yacht. The helicopter was securely tethered down, attached to a grove of palms, between the camp fire and the water, a safe distance from the tree line.

Captain Anderson circled around the helicopter, to make sure it was okay. He looked up at the stars which seemed so strange – no recognizable constellations – no familiar planets. No north star, no Cassiopeia, no Big Dipper. Yes, this must be, as Isis had suggested, an alternative universe – only the moon was familiar.

He came back to the group and sat down next to V, keeping his eyes wide open, scanning the beach, the tree line, the water.

He listened to the soft, even breathing of V, the vampire – the weird, beautiful, dangerous creature lying on her side next to him.

V opened her eyes, put her hand on his thigh, and then closed her eyes. The warmth of her touch was reassuring. It and the soft breeze and the gentle roll of the sea made all the violence of a few hours before – the thunder, rain, hail, tornadoes, and waterspouts– seem unreal. It was as if they were on a normal planet, in normal times, on a vacation in some magical and privileged spot as yet unspoiled by civilization. Captain Anderson yawned. Tomorrow they could go for a swim and do some fishing. They would need food, and …

Then he heard it – a sound … the sound of drums, drums beating deep in the forest. He picked up his submachine gun and stood up.

V's eyes flickered open.

Isis lifted Guy's arm off her waist – very gently, so she wouldn't wake him – and she stood up.

As if by magic, silently, Isis and V and Sergeant Eve Schmidt were standing next to Captain Anderson, V with a submachine gun, and Eve with a machine pistol in her hand.

"So," whispered V, "we are not alone."

"Those are human sounds at least," said Eve.

"Yes, but it sounds like drumbeats from the distant past," said the Captain.

"I think," said Isis, "I think that maybe it's the sound of the future."

"The future," said V, "the future?"

"A different future," said Isis, "In a different place. Not all time is foretold, and time is not linear, every instant time branches out, in an infinity of directions, or so I have been told."

"Parallel universes?" V raised an eyebrow, "Alternative universes?"

Isis gazed at V and nodded. "Yes."

It was dawn, almost dawn.

"Maybe a reptilian demon will frighten them," said V, "That is, if we are going inland to pay the natives a visit."

"Yes," said Isis, with a grin. "In demon form you do indeed strike terror into the hearts of men – and even women too, for that matter."

"Thank you, Isis, love." V allowed her gaze to linger on Isis, such a beautiful child, and, in centuries past, her greatest, closest friend.

"It's a good idea," said Eve Schmidt, "What do you think, Captain?"

"Yes, it's a good idea – do it, V, if you think it is the best way to present yourself to the natives, whoever or whatever they are."

"Yes, good: I'll present myself as the demon, then."

Turning her back on her companions, V took off her clothes, folded them neatly, put them into the backpack, and – in a twinkling – morphed into demon form.

"Wow," said Annette Brighton.

"Yeah," said Federico Harvey. "I'd like to see her do that again."

"You probably will," said V, glancing over her shoulder.

Shortly after dawn, Captain Anderson, V, Isis, and Eve Schmidt headed inland to see if they could contact the natives, while Annette Brighton, Federico Harvey, and Guy Vargas stayed behind to guard the helicopter and the yacht.

The rear guard set out a perimeter on the beach and they had it covered with submachine guns. The order was not to engage the natives unless they proved hostile, and to do everything to keep the natives from becoming hostile. But, above all the helicopter and the yacht had to be protected. Without the helicopter and the yacht, there might be no way out of this alternative or parallel universe or whatever it was.

"Maybe these natives are not even human. Who knows? I mean, other creatures, creatures that aren't human, can beat drums, right?" said Captain Anderson.

"That's quite possible," said V. "Even I can beat a drum."

"Let's rock, and let's roll," said Eve.

"V was great with a lute, too," said Isis, "though I couldn't hear a thing in the old days since I was totally deaf. But V charmed all the servants in the House of Marcus. Even I could see that. They would laugh and sway to the rhythm of her playing."

"Maybe we can put together an ensemble," said Captain Anderson.

"Good idea, Captain!" The glittering turquoise reptile, favored him with a big reptilian smile, making the captain feel all warm and fuzzy.

And so, the four explorers headed inland.

The air was full of sounds and sweet airs, alluring perfumes, and strange forms of music – calls of birds, screeches of distant animals, the melodic yodeling of beasts that had no earthly names.

A large snake curled around one low-hanging tree branch, and slowly came down, to have a look at V. Their color schemes almost matched. Their reptile eyes blinked at each other. Then the snake hissed, in a not unfriendly fashion, and V hissed back. This conversation continued for about a minute, and then the snake curled its way back up onto the branch and away into the tree where he quickly became invisible.

"Not poisonous," V said, "and he's a vegetarian."

"How do you know?" Eve Schmidt had watched with fascination as V and the snake exchanged hisses.

"He told me," V said, and winked a reptilian wink.

"You are not serious," said Eve.

"Yes, I am," hissed V softly, "I'm a reptile, remember." She laid a claw on her friend's arm, "but look at that!"

Emerging from a bank of thick vegetation were overturned statues which had once stood on pedestals, equally overturned. The statues and pedestals were all moss-covered and entwined in vines, half buried in the clayey earth. The statues were of tortoises, monkeys, birds, and fish.

"There are some kinds of birds and fish and plants here that I have never seen before," said Captain Anderson.

"Me neither," said Isis.

"I don't know if any of these plants ever existed on earth," said Eve Schmidt, who had studied biology before opting for a military career, "I don't think so."

"Maybe, in fact, we are in the distant, a very distant, future," said Captain Anderson, "Just as Isis suggested, or an alternative universe, as she also suggested, or both."

"I do think this is an alternative universe," said Isis. "But I'm not really sure; and, yes, of course – this could be the future, but a very, very distant future, if plants and animals have evolved to be so different, and if the stars have lost their patterns."

There, amid the trees, rising out of the thick, tangled vegetation, covered in vines and with trees growing in the midst of it, was an enormous wall, made of huge blocks of stone. It towered up, perhaps thirty feet.

"A temple," said Isis. "It looks like a temple."

They followed the wall for about fifty yards, pushing through the underbrush, climbing over vines, and detouring around the giant tangled roots of trees, and found an entrance – it looked like an entrance.

Inside the walled enclosure was an enormous temple, set up on a giant platform about three yards above ground level.

It was approached by going up steps and then passing between columns – a rough Doric style – and then approaching what looked like an enormous open door.

"It's like going into Saint Peter's in Rome," Eve whispered, drawing her pistol. "Awesome."

Carefully, looking left and right, and with their weapons at the ready, they climbed up the steps and entered the temple, glancing in all directions. The walls soared up and were built of huge stone blocks. They had been weathered by the ages, moss grew on the granite; much of the mortar had crumbled, leaving cracks and open spaces, a few huge blocks of granite had tumbled away, and lay on the buckled marble floor of the building; light streamed down through the arched, shattered roof. An enormous tree had grown up against one wall, pushing aside the floor stones, as it reached towards the light. There were pools of water where rain had come through cracks and gaps in the roof. Birds took flight, with a whirr, their wings sparkling white in a beam of sunlight; the temple was empty, no chairs, no pews, no monuments or tombs that they could see – but, at the far end of the long vaulted space was a giant brightly colored statue, standing proudly, defiantly, on a high altar.

"Oh, bother," said V, "look at that!"

"My God," said the captain.

"It's an exact likeness," said Eve, "It's you."

"So, you are a goddess," said Isis, giving V a poke, "like me – only better, and certainly bigger!"

V stood there, her claws on her hips, her reptile brow arched in a quizzical expression. "This is annoying!" She frowned. Being a goddess would certainly bring lots of obligations and duties. It would be more trouble than it was worth. "Oh, bother!"

In front of them, on a high platform, set against the temple wall, was a giant statue. It was an exact, detailed, likeness of V in her reptilian version, towering up, at least four times life-size, perhaps eight meters tall: the statue's arms were on her hips, echoing her V's posture, her eyes, painted or inlaid gold, blazed with an inner light, her fangs, perhaps made of ivory, brightly reflected the dusky twilight in the temple. On the high pedestal, just in front of the statue, was a large stone table that looked like a sacrificial altar – runnels ran from a central basin.

"Runnels to carry blood," V said.

"Yes, it looks like a place of sacrifice," said Isis, "sacrifice to you!"

"It's you, no doubt about it," said Eve.

"Well, I'll be damned." Captain Anderson scratched his head.

"I'm not sure it's me, but it certainly does look like me," V climbed the steps leading up to the statue. She saw there was a space behind it, so she walked around the statue. She reached up and touched it – just caressing the ankle. Her eyes and the tips of her claws agreed: her skin scales were reproduced in exact sculptural detail. The statue had been painted vividly, undoubtedly long ago, and the colors were still there, in some places, and the colors were …

"It's exactly your color scheme, even down to the –" captain Anderson was staring up at the idol's face.

"Even down to the gold stripe above my snout! Yes, damn it!" V stared up at the face of the idol. It was indeed her exact likeness. She looked at the foot-claws. She counted the toes. Yes, exactly eight claw-like toes. She went around to the other side, where, under her right arm she had a small tear-shaped blue mark: yes, it was there!

"Either this is me," she said. "Or it's my double."

"Whoever built this," Eve said, "built it a long time ago and it has fallen into disrepair – for a long time, perhaps 50 or 100 years or more, maybe much more."

"A civilization in decline," Isis glanced around. "Or maybe they just moved on – went somewhere else or changed their religion."

"Yes, but who would worship you," Eve turned to V, "and why?"

"Well, I can think of any number of reasons to worship me, actually," said V, flicking her tongue at Eve, "after all, I am so very goddess-like – don't you think?"

"Absolutely!" Eve laughed. What a weird world! Her newest best buddy was now a hybrid, not only that – but the original hybrid, founder of the race of hybrids. "Yes, in fact, you are rather a goddess princess, aren't you?"

"Definitely! But," V frowned and ran her claw over one of the foot-claws of the statue, "Your question is a good one. I don't know why I should be worshipped or by whom or where, or when. I really don't have a clue."

"If this is the past, then, when would someone worship you?"

"And if it's the present, where are we?"

"And, if it's not the past, and not the present, then …?" captain Anderson let his question hang in the air.

"The future," breathed Eve Schmidt, "we are in the future, a distant, alternative future."

"Maybe."

"Yes, maybe."

"And now, V, the goddess, has returned to her ruined temple," said Isis, blinking at V. "Perhaps, sensing you are here, the worshipers will return too."

As if on cue, again, drums began to beat – a distant chanting that echoed in the high empty ghostly temple.

"Oh, oh, those drums are closer than last night," Eve Schmidt looked around.

"Much closer," said Isis.

"They know we are here," said V.

"What do we do?" Captain Anderson drew his pistol.

"Well," said V, "I believe you all should throw yourselves down on the ground and prostrate yourselves before me and worship."

"Worship?" said Eve Schmidt.

"Prostrate ourselves?" said Captain Anderson.

"That's an excellent idea," said Isis.

"Yes," said Anderson, "I see your point; yes, it is a good idea."

"Down on your knees," said V, "Otherwise those fellows – the ones with the poisoned spears and sacred hatchets – might get the wrong idea. Now, Eve, down on your knees! I want to see you down on your knees!"

"Shucks, okay, boss goddess," said Eve Schmidt. She got down on her knees.

Then, when V glanced towards the entrance, she saw them.

Standing in the doorway to the temple, outlined in streaming sunlight, were three men with spears. They appeared to be dressed entirely in feathers, and had elaborate headgear, feathers sticking straight up.

"Oh, Great Goddess V, from whom all proceeds and to which all in the end will flow, please accept my prayers and my supplications," Eve Schmidt, on her knees, extended her arms to V, praying to V, and wailing in an excellent pious manner, but keeping her pistol, laid sideways, ready, in her extended palms. "This could be fun, fun, fun," she trilled loudly, "fun, fun, fun!" She frowned. I hope these people don't speak English, and so she warbled, in fine ecclesiastical style, "This, this, this, is, is, is, fun, fun, fun!"

V stared at the others. "Well," she said, hands on hips, in the regal or godly posture.

"This is great," said Isis, kneeling, reaching her arms out in supplication, and she wailed in a high-pitched rhythmic ululation. "You are finally getting the recognition you've always craved."

"Yes, Oh Goddess," intoned Captain Anderson, getting down on his knees, "Oh, Goddess, have mercy upon us – make the sun we worship shine, please! Make the moon rise! Keep away the mosquitoes!"

"Oh, Goddess, have mercy upon us," said Isis, shuffling on her knees, and then throwing herself down, flat on the floor, prostrating herself completely, "Let the moon rise, please! Pretty Please! Make the good old moon rise!"

"You exaggerate, Isis," sang Eve, "You exaggerate, Isis," but she followed the girl's example and threw herself down, full length, being careful to keep her pistol ready and trying to keep an eye on the warriors or priests or whatever they were who standing at the entrance to the temple and who, she noticed, had taken off their headgear.

And so it was that they all lay down flat, faces facing the sand that was strewn on the shattered floor of the great temple, wailing supplications and jokes.

V strutted back and forth. She muttered some mumbo-jumbo she had picked up in a fairground in the early twentieth century in Milwaukee and then she decided that perhaps, as a goddess, she should make some real noise; maybe she could sing something. So, pitching her reptilian voice low, she conjured up a tenor solo from Aida, *Celeste Aida* ...

The temple echoed with her voice.

The men in feathers fell to the floor, prostrating themselves before the goddess.

"Well done," whispered Eve Schmidt, still prostrate on the floor, "Well done, oh, Goddess! Oh, thou art truly divine!"

So it was that V became a goddess.

V, the goddess, had returned. She had been long absent; and her people had longed after her for many moons and many suns – her absence had left her people impoverished, melancholy, as if laboring under a perpetual curse.

The helicopter was presented as a sacred bird. The Great High Priest – and he alone – was taken up for a short flight.

A Flight of Fancy was presented as the sacred vessel of the goddess; it had brought her from across the Great Water. No canoes were to go near it and the Great High Priest, who was treated to a dinner of Mars Bars and a bottle of chilled pinot grigio on board, stationed other canoes near the yacht, so that it would not be disturbed or visited by anyone except by the goddess and her celestial attendants – Captain Anderson, Guy, Isis, Annette, Federico – and Eve.

V stayed in reptile form. She performed a few miracles – she healed the scrofulous son of a rich villager; she cured three cases of blindness; she restored the limbs of a young man who had broken both legs tumbling down a mountainside.

They were very intelligent and quick, these people. They had gold-colored skin, they were handsome but not very tall; they were slender, and their hair was short, jet-black, and straight. They were, to V's eye at least, very similar and very pretty. The women had fine waists and large breasts.

The New Temple – which had replaced the old ruined temple – was where V was to perform. It was farther inland – and it consisted of a high platform out in the open air, towering above the worshiping multitude, and reached by steep ascending steps, and with rooms behind the sacrificial altar for priests and preparations.

The priests offered to V criminals and young people.

V signaled that she preferred the criminals.

V used her mind to communicate directly with the priests and, mobilizing her hybrid mind-power, she could plant thoughts in their minds, and she was able to discover and explore their beliefs. She brought offerings to her friends.

V and her celestial companions camped near the beach in a temple complex set aside for them. Sitting Indian-style on the sand, V said, "I'm not sure how long I can play goddess. I must perform a sacred dance every evening towards dusk to make sure the sun will come up in the morning. I don't know how they got along without me. Who got the sun up in the morning before me?"

"You're enjoying it," said Isis. "Admit it, you like being a goddess."

Isis, in her tunic, and with her short curly dark hair, which made her look like an especially beautiful boy, was usually required to act as an assistant to the officiant at the sacrificial ceremony. If she was not available, Eve Schmidt, who was, by now, tanned an even honey-gold and whose wardrobe had been reduced, by a series of unfortunate accidents, to a loincloth, stood in for her, showing remarkable theatrical talent, something she had never expected to discover within herself. Both Isis and Eve were extremely popular, particularly with the Great High Priest who took to ruffling their hair, patting them on the shoulder, and referring to them, both of them, as "my children."

V was required to feed in the temple. And, as she carried out the rituals, she wondered. Maybe the Goddess really was her. Or she was really the Goddess. Perhaps this voyage, right now, was the creation myth, and history here in this universe, circled around on itself, like a mythical serpent biting its tail. And, if she was the Goddess, where had she disappeared to, where had she gone for all these eons, abandoning her chosen people? And when had she disappeared? And why had she disappeared? Of course, gods did, generally, have a habit of abandoning the faithful, from time to time, leaving the poor folk desperate and bereft and feeling guilty, and of skipping off nowhere in particular, while often promising, or threatening, to come back. Maybe the divine V had been following – imitating – an age-old sacred marketing pattern of intimidation, enticing promises, blackmail, and absence. In spring and summer, planting and harvesting, *poof*, you are here, and in autumn and winter, with sterility and dearth, *poof*, you are gone. Only, perhaps, here, there was no winter. In any case, make yourself scarce, deity, and you will be a more valuable commodity. Familiarity breeds contempt. Absence makes the heart grow fonder.

The priests enjoyed V's performances.

Her show was absolutely authentic – at last, they had the real thing, the true Goddess – and the performances were extremely profitable. All the villages, up to, and beyond, the great smoking mountain, sent many of their people, men, women, and children, to see the Goddess in person, and all brought offerings.

Having deciphered the sacred routine by reading the priests' minds, V was able to fulfill, to the letter, the scenario they had in mind: The High Sacrificial Mass for the Goddess.

V danced with the victims, who were usually in a drug-induced trance and delighted to interlace their limbs with those of the Goddess. She caressed the victims, and then, reading each victim's mind to be sure the victim was "worthy" of sacrifice – sufficiently a doer of evil to be fodder for a discriminating vampire of refined and ethical tastes such as she considered herself – she would either reject the sacrifice, saying, "This one is not pure and must return to his – or her – family!" Or she would accept, chanting, in the language of the people – which was, grammatically, a greatly simplified language with what seemed to be distant echoes of Spanish and English and Indonesian with bits of Swahili and Mandarin and German and French – that "This one is worthy; this one is ripe. This one I shall consume!"

And she would – after an appropriate pantomime – plunge her fangs into the victim's neck and drain him – and occasionally her – dry until she was sure, "You are dead, truly dead, and you shall not rise again."

The blood sacrifice ritual did sometimes create difficult situations, because some of the offerings wished to be sacrificed, and, in one case, behind the scenes, in the inner sanctum, V had a tremendous struggle, and then a fight, with a young girl who insisted on being offered up, and drunk dry, and left as a carcass to be dismembered and then burnt, as an offering, with the ashes rising, as smoke in the evening or in the morning light to the heavens where she was convinced she would be reunited with her ancestors and with the boy she had loved but who had died two moons earlier in a hunting accident …

V said, "No, you are not ripe."

"I am ripe, goddess! You have no right to stop me."

"How old are you?

"Sixteen seasons have come and gone. I am a woman, I am ripe. My blood flows with the moon. If my love had lived, I would now be preparing to be the mother of many children."

The girl had marvelous clear skin, dark passionate eyes, and … She fell on her knees, supplicating V.

"I refuse you; you are not ripe," V turned her back.

The girl threw herself on V; she clasped her arms around V's waist, "If you do not accept me, they will burn me in the fire. If they do not burn me in the fire, I will throw myself off the cliff, onto the rocks below, there I will die in agony, and the agony will be slow and long, and my suffering infinite, my broken bones, my shattered spirit, my homeless soul, destined to wander forever alone, forever cold, forever a prisoner of the air, a chilly nomad riding the breeze, and this my lost and wandering spirit will reproach you and curse you and hate you forever, oh, Goddess."

"Oh, well, if you must insist, idiot child, but you are the most exasperating sacrifice I have ever met," said V, frowning, turning around to face her victim. The girl was indeed a delicious morsel, nut-brown, golden-hued skin, sparkling bright defiant eyes, a supple fresh body, bright teeth, and lustrous jet-black hair. Her blood would be rich, passionate, high-spirited, and altogether tasty.

"Oh, thank you, Goddess, thank you!"

"First, annoying child, you must drink with me the sacred potion."

And so they drank the sacred potion. V hoped that when the girl got tipsy she would rediscover – as melancholic creatures occasionally do when they get drunk – that life was too delightful to be abandoned, that death was really not such an enticing prospect, and that, perhaps, thinking it all over, looking at it from a wider perspective, it was better to go on, to continue, and to see the sun rise and set and to feel the breeze and watch the moon … But, no, no, no, no! The girl, who was otherwise a splendid conversational companion, telling V many wonderful anecdotes of village life, became, on the topic of sacrifice, more and more boring and more and more insistent, "I must die, Goddess, I must die and you must consume me!"

Finally, after pouring the girl a last libation, V shrugged her divine shoulders and sighed. "Well, I give up, you win, my beautiful sacrifice."

"Oh, thank you, Goddess!"

"But I shall keep your spirit for myself for a time because it is such a delightful spirit, and I do not want you to disappear, entirely, from this earth. So, you will reside within me to the end of time."

"I am honored." The girl bowed her head.

V caressed the girl's neck and shoulders; she carefully pinned up the girl's hair so that strands of hair would not intermingle with her feeding, which was something she abhorred.

Together they went out onto the platform, where the priests, who had been waiting impatiently, for it was past midnight – dawn and the rising of the sun were not too far away – were overjoyed.

Isis, who had been keeping the Great High Priest amused by talk of how divine V was, raised her arms to the sky, and bowed to the Great High Priest, who bowed back towards Isis.

Then, between Isis and the Great High Priest, on the altar, high up above the crowd, V leaned over the girl, and caressing her long neck, V made the ritual signs, that she had conned from inscriptions on the walls of the temple – hieroglyphics of a kind – and from the priests' minds and musings – and then slowly – making a great show of glittering ivory and allowing bursts of light to flare from her eyes and flash towards the multitude below – she plunged her fangs into the girls' neck, and began to drink.

The audience, the profane, the believers, hundreds and hundreds of them, some of whom had not seen the Goddess perform before, let out a sigh of awe.

All faces were turned upwards; all arms were outstretched.

"Yummy!" V drank deeply; she sucked up every last drop of the girl's deliciously rich and bubbly young blood, and she absorbed with the blood, the girl's spirit, and saying unto the girl's body V pronounced the words:

"Now you are dead, you are truly dead, and you shall not rise again,"

And V said, inwardly, unto the girl's spirit, "Now you are mine! Now you are dead! Are you happy?"

And the girl's spirit answered unto V, "I am at one with you and I am in an ecstasy here in the darkness. I am at one with you for all eternity! I am indeed happy! I am in paradise!"

Cradling the girl's limp body in her arms, V turned her bloodied fangs and lips, her blood-dripping breasts, to the vast crowd.

She laid the loose-limbed, bloodless body – now white and chalky and cold as ancient marble – on the altar.

V raised her bloodied arms to the heavens, exposing her blood-coated jaws and breasts to the multitude, and just as she did so, the sun rose, painting everything scarlet and crimson, and the multitude rose as one and cried out the local equivalent of hallelujah.

"Praise the Goddess! Praise the Goddess! Praise the Goddess!"

V stood as still as a statue, accepting the adoration.

For that particular performance, V got three bushels of corn and two cartloads of something like wheat, and all the wine she and Isis and Captain Anderson and Eve Schmidt could carry in amphora-like vases back to the beach where Guy and Annette and Federico kept the base camp active and were zealously protecting the helicopter and the yacht.

"I shall never forgive myself," V grumbled.

"Yes, you must forgive yourself," said the girl's voice, a beautiful and musical voice, as it faded into nothingness, "I am here, I am happy, I am one, I am reunited ..."

And then she was gone – but only for a time. Every once in a while, for centuries and centuries, she would return, always amused, always delightful, always, eternally, grateful.

Being a goddess did have its perks; but it presented other challenges in addition to dealing with stroppy sacrifices who insisted on being sacrificed.

V had to watch her diet. Human sacrifice was the local form of mass – instead of bread and wine, it was flesh and blood, real, live, human flesh and blood. Of course, theologically speaking, from the transubstantiation point of view, this was the same thing – but, somehow, to V, it seemed different. She did wish that her old friend, the late Father O'Bryan SJ, could have been with her on this voyage. She and Father O'Bryan and the goddess Iris – and perhaps the others – could then have held a very interesting seminar on the original nature of sacrifice, and on the mysteries of transubstantiation, and how, in a sense, all more recent forms of ritual sacrifice were sublimations of the original bloody sacrifices – of enemies, of prey, or of children – practiced by allegedly more primitive societies.

One little problem as this: V was a spectacular incarnation of divinity, truly a crowd-pleaser and worshipper magnet. The priests, who knew a good thing when they saw it, wanted her to perform at least twice a week.

The more sacrifices were made, and the more ceremonies were held, the more offerings the priests gathered in.

The Great High Priest had explained to Isis – who like V had used her mind-reading capacity to learn the language – and teach elements of it to the others – that the return of the Goddess would mean the return of the Greatness of the Tribe, which had been a Lost Tribe, lost in darkness, and condemned to a fallen and sinful and wandering existence, which could only be redeemed by continual sacrifice.

Once, he told Isis, men could fly.

Once, he told Isis, men could cross the great waters.

Once, he told Isis, men lived in great villages called cities.

Once, he told Isis, men could read the signs written on the walls.

Once, he told Isis, eyeing her carefully, love was free.

Now, he told Isis, men crawled on the ground, could not sail the great waters, lived lost in the forest, and did not know the meaning of the signs written on the walls; now, he told Isis, love is in chains, love is dead.

"That is very interesting, Great High Priest," said Isis, gently and most respectfully lifting the Great High Priest's hand from her left breast.

"I am going to suffer indigestion and ruin my figure." V burped. "Isis, can you perform some miracle for them, something that would give me a rest. I usually feed every two weeks. Twice a week is too much. I'm putting on weight and I'm going to lose my hourglass figure of which, you know, I am vain and inordinately proud."

Time passed. V ate and ate.

But her hourglass figure remained as it was – hourglass, forever hourglass, hopelessly hourglass.

"We've been here three months now. We should be back fighting the Puppet Master," said V, gloomily poking at the fire. She stayed in demon form all the time since she was a goddess and had to make sure that she inspired the appropriate awe and that none of the natives spotted her changing into merely human form – though when she reflected upon it, perhaps doing a metamorphosis would add to her appeal – but she had a good thing going, and, as she put it to Eve and Isis and Guy one evening when they were waiting for the Great High Priest – he was a decent chap, really, and highly intelligent, and he did have the best interests – survival and regeneration – of his people at heart, "I don't want to upset this particular applecart."

"Back in the old world, there may be no humans left," said Guy, "maybe everybody's a zombie now."

Isis who was pouring fruit juice into Guy's mug said, "I think time may not have passed at all back there; maybe, when we will return, it will be only five minutes after we left, or even less."

CHAPTER 39 – THE UNDERWORLD

Then one morning …

"The time has come," Isis bowed towards V, "I must take you there."

"Take me where?"

"I must take you where you will fight for all of us."

"Okay," said V, "I'm ready, take me."

"Good luck," said Eve.

"Yes," said Captain Anderson, "Good luck. We'll be waiting for you when you get back – both of you."

At the temple, the Great High Priest bowed, "Yes, I too have heard the call," he said, "The Goddess must go to the underworld, to do battle. Three days journey it is to the place of darkness, away from the sea, away from the light. When she will return, we do not know; no one knows."

When V and Isis were away from the settlement, V changed into human form. "I need a break from being a reptile-demon-goddess." She pulled the slick skintight black armored catsuit out of her backpack and slipped into it and pulled on her military boots.

"Handsome," said Isis.

"I like it too," said V, "It's my sleek, girl-warrior look."

V and Isis pushed their way through the stalks of jungle growth, the vines, the trees towering overhead, the serpents poised on every branch and coiled under every leaf, fangs dripping poison; and spiders, giant spiders, some two feet in breadth, that spun webs that hung between the trees, thick gooey webs, glittering in bright golden shafts of sunlight; but none of these creatures attacked Isis or V and many, humbly, made way for them.

While Eve and the captain stayed with the High Priest in the New Temple, Guy and Annette and Federico stayed on the beach to protect the helicopter and the yacht.

On the third day V and Isis reached a mountain which soared up before them, rising into the clouds. Upon the mountain side were the ruins of what looked like a group of temples – columns and facades and shattered walls. In the distance was a giant volcano, perhaps four miles tall; its flames were reflected in the clouds and in the smoke that rose from its summit.

"Here it is," said Isis, pointing to a miniature triumphal arch that crouched against a parapet of rock, surrounded by ivy and ferns.

"That's it?" V stared at the broken arch; it looked like once it had been a temple, now it looked like a broken gateway; but it was a miniature silly little thing, like a toy triumphal arch in the ruins of a toy city or mockup of Rome or Petra; it was barely high enough to crawl under. V did not particularly like the idea of crawling belly down in the dust through that little opening, "It hardly seems worthy of the fuss and bother, such an undignified little tiny itsy-bitsy gateway."

"Well, that is it," said Isis, "What lies within, I do not know, but I shall wait for you here – however long it takes, I shall be here."

"So, this is the way down, then." V hesitated. The arch obviously led to a tunnel, obviously a tunnel leading to the nether world, to the world below the temple complex, to the world below the world. "This is one of those bloody tunnel-like places, sort of vaginal passages, and womb-like tombs, where you are supposed to die and be reborn, I imagine." V grimaced. She'd always thought being born once was enough, "Oh, well, into the breach, dear Isis, into the breach!"

"You'll have fun," said Isis, with a grin.

"You bet," V unbuckled her belt and, opened it, and slipped out of her armored catsuit; she handed both to Isis, and instantly morphed into her demon reptilian self.

"You'll watch my stuff, right?" said V, a shaft of sunlight burnishing her turquoise and gold shoulders.

"I will," Isis was already busy. Kneeling, she carefully folded and packed V's clothes and weapons into V's backpack. "If anything happens to me," Isis looked up, "your things will be here." She stuffed the backpack into the hollow of a gnarled and ancient tree that leaned darkly – like an evil patriarchal Biblical prophet or old-time sorcerer – over the entry to the tunnel.

"Nothing will happen to you," said V. "Nothing must happen to you!"

"This hollow tree is ugly," said Isis, "but at least it's clean; it's not a nest for snakes, just the usual swirling bacteria and crawling bugs, centipedes, snails, beetles."

"Ugh," said V, grinning at Isis.

"Yes, ugh," said Isis.

"Well, the moment has come," V held Isis close for a moment, admiring, as always, the neat pristine precision of this young person, in her simple tunic, tied with a simple belt at the waist, in her simple sandals.

"Good luck, V."

"Good luck, Isis! I'll see you anon!" V kissed Isis, gazed at her, her one true ancient love, and then got down on her belly, and, with her trusty machine pistol in one claw, she wiggled and squirmed her way under the small broken stone arch, half expecting to meet a fox or some other burrowing animal, but instead, as she wiggled and wiggled, pushing herself forward deeper into the dark dank musty space, she came to a muddy opening. It yawned like the mouth of darkness itself and it smelled of sulfur.

Yuk," V muttered.

With a grimace of distaste, her fangs bared, she crawled headfirst into the dank dark hole, and slithered her way down, deeper into the downward sloping muddy tunnel.

It was less than three feet wide and it went down at an angle of about forty degrees. It was slimy and viscous and totally dark. V's night vision gave her only a vague image of what was in front of her.

Pushing the pistol ahead, ready to shoot, she kept going, crawling ahead, and digging her claws into the soft clay, pushing with her claw-feet. It was like swimming in super-thick rather warm molasses.

She heard echoes of groaning. The earth was giving birth to something, something monstrous and primeval.

"Hmm," she muttered, "I am in the very womb of time; I am in the very womb of time."

She was not entirely sure this dark, clammy, death-and-rebirth caper was a good idea.

Maybe she should double back.

She gritted her fangs. "No, V, you must keep on. It is a question of honor and of destiny. Besides, there was the small matter of the human race – it needed saving. A world of zombies would be definitely unappetizing. Besides, she had sworn her sacred oath to her father Marcus – defend the human race, at all costs!"

It was so muddy she had to keep wiping her snout with the back of her claw to keep her nostrils open.

The air was clayey, and smelt of soft muddy things, nameless things that lie on the fine line that divides the living from the dead, the vital from the inert, and the beautifully vivacious from carrion.

The tunnel levelled out and became more spacious, giving V a tiny bit of elbow room. Stubbornly, she kept going. She saw a glow of what looked like light at the end of the tunnel.

Oops! Bad news!

An ocean of liquid mud splashed and oozed out of nowhere and began to pour into the tunnel, sloshing, gurgling; soon it would flood the whole thing.

Oh, horror! She was going to drown in a sea of goop and gunk!

She hurried up, pushing forward, elbows and knees pumping, driving her forward, her belly sliding and wiggling through the rising tide of oozy warm sludge. Yes, she was amphibious, an aquatic creature as well as terrestrial, and could breathe underwater, but this thick gluey sludge would be too viscous for her gills. It would clog them beyond repair.

She would suffocate and drown; the very idea was disgusting!

The mud crept up, flooding over her shoulders and her back and then up over her neck. V pushed on as fast as possible, sloshing ahead blindly, concentrating, ordering her gills to stay shut, knowing they would choke up and strangle her if they tried to breathe. The guck was thick and clingy like a bloody ocean of glue.

The gills obediently stayed shut.

V grimaced. The wonders of this alien body were of course a life-saver, just as her father Marcus had told her. You never knew what the reptilian demon body could do, until you put it to the test and tried. She was controlling an involuntary process by using her willpower, by turning it into a voluntary process. But there were limits.

The mud sloshed up to her nostrils.

V knew she could survive for maybe ten minutes without oxygen, maybe more, but she didn't want to push that limit. Her demon body was after all a body, a biological entity, and it did need oxygen. Her eyes were still above the slime.

She was by now afraid, very afraid, and more afraid when the tunnel widened slightly and she saw, rising out of the mud in front of her, two wide brightly glowing reptilian eyes.

"Oh, hello," she thought, "who are you?"

The thing reared up and V's night vision gave her the picture. The thing consisted of massive coils of muscle, scaly skin, its body about a foot thick, something like a python, but different, it had more intelligence, a cunning intelligence that was more than reptilian.

"Are you a girl monster or a boy monster?" V asked, mentally, testing the thing's mind to see just what sort of entanglement and relationship she was going to get into here.

"I'm a boy monster, lover-girl!" The thing answered from some dark pit of satanic macho intelligence; it was not a friendly answer; it was not a declaration of love or amorous intent; it was not the opening gambit in a courtship. Lust there was, though, but it was bloodlust. V could sense it and feel it, hot, slimy, obsessive – infernal. It was killer lust.

"Not my sort of fellow at all," thought V, rather miffed that her demonic and reptilian charms were impotent down here in the slime, even with a giant phallic purely male and very macho python-like monster.

V's nostrils were now under the mud. They shut themselves automatically. She was running on stored oxygen – she didn't have much time.

She tried the pistol – a sluggish click, click, click, was all she got.

It was clogged. She should have brought the AK-47. Her old friend Mikhail Kalashnikov had invented in the 1940s a weapon that was almost indestructible. You could abuse it and abuse it, throw it into mud or water or sand, and still it would fire.

Back the pistol went into its holster; she shoved and squished it in; it was difficult to do because of the mud.

She would have to fight this thing alone – no technology, no fancy human gadgets, just animal against animal, vampire demon reptile against a satanic serpent.

The darkness was almost total, and if it weren't for her night vision, V would have been utterly blind. She blinked away the mud and stared. The python's yawning jaws sloshed up above the mud; the fangs were long and sharp; the sleek flat head, mostly eyes and nostrils, was flat enough that it could fit between the surface of the mud and the roof of the tunnel – so that it could keep its infernal nostrils above the mud.

"This is not cricket, not cricket at all: it can breathe, and I can't, damn it!"

"I shall crush you, female," said the serpent's mind.

"No, you won't!" replied V.

"Oh, yes I will!" The thing reared up as far as it could, its head touching the roof of the tunnel, and it slithered forward, plunging straight at V.

V swiveled aside, sloshing over on her side deeper into the mud, blindly grabbing for the beast's mouth, closing her claws on its jaws, and twisting its head away and holding the head under the mud level.

"Let's hope you can't breathe under mud," V thought, as the serpent twisted its muscular coils around V, and the two of them, entwined in a deadly fluid, slippery, serpentine embrace, swirled and sloshed and wrestled, limb entwined with limb, twisting and turning under the clayey slime, V's limbs entangled with the monster's coils, the monster trying to break V's hold on its jaws, desperately heaving upwards, straining with every muscle, trying to free its head to breathe and to bite, and trying to twist itself around V to lock and crush V's limbs in a fatal embrace, its body curling around V's torso and legs. Finally, in a mighty heave of its coils, it managed to flip V over – slow motion – in the sludge, freeing its jaws from her grasp and sending V squishing down in the gooey morass, pinning her to the bottom of the tunnel, crushing her deep under the mud against the tunnel's solid floor.

V squirmed, she kicked, she wiggled, and writhed. She pressed up her hips, twisting, thrashing, desperate to break the serpent's vice-like hold.

Finally, it seemed after an eternity, in which V could not breathe, levering herself against slippery wall of the tunnel, V flipped herself over on top of the serpent, twisting him around, straddling his thick writhing body, clamping the serpent's round muscular heaving slippery delicious phallic torment between her clenched super-muscular thighs.

"Ah, got you!" she pinned him down. He fought to slip out from her grasp, he bucked; he curled upwards, levering against the tunnel's floor, and heaving himself against the roof; he swished down, he whip-lashed around, with snapping knife-like motion. V had to watch out for his head, for his giant jaws and razor-sharp teeth – they could do some real, perhaps fatal, damage.

"You are a wonderful bronco buster, V, you are the true Queen of the Wild West frontier," she thought, almost choking, with her mouth full of mud – phew!

A muffled, outraged hiss answered her inner rodeo joke.

"Ah, so you do read my mind – and you have no sense of humor!"

"No, I don't," the monster hissed, squirmed, thrashed between her thighs, pushing her upward like a wild bucking stallion in a rodeo.

"Get along little cowboy, get along. I shall tame you yet, you over-sized worm!"

The monster hissed. It curled closer around V, tightening one knot, then another, then another, bucking, tying itself in knots, a bucking bronco of a python, trying to escape the vice-like embrace of V's muscular demon thighs, while wrapping her in its coils. "You absolute turd," thought V, trying to insult the serpent, trying to penetrate its snake-like mind, trying to make it mad. She figured if it lost its temper, it would make mistakes.

But …

Maybe making it mad was not such a bright idea.

Silently the python coiled tighter, around V's ribcage, around her breasts, forcing the oxygen out of V's lungs – *Oooofff!* V spluttered, bubbling out her air supply, mud bubbles rising through the slime.

If she exhaled all the air, then she would be forced to breathe, and she'd fill her lungs with mud, and she'd die. Yes, even she could die. She wanted to sneeze. Hold on, V, hold on! You keep forgetting that you are, potentially, mortal. Your pride, V, and your vanity, will be your doom – just remember that!

Claws extended and grasping, she freed herself from the knots – so slippery they couldn't hold her – and she felt her way, claw-over-claw; she climbed blindly up the slippery squirming foot-thick rope-like body – he must be at least 15 feet long, maybe 20!

It seemed an eternity.

It all happened, squirming, fighting, and climbing, in mud-sealed blindness, blindly sloshing, groping, feeling, climbing along the monster's greasy scales.

Finally, she again found his head, pressed the points of her claws into the serpent eyes – blind him, blind him, blind him.

The jaws snapped; he tried to seize her; he tried to snap his jaws down on her claws, trying to cut her arms off – amputate them – at the wrist.

Flashing her claws this way and that, V evaded his razor-sharp teeth. She twisted the serpent's head back, and then, letting him open his jaws for an instant, she seized the upper and lower jaws forcing them apart, and the serpent coiled tighter around her pinning V's legs together, and using its long muscular body to twist and break V's back.

She pulled, levering, the jaws apart.

They forced themselves shut, almost trapping her claws.

"Bugger, absolute bugger!" she muttered, silently, mentally.

She was running out of oxygen, and she was running out of strength.

In this black glue, everything went in slow motion, everything was in the blindness, darkness; everything was viscous, primeval, elemental, body-against-body, reptile against reptile, scales against scales.

V inserted her claws between the beast's fangs, she pushed inward and then she pulled and pulled, prying the two jaws apart. It was slow, but slowly she brought them up, levering them apart, pushing, pushing, pushing, until …

He forced his jaws shut again, almost, but V stopped them just before they closed.

She could feel her own muscles bulging, straining, oxygen being consumed and burned, disappearing; she was desperate to suck in air!

But there was no air, just thick blind slimy unbreathable guck.

She pulled and pulled. Now the jaws were opening again … she pulled and putting every ounce of her super-human strength into the effort, she pulled …

Until …!

Snap … crack …

SNAP!

The hinge snapped; V tore the serpent's head into two pieces; the bones shattered; its jaw muscles severed, limp, helpless, gaping – two halves of a jaw.

The serpent went into a twisting spasm. It tightened itself around V's body in one last effort, pressing down on her rib-cage and stomach muscles, levering back, trying to tear one of V's leg upwards from her torso, bending it back, and back, until V felt her muscles about to snap, her leg and hip about to break – and then, suddenly, the giant went limp – a long twisted cable, now dead, inert, its furious snake-thoughts, a jumble of cannibalistic and hellish images fading, fading, fading – and then, nothing …

Still under the surface, still unable to breathe, still blinded by the mud, V disentangled herself from the knots of the giant's mud-slick body.

Finally, she freed herself; she pushed herself along the tunnel over the dead slimy body and got her head above the sloshing sticky surface. She opened her mouth wide – her nostrils were coated in mud – and gasped for air.

She swam, pushed, crawled, and, finally, covered in black slime, she pushed herself up out of the tunnel, blinking, gulping oxygen.

"At last!"

She shook herself, while muttering an angry hissing soliloquy – almost certainly in Shakespearean iambic pentameter – about being absolutely disgusted and disgusting and utterly filthy and needing a shower, and "Why do I put myself through this? Why don't I just retire to some desert and feed on passers-by – the occasional delicious truck driver, for instance, or foolish hitchhiker or backpacker?" She was being irrational, and she knew it. Outside, far away, somewhere, the world was coming to an end. There would be no more delicious hitchhikers, backpackers, or truck drivers.

She climbed out of the tunnel entrance – a sort of muggy, viscous hole in the ground – and wiped the mud from her eyes and snout with the back of her claws and looked around. Where the deuce was she?"

The space was huge. It must, she thought, be an enormous underground cavern, part of a temple complex. What looked like human bones and skulls were piled up against the walls and torches were burning and there was what looked like an altar at the far end.

V crouched down on her haunches. The floor of this immense space was tiled with red shining tiles.

Only now did she realize that she still had the foot-thick body of the serpent draped over one shoulder and that she had lost her pistol, of course.

The holster had been ripped off in the struggle.

She slipped the coil of slippery muscle off her shoulder and dropped the serpent into the tunnel's mouth.

Slowly the loops of scaly muddy muscle sank out of sight.

"So long, lover," V sighed. She replayed in her mind some of the more sensual moments of the struggle. What a phallic fellow he was! He would, if he had had a better temper, been a beautiful pet, a wonderful addition to her Tuscan villa, a conversation piece. Just think the mischief they could have gotten into! She wiped more mud from her snout and sneezed.

Ah, that was better!

Beyond the altar was darkness, but then the darkness filled, and a spiral galaxy shone, red and yellow and silver stars in a vast and smoky swirl of light.

Infinity!

Yes, where the devil was she?

She set off and walked until she came to a river.

She stepped into the river. The water was dark and deep, and she waded in and splashed around near the shore, got down on her hands and knees, rolled around, plunged under, and scooped up water, cleaning off the slime from the tunnel.

Finally, she splashed out of the river and walked along the bank.

She came to a creaky-looking, moss-covered, moldy old wooden pier that stuck out into the water and where a sleepy boatman was dozing on a rickety black wooden rocking chair under a feeble overhead reading lamp. The boatman was wearing a black skipper's cap and a high-collared black mariner's jacket with brass buttons; he stood up and stroked his salt-and-pepper beard and stared at her. "You don't want to go across there, do you, lady demon?" A thick hardback book had fallen by his chair, and was lying, V noticed, with its pages open.

"Yes, I do want to go across."

"I can take you, but I am not sure you will ever come back."

"So be it, boatman, if I don't come back, I don't come back."

"If that's the case, let us go."

The boatman polled the boat – which was very much like a Venetian gondola and lacquered entirely in glossy funereal black – across the river and delivered V to the other side, and then he said, "Whatever you do, my demon friend, do not fall asleep!"

"I shall try to stay awake, boatman."

"Do that. The gods be with you!" He shoved off and within seconds he and his sleek silent gondola disappeared into the foggy darkness.

V set off across a vast plain – under the vaults of stone. It was a very strange place, a whole dark desolate endless landscape trapped underground.

V blinked: What the hell?

Suddenly she was surrounded by bright light bulbs on strings and fairground organ music coming from every direction.

"Step right up!"

"Step right up, ladies and gentlemen!"

"Damnation!" V was in a fairground, she could see a roller-coaster going up and down and a Merry-go-Round spinning round and round and there were strings of colored light bulbs, and there was an immensely fat woman behind a small brightly painted wooden cart selling candy floss and candied apples, and there were barkers and one was shouting, "Step right up, ladies and gentlemen, step right up and get your fortune told, Madam Stavropoulos, the Psychic knows all, foretells all, though she is blind and deaf and wears a veil she can tell you what the future will bring!"

Another barker, a short stout man in a brown raincoat, was shouting, "See the wonders of the world, the pyramids, the world's wonders brought to you, right to you, right here!"

V turned a corner and saw a tall skinny man with buck teeth prancing on a small stage shouting, "Step right inside, folks, step right inside, and you will see these pitiful wonders of nature, these freaks, the bearded lady, the turtle man, the bird lady, the tattooed dwarf, the duck lady, the mad man of Borneo, and step right up, you will see the reptile woman! How about you, lady, how about you, would you like to see these wonders of nature, you look like a respectable woman, you know, but however respectable you are, my dear lady, you have to learn to look the facts of life in the face, you have to stare wickedness and cruelty and horror in the eye, boldness is what it takes, lady, step right up, come right in, come right in!"

V pushed her way in through the curtains and found herself in the dank clammy interior, with its garish posters and heavy curtains. A monstrous clown surged up in front of her. "Ha, ha, got you now, Madam, curiosity killed the cat, you know, you just step out of your gated community, out of your comfortable little suburban oasis, out of your high-class condo, and what do you see? You see horror, that's what you see, you are plunged into horror, and you become horror, and you know, finally, you finally realize, that the true freak is you, you are the true freak, ha, ha, ha! You! You! You!"

He screamed. His clown mouth was huge. His red lips, like his nose, were bulbous. He had giant teeth, fangs really; his round scarlet nose glowed, and he had a flower, a large daisy, in his button hole, and from it he squirted water, catching V in the eye, "Ha, ha, ha, got you, lady," he shouted, "Every proper clown has a flower in his buttonhole," he leaned forward, suddenly confidential, intimate, whispering into her ear, "Every proper clown is a true and rakish dandy!"

V sputtered, wiping the water from her eyes.

"Now, lady, over there is the living doll, you see her, up against the wall, she wandered in here one night, laughed at the freaks, and presto, the freaks took their revenge, they turned her into one of them, and – abracadabra – she became a doll, proper only to be propped up against a wall, as you can see, and as you can also see, just one tear traveling down her painted cheeks, that's all that remains of what she once was, of all her humanity there is now only one little wandering tear, ha, ha, ha … and over there is the monkey man, well, once he was a man and now he's a monkey, or a man-like monkey, or a monkey-like man, isn't that clever, and you might ask, how did he manage such a thing, well he got drunk one night, he was a sailor, and sailors do tend to get drunk, and the wicked witch had her way with him, in the dark, you know, and his performance, she thought, left something to be desired, didn't live up to the sales pitch if you know what I mean, and so there he is, hirsute, hairy, and horny as hell, perpetually scratching under his armpits – Stop that! – and over here is the tattooed lady, well, she speaks for herself doesn't she, a living work of art, she could be hung in a museum, and then, over here is the giraffe lady, she is truly exceptional, and beyond her, there, you see it, the best part of our collection, the reptile lady, poor thing, she has great difficulty finding suitors, let me tell you, perhaps you could give her some advice, you seem to have no difficulty finding suitors, do you, but then not all of us are equal, are we? No, no, don't go, please don't go!"

V pushed her way out of the stifling tent. Inside had been, yes, a disquieting experience. The reptile woman was V, the spitting image of V, but smaller, much smaller, only about two feet tall, but alive, apparently alive, for she had bowed, this miniature V, she had bowed towards V, and stared at V with sparkling diabolic reptile eyes, and at that point V decided that, reptile or not, demon or not, goddess or not, she needed some fresh air.

Outside, she found herself next to the Hall of Mirrors, and the barker, dressed in a silver suit, was in the full thrust of his spiel, "Now, step right up, don't be shy, you live in a shattered world, come in! See yourself as you truly are!"

V pushed through the door; it was like a leather curtain, it softly heavily swished aside, musty and tepid.

She was inside the Hall of Mirrors and she saw herself, V, reflected back, a turquoise humanoid reptile, on all sides, and V in infinite regression, reflections reflecting in reflections reflecting in reflections, and she wanted out of there right away, it was too much, but it took her a long time, it seemed years, maybe decades, to find the true exit, there were so many false exits, so many dead ends, so many illusions and mirages. Finally, a mirror dissolved, and she was once again out in the open air.

It was dank and dark. All the light bulbs – red, green, blue, white, and purple, suspended on strings – lining the trailers and stalls – shone in a slowly drifting fog that covered and clung to everything reducing visibility to a few feet. She could barely see her claws.

V was exhausted.

She began to suspect that perhaps this matrix, this place, was inside her own mind, that it was all an illusion, that she was trapped inside her skull. The mind, after all, is a circus, and, truth be told, a freak show. If so, if she was really inside her own cerebellum, when had the illusion begun? Was it *all* an illusion – Isis, Eve, the helicopter, the *Eden of the Seas*, the president, the …?

But this was no time for metaphysics and self-doubt. She walked out of the circus, leaving behind the hurdy-gurdy music, the barkers' cries, and the melody from the Merry-go-Round.

Suddenly, she found herself in a ruined city. The buildings had tumbled down, grass grew in cracks in the sidewalks, the windows were all broken, the subways – as she saw when she peeked into the stations – were flooded full of sea water, the streets were empty, and when V explored the neighborhoods, and the avenues, and the little courtyards and alleyways, she saw no one, not a single person. Everything was gray, even the grass, as if covered in ashes or dust; all the color had been drained out of this particular world.

She climbed up a rickety wooden staircase that was attached to the side of a derelict stone building; all the windows were arched and broken and dark; it was an ancient building, or so it seemed; she came to a room that she knew was her room, a rented room, her own little refuge; but she discovered that it was no longer her room; everything was dusty and gray and dull brown, as if it not had been lived in or cleaned or polished or cared for, for centuries, perhaps for millennia. So she left the room, and climbed back down the rickety wooden staircase.

Other than the grass – and it was withered and brown – there was no sign of life anywhere, no life of any kind. It was a city and landscape of stone. There were no people. V knew, somehow knew, that all the people were dead; they had been dead for a long time; this was a dead city, a city of the dead. Perhaps it was peopled with ghosts; she didn't see the ghosts; but she felt, from time to time, their eyes upon her. She closed her eyes.

Now she was again in a cave, an enormous cave.

She felt drowsy; she sat down by a towering stalagmite. "Just for an instant, I'll just rest for an instant. Her eyes fluttered.

V fell asleep …

"I know the boatman told me not to fall asleep," V yawned, "But I can't resist. I'll just rest a minute or two here, and then I'll go on, and I'll …"

CHAPTER 40 – THE SOUL EXHANGE MACHINE

V woke up and tried to yawn, tried to stretch, tried to stand.

But she was already standing.

She was erect, on her feet, but frozen, could not move a muscle, could barely blink her eyes, her lips and cheeks felt numb. What had happened to her? It was a dream … No, it was like a nightmare.

It *was* a nightmare.

She was a statue, carefully posed, her arms up, pointing, and rigid as stone. She was, she realized, the image of the goddess in the temple. She was in the same pose; she was frozen, on a pedestal, now, in stone.

The high metallic arches of this place, whatever it was, glimmered, pure steel or something like steel. This, she realized, must be the secret underworld place where the Puppet Master resided and worked his evil magic – turning humans into beasts.

She heard a voice, and she saw a small creature, a man, well, it seemed like a man, or perhaps a child, or a monkey-like thing. It was very small, and it came ambling along, nonchalant, shuffling sideways, towards her.

The creature was chalk-white, well, more a blotchy, whey-colored, off-white, a sort of rotten-goat-cheese-crust white. It was male, that much was clear. It looked like a naked monkey, completely hairless, with an over-sized bulbous head, twisted limbs, and it walked with difficulty, swinging along the floor, its arms too long for his body, his knuckles dragging on the ground.

He …

Yes, it was a he.

The creature came to the base of V's pedestal and stopped and, slowly looked up at her, peering at her from watery baleful eyes. "Ah, she is awake, the vampire goddess is awake!" His voice was high, raucous, and grating – very unpleasant.

He shuffled closer, stopped, and gazed up at her. With one oversized gnarled hand, he stroked his pointed fetus-like chin, "You are exactly what I've always wanted."

V's tongue and lips wouldn't move. She wanted to say, "Who are you?" or, maybe, something more like, "Piss off and leave me alone!"

She tried to read his thoughts, but her mind, like her body, was paralyzed; it seemed to be blocked in an ocean of glue; she couldn't transmit thoughts and she couldn't read thoughts. Even thinking had become difficult – one idea struggling mightily to follow another idea, and by the time idea number two arrived, the first idea, the idea it was to be connected with, had been forgotten. Her mind was a stagnant, deepening fog.

"I imagine, V, you are wondering who and what I am." He scrambled up a stepladder, which had suddenly materialized, with a neat little wooden platform at the top, so his face was facing hers. His nose – dripping silver drool – was only inches from her snout.

He licked his fleshless lips. "What, V, you are mute? Can you not speak? Oh, I love it! I love to see you standing there, helpless, unable to move! You, the glittering demon, transformed into my own personal work of art, my own bit of statuary! Why Michelangelo himself would paid his weight in gold to have possessed you. What a dream! Well, V, I am Dmitry."

V thought, laboriously. Her thought, the image, the concept, struggled sluggishly to be born, her mind was locked in slow-motion, dreadful, sickening slow-motion, the words coming drip-by-drip, swimming, slogging, through glue-like treacle: "But that is impossible! Dmitry is dead, Dmitry ..."

With long bony fingers, he scratched his scrawny armpits. His oversized sex, giant sausage-like penis and swollen misshapen elongated testicles, dangled between his legs, hanging down beyond his crooked bow-legged knees. "Yes, yes, I know what you are thinking: Dmitry is dead; he was killed by Sabrina, your sister; he was emptied of every drop of blood, and he was, as you love to say, and as dear Sabrina, methodical in all things, did truly say, "Dead, truly dead, and will not rise again!"

Helpless, immobile, she stared – even her reptile eyes unable to move.

"Well, my goddess," he cackled and then coughed and spit up a huge white gob of phlegm, which he caught in his paw, and wiped on his chest, patting it down, "Bodily fluids," he cackled, it was like listening to a crow caw, "I love bodily fluids, particularly my own bodily fluids, I adore them, I really adore them. Don't you adore bodily fluids, V?" He coughed again, in a rippling obscene cackle, his long dirty pointed teeth bared in a grin, "I am sure you adore blood, in fact you worship blood. It is your only religion!" He cackled again, dancing up and down in glee, his sex wagging heavily, a long flaccid length of thick hose pipe attached to two huge, wrinkled, sagging udders.

"Yes." He reached out and touched her, stroking her scales, "Oh, divine, divine, so divine!"

V felt the rough moist fingers – long discolored sausage-like appendages with pointed yellowish dirty broken nails – stroke her scales. Inwardly she recoiled, but she couldn't move; she couldn't protest.

"Well, now, V, you see what I have done. I have performed a miracle! I have created a race of zombies! And this is just the beginning!"

V yearned to scratch his eyes out. Her claws refused to budge.

"In fact, V, the whole human race will soon be zombies. They will be the slaves of the Puppet Master. They will be the slaves of Dmitry. Most of them will die, of course; but no matter, others will survive. They will eat garbage and perhaps small animals. And it will still be possible to drink their blood, so there's no worry there – food will be available, food and fodder in abundance.

V raged. Her first duty, her primal duty, was to defend the human race – and she had failed, she was failing; she would fail. How stupid she had been – to fall asleep, to doze her way into oblivion and damnation! The boatman had warned her! But, no, she thought, I will not surrender, I will win. I will not fail!

"But I imagine you are curious about me, V, well, you see, you were quite right, Sabrina did kill Dmitry, she did kill me, and she drank the blood of Dmitry's body – Oh, his magnificent body, I was very proud of that body – well, she drank the blood right down to the last drop, so that he would be dead, truly dead, and not rise again. She did her duty as a hybrid and as a vampire, she truly did. She followed your instructions to the letter. She enacted your DNA – and Claire's – literally to the last syllable. And she was diabolically clever, of course, Sabrina, since she disguised her intelligence so effectively, wondrously treacherous wench that she is, and I – the old Dmitry, the human Dmitry – I thought I had reduced her to a simpering slave, a mere speechless animal, an idiot, while, all the time, she was pretending to be a cowering mindless animal and scheming her revenge. It was admirable. I myself could not have arranged it better."

V tried to move – but she couldn't. How had Dmitry survived, if he had? And what did this monster have to do with Dmitry, Dmitry the handsome urbane sadistic devil, what did this shrunken specimen have to do with Dmitry?

"Well, yes, so, you see, beautiful Sabrina did kill Dmitry. But Dmitry had taken a precaution, he had designed an experiment, and he had chosen himself to be the first guinea pig. Now, you, oh exquisite one, you will wish to know what that experiment was. Yes, don't deny it!" He sat back on his haunches and gazed at her. "Oh, how exquisite you are! And how intelligent you are – how curious about all things!"

Inwardly V swore and stormed about in a rage. But outwardly, she was a statue, a thing, a monument of marble. She couldn't move. There was absolutely no expression on her face. It was as if she had been carved in stone or cast in bronze. Damnation! She seethed.

"You see, my dear V, Dmitry had downloaded his personality into a new kind of bio-memory bank, before going out to meet and collect Sabrina in her new reptilian form. And then, though he was officially dead, he had arranged – post-mortem as it were – to download the memory bank, his personality, his memories, his desires, into a body."

He hesitated and coughed violently and wiped the foam of phlegm on his arm. "It was supposed to be a beautiful body, a sublime body, the body of a champion swimmer and athlete, a fellow Dmitry had murdered and stored in the deep freeze precisely for the moment of his own resurrection. But there was a screw up. The strain was too great. The scientists, who had been charged with carrying out Dmitry's desires, botched the operation!"

He cackled, "What a joke, eh, what a joke! And so here I am – as they made me! This is me, Dmitry reborn! Am I not beautiful?" He pirouetted around on the small wooden platform. "Those scientists suffered, I can tell you; they died, slowly, very slowly, in the most painful, most horrible, most grotesque ways I could devise. Perhaps I exaggerated; perhaps I should have been more forgiving. My brother also died, with his family, but you know that …"

V thought, "So I was right, Sabrina was right. You did murder your brother – and his family." But the thought was silent; it was buried; V did not move, she could not move, not even scowl, not even twitch.

"So I have been trapped in this body, a travesty, I must say, a travesty, I do not like to pass mirrors, well, let me correct that: I didn't like to pass in front of mirrors, but now I delight in my deformity, I delight to gaze upon myself, and cast my lurching shadow on every lurking wall – I delight in my deformity and in my passion – for evil." Suddenly, beside him, there was a lamp. It cast his shadow on the wall of what seemed to be a temple.

He made patterns with his hands, a duck, a top hat, a racing car; the lamp cast giant shadows on the wall, perfect shadow images of a duck, a top hat, and a racing car, "You see, V, Dmitry was an artist, and I am an artist. Can you not see that? Oh, I hope you can! I hope you can appreciate how beautiful it is to be me! Because, soon, you will be me and I will be you."

V's reptile eyes were expressionless.

The Dmitry creature reached out and with his calloused hand caressed her thigh; he moved his fingers over her belly. "Ah, how sweet you are, how sublime you are!"

His tongue was hanging out, at least two inches, dripping saliva. He was gazing at V, almost worshipfully.

"Now how did I do what I have done, being what I have now become? Well, I did it by lying low, pretending to be harmless, pretending to be the court buffoon, the clown, and, oh, I was a witty fellow, hidden in the heart of one of Bio-Prom's subsidiaries, lost in the Caucasus Mountains, I must say, full of zest and bon mots and practical jokes, a true jester I, I bided my time. I secretly took over Bio-Prom, which after all already belonged to the old Dmitry, that is, to me, and I created a secret program, the Zombie program. The Advanced Coordinated Puppet Master Slug Virus – ACPMSV-3B – is one of my masterpieces. Sabrina and her experts thought at first it was the Korean virus, or one of the North Korean knock-offs. Not at all, not at all, my darling V! But it was designed to look like the Korean virus, to throw the hunters off the scent. And, then, I only needed that foolish vice president of the United States and a few of his cohorts and, voila, presto, abracadabra, the end of the world – well, the end of the human world!"

The little fellow danced up and down and kicked out his twisted legs, his shadow, enlarged by the lamps, stretched across the stone wall, a giant – a shadow giant kicking up his heels.

"Now, I will soon have mastery of a large part of the world – and then, of course, the whole world. You, V, were the danger, the principle danger and threat to my plans, and now I will eliminate you. But not only that, V, not only that! You see, V, I think that perhaps I need a more suitable form for my mind and my personality – now that I am going to be master of the world. I need a suitable costume for my new role! And that is one reason you are here, dear V, you are here to become my body. Your body will be my new terrestrial envelope. And as you, in your body, with your abilities, I shall become a god – or rather goddess. Isn't that just giggly? I am going to download me into you! Oh, yes, oh yes! I'm sure you find that delightful!"

V could not move, could not speak. But her mind, now, was racing. The adrenaline of fear – of terror – could come in useful, she thought, even for demons. The thinking logjam had broken. The fog flew away. Pure terror will do that.

V was terrified.

All the chemicals of fear and terror pumped into her blood.

The Dmitry creature pranced away, and then came dancing back, his giant sex joggling, dragging on the surface of the platform, stirring up miniature whirlpools of brown dust.

V's reptilian eyes stared at him. She must break out of this paralysis, but she could not move. She was horrified: Was her body going to become the vessel for this obscene and evil maniac? It could not be! No, no, no!

"But, don't worry, V, I shall find a home for you. I am going to put you in my body, this body. I will be the new you. And you will be the new me! I am going to downgrade this body radically, so that you will be more or less powerless, even weaker and more grotesque than I, but you will continue to exist, even to think, but you will be locked in this body – is it not beautiful? – But of course you will be without any of the powers that might make you dangerous. You will have no powers at all. You will be lower than the lowest of the low. You will be impotent, V, impotent. And I will rule the world!" He giggled hysterically.

V strained to break the spell, whatever it was, that held her fast. How was he going to do this monstrous thing? He would be extraordinarily dangerous if he acquired her powers; if he had his diabolic way, he would be a nightmare – even for the mindless beasts that humanity would have become.

And then the thought of becoming *him* made her shiver inwardly. If she could break out in a cold sweat, she would have broken out in a cold sweat. She tried to evoke her Avatar. She concentrated. Maybe the Avatar could save her. But the Avatar did not answer. This Dmitry monster – obviously an expression of some deeper and even more horrible force – had deadened her mind, so not even her Avatar could hear her. She was his prisoner. She concentrated: "Claire, Claire, I need help! I've been captured! I'm helpless!"

V was proud. She was vain about her status as the head of the pack of hybrids. Calling for help was shameful; but, if she had to get down on her knees, she would get down on her knees. "Claire! Please help me! Please hear me!"

But Claire, wherever she was, was silent.

No one could hear her, no one anywhere.

Of course, they were in a different time, thousands of years, perhaps hundreds of thousands of years, away from help. Perhaps, too, as Isis said, they were in a different, alternative universe, sealed away from everyone and everything they had ever known.

"Let us begin," said the Dmitry Doll, that's how she thought of him, he was a little puppet-like creature, a doll. But in truth, she knew she was deluding herself. He was not a puppet – he was the Puppet Master, he was pulling the strings, and he was the expression, the incarnation of a powerful ghost, an evil spirit, who was himself, probably, an expression of something deeper, the Evil Force, the Dark God, the Eternal Enemy. He was an emanation of Evil, sulfurous and infinite Evil.

If she could have spoken there were all sorts of questions she wanted to ask him. V's curiosity was always – almost always – greater than her fear.

But now she was truly terrified.

"Let us begin," the Dmitry Doll said, in his cackling, static-riddled voice, "I know you are eager to get started, V, I know you are eager to know what it is like to be me! So I shall show you – you shall be me, and I shall be you."

He twirled around, and then he put a gnarled fist to his chin and struck the thoughtful pose of a deep thinker. "Ah, I wonder, V, will you be you, when you are me, or will you become *me*, with all my hatred, all my bitterness, all my vitriolic bile, and my infinite hatred and desire to do evil?"

V then noticed that two people – were they people? – they looked like zombies, robotic zombies – had appeared, out of nowhere, with a huge apparatus with electronic equipment and devices, and two tanks, a sort of liquid baths for bodies. The apparatus towered up, it had pipes and channels, and wires and lights and wheels and cogs and steel ladders and conveyor belts and gears and rods and pistons and steam rose out of one part of it, *huff puff, huff puff*, and dials trembled and it seemed to reach up fifty or sixty or one hundred feet, and for some reason she presumed that the two tubs down at the bottom filled with bubbling smoking liquid were the containers where bodies – and souls – were placed – and transformed!

"This," said the Dmitry Doll, "is the Transformer of Souls. Or you could also call it the Soul Exchange Machine."

V concentrated. If only she could communicate with him, maybe she could upset him enough, and he would make a mistake. She concentrated on transmitting the thought: "You are a fake, you are not Dmitry! You are just a puppet!"

She got no reaction.

So she concentrated all her mental might and she felt that she was receiving strength from some source beyond her, she was not sure what, but she thought again, spelling it out, slowly, coldly, "You are a fake. You are not Dmitry. You are a puppet! You are a doll. You are a floppy little counterfeit doll!"

This got him.

Suddenly he stopped. His pale rheumy eyes – they looked, she thought, like pools of snot – stared up at her. "You are a fiction," V added, "You don't even exist."

His lipless mouth dropped open, saliva drooled, and his crooked, pointed, widely spaced, rotten and broken teeth glinted. "You," he screamed, "You are a false thing. You are saying a false thing! It is not true! I am Dmitry. I am the incarnation of Dmitry! I am the true Dmitry. You're a liar!"

He screamed – as if he were in pain.

He hopped up and down, waving his skinny bony arms, with their pip-squeak elbows. His oversized sex jiggled between his bow legs like it was a two huge bags of potatoes attached to a dangling May pole. "I am Dmitry," he screamed. He hopped up and down; he danced around in fury, spittle sprayed.

"You are a pathetic bug!" V concentrated the thought and loaded it up with vivid high definition three-dimensional mental images of centipedes, beetles, creepy-crawlies slithering out from under rotten logs and overturned rocks, slimy gooey indecent formless things.

"You, you, you, you monster!" he screamed.

"You hopeless turd," she answered.

"No, no, no!" he hollered.

"You loathsome figment of a diseased mind, you fatuous bag of putrescent wind, you useless excrescence of a pus-filled wart, you pantomime of shit, you dog's vomit of …"

"Wheel her into the machine," he shrieked. "Let us get this done. Let us see what she does when she is an impotent misshapen dwarf hopping about on broken arthritic limbs and feeling pain with every breath, let us see how she behaves when she becomes me!"

He screamed so hard he was choking on his own screams, on his own saliva.

V hoped for a moment that he would enter into convulsions and die, and at the same time she thought that it was uncharitable and cruel to think such a thought. He rolled on the platform, foaming at the mouth, spraying spittle, and kicking at the air and at the floor with his dusty little heels, and the two zombie-like humans were standing next to V; and V, still frozen like a statue, tried to transmit the thought, "Set me free, let me go, don't do this," but the zombie-like humans seemed indeed truly mindless; their eyes were as empty as pure white mist; their mouths were as slack as dangling rubber bands drooling rivers of saliva; their arms hung limp at their sides, their fingers twitched. They tilted the pedestal on which V stood and which appeared to have wheels; V was still as rigid as a statue, unable to budge, unable even to tumble off the pedestal. They rolled her over to the Soul Exchange Machine, and tipped her on her side, slipping her off the pedestal, and lowering her slowly into one of the salt water baths, a warm greasy saline bubbling concoction, and pushed her under. Her gills opened so she could breathe. At least it was not oxygen-starved fluid as she had feared. The two robot-zombies began to attach electrodes to parts of her body, her breasts, thighs, shins, feet, belly, shoulders, and back. Her body had become flexible now, but paralyzed, floating freely, inert. They encased her head in a sort of one-piece black rubber mask and helmet, which clicked and locked into place. Now, even mobilizing all her extra senses, she couldn't see anything, or feel anything. Her gills inhaled deeply. "Oh, Marcus, I wish you were here, I wish you could hear me, I wish you could help me, in this my hour of need." And then there was silence and darkness and …

And suddenly V was out on a barren, heath-like place, with long tendrils of waving grass, or it seemed like grass, but it was alive in a way grass is not alive, it was conscious, and even the ground under her feet was conscious and she was aware of a humming sound. Flashes of lightning lit up the landscape, a gently rolling plain of this living land, this living, seething earth, and in the distance black mountains rose towards a moon that had the form and face of a skull. Dmitry was standing, not far away. He grinned at her. It was the old, handsome Dmitry. He came towards her, and he opened his arms, and he whispered, but his whisper was like thunder. "Oh, I love you, I have always loved you, V, I have loved and worshipped you from afar, you have been my idol and my goddess, and now, now, V, we can consummate our love!" As he came close, she smelt his breath. It was foul, like a pile of rotting corpses, like a mountain of offal, like an open sewer. It had the sweet sickening rottenness of Hell itself. She tried to move. She tried to draw back. But she couldn't speak; she couldn't budge, not an inch. Then, against her will, she was kissing him, embracing him, worshipping him. He changed. He became the deformed dwarf, on his hands and knees, facing her, and he pounced on her, and she was lying face up, and his mouth was open above her and drooling onto her face. She tried to turn her head aside, but she couldn't and the drool, his drool, thick and gluey drool, dribbled and streamed onto her face, and it covered her eyes, and then her mouth. She couldn't see and she couldn't breathe. Her face became a glutinous formless mask. She wanted to cry out, mentally or physically; she wanted to move, and spring away, but she couldn't. She had become as immobile and silent as death, and then she blinked open her eyes and ...

She blinked open her eyes and she was lying flat on some sort of surface, and the liquid was no longer there and she tried to get up and she found it was painful, there were aches and pains everywhere. She had forgotten what pain and aches were like – it took her a second to realize what she was feeling. She struggled to her feet and she looked down and saw that her arm was a bony, misshapen spindly chalk-white appendage.

She shrieked.

The shriek came out as a spittle-laden, muted, throaty cackle. She was drooling; between broken teeth she was drooling. She looked down at the floor and at herself. The floor, made of white marble, was closer than it should be, and she, well, she was a tiny creature, and her body sagged, and she was ... male!

Ugh!

The grotesque oversized male sex dangled between her skinny bow legs, sticking out, enormously below her swollen wrinkled little belly, and the turgid sex was hanging down, far beyond her bony bulbous knees.

Ugh! Ugh! Ugh!

She hobbled towards a full-length mirror she saw hanging on the wall. Her arms were swaying and dangling, her knuckles brushing the cool white marble; every step was an immense effort, heaving the misshapen little body painfully forward, step by agonizing step.

And in the mirror she saw not herself, not V the glittering turquoise exquisitely fashioned hybrid, but *it*, the Dmitry Doll, the dwarf! She cried out, and the cry was like a crow's raucous caw; spittle sprayed from the dried thin lips! Oh, horrible, most horrible!

V stared at what she had become. Her rheumy colorless misshapen eyes stared. Her lipless mouth, with saliva dripping from between the pointed broken teeth, hung comically open. Her legs, bowlegged, barely supported her skeletal, parchment-dry body. Its crooked ribs stuck out. Her sunken chest and little round pot belly were a mockery. Her skinny arms hung uselessly at her sides.

She heard a voice, a suave female voice with a slight hiss and lisp say, "So, V, how do you like your new home?"

V turned to see herself, the demon V, leaning nonchalantly against the Transformer of Souls. She hopped painfully over to the suave demon. She looked up at the goddess-like creature and she croaked, in a petulant, childish falsetto croak, "Give me back me, Give me back me, Give me back me!"

The iridescent demon pirouetted gracefully, playfully, and said, "Now, why ever should I do that? I am perfectly happy where I am! I feel just perfectly gorgeous being me, I mean being you being me, or me being you! Here I am, in the perfect body, immortal, me being V, a goddess, what I've always dreamed of being! I am perfectly happy with my new home and its new super-powers. I shall remain just as I am forever. And you shall remain just as you are, as long as that miserable little body survives, which, my dear, I am afraid, will not be very long – Or, no, perhaps I shall preserve you, keep you, perhaps in a cage, or parade you on a leash, from time to time, for all eternity!"

The dwarf V raged. It danced up and down. "Give me back me, give me back me, give me back me!" Its outsized sex, the testicles and penis swollen in rage, flipped and bounced, up and down, and slapped against the creature's bony shriveled thighs, bounced, again and again obscenely slapped against the creature's thighs, and slapped, and slapped, and slapped.

"I love it when you rage, stupid little insect," the reptile demon blinked its eyes flirtatiously, "You are so cute and so grotesque when you are angry!"

"Give me back me, Give me back me!" The little one bounced up and down, making splashes in the dust.

"Oh, this is just divine," lisped the turquoise reptile demon, "oh truly cute!" The reptile demon strutted back and forth, swaying its hips, sashaying to-and-fro hands on hips.

It stopped and gazed with rapture into the full length mirror, "Oh, I am positively gorgeous! Don't you think I'm divine? And, you know, darling, the most wonderful thing is, with these new powers, I can drive my puppets faster, and faster, and faster – soon there will be no humans left except those I keep in cages – to feast on, of course …"

V, trapped in the tiny deformed body, whimpered. She was lost. She had lost the war – defeat, utter defeat, loomed, and not only for her.

CHAPTER 41 – SAMANTHA UNLEASHED

In the Volpe Tower in New York City, Bill Brothers wiped his forehead.

"Now, this is horrible, truly horrible" he said. "Replay that please!"

On the screen, tied up in her mummy duct tape, Sam, who had been silent for almost fifteen minutes, suddenly screamed, "Ugh, Ugh … Grrhh, Charlie battle now on, and battle, battle for end, battle for victory. Puppet Master will be Master of World, Master of World! Cannot let happen, Grrhh, end of all things, Charlie, end of time, end of time now to be decided, now, now, now … and now, all is lost, Charlie, all is lost, darkness descends, Charlie, darkness descends, there is no hope, Charlie, all is lost, all is darkness …!" Sam thrashed and foamed and tore at the duct tape and her green eyes flashed like lightning. "Oh, kill me now, Charlie, kill me now … Please kill me now!"

"Now, Sam, calm down. Things will get better."

Sam whimpered. Then she screamed – "No, no, no, the Puppet Master has won, he has won."

"Won?" Charlie said, "What do you mean, won?"

"He has conquered the Goddess."

"The Goddess?"

"He has conquered the Serpent Goddess, the turquoise beauty, the scaly wonder, the vampire, who is the protector. She is the shield. She is the salvation of humans … of us … of humans … of those who are still human … She has sworn to protect us …"

"So, this Goddess, this vampire, you say …"

"Only, grrrh, only barrier to universal damnation, Charlie, is the Goddess."

"Wow, Sam, this is new."

"The Goddess has fallen into a pit of darkness. She is no longer …" Sam began to writhe and twist and turn, thrashing this way and that.

She broke free of her duct-tape bonds and she tore the duct tape from her body, sticky bits of gold tape flying here and there, sticking to the walls, to the child's drawings, to the bedside lampshade, except some stubborn thickly wound tape, silken black, that still entangled her legs; the last stands of hair flew from her head …

And now, utterly hairless, she rolled over and over, came to the edge of the bed, teetered for an instant, and, then, like a fish flipping out of a fisherman's net, she flopped off the bed, and fell with a thump on the floor.

"Hey, Sam, what are you doing, Sam! Hey!" Charlie was afraid, if she got loose and sprayed the stuff all over that he would finally catch the zombie virus and be of no use to anybody. But he decided to stand his ground come what may and so he came closer and trained the camera on Sam.

She was flopping and wiggling like a mermaid out of water and she twisted and turned and then she tore away the last sticky bits of duct tape that bound her ankles and thighs and she was now on her hands and knees.

"Oh, oh," said Charlie, keeping the camera steady.

Sam looked up at Charlie with phosphorescent green eyes and, she made a baying sound, like a wolf in heat. Slowly, unsteadily, she stood up and stretched and she howled again, like a banshee in the wild.

Charlie said, "Okay, Sam, keep going!"

"Charlie, Grrrhhh, Charlie, Grrrhhh, brave, gallant, heroic Charlie, Grr-rhhhhhh, the Goddess, the Goddess, Charlie, she is in the pit of darkness, grrrh! She has been possessed, but now … Charlie, now … Charlie …"

"Yes, Sam," said Charlie, backing up so he could keep Samantha, from the shoulders up, fully in the frame.

"Charlie, grrrh," she said, coming towards him, reaching out her arms, "Charlie, grrhhhh, I … Charlie … grrhhhh," foam spilled from her mouth, flowed down her chin, "Charlie, zombies now on the march, cannot be stopped, Charlie, grrhhhh, cannot be stopped … grrhhhh!" She sprayed more goo; some of it caught Charlie on the cheek, "grrhhhh, whole world now, grrhhhh, no end, world without end, no light, Charlie … grrhhhh!" The foam dripped from her eyes, cascaded from her mouth, "grrhhhh, Charlie, and, Charlie, grrhhhh, I love you, Charlie … grrhhhh … I love …"

Sam's face filled the screen – and then the sound was, clatter, clatter, "grrhhhh." The screen went dark.

"Well," said the General "well, well."

"Communications with Charlie and Samantha broke off at this point, just a few minutes ago." Bill Brothers ran a handkerchief over his forehead, sweat was gathering, the air-conditioning was still dead. "General, what do you make of what Samantha said about the Goddess? What Goddess? What is she talking about?"

"Well, Bill, we are in an exceptional state, right now, a state of emergency is the least we can say about the state we are in. So, Bill, I will confide something."

"Yes, General, confide."

"Well, as we discussed earlier, Biological Creations, the earlier model BIOCs, and the more advanced synthetic individuals, or SINs, both really different versions of synthetically created human beings, are apparently immune to the zombie virus and have been in the front line of the fight against the zombies."

"Yes, General. We've seen several examples of that in the footage – or so it seems."

"Yes, like the charming young lady in the French waitress's costume, who was quite possibly a SIN and thus immune to the zombie virus."

"You like that one, don't you, General?"

"Well, Bill, at my age I am allowed to like what I like because I rarely get a chance to do anything about it. But, were I several wars younger, I tell you …!"

"Ah, General, I'm sure you continue to make conquests to this day."

"Nice of you to say so, Bill, nice of you to say so: but to get to the point, hybrids are also, I would imagine, immune to the virus."

"Hybrids – like the reptile man, the murderer …?"

"Yes, like the reptile man."

"What has that got to do with …?"

"Well, Bill, for many decades there has been a rumor in intelligence circles about a hybrid, a female, a sort of reptile demon, like the reptile man, but this female does good, on the whole, she does good."

"And this female hybrid, she's the Goddess?"

"Some intelligence documents do refer to her as the Goddess, yes."

"My God, this is …"

"Astounding, I know, Bill, I know. But she could indeed be the Goddess that Samantha is referring to. Now, Bill, you and your viewers are too young to remember, but in the great events of 2027 –"

"The earthquakes, the volcanic eruptions, the tidal waves …"

"Exactly!" the General leaned forward. "Well, at that time the world almost came to an end, and then, suddenly, everything stopped. The catastrophes ceased."

"It was mysterious."

"Yes, it was mysterious – and the weird shifts in the electromagnetic and gravitational field were similar – but worldwide – to what we have seen in southern Florida right now, and what we are seeing."

"So ..."

"Well, at the time there was, well, there was a woman, a woman reptile, looked like a demon, reported to be quite sexy, though, a sort of hybrid, and she was rumored, well, more than rumored, she was reported by various agencies, very hush-hush, you know, top secret, to have stopped the terrorist attack that was behind the disasters."

"Seriously?"

"I know it sounds far-fetched, Bill, but I have seen documents, and I believe that in fact we have an invisible ally, with the occasional code name 'The Goddess,' a hybrid human-alien, or something like a hybrid, and that this hybrid, who is a woman, often works with our intelligence services, ours and those of our allies, she is very powerful, apparently, and she comes into the fight when the going really gets tough, like it is now, and she comes to our aid, and she helps us, and, sometimes, Bill, sometimes, goddamn it, sometimes she saves our bacon, Bill, goddamn it, she saves our bacon."

"So, if, as Samantha suggests, this hybrid, this Goddess, has been destroyed ... or defeated ... then ..."

"Then it is bad news for us, Bill, and it is bad news for the human race," and, as the camera zoomed in on him, the General, for once, did not flash his famous smile.

CHAPTER 42 – TRANSCENDENCE

Trapped in the tiny dusty ancient contorted male body, crouching bitterly on the floor of the immense cavern, her knuckles dragging in the dust, monkey style, and, bent over like a tortured broken twig, V watched the performance of the glittering female demon that had once been she.

V drooled envy. Ribbons of silver saliva spilled from her chapped and twisted lips, from between her crooked and broken teeth; she was filled with envy and horror – and fear …

That monster was dancing in her body. He is in *my* body, he has taken possession of *my* body and *my* powers, and I am trapped in his, and forever, this is a punishment beyond all punishments, this is cruel, this is undeserved, this is, this is …

Then, suddenly, she stopped.

She stopped and a light dawned.

Ancient lessons floated up from all the sages and ancient books. Buddha, Jesus Christ, Marcus Aurelius …

She stopped and she thought:

I am what I am. I will be what I will be.

Nothing can change that.

Yes, I should not be envious; I should not hate Dmitry; I am uncharitable; Dmitry has suffered; he has his own form of madness; he is trapped inside himself – even if he is in my body, even if he has acquired my powers, he is still trapped inside himself. Indeed, he is undoubtedly an instrument of something much greater than he. He is a tool merely, exploited as we can all be exploited.

Yes, towards Dmitry, I am being uncharitable; I am binding and blinding myself in ignorance. I am limiting myself to myself. I am not thinking clearly. I have put barriers between my mind and what is truly important. I am thinking in a petty and cruel and egoistical manner. I must liberate Dmitry, not imprison him.

Yes, the angelic voices said: Do onto others … There but for the Grace of God go I. Put yourself in the other guy's shoes, goddamn it, V! Put yourself in the other guy's skin. Detach yourself from yourself, V, free yourself from the chains, let the ego die, V, free yourself from the chains of desire, of fear, of pride, of vanity, of ego! Relax, V, dissolve the self, the ego, let yourself melt away, into the vast ocean of what is, was, and shall forever be …

And V became calm.

The small dusty aged body became calm.

What is, is; what shall be, shall be.

Visions flooded her mind: she saw Isis, sitting on a tree branch, just outside the cave, patiently waiting – and her heart filled with love for Isis.

She saw Sergeant Eve Schmidt, as she had first glimpsed her, with that tight brave smile, her golden hair pulled back in a tight bun, her hand curled next to her pistol, willing to face death, willing to face annihilation, and asking V in a curious and humane way, one being to another, "What are you, what are you really?" And her heart filled with love and admiration for Eve Schmidt.

She saw Monica, so brave, so calm, transformed into a hybrid, and giving birth, with Doctor Mansoor and Colonel Siebert risking their lives to help her. And her heart filled with love for Monica, for Doctor Mansoor and for the Colonel.

She saw Sabrina, object of so much hatred and envy, worried, tired, working endlessly to keep the fight going, to save *Andromeda II*, to save humanity. And her love for Sabrina, which was already great, was reborn, and redoubled in strength.

She saw the Captain of the *Eden*, Magnus Olsen, talking to a zombie, a woman, "Ingrid," he was saying, "I believe both of us could use a coffee," and the zombie woman, a young woman, her eyes flicking shadows of green, answering him, "Yes, Magnus, I shall make us some coffee. Thank you, Magnus." And her heart was flooded with love for Magnus and Ingrid, for their calm and for their dauntless courage.

V saw the president, so elegant and cool and brave under pressure, and then so delightfully crazy as a spoilt-teenage freshly invented hybrid reptile girl.

She saw Alex, so serious and determined to save everyone; she saw the little girl, Aaloka, Alex had rescued, delightful Aaloka. She saw Helen, whom she had always loved, from the first glimpse, and her heart filled with love for Helen.

She saw Sarah James, resigned to her fate as a black-and-red reptilian hybrid, concentrating on saving people, and cracking jokes about how she would get even with V. Ah, Sarah, my love! How funny you are!

She saw a woman she didn't know, a zombie – she looked like that famous actress Virginia Lily – with a rigid crest of platinum hair and glowing green eyes, but this zombie was different, she was holding a young boy, and they were friends, and she felt the trust and love and courage flow between them, and the zombie was saying, "We're going to make it, Jake, we're definitely going to make it!"

She saw a heavily pregnant – utterly beautiful – young woman in a swimming pool, up to her neck in water, surrounded by zombies, all standing at the edge of the pool, all staring at her, and she could feel the young woman's desperation and anger, she could hear the young woman say, "I'm not going to put up with this anymore! I have had absolutely enough!"

She saw a truck driver, trapped in the cabin of his truck, surrounded by zombies, staring in through the windows, hungry for him, and there he is, all alone, sweating it out, and he is thinking, "How the hell do I get out of this? I've got to make sure Mary Loo is okay! I can't sit here all night!"

She saw a bus full of zombies, just outside Lincoln Tunnel – Oh, no, oh, no, she thought – and the zombies, all Japanese, were climbing out of the bus, and, led by their tour guide, a Japanese lady from Osaka, they were entering the Tunnel which was blocked by a huge traffic jam. The zombies were going to get into Manhattan, and, with its highly concentrated population, all on an island, oh, boy! It will be a zombie explosion!

She saw a thin, good-looking, deeply tanned woman, her face dripping with water, staring into a mirror and saying to herself, "I am a real bitch. I killed that girl. I killed her."

She saw a girl, well a woman, it looked like a woman, naked crawling on all fours, then leaping up, eyes glowing phosphorescent green, she was a zombie, and she was screaming, "The Goddess has lost, all is lost, Oh, Charlie, Oh, Charlie, I love you, Charlie."

And V thought, so much depends on what every single person chooses to do, each instant of each and every day. She felt the courage, the love, the good humor, the intelligence, the skills, the talents, and the dogged determination of hundreds, of thousands, of millions of people, of hundreds of millions …

And she saw Claire …

Claire, my daughter, my sister, my love …

Yes, I love you, I love you all.

V's mind expanded. The little body she inhabited was still. It sat down, crossing its legs, yoga style, the giant swollen sex lolling between its thighs, and V had to laugh, "So this is me – this is what I have become. Well, now I know, and so …"

She felt an overwhelming joy.

All the mystics and all the sages and all the prophets …

So now I know! Her mind expanded still more, in all times and all directions. She was made of atoms from the stars. The air and the sea contained atoms of which she had been made and which had passed through her and rejoined the universe. Her consciousness made her part of everything, of all time and all space, from the beginning of time and before the beginning of time, the small infinitesimal point, from which all that was or would be exploded outward in a vast unending explosion and then expansion and the birth of stars and the creation of the elements, and the gathering of cosmic dust that created the earth, and the ignition of a nuclear reaction at the center of the gathering of the earth that welded all into one, the planet earth, our home, and the birth of continents and oceans, the salt water and the plants and animals, and the first gods, born obscurely in dark caves and open plains, in forests and deserts, the gods and spirits that gathered together to make one God, or Goddess, or many gods and goddesses, nymphs, satyrs, and dryads, elves, pixies, and dryads, mountains, fountains, rivers, lakes, and trees, animals and fish and birds, a cornucopia of sacredness, and the farthest stars and the smallest fragments were part of her …

Encompassing all, she possessed all.

Being without desire, she was fulfilled with bliss.

Being without fear or hope, she was outside time, timeless.

Being tiny, she was everything.

All barriers, all surfaces dissolved.

A blessing, she thought, this is a blessing.

She looked down at her gnarled oversized arthritic hands, palms upwards, twisted fingers curled, relaxed, welcoming the heavens.

Hold eternity in the palm of your hand …

To see a world in a grain of sand

And a heaven in a wild flower
Hold infinity in the palm of your hand
And eternity in an hour.

V sighed in pleasure.

I am what I am ...

V felt an immense force ...

A surge of explosive energy swept through her, sparks exploded from the pale stick-like fingers.

And all the walls came tumbling down.

When Humpty Dumpty fell ... not all the King's horses ...

A wave of joy swept through V.

The whole world trembled, the platform on which she sat, and the air itself.

A suave mechanical female voice said: "This protocol is going to be ..."

Sparks!

"This protocol is going to be ..."

"This protocol is going to be terminated; this protocol is going to be terminated; this program is going to be terminated; this program is going to be terminated ..."

"No, you cannot!" a voice screamed.

"No, I won't let you!" the voice screamed again.

And the little V dwarf, and the statuesque Dmitry demon were frozen, in time, and the statuesque reptilian V began to disintegrate, and fall apart, only slabs of V's iridescence remaining, and then slipping and sliding, dissolving into scintillating dust and falling down through a deep blue emptiness that seemed to lie below and beyond and within all things, where nothing is everything and everything is nothing, and then there was just darkness and V felt her gills breathing and she focused and she moved her limbs and she ...

"This protocol ..."

There were huge screams, wails of agony, screams of despair, worlds seemed to tremble, dust fell from far above; machinery exploded, stars imploded, galaxies turned to whirling dust, and darkness.

More screams. "No, no, no, you can't, you are not allowed, you can't, you cannot! You cannot, absolutely not, no, no, no ..."

"This protocol is being terminated; this protocol is being terminated; this protocol ..."

V moved her limbs. She focused her mind on the machine, on what it might be doing, and she sent from her mind a surge of energy into the circuits and programs, and she saw a universe of cart-wheeling galaxies, and the galaxies all became smaller, and then they disappeared and it was all an outward expanding glowing dust, and then there was a huge blinding flash, and then the flash shrank and shrank until it became at tiny glowing point, and then it disappeared, and then there were tendrils and faces and a sort of singing voice as if V were entering into a temple …

In the distance, from somewhere, there were screams, more screams.

Is that me? V wondered. Is that me, screaming?

"This protocol is being terminated; this protocol …"

No, no, it is not me.

Who is it, then, who is screaming?

The screaming continued, "No, no, no, no, she cannot do this; it is not allowed, no, no, no … She cannot repossess … It is the end of everything!"

"This protocol …"

And then she saw it, a white marble temple, just as the Greeks used to build, a white marble temple, in the simple classic Doric style, the simplest and the purest. The temple was on a table-top plateau, a mesa, a flat-topped outcropping like the Acropolis, and she stood gazing at it and then she walked towards it and she realized she was in human form, her old human form and she was wearing the sort of robes the Ancient Greeks used to wear, but shorter, a sort of simple tunic, tied at the waist, like the tunic Isis was wearing, except this one was pure dazzling white, and she walked, barefoot, up the marble steps, warmed by the sun, and she walked under the colonnade, which was very high, the spotless white Doric columns towering above her, and she entered the open temple door; and, within, the temple was bright, one vast bright pure white room, with lateral colonnades, all Doric columns, down both sides, and no altar, no platform, no seating, no icons, just light streaming in from above at the far end of the temple, and she walked forward and she saw …

… Isis standing at the center …

… and …

… Claire standing to one side, and then Marcus on the other side, and Marcus and Claire came towards her and Marcus opened his arms, and Marcus said, "All life is one, V, and all life shall dissolve."

And Claire was smiling and reached out her arms, "All life is one, V, all life is one! You are me, and I am you – and together we are nothing – and we are infinity!"

Isis smiled and blew her a kiss.

Thunder and lightning flashed outside the temple.

Infinity …

Infinity is now …

And Marcus and Claire and Isis and V stood there, smiling, facing each other, and then the temple and Marcus and Claire and Isis faded and faded …

And there was a sound of wind, and then of waves. V was sitting alone, on a ledge of black stone, above a rocky shore with the trees of a tropical jungle behind her, and below her, a sandy beach stretched off, pure white sand, and the sea, a vast ocean, in front of her, and a blue sky. Clouds were scudding low along the horizon, cumulus clouds, catching the sun, bright white high towering clouds, but the clouds were far away, tiny, and crushed by the pure blue above. The sea rolled in, and the spray, warm salty spray, touched V's face, and bathed her flimsy robe – still that skimpy tunic she had been wearing when she approached the temple. V stood up and carefully took off the tunic and folded it neatly on an sun-drenched outcropping of rock, and following a twisting gentle path, she went down a series of stone steps, down to the sand, to the beach, a small beach sheltered in a fold of the rocks, and feeling the hot fine pure white sand beneath her feet, V walked into the glittering deep dark sea …

"This protocol …"

"This protocol will be terminated; this protocol …"

She heard more screaming, "No, No, No, I will not permit it, not now, not now that I have gained it all, not now …"

And V thought: whatever I am, I am nothing, and, being nothing, I am open to everything, and being open to everything, I am neither here nor there, neither in this body nor in another, I am neither today nor tomorrow nor yesterday – I am, I am, I am … Thank you, whoever whatever you are, for the fact that I am, merely, that I am …

Thank you!

And V walked into the sea, over her head now, breathing easily, and dissolved into water, dissolved into the whole universe now, a drop of water, in an ocean stretching to the horizon …

The screaming now was huge, a bellow, a shriek, it echoed through the whole universe, it rebounded; it was an earthquake, a tsunami, a … shock wave …

WHAM!

"This protocol will be …"

WHAM!

V then felt she was in over her head, she was losing her footing, she was drowning, she thrashed in the water, she sputtered and blinked her eyes and realized she was suffocating and realized she was encased in a mask and hood. She felt for the buckles and clips and opened them. She pulled off the hood and mask and realized she was still underwater in the salty ocean, no, not in the salty ocean! *I'm not in the ocean at all!* She was in the saline solution. She was in the the Soul Exchange Machine and the Soul Exchange Machine was trembling, and bits and pieces were popping off, the machinery was breaking apart, and electric sparks were everywhere …

"This protocol will be terminated …"

V reached out and saw that her arm was her usual glittering reptile arm and she tore off the electrodes, ripping them from her belly and breasts and thighs and back. She levered herself up out of the saline bath. Dripping the gooey salty solution, she pushed herself out of the thick rubbery lips of the immersion basin, and stepped out of the Soul Exchange Machine. The vast machine was vibrating and trembling. V looked around. Inside her head, she heard a voice, "Help, Help, help me!"

"This protocol is terminated," the lights of the great machine went off; the trembling stopped; the sparks dissipated; smoke rose from overheated metal; dust drifted down; a few pebbles fell, from far above.

V heard the small voice, "Help, help, help me!"

She went to the other saline bath, parted the rubbery lips of the immersion basin.

The Dmitry Dwarf was convulsing, its arms and legs were flailing, thrashing.

V reached in and unhooked the hood and the collar and then opened it up, peeling it away, the head of the dwarf was now enormous, or so it seemed, like the head of a tiny but monstrous baby, and the mouth was contorted, and now toothless, in a wild convulsion of pain or fear or desire. The eyes stared up at V. V lifted the limp body out of the dripping warm saline solu-tion. She cradled the tiny body. "Now, now, don't be afraid, don't be afraid, hush, hush, hush, Little Dmitry, hush, hush!" The creature made a mewling sound, looking up now with its toothless baby mouth, the lips gaining color and definition, the body growing plump, and it reached out its spindly arms now filling in with baby fat, the dry aged skin becoming pink and glowing and damp and it shrank and shrank to the size of a small baby, just born, just pulled from the womb. Its chubby fingers closed on one of V's breasts and it brought its mouth, puckered, toothless, ready to suck, to her breast and closed on the nipple and began to suck, and V thought, "Gosh, I have milk," feeling it course through the nipple. "I have milk, the reptile has milk, lactation without even being a mother and with no stimulus whatsoever, wonders will never cease!" Inside V`s mind there was a small voice, a distant voice, crying out, "Help me, help me, help me!" And, while cradling and rocking the newly-born baby, V said, in her mind, to the small distant voice, "Welcome Dmitry, welcome," and the little voice cried out, "Where am I, where am I," and V whispered silently, "You are home now, Dmitry, you are home, go to sleep now, go to sleep."

"I am home now, really home?"

"Yes, Dmitry, you are home, you can relax now."

The tiny voice, become childlike and trusting, said, "Yes, I will sleep now, thank you, I will sleep now, all curled up and very small, invisible even, I am like a little worm. Will you sing me a lullaby?"

"Certainly, I will sing you a lullaby, Little One," and V began to hum a lullaby and then she sang the lullaby, without really thinking about it, she sang, a strange and sweet song in a language she really didn`t know or understand, and she sang a melody she remembered from her deepest past, the melody her nurse, Lalla, had sung in North Africa, twenty-five centuries in the past, the language Lalla spoke to her and sang to her, the language of Marcus, her father, the language that came from the stars, and, as the voice within her shrank and shrank and shrank and became nothing, V cradled the sucking baby, its round mouth gulping down her milk, and she looked into its round candid blue eyes that stared up at her with love, and, pausing for a moment in her singing, V said, *And, so, now, little one, who are you, then, who are you, who are you really?*

CHAPTER 43 – ON THE ROAD

It was damned hot for two o'clock in the morning. Billy Wayne Penn was sweating like an overweight suckling sow caught afterhours in an overheated Laundromat.

The cicadas were making a damned racket too, goddamn it, raspy music to the ears, but music just the same, music of the shimmering lazy hazy heat, if you are snuggled down with a fan blowing the sweat off your pores and an ice-cold beer in your fist and your honey, maybe stark naked and beaded in sweat, all worshipful, by your side. But out here, all alone, no, the cicadas were just a fucking annoying soundtrack and backdrop.

It was not the best time to be stuck on the side of the road in the middle of nowhere in Louisiana, trying to fix the goddamn motor of the tractor-trailer.

But, finally, after forty-five minutes fiddling with the sparkplugs and the carburetor, hands now greasy as hell, the engine had agreed to kick over. Everything, these days, seemed to be falling apart; but now, the old engine, and it was a very, very old engine, sprang into life. It was a godsend when you had something you could damned well repair for yourself instead of having to wait for a computer or robot to do it for you!

"Well, thank the Living God for that!" Billy Wayne Penn slammed down the hood, wiped his hands on the oil cloth, stood, for just a few seconds, looking around, feeling a chill of fear skitter up and down his back for some unknown fucking reason, and a funny eerie uncanny ripple moving along his nerves, like there was somebody watching him, or some ghostly memory or inkling inside him, whispering about dangers lurking close by, then he said, "Fuck it," and climbed into the cabin, slammed the door shut, put the rig in gear, glanced in the mirrors – nothing but asphalt, the white line under the moon, and encroaching forest dark as hell – and pulled out onto the road, damned empty road tonight, not a single sign of life, like only the ghosts from the bayous were about, and he turned on the radio, good old-fashioned radio.

Big Band dance music from back when America was great. What did they call those people who wandered their way through the Great Depression – rode the rails – and fought their way through the Second World War from Midway to Tokyo and from the beaches of Normandy to the bloody Kraut capital Berlin, all smoke and rubble, where the Russians were waiting for them? *The Greatest Generation*, that's what they called them. That was a fucking long time ago when your ordinary Joe could be a hero.

Tickertape dreams …

Big Band music, phew …

Too old-time for me!

Click!

Billy Wayne switched stations. Static went in and out, arcs of electricity, flash, flash, buzz, buzz, hiss, hiss. He could just picture them, those great blank white-yellow walls of sheet lightning flickering along the horizon, turning the barns and stands of trees and silos into pale ghosts, lighting up the magnolia trees, turning the sand on beaches into pure silver or gold. The whole atmosphere had gone haywire. The ozone layer, or whatever the fuck it was, was acting up again. Showers of ions or whatever and comets and evil portents of all kinds, or so the soothsayers said, had been seen, so the priests said, and the wacko scientists blogging away as fast as their fingers or vocal cords could spew out their various forms of nonsense. It was all the fucking sun's fault, the sun had spots, solar acne, it was sick, soon it was going to kill us all, one guy said, on that program – what was that program called – Oh, yeah, "Our Worst Fears." Northern lights been seen as far south as Houston, and in Panama City, all year round, flickering, lighting up the whole damned sky, what does this mean? "This, Mary Loo, is the punishment we get, the punishment we deserve, for ignoring the word of God. The fucking world is fucking falling fucking apart," that's what Billy Wayne told his girl, a cute tight bit of ass he'd picked up in the refugee camp outside the watery grave of what used to be New Orleans, she was a nurse, part time, and, well, she was a fine girl, looked like she wasn't wearing anything, somehow, under that white nurse's uniform, made a man hot and bothered and hungry all at once, and soft and tender and eager, it did, a girl like that, looking like that, and so they sat around in her trailer, her in her undies, him in his boxer shorts, shooting the shit, screwing, talking, emptying a bottle or two, and he told her about how God was pissed off, "His patience is running out, Mary Loo, His patience is running out!" She nodded, eyes glazed, thinking, or so Billy Wayne thought she was thinking, that her very own Billy Wayne was a hell of a smart guy.

He pushed more buttons ...

"Zombie sightings reported as far north as ..."

Click!

"The president is back. This afternoon Katherine du Bois Hughes landed by helicopter ..."

Click!

"Zombie reporter for the Volpe Network, Samantha Andrews, is reported to have ..."

Click!

"Fires are said to be burning in the center of ..."

Click!

"Trust in the Lord, with all your heart ..."

"Ah, fuck, this is more like it! Fire and goddamn brimstone!" Billy Wayne slapped his thigh, "that's what we want on a hot summer's night to get the blood boiling." It was the deep sugary voice of the Reverend Slick Roberto and his weekly homily "Trust in the Lord with all Thine Heart."

"Now, ladies and gentlemen, brothers and sisters, we know the end is nigh, we know that the time is ripe, we know the end of time is upon us, the end of days, that the evil spawn multiply, that the plague infects us all, each and every one.

"We know that this time our anger, our righteous anger, will bear fruit, we know that, right now, you, citizens of America, are threatened as never before, we are all threatened, every man, woman, and child, all threatened as never before.

"There are those who will take from us what is rightfully ours. There are those – and you know who they are – I don't have to name them – you know who I mean – there are those who will take way our livelihoods, who will violate our bodies, who will desecrate our beliefs, who will pollute our blood, who will destroy our communities, those for whom nothing is sacred, those for whom power has no limits, those who work in the shadows, those who have sown the wind and who now will reap the whirlwind, those who, through their arrogance and their godlessness, have brought us to the edge, to the precipice, to the very eve of the apocalypse, the apocalypse, the revelation, when Evil and Good, when Satan and God will confront each other, this is the final battle, this is Armageddon, when all will be unveiled, and all will be set right. Now, the cries for help, the lamentations, and the cries of distress rise from everywhere in the land.

"This is because, brothers and sisters, we humans have made a pact with Satan. We asked for the power of science, and Satan gave us the power of science, evil atheistic science! It is godless science that dissolves all the sacred bonds, that destroys and liquefies everything it touches, the family, the individual, and even the most holy concept of the human person, made in the image of God, aspiring to the Love of God, and never, even in his or her darkest moments, forsaken by God.

"We asked for freedom, and Satan gave us freedom.

"And, Oh, brothers and sisters – How we misused and abused this freedom!!

"We fornicated, we blasphemed, we sinned, oh, brothers and sisters, we strayed from the path of righteousness; we strayed from the Way of the Lord. The straight and narrow is something we shall never see again. We worshipped the idols of power, of science, the arrogance of the human mind – Oh, the arrogance of it, thinking, you puny creature, you, thinking you can conquer all, thinking you can master the secrets of the universe, the secrets which are God's alone. No, the secrets are sacred, and shall forever remain buried, hidden! Only in the final days, in the final reckoning, in Armageddon, the final battle will Good and Evil be fully revealed, will the truth be unveiled – in Holy and Infinite Revelation. Oh, brothers and sisters, we must return to the true faith, the faith of our fathers, the faith in a loving and righteous and vengeful God. We must abandon the path of wickedness. We must forsake the false idols of freedom, of individuality, of relativism, and of perverted science. Let us pray."

And the music began. It was something like "The Old Wooden Cross."

"Now that is what I call entertainment!" Billy Wayne Penn slowed down for a particularly difficult turn, and he was just coming out of the turn when something slammed against the windshield, and Billy Wayne instinctively ducked away, lifting up his arms to protect himself, letting the wheel go for just a second, but the great truck kept going, steady, and Billy Wayne, thinking quick, put his hands, both of them, solidly, on the wheel again, and tried to steady himself, because, to tell the truth, the situation was unsettling: lying on the hood, and half-plastered against the windshield, making it difficult, in fact making it impossible, to see what was ahead, was a body, or part of a body, and its face was squashed up against the glass, facing Billy Wayne, and its goddamn eyes were glowing, green phosphorous. It was a zombie, a goddamn zombie!

And there were more of them, slamming against the cabin of the truck. The trouble was, Billy Wayne could not see a goddamn thing and that made it dangerous, maybe fatal, to accelerate, to try to make a run for it.

And what were the zombies doing here? They were supposed to be down in Florida. He pushed a button – changing stations – and at the same time he slowed down, there were lots of curves, lots of ditches, so he slowed down, but if he slowed down too much then the goddamn zombies could grab on, and what then …?

"… the senator stated that the zombie invasion was apparently out of control and asked what the government intended to do about it … A spokesperson for the Pentagon said that electromagnetic disturbances had interrupted defensive …"

WHAM!

A zombie slammed into the side of the cabin, right beside Billy Wayne. It held on. It was hammering on the window; it was trying to open the goddamned door!

WHAM!

"Oh, Jesus," Billy Wayne glanced in the side mirror and what he saw made him feel sick: zombies were clinging to the sides of the trailer and to the cabin, must be dozens of them. They were using his goddamn truck like a bus. Where the hell did they come from?

"… reports from New Jersey say that at the entrance to the Lincoln Tunnel …"

The motor suddenly failed.

"Oh, Jesus," Billy Wayne pushed the emergency button that would put him in direct contact with the highway patrol and emergency services.

"… the threat to Manhattan is for the moment …"

The emergency line answered: "All our lines are busy right now, please call back later."

"Fuck that!" Billy Wayne could feel sweat breaking out on his brow and bubbling up and dribbling down his back.

"All our lines are busy right now, please call back later."

The radio sputtered and went dead.

The tractor-trailer glided to a stop as Billy Wayne steered it carefully, at least as much as he could see to do so, to the side of the road.

Then it was silent.

The zombies were glaring at him – the dead one, apparently dead, was still lying on the hood. No, it was not fucking dead at all. It was clawing, with the stump of one arm, at the windshield, leaving a smear of blood. The others now gathered closer.

Billy Wayne let out a whistle. "What the hell do I do now?"

CHAPTER 44 – ASHLEY FIGHTS BACK

"This is intolerable. This is absolutely unacceptable," Ashley Samos, up to her neck in the swimming pool, was furious; enough was enough! The whole day had been just one thing after another!

The squiggling serpent of goo spittle – a regular snake, it was – sent skittering toward her courtesy of the Reverend Hubert Fish Zombie – who had spat it with great vigor into the pool – and that had tried to attack her was bad enough.

She had grabbed it, held onto it, though it was slippery and disgusting and wiggly and had kept trying to slip down headfirst into her dress or flip its head back up and get at her mouth, she had managed to hold the twisting slippery little monster away from her and she had thrown it out of the pool, and over the fence, into the neighbors' backyard, for which she felt a tiny bit guilty, but she was sure the neighbors were not home, and maybe on the stones of the patio the thing would curl up and die.

Uncharitable thought!

Be kind to all living things!

But was that little bastard alive or only pretending?

Ashley was still trapped in her backyard pool. She was still thinking that she was going to die or to be transformed into a zombie. She was still worried about Kevin for whose sanity and life she feared. The zombies were still standing around the pool, staring at her, and the afternoon had drawn to a close. Night had come. The pool and patio lights had gone on. Ashley did not particularly relish staying all night immersed up to her neck in the water; above all she was worried about the effect this might have on the baby. The water was still warm, and it was buoyant, supporting her big ripe belly very nicely, like she was all wrapped in warm amniotic fluid, but …

Enough was enough!

To be trapped in your own backyard pool!

It was outrageous!

And she was eager to get to work on her lecture on Kandinsky – being forced to do nothing while trapped in the pool had, weirdly enough, stirred up her creative juices. She had some new, exciting ideas, and, damn it, she wanted to write them down, zombies or no damned zombies!

Then, at about 8:00 p.m. to judge by Ashley's waterproof wristwatch, the Reverend Hubert Fish began to change. His features went blurry, tentacles erupted out of his arms and ears and chest.

Ashley rubbed her eyes in disbelief.

The Reverend's face went furry, or was it feathery, all sorts of spindly excrescences in any case, and he began to melt, and dissolve, and he became, within, well, within about three and a half minutes, a sort of plant …

It was like watching Georges Braque or Salvador Dali at work – the Reverend Hubert Fish fell apart into a series of zigzags, rather cubist, then he melted, becoming fluid, entering the surrealist movement, then he reformed, he gelled, and – dribbling – he approximated a Jackson Pollock, or, regarding some of the more spindly appendages, perhaps, the little twig-like networks, or branchings could make one think of a Cy Twombly or …

And he became a plant – a vegetable creature, a fruit and veg mashup; something Giuseppe Arcimboldo might have dreamed up – but not really, because this was a plant such as the earth, Ashley was fairly sure, had never seen before. This was no ordinary stalk of tomatoes.

The Reverend, normally the meekest of men Ashley thought, turned out to be a hungry, voracious, aggressive, flesh-eating plant, apparently, because one of his flowers, and he had these bright crimson cabbage-sized flowers, suddenly opened its petals, which were quite thick, and chomped on Mrs. Henry Elliot's arm, cutting it off just above the elbow.

The old lady looked down at the stump, which gushed red blood and spurted a stream of green fluid, and then looked up, and yowled like she was baying at the moon, though there was, as yet, as far as Ashley could see, no moon in the sky.

The Reverend Hubert Fish Cannibal Plant now put tentacles, with mouths, well, they looked like mouths, gaping mouths, toothy gaping mouths rather like the mouths of a poisonous serpent, it now put three of these tentacles into the water, and they headed towards Ashley; and it was at this moment that Ashley heard her friend, Michelle Bruni, shout:

"Ashley, are you there? Are you okay Ashley?

And then:

"Help, Ashley, Help!"

And Ashley decided finally, gentle and accommodating as she usually was, and patient and diplomatic to a fault, that she had had enough; that she was going on the warpath.

If anything bad happened to Michelle she would never forgive herself.

She swam quickly to the shallow end of the pool, the tendrils of the Reverend swimming quickly behind her, one of them grasping at the remains of her pajama top, but she kicked it away, and she climbed dripping out of the pool, and she pushed two zombies, who stumbled towards her, into the pool, where they screamed – they didn't like water it seemed – and where the Reverend Poisoned Plant's tentacles attacked them, but of all this Ashley was only dimly aware, because ...

She didn't have time to stand around gawking ...

She made a dash for the tool shed, with three zombies stumbling behind her; she kicked one of them away; she smashed open the door to the tool shed, and she rushed inside, slamming the door behind her, hoping it would hold. Turning on the light, she grabbed the gas-powered chainsaw, which she generally considered a really evil and dangerous instrument liable to inflict injury and death on whoever touched it.

She flicked the switch.

And, yes, there is a God! The chainsaw roared into action at the first touch.

Ashley held the power saw out in front of her and she kicked open the shed door and she came out swinging the saw in front of her and she cut off three heads and two legs and a couple of arms within one minute flat, and pushed two more zombies into the pool and then went to the back gate in time to see her friend, Michelle Bruni, her back against the wall, fighting off two zombies, and Ashley, the gas-powered chainsaw making a great racket, headed straight for the zombies, intending to lop off their arms, heads, legs, torsos, or whatever it took to save Michelle, when, suddenly, just as she was about to cut into them with a roar of the spinning rotating chain blade, the two zombies fell to the ground and lay there inert, totally still, as if unconscious.

"Whew," she said, looking down at them. "Are you okay, Michelle?"

"Yes, I'm okay, but nobody else is. Everybody is crazy or dead," said Michelle, blue eyes blinking, running one hand through her blond hair. "I guess I'm immune."

"Yes, I guess I am too," said Ashley. "Let's get back into the house, come with me, maybe we can defend the house. There's another chainsaw in the shed – Kevin collects these things – and anyway, I'm hungry, I think there is some lasagna in the fridge we can heat up, and let's just hope we survive the night."

"We will, Ashley, I'm sure we will."

They left the two zombies lying in the alleyway and went back into Ashley's backyard, with Ashley leading, and the chain saw still roaring. All the zombies, except the Mrs. Henry Elliot Zombie, were standing utterly still, inert, like statues, and the Reverend Hubert Fish Cannibal Plant looked dead – its tendrils and tentacles all withered and brown, like empty husks.

"What in the world has happened to them?" Ashley looked at Michelle.

"They look dead."

"Or asleep," Ashley noticed the zombies were breathing; chests were rising and falling. The Mrs. Henry Elliot zombie was moving the stump of her missing arm back and forth and she was cradling it with her other hand.

"Let's eat. I'm starving."

"Right let's eat," said Ashley. But she couldn't resist, she went up to the old lady, who was now holding the stump of her right arm which had been chomped off by the Reverend Hubert Fish but which now seemed to have stopped bleeding and she put her face right in front of the old lady's face, the empty shell that had once been Mrs. Henry Elliot. "Are you okay, Mrs. Eliot?"

The old lady's face remained slack, without any expression. The glow in the green eyes was less lively now, and something of the old eyes, her old pre-zombie eyes, gray and hazel, seemed to be re-emerging. The old lady said, in a distant mechanical voice, "The voice has stopped, the voice has stopped, the voice has stopped ..."

The remaining zombies stood like statues.

"It's like somebody pushed the off button," said Ashley.

"Well, whoever did it, I hope they did it everywhere and for all of them!"

"Let's get inside. This might not last."

CHAPTER 45 – I AM THE VOICE

Billy Wayne Penn was about to open the cabin door, leap down, and make a run for it – he didn't know where he'd run because the goddamned zombies seemed to be everywhere and he was stalled – the motor dead and for no reason he could figure out – and he and his 60-foot tractor trailer were trapped in the midst of goddamn nowhere on a long stretch of narrow isolated rough asphalt road in bayou country – serves you right, Billy Wayne, for taking a short cut – with only swamps and alligators and python-infested canals on either side, and it was dark out there, still night or deep in the night, Billy's watch had ceased to tell time; he was getting goddamn antsy sitting inside, like a monkey in a glass cage, with all those zombies staring at him with their green eyes, and he thought he had to get to Mary Loo and make sure she was okay; he'd tried to raise her on his U-Tab but no go; he'd tried the cabin's computer Internet connection, but no go there either; he'd tried checking with GPS coordinates, just for the fun of it, and there was nothing doing there either, just a blank, coordinates were, 00:00;00. It was like the satellites and computers and Internet and everything had been fried dead by some extra-terrestrial catastrophe, or by one of those weird electro-magnetic storms they'd been talking about on "Our Worst Fears," maybe this was the aliens and the hybrids, maybe they were behind the zombies, he'd just like to get his hands on one of those fucking aliens or hybrids! He tried the old-fashioned radio, for which he had great affection, and twiddling the dial all he got for his pains was static and a dead whistling sound. And, so, here he sat, as red-blooded an American as could be, trapped by a bunch of folk who'd gone and turned themselves into zombies. One of them, the remains of the woman, was still lying on the hood, her face squashed up against the windshield, phosphorous eyes glowing like two devilish jelly fish, and her tongue, which she occasionally wagged when she winked at him, seeming about a foot long, and she flipped occasionally and shifted her position like she was a fish out of water and not so comfortable. Then there were the three or four zombies hanging onto the doors and just staring at him. One looked scholarly and erudite like a cartoon professor with round glasses and green eyes that were somehow like the eyes of an owl and wearing the remains of a bowtie – a fucking bowtie! Another was a big heavy good ol' boy, with the remains of a shock of blond hair combed forward over his forehead and a big square jaw and teeth which were set in a big good ol' boy grin, like the sort of grin that bedded the girls down on Bourbon Street in New Orleans in the good old days and got you what you wanted without you ever having to pay for it and the good ol' boy just stared at Billy Wayne with those green lantern eyes like he wanted to eat Billy Wayne up, down to the last mouthful and spit him out though those beautiful well-tended, well-cared for, very expensive teeth. Then there were all the zombies who had latched onto the trailer and were hanging there like flies on sticky paper, silent, waiting, not even buzzing. If he did jump out and run for it, he would have a whole herd of hungry zombies on his tail, which was not such a delightful image when he conjured it up, him hightailing it, and the zombies racing after. No, that was not a pleasant prospect at all. He pulled a power bar out of the lunch pail, unpeeled the wrapping, took a bite and thought, well, better make a stand, a stand for human rights, for American Freedom, and not die like a rat cowering in a cage.

He pulled the shotgun, a double-barreled, pump-action, multiple-load baby, out from its rack just beside his couch, which was up behind the driver and passenger seats, and he checked that it was fully loaded, all greased up, smooth and easy as an eager whore down on center and main, and all ready to go.

Billy Wayne muttered to himself, "Okay, now, boys, the Marines are coming, the United States of America Marines are goddamn coming, the Star Spangled Banner is unfurled, and you'd better get the fuck out of the way," and thinking of Mary Loo, well, not thinking, really, not thinking, but seeing Mary Loo in that cute nurse's uniform, or in the fishnet elastic teddy she liked so much or, even better, barefoot, naked, washing the dishes while he dried, glancing sideways at him with love or lust in her eyes – "Ah, easy to confound the two, love and lust, ain't it Billy Wayne, and who cares if you do confound the two, eh, Billy Wayne, I mean, lust and love, two of a kind, right …?"

Billy Wayne clicked the lock off, pushed open the cabin door, pushed himself out, the shotgun in front of him, his fingers eager to do their work, and the two zombies, clinging to the door, fell off the door, fell down, wham, on their backsides on the asphalt and they slowly got up, and then they came rushing at him, but Billy Wayne was already hightailing it down the road, and, glancing back, he noticed, behind him, in the moonlight, the torso on the hood of the goddamned truck, had slid off and was wiggling on the pavement trying to chase after him, and, wondering at the spirit of it, Billy Wayne looked ahead, and then glanced back again, the zombies running behind him now, and he kept running, thinking, at some point I'll just swing around and let them have it and that'll delay them a bit.

He had filled his vest as he always did with refills so he could reload and then start all over again, and then, goddamn it, looking ahead of him he saw more zombies, making a line across the road and coming towards him, and he thought, where the hell did these fellows come from, Oh, Billy Wayne Penn, you are going to be in the fight of your life shortly, and you'd better give a good account of yourself, be a hero for once, fight the good fight, eh, for us, the underdogs, the true folk, the real people, let's hear it for Billy Wayne Penn, he knew when the chips were down and he stood his last stand like General George Armstrong Custer at Little Bighorn, still wearing his hat, the flag still flying, or me, fighting to the last on the walls of the fort, at the Alamo, we stake out our destiny, we do …

And now the zombies were close on both sides, two lines of zombies approaching, blocking the road in front and the road behind, no way to advance, no way to retreat, and Billy Wayne was just considering zipping sideways into the swamp – and into God only knew what goddamn perils – when suddenly the zombies stopped advancing.

They stopped.

They just stood there.

They all just stood there, their mouths open; they drooled spools of that goo they seemed to drool; and they were staring at him, or at something beyond him.

They just stood there, silent, not moving.

Billy Wayne thought, Maybe they just want to draw out the suspense; maybe they just want me to suffer a little extra bit before they tear me apart; or maybe they are afraid of the shotgun, maybe they are afraid of being blown to little shredded bits of zombie flesh. But, no, that didn't seem reasonable: the zombies – in Billy Wayne's limited experience of zombies, but, hey, you have to generalize don't you, otherwise you can't say or think a single fucking thing – in his limited experience, the zombies did not seem to think things through, they just *did*; they didn't sit around musing on what to do. The zombies, generally, feared nothing; they just charged, they went straight into action, those zombies.

"Hey, zombies, hey!"

No answer.

"Hey, you guys, you there – what the hell do you want?"

They just stood there; they didn't even seem to hear him. Their mouths were open, their green eyes were blank, their arms hung limply at their sides. Most of them didn't have much in the way of clothes on and it would be funny and in some cases pretty erotic except that they all looked so disgusting, cadaver-white and green, and filthy, smeared with blood and guts and zombie goo and most of them missing most of their hair.

"Okay, zombies, I am coming through," Billy Wayne said, but without moving, "I am coming through."

They didn't move; they didn't flinch.

Billy Wayne walked slowly up to the line of zombies; he held the shotgun ready. Now, there he was, face-to-face with one of the zombies. I am a goddamned fool, he was thinking, I am a goddamned fool, and he said, "Okay, zombie what's bugging you, eh? Fess up, you can talk to old Billy Wayne!"

Tears, green tears, were streaming down the zombie's cheeks.

"Voice," it said, "Voice is gone."

"Voice," said Billy Wayne, "Voice is gone, huh?"

"Voice is gone," and more tears flowed and the others muttered, and wailed, "Voice is gone! Voice is gone! Voice is gone!"

"Well, then, zombies," said Billy Wayne, "I am the voice. I am the VOICE! So I am the voice and I'm telling you to get off the road, to go stand over there, on the side of the road! This is the VOICE speaking!"

There was a moment's silence.

Nobody moved; nothing moved.

Then …

They did it!

They nodded and shuffled and moved off the road, so both lines were off the road now, standing on the side of the road, facing towards the road, like a silent crowd waiting to see the king or the Pope or the president or a funeral procession.

They did it!

"Well God's Little Acre!"

They did it!

Billy Wayne felt like he had invented a new religion and he was the Savior and the Prophet and maybe the Holy Ghost even God Himself Almighty. Now, I'm mustn't let this go to my head, he thought, and he remembered, in all the stories he'd seen and all the tales he'd been told, that it was just when the hero – or villain – was really sure of himself, or herself, just when you think you've gotten out of the shit, it is precisely at that moment that the shit really hits the fan and pride is punished and hubris turns in the blink of an eye into nemesis and the hero or heroine is dead, a goner, or loses the girl of his dreams, or the kingdom and the gold, and becomes a blind homeless hopeless beggar wandering the earth forever – or was it wandering the water forever – like the Flying Dutchman or buried in some unmarked grave and turned to ashes and to dust …

Keeping the shotgun cradled in his arm Billy Wayne walked slowly back toward the truck. The zombies didn't move. Billy Wayne felt like he was passing the troops in review – "Present Arms!"

The torso woman had crawled off to the ditch. She lying there like a grounded limbless seal, pawing at the dust with her stumps, watching him with green eyes, but now those eyes didn't seem baleful or threatening; no, they seemed to worship him, to worship Billy Wayne Penn! Poor old hag, Billy Wayne thought, poor old hag, maybe she wasn't even a hag a few hours ago. Maybe she was a beauty.

And again he thought of Mary Loo – and his stomach knotted up: was she alive, was she alright, was she human – was she a zombie?

Billy Wayne popped open the hood.

He looked inside, while keeping a sharp eye all around him, the shotgun ready to pump lead faster than you could say Jack Robinson.

He spotted the problem – a loose wire, easy to fix. Yeah, but – hmm – how had that happened, he wondered. And, watching carefully, Billy Wayne fixed the connection. Then he slammed the hood down, thinking, I hope that was the only problem, and he climbed in the cabin, checking first to see that there were no friendly dwarf zombies hiding in the cabin – but no, there weren't – and he inserted the key, and turned it, and the motor roared into life, and Billy Wayne put her in gear, and slowly he accelerated, and he looked in the mirrors and there were no zombies clinging to the trailer, not that he could see.

He drove past the line of zombies, now lit up in the headlights.

There they were, standing in a line, staring out at the road; and, picking up speed the tractor trailer roared past the zombies and left them behind, standing like living statues in the bayou on the side of the road.

"The Voice is gone," muttered Billy Wayne Penn; he clicked on the U-Tab and he tried for Mary Loo.

CHAPTER 46 – SAMANTHA AROUSED

"Grrrh, I'm so sorry, Charlie, grrrh, slobber, drool, grrhhhh, I'm sorry, I'm sorry, I'm sorry, Charlie, I'm really sorry!"

Samantha Andrews had flipped herself off the bed, had freed herself from all her duct-tape bonds and had strode with great deliberation towards Charlie, and then she had jumped him, really jumped him, forcing Charlie to flick the camera and microphone off and to throw the camera towards the bed, where, happily, it landed and bounced without falling off, so Charlie thought, in the brief moment in which he was able to think anything, that the camera would probably survive.

"Grrrh. Grrrhhhhhh. Oh, oh, oh, so sorry, Charlie ... Grrhhhh ..." Samantha was dribbling green goo down onto Charlie and she was sprawled, stark naked on top of him, her legs pinning his legs down, and she was caressing with the palm of her hand the side of his face and she was kissing him, drooling kisses, spongy kisses, but kisses they were, on his forehead and on his cheeks and on his lips.

"Now, Sam," Charlie was saying, trying to wipe the goo out of his eyes, "Now, Sam, there's nothing to be sorry about, you're not doing anything wrong."

"Grrhhhh, love, Charlie, grrrh, slobber, grrrh, goo, love, Charlie ... I love ... Charlie I'm sorry, sorry, sorry, grrrh, but I love, Charlie ... I love ... you, Charlie ..."

"Now, now, Sam, I'm old enough to be –"

"Grrhhhh, shhhh, shhhh, shhhh, Charlie," Samantha put her finger to her lips and she put her hand over Charlie's mouth – he had a moustache of drying green goo left by her kisses and she said, "Grrhhhh, not another ... grrhhhh, not another word, Charles Edward Parr, grrrh ..."

"Sam!"

"Charlie!" Sam sat upright, astride Charlie's midriff, popping open his buttons, ripping off his shirt, and unbuckling his buckle and opening his belt and then she stood up, and pulled his belt up with her, slipping it out of the loops. She snapped it like it was a whip and then she knelt next to him and concentrated on unbuttoning the buttons of his jeans, and she pulled at his jeans, and Charlie said,

"You are bloody strong, Sam!"

"Grrrh, super zombie, grrrh, Charlie, grrrh, super zombie, did you think … just think, Charlie … I worked out on the grrrh Nautilus Exercise machine and did forty push-ups grrhhhh and ate those grrhhhh awful … grrrh … protein shakes … without … getting grrrh, these zombie results, Charlie … Stand up, Charlie …"

Charlie stood up, holding tight to his jeans, and he said, "Now, maybe Sam, just maybe, we should think …"

Sam stood up and put her hand on his hand. "Grrrh … zombies don't think, grrrh, Charlie, zombies act, zombies do, zombies accomplish, here, Charlie let go!"

Charlie sighed. He let go of his jeans.

Sam pulled his jeans down until they were around his ankles, and she said, "Socks, Charlie, underwear Charlie." She was on her knees in front of him.

And Charlie said, "Now, maybe, Sam …"

She was pulling down his underpants. "Grrhhhh, yes, Charlie, grrrh … I know, I know … grrrh, you are going to say, grrhhhh that we need a shower … grrhhhh, yes, Charlie … yes, yes, yes, a shower, together, Charlie, together …"

"Well, Sam, now that you … mention … it …"

The shower was large enough, just right, for both of them.

Sam was by this time completely hairless and smooth, a disconcerting but strangely exciting sight; Charlie wondered, not for the first time, if he were extraordinarily uniquely perverse, or just normally run-of-the-mill perverse, perverse like virtually every other male of the species, "Now, now," Charlie said, speaking as much to himself as to her, "Now, now, now …"

"Grrhh … Charlie … grrrh," Sam was reaching up and shampooing his head – she was about five inches shorter than Charlie. "You – gggghhhhhh – have enough hair for both of us, Charlie, and, Charlie," she said, tilting her face up to his, her eyes, now human but still glowing green, "Charlie, the Goddess, Charlie … the Goddess is back …" Cool green delicious gruel ran from her lips.

"The Goddess is back," Charlie said.

"Yes, gggghhhhhh, the Goddess is back," Sam said, and she wiped her lips free of goo with the back of her hand and she put her lips to Charlie's lips and she kissed Charlie and it was a long deep intense kiss, a zombie to human kiss, and Charlie didn't mind at all, though he was thinking that Sam at the present moment, although utterly charming, was totally insane; and that he had to keep this thing under control otherwise Sam would wake up fully human tomorrow morning and totally regret what she had done with Charlie in her drunken euphoric zombie state; and that right now, while absolutely insane and libidinous in a wonderfully free-ranging zombie way, she was just feeling grateful to Charlie because he had stuck with her, saved her life, just maybe, even though he wouldn't put it that way, and because, like old war veterans and comrades, they had gone through lots of incredible stuff together, battles and madness, and this can cement friendship like nothing else, and arouse libidinous cravings, like when soldiers are just going to war or in the London Blitz more than a century ago, so Charlie was telling himself, be careful Charlie, be careful …

Be careful, Charlie, be careful …

As the water poured down, Sam pressed her slick, slippery, stark-white, utterly naked body against his body and nibbled at his ear – using her four incisors most artfully – and ran her fingers through his hair and put one hand around behind him to press, hard, on the small of his back, and as she whispered, "Grrrh, grrrh, grrrh, Charlie, Oh, grrrh, grrrh, grrrh, Charlie," her breath now perfumed by cool mint toothpaste and heavenly azure mouthwash, and …

And the hot water splashing over them, and …

And she had, in spite of his best intentions, a fairly strong effect on Charlie, who was feeling his animal self, aroused and taking over, and Charlie, though wrinkled and grizzled was a lean, muscular, tough, finely-tuned male animal of the human species, and he said …

"Now, now, now, Sam, we must be cautious, we must be careful," and he let his lips rest, once again on hers and they kissed, and she said, nuzzling against his stubble, nibbling on his lips …

"Cautious? Charlie? Why, Charlie? We have gazed, together, you and I, into the heart of darkness, Charlie, we have voyaged together, hand in hand, through the Valley of Death, Charlie, so what limits should we now put on our foolishness, Charlie, you and I, finally freed of all bounds, and we must seize the fleeting instant, carpe diem, seize the day, make whoopee, gather ye rosebuds – "

She suddenly stopped and blinked and gave him a quick kiss on the lips.

"Yes?" Charlie said, looking into her eyes, now suddenly clear, now blue, and realizing that she had stopped growling.

"There is something we must do, Charlie."

"Right, Sam, something we must do ..."

"We must tell the world."

"Of course, we must tell the world ..." Charlie had been through some cold shower treatments in his life, but this quick change of gears was a very cold shower indeed, and he was both relieved and, ah, disconcerted; hot soapy water continued to cascade over them, and Sam was still holding Charlie tight, her fingers exploring the small of his back and in particular fiddling with one small rigid lip-like shrapnel wound – souvenir of a roadside Improvised Explosive Device – which she stroked – fingertips going back and forth, back and forth.

"Let's go," she said.

"Whatever you say, Sam," Charlie said looking down at her with a wry grin.

She caught the grin, gave him a quick wet peck. No goo this time, Charlie noticed, no slime, no gruel – and she flashed her own grin back at him, looking suddenly about five years old, and she said, "Quick, Charlie, quick!"

They tumbled out of the shower, Charlie turned the shower off, and Sam said, "Just wrap a towel around your waist, Charlie, this won't take a moment!" And, while Charlie wrapped a towel around his midriff and got the camera set up, Sam toweled herself down, and got rid of the last bits of sticky stuff from the duct tape that had been clinging to her legs and tummy and she glanced at herself in the mirror. "Wow, I look like an extraterrestrial! Charlie, how in the world do you like me? You do like me, Charlie, don't you?"

Charlie cleared his throat. "I ... ah ... adore you." He'd never stated desire and admiration and love so blatantly in his whole long carefully guarded life; he was thrilled, appalled, subjugated, and he thought: I must protect her from me; I must protect myself from her; I must protect both of us from, ah, from both of us.

The expression 'folie à deux' zipped through Charlie's mind: yes, contagious madness, couple crazy, crazy couple, 'l'amour fou,' or crazy love, or whatever ... And, of course, there's no fool like an old fool.

It was delicious but dangerous.

Sam had wrapped one light bit of sari-like turquoise semi-transparent cotton she had found draped over a lounge chair around her still-damp body, making a curve-revealing alluringly semi-see-through sari, and she had wrapped a small towel around her head, making a turban, and she had applied some makeup she found, to her face, creating eyebrows where there were no eyebrows, and lots of eye shadow and a good dose of crimson lipstick.

"Wow," said Charlie.

"Let's roll, Charlie," Sam said, sitting down in a straight-backed chair.

"Okay!" Charlie fiddled with a few dials, tapped on his keyboard, and miracle-of-miracles, got straight through to Shelly Nixon in the Volpe Octopus Tower. "Okay, Shelly, Sam's ready with her latest update," Charlie said.

"Oh, thank God – how is she!"

Charlie said, "Well, Shelly, she is, ah, amazing."

"Great, okay, let's roll," said Shelly, "Oh, tell her …"

"Yes?"

"Tell her I love her and I beg both of you to forgive me."

"It's already done, Shelly. The kid worships you, you know."

"You are an angel, Charlie! Even your lies become you."

"All the girls say that."

"Okay, let's roll."

Sam and Charlie again broke records and the ratings soared. Sam sat very erect in the straight-backed chair, looking like a goddess or a queen of Egypt or like the empress of some ancient hieratic empire, and she announced to the world that the Puppet Master had been defeated; that the zombies were going to come screeching to a halt because they no longer had the voice telling them what to do; that the voice had died, but would be reborn in innocence and that the Goddess – our mysterious savior had won. "Our mysterious savior, the Goddess, has delivered us from this evil – she has consumed the evil and taken it upon herself. As all divine mother goddesses do! She had eaten and consumed the evil, transforming it into innocence and good!"

"How do you know this, Sam?" said Shelly in Sam's ear.

"I know this, Shelly, because, and I know it will seem strange, I know this because in my mind I was with the Puppet Master when he died, when he lost control of the voice, when he was defeated by the Goddess, and so I lived, and again I know this sounds really strange, I lived his defeat and his death with him. I was part of him and he was part of me. At first it seemed like he had won, but then, suddenly, the tide turned, the Goddess took a deep breath, she surrendered her will, she surrendered her ego, she became, well, something like the Buddha I guess, or Jesus, or a stoic philosopher or mystic, something like Marcus Aurelius or Confucius, or William Blake, or Walt Wittman, or John Keats, perhaps. She accepted everything. She opened herself to everything – I know this sounds mystical and I guess it is – she opened herself to the whole wide universe and to every living thing and even to the stones, and, thinking perhaps of Jesus, she became forgiving, infinitely forgiving, and so, in that instant, she broke out of her chains, she transcended herself, and she was reborn, and she defeated him, and she vacuumed the Puppet Master up like he was dust on a staircase. But she has given him rebirth, rebirth in child-like innocence. Don't ask me to explain this. I lived it. But I don't understand it. The Goddess is great, that's all I know. And when I use the word 'Goddess,' it is a metaphor; she would insist on that, she would say she is not a goddess, but a moral, an immortal mortal."

"What happens now with the zombies?"

"The zombies will remain in position. They need to be cured, Shelly. Some, the least infected, will cure themselves – I think I am one of those. Others, they will need help, they will need an antidote, and, I don't know how I know this, but I know help is coming."

"This Goddess, who or what is she?"

"I have seen the Goddess – again in my mind. She is, I think, half-human, half-alien, she is turquoise and gold and glitters. She is very beautiful, part reptile, or that's what it looks like. She is a predator, but she is – how shall I put this? – She is a good predator."

"It sounds like she is a hybrid."

"Yes, I think she is a hybrid."

"So we humans have been saved by a half-alien, by the aliens."

"So, yes, Shelly, we humans have been saved by a half-alien, by a hybrid. But, I see too a great darkness, a sort of Dark God, but whether he is a god or not, I can't really tell, but he is alien too ... I think we are – we have become – pawns, in a great battle ... between Light and Dark, Good and Evil ..."

"Maybe it has always been so."

"Yes, Shelly, you are right. Maybe it has always been so. Now," Sam said, staring straight at the camera, "The important thing is to cure the zombies. They want to be released. I know, as you saw, I was one, I have been one, I know what it is like. The zombies too want their freedom! And I think their freedom is coming – soon!"

Sam unwrapped her sari, unspooled her turban, walked naked into the kitchen, opened the refrigerator, and saw that, in the cooler section there was a bottle of chilled rosé, and she said, "Charlie, let's go out onto the terrace."

Charlie, with the towel wrapped around his waist, watched her carefully. "Yes, Sam, whatever you want, Sam."

On the terrace the evening was soft and balmy and the air close and caressing. Sam took a mattress from one of the deck chairs and laid it on the terrace next to the pool, and she somehow found a box of matches and she lit the candles which were ready, in holders, around the terrace, and she poured glasses for both of them and they drank and Charlie said, "Sam …"

Sam put her finger to his lips and said, "Shhhh, Charlie, shhh!" She knelt in front of him, and she gently pulled the towel away from him, and indicating the mattress, she said, "Charlie, lie down next to me, Charlie, and, no, Charlie, don't worry, I'm an adult, I've been around, I will not regret anything, I promise you that, Charlie, I will not regret, not a thing, not a moment, Charlie, just come to me, gently, Charlie, come to me, gently, gently, Charlie, gently …"

CHAPTER 47 – TURN OF THE TIDE

In the Volpe Octopus Building in New York, Bill Brothers wiped at the sheen of sweat that glittered on his forehead, turned from the camera to his guest and said, "Well, General, we've heard from Samantha, who seems to have survived her ordeal. She tells us that the Goddess has won. What do you make of such a strange statement, General?"

"Well, Bill, Samantha has been in the front line and she has been, as it were, inside the beast, in direct communication, spying, as it were, on the enemy, so I think she has a direct line to what is happening. So, somewhere, somehow, there was, it seems, a great battle going on, off stage as it were, invisible to the rest of us, and that battle, for the moment at least, has been won."

"It was a close thing, I believe, General."

"Yes, Bill, at one point, and you'll remember, Samantha was in despair, it seemed the battle was lost, the Goddess had been beaten. But, then, there was a turn of the tide, and victory, for the moment, is ours. You know, Bill, the forces of both good and evil can be fooled by hubris – they think they've won – and that is the moment in which, letting arrogance take over, letting their guard down, they lose, and sometimes they lose forever, irrevocably. We don't know if that is the case now, so we must not let our guard down, but for the moment things are looking good."

"What are the implications, General, of the victory of the Goddess?"

"Well, Bill –"

"Ah, just a second, General, we've got reports coming in …"

"Yes …"

"Reports saying that, yes, that the zombies seem to be … stopping their offensive action, stopping, and standing still. What do you think of that, General?"

"Well, Bill, up until now, the zombies have been on a rampage, and they seemed to know what they were doing – they had orders, apparently, and they were clearly carrying them out – they appeared in Houston, and they got there by plane, they were in New Jersey and about to enter the Lincoln Tunnel, they were in Louisiana, and so ..."

"Unstoppable."

"Yes, Bill, the epidemic, or invasion, looked unstoppable."

"But now ..."

"Well, Bill, if, as Samantha has just told us, the Goddess has won, and if as reports suggest the zombies have suddenly stopped, and are standing still or wandering around aimlessly, then that confirms it. As Samantha told us, the voice has ceased, the zombie army is leaderless, they are no longer receiving orders, and the Goddess has certainly, as Samantha said, conquered the Puppet Master!"

"Just a second, General! We have another news flash here. Renée Scott, the President's Press Secretary, who was reported missing after the *Eden of the Seas* attack, is going to give a press conference, we'll go live, right now, here is President Katherine du Bois Hughes' Press Secretary, Renée Scott, live from somewhere near Miami."

"Renée alive, Bill, that's great news!" The general slapped his thigh. "Wonderful news! She's a great girl, Renée!"

"Indeed she is. Maybe for the radio audience – we have radio and audio net as well as visual – you could describe this scene, General."

"Okay," said Bill Brothers, "Here she is, Renée Scott – from Miami."

"Well, yes," said the General, "You can see, now: Renée Scott – her head is shaved apparently, like the President, so Renée must have been decontaminated too, she's wearing a baseball cap, and she's wearing what look like worker's overalls or laboratory overalls; she is standing on the roof of a building and behind her we can see a background of burning and smoking buildings. Okay, Renée – she's an old friend, by the way – is about to speak. Here she is, Renée Scott."

"Good Evening. I'm Renée Scott. The president has asked me to give you a briefing from the front line in the zombie war, here in Florida. Incidentally, I have a new haircut, just like the president, because a group of us, escaping from the *Eden of the Seas*, had to be decontaminated to make sure we weren't carrying the zombie virus with us. It was exciting, I can tell you. Well, the tide has turned. An antidote to the virus has just been discovered and is being mass-produced and in a few hours, well, right now, actually, we are applying the antidote to victims of the virus and bringing them back to themselves. We are turning zombies into human beings. Here's a brief clip, just taken a few minutes ago, outside our laboratory, only a few streets away. As you can see, M-J, the young woman in overalls and baseball cap in the images you see, is spraying the young woman – a zombie, you can see from the green foam and the green eyes – with the antidote, and, suddenly, as you can see, the young woman blinks her eyes, goes berserk for a second or two, collapsing, falling down, and then she gets up, and suddenly she comes to herself, like she is waking from a bad dream; Let's listen in! Here is M-J, explaining to the woman …"

"What happened to me?"

"You were infected with the zombie virus, but you are okay now."

"The zombie virus, how can that be? Oh, now, I remember. Oh, God, where's my son, where's my boy?"

"We'll find him! We'll find him for you!"

Renée reappeared, holding the mike. "As you can see with this clip with M-J – Marie-Josée is her name by the way – the cure can be quick and efficient, but huge damage has been done – people have been lost, people have died, and – I'm afraid – some people will never be cured.

"And as you can also see from the clip with M-J, there will be lots of social work, lots of therapy, and lots of search-and-rescue operations coming up. Families have been divided and loved ones have been lost. Clean-up operations have just begun. The suffering is not over. We all need to work together. And the president has asked me to tell you – and M-J has given her permission, the president has asked me to tell you that M-J, whom you have just been watching, is a synthetic individual, or SIN. SINs are immune to the virus, and this has been a godsend. M-J has been working, as a volunteer, from the beginning with us, to fight the zombie virus; and the president asked me to tell you all, that SINs and other bio-creatures have been absolutely essential in the fight against the zombie virus and that we owe them a debt of gratitude. I can say, personally, that in the last two days, M-J saved my life twice and that she and I have become close friends. One more clip; this is an interview I taped a few minutes ago with Colonel Jefferson Siebert of the Marines – he's leading the fight to distribute the antidote here and you can see in the background armored cars and SUVs being used to get the antidote out to people and zombies as quickly as possible.

"Colonel, how is distribution being organized?"

"Renée, we using my Marine units, human and BIOC and SIN volunteers like M-J, and like those two Chinese girls – Fang and Fei Wang – they are fully human but also immune to the virus – and you see them over there treating those two zombies. Working with them we have militia volunteers from BLACK MURK and other security companies. Everybody, right now, is on the same team, I can tell you. We are widening the perimeter here and we will be soon getting supplies out to all the infected parts of the country. The hover-jet you see in the background, Renée, is from Andromeda Corporation – Andromeda and its Miami affiliate Bio-Futures developed the vaccine by the way – and the hover-jet is getting supplies out to infected zones already. We are now winning this war, definitely."

"Thank you, Colonel Siebert. There will be more details to follow. Web addresses for additional information are on your screens. One big battle has been won, but the war is not yet over. This is Renée Scott, speaking from Miami on behalf of President Katherine du Bois Hughes. Good luck to us all and God Bless you all and God Bless America. Thank you!"

"Well, General, what do you make of that?"

"Bill, I don't want to toot my own horn, but I will say that I feel vindicated. The SINs have been helpful, indeed, as Renée and the president say, they have been essential in the fight to conquer the zombie virus. And you and I were wondering, if you remember, Bill, about the young lady – the waitress on the *Eden* – well, there she is, the young lady from the restaurant, and she is indeed in the front line. She is probably a European SIN. I'd imagine EURO-BIO product. I'm glad she is on our side, Bill, and I'd like to pin a medal on her myself."

"So, we are winning the zombie war."

"Yes, Bill, if things go as they seem to be going, I would say this war will be won!"

Shino Mori, a twenty-five-year-old Japanese tourist guide, had been leading tours of Japanese executives and their families for four years now and this was the strangest thing that had ever happened to her.

They were supposed to be touring Charleston, South Carolina, where she was going to show the Tojo Corp executives some of the many sights of Charleston and then they were going to have lunch at a typical …

But somehow she woke up and found herself now, half-naked, with a group of bloodied, insane, half-naked – or fully naked – executives and their spouses, milling around, aimless, with lots of other bloodied, aimless, half-insane people, most of them just standing with their arms dangling, and their eyes glowing green, just looking paralyzed and bewildered, at the entry to Lincoln Tunnel where all the traffic had stopped. Shino had woken up holding her little flag-sign, and apparently leading her flock towards Manhattan. Looking at herself, she discovered that she was wearing panties and high heels and nothing else.

She wondered how in the world they had ended up at the entrance to the Lincoln Tunnel. Then she remembered that a strange man had arrived at their motel; he had glowing green eyes; and he had been spitting out some sort of green mist, and … where had he come from …?

Perhaps he carried some form of madness.

Well, there was the bus. She went to Tojo Heihachiro, the CEO of Tojo Corp, who was standing there in his underwear, covered in blood and what looked like green goo of some kind, and she said, "Tojo san," and bowed. He just stared at her out of dead green eyes. She noticed he was wearing the driver's cap. He must have stolen it. She repeated, "Tojo san!" He remained standing there, no reaction. Hmm. So, she said, in a very loud commanding voice, "Now, into the bus, into the bus immediately!"

Tojo san snapped to attention, bowed, and headed towards the bus.

The others gathered slowly behind him and marched like sheep, staring into space, into the bus where the bus driver was sitting, dead, behind the wheel; his head had been cleanly chopped off, and green tendrils or vines that looked something like wisteria were growing out of his neck, up over the windshield, and some of the vines, were already in flower, a nice mixture of mauve, purple, blue, and, strangely, burnt sienna. One vine had climbed out the side window which was open and wrapped itself around the rearview mirror.

"Oh, oh, another problem," thought Shino. She had liked the man. But this was not a time to mourn or to hesitate. She did know how to drive a bus. She pushed the driver out of his seat, and, with the help of Tojo san, who seemed to realize she needed help, she propped the driver's body up in an empty front seat, and strapped him in. She then tore away the vines and flowers and tossed them out the door of the bus.

"Okay, now," she said to herself. She sat down in the driver's seat, though it was a bit sticky with blood and other nameless fluids. She looked out the window, and she saw that there was an opening in the traffic jam, so she clicked on the speaker and said, "Now, honored gentlemen, honored ladies, we will be shortly heading for Charleston, South Carolina." She put the bus in gear, and slowly turned it around, maneuvering it out of the jumble of stopped cars. She would see, too, if she could communicate with the American authorities, so she pushed the automatic telephone connection for the traffic police, "All our lines are busy right now, all our lines …"

Shino was feeling hungry; they had vouchers for McDonald's.

She saw one in the distance.

"So," thought Shino Mori, "there is life after death. And hamburgers and French fries, too." She shifted gears. The bus rumbled forward.

Kaitlin Wagner had listened to Renée Scott on her U-Tab. It had been a close call; but it looked like things might be about to get better. She put her hand on Doug Serra's forehead. He opened his eyes. "I'm feeling stronger," he said. "I think I'm going to beat this thing."

"I know you will."

"It's been a close call," he said.

"Yes, a close call," said Kaitlin, thinking back to only a few minutes before and how she had watched, through Doug's binoculars, as the helicopter gunship that was supposed to save them, came in low over the Everglades, over the dark trees. She watched as it came, out of the night, and she watched as, suddenly, the floodlights under the gunship went on, and how they lit up the whole roadblock, the burned-out cars, the overturned oil drums, the scattered bodies, the blood- and fire-stained asphalt; and she had watched as the bombs were dropped, incendiary bombs, incendiary shells; and she had watched as the whole roadblock, and the forest around it exploded into a wall of flame. The gunship then swung around and again passed over the roadblock, dropping more incendiaries, and then, in a third pass, it came down even lower, using its Gatling guns to shred everything and anything that might have escaped the flames.

Fluff was perched on Kaitlin's shoulder and the flames were reflected in his eyes.

"So you were right! Of course, you were right," said Doug Serra, who seemed just a bit better and who was lying on his side.

"We were both right," said Kaitlin. "How do you feel?"

"Better, better," he said, "I think that the zombie thing is fading."

"It was never very strong with you," Kaitlin said, thinking it was sure lucky the wheelbarrow was there – it had been used to transport Molotov cocktails – and she'd been able to load Doug Serra onto it, and she'd been able to wheel him away from the roadblock, so that by the time the helicopter gunship came they were about half a mile away and hiding in the edge of the forest, just off the roadway. They'd left the patrol car behind because it would have been missed, and, as Kaitlin guessed, it had tracking devices on it which would have made it easy for the gunship to track them and bomb them.

"They're playing it safe," said Doug Serra.

"Yes," said Kaitlin. She was beginning to feel like she needed to sleep and needed to sleep for a long time.

"What do we do now," Doug Serra asked, and he coughed blood, but not much, just a little bit.

"We have to get you to a hospital or a doctor or something," said Kaitlin.

"And how are we going to do that?"

"I don't know," said Kaitlin, "I don't know." She glanced at Fluff. Fluff blinked at her. The fires were still reflected in his eyes. "But I'll find a way," Kaitlin said, "Somehow it seems I always do!"

CHAPTER 48 – REBIRTH

V was holding the baby, looking down into its candid blue eyes.

The inner voice, the Dmitry voice, had calmed down, and started saying things like "goo, goo, ma, ma, goo, goo," and then it faded away.

BANG!

WHAM!

CLATTER!

The Soul Exchange Machine rumbled, and puffed, and groaned and creaked, and then, suddenly, it exploded. It broke entirely apart. Wheels, gears, pulleys, levers, cables, slabs of metal, screws, braces, vats of chemicals, all came crashing down, bouncing, rolling, and exploding in a huge cloud of dust and smoke. And then the dust settled.

And then – there was nothing, nothing at all.

The night that had been filled with distant galaxies faded. What had been as vast as infinity became a wall of rock.

"Well, that, I guess, is that!" V cradled the baby. "Let us go, then, you and I, when the stalactites are spread out against the sky, and the smoke of many fires darkens all the heavens and …" She glanced down at the innocent little face. Its blue eyes blinked back at her. And so, cuddling the baby, V trekked across a dark plain that seemed infinite except that it was under the towering overreaching arcs of rock, immense stalactites hanging down.

Dust rose in swirls at her feet.

Distant cries echoed; and bats swirled high overhead; they were giant bats, and some of them swirled down close, to greet V. And V returned their greetings in the ancient language of bats, the high-pitched, ultra-sonic squeaks, that she had picked up when sleeping in caves long ago in North Africa on her journeys with Marcus, when she was still vulnerable to the sunlight, and when Marcus would wait for her, patiently out in the fresh air, in the desert, with the sun burning down, waiting for her until dusk had come, cool friendly dusk, and then night, so she could walk free, with her father, under the stars.

There was wailing too, distant wailing, as if spirits were calling out from Hell, from some Hades buried deeper in the rock.

Finally, V and the baby came to the shore of the dark river – here was the watery passageway back to the world of the living.

"Here we are," said V, walking out onto a rickety black wooden dock and feeling the boards and planks tremble and groan under her feet. Mist and darkness swirled around her. It rose off the silken black water; glimmers of light flashed from mysterious distant sources; V cradled the baby close.

"So, lady demon, you want to leave, then?" The boatman roused himself, blinked, and stood up. He had been snoozing, waiting for her on this side of the river, slouched back in a chair under a single crooked lamppost, the big thick book open on his chest.

"Yes, we want to leave."

"No one ever leaves," said the boatman, "or hardly."

"Well," said V, her gold eyes flaring, "There's always a first time."

"True, true," said the boatman; he chewed his lip thoughtfully. He had a long crafty sly face, creased with age and care, chin sticking out like a shovel, and gray hair hanging out over his forehead; somehow V wanted to sit him down by a spittoon in some ancient hardware store, watch him chew dark tobacco and spit loops of the stuff straight into the spittoon, and listen to him spout cracker-barrel wisdom and discuss with him, on endless wintery nights, the wisest thoughts of Aristotle and Plato and the ways of the world.

"So, here we are," said V, her turquoise scales catching rippling flashes of distant light; her eyes sparkling luminous gold.

"Few come, fewer return," said the old boatman, glancing down at the book he had been snoozing under. It was *The Farmer's Almanac*, 1854 edition. He looked up again, "In fact, no one mortal has ever really returned, so this is one for the record books, I reckon," he tucked the book under his arm and stepped down into the gondola.

"Well, I am happy to return," said V, as the boatman reached out a hand to help her into the boat. "I am eager to see the sun and the moon."

"Welcome aboard, then" he said, handing her into the gondola. "Oh, I see you have a young one with you!"

"Yes, I do."

"Unusual, most unusual," the boatman said, gazing down at the child.

"Yes," said V, offering the baby up for inspection.

"Well, do not worry: He will be a fine fellow and worthy of you and you can rest assured that all the evil has been washed and cleansed out from within him, ma'am, and is no more than what is found in the usual feisty hungry young masculine thing born on earth to womankind."

"No sulfurous odor, then?"

"Not a whiff," said the boatman. "No more than the usual."

"I am indeed pleased," said V.

"Well, it is a miracle, I must tell you, ma'am, but since it is so, we can be on our way. Will you please unhook the rope there, yes, thank you, ma'am, I am most obliged!"

The boat, gliding smoothly like a black, highly varnished Venetian gondola, funereal and elegant and silent, moved off across the dark water, the old man polling it forward, and there were lights on the water like distant stars and the old man said, "I suppose you realize, my fine reptilian friend, that all of this, like the whole world itself, is an illusion and that we are all figments, perhaps, and that some great mind, half asleep, perhaps digesting its lunch or dinner, and, drifting between wake and sleep, is dreaming this world, and dreaming us too, fluttery phantoms and ghosts of its imagination, between waking and sleeping, I imagine, in some dusk – perhaps with a cool breeze – some star-filled, perfumed dusk, so magnificent we cannot even imagine its magnificence, or so it seems to me, from time to time, when I allow my mind to wander, and when I gaze back into the deep dark backward abyss of time, and think of all the things that have been and that are no more, not even the slightest trace remaining."

"Yes," said V, noticing the baby was once again hungry.

"Mind you, these are just the ravings of an old man who gets lonely, who has too much time on his hands, mind you, and who cannot for the life or death of him stop thinking."

"Yes," said V, the baby's toothless mouth closing on her nipple.

"I read so as not to think," said the old man, "Always a book in my hand, always. I swear by the stars and the prognostications, I do."

They came to shore and the old man handed V and the baby out onto the rickety pier, made of wooden pilings and rough-hewn wooden planks.

"No, no coin, my lady demon, there is no need for coin, as you are naked and have no coin or purse or wallet, or so it seems to me."

"Indeed, I am naked – I am what I am, nothing more."

"And nothing less! Yours is the way and the state of holiness, one might say," said the boatman, tipping his black broad brimmed hat, "You walk as innocent and as naked now as you were when you entered the world."

V bowed. "Thank you, boatman."

"It has been a pleasure serving you, demon lady." The boatman stroked his beard, "and your young one, he is indeed a healthy baby, now, and hungry, isn't he, well good night, or good morning, or whatever it is up there in the world people are pleased to call the real world, good-bye, good-bye, good-bye."

And, as his gondola drifted off into the night, and, echoing among the dark stalactites and stalagmites, his voice faded, "good-bye, good-bye!"

V found the tunnel easily. It was no longer flooded with mud but was now only a bit muddy with streaks of half-dried clay here and there.

There was no sign of the body of the giant serpent V had fought not so long ago – how long ago was it, really, she wondered.

Holding the baby close, V crawled through the tunnel, and then, during the last stretch, where the tunnel narrowed to body-width, she wiggled her way through the muddy slush, this time on her back so she could hold the baby up and protect him from the clayey sludge, and then, suddenly free, she wiggled out from under the little stone arch, and she found Isis, who was sitting just outside the opening, perched on the low branch of a tree, preparing a short stick or twig for whittling by peeling off its bark.

"Welcome back, V. I see you have brought a friend."

"Yes, Isis, now we are three." V held up the baby.

"You two, human and reptile, are disgracefully dirty." Isis peeked at the baby and offered it a finger which it immediately grasped, gazing up with blue eyes at Isis's dark eyes. "There is a waterfall over there. Let us go. I too need to shower."

Isis took V's backpack out of the hollow of the tree and hoisted it on her back; it matched her tan-colored tunic perfectly.

"Yes, let's go," said V, and, holding out the baby, she added, "Isn't he splendid!"

"Yes, he's a pretty fellow," said Isis. "He looks like innocence reborn – I won't ask how you got him."

"No, don't ask, not now, later maybe."

"And now you are back," Isis grinned, "It fills my heart with joy!"

"How long have I been in there – I've lost track of time."

"About four weeks, local time," said Isis.

"I thought it was four hours," said V, cradling the baby.

"Everything is relative," said Isis.

"And back in that other dimension, back in the old humdrum twenty-first century world," said V, stroking the baby's head with her claw, "I wonder how much time has passed."

"Maybe five minutes, maybe 1,000 years," said Isis, pushing aside a thick veil of vines and creepers, "So now you are a mother, and nursing him, I see."

"Yes. Drink, baby, drink," said V to the gurgling fellow who was busy at her breast, then, glancing through the opening Isis had made, "Oh! I like this waterfall – how beautiful!"

"Just for you, just for him, just for us," said Isis.

Water plunged in silver ribbons down a high cliff that reached up above the clouds, and the water landed, bubbling and clear, in a shallow pond sur- rounded by giant ferns and trailing vines and flat rock ledges that seemed made for sun bathing.

"Have you noticed, Isis, how strange the plants are? They are different, in many ways, large and small, from the plants of earth – earth as we know it."

"Yes, Eve was saying the same thing. I think we all noticed it. Time has passed, I think, maybe hundreds of thousands of years, so even if we are in the same universe, things will have, what is the expression, *evolved*," said Isis, "as I believe I have heard. In the nineteenth century, a fellow called Charles Darwin …"

"Let's not discuss theology now," said V, "Let's just enjoy!"

Isis gave V a look, stuck out her tongue, undid her belt, and let her chamois-tan tunic drop gently away onto the smooth black basalt, sun-dried, stone ledge which looked ideal for sun-bathing.

They showered under the crystalline cascading waters. And, as they showered, including the baby, who sputtered and spit and waved his little arms and legs and seemed to like it, V had a vision: Sergeant Eve Schmidt, covered in blood, her belly split open like a peeled banana, agonizing, while crowds of worshippers cheered and exulted.

V sputtered, "I think we have to get back. Our friends are in trouble."

"Let's go, then," said Isis, stepping out of the water, and slinging her tunic over her shoulder, "I'll put it on when I'm dry," she said, responding to the quizzical glance of V's golden reptile eyes.

And so they set off through the jungle, V, the baby, and Isis, leaving the towering mountains, the smoking volcano, and the entry to the Underworld behind.

CHAPTER 49 – SACRIFICE

"It would be an honorable and a glorious death, for such a lady," said the Great High Priest, holding the glittering scimitar out to Eve Schmidt.

The vast crowd shouted its approval. "Death, Death – Glorious Death!"

The Great High Priest raised his arms.

The vast crowd shouted again, "Death, Death – Glorious Death!"

For the last four weeks, at the request of the Great High Priest, who said the public was getting restive and needed some sort of flashy spectacle to compensate for the absence of the Turquoise Goddess, Sergeant Eve Schmidt, whose totem name had been decreed "Salamander," covered in palm oil and sporting a knotted loincloth, and Captain Anderson, known in totem terms as "Frog," equally oily, garishly painted, and skimpily costumed, had been performing, on the great granite outdoor sacrificial platform of the Great Temple, a ritual erotic sacred dance – a mixture of waltz, tango, and twist that they had cooked up one night in desperation over the campfire. This dance they performed each day at high noon and again at dusk – to the accompaniment of drums.

It was fun, Eve Schmidt thought, and besides, Captain Anderson was a cool, very muscular guy, and he could toss her around like ...

Guy the pilot, totem name Wild Goose, and the two soldiers, Annette, or Lamb, and Federico, or Turtle, resurrected by Isis, performed a chorus routine – roughly based on something called the French cancan, which Guy had once seen at a place called the *Folies Bergère* – and they officiated at the sacred ablutions – rubbing of oil, combing of hair, and painting of bodies – for the star dancing pair.

But the crisis had finally come, and suddenly.

"It is fine stuff," the Great High Priest put on his most thoughtful expression, "and I am greatly in your debt; but, after four long weeks deprived of the Goddess, it is perhaps not enough to keep the worshippers happy."

"Oh," Eve said, downcast. She thought they been doing great.

"It is no reflection on your dancing," said the Great High Priest, quickly, not wanting to hurt Eve's feelings. "It is, rather that the people are a many-headed unstable mob and there are rabble rousers, sceptics, unbelievers, and apostates, as well as fundamentalist fanatics and potential terrorists, among them. The agitation is reaching a boiling point. I am not sure I can keep the lid on – there is talk of killing all of you and of destroying your sacred bird and of burning your sacred vessel that rides so lightly on the waves."

"Oh," Eve said. She wiped her forehead with the back of her hand, being coated in oil and war paint made a sultry night even sultrier. "I see the problem. Yes, this is serious! Gosh!"

"Perhaps," the Great High Priest intimated, eyeing Eve's legs and midriff and breasts, "a human sacrifice would be in order."

"Oh." Eve blinked at the Great High Priest. Was the man serious?

"Oh," said Captain Anderson who had been listening with rising disquiet. He was miffed, almost insulted. The night before he and Eve had concocted a brilliant Fred Astaire-Ginger Rogers routine, lifted from imperfect memories of an ancient video called something like *Flying down to Rio* – and he was sure it would wow the crowd.

"I believe Salamander should be the sacrifice," said the Great High Priest, bowing slightly towards Eve, "She is most magnificent. The worshippers idolize her. She is a true star!"

"Do you really think, Great High Priest," said Eve, "that I am worthy of ..."

"Have no fears, Salamander," said the Great High Priest, giving her his best smile. "You are worthy; you are more than worthy. And, to make the ceremony special, to give you top billing, as it were, it can take the form of self-sacrifice, so you won't have to share the stage with an executioner. You, who are a sacred and beautiful and worthy female supernatural and extraterrestrial person, can immolate yourself." The Great High Priest gazed at her, adoration and admiration blazing in his eyes – she was truly magnificent, this extraterrestrial supernatural being.

"Immolate myself ...?" Eve gave him her best smile.

"Yes, by the most honored method, Salamander," said the Great High Priest, "by the method only granted to true warriors and high priests – by means of a razor-sharp scimitar, hara-kiri-style, by cutting out your belly, thus, and thus, backwards, forwards, and sideways, and thus, and then ripping it open, upwards, like this, to the lungs and heart, and then, swirling the blade, like this, twist, twist, twist, carving out an empty, twirled, space behind your rib-cage, vacating the heart and lungs, which then spill onto the altar. It's simple, really."

"I don't really think I want to do this," murmured Eve, or Salamander, sweating under the oily gleam. It was true. She did look magnificent, truly worthy of sacrifice – three months of tropical outdoor jungle and beach life and calisthenics and dancing had done wonders for a person who was already tanned and splendidly fit and stunningly handsome. Eve was feeling good. She did not particularly want to die, not just yet – besides, they still had to save the human race and she wanted to be there for the finale.

"I'm not sure this is such a terrific idea," said Captain Anderson to the Great High Chief, "I mean, it may just whet their appetite for more, if you see what I mean."

"That is a good point, Oh, Frog," said the Great High Priest, "but without some tidbit, without some morsel, without some sort of action, they will get impatient, run out of control, and kill everyone, possibly even me, and, as I said, burn your ship and your sacred bird that is sitting vulnerable and ready for sacrifice on the beach."

"And then," said Captain Anderson, "Who will I dance with if Eve is gone? I mean the act will suffer. And we've prepared a really spiffy –"

"Enough, I have decided," said the Great High Priest, "I have decided with regret, Oh, Frog, I have decided with grief, Oh, Salamander, but I have decided; and, that is that." He pressed the scimitar onto Eve – while thousands of voices below, in the vast open space, clamored, "Yes, Yes, Yes, Death, Death, Death, Now, Now, Now ..."

Eve accepted the scimitar. Now what should she do?

She decided that she'd better do it – otherwise the worshippers would run amok and kill everybody and destroy the yacht and the helicopter, and if they did that, then who would save the human race?

"Okay, boss," she said to the Great High Priest, and, daringly, she leaned over, and kissed him, warmly, on both cheeks. His heart was in the right place; she really did like the Great High Priest – he had, from the beginning, been their ally and protector.

She held the scimitar aloft, and, thinking maybe the ceremony needed a melody, and remembering a wonderful old Lena Horne number, she intoned, "Stormy weather ..."

By now the worshippers were in ecstasy. The crowd was screaming, wailing, jumping up and down. People were throwing themselves into each other's arms.

The time had come.

She must plunge the knife.

She noticed that Captain Anderson and Guy – their muscles tensing, their expressions grimly determined – were getting ready to leap on her, to stop her from making the sacrifice and disemboweling herself. She glanced at them – a fiery glance of command – and shook her head. No, they must not risk the whole mission, they must not let the helicopter and the yacht be destroyed, V and Isis must have a way back to earth, earth as it was, or had been, or was to be, wherever, and whenever it was, and, if she, Sergeant Eve Schmidt, had to die, well, so be it! She raised the knife ...

Now ... now ... now ...!

As Eve Schmitt raised the knife, the Great High Priest watched with sadness, trying to control his expression, fighting back a sob, trying to keep his gaze grave and indifferent – he was, he knew, in love with the beautiful alien female supernatural creature. But higher interests must prevail. The peace of the tribe was threatened. If the people revolted, if they destroyed the sacred bird and the sacred vessel, then the Goddess would be angry, and, even worse than the Goddess, the Great Volcano would be furious, and would take its revenge, as it had in the past, and bury many villages in flames – and consume many hundreds – indeed thousands – of lives in frightful agony.

Captain Anderson watched in horror – he was tempted to intervene, to leap forward and save Eve, and he began to move, but then he saw Eve's fiery glance and felt her command – and he felt Guy's hand on his arm, and he knew that Eve was right, that Guy was right, that the Great High Priest was right – if Eve did not sacrifice herself, then, disaster would befall them all, and death, and worse.

Guy bit his lip. He didn't know if he could watch this. He didn't know if he could stand it; he laid his hand on Captain Anderson's arm; he knew the Captain, and he knew that, if he didn't remind the Captain of the situation, well, then, the Captain would leap forward and knock the scimitar from Eve's hand ... But the hint worked; the Captain's arm muscles relaxed; the Captain was resigning himself; the moment of danger had passed. Guy closed his eyes.

Eve Schmidt plunged the knife downwards, thinking, well, it's been a good life, and if now I die, perhaps I will have saved my friends and maybe lots of other people too, and it's not so different from dying on the battlefield, and lots of my friends have done that too, and I've seen them die, and held their bloodied bodies in my arms and closed their eyes with my own hands …

Time seemed to slow down.

I just have to make sure I do it right. We have had great reviews here so far, with our sacred dances, the shimmy, the twist, the waltz, the cha-cha-cha, and we've held the beastly believers at bay for four weeks, almost for four weeks, and it would be a shame for a slip of the scimitar to ruin the whole thing and spoil the sacred effect; and also, it would disappoint the Great High Priest who gave me such careful instructions on how to do it correctly.

Remember, just remember, straight down, sideways, upwards, and the final double twirl and twist of the point of the blade, with just the right pressure!

Time was still slowing down. The scimitar was on its way down to Eve's stomach, precisely aimed, at exactly the right angle … Eve wondered at this strange sensation, time switching into slow motion; time was decelerating, going slower and slower; it was as if she were plunging the knife down through a gluey fluid; the moment was being stretched out and out. She wondered: Was this about death? If the mind died at the moment of death, and therefore no longer experienced anything, then it might be that, as the mind approached that barrier, the nothingness barrier, as it approached the limit of all experience, it slowed down, and down, and down, and then maybe came – what a horrible thought – it to a full stop, so that, in the moment of your death, you were left stuck, for all eternity, with that instantaneous last snapshot of experience, the moment of death – forever, and ever, and ever.

Was that Heaven, or was it hell?

Hell, Eve figured, it must be hell, frozen there, repeating the gesture, over, and over, and over, yuck – ripping my own guts out, for all eternity, heart, lungs, intestines, bowls, stomach, spilling out, forever!

"Baby!" shouted V. And she handed the baby – well, tossed it – to Isis who caught it nicely and neatly and gently and pressed it against her tunic and held it tight, while staring with her dark mysterious eyes at V and then at the scene before them.

They had just come out of the jungle, and entered the stone gates, and the sight that met them in the vast sacred space was scary and magnificent. It reminded V of massive political rallies in a place called Nuremberg more than 100 years before – well, 100 before the present, V's present, not counting whatever present, past or future, or dimension, or universe, they were in now, which was possibly, as Isis had suggested with her reference to Charles Darwin, hundreds of thousands of years in the future. Or maybe it was an alternative future, one that might never come to pass. Who knew?

Banners hung limp and straight in the still evening air. Great fires and torches flared up on either side of the multitude. And it was a multitude – perhaps 7,000 people, maybe 8,000 – it was hard to tell – all wearing loincloths, many with their bodies oiled and painted in garish colors, many, particularly the women, with their hair braided and caked in oil and black clay, many holding spears and machetes and banners. And the smoke rose straight up from the torches and the flames made that flickering rippling sound, like flags flapping in the breeze, whap, whap, whap.

Eve Schmidt – just as in V's vision – was standing up on the platform, next to the High Priest and to Guy and to Captain Anderson.

Eve had raised the knife – and she brought it plunging down.

V leapt into the air – a glittering flash of turquoise and gold – and, as she leapt, she willed time to slow down, she willed time to give her just that extra second or two she would need, just an instant – she had taken a great liking, more than a liking to Sergeant Eve Schmidt – and she was determined not to lose her.

V landed on the platform, just as the point of the scimitar was about to break Eve's skin and with a swish of one claw she grabbed Eve's wrist, and stopped the scimitar, stopped it cold, and, as Eve staggered back, shocked by the sudden apparition, shocked by the thudding acceleration of time, shocked by the shuddering stop of the scimitar, the scimitar which V lifted from Eve's limp hand, and held high in the air, as she swung around, standing astride the altar, the conquering turquoise and gold Reptilian Goddess, facing the multitude, which raising thousands of arms in the air went …

"Ohhhhh!"

"Ohhhhh!"

And with the other claw V grabbed Eve, who, in a state of shock was falling backward, grabbed Eve under the waist, and lifted her up, so V stood there, glittering, magnificent, holding the scimitar aloft with one claw, and holding Eve Schmitt's limp, glittering, golden body aloft, high in the air, with the other.

"Ohhhhh!" the crowd breathed out – awe, pure awe …

429

And V lowered Eve down and bent close over Eve, her fangs less than an inch from Eve's lips, and whispered, "I'm going to give you the gift of eternal life!"

"Must you really?" Eve breathed. She was not sure she liked the implications ... of ... eternal life.

"They need another miracle," V whispered in a hiss.

"Wasn't this enough?" Eve's blue eyes were now looking straight into V's golden serpent eyes, "I mean you appear out of nowhere, you bound down on the stage, you stop time, you ..."

"No, they're still restive," V's eyes blinked; her fangs were glowing, tingling even; out of the corner of her eye she saw the Great High Priest; he nodded: Yes, they need more!

"They need an encore, you're sure?" Eve sensed V's tingling excitement. It was contagious, the tingling spread to Eve's limbs. "Really?"

"Yes, yes," said V, "I'm sure. A mere rescue is anticlimactic. In the Colosseum they always killed a few gladiators. Otherwise, I mean, what's the point? Religion is a blood sport, right?"

"That's true – so what do you mean 'eternal life'?" Eve's eyes were half closed. Hanging in the air, held out at arm's length by V's claw, which was planted firmly in the small of her back, with her head flung back, arms and legs dangling passively, was somehow – it made her sleepy somehow, it was, ah, sort of ... delicious. No, that was not the right word. It was sort of, ah, voluptuous, yes, it voluptuous.

"You become like me, but right away – wham, bang – it will be impressive: beautiful goddess-like alien mortal transformed into a total 100% goddess – abracadabra – poof – alakazam – puff – presto – before their very eyes."

"Oh, boy, did I sign up for this?"

"A soldier's life ..."

"Right, okay, V, I volunteered, I see your point; you're right. I have a duty to the flag, to the president, to the Marine Corps. Do your best, do your worst!"

"Okay, offer up your neck."

"It's already offered up, you fool!"

"Right! Of course. I should have noticed." V held Eve further aloft, up towards the heavens. Eve's oiled limbs glittered in the smoky light of the giant torches.

"Ohhhhh!" The crowd exhaled.

V knelt and brought Eve down, now sprawled, limp, across V's lap, in one fell swoop, recreating the image, instantaneously, of Michelangelo's *Pietà*, and

V looked down, with compassion, upon the limp figure, and she winked at Eve, who, eyes open, and curious as to what would come next, winked back, and, with the winks still echoing in the air, still fading in the onrush of time, V plunged her fangs down towards Eve's freely offered jugular, and, following a recipe she had discussed at length, years ago, with Father Michael O'Bryan S J, her very favorite expert in witchcraft, black magic, and all things esoteric, she made one quick prick, injecting a quick one-time spurt of Vampire-Alien fluid directly into Eve's veins, and then she withdrew slightly and sealed the prick with a cross-shaped scratch, and a filmy spurt of Vampire-Alien fluid to coat the resulting scratch, which began to glow like a fiery ember, and then V stood up and she lifted Eve up, still limp, still human; and she placed Eve, supine, on the high altar stone, like a high table, and she stood back, for just a second, holding the scimitar with her right hand, and gesturing, with her open claw, to Eve, sprawled on the high altar table, with her left.

For a short but perceptible moment nothing happened.

V held her breath, hoping that she and Father O'Bryan had been right in their speculations about combining rituals and symbolisms and about bringing about instantaneous transmogrification without the diabolic shaggy monstrous degradation-to-pure-beast side effect which would indeed be unfortunate. "Of course, this is pure speculation, V," Father O'Bryan had said, "But I think we can say with some certainty, V, that under certain hypothetical conditions, if you follow the recipe exactly, then the timing should be …"

Dear Father O'Bryan!

Isis, holding the baby and letting it play with her finger and with the neck-line of her tunic – clever little fellow – stared at the distant altar. She could feel the building expectation, she could feel the charged atmosphere; she could feel that the crowd's mood was suspended on a knife-edge, between awe and massacre. "I do hope V has got this one right," she whispered to the baby. He looked up at her, smiled and said, "Goo!"

Then …

Eve's body began to glow, sparks flew, smoke rose, a shimmering light shone straight upwards from her body, from the altar, a beam of light that seemed to pierce the clouds, and then, wham …

WHAM!

In an immense flash and a great puff of smoke, a golden demon appeared, lying on the altar, pure gold she was, shining like the sun, glittering limbs loosely, limply, dangling.

Smoke rose from the freshly-minted demon. Flames flickered on the stone. Sparks littered the air and drifted upwards into the flow of the damp night. Bits of fabric, motes of ash, remains of Eve's loincloth, drifted above the crowd. Hands reached out to seize a holy fragment, a wisp of magic.

Eve had disappeared.

Salamander had disappeared.

There was only the golden demon, lying limp on the altar, golden arms dangling, golden claws offered, and open to the sky.

The Great High Priest looked at the altar, looked at V, looked at Guy and Captain Anderson with wide open eyes.

The demon did not move.

V whispered, "Stand up!"

"Why?"

"It's done."

"Really? I hardly felt a thing."

"Yes, stand up!"

"Okay," Eve levered herself up, slipped off the altar, looked down at herself and whispered, "Holy Cow!

"Bow!" hissed V.

Eve was still staring at herself, "Jesus Christ Almighty!"

"Bow," hissed V again, who was facing the multitude, her arms raised in a "Victory" sign and favoring the startled uplifted faces with a reptilian smile.

"Right, bow," Eve bowed, then she raised her arms in the "Victory" sign, then she joined claws – claws, she realized, Holy Cow! Jesus Christ Almighty! – She joined claws with V.

The vast crowd began to sing the equivalent of hallelujah, a thunderous rendition that echoed against the very mountains.

"Whew," said Isis, looking down at the baby. "Well, young fellow, I guess we live to see another day!"

"Can I change back?"

"Not yet, not now," said V, tossing a log into the fire.

Eve, Golden Dragon II, was sitting cross-legged on the sand next to Captain Anderson, "Okay, I guess I can get used to this."

"I'm not sure I can," said Captain Anderson, "I was getting used to the holding the human you in my arms – and now there's this new version of you."

"Oh, you'll get used to it," said Eve, "won't he, Guy?"

"Eve, I'm already used to it. I'm sure the Captain will see the light. Now that we have two goddesses – maybe three if you count Isis – it's becoming run-of-the-mill."

"Well, I wouldn't say we are run-of-the-mill, exactly," said V, flashing her fangs, in friendly fashion, at Guy, and crouching, concentrating, her turquoise thighs glittering in the firelight, and stuffing some twigs under one of the burning logs, "I actually think we are rather special, actually, all things considered, when you look at the bigger picture, I mean."

"Yes," said Eve, "I think we are rather special. I mean, very special, I mean, especially special, I mean, who else has such claws," and she curled her claw and examined her nails – long, pointed, golden, and deadly.

The surf was rolling in a few feet away and was silver in the light of the moon which was now full once again.

Isis, cradling the baby in her arms, was walking, ankle deep in the foaming surf, with Annette and Federico.

"I like it here," Federico said.

"Yes, but we can't stay here," Annette took his arm, "What do you think, Isis, you are the goddess who helped bring us here."

"Hmm, what do I think?" Isis led them back to the fire to join the others. She was peering down at the baby's moonlit face; she said, over her shoulder, to Federico and Annette, "No, I don't think you can stay here, and neither can I. The old world calls us. We all have to go back. Even I have to go back. We all have to go back."

"The Great High Priest will miss Eve and V," said Captain Anderson, pushing another log into the fire.

"And you and your dancing," said Guy, poking the Captain in the ribs.

"So how are we going to get back?" said Eve, stretching her golden limbs – boy, this was cool; she really did want to go back to being human, but on the other hand, to be as powerful as Superman, to sparkle like a diamond, or like a pure gold, to strut around naked without bothering with clothes …

"Ah," said Isis, coming up close to the fire, "there is a tide in the affairs of men …"

"In our end, is our beginning," said V.

"In our beginning, is our end," echoed Eve.

Isis raised an eyebrow. "Ah," she said, "Yes, it is so: that is the recipe: we return to where we were – and then, perhaps, if they are really clever on the other end, if your friends are really clever, V, if they establish the beacon, if they map the matrix, if they precisely locate the gateway, and at precisely the right moment, then the force will guide us home – well, your home. My home, and I greatly regret this, lies elsewhere, far from you, far from all of you."

CHAPTER 50 – EQUATIONS

Kate Thornhill – her body a rippling zebra-like pattern of black stripes and white stripes – held a piece of old-fashioned white chalk against the old-fashioned blackboard that had been set up in the Control Room of *Andromeda II*. She stared at the mass of equations that she had been able to construct from the information Claire had plucked from the distortion of the space-time continuum, the twisting of its coordinates and of the gravitational field, that had apparently snatched away the helicopter gunship and the yacht *A Flight of Fancy* and projected or carried them into some distant place or some distant time or perhaps both – or which had, perhaps, merely evaporated them.

But Kate was confident that V and the others still existed – somewhere, in some time or in some universe – the trick would be to find them, and to see if *Andromeda II's* computers and information systems could piggyback on the cosmic forces – the distortions – to bring them back to where they came from, to bring them back to the here and the now.

"We will be a beacon," she said, half to herself, half to Anthony Garcia who was standing next to her staring at the wall of equations: It was a marvel, he was thinking, what came out of this girl's head – of course, she wasn't a girl, she was …

Ted and Audrey were perched on a chair near the blackboard. Audrey reached out with a tentacle and indicated a square root sign and squeaked.

"Yes, of course, you're right, Audrey, it's a cube root," said Kate, and she changed the square root to a cube root, "Is that better?"

Audrey and Ted squeaked simultaneously; Antony Garcia shook his head, "You guys! And I can hardly check the bill in a restaurant."

"You know that's not true," said Kate, poking him gently.

In Kate's earphone, Sabrina's ancient voice, croaked, "You know what I think?" the clogged raspy voice cleared itself of an accumulation of phlegm – a young woman transformed into a tottering hag in a few seconds … Brrrh … how horrible!

Tended to by Marit, who was infinitely patient, and who strangely was treated by Sabrina with great respect, Sabrina was hiding away in her private suite, but she was following everything from there – crouched over a computer terminal. The image of Sabrina's transformation into a grotesque crone made Kate's blood run cold. Is that what waits for all of us, she wondered. Sabrina was growing increasingly, willfully, crotchety. She seemed to be taking great pleasure in being the most obnoxious old lady possible, except to Marit. But then, Sabrina, underneath her usual cool stylish exterior, was eccentric – and quite possibly mad, absolutely mad. "You know what I think?" Sabrina's ancient voice repeated.

"Are you okay?" asked Anthony, and Kate nodded that, yes, she was okay, shaken, but okay.

"I think you think what I think," said Kate into the mike.

"And what is that, then?" the ancient Sabrina voice said, and coughed and cleared its throat.

"They didn't go into the past," said Kate.

"No, I don't think they did," said the ancient voice, "not into the past."

"They went into the future – 350,000 years, roughly," said Kate, "perhaps with a twist sideways into an alternative version of the future, a different version of our universe."

"Roughly, yes, I'd say, roughly." The crone's voice coughed, "Alternative maybe, maybe a smidgeon of alternative, or more."

"And they are somewhere in what is now Indonesia, but in the future."

"In the future it could be anything," the Sabrina voice cackled as if being anything were an amusing idea, "Everything could be anything – or nothing."

"Yes, it could be nothing – travel to the future and it's a desert, or a meteorite has hit us, or volcanoes have erupted, or … we have evolved – slightly – or redesigned ourselves – or become extinct, or –"

"Ha, ha, ha," cackled the old voice, "But, you know, V is alive, I sense it, I know it, and she will come back, somehow."

"In fact, I think," said Kate, "that they have gone to one of the possible futures that the future, ah, may hold."

"One of the possible futures," cackled the crone's voice, "Ha, ha, ha, one of the possible futures – I think, in fact, that you, ha, ha, ha, may be right, Kate, ha, ha, ha. Alternatives futures, as you said. Many possible futures are possible and at each instant, ha, ha, ha, each nano-second, events occur, trillions upon trillions of them, a fly landing on a wall, or buzzing towards a light bulb, an electron settling here instead of settling there, all of which makes the future split and split and split again and again and again, into an infinity of possibilities, ha, ha, ha, ha … So there are as many futures as there are possibilities; this means infinity, endlessness. All is written, and nothing is written, ha, ha, ha, ha!"

"You are laughing a lot, Sabrina. Do you find this funny?" said Kate, putting a smile into her voice and glancing nervously at Anthony.

"Ha, ha, ha, ha," cackled the old voice, "Yes, ha, ha, ha, well, Katie my girl, and I love you, you know, now that I am suddenly and impossibly ancient, I mean, really ancient, a hag, a crone, an obscene crooked old fairy-tale witch – possibly with evil magic powers – it's a new perspective, and, well, I just find everything funny, my dear, ha, ha, ha, ha …You know what they say …"

"No, Sabrina, what do they say?"

"A change is as good as a holiday, ha, ha, ha!"

"Yes," said Kate.

"One thing I'm going to do – just for fun!"

"Oh no, what are you going to do?"

"I'm going to try Claire's patience. I like to see her riled. Sparks come off!"

Kate looked at Anthony and raised her eyebrows and then she said, "Well, that sounds like fun, Sabrina, but now we have work to do!"

"Yes, yes, we have," said the ancient voice. "I'll torture Claire later."

Claire was out on deck, leaning on the railing, one claw clenched around the round cool metal, staring at the wall of white mist to the south where, twenty minutes ago, the yacht and the helicopter had disappeared. It seemed like a living thing, the mist or fog, living, beautiful – and, strangely malevolent, as if it had thoughts of its own, as if it were a living thing, a beast, not merely water droplets.

Gail McCoy, Claire's model, friend, and folksinger of worldwide fame – a beautiful, haunting, androgynous voice, like a child, and lyrics and melodies of a depth and passion that made people swoon – was barefoot and wearing a black kimono belted high at the waist and standing next to Claire as Claire mused, "I wonder if we just sailed into that mist, would the time-machine take us too?"

Gail laid her hand on Claire's reptilian arm and stroked the smooth black scales. "Do you want to try? I mean, I think it would be pretty scary, but it would be a great adventure."

Claire turned her golden eyes and moistly gleaming red-and-black quivering snout to Gail, "Yes, it would be a great adventure; but we have to stay here – we have to help bring them back, though how we can do that I don't know and ..." Claire trailed off; tears ran from her golden eyes. Gail reached out and captured the tears with her fingertips.

"You are thinking of Sabrina," Gail put her arm around Claire.

"She sacrificed herself for me," said Claire, staring out at the veil of mist that seemed to shimmer in the late afternoon light, a wall of haze, then wisps of mist or fog reaching out over the ocean like tentacles of some monstrous beast, exploring, probing, testing ...

"You love her," Gail stroked Claire's shoulders which she knew the reptile girl absolutely adored and which would cause her, normally, to lose control and to purr shamelessly.

Claire shivered with pleasure, "Marit is looking after Sabrina, seeing to her needs, and keeping her amused, but V is the only one who can save Sabrina, and so it's another reason to get V back – there are a gazillion reasons to get V back," and Claire couldn't help it but she wiggled and began to purr with pleasure, "I love V."

"Yes, we all love V, I think," said Gail, who always for some reason pictured V, alone, on a misty road, at night, in human form, wearing a dark raincoat with the collar turned up, and maybe a fedora, the brim snapped down over her eyes, walking down that road, alone, between two brick walls, perhaps, like it was a country lane in England, or out west on a flat road in the dust bowl, a road leading everywhere and nowhere, and she was thinking of the lyrics for a new song about lonely love and about sacrifice and about giving simple animal pleasures – touching, stroking, feeding, drinking – to your lover or your friend, out on some lonely farm or in some solitary abandoned place where the only possible pleasures were the simple ones – a word, a touch, a glance, a gesture ... and food or sex or drink and maybe watching a field of ripe golden wheat waving in the hot breeze in the sun.

"I like the idea of that song," said Claire, who was finely attuned to Gail and could read her thoughts even when she didn't intend to, and who was shivering again from the caressing pleasure rippling down from Gail's fingers working their way across her shoulders, "It will be yet another top ten hit for

Gail McCoy," she said and she turned her snout to Gail and gave her a reptilian kiss – a quick lick of the forked tongue – and she said, "Maybe you could call it, 'Touching in the Dark.'"

"I like that," said Gail, "Or maybe 'Touching Strangers,'" and she gave Claire another nice languorous long stroke across the shoulders.

"Hmm, yes," said Claire, wiggling and shivering. "That's more suggestive, maybe, hmm, yes, you're right, that's better." She rippled with pleasure, closing her eyes, turning her head up to the light, basking in the sun, lolling in the luxury of being patted and stroked. She purred.

"You are so beautiful," said Gail.

"You too," said Claire, opening her eyes, gazing at Gail for a long shimmering sensuous moment, and then, blinking, "Well, now, back to work, I guess." She gave one last shiver of pleasure, and a little high-pitched parting fanfare purr, a flourish, which was almost a puppy's yip.

"Yes, back to work," said Gail, "See you later, alligator."

"In a while, crocodile!"

While Gail went back to the design studio to model Claire's inventions for Claire's assistants, Claire headed back to the Control Center to see if Kate Thornhill had used the information Claire and Ben had snatched from the cosmos to come up with the magical formula that could lock into the forces that had carried V away, and, somehow, magically, bring her back – an electronic beacon to bring V and the others home.

CHAPTER 51 – GOODBYE, GODDESS

The High Priest was on the shore, in his best regalia and most magnificent helmet, and his retinue – and a huge crowd of worshippers. The worshippers waved at the departing Goddess. Banners floated above the beach. A huge bonfire flickered in the brightness of the brilliant blue day.

"I'm sorry to leave them," said V.

"I could have stayed there forever," said Federico.

"Me too," said Annette, "with you, Federico, I could have stayed there with you."

"Oh, you lovebirds," said Isis, with a sigh, her head tilted slightly to the side, she was barefoot, her tunic fluttering, and she was pulling on a rope, playing her role as a regular skilled little sailor, swinging the mainmast around, catching the light off-shore breeze. The sail snapped to. *A Flight of Fancy* shuddered, seized the wind, and began to cut through the waves. The breeze flattened Isis's thin tan tunic against her lithe young body.

So it was that *A Flight of Fancy* upped anchor and sailed out to the exact spot – or as closely as they could reckon it – where she had been when the time shift had occurred. The helicopter too had taken off and was positioning itself in a spot, almost two kilometers farther from shore, as close to where it had been when the bolts of lightning had plucked it out of the "present" and tossed it into some distant future or unfathomable past.

"Okay, let's adjust our position."

"Yes, okay."

The helicopter moved a bit closer and the yacht moved a bit farther away from the coast.

"Will this work?" Isis was standing next to V on the deck of the yacht.

"Yes," said V.

"Hold me," said Isis, "just for a moment, hold me."

In the helicopter gunship, Eve was back in her old position, though still in her golden reptilian version, with Captain Anderson and Guy, the pilot. "Well, let's see if this works, Eve," said Captain Anderson, eyeing his former dancing partner, "By the way, you fully deserve to be a goddess – you were willing to sacrifice yourself and …"

"And you and Guy were willing to save me, for which, thanks, guys, and I apologize for not accepting your help, but you know in the end it was the right decision, and now," she blinked her golden eyes flirtatiously – fully exploiting that intriguing black slit pupil and long fluttering black lashes, "let's see if we can get home."

"Home! God, how long has it been?" Captain Anderson could hardly keep his eyes off Eve, even though, being all gold, she was blindingly bright, catching and reflecting every nuance of sunlight, every ripple of light from every wave. God, he sighed, she is damned beautiful as a reptile – just as she was damned beautiful before – as a human being. "We made a great dancing couple, Sergeant Schmidt," he said.

"We sure did, Captain, we sure did," and she laughed and laid a claw on his arm and leaned over and gave him a tickling touch of her forked tongue, right on his cheek, a goddess-reptile kiss.

"We're about in position, Captain," said Guy.

"Great, Corporal, great, now we'll just see what –"

A huge bolt of lightning flashed out of the empty blue sky; the helicopter shuddered as if it had been hit by a shock wave; the world turned dark, rain, a torrential, tropical rain began to hammer at the helicopter's rotor blades and canopy and then, just as Eve was leaning forward, straining her seatbelt to get a glimpse of what was going on, to see if she could catch sight of *A Flight of Fancy*, just at that instant, as she was putting her claw against the Plexiglas to clear away the sudden fog, the sudden humidity, just at that instant, everything evaporated and she felt herself dissolving too, looking down at herself, just for an instant, and she felt and saw herself, a few golden scales, a thigh, a hipbone, one breast, dissolving, disappearing, vaporizing into mist and then into nothing …

CHAPTER 52 – RECKONING

President Katherine du Bois Hughes stood in the Oval Office, in front of her desk, leaning against it. She was still in the black jeans and black T-shirt, though she'd taken off the baseball cap and she had changed the military boots for something comfortable, slow slung sandals, and she was smiling at the vice president as he came into her office, but she did decline, and some of the aides noticed this before they left the room, she did decline to shake his hand.

"Terrible, terrible times," said the vice president, "times of judgement."

"Indeed," said the president; there seemed to be an edge to her voice and to her smile – all that white teeth, the full lips ever so slightly rigid, "Times of judgement."

"You look good, Madam President, after your horrible ordeal inflicted by these cowardly ungodly terrorists who are out to destroy the United States of America and true freedom and democracy and to defy the edicts of God."

"Sit down, Joseph."

"Yes, ma'am, certainly ma'am," the vice president folded his tall lanky frame, being careful to keep the crease in his Savile Row trousers, into one of the sofas; he didn't like sitting if somebody else was standing; he felt it diminished him and took away the advantage conferred upon him by his God-given height, which was six-feet-and-four inches, height which had been conferred specifically upon him by the Creator so that he could impose upon others, and look down upon them and speak to them from a great and prophetic height, and thereby do the Lord's Good Work in this Fallen World by getting his own way on almost everything almost all the time; it was for the same reason that God had given him a deep resonant voice, a beautiful smile, a full head of hair, a large vocabulary, a good command of English syntax, a virtuoso mastery of universal bullshit, and, largely thanks to his wife, a substantial fortune invested in oil, gas, beer, coal, guided missiles, killer drones, automatic weapons, and casinos, and it was for the same reason that God had arranged for the Big Bang and for the delicate balance of Cosmic Forces, the fine-tuned universe with its perfectly honed fundamental laws of physics, such as the law of gravity, the strong force, the weak force, and electromagnetic force, and the second law of thermodynamics, keeping time's arrow on course, making one thing happen after another, so life could come into being, with the express purpose that, finally, he, Joseph Humility Ebenezer Jackson, would see the light of day, could keep his feet on the ground and could come into existence, precisely and exactly as he was, perfect, and at the right time, and worship the Lord and do his Good Works on Earth – and be president which he should have been except for this goddamned woman, who had outmaneuvered him at every turn, and who seemed to have the seven lives of a cat and must have sold her goddamn soul to the Devil she was so goddamned successful. He clasped his large handsome hands together thoughtfully, wondering what the woman had in mind.

"We've known each other for a long time, Joseph, haven't we?" she said, she was standing close now, looking down at him.

He glanced up, almost sheepishly, feeling like a school boy about to be scolded by the schoolmarm; and, My God, she did look in good shape; her skin positively glowed; she was indeed a sexy, vital, intelligent, appealing woman; it was amazing – the ordeal seemed somehow to have given her extra strength. This was backfire and backlash in a big way. The Lord had a lot to answer for here. He had let the ball drop, the Lord had. He had definitely let the ball drop. The Lord had screwed up, horrible as it was to say or admit it. The Lord had screwed up royally, big time – otherwise this woman would be dead or insane, bug-eyed, foaming at the mouth, and feasting on the bones, say, of her Press Secretary, that blaspheming apostate Renée Scott.

"Twenty odd years, maybe twenty-five, Madam President," he said, still looking up at her, still looking up at those beautiful eyes, so beautiful and so – ah, friendly and all-understanding – that they were almost hypnotic; you sure could understand how she could get anybody to confess to anything; but how the hell had she escaped from the *Eden of the Seas*, the thing was impossible! Right now she should either have been vaporized atoms, courtesy of the tactical nuke that should have hit the *Eden*, or a cadaver, food for the fishes, or she should have been crawling on all fours, drooling green goo, and devouring her neighbors.

"Yes, we've known each other a long time, Joseph," the president smiled again and then she sat down on the couch opposite and just stared at him, in a friendly way, without any judgement in her eyes, and she let a long moment pass, a moment that became increasingly uncomfortable for Joseph Humility Ebenezer Jackson.

"Why did you do it, Joseph?"

The vice president hesitated for a long time, he tried to keep his eyes focused on her eyes; he found it was difficult to do so. Finally, he cleared his throat, tried to flash his trademark big-tooth smile, and said, "Do what?"

"Oh, Joseph," she said with a big wide but sad smile; the smile of a mother who, though she understands the sins of her wayward child is, when all is said and done, disappointed, dreadfully disappointed.

The vice president didn't say anything; he was wondering: What was she talking about – was she talking about his firing most of her cabinet, was she talking about his having many of her key people arrested, was she talking about the witch hunt he had launched for journalists, SINs, hybrids, and other ungodly creatures, was she talking about the newly opened outdoor holding camps – with resident firing squads – in the dustbowl desert, was she talking about the arrest of scientists and the closing of bio-tech companies, was she talking about the attempt to nuke the *Eden of the Seas*, the missile attacks on *Andromeda II*, the machine-gun helicopter gunship Gatling-gun massacre of thousands of innocents on Karl Rove beach, was she talking about …?

"I have a recording, Joseph. I have a recording of several telephone conversations you had …"

"Recordings? Telephone conversations? How did you get them? Wire-tapping is illegal, it is unconstitutional, it is …"

"No it isn't illegal, Joseph; you made it legal, remember?"

"I did?"

"Yes, you did."

"The Ways of the Lord are mysterious."

"What?"

"Sometimes out of evil good will come."

The president smiled pleasantly, "Perhaps you'd like to explain your sermon, Joseph, do a little gloss on it – give me the skinny?"

"I did what I did because I had to do it."

"Oh, I see," the president glanced out of the windows – the garden was in full bloom, the roses were visible, the leaves were heavy, rich, lush and lustrous green, thick foliage on the trees. She would like to wander off and walk barefoot across the grass. She would like to raise her face to the sun, to the breeze, to the moon and the stars. She would like to sit down and read a story to some kids and watch as delight lit up their eyes. She slipped off her sandals and wiggled her toes in the thick carpet; it felt nice.

"Many people have died because of what you did, Joseph," she said, softly.

"I had to do it because you are too soft."

"I'm too soft," the president blinked at him, gently.

"Yes, you did not proceed with the vigor required by the situation – you are a hypocrite, you talk the talk but you don't walk the walk. You allow yourself to be swayed by womanly emotion, by misguided pity, you have an atavistic memory of what it is to be a slave, and so you identify with what you think is the underdog, you are vacillating and weak, and you did not do what you should have done to defend the human race because, being the great, great, great granddaughter of slaves you don't fully identify with humans or with the human race and its divine mission, and you have not prosecuted and oppressed and eliminated with the required vigor those who would destroy us – the hybrids, the SINs, and the scientists such as that evil godless Sabrina Jacobs ..."

"Perhaps being a slave, being denied one's humanity, makes one aware of how valuable our humanity is," the president said softly, "You only know what things are truly worth when you lose them."

"Could be, could be!" Joseph grimaced.

"And so?" the president was smiling patiently; she curled her toes in the thick cool pile of the rug, comforting, voluptuous, touching things ...

"And so ..." the vice president let his words hang in the air; he merely gestured.

"And so, Joseph," said the president, still smiling, and she leaned forward and pushed a button on a small recording device, and the vice president's voice was clearly heard, saying "She will die." And then she pushed another button. And, there it was, the conversation:

Vice President: "Is this line secure?"

Other voice: "Of course, Joe, of course it's secure."

Vice President: "So, what the hell is happening? The *Eden* was supposed to go out to sea."

Other voice: "Well, Joe, there's been a change of plan."

Vice President: "What change of plan?"

Other voice: "Well, Joe you just wanted to scare America, right?"

Vice President (pause, then choked voice): "Yes."

Other voice: "You just wanted to kill the president, right?"

Vice President (pause): "Yes."

Other voice: "Well … Our fellows, our friends, you know: well, they have a different idea, Joe."

Vice President: "And what precisely is that idea?"

Other voice: "Well, Joe, it turns out they don't want to scare America, they want to destroy America."

Vice President: "What? Are you crazy? Are they crazy?"

Other voice: "Well, maybe they are, but they don't care if they die, they don't care if everybody dies. They don't even care if you die. Do you want to die, Joe?"

Vice President: "What the hell …What the …"

The other party hung up; the recording ended.

The president just stared at the vice president, thinking, yes, indeed, he is a handsome man, and, by his lights, he thought – and he still thinks, even now – that he was doing the right thing.

"What do you intend to do, Madam President?"

"Joseph, I think, after an appropriate time, say, a week, you should resign."

"What else?"

"I think perhaps you could be named Ambassador somewhere, or just retire to your ranch, as you like; it depends on you; you could say you want to dedicate more time to spiritual pursuits."

"Spiritual pursuits," the vice-president's big handsome tanned hands were hanging between his legs, limp at the wrist, defeated; his wife was about to file, or had already filed, for divorce; without her money, his fortune, though considerable, would be much reduced. His dream of building the New Jerusalem was shattered; his enemies would be in power; the human race and its divine mission were now compromised, lost, forever lost, "And what about the hybrids, the SINs, the BIOCs, the biologically designed creatures, those devilish inventions of biotechnology?"

"To tell the truth, Joseph," the president leaned forward, "To tell the truth, I have changed my opinion of those creatures – and I've changed my mind about the science."

"Oh?"

"The hybrids and the SINs and the scientists you hate – and I hated, I must admit – they helped us, they helped us more than anyone can know, in the struggle against the zombie virus. And we will win. Science can be used for good or evil, that's true, and SINs and hybrids can be good, or evil, like humans. So you changed my mind, Joseph. What you did made me change my mind."

"Me."

"Yes, you changed my mind and you changed me – you changed me, profoundly, and now I can't change back. The truth will come out shortly, but I want to thank you."

"You are welcome, Madam President," the Vice President said, staring at her with steely eyes.

"One thing, Joseph; if anything happens to me, anything at all, an accident, an illness, an assassination, death, incapacity, then the tapes – and much more – will be released that show that you are a mass murderer, that you are, personally, responsible for the death and maiming of tens of thousands of American citizens, men, women, and children. And not only Americans, I might add, there were victims of almost every nationality on the *Eden of the Seas*. So you will not have many friends, Joseph. There will be no place on earth for you to hide. Do I make myself clear?"

"You do."

"Good. Now, go on holiday for a few weeks – to your ranch. You will be accompanied by the Secret Service – people I will personally assign. And don't talk to anybody, except your wife, or your immediate staff. If I catch the slightest whiff of a plot or of talk of a plot, then …"

"Then you will take action."

"Yes, then I will take action."

The president stood up, and in spite of all, she reached out her hand – and she was still smiling.

The vice president hesitated and then took her hand and shook it.

"Good-bye old friend," said the president, "We did do some good things together. And, Joseph, when all is said and done, I will … I will miss you."

"Goodbye, Madam President."

CHAPTER 53 – SOFT LANDING

On *Andromeda II*, a strategy was being elaborated.

"You see, what I think will happen, is this: if they can put themselves, very roughly, back in the position they were in, relative to each other, and relative to their arrival point, then, perhaps, the manifold will reverse itself, and the space-time continuum will unravel but backwards this time, and plop them right back where they came …" Kate pointed with the piece of dusty chalk to the blackboard and a massive squiggle of arrows, loops, circles, squares, ellipses, and equations.

"Yes," said Claire, "We can do it."

Ted and Audrey applauded.

Antony Garcia thought that perhaps all of this would have a happy ending.

"Plopped right back where they came from," cackled Sabrina's cracked old voice over the speaker. "That'll take the cake – Ha, ha, ha!"

"Now, now, Sabrina," Marit's soothing voice was heard in the background. "Don't rile people up."

"I think I preferred the old serious scientific you, Sabrina," said Claire. "The you who was my sister, my mother, my love."

"Ha, ha, ha, well you got the new old me now! Baby Claire, ha, ha, ha!"

"Boy, oh, boy, oh, boy," Claire bared her fangs and hissed at the screen from which the crone was staring at them. Sabrina stuck out her furry old tongue; Claire stuck out her forked tongue and hissed again.

"Girls, girls," said Kate.

"Yes, listen up, people!" shouted Anthony, using a good strong masculine voice. Kate the zebra girl flashed him a grin. Boys came in useful, sometimes.

"So," Kate said, "Now, if we draw a line from here, to here, assuming that dark matter is operating as a sort of … transmitting agent, then we may get a result. Can you do it, Claire? Can you map these coordinates onto the system?

If you can, then the coordinates we transmit may, if the force is activated from the other side, act as a sort of beacon. So we set the beacon, and it will be there, waiting for them, and if they make the right moves – then, just maybe …"

"I can do it," said Claire, "Come on, Ben, let's get to work – you set it up and I'll plug myself in and I will become the matrix and I will map the coordinates onto the dark energy configuration and set it up so it will be there, the beacon, and we shall see."

It took about twenty minutes to set up.

Ben Kamu adjusted the computer and transmission settings.

Claire concentrated, eyes closed, snout pressed against the computer screen.

There was silence; everybody waited. Even Sabrina, watching from her private suite, was silent, waiting – so much depended on what would happen next.

The silence continued. Air-conditioning whirred; the engines of *Andromeda II* were faintly audible. Somewhere, out on deck, somebody was whistling, just snatches of a song, "Oh Sole Mio!" and a small rotating fan, on one of the desks, rustled some paper. A routine signal – a low, mournful horn – was heard from one of the escort ships, maybe the Chinese missile launcher, or the American destroyer that had just joined it, and somehow the sounds made the vastness of the summer afternoon, turning towards evening, somehow it made the peaceful shimmering vastness of the summer afternoon tangible inside the Control Room.

"It's done," said Claire, "I've mapped it – it's there, the beacon."

Nothing happened. The fan rustled some more papers. Sabrina's voice coughed, the cough amplified by the speaker system. The American destroyer – or the Chinese missile launcher – they sounded alike – let out three short blasts: routine communications.

"Maybe they're not in position," said Ben Kamu.

"Maybe we'll have to adjust," said Kate, "maybe we'll have to …"

WHAM!

WHAM!

WHAM!

The whole room swayed.

Anthony caught Kate as she almost fell over. "There, there," he said.

Kate looked up at him, her eyes blinking, her skin rippling black-and-white stripes, a beautiful kaleidoscope human zebra. She touched the side of his face. "Oh, Anthony," she whispered.

Claire lifted her snout from the computer screen, golden eyes blinking. Ben Kamu flipped a couple of switches.

WHAM!

WHAM!

"They are back," cackled Sabrina's voice, "I'll bet apples to donuts they are back – that is the shock wave of a time-bubble bursting, ha, ha, ha," and she reeled off into an incredible fit of coughing – "Ha, ha, ha!"

"It's changed her whole personality," said Claire.

"Ha, ha, ha, you bet it has, baby Claire," cackled Sabrina, "You thought I was difficult before, ha, ha, ha!"

"Oh, come on, Sabrina!" Marit's voice was saying.

"But I bet she's right," said Kate, "They are back."

"Behave, Sabrina!" Marit's voice was saying.

"Yes, I think they are back," said Ben Kamu. "I'm just going to check something." He flipped a few switches.

"Well, let's go and see, ladies," said Anthony Garcia.

"The wall of mist is giving way on the radar," said Ben Kamu, leaning over another screen, "I think they are back. Or something is back."

"That's right," said Claire, "A beacon might beckon to any creature, to any … monster …"

"But not with the same or similar configuration," said Kate.

"Apples to donuts!" cackled the old voice.

"You are wicked, Sabrina!" Marit's voice was saying, "And you are so funny!"

WHAM!

WHAM!

WHAM!

It was late afternoon and the helicopter was hovering about a mile and a half from the yacht, *A Flight of Fancy*.

"Gosh," said Eve Schmidt, thinking, "It's like no time has passed at all, it's like we never traveled in space or time; it's like maybe it didn't really happen." Then she looked at Captain Anderson, tanned like he had not been tanned before, and his uniform, tattered by jungle and by months of wear and tear, and then she suddenly saw her own arm and realized that she was – Wow! – covered in golden scales and had claws … she was a … hybrid.

A golden goddess, that's what I am, she thought, I wonder if this merits a promotion – I think I'll go on leave for a while, if they will let me.

"Well," said Captain Anderson.

"Well, well," said Eve.

"You are still a goddess," said Captain Anderson.

"Thanks," said Eve, blinking her gold and anthracite eyes, and casually crossing two golden legs. "I wonder what goddesses do in the modern world – advertise for a god online or in the *New York Review of Books*?"

"You already have, ah, admirers, you know," said Captain Anderson, and looked down and blushed.

"We are back, folks, I think we are back," said Guy, "I have *Andromeda II* on my radar; I can even see *Eden of the Seas*, and the coast of Florida, right where they should be, and the GPS is working and the radio waves are full of stations gabbing away."

On the deck of *A flight of Fancy*.

"You are back," said Isis, "I can leave you now."

"You can't leave," said V, cradling the baby and steering the yacht, as Federico and Annette manned the sails.

"Oh, yes, I can, I must. I cannot stay."

"But, what will I do without you?"

"Everything, V, you will do everything," said Isis.

V let the wheel look after itself: the wind was gentle and they were on course. She wrapped her arms around Isis. The girl was perfect, she was a dream girl – a dream friend – and they shared so much, over the centuries, they had shared so much, so many things that V could share with no one else.

"Besides," said Isis, "I may come back. I am, after all, the goddess of rebirth. And, you know, V, I am in your heart, and like your very own Avatar, I shall be with you, in your heart, always, and you in mine."

V kissed Isis on the forehead.

Isis stepped back and she cried out, "Federico! Annette!"

They turned towards her, both of them tanned, the afternoon sun gleaming on their shoulders.

"Good-bye Federico, Good-bye, Annette – it has been a great pleasure knowing you and knowing the baby, the little one, too, of course." Isis offered her finger to the baby and she kissed the baby on the forehead and then she kissed V on the lips, a brief quick playful kiss, and then she walked into the cabin and turned and waved and then she was gone.

When, a few minutes later, Federico went into the cabin, there was no one there.

Not a sign she had ever been – except ...

Except, on the desk – the girl's bracelet lay on a small square of velvet. Federico picked up the bracelet. It was engraved: "To V with love forever – Isis."

Federico went back on deck and handed V the bracelet.

V took it, read the inscription, a tear trickled down her reptilian cheek. She put the bracelet around her wrist, locked it, and then, blinking the tears away, she looked up at the sun and at the clear blue sky, and, quietly, she said, "Set sail for *Andromeda II*."

CHAPTER 54 – DEATH

"Present arms!"

"Forget the fucking formalities, just set the things up!"

Blind and half deaf, Sonia Davies, the president's former National Security Advisor, heard the orders, muffled by the full hood she was wearing, and wondered, vaguely, what they meant. She was sure she was going to faint. They had been walking for hours across what must be desert under the burning sun. Her shoes had given up and blindly she had to kick them off, though it was difficult to kick with her ankles chained close. The ground was rough and the dust and dirt were hot and some of the pebbles and stones were sharp and as she shuffled blindly along she imagined that the soles of her feet were torn and bloody; they certainly felt torn and bloody; each shuffling step was agony. She yearned to breathe, just to breathe the cool air. Her face was coated in a lather of sweat and grimy dust, she could taste the dirt on her lips, in her mouth – which was bone-dry, her saliva seemed to have run out or dried up – and she thought, if this goes on much longer, I'm going to die, I'm just going to suffocate and die, I'm going –

"Okay, bitch," somebody unzipped the hood and ripped it off, and Sonia blinked, suddenly in the brilliance of the light, she was blind, it was all blurry, her eyes were coated in grime and dust; she blinked, she blinked again …

The breeze, a very light hot breeze, but it felt cool, oh, God, it felt so good, it felt so good, so cool on her skin, and for some reason, the touch of the breeze it must have been, Sonia had a flash memory from the TV images of the president, stepping out of the helicopter, onto the deck of the *Eden of the Seas*, in the brilliance of the sunshine – a scene she had watched in the large screen in her office in the White House, only yesterday – had it been only yesterday?

And now the world is changed – the president is dead and …

Sonia blinked; her vision cleared; and then she saw …

About twenty yards away …

A machine gun, two machine guns, heavy machine guns, on tripods, were set up facing the line of people, perhaps a hundred people, all in the orange overalls of prisoners, machine guns facing her, too, facing me, she thought, facing Sonia Davies, the president's press secretary, the dead president's press secretary.

The men and women standing around the machine guns were wearing Black Murk uniforms; they were talking, arguing apparently.

The breeze touched Sonia's hair.

God, they are going to kill us, they are going to murder all of these prisoners; she thought of running. But, of course, we can't run, we are all chained together!

She looked sideways along the row of prisoners, perhaps a hundred people, maybe more – the hoods had been taken off, people were blinking in the sunlight, trying to get their bearings – and Sonia saw people she knew, some of them famous, Doctor Rosenthal the biologist, Henry Blake a security advisor, Susan O'Connell a biologist and President of the American Academy of Sciences, Ed Klein, an economist, and others, and more and more …

And Sonia saw, out of the corner of her eye, behind them, just two yards behind her, a long deep freshly dug trench, it matched, almost exactly matched, the length of the chain gang.

"That is our grave," she thought, "that is where they are going to shovel our bodies," and she saw, down at the end of the trench, the small Black Murk bulldozer – a man, a dark silhouette against the bright sunlight, probably the bulldozer operator, was standing beside it – waiting for orders, Sonia thought, waiting for the moment when he will bury us.

"To die like this," she thought, "for nothing, for –"

A shot rang out.

Sonia blinked; she saw the Murk people were fighting. More shots rang out. There were scuffles. One guy was running towards one of the heavy machine-guns; the barrel of the machine gun was aimed straight at the line of prisoners.

"Into the trench," Sonia shouted, "back up. Let's fall into the trench."

The man on her right looked at her, blinked, and said, "Good idea!"

"Right," said the man on her left, "Excellent idea!"

Somehow the idea spread

They shuffled backwards, chains clinking, ankles chaffing, feet bleeding, they shuffled, and shuffled, and, "Okay, now!", they fell into the trench, just as the machine gun began to fire. It went on for a long time, firing, firing, firing.

"Ms. Davies! Ms. Davies!"

Somebody slapped her.

"Ms. Davies! Ms. Davies!"

Sonia blinked; somebody was standing over her, against the glare of the sky, and she, Sonia was lying on her back, and then she realized, she was lying at the bottom of the trench and she was still chained, still with her wrists chained behind her back, her ankles chained close, and she had dirt in her eyes. She blinked again. A black woman was standing above her. The woman leaned down, "How you feeling, Ms. Davies?"

"Okay," said Sonia, "Alive, I guess."

"Absolutely, you are indeed alive," the woman said, "You're lucky, not so many made it, you know."

"Not so many?"

"Only about twenty-five made it. The rest, well, they were shot before we could stop it. Here, turn over, I'll get you free there, just on your right side, like that, right, that's good, just like that," and Sonia turned on her side, and she could see down the trench, some people, the ones close to her, were alive, but others, farther down, their bodies had been – exploded, it looked like … the trench was a mass of blood, red blood, pieces of bodies.

"After the machine gun, they used grenades, they did," said the woman, "at the last, before we could stop them, and, I tell you, we had to kill them, we had to kill them all, every single one, to stop them. There, that's the handcuffs, now I'll do the ankle cuffs and I'll have you free in a jiffy, Ms. Davis. I got a call that the president wants to see you back at the White House as soon as possible – if you think you are up to it – we've got helicopters coming in."

"The president – she's alive?"

"Yes, why, you didn't know, of course you didn't. She's not only alive, she's back in Washington and she's leading the fight. God forgive me, but I must say I am proud of that woman!"

"Me too," said Sonia; blinked at the woman. "Thank you," she said.

"You are very welcome," said the woman, "Now, I'll just get these chains off you, and you and Mr. Fredericks here will be free."

"As for the White House," said Sonia, "I'm up to it, yes, I'm up to it; I'm sure I'm up to it!"

Shortly after 9 pm on Day Two; after defeating the zombies and just after revealing the discovery – *Eureka* – of the antidote, Virginia Lily fell into a deep coma.

"Exhaustion," said M-J, "Or is it something else?"

"I don't know what it is – this is a really deep coma," said Alex.

"We've tried just about everything," said Henry Cheng.

"You have to save her!" Jake stared at Virginia; tears streamed down his face.

"Jake, you have to be strong; I think she will come back by herself. Virginia is a very strong girl – she's a super heroine, remember that!" said M-J, and put her arm around Jake.

Meanwhile Bio-Frontier machines were churning out the antidote based on Virginia's saliva and they were churning out a vaccine – which, when tested, worked – and which was based on the antibodies taken from Jake and Aaloka, Fei and Fang.

All that night, Jake sat by Virginia's bedside.

Virginia's coma was deep.

Her mind was still there, but …

By nine a.m. the next morning, Jake was falling asleep, his eyes were closing, then he'd snap them open, then they'd close again, then he'd snap them open. His head tilted down; the lamplight shone on his hair.

M-J was standing over him, "Come on Jake, you'd better go to bed."

"I'm not going to leave Virginia."

"Tell you what, Jake," M-J put her hand on his shoulder, "I'll set up a camp cot, right here, next to her, okay?"

"Okay, I'll wait just another fifteen minutes, and then I'll sleep, but next to Virginia."

A few minutes later, Jake had almost nodded off when he felt M-J shake him, gently, by the shoulder. "The cot is ready, Jake," said M-J, "I'll check in on you both later." She leaned over and gave Jake a kiss on the forehead and patted his hair.

"Thanks, M-J," he said; M-J had become, with Aaloka and Black Dragon and Alex and Helen and Henry and the twins – Fei and Fang – so many others, like his family, his real family; they were his most favorite people in the whole world. Everybody came to see how Virginia was doing, everybody stopped to talk with Jake.

Jake was just about to get up and give a good night kiss to Virginia when he noticed her eyes were open and they were clear and blue and she was lying on her side and she was looking straight at him and her eyes blinked.

"Virginia," he said.

She didn't say anything, she just reached out an arm and her hand caressed the side of his cheek, and then tousled his hair, curling one strand around her finger, and he said, again,

"Virginia?"

She said nothing; her eyes just stared, and there was a suggestion of a smile on her lips.

He thought: what if she doesn't remember, what if she doesn't remember anything, what if she doesn't know who I am, what if ...?

"So, Jake," she said, "What's the square root of 64?"

"Eight," Jake was almost crying but he didn't want her to see tears in his eyes, so we wiped at his eyes with the back of his hand, and he said, "Eight, Oh, Virginia."

"Jake, we're going to stick together, right?" she said, and she began to sit up, and then felt a bit dizzy, and she put her hand to the side of her head, and then she said, "No, I'm okay, I'd just better go a little slow here. Is that okay?"

"Okay, Virginia," said Jake, "Whatever you say is okay."

CHAPTER 55 – HOME

It was warm, dusk, in Italy – a milky dusk that turns every shadow into a ghost and every vista into a promising memory and an enticing dream. Just over that hill, you think, perhaps, just over that hill lies happiness, just beyond that valley lies paradise, lies Eden.

Two shiny black SUVs with dark smoked windows turned into the long driveway, and drove down the dusty unpaved road, between the cedar and cypress trees, and pulled up to stop in front of a large, low-lying, ancient villa built on the edge of a cliff overlooking the Mediterranean. The villa's thick gray stone walls were covered in climbing ivy, and fronted by thick, flowering magnolia and bougainvillea bushes. The air was rich with the perfumes of evening.

At the door, a thin, tall, distinguished, very muscular, but ascetic-looking man, dressed in a black jacket, trousers, white shirt, and red tie, was waiting. He opened the passenger door on the first SUV and said, "Welcome home, Madam V."

"Hello, Jeeves," said V "and thank you." V was in human form and dressed in one of her favorite outfits, a charcoal-black Armani-type pleated skirt and narrow-shouldered narrow-lapelled jacket, a white silk T-shirt, dark stockings, high heels, and dark, wrap-around glasses. In her arms, wrapped in a blanket, she was carrying baby Alex, who was fast asleep with his thumb in his mouth, "And how are things on the home front, then?"

"You call him Jeeves?" said a burqa-clad figure, who was just stepping out of the SUV, "You call him 'Jeeves'?" said the muffled voice; black rimmed golden serpent eyes, with long black lashes, peered out from the narrow slit in the voluminous black cloth.

"Yes, indeed, Madam V does call me Jeeves. She likes her little jokes," said the butler, turning to the black burqa "She is under the illusion that I am unflappable, imperturbable, and competent beyond belief, as well as being over-generous with elaborate and sage advice even when it is not requested, and so she has baptized me Jeeves. You may call me 'James' if you wish, Madam, or Jeeves, whichever. I take no offense."

"And can I finally take this thing off?" said the burqa.

"Of course," said V, "Jeeves, I can see, is curious."

Lieutenant Eve Schmidt peeled off the burqa, revealing a naked golden hybrid.

"Splendid," said Jeeves, "most impressive and one of the most unique designs. Dare I ask if you traveled like this?"

"I had to, Jeeves, I mean, James. V has not yet figured out how to reverse the transformation. For now I'm stuck in gold. Call me Eve, please, by the way."

"Madam Eve, you are, I dare say, a true goddess, it is an honor to meet you," said Jeeves, bowing, "And, Madam V, you asked about the home front."

"Yes," said V, who had walked back to the second SUV where Kate Thornhill and Anthony Garcia and Marit were helping Sabrina, the ancient Sabrina, but she was not now so ancient as she had been (V had laid on hands several times already), and, looking back at Jeeves, V asked, "Yes, what is happening here?"

"There is a Jesuit priest, Father Patrick O'Connor O'Bryan …"

"Yes, Father Michael Patrick O'Bryan's nephew."

"Indeed," Jeeves bowed, while coming around, with Eve, to watch Sabrina being helped into her wheelchair – Sabrina was now a handsome old woman, perhaps eighty or ninety years old, to judge by the looks of her, and she was saying, to Kate Thornhill and Anthony Garcia, "Thank you, Kate, thank you Anthony, thank you, Marit, you are being most kind, ah, and hello, Jeeves, my old friend, how are you?"

"I am well, indeed well, Doctor Jacobs, and I see you are indeed well."

"I've seen better days, Jeeves, but I'm getting better every day, with the help of V, here, and Sabrina patted V's hand with her mottled and bony fingers, "Soon I shall be a teenager."

"To continue," said Jeeves, turning back to V, "Father Patrick O'Connor O'Bryan has been here for several days now, doing research in the papers you and father O'Bryan prepared together. I have put Father Patrick O'Connor O'Bryan in the Ochre Room."

"Very good, Jeeves, that is perfect," said V, turning to Eve, "Father O'Bryan wanted Patrick to go over the papers we wrote together and the background research – on witchcraft and witch trials in the sixteenth and seventeenth centuries, magic incantations, and alchemical transformations, so I told him he could come anytime and stay as long as he wanted."

"So this is like a seminar, a monastery," said Eve, blinking her serpent eyes.

"Well, it's not exactly a monastery," grinned V.

"Yes, we are not quite monastical," said Jeeves, "And, to continue, Doctor Jed Baker the criminologist arrived from Cambridge this afternoon. He said you and Maria wanted to consult with him on some criminal matters so he thought he'd come in person and, as he put it, 'get in some swimming and eat some good Italian food.' I put Doctor Baker in the Amber Room."

"Perfect, Jeeves, perfect," V had slid her dark glasses up onto her head – her hair was now something like a very short brush cut, and, still cradling the sleeping baby, she had slid her arm under Eve's arm, and the three of them – Jeeves, V, and Eve – followed Kate and Anthony, as Marit pushed Sabrina's wheelchair along the flagstone path towards the front door.

"I'm not sure I want Jed to see me like this," said Sabrina.

"He will love you in whatever form you appear," said V, and added, to Eve, "Sabrina was the great love of Jed's life when he was a young impressionable person. And, in any case, Sabrina, you will soon be back to where you were before."

"Then," said Jeeves, "There is …"

"There's more?" said V, smiling and leaning against Eve's golden arm, and golden shoulder.

"Yes, there is a delightful and high-spirited young Mexican person in an advanced state of pregnancy. She arrived here with a small army of body-guards, saying that you had said …"

"Oh, yes, of course, Callida, yes, I offered her refuge and protection."

"She and her husband, the governor, apparently decided that your offer should be accepted," said Jeeves, bowing slightly and smiling. He was always pleased at V's generosity in coming to the aid of the innocent and the threatened. He often felt he was working for a female Don Quixote, albeit a vampire; and that, together, they were engaged in a heroic tale of romance and adventure, "I put the young lady in the Pink Room. And two of her guards are staying in the Blue Room."

"Perfect," said V, "And here we are!"

"Yes," said Jeeves, "And welcome Doctor Thornhill. It is a pleasure to see you once again."

"Thank you, James," said Kate – she was now totally calm, totally without motion picture tattoo effects, "And this is Anthony Garcia, James; Anthony saved me when I was in great danger."

"It is a pleasure, Mr. Garcia," said Jeeves.

"The pleasure is all mine," said Anthony.

"And of course, Ted and Audrey," said Jeeves, to the two extra-terrestrials, who had been riding on Anthony's shoulders, and both of whom offered Jeeves a tentacle to shake. "It is a great pleasure to see you both again," said Jeeves. "It has indeed been too long. And Marit! I have heard so much about you, Marit!"

Marit bowed, and smiled a glorious smile. "And I have heard tales of you, too, James, and of this wonderful place."

"Now, the problem of evil, Eve," Father Patrick O'Connor O'Bryan, was saying, and tapping his hand, to make his point, on the golden reptilian arm of Eve, who was seated on his right and who was holding a glass of Barolo with her other claw, and following the Jesuit's every thought with her serpent eyes. She liked him. None of his thoughts were trivial; he was profound; and he was truly a good man. "Now, the problem of evil is complex, Eve. I really don't think we've sorted it out entirely. Is it a result of …?"

V, at the head of the table, was sipping the Barolo, from a very fine goblet of Venetian glass, and she was just listening.

"Criminal psychology, Sabrina, is infinitely fascinating and infinitely seductive, you know, and …" Jed Baker was saying – and then he stopped and just gazed at Sabrina. She could be a thousand years old and his heart would still throb.

"Yes," said Sabrina, who already looked younger, perhaps in her mid-seventies, "Go on, Jed! Go on!"

"It was you that got me into the study of the criminal mind?" said Jed.

"Me? Oh, yes, I remember."

"I was so obsessed with you I began to have all sorts of criminal thoughts about you – kidnapping you, carrying you off, slung over my shoulder, and worse, and much, much worse."

"Yes, I remember, Jed. You confessed your evil sadistic erotic cravings to me many years ago."

"And I decided I should study the criminal mind to see if other minds were as wicked as mine."

"I'm delighted to have been your muse, Jed." Sabrina gazed at him fondly; Jed had aged, but he had aged very well, now he was very distinguished looking; it was strange how that happened to some men; they looked goofy when they were young, and they looked like Aristotle when they grew old; how things change! A week ago she looked fifty years his junior, she thought, wryly, taking a careful sip of the pinot grigio. Now, she could be his mother, and next week she would be ...

A few seats down, Callida was explaining to Marit and Kate and Anthony – and to Ted and Audrey who were both perched on the back of one chair – how V had saved her from Don Juan Miranda-Fernandez, how V had virtually danced him to his grave, drinking him absolutely dry, and then how V, humbly, with pail and mop, and with a cloth, down on her hands and knees, had cleaned up the mess, and then, after a quick shower, had insisted on preparing for Callida a most delicious omelet. "She was magnificent! You should have seen her!"

"But, father," Eve was saying, "Does the distinction between good and evil apply to creatures that are not human? I mean, look at me, I am no longer fully human, and I certainly don't look human." She blinked her golden eyes at him, and the candle light made the gold of her eyes – and the black slit pupil and long black lashes – doubly seductive.

"Do you feel you can distinguish between good and evil, Eve?"

"Yes, I do, just as I did before."

"Then, certainly, the moral sense is present in you," said Father O'Bryan, "I don't think humanity is to be defined by external appearances. You have golden scales and golden eyes and claws but ..."

"And I look like a demon."

"Yes," Father O'Bryan laughed. "You look like a demon – a most beautiful demon – and you have some of the powers of a demon or of an angel, but you are, in fact, a delightful young woman and you have the heart of an angel!"

"And everyone is capable of evil," piped up Jed Baker, who, as one of the world's leading criminologists was presumed to know what he was talking about.

"Yes, I think evil lurks the hearts of us all," said Father Patrick O'Bryan.

"The doctrine of original sin," mused Eve.

"Do we do evil when we think what we are doing is good?" Father Patrick

O'Bryan toyed with his wine glass, "Or do we do evil knowing what we are doing is something evil and still choosing to do it? Is evil a form of ignorance? Is redemption possible here on earth – or must we be saved by a Redeemer, by Christ, by the Grace of God, for instance, these are questions that ..."

Maria entered at this point with her assistant cook carrying a tray laden with hot dishes, "And here we are, here we are, at last, for those who eat, the food is here!"

"Socrates argued that evil was ignorance of what was good and that if men – or women – only knew 'the good' they would pursue it," said Eve, who had studied philosophy – and written a long essay on Wittgenstein – before shifting to biology and then joining the Marines.

"I read about that," said Marit, the SIN, who had had a great deal of philosophy programmed into her. "But how could one do things that are bad, knowing they are bad? Wouldn't that mean you were divided against yourself?"

"I have done things that are bad, knowing that they were bad," said Jed, glancing at Marit, who was, certainly, someone's very precise – and extraordinarily successful – idea of perfection.

"Me too," said Sabrina, "I was very naughty to Claire and yet I love her; I did then, and I do now. Love makes us do strange things."

"Yes, it certainly does," said Marit, staring into her wine glass.

"It does indeed, Sabrina," said V, "But Claire has forgiven you!"

"She always does," said Sabrina, "She always does."

CHAPTER 56 – MOONLIGHT SERENADE

Oh, boy, was it a perfect evening!

Mary Lou turned out all the lights. Out on the backyard hardwood deck, she had the hot tub all hot and bubbly, the water swirling around, the steam rising gently into the balmy misty evening.

It really was a perfect evening, smoky and sultry evening, full of beautiful perfumes, the sort of evening that gets under your skin, giving you that itchy feeling of being all alive, that feeling of bursting with life and just having to revel in all that pressure for pleasure.

Mary Lou had bought two bottles of that rosé wine, which for some reason made her and Billy Wayne Penn particularly mellow, especially if prepared for or chased down by some good old Southern Comfort and spiced up with some hot Indian curry, which Mary Lou had prepared herself.

Mary Lou lit the last of the candles that surrounded the hot tub; she slipped out of the towel she had wrapped around her waist, and she lowered herself into the hot tub, Oh, oh, but that was good!

She reached out, took the glass of rosé. It was a plastic glass so they couldn't break and nobody'd get hurt. Mary Loo had a continual acute sense of disaster impending; and she'd seen enough suffering as a nurse that she didn't want to add to the total! So plastic cups it had to be and they were just as elegant and fine, she thought, as those fancy glass ones.

She took a cool careful sip, just with the edge of her lips and lapping at it a bit with her tongue and she called out softly, "Billy Wayne, Billy Wayne, where are you?"

And like magic, Billy appeared, a towel around his nice tight midriff – he was a neat package, Billy Wayne was, and he had the neatest most muscular ass, perfect glutes, positively sublime glutes, which was a wonder, since he sat in that goddamn truck all day and often through the night sometimes going twenty-four or more hours at a stretch which should have been against the law but all the regulations had been repealed years ago so there was no limit now on the hours a man or a woman had to work, and it made humans as cheap as self-driving auto-pilot – and there he was and he had the radio U-Tab with him, a thing which rarely left his presence.

"Are we going to listen to music, Billy Wayne?"

"No, I figured, 'Our Worst Fears' would add some spice."

"Our Worst Fears!" Mary Lou pretended to shiver and shake. She was not sure terror and paranoia created the most erotic of moods, but Billy Wayne did have a great sense of theatre, and sometimes a good scare was a real stimulus to the most creative forms of mischief that two people could …

"Yep, the thing is," said Billy Wayne Peen, dropping his towel, crouching down, and setting the U-Tab radio carefully in place, tilted on its little stand, "the thing is, Mary Lou, it makes it even sexier if we listen to the spooky stuff and get scared while we're making out. It's like we're out in the jungle. The world is coming to an end – and it's just you and me!"

"Haven't we been scared enough, Billy Wayne," said Mary Lou – she had spent three hours of pure horror hiding in the attic of the farmhouse next to the trailer park and watching through the cobwebs of a dormer window a bunch of zombies wandering up and down looking for people to turn into zombies and wondering, as she ate from a bag of peanuts she'd managed to grab as she hightailed it to the attic, wondering how the hell the zombies got to Louisiana since they were all supposed to be down in south Florida eating snowbirds, and worrying herself sick about her man, Billy Wayne – was he still human, had he survived …? "I mean, Billy Wayne, you spent hours surrounded by zombies. Isn't that enough?"

"Well, yes, that was pretty exciting, but I always like hearing what George Apostolou has to say for himself," and Billy Wayne, switched the radio on and he slipped naked as when he was born into the hot tub beside Mary Lou and he took her slippery smooth body – oh, boy, she was a total woman, she was – a real handful in all the right places – in his arms and he put his lips to her lips and he said, "Hey that wine does taste mighty good, Mary Lou," whispering the words almost inside her mouth, the sweetness of his breath mingling with hers and Mary Lou whispered back, in a sort of low purring murmur, "You always have your way with me, Billy Wayne, and you know it, so let's be scared together," and she gave him a good hard kiss and ended with a little nibble on his lips, "So let's listen to scary old George What's His Name and see what mischief we can get into," and she pressed herself closer to Billy Wayne while thanking her lucky stars she'd somehow happened upon a man who was a real man and who was kindness and courtesy itself and who had a real sense of humor. "Oh, Billy Wayne," she sighed. He sighed right back, "Oh, Mary Lou!"

The candles flickered and flared, casting their warm light and ghostly shadows across the hot tub, and Billy Wayne and Mary Lou pressed their bodies together and exchanged a deep, passionate kiss.

And, as the spooky signature music wound down, George Apostolou's voice, a deep, comfortable voice, began:

"Hello friends out there in the dark, in the night, this is 'Our Worst Fears,' and tonight I've got two guests – maybe even three, I've been told there's a third, but the third guest, if he or she appears, is a secret even to me. Our first guest is our old friend, Greg Erdman, who is author of the best sellers, 'Alien Invasion,' and the 'Aliens are Among Us.' Hello Greg!"

"Glad to be back, George."

"And we have another guest, a first timer for us, Claire V. Jacobs. Now, if you don't know who she is, Claire is a fashion designer, she's also on the board of one of the largest biotech companies in the world, Andromeda Corporation. Is that right, Claire?"

"That's right, George, and by the way, I am delighted to be here, and in particular to meet Professor Erdman. I've read all his books with great interest."

"So, Claire V Jacobs, why did you come to my radio show? I mean we are not your usual effete cappuccino sipping Left Bank Parisian fashionista crowd out here. We're real folks, simple, down-to-earth."

"Well, I like your moustache, George, and I love your voice."

"Thank you, Claire! Now, folks, you all know Prof Erdman, but I must describe for you our new guest. She is a stunning young woman, a blonde with blue eyes, tall, and she's a model and designer ... real famous in New York and Paris and Berlin and London and Moscow and Tokyo and Shanghai ... and so what's she's doing on my program – we're populist mid-west nighthawks and road-prowlers, people of the Heartland, not your usual fancy Paris Euro public."

"Well, George, I'm here because people trust you."

"That's nice, thank you."

"And also – since what I'm going to do is something you really have to see to believe. So doing it on the radio is like a teaser."

"People will get curious and want to really see you do your trick?

"Yes, that's exactly it."

"You are totally successful, a fashion designer, and you are well known, all over the world, so what trick are you going to show us? By the way, listeners, we have a webcam set up here, so you can in fact check out visuals of Claire's trick – whatever it is – to make sure we are not cheating here."

"Well, my trick – and it's actually not a trick, it's for real – is that I'm going to reveal, George, I'm going to reveal, for the first time, on your show, I'm going to reveal to the world that I'm a hybrid."

"You're a hybrid. You're joking. What do you mean by hybrid? You mean you're a hybrid like the reptile man? A hybrid like we heard rumors about during the zombie plague?"

"Yes, like those rumors and like the reptile man, except I'm not a killer like him. I'm an alien, I'm part alien. I'm one of those creatures Greg has been warning us about."

"You mean, you immigrated from somewhere else. I think you've got UK and EU passports, right?"

"Yes, I have those passports," Claire laughed, "but that's not what I mean."

"You mean you're an alien, as in alien-alien?"

Claire laughed. "Yes, like in alien-alien. I'm the sort of alien Greg writes about, particularly in volume three of the 'Hidden Eyes' series. Greg is right: aliens have paid us a visit and I can prove it, because I'm the result of one of those visits – but it happened a long time ago."

"Like in from outer space, like in the invasion of the body snatchers."

"That's almost exactly it. I was born here. Well, more exactly, I was cloned here."

"Cloned?"

"Yes."

"I find this hard to believe."

"Well, it is true. But you'll see in a moment."

"So this is dangerous – because if you are a hybrid, you know there was a sort of … There was – is – a sort of witch hunt, particularly just before the zombie invasion – and for a bit of a time after."

"I'm not sure, George, that I'd call it a witch hunt," said Claire.

"Would you call it a witch hunt, Greg?"

"No, not exactly, I think people were frightened and are frightened still. And I think we humans have to defend ourselves from invasion and from the monsters we ourselves have created, the BIOCs and the new version SINs, the Synthetic Individuals, even if, as I have heard, and I have even seen, and to be fair, it seems the SINs and BIOCs, like that famous girl, M-J, and even maybe hybrids helped fight the zombie plague. But, Claire, you look entirely human to me."

"Well, Greg, I feel entirely human – right now, but you'll see in a moment. And I agree with you. I think witch hunt is maybe not the right expression, because, Greg, you are right, people are afraid, they want to defend them-selves, they have a right to defend themselves, and it's difficult to know who is an enemy and who is a friend."

"Are you a friend?"

"Of human beings, of the human race?"

"Yes."

"Absolutely," Claire gave him her best smile, "but I'd say, yes, I want us – and I mean us humans – I'm speaking from my human side now – I want us to be free, successful, and happy. I want us – humans and hybrids – to survive. That's why I'm here – I want us to be friends, I want us – and SINs – to work together."

"What does your alien half say?"

Claire laughed. "My alien side has exactly the same opinions as I do, as my human side. She looks different and she can do a few different things; that's all."

"She can do different things?"

"When I'm in my alien form, I'm physically stronger, faster, stuff like that; and I sort of look like a demon."

"You look like a demon – you?"

"Yes, scales, red and black color scheme, claws and fangs, stuff like that."

"What? Really – claws and fangs?"

"Right."

"Well, let's see this. You are going to show us."

"I should take off my clothes. It's really bad on my wardrobe when I change or morph; the change sort of disintegrates, explodes clothes – and I do like this dress."

"This is radio."

"Okay. So I can do my strip-tease?"

"Absolutely, Claire this is libertarian radio, frontier radio, freedom radio, we are individualists, with the pioneer spirit, this is true America – you can do what you want to do!"

"Great! Now I've brought a friend with me, to assist with the clothes. She's the surprise mystery guest I promised you. She's just outside. Can she come in?"

"Sure, Claire, the more the merrier: so this is the mysterious extra guest Greg and I have been wondering about?"

"Yes, indeed, this is the secret mysterious guest I promised."

"Bring her in!"

"Hey, Gail, you can come in!"

"My god," George's voice went up an octave, "that's Gail McCoy! Are you Gail McCoy?

"Yes, George, I am! Hi folks! Hi Greg! Hi George!"

"You are one of us, I mean, ladies and gentleman, we now have two gorgeous girls here, and one of them, Gail McCoy, why, she's a genuine down-home girl, the real McCoy if I may say so, a red-blooded American girl, if there ever was one, five great albums that have topped the charts, some songs to break your heart, and one of the top models in the world! We are honored, Gail, we are totally honored and even flabbergasted, but honored to have you with us tonight."

"Thanks, George, I'm the one that's honored: many's the time you have kept me company, George, and you Greg too when you two night owls have been together, many's the time you've been with me those lonely nights, driving cross country, you know, stopping off in locations where we were doing a fashion shoot or where I was doing a gig – or touring – and you know, lying awake in those motels, listening to the two of you – well, for me, you're like family! So when Claire said she was going to try to get on your show and she wanted me to come along – well, I was absolutely thrilled, George!"

"Gail, thank you for that, I'm sure all our folks out there will thank you for that, right Greg?"

"Absolutely! I'm a fan, Gail, right from the first moment I heard the 'Wandering in the Mist' ballad, I mean, it is awesome!"

"Now, Gail, you are here to help Claire with this bit of magic she's going to pull off – revealing she's a hybrid and all – do you believe it?'

"Well, George, I work with Claire all the time. And – first let me say I am one hundred percent human, not a drop of alien in me – I'm a girl from the heart of the Appalachians – and I not only believe it, I know it."

"So you've seen the alien in Claire?"

"I model Claire's designs, very often ..."

"Yes, I saw you, high-stepping it in Paris, New York."

"Gail is my inspiration," said Claire, "She's the inspiration for lots of my fashion work – lots of ideas I get – in fact, we get them together – without her I couldn't do half, three quarters of the stuff I do."

"Claire is very kind. She likes to flatter me, it keeps me happy. Anyway, Claire likes to work in her demon – or hybrid form – and so I see her that way even more than I see the human side. So when she does her human thing, like she is now, you know, blond and blue-eyed, then I say, 'Whoa! Who's this girl – do I know her?'"

"Wow, ladies and gentlemen – do you hear this?"

"Usually, when she's inventing new designs, Claire dresses – and undresses me – and so tonight, on your show, we are reversing the roles. I'll undress Claire. Is that okay, George? Is that okay Greg?"

"Sounds great to me!"

"No problem!"

"As Greg says: absolutely no problem!" George Apostolou cleared his throat. "Now, we'll focus the webcam on the two of you, so that you can't play any tricks. And Greg and I and the whole world will be watching. For those who are not on the webcam we'll describe events here on 'Our Worst Fears'!"

"Okay," Gail flashed a huge smile at Greg and George. "I'll help Claire off with her dress, and from now on I'll shut up and Claire can comment on what she's doing."

"Thanks, Gail! Now, gentlemen, when I morph into my alien form, my voice will change a little bit."

"Why?"

"My tongue is forked."

"Wow! Did you hear that, folks, did you hear that, Greg? Her tongue is forked!"

"It's sort of cool when you get used to it."

"Okay, I'm sort of getting skeptical here. I mean we're doing a lot of talking, let's see some action here."

"Okay, guys; don't scream. Don't try to kill me, okay?"

"Well, okay, now, folks, with Gail McCoy's help, our young guest is taking off her clothes. She's got a little towel Gail is using to shield Claire a bit from Greg and me and from the guys and girls in the control room and from the webcam, but it is an itsy-bitsy tiny teeny towel. You are a very beautiful young woman, Claire – wouldn't you say, Greg?"

"Yes, she certainly is – it's two beautiful and extraordinarily talented young women we have here tonight."

"Thank you gentlemen, you are very kind. Now Gail has got all my clothes – there's nothing left here, behind the towel, but me."

"This is kind of exciting, wouldn't you say, Greg?"

"It sure is – reminds me of when I got my first telescope!"

"So now we are going to see this magic act, Claire. You are going to reveal your alien side and you are going to prove that Greg here is right, that aliens have visited the earth."

"Right."

"Ready?"

"Ready."

"Oh, my God!"

"Unbelievable, My God!"

"Are you seeing what I'm seeing, Greg?"

"Yes, George, I believe I am. It is incredible."

"Gail, you mean, you've worked with this … with her?"

"All the time, George, virtually every day I'm not on tour!"

"Amazing! I mean …"

"Ladies and gentlemen, folks out there, let me try to describe what we've got in front of us … ah … do you mind if I describe you, Claire, uh, it is still you, Claire, right, it's not something else, it is you …?"

"Yess, it'sss me … you can hear the hiss, right?"

"Right.

"I apologize for that. I can't help it. It comes from the forked tongue – and I guess from the fangs too. And go ahead, describe what you see. Do you want me to stand up, to turn around?"

"Okay, this is Gail talking – I'm pulling away the towel. This is like the dance of the Seven Veils, Claire, only quicker – one towel instead of seven veils."

"Ah, yes, I mean, yes, well, folks this is extraordinary. What do you think, Professor, I mean, Greg … What do you think?"

"It's unbelievable. I mean, I wrote about this, but I never … I never thought I'd … I don't know what to say …"

"Well, folks, Claire is here with us, and we were watching when she transformed herself, in the blink of an eye into, well, how would you describe it? No, I'll try. She's a voluptuous young woman in form."

"Thanks for the voluptuous."

"Yes, I mean, I think you are more, ah, statuesque."

"Yes, that's right. I checked the measurements with Gail. We measured a bunch of times – always got the same result ... bigger tits, if I may use the word, bigger hips and etcetera."

"But that's not the most amazing."

"Yes, she's ... well ... she's ..."

"She's ... she's, well, she's covered in black-and-red scales, looks like a ... Claire ..."

"Like a reptile, you can say it, George, that's what I call myself, or a demon. I sort of look like those images of devils, you know, the ones you see in those old medieval manuscripts. When she wants to get my attention, Gail often shouts, 'Hey, demon!'"

"Yes, you've got two fangs, and claws, I see your claws are yellow and pretty long. You look dangerous."

"Well, yes, I can be dangerous. But I'm very peaceful."

"You've kept your human personality."

"Yes. If you look at my eyes, you'll see they look like reptile eyes."

"Yes, folks, the eyes are gold-colored, and they have a sort of slit or lozenge, which is black or maybe the slit is deep brown, it's hard to tell."

"Yes. It changes according to the light. And in fact, I see things differently this way, I've got a wider range, and it's a bit more three dimensional. The colors are very strong too. The eyes have good night vision, and optional infra-red ability – I can turn the features – like infra-red vision – on and off. There are features – capabilities – of the hybrid body I haven't really explored at all."

"What do you say, Greg?"

"Well, I'm amazed. May I touch you, ah, Claire?"

"Yes, Greg, of course! Go ahead."

"Well, yes, she's got skin or scales and she's warm ... warm blooded ..."

"Yes, I'm warm blooded ... reptilian mammal, actually."

"And these claws ..."

"They are retractile – I can draw them in, so that I don't scratch things."

"And the fangs ..."

"They can bite, and I'll show you something I'm not entirely happy about, but it's part of the design, these fangs, here, look, I'll open my mouth, these fangs have little channels or tubes."

"What are they for?"

"Drinking blood."

"Drinking blood – like a vampire?"

"Yes, like a bat, or like a vampire."

"Human blood …"

"Yes, but not necessarily."

"My God, my God …"

"I told you I was going to tell you the truth."

"Yes, you did."

"So, you can be a killer."

"I can … absolutely; but then so can you, Greg, or George here, or even Gail, though she wouldn't hurt a fly. Any of us can be killers. We humans – if I may refer to myself as human – since I'm half-human at least – we humans are very efficient hunters and predators; and therefore, we are killers."

"That's true, but what about morality, do you feel you are human?"

"Yes, even now, I feel totally human, and I mean, look at me – I don't look human."

"Well, you do, in your form, your shape … look *very* human."

"Yes, thank you George. I love you two gentlemen, you are so … well, considerate, and gentle, and gallant."

"So do you feel human … in spite of … what you are?"

"Yes, I do. I mean the words we are using, those are the words I think with, the good old English language, so my thoughts are human thoughts, and when I make decisions, I think in human moral terms – is this a good thing to do, or a bad thing, is this better than that, will this make a person happy, or sad, hurt them or help them … I imagine I think just like you think, George, or you Greg or like Gail – I try not to hurt people or their feelings."

"Christianity? Do you believe in the moral precepts of …?"

"Judaism, Christianity, the religions of humanity … Buddhism … Yes."

"Are there many of you?"

"No, just a handful: less, maybe a dozen."

"Are you planning to take over the world?"

"No, absolutely not. We want to avoid that – that's why, so far, we have not reproduced – or only in the most limited way."

"What about the alien society, the society you come from?"

"Well, strange as it may seem, George, I don't know much more about it than you do. I was cloned. But even the oldest of us, she doesn't know much either. None of us have been to another planet or anything like that. I don't speak alien, whatever it is, if you know what I mean."

"So tomorrow you are doing this again, live, on TV."

"Yes, I'm going to be on Katherine du Bois Hughes' old program, hosted now as you know by Fajah Jackson, and they've told me I can announce there will be a surprise guest."

"A surprise guest – not Gail?"

"Gail will be on the show, but the surprise guest is not Gail – no."

"You can't tell us, I guess."

"No, George, it wouldn't be a surprise then, would it?"

"So, Claire, can you stand and move around, so the web cams can get a good look at you?"

"Of course, George!"

"Do you believe this?" said Mary Lou, her legs were locked around Billy Wayne's waist and she was leaning back and sighing, and just in ecstasy if that was what it could be called, being so relaxed and all, feeling at one with Billy Wayne, as if they'd somehow merged into one person, and Billy Wayne pulled her to him, and kissed her on the lips, and she sighed again, and Billy Wayne reached out and pushed a button and the U-Tab picked up the webcam broadcast and Mary Lou glanced at it, and said, "Put it on Hologram, Billy Wayne," and Billy Wayne said, "Hologram, please," and a miniature hologram image of Claire V Jacobs appeared, in demon form, brilliantly illuminated, turning gracefully around, displaying herself, on the edge of the hot tub, and Billy Wayne said, "I think I do believe it, Mary Lou," and Mary Lou, her legs still locked around Billy Wayne, glanced sideways at the small bright figure, and she said, "Yes, I believe it, why would the girl lie, and then she's there with Gail McCoy, and Gail is as honest I bet as the day is long," and Mary Lou took a closer look at the hologram, and she said, "She's very pretty, I mean it would be nice to have a little statuette of the demon or something."

"Maybe I'll try and get you one. I bet they try to market these things. I mean, she's in the fashion business, isn't she?"

"She is," said Mary Lou.

"Oh, Mary Lou," said Billy Wayne, and he lifted her out of the water and both of them rolled onto a towel, and Billy Wayne said, "It's time for some more love-making, I figure, Mary Lou, and he took her in his arms, and pressed her down on the thick warm towel, while the candles flickered and flamed around them, and while the little demon figure danced just next to them, saying ...

"So this is what I look like."

"Stunning, I think, don't you, Greg?"

"I do – but Claire – are you aliens friendly or are you hostile? I mean, are you signaling the end of the human race here – or something else?"

"That's a good question, Greg. I'm a hybrid, not an alien, so I was born here, so, as I said, I don't know the alien civilization – or its intentions. I did meet my father, the father of the source of my alien DNA, and he calls me his daughter, which in a sense I am. My father is an alien, but he looks totally human, like an army officer, really, very distinguished. And he said our job here is to try to help protect the human race."

"Help protect the human race?"

"Yes, as you've heard, there were some hybrids in the front line of the battle against the zombie invasion, I can tell you that. But my father, he also said that there are forces – on earth and elsewhere – that are not friendly to human beings. So I'd say, we hybrids want to do our bit to defend human beings – we want to be part of the team. We want to be part of an alliance with SINs and humans that protects the human race, because, in the end, we are part of the human race."

"What do you think, Greg?"

"I don't want to doubt the word of such a beautiful young woman or hybrid – I think we'll have to wait and see ... But, I'll tell you, George, I've seen things here tonight that I never thought I'd live to see."

"That's fair, I think," Claire said, "and I have a suggestion, Greg, if you and George agree – Gail, I think would be willing to sing one of her new songs. She told me if I was very, very good, she might do it for us."

"Fabulous, Claire! That is great – you agree, Gail?"

"I'd be delighted, George, and Greg."

"Okay!"

"This is a song I'll dedicate to my friend Claire. We were actually in the middle of the zombie crisis when I thought of it and I was working with Claire. Claire and I brainstormed a bit for the title. Here it is "Touching Strangers.""

"I like those girls," said Mary Lou.

"Me too," said Billy Wayne, "I heard rumors, you know, as to how those hybrids and of course the SINs – like that general said on TV – helped fight off the zombies. I say we give the girl a chance."

As Gail McCoy sang her song, "Touching Strangers," shortly to be an international hit, Billy Wayne and Mary Lou made love, slowly, gently, and whispered old secret forms of human tenderness to each other, and breathed the smoky wonderful soft air of that great old planet, Earth.

On the Fajah Jackson show, the next evening, the "secret guest" who appeared after Claire V Jacobs – who did her transformation strip-tease – and after Gail McCoy and the Actress Virginia Lily had warmed up the audience up, with Samantha Andrews acting, with Fajah Jackson, as co-master of ceremonies, well, that "secret guest" turned out to be the president of the United States, Katherine du Bois Hughes.

There she was, appearing on her old show, to tell the story of the fight to stop the zombie epidemic – she left out the role of the vice president. He was on his ranch in Texas, mulling over his destiny and playing poker with his Secret Service guards.

She revealed that, in order to survive the zombie assault, she had become a hybrid. She joked about it, and told stories, and had the audience laughing and eating out of her hand.

The shock waves from the revelation were felt around the world.

With flashbulbs flashing and cameras whirring at the Paris Fashion Show, and in front of a world-wide and absolutely awestruck TV and Internet audience, Claire V. Jacobs and Gail McCoy strode down the runway together, the glittering naked reptile-hybrid, wearing only CVJ accessories, and the gloriously, sumptuously clad human, wearing a stunning CVJ slinky reptile-hybrid fabric gown. And, along with them, was Nobel Laureate Kate Thornhill, a human zebra, modeling a whole series of daring CVJ dresses and catsuits.

Hybrid Mania, as it came to be called, swept the world – and accessories in hybrid design, together with hybrid dresses, and suits, and make-up, gave CVJ its most profitable year by far.

Claire began, occasionally, to go to restaurants or gallery openings in her hybrid form, and, if she wasn't careful, she was mobbed by fans wanting autographs.

"I'm going to throw a jealous fit," Gail McCoy grinned, one afternoon in Shanghai when both of them, after a luncheon for the Shanghai Chamber of

Fashion, were sitting at an autograph signing table, being besieged by young fans.

"I think we've got equal billing," said Claire, and she used her right claw to sketch out a particularly brilliant scrawl of an autograph for the mayor's daughter, "And I'm just an oddity; you're a star. They love you; they're curious about me."

After the Supreme Court ruled that she was not, because of her hybrid nature, barred from serving in public office, and that she was eligible to run again, Katherine du Bois Hughes was re-elected president of the United States, for her second term, taking all 50 states.

Monica Fabritz discovered, in her fifth month as a reptile, on the eve of her 21st birthday, which was about to be celebrated by a lavish party on *Andromeda II*, that she could shift back to being human – appearing exactly as she did before.

And, as soon as she shifted, the baby shifted too. "Well, we are in synch, then, my dear little Anton," she said, and, turning to her father and mother, she said, "See, Daddy, see Mommy, I really am me!"

Monica decided she would continue her post graduate work at M.I.T., with Doctor Kate Thornhill; and sometimes, if she was, say, invited to Kate's for dinner – which happened often – Anthony Garcia was, among other things, an excellent cook – Monica would shift to reptile hybrid mode, with the baby, just for the fun of it, among family and friends as it were. Baby Anton was a hit, in particular, with Audrey and Ted.

Virginia Lily adopted Jake. They split their time between the west coast and Manhattan. Virginia co-produced and starred in the new series *Zombie Crusade* and Harvey Finkelstein, lighting up a huge cigar, said to Jake, "I think, Jake, my boy, this is her greatest role yet, it's certainly her greatest hit!" And Virginia said, though they were out on the terrace overlooking the Pacific and the gentle breeze was carrying the stench out to sea, "Harvey, those disgusting things will be the death of you!" Jake was, of course, precocious, and would soon be going to university.

"I will want to inspect your girlfriends," said Virginia with a stern grin, "each one, very carefully."

"Oh, Virginia," said Jake; he blushed.

Professor Kevin Harris was found wandering in the Everglades. He was difficult to capture and when captured he was found to be dangerously insane – not human any more – growling and slobbering and snarling and yowling. He was incarcerated in a straw-strewn cage, alone, in a special isolated pavilion, in an institution for the criminally insane. Each year, on his birthday, he received a visit from a beautiful young woman; he yowled and stared at her and sniffed the air and grasped the bars of his cage, but had no idea who or what she was.

Colonel Jefferson Siebert was asked by President Katherine du Bois Hughes to set up a special highly mobile special operations anti-terrorism unit – to be used at home and abroad. After some discussion, Freddy the reptile man was integrated into the unit. Freddy's help proved invaluable.

Aaloka was adopted by Gold Dragon and Silver Dragon. Black Dragon became, as it were, her Godmother, with Virginia Lily and Jake present at the ceremony. Aaloka lived much of the year with Alex and Helen on *Andromeda II*. She was everybody's favorite, had her own tutor, and was soon quickly growing up to be a very beautiful and talented young woman.

Special Secret Agent Sarah James now worked at the White House on national security with Sonia Davies. V had finally released Sarah from her locked-in reptile state. "But only if you come and spend at least one holiday a year at my place in Italy!"

Sarah would sometimes go and stand by a cage at the Washington Botanical Institute, where there was a very exotic plant called the "Madison Chloe Brown Climbing Vine" – "It's a highly intelligent plant," the keeper insisted.

Sarah would stand close to the bars and the plant would reach out a tentacle, with its suckers and wrap itself around Sarah's arm and, for a time, Sarah James and Madison Chloe Brown would reminisce, silently, mind-to-mind, about old times.

The *Eden of the Seas* was cleaned up and repaired and readied itself for the coming season. Magnus Olsen stayed on as captain and he and Ingrid became famous for saving the *Eden*.

Ingrid Carlstrom remained for two years as his executive assistant, while working on her Ph.D. in naval history at Uppsala University. The bullet lodged in her brain had left her intelligence intact but had left her, too, with a very limited range of feelings – adoration for Magnus Olsen was one of them. Magnus was worried and he mentioned the problem to the Andromeda Corporation lawyer, Helen Guerrera, and Helen said, "Let her stay with me for a day or two."

When Ingrid returned from *Andromeda II*, she was cured, and with her brilliant smile from the old days. "I'm no longer a zombie, Magnus, but I still adore you!"

AFTERMATH

1,432,562 people died in the Zombie Plague, and several thousands more were injured, some of them maimed or wounded for life.

In the weeks following the plague, several strange creatures – half animal, half vegetable – washed up on the beaches of Florida and it turned out they were victims of the zombie plague who had been turned into half-plants. They were added to the collection taken from the *Eden of the Seas,* and they all found homes in the municipal botanical gardens of a variety of cities.

CODA

It was some time after dusk and the Mediterranean was quickly darkening.

"The moon will be up soon."

"Ah, yes, that might help."

"Do you think she got it, Giuseppe?" Mario was peering over the edge of the fishing boat trying to see down into the dark water. It was just past sunset. The air was dusky and purple. They were about a mile out and two miles down the coast from their village which was just next to the grounds of V's villa. They were fishing for squid by lamplight. This was the spot where three nights ago they had lost an engraved anchor that had been in the family for five generations.

Mario squinted into the water. It was several hundred feet deep, with rocky ridges, and large boulders and an underwater cliff, not much farther out, plunging down almost 800 feet.

They had seen V swimming near shore – twilight was her favorite swimming time – that and just before dawn – and asked her if she could help – she was the local mermaid, and she was, also, and had been in centuries past, the benefactor and protector of the village.

"She'll get it, I'm sure. Has the signora ever failed yet if she says she's going to do something?"

"No, you are right. She has never failed yet."

Three hundred feet below them, using a powerful underwater flashlight and her own very sensitive night vision plus a metal detector and after being misled by other ruins – several barrels of oil from a 1943 oil tanker sinking, two amphora from the time of Ancient Greece, and a bronze statue from the Roman Imperial period – V had located the missing anchor.

It was lodged on the cliff edge, wedged between two outcroppings.

V had a steel and plastic cable attached to a belt around her waist. It led up to a winch on the fishing boat.

The water was cold down at 300 feet but for V not at all unpleasant. Exploring the murky depths was one of her favorite things; she sometimes suspected that her alien side was more aquatic than terrestrial – the underwater world was mysterious and alluring.

She hooked the steel and plastic cable to the anchor, and pulled on it to make sure the link was solid.

Below, the cliff plunged down into mysterious depths. Down there, somewhere, was a sunken cargo ship that V intended, someday, to explore. It would have to be done carefully as she would have to work her way down slowly to adapt to the pressure.

She tugged on the anchor and lifted it free of the two outcroppings where it had been jammed and then she sent a very strong mental message up to Giuseppe and Mario: "I've got it; you can turn the winch on now!"

"Did you hear that?" said Giuseppe

"I did."

"It's amazing how the signora does that," said Giuseppe, flipping a switch so that the motor began to whir, the barrel to turn, and the steel and plastic cable to pull upwards, wrapping itself neatly around the turning barrel, "I mean, transmitting thoughts like that!"

"My great grandfather used to tell the story of how, sometimes, during the eighteenth century, she would warn our people when the brigands were on their way, so we could prepare. And he told me that long before that she had helped protect the village from raids by the Saracens, that must have been, what, 1,000 years ago!"

"We have been lucky to have her!"

"And the doctor, when he has a problem, he calls on Jeeves, and Jeeves brings the signora, if the problem is serious …"

"Yes, she does have healing powers … I've seen it myself. When my youngest, Laura, oh, sweet Laura, was sick with the …"

V followed the anchor up towards the boat, and then, as the anchor got to the boat, she emerged. Her reptile face came out of the water and she put one claw against the side of the boat. Giuseppe was looking down at her and he said, "Signora, you are an angel. Do you want to come aboard for a drink – only if you have time, signora!"

"Perhaps another evening," said V, "I have guests tonight, and I'd better get back."

"There'll be a basket of fresh fish for Jeeves, tomorrow," said Giuseppe, "for your visitors."

"Thank you," said V, "Jeeves and my visitors will be delighted with the fish. Thanks again. Good-bye Giuseppe, Good-bye Mario."

She waved and then plunged and swam straight down into the dark depths and headed towards shore.

As V skimmed along the bottom, now mottled with moonlight, she felt that a new presence was waiting for her, a friendly presence.

She came up out of the water just next to the beach, and beside a rocky out-cropping and, sure enough, holding a glass of whiskey, and looking down at her, his hair and shoulders lit up by the moon, was her mentor, her father – Marcus.

"Marcus," V said, as she climbed out of the water and up on to the rock and he reached out to embrace her. He was as handsome as ever, with the tanned skin, the slightly greying blond hair, the small scar over his eyebrow, the solid muscular body.

"But I'm all wet!"

"These jeans and this T-shirt will recover if you hug me," he said, "but I won't, if you don't."

"Blackmail, Marcus, blackmail!" V pressed herself against him; she instantaneously felt all the old love and admiration flood up and all the memories of centuries and centuries ago when she was just a girl and learning to be a demon and learning to be a vampire – and, yes, learning to be human, and when Marcus, her father, her mentor, had taught her how to be all of those things, and how to survive.

"Oh, Marcus," she breathed.

"I'm very proud of you," he said, "as always."

"Thank you, Marcus."

"You are the luckiest thing, V, and the best thing that has ever happened to me."

At one point, V asked, "And Isis, she …?"

"Ah, Isis," said Marcus, "Well, she was sent, undercover as it were, to help you – she is, ah, how shall I put it, she is Asherah of course, the original Asherah you knew back when you were a young woman, but she is also your cousin, V, a younger cousin."

"My cousin – she's my cousin!"

"Yes, delightful girl, too, still is – mischievous as hell when she wants to be. She sends her love, by the way."

"For me, it was love," said V, "at first sight!"

"It was mutual," said Marcus, "mutual."

As they walked, under the silver moonlight, up the winding stone staircase to the villa, Marcus told V of coming struggles, of a civil war in the Empire, of a cosmic struggle which would decide the fate of them all, and he told her too, that Dmitry had acquired such incredible powers, if only briefly, because he had tapped into the powers of the enemy, of the evil force, a mysterious force, which threatened the Empire and which also threatened earth and all the creatures on it.

"We will have to work together to survive," said Marcus.

"I'm ready," said V, "I will do whatever you say needs to be done, Marcus."

"And not only you," said Marcus.

"Yes, and not only me; we have many friends now, Marcus."

At the top of the staircase stood Callida, the young Mexican V had rescued from rape and murder. She was holding two babies in her arms, her own, and V's. "Oh, how wonderful, your father found you, V, I'm so happy to have met him! He is so charming!"

"Callida told me you had gone swimming and Jeeves told me that dinner would be served, right about now," said Marcus, glancing at his watch, "and that you have guests – a golden Hybrid, Eve, Sabrina, who now looks about 25, Jed Baker, Kate and her charming young man, and Ted and Audrey, and Marit, a most fascinating and beautiful SIN, and Father O'Bryan's nephew."

"Yes, everybody decided to stay for a while; it's not as solitary as it used to be."

"Delightful," said Marcus, bestowing a broad smile on V and Callida.

"Let us go, then," said V, taking Marcus by the hand, and her heart, as always when she touched him, was flooded with utter happiness.

So, indeed, this little patch of our sweet planet, Earth, offered, for now at least, a glimpse of humanity's dream through the ages – paradise – otherwise known as – Eden.

NEXT: VOLUME 5 IN THE
ADVENTURES OF V

EXTINCTION

BOOK 1

GIRL WITH THE GOLDEN EYES

by
GILBERT REID

TWIN RIVERS
PRODUCTIONS

EXTINCTION BOOK 1:

GIRL WITH THE GOLDEN EYES

"Shoo! Damn! Shoo!" Miranda Hughes batted a floating string of burning flesh. "Go away!"

Explosions echoed.

Death was everywhere.

The string of sizzling skin lingered in the smoky air – its ember points sparkled like rubies, bubbles of burning fat. It hovered near Miranda's cheek. "Damn! Go away!"

Huge fires lit up the crash site.

"They are going to *eat* us, mother," Miranda sniffed the air and glanced around at the wreckage.

"Eat us? Who's going to eat us?" Nikki Hughes stretched, arms up in the air. She wiggled her shoulders, working out the stiffness.

"Mutants. They're getting close." Miranda stared at the granite walls of the ravine, lit up by the burning wreckage of Presidential Super-Liner Airship 47. From beyond that cliff, Miranda somehow knew, weird creatures, strange misshapen shapes, were hurrying forward, hobbling, leaping, hopping, crawling, and slithering – ever closer.

Death was a heartbeat away.

"Sorry, Miranda. I was distracted. Who is coming to eat us?"

"Mutants! They're coming fast."

"Ah, mutants!" Nikki Hughes glanced at her daughter, narrowed her eyes, and smiled. "So, these mutants intend to eat us?"

"Yes, mother."

"You don't say!"

"Yes. I do say!"

Nikki, her hands her on hips, nodded, and with a thin smile, said, "Well, just let them try!"

"Mother! This is serious!" Miranda fumed. Such casual insouciance was so typical of Nikki! She was so ultra-cool. About absolutely everything! Sometimes, it was frustrating. Miranda frowned and kicked at a pebble. It was puzzling. She had absolutely no idea how she knew mutants were galloping towards them, or how she knew they were eager to feast on her and her mother's élite Cosmos first-class flesh, and drink their élite champagne-quality, first-class Cosmos blood. But she knew it – she *felt* it. She could *see* it. She *heard* them, their growling acidic stomachs, their drooling jaws, their clamorous inchoate whispery thoughts, like the rustling of leaves.

It was *weird*, totally *weird!*

Miranda and Nikki Hughes were alone, the only survivors of the crash, just the two of them, in the Dead Land's desert a thousand miles from civilization. How could such a thing happen?

Miranda, who was just two weeks short of her fourteenth birthday, stared at the burning wreckage: Well, on one level, *how had it happened* was a stupid question!

They had crashed – as simple as that!

Around them was burning wreckage. Miranda suddenly had a *vision* – of what the last few seconds must have looked like from the ground. It was awesome, that's what it was!

The monster aircraft, Presidential Super Liner 47, had screamed out of the night, its engines aflame, its wings immense dark shadows, swooping earthward at a shallow angle – out of control, doomed.

When the wings smashed into the walls of the gully, they snapped off, scything, somersaulting, like giant knives.

The motors flew away, skittered, careened, along the stony escarpment, plowing into the ground, spawning waves of flame, coating the floor of the ravine with liquid fire.

The fuselage thumped, belly down, skidded, and exploded, breaking into four giant pieces, fragments smashing into rocks and outcroppings, spinning, rocketing everywhere. Behind the hurtling hunks of fuselage came a flooding wall of fire.

ACKNOWLEDGMENTS

Thanks to the many people who made the *Adventures of V: Return of the Goddess* possible: Adrienne Clarkson, Andra Sheffer, André Kirchberger, Anna Porter, Bernice Landry, Bernie Lucht, Beverly Topping, Bob Ramsay, Chuck Shamata, Claudia Neri, Denise Jacques, Diana Leblanc, Diane Shamata, Dianne Rinehart, Dorothy Vreeker, Duncan Derry, Ed Cowan, Elena Solari, Florence Treadwell, Heather Reid, Irene Spampinato, Irene Tudisco, Jacqueline Baker, Jacqueline Park, Jacqueline Swartz, Janie Yoon, Jennifer Hambleton, Jennifer Puncher, Jim Downs, John McGreevy, John Pearce, John Ralston Saul, Josephine Khu, Jules Cashford, Julia Belluz, Julia Hambleton, Marie-Christine Dunham-Pratt, Mark Fenwick, Martine Matus Siebert, Norm Barber, Norm Christie, Nuala Fitzgerald, Paola Pugliatti, Peter Williamson, Ramsay Derry, Sandra Martin, Simona Barabesi, Susan Mahoney, Susan S. Senstad, Tony Robinow, Trisha Jackson, Wendy Trueman, and many others too numerous to name. I owe an infinite number of literary debts, too, but in particular to Joyce Carol Oates, Justin Cronin, and Stephen King.

TITLES IN THE
ADVENTURES OF V

WORKS BY
GILBERT REID

SHORT STORIES
So This is Love: Lollipop and Other Stories
Lava and Other stories

GRAZIA SERIES
Son of Two Fathers (with Jacqueline Park)

ADVENTURES OF V
Vampire vs Vatican
Vampire Clone
Pandemic Book 1: Party Balloons
Pandemic Book 2: The Gateway
Extinction Book 1: Girl with the Golden Eyes
Extinction Book 2: Revolt of the Angels
Extinction Book 3: Elysium

GWENDOLINE SERIES
By Gwendoline
The Shaming of Gwendoline C
Gwendoline Goes to School
Gwendoline Goes Underground

To receive a free book or novella
And to learn more about V and get notes on writing and other topics:

Sign up at

https://gilbertreid.com

Please write a short review!
Just two or three lines.
And post it to Goodreads or Amazon
or any other book group you may belong to.

Or send it to me!
At: gilbert@gilbertreid.com

GILBERT REID is the author of two short story collections: *So This is Love: Lollipop and Other Stories* (2004, 2019) and *Lava and Other Stories* (2019). He also co-authored, with Jacqueline Park, the historical novel *Son of Two Fathers* (2019). He has written extensively for television and radio. Most notably he researched, wrote, and narrated two five-hour radio series: *Gilbert Reid's Italy* and *Gilbert Reid's France* for CBC's flagship radio program IDEAS. His many television series include *Paths of the Gods*, *For King and Empire*, *For King and Country*, and *Sir Peter Ustinov in Burma: Road to Mandalay*. After thirty years in Europe working as an economist, university lecturer, diplomat, script doctor, journalist, and adventure travel guide, Gilbert now lives in Toronto.

www.ingramcontent.com/pod-product-compliance
Lightning Source LLC
Chambersburg PA
CBHW050119030726
47505CB00007B/1953